Praise for Harry Turtledove and *Colonization: Aftershocks*

"If only there were another five books in the series to look forward to."
—*Booklist*

"Turtledove has proved he can divert his readers to astonishing places. He's developed a cult following over the years; and if you've already been there, done that with real-history novelists Patrick O'Brian, Dorothy Dunnett, or George MacDonald Fraser, for your Next Big Enthusiasm you might want to try Turtledove. I know I'd follow his imagination almost anywhere."
—*San Jose Mercury News*

"Turtledove, like Stephen King . . . can still deliver quality, page-turning entertainment."
—*Contra Costa Times*

"Harry Turtledove [is] probably the best-known practitioner of alternate history working today."
—*American Heritage*

"Turtledove has established himself as a grand master of the alternative history form."
—POUL ANDERSON

Books by Harry Turtledove

The Guns of the South

THE WORLDWAR SAGA
Worldwar: In the Balance
Worldwar: Tilting the Balance
Worldwar: Upsetting the Balance
Worldwar: Striking the Balance

COLONIZATION
Colonization: Second Contact
Colonization: Down to Earth
Colonization: Aftershocks

THE VIDESSOS CYCLE
The Misplaced Legion
An Emperor for the Legion
The Legion of Videssos
Swords of the Legion

THE TALE OF KRISPOS
Krispos Rising
Krispos of Videssos
Krispos the Emperor

THE TIME OF TROUBLES SERIES
The Stolen Throne
Hammer and Anvil
The Thousand Cities
Videssos Besieged

Noninterference
Kaleidoscope
A World of Difference
Earthgrip
Departures

How Few Remain

THE GREAT WAR
The Great War: American Front
The Great War: Walk in Hell
The Great War: Breakthroughs

American Empire: Blood and Iron

COLONIZATION: AFTERSHOCKS

Harry Turtledove

BALLANTINE BOOKS • NEW YORK

A Del Rey® Book
Published by The Ballantine Publishing Group
Copyright © 2001 by Harry Turtledove

All rights reserved under International and Pan-American Copyright Conventions. Published in the United States by The Ballantine Publishing Group, a division of Random House, Inc., New York, and simultaneously in Canada by Random House of Canada Limited, Toronto.

Del Rey is a registered trademark and the Del Rey colophon is a trademark of Random House, Inc.

www.delreydigital.com

ISBN 0-345-43024-7

Manufactured in the United States of America

First Hardcover Edition: February 2001
First Mass Market Edition: March 2002

10   9   8   7   6   5   4   3   2   1

COLONIZATION: AFTERSHOCKS

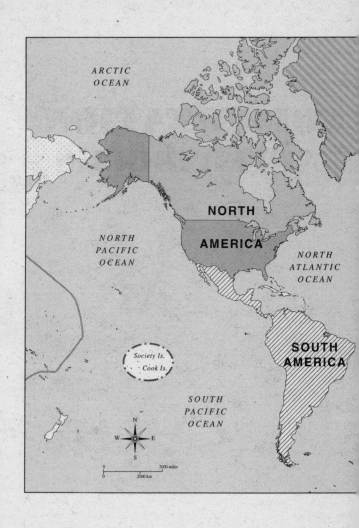

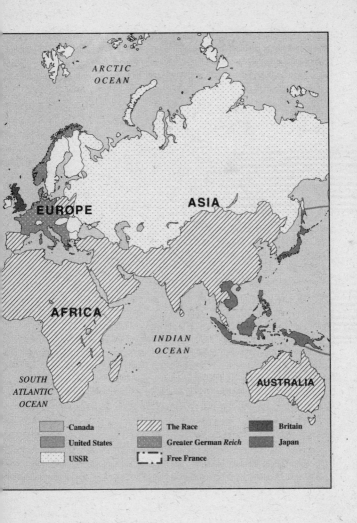

☆ **1** ☆

As the jet aircraft descended toward the airport outside the still slightly radioactive ruins of Nuremberg, Pshing asked Atvar, "Exalted Fleetlord, is this visit really necessary?"

"I believe it," the commander of the Race's conquest fleet told his adjutant. "My briefings state that a Tosevite wise in the political affairs of his kind recommended that a conqueror visit the region he conquered as soon as he could, to make those he had defeated aware of their new masters."

"Technically, the Greater German *Reich* remains independent," Pshing pointed out.

"So it does—technically. But that will remain a technicality, I assure you." Atvar used an emphatic cough to show how strongly he felt about that. "The Deutsche did us far too much harm in this exchange of explosive-metal weapons to let their madness ever break free again."

"A pity we had to concede them even so limited an independence," Pshing said.

"And that is also a truth," Atvar agreed with a sigh. He swiveled one eye turret toward the window to get another look at the glassy crater that filled the center of the former capital of the Greater German *Reich*. Beyond it lay a slagged wilderness of what remained of homes and factories and public buildings. Conventional bombs had devastated the airport, too, but it was back in service.

Pshing said, "If only we had some means of detecting their missile-carrying boats that can stay submerged indefinitely. Without those, we could have forced unconditional surrender out of them."

"Truth," Atvar repeated. "With them, though, they could have inflicted a good deal more damage to our colonies here on

1

Tosev 3. They will be surrendering the submarines they have left. We shall not allow them to build more. We shall not allow them to have anything to do with atomic power or explosive-metal weapons henceforward."

"That is excellent. That is as it should be," Pshing said. "If only we could arrange to confiscate the submersible boats of the United States and the Union of Soviet Socialist Republics as well, we would truly be on our way toward a definitive conquest of this miserable planet."

"I merely thank the spirits of Emperors past"—Atvar cast both his eye turrets down to the floor of the aircraft that carried him—"that neither of the other powerful not-empires chose to join the Deutsche against us. Together, they could have hurt us much worse than the *Reich* alone did."

"And now we also have the Nipponese to worry about," Pshing added. "Who knows what they will do, now that they have learned the art of constructing explosive-metal weapons? They already have submarines, and they already have missiles."

"We never did pay enough attention to islands and their inhabitants," Atvar said fretfully. "Small chunks of land surrounded by sea were never important back on Home, so we have always assumed the same would hold true here. Unfortunately, it does not seem to be so."

Before Pshing could answer, the aircraft's landing gear touched down on the runway outside Nuremberg. The Race's engineering, slowly refined through a hundred thousand years of planetary unity, was very fine, but not fine enough to keep Atvar from feeling some bumps as the aircraft slowed to a stop.

"My apologies, Exalted Fleetlord." The pilot's voice came back to him on the intercom. "I was given to understand repairs to the landing surface were better than is in fact the case."

Peering out the window, Atvar saw Deutsch males in the cloth wrappings that singled out their military drawn up in neat ranks to greet and honor him. They carried rifles. His security males had flabbled about that, but the *Reich* remained nominally independent. If some fanatic sought to assassinate him, his second-in-command in Cairo would do . . . well enough. "What was the name of the sly Big Ugly who suggested this course?" he asked Pshing.

"Machiavelli." His adjutant pronounced the alien name with care, one syllable at a time. "He lived and wrote about nine hundred years ago. Nine hundred of our years, I should say—half as many of Tosev 3's."

"So he came after our probe, then?" Atvar said, and Pshing made the affirmative gesture. The Race had studied Tosev 3 sixteen hundred years before: again, half that many in Tosevite terms. The fleetlord went on, "Remember the sword-swinging savage mounted on an animal the probe showed us? He was the height of Tosevite military technology in those days."

"A pity he did not remain the height of Tosevite military technology, as we were so confident he would," Pshing said. "When we understand how the Big Uglies are able to change so rapidly, we will be able to prevent them from doing so in the future. That will help bind them to the Empire."

"So it will . . . if we can do it," Atvar replied. "If not, we will wreck them one not-empire at a time. Or, if necessary, we will destroy this whole world, even our colonies on it. That will cauterize it once for all."

One other possibility remained, a possibility that had never entered his mind when the conquest fleet first reached Tosev 3: the Big Uglies might conquer the Race. If they did, they would next mount an attack on Home. Atvar was as sure of it as of the fact that he'd hatched from an egg. Wrecking the world would prevent it, as a surgeon sometimes had to prevent death by cutting out a tumor.

With the *Reich* prostrate, the Big Uglies would have a much harder time of it. Atvar knew that. But the worry never went away. The locals were quicker, more adaptable, than the Race. He knew that, too; close to fifty of his years of experience on Tosev 3 had burned the lesson into him again and again.

Clunks and bangings from up ahead came to his hearing diaphragm: the aircraft's door opening. He did not go forward at once; his security males would disembark ahead of him to form what was termed a ceremonial guard and amounted to a defensive perimeter. It would not hold against concerted attack; it might keep a single crazed Big Ugly from murdering him. Atvar hoped it would.

One of those security males came back to his seat and bent into the posture of respect. "All is in readiness, Exalted Fleetlord," he reported. "And the radioactivity level is acceptably low."

"I thank you, Diffal," Atvar said. The male had headed Security since midway through the fighting. He wasn't so good as his predecessor, Drefsab, but Drefsab had fallen victim to Big Uglies with even more nasty talents—or perhaps just more luck—than he'd had. Atvar turned an eye turret toward Pshing. "Come with me."

"It shall be done, Exalted Fleetlord," his adjutant said.

Atvar let out a hiss of disgust at the weather outside, which was chilly and damp. Cairo, whence he'd come, had a reasonably decent climate. Nuremberg didn't come close. And this was spring, heading toward summer. Winter would have been much worse. Atvar shivered at the very idea.

As he emerged from his aircraft, a Deutsch military band began braying away. The Big Uglies meant it as an honor, not an insult, and so he endured the unmusical—at least to his hearing diaphragms—racket. The security officials parted to let a Big Ugly through: not the *Führer* of the Deutsche, but a protocol aide. "If you advance to the end of the carpet, Exalted Fleetlord, the *Führer* will meet you there," he said, using the language of the Race about as well as a Tosevite could.

Making the gesture of agreement, Atvar advanced to the edge of the strip of red cloth and stopped. His security males kept him covered and kept themselves between him and the ranks of the Deutsche. The Tosevite soldiers looked fierce and barbaric, and had proved themselves formidable in battle. *They are beaten now,* Atvar reminded himself. They didn't seem beaten, though. By their bearing, they were ready to go right back to war.

Their ranks parted slightly. Out from among them came a relatively short, rather stout Big Ugly in wrappings related to those of the soldiers but fancier. He wore a cap on his head. The hair Atvar could see below it was white, which meant he was not young. When he took off the cap for a moment, he showed that most of his scalp was bare, another sign of an aging male Tosevite.

As the Deutsche had parted, so, rather more reluctantly, did Atvar's security males. The Big Ugly walked up to Atvar and shot out his arm in salute. Being still formally independent, he did not have to assume the posture of respect. "I greet you, Exalted Fleetlord," he said. He was less fluent in Atvar's language than his protocol officer, but he made himself understood. "I am Walter Dornberger, *Führer* and Chancellor of the Greater German *Reich.*"

"And I greet you, *Führer.*" Atvar knew he made a hash of the

Deutsch word, but it didn't matter. "Your males fought bravely. Now the fighting is over. You shall have to learn that fighting bravely and fighting wisely are not the same."

"Had I led the *Reich* when this war began, it would not have begun," Dornberger replied. "But my superiors thought differently. Now they are dead, and I have to pick up the pieces they left behind."

That was Tosevite idiom; the Race would have spoken of putting an eggshell back together. But Atvar understood. "You shall have fewer pieces with which to work henceforward. We intend to make certain of that. You did too much harm to us to be trusted any longer."

"I understand," Dornberger said. "The terms you have forced me to accept are harsh. But you and the Race have left me no other choice."

"Your predecessors had a choice," Atvar said coldly. "They chose the wrong path. You are obliged to live with their decision, and with what it has left you."

"I also understand that," the Tosevite replied. "But you can hardly deny that you are wringing all possible advantages from your victory."

"Of course we are," Atvar said. "That is what victory is for. Or do you believe it has some other purpose?"

"By no means," Dornberger said. In tones of professional admiration, he added, "You were clever to set France up again as an independent not-empire. I did not expect that of you."

"I thank you." The fleetlord had not imagined he might know a certain amount of sympathy for the Big Ugly who now led the not-empire that had done the Race so much harm. "Little by little, through continual contact with you Tosevites, we do learn how to play your games. You should be thankful we left you any fragments of your independence."

"I am thankful to you for that," Dornberger answered. "I suspect I should also be thankful to the Americans and Russians, who would not have taken it kindly to see the Greater German *Reich* disappear from the map."

The Tosevite was indeed professionally competent. Both the USA and the Soviet Union had made it very clear to Atvar that their fear of the Race would increase if the *Reich* were treated as an outright conquest. After what he had suffered fighting Germany, he did not want the other not-empires excessively afraid;

it might make them do something foolish. He hated having to take their fears into account, but they were too strong to let him do anything else. His tailstump quivered in irritation.

Pointing at Dornberger with his tongue, he said, "We no longer need to worry so much about the opinion of the *Reich*. And we shall do everything possible—everything necessary—to make sure we never have to worry about it again. Do you understand?"

"Of course, Exalted Fleetlord," Dornberger answered, and Atvar wondered how—and how soon—the Deutsche would start trying to cheat him.

Sweat ran down Colonel Johannes Drucker's face. Everyone knew the Lizards preferred their weather hot as the Sahara. As the German sat, a prisoner of war, in a cubicle aboard one of their starships, he scratched his bare chest. The Lizards were scrupulous. They'd returned to him the coveralls he'd worn aboard the upper stage of the A-45 that had lifted him into Earth orbit. They'd even washed them. But he couldn't bear the thought of putting them on, not when he felt about ready to have an apple stuck in his mouth even naked.

He sighed, longing for the fogs and chill of Peenemünde, the *Reich*'s rocket base on the Baltic. But Peenemünde was radioactive rubble now. His family lived in Greifswald, not far to the west. He sighed again, on a different, grimmer note. He prayed that they weren't radioactive dust, but he had no way of knowing.

The chair on which he sat was too small for him, and shaped for a backside proportioned differently from his. The sleeping mat on the floor was also too small, and too hard to boot. The Lizards fed him canned goods imported from the lands they ruled and from the USA, most of which were not to his taste.

It could have been worse. He'd tried to blow up this starship. Its antimissiles had knocked out one of the warheads he'd launched from his upper stage, its close-in weapons system the other. The Race had still accepted his surrender afterwards. Few humans would have been so generous.

He got up and used the head. Every so often, Lizard technicians came in and fiddled with the plumbing. It wasn't made for liquid waste; the Race, like real lizards, excreted only solids. From trying to blow the starship to a cloud of radioactive gas, he'd been reduced to causing problems in its pipes. That was funny, if you looked at it the right way.

Without warning, the door to his cubicle slid open. He was glad he'd finished pissing; getting caught in the act would have embarrassed him, even if it wouldn't have flustered the Lizard who caught him. He'd seen this fellow before: he recognized the body paint. "I greet you, superior sir," he said. Anyone who flew in space had to know the Lizards' language.

"I greet you, Johannes Drucker," the Lizard named Ttomalss answered. "I am here to inform you that you will soon be released."

"That is good news. I thank you, superior sir," Drucker said. But then his mouth twisted. "It would be better news if it did not mean my not-empire had been defeated."

"I understand. I sympathize," Ttomalss said. Perhaps he even did; he showed more knowledge of the way people worked than any other Lizard the German had met. Drucker wondered how he'd acquired it. Ttomalss continued, "But you will have the opportunity to help repair the damage."

I'll have the opportunity to see the damage, Drucker thought. He could have done without that opportunity. He'd been a panzer driver, not a spaceman, when the *Reich* detonated an explosive-metal bomb to derail a Lizard attack on Breslau. He'd cheered then. He wouldn't be cheering now.

"Can you drop me near Peenemünde land?" he asked. "That is where my . . . mate and my hatchlings live—if they live anywhere at all."

But Ttomalss made the Race's negative hand gesture. "Captives are being exchanged outside Nuremberg, nowhere else."

"Very well," Drucker said, since he couldn't say anything else. From Bavaria to Pomerania through a war-ravaged landscape? Not a journey to look forward to, but one he would have to make.

"Eventually, a shuttlecraft will take you back to the surface of Tosev 3," the Lizard told him. "In the meantime, now that hostilities have concluded, I have gained permission to inform you that you are not the only Tosevite presently aboard this starship. Are you interested in meeting another member of your species?"

After weeks with nobody but Lizards to talk to? What do you think? Aloud, Drucker said, "Yes, superior sir, I would very interested be." He used an emphatic cough, then added, "I thank you." Did the Lizards have a beautiful spy waiting to try to charm secrets out of him? Not likely—not that he'd be much interested anyhow, not when he hadn't the faintest idea whether Käthe was alive or dead. Had he watched too many bad films and read too many trashy novels? That struck him as very likely indeed.

Ttomalss said, "The other male is from the not-empire of the United States. He is here on a . . . research mission, I suppose you would describe it."

Something in the way he hesitated didn't quite ring true to Drucker, but the German was hardly in a position to call him on it. And the Lizard had used the masculine pronoun. *So much for beautiful spies.* Drucker laughed at himself. "All right," he said. "No matter who he is or where he is from, I look forward to meeting him."

"Wait here," Ttomalss told him, as if he were liable to wait somewhere else. The Lizard left the cubicle. Ttomalss could leave. Drucker couldn't.

After about forty-five minutes—his captors had let him keep his watch—the door slid open. In came a young man with a shaved head and with body paint on his chest. He nodded to Drucker, ignoring his nakedness (he wore only denim shorts himself), and stuck out his hand. "Hello. Do you speak English?" he said in that language.

"Some," Drucker answered in English. Then he shifted: "I must tell you, though, I am better in the language of the Race."

"That suits me fine," the American said, also in the Lizards' tongue. *He's very young,* Drucker realized—the shaved head had disguised his age. He went on, "My name is Jonathan Yeager. I greet you."

"And I greet you." Drucker shook the proffered hand and gave his own name. Then he eyed the American. "Yeager? It is a German name. It means 'hunter.' " The last word was in English.

"Yes, my father's father's father came from Germany," Jonathan Yeager said.

In musing tones, Drucker said, "I knew an officer named Jäger, Heinrich Jäger. He was a landcruiser commander. One of the best officers I ever served under—I named my oldest hatchling for him. I wonder if there is a relationship. From what part of Germany did your ancestor come?"

"I am sorry, but I do not know," the young American answered. "Maybe my father does, but I am not sure of that. Many, when they came to America, tried to forget where they came from so they could become Americans."

"I have this heard," Drucker said. "It strikes me as strange." Maybe that made him a reactionary European. Even if it did, though, he was a wild-eyed radical when measured against the Lizards. He asked, "What sort of research are you engaged in here?" The unspoken question behind that one was, *Why would the Americans send a puppy instead of a seasoned man?*

To Drucker's surprise, Jonathan Yeager blushed all the way to the top of his shaved crown. He coughed and spluttered a couple of times before answering, "I guess you could call it a sociological project."

"That sounds interesting," Drucker said, hoping Yeager would go on and tell him more about it.

Instead, the American pointed an accusing finger his way and said, "And I know why you are here."

"I have no doubt that you do," Drucker said. "If my attack had been a little more fortunate, we would not be having this talk now."

"That is a truth." Jonathan Yeager sounded surprisingly calm. Maybe he was too young to take seriously the possibility of his own demise. Or maybe not; he went on, "My father is an officer in the U.S. Army. He would talk that way, too, I think."

"Professionals do." Drucker started to say something else, but checked himself. "Is your father by any chance the male who understands the Race so well? If he is, I have some of his work in translation read. I should have of him thought when I heard the name."

"Yes, that is my father," Jonathan Yeager said with what sounded like pardonable pride.

"He does good work," Drucker said. "He is the only Tosevite who ever made me believe he could think like a male of the Race. Why are you here instead of him?"

"He has been here," the younger Yeager answered. "I first came here with him, as his assistant—I still wear the body paint of an assistant psychological researcher. But I am . . . better suited to the research for this part of the project than he is."

"Can you tell me why?" Drucker asked. Jonathan Yeager shook his head. Seeing that gesture instead of one from a scaly hand made Drucker feel at home, even though the American had told him no.

Yeager said, "I am told you will be able to go home soon."

"Yes, if I have any home left," Drucker answered. "I do not know whether my kin are alive or dead."

"I hope they are well," Jonathan Yeager said. "I look forward to going home myself. I have been up here since the war began. The Race judged it was not safe for me to leave."

"I would say that was likely to be true," Drucker agreed. "We fought hard."

"I know," Yeager said. "But did you really think you could win?"

"Did I think so?" Drucker shook his head. "I did not think we had a chance. But what could I do? When your leaders tell you to go to war, you go to war. They must have thought we could win, or they would not have started fighting."

"They were—" Jonathan Yeager broke off, shaking his head.

He'd been about to say something like, *They were pretty stupid if they did.* Drucker would have argued with him if he hadn't felt the same way. The crisis had started while Himmler was *Führer,* and Kaltenbrunner hadn't done anything to make it go away. On the contrary—he'd charged right ahead. *Fools rush in,* Drucker thought. He wondered how General Dornberger would shape up as the new leader of the *Reich.* He also wondered how much trouble the SS would give the new *Führer.* Dornberger hadn't come up through the ranks of the blackshirts; he'd been soldiering since the First World War. The secret policemen might not like him very well.

Drucker had no sympathy for the SS, not after they'd tried to get rid of his wife on the grounds that she had a Jewish grandmother. If all the blackshirts suffered unfortunate accidents, he wouldn't shed a tear. With SS men in charge of things, his country had suffered an unfortunate accident—except it hadn't been an accident. Kaltenbrunner had started the war on purpose.

Something else occurred to him: "Is it true what some males of the Race have told me? That France is to be made independent again, I mean?"

"Yes, that is true," Jonathan Yeager told him. "From the news reports I have seen, the French are happy about it, too." He sounded pretty happy himself. He was, after all, an American, and the USA and Germany had been at war when the Lizards came. They still didn't get along very well, and gloating at a rival's misfortune was a constant all over the world, and probably among the Race as well.

"I do not care whether they are happy or not," Drucker said. "It will mean a weaker Germany, and a weaker Germany means a stronger Race." He was sure the Lizards were recording every word he said. He didn't much care. They'd captured him. They'd beaten his country. If they thought he loved them because of it, they were crazy.

Back in the cubicle Jonathan Yeager shared with Kassquit, he said, "Strange to think I was just talking with a male who could have killed both of us."

When Kassquit made the affirmative gesture, she almost poked him in the nose. As far as Jonathan was concerned, the cubicle would have been cramped for her alone; being smaller than people, Lizards built smaller, too. But she was used to it. She'd lived in a cubicle like this her whole life. She said, "You can take off those foolish wrappings now. You do not need them any more."

"No, I suppose not. I certainly do not need them to keep me warm." Jonathan used an emphatic cough as he kicked off the shorts. The Lizards kept the starship at a temperature comfortable for them, one that matched a hot summer's day in Los Angeles. Even shorts made him sweat more than he would have without them.

Kassquit was naked, too. She'd never worn clothes, not after she'd got out of diapers. The Lizards—Ttomalss in particular—had raised her ever since she was a newborn. They'd wanted to see how close they could come to turning a human into a female of the Race.

Jonathan shaved his head. Plenty of kids of his generation—girls as well as boys, though not so many—did that, aping the Lizards and incidentally annoying their parents. Kassquit shaved not only her head—including her eyebrows—but all the hair on her body in an effort to make herself as much like a Lizard as she could. She'd told him once that she'd thought about having her ears removed to make her head look more like a Lizard's, and had decided against it only because she didn't think it would help enough.

She said, "I wonder if I will be allowed to meet him before he returns to the surface of Tosev 3. I should learn more about wild Tosevites."

With a chuckle, Jonathan said, "I think he would be glad to meet you, especially without wrappings." The Lizards' language had no specific term for clothes, which the Race didn't use, but could and did go into enormous detail about body paint.

"What do you mean?" By Earthly standards, Kassquit had a remorselessly literal mind. "Do you mean he might want to mate with me? Would he find me attractive enough to want to mate with?"

"Of course he would. I certainly do." Jonathan used another emphatic cough. He always praised Kassquit as extravagantly as he could. She unfolded like a flower when he did. He got the idea the Lizards hadn't bothered—or maybe they just hadn't known people needed such things. Whenever he thought Kassquit acted strangely, he had to step back and remind himself it was a wonder she got even to within shouting distance of sanity.

And he hadn't been lying. She was of Oriental descent; living in Gardena, California, which had a large Japanese-American population, he'd got used to Asian standards of beauty. And by them she was more than pretty enough. Her shaved head didn't put him off, either; he knew plenty of girls at UCLA who shaved theirs. The only thing truly odd about her was her expression, or lack of expression. Her face was almost masklike. She hadn't learned to smile when she was a baby—Lizards could hardly smile back at her—and it was evidently too late after that.

She asked, "Would you be upset if I decided to mate with him?" She didn't have much in the way of tact, either.

To keep from examining his own feelings right away, Jonathan answered, "Even if he finds you attractive, I am not sure he would want to mate with you. He is concerned with his own mate down in the *Reich*, and does not know her fate."

"I see," Kassquit said slowly.

Jonathan wondered if she really did. She hadn't known anything about the emotional attachments men and women could form . . . *till she started making love with me,* he thought. He hadn't wanted to explain to the German spaceman the sort of sociological research project in which he was engaged. It was really more the Lizards' project, not his. He was just along for the ride.

He chuckled. *They brought me up here and put me out to stud.* He wondered how much they'd learned. He'd certainly learned a lot.

He went over to Kassquit and put a hand on her shoulder. She squeezed him. She liked being touched. He got the idea she hadn't been touched a whole lot before he came up to the starship. Touching was a human trait, not one the Race shared to anywhere near the same degree.

"He will be going down to his not-empire before long," Kassquit said.

"Truth," Jonathan agreed.

"And you will be going down to your not-empire before long," Kassquit said.

"You knew I would," Jonathan told her. "I cannot stay up here. This is your place, but it is not mine."

"I understand that," Kassquit answered. She spoke the language of the Race as well as someone with a human mouth possibly could. And why not? It was the only language she knew. She went on, "Intellectually, I understand that. But you must understand, Jonathan, that I will be sorry when you go. I will be sad."

Jonathan sighed and squeezed her, though he didn't know whether that made things better or worse. "I am sorry," he said. "I do not know what to do about that. I wish there were something I could do."

"You also have a female waiting for you on the surface of Tosev 3, even if she is not a female with whom you have arranged for permanent exclusive mating," Kassquit said.

"Yes, I do," Jonathan admitted. "You have known that all along. I never tried to keep it a secret from you."

He wondered if Karen Culpepper would still be his girl when he came home. They'd been dating since high school. When he'd come up to the starship, he hadn't expected to stay, and he hadn't thought he would have that much explaining to do once he got back. He hadn't really believed the Nazis would be crazy enough to attack the Lizards over Poland. But they had, and he'd been here for weeks—and he'd almost died a couple of times, too. Karen would have an excellent notion of where he was and why he'd come up here. He didn't think she'd be very happy about it.

"You will go back to her. You will mate with her. You will forget about me," Kassquit said.

She didn't know it, but she was reinventing the lines everyone who'd ever lost a lover used. "I will never forget you," Jonathan said, which was the truth. But even if it was, he doubted it consoled her much. Had someone told him the same thing, it wouldn't have consoled him, either.

"Can that really be so?" she asked. "You know many other To-sevites. To you, I am only one of many. To me, you are the most important Tosevite I have ever known." She let her mouth fall open, mimicking the way Lizards laughed. "The size of the sample is small, I admit, but it is not likely to increase to any great degree soon. Why, if I meet the Deutsch male before he leaves the ship, it will go up from two to three."

She wasn't trying to make him feel sorry for her. He was sure of that. She didn't have the guile to do any such thing. No doubt because of the way she'd been raised, she was devastatingly frank. He said, "You could make it larger if you came down to visit the United States. You would be most welcome in my . . . city."

He'd started to say *in my house*. But Kassquit wouldn't be welcome in his house. His father and mother—and he, too, when he was there—were raising a couple of Lizard hatchlings who were Kassquit's exact inverses: Mickey and Donald were being brought up as much like human beings as possible. The Race wouldn't be delighted to learn about that, and Kassquit's first loyalty was inevitably to the Lizards.

"I may do that," she said. "On the other fork of the tongue, I may not, too. Is it not a truth that there are Tosevite diseases for which your physicians have as yet developed no vaccines?"

"Yes, that is a truth," Jonathan admitted.

Kassquit continued, "From the Race's research, it appears that some of these diseases are more severe for an adult than they would be for a hatchling. I do not wish to risk my health—my life—for the sake of a visit to Tosev 3, interesting as it might otherwise be."

"Well, I understand that." Jonathan made the affirmative gesture. "But surely other Tosevites will be coming here to the starship." Getting away from the personal, getting away from guilt he couldn't help feeling at leaving someone with whom he'd been making love as often as he could, was something of a relief.

"I suppose so," Kassquit answered. "But still, you must understand, you will be the standard of comparison. I will judge every other Tosevite I meet, every other male with whom I mate, by what I have learned from and about you."

So he couldn't get away from the personal after all. Stammering a little, he said, "That is a large responsibility for me."

"I think you set a high standard," Kassquit told him. "If I thought otherwise, I would not want to share this compartment with you and I would not want to go on mating with you, would I? And I do."

She put her arms around him. She was as frank about what she liked as about what she didn't. He kissed the top of her head. An American girl would have tilted her face up for a kiss. Kassquit didn't. Kisses on the mouth, and especially French kisses, alarmed rather than exciting her.

They made love on the sleeping mat. It was harder than a bed would have been, but far softer than the metal flooring. Afterwards, Jonathan peeled off the rubber he'd worn and tossed it in the trash. He didn't flush such things; he had no idea what latex would do to the Lizards' plumbing, and didn't care to find out the hard way.

Kassquit said, "I think I begin to understand something of Tosevite sexual jealousy. It must be close to what I felt when, after the colonization fleet arrived, Ttomalss began paying much less attention to me because he was paying much more attention to Felless, a researcher newly revived from cold sleep."

"Maybe," Jonathan said. He didn't know what Kassquit had felt then. He supposed it was something strong, though, because Ttomalss had been—still was—as close to a mother and a father as Kassquit had.

"I think it must be," Kassquit said earnestly, "for I know much of that same feeling when I think of you mating with that other female down on the surface of Tosev 3. I understand that this is not rational, but it does not appear to be anything I can help, either."

Jonathan wasn't nearly sure Karen would want to mate with him after he got back to Gardena. But if she didn't, some other girl—some other girl who not only was but wanted to be a human being—would. He had no doubt of that. While Kassquit . . . Now she knew more of what being human was all about, and she would go back to living among the Lizards.

"I am sorry," Jonathan said. "I never meant to cause you pain or jealousy. You were the one who wanted to know what Tosevite sexuality was like, and all I ever wanted to do was please you while I showed you."

"I understand that. And you have pleased me." Kassquit used an emphatic cough. But then she went on, "You have also shown me that there are times when the pleasure cannot come unmixed with pain and jealousy. From everything I gather about the behavior of wild Tosevites, this is not uncommon among you."

However alien her background and viewpoint, she wasn't a fool. She was anything but a fool. Jonathan had discovered that before, and now got his nose rubbed in it. She'd just told him something about the way love worked that he'd never quite figured out for himself. He assumed the posture of respect before her, and then had a devil of a time explaining why.

Armed guards stood outside the compartment housing the Deutsch captive. Kassquit hoped the males would never have to use their weapons; the thought of bullets tearing through walls, through electronics, through hydraulics, through spirits of Emperors past only knew what all, was genuinely terrifying.

She used an artificial fingerclaw to press the recessed button in the wall that opened the door. After it slid aside, she stepped into the cubicle. "I greet you, Johannes Drucker," she said, pronouncing the alien name as carefully as she could.

"And I greet you, superior female." The wild Big Ugly stood very straight and shot out his right arm. From what Jonathan Yeager had told her, that was his equivalent of the Race's posture of respect.

The strange gesture made him seem wilder than Jonathan Yeager. He looked wilder, too. He was hairy all over, with short, thick, brown hair streaked with gray growing on his cheeks and chin as well as the top of his head. No one had given him a razor. And he spoke the Race's language with an accent different from, and thicker than, Jonathan Yeager's.

He seemed to be trying not to study her body, which was covered only by the body paint of a psychological researcher's assistant. Kassquit remembered both Jonathan and Sam Yeager behaving the same way at their first meeting. Coming right out and staring was evidently impolite but difficult to avoid.

He said, "They told me I would another Tosevite visitor be having. They did not bother telling me you would a female be."

"Tosevite sexes and sexuality are matters of amusement and alarm to the Race, but seldom matters of importance," Kassquit answered. "And, though I am of Tosevite ancestry, I am not precisely a Tosevite myself. I am a citizen of the Empire." Pride rang in her voice.

Johannes Drucker said, "I understand the words, but I do not think I understand the meaning behind them."

"I have been raised in this starship by the Race from earliest hatchlinghood," Kassquit said. "Until quite recently, I never so much as met wild Big Uglies." She hardly ever said *Big Uglies* around Jonathan Yeager. When speaking to this much wilder Tosevite, it came out naturally.

"I . . . see," the captive said. His mouth twisted up at the corners: the Tosevite expression of amusement. "Now that you have started us meeting, what do you think?"

Kassquit couldn't imitate that expression, try as she would. She answered, "The ones I have met are somewhat less barbarous than I would have expected."

With a loud, barking laugh, the Deutsch captive said, *"Danke schön."* Seeing that Kassquit didn't understand, he returned to the language of the Race: "That means, I thank you very much."

"You are welcome," Kassquit answered. Only after the words were out of her mouth did she stop and wonder whether he'd been sarcastic. To cover her confusion, she changed the subject, saying, "I am told you came close to destroying this starship."

"Yes, that is a truth, superior female," he agreed.

"Why?" she asked. War, whether carried on by the Race or by Big Uglies, still seemed very strange to her. "No one aboard this ship was trying to do the *Reich* any particular harm. Most males and females here are researchers, not combatants."

She thought that a paralyzingly effective comment. The wild Big Ugly only shrugged. "Do you think all of the Tosevites in the Deutsch cities on which you dropped explosive-metal bombs were doing nothing but fighting the Race?"

Kassquit hadn't really thought about that at all. To her, the Deutsche had been nothing but the enemy. Now that Johannes Drucker pointed it out, though, she supposed most of them had just been going on with their lives. That made her examine her own side in a way she hadn't before. "Why?" she said again.

"Anything that the enemy serves a fair target is," Johannes Drucker replied. "That is how we fight wars. And we have seen that the Race is not very different. No one invited the Race to come here and try to conquer Tosev 3. Do you think it is any wonder that we as hard as we could fought back?"

"I suppose not," admitted Kassquit, who hadn't tried to look at things from the Tosevite point of view. "Do you not think that you would be using explosive-metal bombs on one another if we had not come?"

"We?" The wild Big Ugly raised an eyebrow in what she'd come to recognize as a gesture of irony. "Superior female, you have no scales that I can see."

"I am still a citizen of the Empire," Kassquit replied with dignity. "I would rather be a citizen of the Empire than a Tosevite peasant, which I surely would have been had the Race not chosen me."

"How do you know?" Johannes Drucker asked. "Are you happy here aboard this starship, living with nothing but males and females of the Race? Would you not be happier among your own kind, even as a peasant?"

Kassquit wished he hadn't asked the question that particular way. The older and the more conscious of her alienness she'd become, the less happy she'd grown. Some of the males and females of the Race were only too willing to rub her snout in that alienness, too. She answered, "How can I know? How does one find an answer to a counterfactual question?"

"Carefully," the wild Tosevite said. For a moment, Kassquit thought he hadn't understood. Then she realized he was making a joke. She let her mouth drop open for a moment to show she'd got it. He went on, "Everyone's life is full of counterfactuals. Suppose I this had done. Suppose I that had not done. What would I be now? Dealing with the things that are real is hard enough."

That was also a truth. Kassquit made the affirmative gesture. She said, "I am told you do not know what has happened to your mate and your hatchlings. I hope they are well."

"I thank you," Johannes Drucker answered. "I wish I knew, one way or the other. Then I would also how to go ahead know. Now I can only at the same time hope and worry."

"What will you do if they are dead?" Kassquit asked. Not until the question was out did she think to wonder whether she should have asked it. By then, of course, it was too late.

Though still imperfectly familiar with the facial expressions wild Big Uglies used, she was sure Johannes Drucker's did not show delight. He said, "The only thing I can do then is try to put my life back together one piece at a time. It is not easy, but it happens all the time. It is certainly all the time in the *Reich* happening now."

"Males and females of the Race are also having to rebuild their lives," Kassquit pointed out. "And the Race did not start this war. The *Reich* did."

"No matter who started it, it is over now," the wild Big Ugly said. "The Race won. The *Reich* lost. Putting the pieces back together is always easier for the winners."

Was that a truth or only an opinion? Since Kassquit wasn't sure, she didn't challenge it. She asked, "If your mate is dead, will you seek another one?"

"You have all sorts of awkward questions, is it not so?" Johannes Drucker laughed a loud Tosevite laugh, but still did not seem amused. Kassquit did not think he would answer, but he did: "I cannot tell you that now. It depends on how I feel, and it also depends on whether I meet a female I find interesting."

"And what makes a female interesting?" Kassquit asked.

The wild Big Ugly laughed again. "Not only awkward questions, but questions different from the ones the males of the Race, the military males, have asked. What makes a female interesting? Ask a thousand male Tosevites and you will have a thousand answers. Maybe two thousand."

"I did not ask a thousand male Tosevites. I asked you," Kassquit said.

"So you did." Instead of mocking her, Johannes Drucker paused and thought. "What makes a female interesting? Partly the way she looks, partly the way she acts. And part of it, of course, depends on whether she me interesting finds, too. Sometimes a male will find a female interesting, but not the other way round. And sometimes a female will want a male who does not want her."

"I think the Race's mating season is a much tidier, much less stressful way of handling reproduction," Kassquit said.

"I am sure it is—for the Race," the wild Big Ugly said. "But it is not how Tosevites do things. We can only what we are be."

Confronting her own differences from the Race, Kassquit had seen that, too. Culture went a long way toward minimizing those differences, but could not delete them. She wondered whether to ask Johannes Drucker if he found her attractive, and whether to use an affirmative answer, if she got one, to initiate mating. In the end, she decided not to ask. None of his words showed he might be interested. Neither did his reproductive organ, which was liable to be a more accurate—or at least less deceitful—indicator. As she left the compartment, she wondered if her decision would please Jonathan Yeager.

He was quiet when she returned to the compartment. He did not ask her whether she'd mated with the Deutsch captive. It was as if he did not want to know. He did not have much to say about anything else, either. Kassquit didn't care for that. She'd grown used to talking with the wild—but not too wild—Tosevite about almost everything. She felt empty, alone, when he responded so little.

At last, she decided to confront things directly. "I did not mate with Johannes Drucker," she said.

"All right," Jonathan Yeager answered, still not showing much animation. But then he asked, "Why not?"

"He did not show much interest," Kassquit replied, "and I did not want to make you unhappy."

"I thank you for that," he said. "I thank you for thinking of me." He hesitated, then went on, "You ought to think of yourself, too, you know."

Kassquit had thought of herself—as a member of the Race, or as close an approximation to a member of the Race as she could be. She'd given little thought to herself as an individual. She hadn't been encouraged to give much thought to herself as an individual. She said, "Does it not seem that wild Tosevites—especially wild American Tosevites—concern themselves too much with their individual concerns and not enough with the concerns of their society?"

He shrugged. "I do not know anything about that. But if the individuals are happy, how can the society be unhappy?"

Big Uglies had a knack for turning things on their head. The Race always thought of society first: if society was well ordered, then individuals would be happy. To look at individuals first . . . was probably the mark of American Tosevites, with their mania for snoutcounting. "Do you know that you are subversive?" she asked Jonathan Yeager.

When his eyes narrowed and the corners of his mouth turned up, she responded to his amusement, even if she couldn't duplicate the expression. *Genetic programming,* she thought. It couldn't be anything else.

He said, "I hope so. As far as we Tosevites are concerned, a lot about the Race could use subverting."

Had he said that when he first came up to the starship, she would have been furious. But now she had seen that he had his own way of looking at things, different from hers. From his sense of perspective, she was beginning to get one of her own. She said, "Well, you are halfway to subverting me." They both laughed.

As a senior researcher, Ttomalss stayed busy on a wide variety of projects, some his own, others assigned him by his superiors. Staying busy was what he got for being an expert on the Big Uglies. Of course, his research on Kassquit remained an important part of his work. Now that she was an adult, though, he did not have to give her constant attention, as he had when she was a hatchling.

He still recorded everything that went on in her compartment. He would do that as long as she lived (unless she chanced to outlive him, in which case whoever succeeded him would continue the recording). She was far too valuable a specimen to let any data go to waste. Even if Ttomalss couldn't evaluate all of it, some other analyst would in years or generations to come. The Race would be a long time figuring out what made the Tosevites respond as they did.

Because he had been involved in her life so long and so closely, Ttomalss still evaluated as much of the raw data as he could. Kassquit's interactions with Jonathan Yeager had taught him as much about the Big Uglies' sexual dynamics as he'd learned anywhere else. Those interactions had also taught him a great deal about the limits of cultural indoctrination for Tosevites.

"Well, you are halfway to subverting me," Kassquit had told the wild Big Ugly a couple of days before Ttomalss reviewed the audio and video. Both Tosevites had used their barking laughter, so Ttomalss presumed she was making a joke.

Hearing it hurt even so, because he feared truth lay beneath it. *You cannot hatch a beffel out of a tsiongi's egg* was a proverb older than the unification of Home. He'd done his best with Kassquit, and had improved his chances of turning her into something close to a female of the Race by not allowing her any contact with wild Big Uglies till she was an adult.

As he pondered, the recording kept playing in his monitor. Before long, Kassquit and Jonathan Yeager were mating. Watching them, Ttomalss let out a small, irritated hiss. He'd known how corrosive a force Tosevite sexuality was. Now he was seeing it again.

He moved the recording back to Kassquit's telling Jonathan Yeager she had not mated with the other Big Ugly aboard the starship. Ttomalss had wondered whether she would; he'd made a point of not mentioning the subject so he could avoid influencing her actions. Since she'd become acquainted with the pleasures of mating, he had rather expected that she would indulge herself. But no.

"Pair bonding," he said, and his computer recorded the words. "Because Kassquit is presently satisfied with Jonathan Yeager as a sexual partner, she seeks no other. These bonds of sexual attraction, and the bonds of kinship that spring from them, create the passionate attachments so characteristic of Big Uglies—and so dangerous to the Race."

The trouble is, he thought, *that Big Uglies calculate less than we do. If they are outraged because of harm that has come to individuals for whom they have conceived one of these passionate attachments, they will seek revenge without regard for their own safety. Preventing damage from Big Uglies willing, even eager, to die if they can also hurt us is very difficult.*

Ttomalss wondered if that hadn't been the motivation behind the *Reich's* attack on the Race. More than any of the Big Uglies' other independent not-empires, the Greater German *Reich* struck him as a Tosevite family writ large. The not-emperors of the *Reich* had always stressed the ties of kinship existing among their males and females. They had also stressed the innate superiority of the Deutsche over all other varieties of Tosevites. Ttomalss, like other researchers from the Race—and like non-Deutsch Big Uglies—was convinced that was drivel, but the Deutsche really believed it.

And, believing in their own superiority, believing in the wisdom of their not-emperors because those leaders were perceived as kin, the Deutsche had charged off to war against the Race without so much as a second thought. Ttomalss wondered if they—the survivors, a decided minority—still relied so blindly on the wisdom of those leaders.

But he did not have to wonder, not with a Deutsch Tosevite aboard this very starship. He paid another visit to the compartment where Johannes Drucker was housed. The Big Ugly who had almost destroyed the ship saluted him and said, "I greet you, superior sir." He did not make a difficult captive, much to the relief of every male and female of the Race aboard the starship.

"And I greet you," Ttomalss said. "Tell me, how do you feel about the leaders of your not-empire who took you into a losing war?"

"I always thought anyone who wanted the Race to attack was a fool," the Big Ugly replied at once, his syntax strange but understandable. "I have in space been, after all. I know, and always did know, the Race is stronger than the *Reich*. I blame my leaders for their ignorance."

That was a sensible answer; a member of the Race might have said much the same thing. "If you believed them to be fools," Ttomalss asked, "why did you and the other Deutsche obey them without question?"

"I do not know," Johannes Drucker said. "Why did the males of your conquest fleet, when they saw Tosev 3 was so different from what they had expected, keep on saying, 'It shall be done,' to your leaders, even after those leaders ordered them to do many foolish things?"

"That is different," Ttomalss said testily.

"How, superior sir?" the Deutsch male asked.

"The answer should be obvious," Ttomalss said, and changed the subject: "What will you and your fellow Deutsche do if your new not-emperor tries to lead you into further misadventures?"

"I do not believe he will," Johannes Drucker said. "I have known him for some time. He is an able, sensible male."

Ttomalss doubted Drucker's objectivity. In any case, the Big Ugly had been too literal-minded to suit him. "Let me rephrase that," the psychological researcher said. "What will you Deutsche do if some future leader seeks to lead you into misadventures?"

"I do not know," Johannes Drucker answered. "How can I know, until a thing happens?"

Seeing he wasn't going to get anywhere on that line of questioning, Ttomalss tried another: "What do you think of the female, Kassquit?"

Johannes Drucker let out several yips of Tosevite laughter. "I never expected a female Tosevite aboard your starship to meet, especially one without any . . . wrappings?" He had to cast about to find the term the Race used. "It made life here more entertaining than I thought it would be."

"Entertaining." That was hardly the word Ttomalss would have used. "Did you find yourself interested in mating with her?"

The Big Ugly shook his head, then used the Race's negative hand gesture. "For one thing, I hope my own mate is still alive down in the *Reich*. For another, I did not think Kassquit was interested in mating with me." Ttomalss wasn't so sure Johannes Drucker was right about that, but gave no sign of what he thought. The Tosevite continued, "And I did not her attractive find, or not very. I like females with"—he gestured to show he meant hair—"and with faces that move more."

"Kassquit cannot help the way her face behaves," Ttomalss said. "That seems to happen when the Race raises Tosevites from hatchlinghood."

"You have it with others tried?" Drucker sounded accusing. Ttomalss hoped he was misreading the Big Ugly, but didn't think so. Before he could answer, Drucker added, "I suppose it is a wonder that she is not more nearly insane than she is in fact."

In a way, that casual comment infuriated Ttomalss. In another way, he understood it. Judged by Tosevite standards, he couldn't have done a perfect job of raising Kassquit, despite his years of effort. He said, "She is satisfied with her life here."

"But naturally. She knows no other," Johannes Drucker said.

"If she did know another life, it would be as a Chinese peasant," Ttomalss said. "Do you think that would be preferable to what she has now?"

Johannes Drucker started to say something, then hesitated. At last, he answered, "I asked her this myself. She could not judge. I do not find it easy to decide, either. If you raise an animal in a laboratory, is that preferable to the life the animal would in the wild have led? The animal may live longer and be better fed, but it is not free."

"You Big Uglies value freedom more than the Race does," Ttomalss said.

"That is because we more of it have known," the Big Ugly said. "Your males of the conquest fleet have seen far more freedom than the males and females of the colonization fleet. Do they not prefer it more, too?"

"How could you know that?" Ttomalss asked in surprise.

With another loud, barking laugh, Drucker answered, "I listen to the conversations you of the Race among yourselves have.

Radio intercepts are an important part of the business. You, now, you know us Tosevites pretty well, so I would guess you are from the conquest fleet. Is that a truth, or not a truth?"

"It is a truth," Ttomalss admitted.

"I thought so," the Deutsch Tosevite said. "You have a good-sized piece of your life here spent. It is natural that we have changed because the Race came to Tosev 3. Is it so surprising that coming to Tosev 3 has changed the Race, too?"

"Surprising? Yes, it is surprising," Ttomalss answered. "The Race does not change easily. The Race has never changed easily. We changed very little when we conquered the Rabotevs and the Hallessi."

"Were those conquests easy or difficult?" Johannes Drucker asked.

"Easy. Much, much easier than the conquest of Tosev 3."

The Big Ugly nodded again, then remembered the Race's affirmative gesture. "You did not need to learn anything from them. When fighting against us, you have had no choice." He paused. His face assumed an expression even Ttomalss, with his experience in reading Tosevite physiognomy, had trouble interpreting. Was it amusement? The look of a Big Ugly with a secret? Contempt? He couldn't tell. Johannes Drucker went on, "You may end up finding that freedom causes you even more trouble than ginger."

"I doubt that would be possible," Ttomalss said tartly. Johannes Drucker laughed yet again. *Ignorant Big Ugly,* Ttomalss thought. Aloud, he continued, "Anyone would think you were a Tosevite from the snoutcounting not-empire of the United States, not from the *Reich*, where your not-emperor has more power than the true Emperor." He cast down his eye turrets at the mention of his revered sovereign.

"We still have more freedom than you do," the Deutsch Tosevite insisted.

"Nonsense," Ttomalss said. "Think of what your not-empire does to those of the Jewish superstition. How can you claim you are more free? We do not do anything like that to members of the Race."

That hit home on Johannes Drucker harder than Ttomalss had expected. The Big Ugly turned a darker shade of pinkish beige and looked down at the metal floor of the compartment: not in reverence, Ttomalss judged, but in embarrassment. Still not looking at Ttomalss, Drucker mumbled, "The rest of us have more freedom."

"How can you say that?" Ttomalss asked. "How can any be free when some are not free?"

"How can you say you are free when you tried to conquer our whole world and enslave us?" the Tosevite returned.

"It is not the same," Ttomalss said. "After the conquest is complete, Tosevites will have the same rights as all other citizens of the Empire, regardless of species."

"Whether we wanted to join the Empire or not? Where is the freedom in that?"

"You do not understand. You willfully refuse to understand," Ttomalss said, and gave up on his interview with the obstreperous Big Ugly.

Sam Yeager called out to his wife: "Hey, hon, c'mere. We've got an electronic message from Jonathan."

"What has he got to say for himself this time?" Barbara asked, but she was waving a hand when she hurried into the study. "No, don't tell me—let me read it for myself." She adjusted her bifocals on her nose so she could more readily see the screen. "He'll be home pretty soon, will he?" She let out a long sigh of relief. "Well, thank heaven for that."

"You said it," Sam agreed. He'd been sighing with relief every day since the Germans surrendered. He hadn't thought the Nazis would start their war against the Lizards. He knew the *Reich* was fighting out of its weight against the Race, and so he assumed the Nazi bigwigs knew the same thing. That hadn't proved such a good assumption. Jonathan had been up in space when the war started. If a German missile had hit his starship . . .

Barbara said, "I don't know how we could have gone on if anything had happened to Jonathan."

"I didn't think anything would," Sam answered. If anything had happened to his only son after he'd encouraged Jonathan to go into space, he didn't know how he'd be able to go on living with Barbara, either. For that matter, he didn't know how he'd be able to go on living with himself. "It's all right now, anyhow." He said that as much to convince himself as to remind his wife.

And Barbara did something she'd never done in all the weeks since the war between the *Reich* and the Race broke out and endangered their son: she put a hand on Sam's shoulder and said, "Yes, I guess it is."

He leaned back in his swivel chair and reached up to set his hand on hers. If she was going to forgive him, he'd make the most of it. "I love you, hon," he said. "Looks as if we're together for the long haul after all."

That *as if* was a tribute to the long haul they'd already put in. Barbara had done graduate work in Middle English before the fighting, and was as precise a grammarian as any schoolmarm ever born. And, over more than twenty years, her precision had rubbed off on Sam. He wondered if they did have as long a haul ahead as behind. He'd just turned fifty-eight. Would they still be married when he was eighty? Would he still be around when he was eighty? He had his hopes.

"So it does." She smiled down at him as he was grinning up at her. "I like the idea," she said.

"You'd better, by now," he said, which made her smile broader. But his own grin slipped. "On the other hand, you know, I'm liable to softly and suddenly vanish away, because the Snark I found damn well is a Boojum."

He spoke elliptically. Whenever he spoke of what he'd found with the help of some computer coding from a Lizard expatriate named Sorviss, he spoke elliptically. He didn't know who might be listening. He didn't know how much good speaking elliptically would do him, either.

Barbara said, "They wouldn't," but her voice lacked conviction.

Sam said, "They might. We know too well, they might. If they do, though, they'll be sorry, because if anything happens to me the word will get out one way or another." He chuckled. "Of course, that might be too late to do me a whole lot of good. The story of Samson in the temple never was my favorite, but it's the best hope I have these days."

"That we should need such things," Barbara said, and shook her head.

"I just wish you hadn't squeezed it out of me," Yeager said. "Now you're liable to be in danger, too, on account of it."

"Think of me as one of your life-insurance policies," Barbara said. "That's what I am, because I'll start shouting from the housetops if anything happens to you. That's the best way I know of to get you out of a jam, if you should get into one. They can't stand the light of day—or maybe I should say, the light of publicity."

"That's true enough," Sam agreed. And so it was . . . to a point. If he and Barbara both softly and suddenly vanished away, she wouldn't have the chance to start shouting from the house-tops. Presumably, those who might be interested in silence could figure that out, too. Yeager didn't mention it to his wife. Any-body could foul up; he'd seen that. A foul-up on the other side's part could well give her the chance to play the role she'd talked about. He said, "We're liable to be worrying over nothing. I hope we are. I'm even starting to think we are. If they'd found out where I've been, I'd think they would have dropped on me by now."

"Probably." Barbara looked poised to say something else on the same subject, but a crash from the kitchen distracted her. "Oh, God!" she exclaimed. "What have those two gone and done now?" She hurried away to find out.

"Something where we'll need to sweep up the pieces," Sam answered, not that that counted for much in the way of prophecy. He got up from his chair and followed Barbara.

He was in the living room, halfway between the study and the kitchen, when he heard a door slam in the back part of the house. He started to laugh. So did Barbara, though he wasn't sure she was actually amused. "Those little scamps," she said. "There they'll be, pretending as hard as they can that they're innocent."

"They're learning," Yeager said. "Any kid will do that kind of thing, till his folks put a stop to it. And we're the only folks Mickey and Donald have."

The shattered remains of what had been a serving bowl lay all over the linoleum of the kitchen floor. Barbara clucked in dismay at the size of the mess. Then she clucked again. "That bowl was in the dish drainer," she said. "They're growing like weeds, but I don't think they're big enough to reach it, not since I shoved it back sideways against the wall there."

Sam examined the scene of the crime. "No chair pushed up against the counter," he said musingly. "I wonder if one of them stood on the other one's back. That would be interesting—it would show they're really starting to cooperate with each other."

"Now if only they'd start cooperating to clean up the messes they make. But that would be too much to ask for, wouldn't it?" Barbara rolled her eyes. "Sometimes it's too much to ask for from Jonathan, or even from someone else I might mention."

"I haven't got the faintest idea who—whom—you're talking about," Sam said. Barbara rolled her eyes again, more extravagantly than before. But when she started for the broom closet, Sam shook his head. "That'll wait for a couple of minutes, hon. We can't let Mickey and Donald think they got away with it, or else they'll try the same thing again tomorrow."

"You're right," Barbara said. "If we read them the riot act, they may wait till day after tomorrow—if we're lucky, they may." Sam laughed, though he knew perfectly well she hadn't been kidding.

Side by side, they walked to the bedroom the two Lizard hatchlings they were raising called their own. Up till a few months before, the door to that bedroom had been latched on the outside almost all the time: the baby Lizards, essentially little wild animals, would have torn up the house without even knowing what they were doing. *Now they know some of what they're doing, and they still tear up the house,* Sam thought. *Is that an improvement?*

He opened the door. Mickey and Donald stood against the far wall. If they could have disappeared altogether, they looked as if they would have done it. Even Donald, bigger and more rambunctious than his (her?) brother (sister?), seemed abashed, which didn't happen very often.

Yeager held up a piece of the broken bowl. By the way the hatchlings cringed, he might have been showing a couple of vampires a crucifix. "No, no!" he said in a loud, ostentatiously angry voice. "Don't play with dishes! Are you ever going to play with dishes again?"

Both baby Lizards shook their heads. They'd learned the gesture from Barbara and Jonathan and him; they didn't know the one the Race used. Neither one of them said anything. They didn't talk much, though they understood a startling amount. Human babies picked up language much faster. The Lizards would have been amazed that the hatchlings were talking at all. Yeager chuckled under his breath. *Barbara and I, we're bad influences,* he thought.

Though behind in language, Mickey and Donald were miles ahead of human toddlers in every aspect of physical development. They'd hatched able to run around and catch food for themselves, and they'd grown like weeds since: evolution making sure not so many things were able to catch them. They were already well on their way toward their full adult size.

Sam remained a towering figure, though, and used his height and deep, booming voice to good advantage. "You'd better not go messing with Mommy Barbara's china," he roared, "or you'll be in big, big trouble. Have you got that?" The young Lizards nodded. They had a pretty good notion of what trouble meant, or at least that it was a good thing to avoid. Yeager nodded at them. "All right, then," he said. "You behave yourselves, you hear?"

Mickey and Donald both nodded some more. Satisfied he'd put the fear of God in them—at least till the next time—Sam let it go at that. He didn't spank them save as a very last resort. He hadn't spanked Jonathan much, either . . . and Jonathan hadn't had such formidable teeth with which to defend himself.

"Maybe the Lizards have the right idea about bringing up their babies," Barbara said as she and Sam went up the hall.

"What? Except for making sure they don't kill themselves or one another, leaving them pretty much alone till they're three or four years old?" Sam said. "It'd be less work, yeah, but we've got a big head start on civilizing them."

"We've got a big head start on exhaustion, is what we've got," Barbara said. "We were a lot younger when we did this with Jonathan, and there was only one of him, and he's human."

"Pretty much so," Sam agreed, and his wife snorted. He went on, "The one I take off my hat to is the Lizard who raised Kassquit. He had to be mommy and daddy both, give her attention all the time, clean up her messes—for years. That's dedication to your research."

"It wasn't fair to her, though," Barbara said. "You've talked a lot about how strange she is."

"Well, she is strange," Yeager said, "and no two ways about it. But I don't think she's nearly as strange as she might have been, if you know what I mean. In the scheme of things, she might have been a lot squirrellier than just wishing she were a Lizard. And"—he lowered his voice; his own conscience was far from clear—"God only knows we're going to raise a couple of squirrelly hatchlings."

"We'll learn from them." Barbara had a lot of pure scholar left in her.

"The Lizards have learned a lot from Kassquit," Sam answered. "I wonder if she thanks them for it." But he didn't wonder. He knew she did. If Mickey and Donald ended up thanking him, maybe he'd be able to look at himself in a mirror. Maybe.

☆ 2 ☆

When Monique Dutourd had fled down into the bomb shelter below her brother's flat, Marseille, like all of France, had belonged to the Greater German *Reich*. She and Pierre and his lover, Lucie, and everyone else in the shelter had had to dig their way out, too, when they ran low on food and water.

She wished they'd been able to stay longer. She might have avoided the bout of nausea and vomiting that had wracked her. But she was better now, and her hair hadn't fallen out, as had happened to so many who'd been closer to the bomb the Lizards dropped on her city. Of course, tens of thousands who'd been closer still were no longer among the living.

But those who survived were once more citizens of the *République Française*. Monique had been a girl when France surrendered to Germany, and only a couple of years older than that when the Lizards drove the Nazis and their puppets in Vichy away from Marseille. But when the fighting ended, France had returned to German hands, and the Germans hadn't bothered with ruling through puppets in the south any more.

Now Monique could walk through the outskirts of Marseille without worrying about SS men. If that wasn't a gift from God, she didn't know what was. She could even think about looking for a university position in Roman history again, and if she got one she would be able to say whatever she pleased about the Germanic invaders who'd helped bring down the Roman Empire.

"Hello, sweetheart!" A man waved to her from behind the table on which he'd set up his wares. "Interested in anything I've got?"

He looked to be selling military gear the Germans who'd survived the explosive-metal bombing of Marseille had left behind when they'd been required to make their way back to the *Reich*.

32

By the way he tugged at his ratty trousers, that junk might not have been what he'd been trying to interest her in.

Since she wanted no more of him than she did of his junk, she stuck her nose in the air and kept walking. He laughed, not a bit abashed, and asked the next woman he saw the same not quite lewd question.

As Monique drew closer to the region the bomb had wrecked, she saw an enormous banner: DOWN BUT NOT OUT. She smiled, liking that. France had been down a long time—longer than ever before in her history, perhaps—but she was on her feet again now, even if shakily.

A lot of Lizards were on the streets of Marseille—the streets on the fringes of town, the streets that hadn't been melted to slag by a temperature on the same order as those found in the sun. Returned French independence was one of the prices the Lizards had extracted from the Nazis in exchange for accepting their surrender. Monique hoped it wasn't the only, or even the largest, price the Race had extracted from the *Reich*.

Back when Marseille belonged to the Germans, a lot of the Lizards who visited the city had been furtive characters. They'd come to buy ginger and often to sell drugs humans found entertaining. Monique had no doubt a lot of them were still here for those purposes. But they didn't have to be furtive any more. Nowadays, they were the ones who propped up French independence. What policeman would want to give them any trouble?

Even more to the point, what policeman would have the nerve to give them trouble? They didn't occupy France, as the Germans had. They didn't carry away everything movable, as the *doryphores*—Colorado beetles—in field-gray had. But France wasn't strong enough to stand on her own even against the battered, enfeebled, radioactive *Reich*. So the Lizards had to prop up the new Fourth Republic. And, of course, they had to be listened to. Of course.

Monique turned a corner and found what she was looking for: a little square where farmers down from the hills around town sold their cheeses and vegetables and smoked and salted meats to the survivors of the bombing for the most bloodthirsty prices they could extort. "How much for your *haricots verts*?" she asked a peasant with a battered cloth cap on his head, stubble on his cheeks and chin, and a cigarette hanging from the corner of his mouth.

"Fifty Reichsmarks a kilo," he answered, and paused to look her up and down. He grinned, not very pleasantly. "Or a blow job, if you'd rather."

"For green beans? That's outrageous," Monique said.

"I have ham, too," the farmer said. "If you want to blow me for ham, we can work something out, I expect."

"No, your price in money," Monique said impatiently. She didn't have to give this bastard anything she didn't want to; he wasn't an SS man. "I'll pay you thirty Reichsmarks a kilo." German money was the only kind in circulation; new francs were promised, but had yet to appear.

"Fifty, take it or leave it." The farmer didn't sound put out that she'd failed to fall to her knees. But he went on, "For once in my life, I don't have to haggle. If you won't pay me what I want, somebody else will—and you won't get a better price from anyone else around."

He was almost certainly right. "When the roads and railroads get fixed, you'll sing a different tune," Monique said.

"All the better reason to get what I can now," he answered. "Do you want these beans, or don't you? Like I say, if you don't, somebody will."

"Give me two kilos." Monique had the money. Her brother Pierre had more money than he knew what to do with, even at the obscene prices for which things were selling nowadays. The Lizards had bought a lot of ginger from him over the years, and Germans and Frenchmen had bought a lot of goods he'd got from the Lizards.

After Monique paid the peasant, she held out her stringbag—a universal French shopping tool—and he poured *haricots verts* into it. When he stopped, she hefted the sack and glared at him. Grudgingly, he doled out a few more beans. Getting cheated on price was one thing. Getting cheated on weight was something else. Hefting the stringbag again, Monique supposed he'd come close to giving her the proper amount.

She bought potatoes from another farmer, one who refrained from offering to take his price in venery. Of course, his wife, a woman of formidable proportions, was standing beside him, which probably had something to do with his restraint. Then Monique headed back to the vast tent city outside of town that housed the many survivors who'd come through even when their homes hadn't.

The tent city smelled like a barnyard. She supposed that was inevitable, since it had no running water. The Romans, no doubt, would have taken such odors as an inevitable part of urban life. Monique didn't, couldn't. She wished her nose would go to sleep whenever she had to come back.

A boy who couldn't have been older than eight tried to steal her vegetables. She walloped him on the bottom, hard enough to send him off yowling. If he'd asked her for some, she probably would have given them to him. But she wouldn't put up with thieves, not even thieves in short pants.

As she'd had to share a flat with her brother and his lover, now she had to share a tent with them. When she ducked inside, she discovered they had company: a Lizard with impressively fancy body paint. He jerked in alarm when she came through the tent flap.

Lucie spoke reassuringly in the Lizards' language. Monique didn't speak it, but caught the tone. She wondered if it worked as well on the Lizard as it would have on a human male. Lucie wasn't much to look at, being pudgy and plain, but she had the sexiest voice Monique had ever heard.

Pierre Dutourd was also pudgy and plain, so they made a good pair, or at least a well-matched one. He was ten years older than Monique, and the difference looked even wider than it was. "How did you do?"

She hefted the stringbag. "Everything is too expensive," she answered, "but the *haricots verts* and the potatoes looked pretty good, so I got them."

"Excuse me," the Lizard said in hissing French. "Is it that these foods were grown in the local soil?"

"But of course," Monique answered. "Why?"

"Because, in that case, they are liable to be in some measure radioactive," the Lizard replied. "Your health would be better if you did not eat them."

"They are the only food we can get," Monique said, acid in her voice. "Would our health be better if we starved to death?"

"Well, no," the Lizard admitted. "But why can you not get more healthful alimentation?"

"Why?" Monique wanted to hit him over the head with the stringbag. "Because the Race has dropped explosive-metal bombs all over France, that's why." She turned to Pierre. "Do you always deal with idiots?"

"Keffesh isn't an idiot," her brother answered, and patted the

Lizard on the shoulder. "He's just new in Marseille, and doesn't understand the way things here are right now. He's been buying and selling down in the South Pacific, till the war disrupted things."

"Well, he ought to think a little before he talks," Monique snapped.

"Who is this bad-tempered person?" the Lizard named Keffesh asked Pierre.

"My sister," he answered. "She is bad-tempered, I agree, but she will not betray you. You may rely on that."

By the way Keffesh's eye turrets swung back and forth, he didn't want to rely on anything. He stuck out his tongue at Pierre, as a human being might have pointed with an index finger. "It could be," he said. Now that he'd started speaking French, he seemed content to stick with it. "But may I rely on you? If you cannot bring in food and have to eat supplies that are possibly contaminated, how is it that you will be able to bring in supplies of the herb my kind craves so much?"

Lucie laughed. Monique didn't know what, if anything, that did to Keffesh; it certainly would have got any human male's complete and undivided attention. Lucie said, "That is very simple. There is little profit in food. There is great profit in ginger. Of course ginger will move where food would not."

"Ah," Keffesh said. "Yes, that is sensible. Very well, then."

Monique shook her head and set down the sack of vegetables. She had no doubt Lucie was right. What did that say about the way things worked in the world? That the coming of the Lizards hadn't changed things much? Of all the conclusions she contemplated, that was odds-on the most depressing.

Rance Auerbach contemplated another perfect Tahitian day. It was warm, a little humid, with clouds rolling across the blue sky. He could look out the window of the apartment he shared with Penny Summers and see the even bluer South Pacific. He turned away from the lovely spectacle and lit a cigarette. Smoking made him cough, which hurt. He'd lost most of a lung and taken other damage from a Lizard bullet during the fighting. Doctors told him he was cutting years off his life by not quitting. *Too goddamn bad,* he thought, and took another drag.

He limped into the kitchen and got himself a beer. "Let me have one of those, too, will you?" Penny called from the bedroom when she heard him open it.

"Okay." His voice was a ruined rasp. He popped the top off another beer. Walking back to give it to her hurt, too. Another bullet from the same burst of fire had left him with a shattered leg. "Here you go, babe."

"Thanks," she told him. She was also smoking a cigarette, in quick, nervous puffs. She grabbed the beer and raised it high. "Here's to crime."

He drank—he would have drunk to anything—but he laughed, too. "Didn't know there was any such thing in Free France."

"Ha," she said, and brushed a lock of dyed blond hair back off her cheek. She was in her early forties, a few years younger than Rance, and could pass for younger still because of the energy she showed. "Now, the next interesting question is, how much longer will there be a Free France now that there's a real France again?"

"You expect the froggies to sail out here with gunboats and take over?" After a long sentence, Rance had to pause and suck in air. "I don't think that's awful goddamn likely."

"Gunboats? No, neither do I. But airplanes full of clerks and cops?" Penny grimaced. "I wouldn't be half surprised. And they're liable to kill the goose that laid the golden egg if they do."

As far as power went, Free France was a joke. It couldn't hold out for twenty minutes if the Empire of Japan or the USA or the Race decided to invade it. But none of them had, because a place under nobody's thumb, where people and Lizards could make deals without anybody looking over their shoulders, was too useful to all concerned. How would that look, though, to a pack of functionaries back in Paris?

Not good. "We came here to get out from under," Rance said in his Texas drawl. "What do we do if that doesn't work?"

"Go somewheres else," Penny answered at once. Her Kansas accent was as harsh as his was soft. "I'm thinkin' about it. How about you?"

"Yeah." He was surprised at how readily he admitted it. Tahiti, with no laws to speak of, with shameless native girls who didn't bother covering their tits half the time, had been awfully attractive—till he got here. One thing nobody mentioned about the native girls was how often they had hulking, bad-tempered native boyfriends. And, with no law to speak of, he often felt like a sardine in a tank full of sharks. "Where have you got in mind?"

"Well, like you said, if the froggies get their hands on this place, they'll squeeze it till its eyes pop," Penny said. "So what I was figuring was maybe going back to France. It's a lot bigger than Tahiti, you know? They won't have half the cops and things they need to keep an eye on everybody, on account of the Nazis have been doing so much of that for so long."

"If I had a hat, I'd take it off to you," Rance said. "That's one of the sneakiest things I ever heard in all my born days. Of course, there's a good deal *to* France, if you know what I mean. You have any place in particular in mind, or just sort of all over the country?"

"How's Marseille sound to you?" Penny asked.

Auerbach made motions of tipping the hat he wasn't wearing and sticking it back on his head. "Are you out of your ever-loving mind?" he demanded. "Do you remember what happened to us the last time we were in Marseille? The Germans almost gave us a blindfold and a cigarette and lined us up against the wall and shot us."

"That's right," Penny said placidly. "So what?"

"So what?" Rance would have screamed, but he didn't have the lungs for it. Perhaps because he couldn't make a lot of noise, he had to think before saying anything else. After thinking, he felt foolish. "Oh," he said. "No more Nazis, right?"

Penny grinned at him. "Bingo. See? You're not so dumb after all."

"Maybe not. But maybe I am. And maybe you are, too," Rance said. "Didn't Marseille have an explosive-metal bomb land on its head?"

"Yeah, I think it did," Penny answered. "But so what again? Some of the ginger dealers'll still be around. And if the place got shaken up good, that gives us a better chance to set up shop there."

Rance thought about it. At first, it sounded pretty crazy. Then he liked the idea. After that, though, he hesitated again. "Going to be plenty of Lizards in Marseille, or in whatever's left of it," he remarked.

"I hope so," Penny exclaimed. "You think I want to sell all the ginger we've got to a bunch of cooks in a restaurant?"

But Rance was shaking his head. "That's not what I meant. You wait and see—there'll be lots of Lizards all over France, pretending they're not telling the Frenchmen what to do. If they weren't there, how long would it be before the Nazis were telling the Frenchmen what to do again?"

"Oh." Now Penny saw what he was driving at.

"That's right," Auerbach said. "If there are official-type Lizards all over France—and you can bet your bottom dollar there will be—they aren't going to be real happy with us. Go ahead—tell me I'm wrong."

Penny looked glum. "Can't do it, goddammit."

"Good." Rance knew he had relief in his voice. The Lizards had arrested both of them in Mexico for selling ginger, and tried to use them in Marseille to trap a smuggler (Rance still thought of him as Pierre the Turd, though he knew that couldn't possibly have been the guy's right name). The Germans had fouled that up, but the Race had been grateful enough to set Rance and Penny up in South Africa—where they'd gone into the ginger business again, and barely managed to escape a three-cornered firefight with enough gold to come to Tahiti.

But Penny still looked discontented. "We can't stay here forever, either, even if the real French don't clamp down on the Free French. We aren't doing enough business; we're too small. And everything is expensive as hell."

"Do you want to try going back to the States?" Auerbach asked. "We haven't done anything illegal there. American law doesn't care about ginger one way or the other."

"If we went home, I wouldn't be worrying about the law," Penny said.

Rance could only nod about that. She'd come back into his life, years after they broke up, because she was on the run from ginger-smuggling associates she'd stiffed; they hadn't been happy with her for keeping the fee she got from the Lizards instead of turning it over to them. And they weren't happy with Rance, either: he'd killed a couple of their hired thugs who'd come to his apartment to take the price for that ginger out of Penny's hide.

He sighed, which made him cough, which made him wince, which made him take another swig of beer to try to put out the fire inside him. It didn't work. It never worked. But he drank an awful lot, as he had ever since he was wounded. Enough hooch and he didn't feel things so much.

Penny said, "If we can't stay here and we can't go to France and we can't go to the States, what the hell can we do?"

"We can stay here quite a while, if we sit tight," Auerbach answered. "We can go back to the States, too, and not have anybody notice us—if we sit tight."

"I don't *want* to sit tight." Penny paced around the bedroom. She paused only to light another cigarette, which she started smoking even more savagely than she had the first one. "All the time I lived in Kansas, I spent sitting tight. That was the only thing people knew how to do there. And I'll sit tight when I'm dead. In between the one and the other, I'm going to *live*, dammit."

"I might have known you were going to say that," Rance remarked. "Hell, I did know you were going to say it. But it doesn't help right now, you know?"

Penny set her hands on her hips and exhaled an angry cloud of smoke. "Okay, hotshot, you're so goddamn smart, you keep thinking up reasons why we can't do this, that, or the other thing—what do you figure we ought to do?"

"If I had my druthers, I'd go back to the States," Auerbach said slowly. "I've got a little pension waiting for me, and—"

Penny laughed a flaying, scornful laugh. "Oh, yeah. Hell of a life you were living back there. You just bet it was, Rance."

His ears heated. He'd had that miserable little apartment in Fort Worth, and he'd been drinking himself to death an inch at a time there. For excitement, he'd go down to the veterans' hall and play poker with the other fellows who'd been left wrecked but not quite dead. They'd all heard one another's stories endless times: often enough to keep a straight face while pretending to believe the juiciest parts of the lies the other fellows told.

If he went back, he'd fall into that same rut again. He knew it. That was how he'd lived for a long time. Life with Penny Summers was a great many things, but a rut never. A roller coaster, perhaps—Christ, a roller coaster certainly—but not a rut.

"Tahiti just won't be the same," he said mournfully. "No matter what happens, it won't be the same. And our gold won't stretch as far as we hoped it would." Down in Cape Town, he'd almost got killed on account of that gold. But it wasn't enough, no matter how much blood had been spilled over it.

"What does that leave, then?" Penny said. "England's too close to the Nazis to be comfortable, and the same people do business in Canada as in the USA."

He pointed an accusing finger at her. "I know what's up. You want to go back to France, and you don't give a good goddamn how stupid it is."

For once, he caught Penny without a snappy comeback, from which he concluded he was dead right. His girlfriend did laugh again, this time ruefully. "If you were younger and dumber, I'd take you to bed with me, and by the time I was through you'd swear going back there was your idea."

"If I was younger and dumber, I'd be a lot happier. Either that or dead, one." Rance drank the last beer in the bottle. "You want to take me to bed anyhow? Who knows how dumb I'll be afterwards?"

Penny reached up to the back of her neck and undid the halter top she was wearing. She pulled down her white linen shorts, kicked them off to one side, and stood there naked. Her body had yielded very little to time. "Why the hell not?" she said. "Come here, guy."

Afterwards, they lay side by side, sweaty and sated. Auerbach reached out with a lazy hand and tweaked her nipple. "What the hell," he said. "You talked me into it."

"How about that?" Penny answered. "And I didn't even have to say anything. I must not know what a persuasive gal I am."

That made Rance laugh. "Every woman ever born is persuasive that way, if she feels like using it. Of course"—he watched Penny cloud up, and hastened to amend his words—"some are more persuasive than others."

The clouds went away. Penny turned practical: "We shouldn't have much trouble getting into France, and our papers probably won't have to be too good. The Frenchies'll take a while to figure out what they're supposed to be doing. We should make quite a killing."

"Terrific," Rance said. "Once we do it, we can retire to Tahiti." Penny poked him in the ribs, and he supposed he deserved it.

Felless was perfectly happy to leave the eggs she'd laid—the second clutch from ginger-inspired matings—in the local hatching room. She hoped she would soon be able to leave the new town in the Arabian peninsula herself. As was her way, she made no secret of what she hoped.

One of the locals said, "You could have stayed in Marseille. That, at least, would have shut you up when a bomb burst there."

"Who addled your egg?" Felless retorted. "A bomb bursting here would have been the best thing that could happen to this place."

That made all the locals in the luggage shop where Felless was trying to find something she liked hiss with derision. She didn't care. As far as she was concerned, the new town was nothing but a small town back on Home dropped onto the surface of Tosev 3. Its males and females certainly struck her as provincial and clannish. They shouldn't have; they'd come from all over the homeworld of the Race. But only a few years on Tosev 3 had united them against the world outside the borders of their settlement.

One of them said, "You do not know what you are talking about. Several bombs have burst not far from here. My friend was right. One of those bombs should have burst on you." His tailstump quivered in fury.

His friend, a female, added, "Look at her body paint. She does research on the Big Uglies. That must mean she likes them. And if liking Big Uglies does not prove she is addled, what would?"

Males and females spoke up in loud agreement. Familiarity with the Tosevites had bred only contempt for them in Felless. To these members of the Race, though, she didn't want to admit that. She said, "They are here. There are more of them than we thought there would be, and they know more than we thought they would. We have to deal with them as they are, worse luck."

"We ought to get rid of all of them, as we got rid of the Deutsche," a male said. "Then we could make this world into something worth having."

"Not all the Deutsche are destroyed," Felless said. "And they got rid of too many of us. How long did you fear this town would be under attack from explosive-metal bombs, as your neighbors were?"

"If you like Big Uglies so much, you are welcome to them," a female said angrily.

There they were, again accusing Felless of something of which she was emphatically not guilty. With such dignity as she could muster, she said, "Since you will not listen to me, what point is there to my even talking to you?" Out she went, accompanied by the jeers of the locals.

The building in which she'd been housed was so overcrowded, it boasted only a few computer terminals rather than one for every male and female of the Race. She had to line up to get her own electronic messages and to send any to the rest of the Race on Tosev 3. And, having stood in line, she discovered that the messages waiting for her were not worth having.

She'd just turned away in disappointment when a ceiling-mounted loudspeaker called her name: "Senior Researcher Felless! Senior Researcher Felless! Report to the unit manager's office immediately!"

Fuming, Felless went. If one of the idiot locals had complained about her because of the argument, someone was going to hear about it. She had every intention of being loud and obnoxious in her rebuttal. When she buzzed the door, the manager opened it. "What now?" Felless snapped.

"Superior female, you have a telephone call here. The caller did not want to route it into the dormitory, but sent it here for the sake of privacy," the manager replied.

"Oh." Some of Felless' anger evaporated. Grudgingly, she said, "I thank you."

"Here is the telephone." The unit manager pointed. "I hope the news is good for you, superior female."

When Felless saw who waited for her on the screen, her eye turrets twitched in surprise. "Ambassador Veffani!" she exclaimed. "I greet you, superior sir. I had no idea you—" She broke off.

"Were not communing in person with the spirits of Emperors past?" Veffani suggested. "When the Race bombed Nuremberg, I thought I would be, but the shelter we built proved better than that of the Deutsch not-emperor. If you think this disappointed me, you are mistaken. Of course, we were also trying harder to dispose of him than of me—or I hope we were, at any rate."

"I am glad to see you well, superior sir," Felless said, though she would not have been too sad to learn Veffani had perished in the war. He was a strict male, and had punished her severely for using ginger. Still, hypocrisy lubricated the wheels of social interaction. "What are your present duties? Are you still ambassador to the *Reich*?"

Veffani made the negative hand gesture. "A military commissioner will deal with the Deutsche for the indefinite future. Since, however, I have considerable experience in the northwestern region of the main continental mass, I have been assigned as ambassador to the newly reconstituted not-empire of France."

"Congratulations, superior sir," Felless said with fulsome insincerity.

"I thank you. You are gracious." Veffani knew a good deal

about fulsome insincerity himself. He went on, "And, with your own experience in the *Reich* and in France, you would make a valuable addition to my team here. I have put in a requisition for your services, and it has been accepted."

Felless knew she should have been furious at such high-handed treatment. Somehow, she wasn't. If anything, she was relieved. "I thank you, superior sir," she said. "Doing something useful to the Race will be a relief, especially after confinement in this refugee center and among the provincials who make up the bulk of the local population."

"Do you know, Senior Researcher, I hoped you would say something like that," Veffani told her. "You are a talented female. You have done good work. I am going to give you only one warning."

"I think I already know what it is," Felless said.

"I am going to give it to you anyhow," the ambassador replied. "Plainly, you need to have it repeated again and again. Here it is: keep your tongue out of the ginger vial. The trouble you cause through your sexual pheromones outweighs any good you can do with your research. Do you understand me?"

"I do, superior sir." Felless added an emphatic cough.

Veffani, however, had known her since not long after she came out of cold sleep. "Since you understand, will you obey?"

Not likely, Felless thought. Even here, even now, with no chance whatever for privacy, she ached for a taste. But Veffani would surely make her rot here if she told him the truth. And so, with next to no hesitation, she lied: "It shall be done."

She was not at all sure the diplomat believed her. By the way he said, "I shall hold you to that," he might have been warning her he didn't. But he continued, "You shall report to Marseille, where you were previously posted."

"Marseille?" Now Felless was startled all over again. "I thought an explosive-metal bomb destroyed the city."

"And so one did," Veffani answered. "But rebuilding is under way. You will use your expertise in Tosevite psychology to guide the Big Uglies toward increased acceptance of the Race."

"Will I?" Felless said tonelessly. "Superior sir, is this assignment not just a continuation of the punishment you have been inflicting on me for the unfortunate activity that occurred in your office in Nuremberg?"

"Unfortunate activity, indeed," Veffani said. "You committed a criminal offense by tasting ginger, Senior Researcher, and you cannot delete that offense by means of a euphemism. You also created an enormous scandal when your pheromones disrupted my meeting and caused the males who had come from Cairo and me to couple with you. Only because of your skills have you escaped getting green bands painted on your upper arms and punishment much harsher than being forced to practice your profession where I order you to do so. If you complain further, you will assuredly learn what real punishment entails. Do you understand *that*?"

"Yes, superior sir." What Felless really understood was that she wanted revenge on Veffani. She had no way to get it, or none she knew of, but she wanted it.

The Race's ambassador to the *Reich*—no, to France now—said, "I do not ask you to be fond of me, Senior Researcher. I merely ask—indeed, I require—that you carry out your assignment to the best of your ability."

"It shall be done, superior sir." Felless even believed Veffani. That made her no less eager for vengeance.

Veffani said, "A transportation aircraft is scheduled to leave your vicinity for Marseille tomorrow evening. I expect you to be on it."

"It shall be done," Felless said again, whereupon Veffani broke the connection.

And Felless was aboard that transport aircraft, though getting to it proved harder than she'd expected. It departed not from the new town in which she was a refugee, but from one that looked close on the map but was a long, boring ground journey away. Even getting her ground transportation proved difficult; local officials were anything but sympathetic to the problems refugees faced.

At last, anxious to be on her way and edgy from lust for ginger, Felless snapped, "Suppose you get in touch with Fleetlord Reffet, the commander of the colonization fleet, and find out what his view of the matter is. He ordered me awakened from cold sleep early to help deal with the Big Uglies, and now you petty functionaries are hindering me? You do so at your peril."

She hoped they would think she was bluffing. She would have enjoyed watching them proved wrong. But they yielded. She was not only sent off to the new town from which the aircraft would leave, she was sent off in a mechanized combat vehicle, to protect her against Tosevite bandits. Even though the Deutsche were defeated, the superstitiously fanatical Big Uglies of this subregion remained in a simmering state of revolt against the Race.

The countryside, by what she saw of it through a firing port, was Homelike enough. That fit in with the weather, which was perfectly comfortable—more comfortable than it would be in Marseille, though that was a considerable improvement over cold, damp Nuremberg.

Herds of azwaca and zisuili grazed on the sparse plants by the road. Felless went by too fast to tell whether the plants were Tosevite natives or, like the beasts, imports from Home. The domestic animals reminded her that, despite the difficulties the Big Uglies caused, the settlement of Tosev 3 was proceeding. As far as physical conditions went, the world was indeed on its way to becoming part of the Empire.

When the aircraft took off, she tried to maintain a similarly optimistic view of political and social conditions. That wasn't so easy, but she managed. With the *Reich* prostrate, one of the three major obstacles to full conquest of Tosev 3 had disappeared. Only the USA and the SSSR remained. Surely they would blunder and fall one of these days, too.

One of these days. That didn't seem soon enough. One of these days, she would get another taste of ginger, too. That didn't seem soon enough, either.

Staring steadily at the ambassador from the Race who sat across the desk from him, Vyacheslav Molotov shook his head. *"Nyet,"* he said.

Queek's translator, a Pole, turned the refusal into its equivalent in the language of the Race. Queek let out another series of hisses and pops and coughs and splutters. The interpreter rendered them into Russian for the General Secretary of the Communist Party of the USSR: "The ambassador urges you to contemplate the fate of the Greater German *Reich* before refusing so promptly."

That gave Molotov a nasty twinge of fear, as it was doubtless meant to do. Even so, he said, *"Nyet,"* again, and asked Queek, "Are you threatening the peace-loving workers and peasants of the Soviet Union with aggressive war? The *Reich* attacked you; you had the right to resist. If you attack us, we shall also resist, and do so as strongly as possible."

"No one speaks of attack." Queek backtracked a little. "But, considering the harm we suffered from the orbital installations of the *Reich*, it is reasonable for us to seek to limit these in other Tosevite powers."

"*Nyet*," Molotov said for the third time. "Fighting between the Race and the Soviet Union stopped with each side recognizing the full sovereignty and independence of the other. We do not seek to infringe on your sovereignty, and you have no right to infringe upon ours. We shall fight to defend it."

"Your independence would be respected . . ." Queek began.

"*Nyet*," Molotov repeated. He knew he sounded like a broken record, knew and didn't care. "We reckon any infringement a major infringement, one that cannot and will not be tolerated."

"That is not an appropriate position for you to take in the present circumstances," Queek said.

"I am of the opinion it is perfectly appropriate," Molotov said. "Are you familiar with the phrase, 'the thin end of the wedge'?"

Queek obviously wasn't. The Pole who translated for him went back and forth with him in the language of the Race. At last, the ambassador said, "Very well: I now grasp the concept. I still believe, however, that you are needlessly concerned."

"I do not," Molotov said stubbornly. "Suppose the Soviet Union tried to impose such conditions on the Race?"

Queek had no hair, which was the only thing that kept him from bristling. "You have neither the right nor the strength to do any such thing," he said.

"You grow indignant when the shoe goes on the other foot," Molotov said, which required another colloquy between the ambassador and his interpreter. "You have no more right to impose such limits on us than we do on you. And as for strength—we can hurt you, and you know it full well. And you will not have such an easy time wrecking us as you did with the *Reich*, for we are far less concentrated geographically than the Germans were."

Queek made noises that put Molotov in mind of a samovar boiling over. The interpreter turned them into rhythmically accented Russian: "Do you presume to threaten the Race?"

"*Nyet*," Molotov said yet again. "But the Race also has no business threatening the Soviet Union. You need to understand that very clearly."

He wondered if Queek did. He wondered if Queek could.

Reciprocity was something with which the Race had always had trouble. Down deep, the Lizards didn't really believe Earth's independent nations had any business staying that way. They were imperialists first, last, and always.

"We are stronger than you," Queek insisted.

"It could be," said Molotov, who knew perfectly well it was. "But we have strength enough to protect ourselves, and to protect our rights as a free and independent state."

More overheated-teakettle noises came from the Lizards' ambassador. "This is an unreasonable and insolent attitude," the translator said.

"By no means." Molotov saw a chance to take the initiative, saw it and seized it: "I presume you have made this same demand upon the United States. What has the Americans' response been?"

Queek hesitated. Molotov thought he understood that hesitation: the Lizard wanted to lie, but was realizing he couldn't, for Molotov had but to ask the American ambassador to learn the truth. After the hesitation, Queek said, "The Americans have also raised a certain number of objections to our reasonable proposal, I must admit."

Molotov was tempted to laugh in his scaly face. Instead, the leader of the Soviet Union said, "Why, then, do you suppose we would acquiesce where they refuse?" He had not a doubt in the world that the Americans' "objections" had been expressed a great deal more stridently than his own.

With an amazingly human sigh, Queek replied, "Since the Soviet Union prides itself on rationality, it was hoped you would see the plain good sense manifest in our proposal."

"It was hoped we would give in without protest, you mean," Molotov said. "This was an error, a miscalculation, on your part. We are more wary of the Race now than we were before your war against Germany. I am sure the Americans feel the same way. I am especially sure the Japanese feel the same way."

"We are most unhappy with the Nipponese," Queek said. "We have never accorded them recognition as a fully independent empire, even though we also never occupied most of the land they ruled at the time of our arrival. Now that they have begun detonating their own explosive-metal bombs, they have begun to presume for themselves a rank above their station."

"Now they too are beginning to be able to defend themselves against your imperialist aggression," Molotov said. "Our relations with Japan have been correct since the war we fought against the Japanese when I was young?"

"They still claim large stretches of the subregion of the main continental mass known as China," Queek said. "Regardless of what sort of weapons they have, we do not intend to yield this to them."

"The people of China, I might add, maintain a strong interest in establishing their own independence once more, and in remaining neither under your control nor under that of the Japanese," Molotov pointed out. "This desire for freedom and autonomy is the reason for their continued revolutionary struggle against your occupation."

"This is a revolutionary struggle the Soviet Union encourages in ways inconsistent with maintaining good relations with the Race," Queek said.

"I deny that," Molotov said stonily. "The Race has continually made that assertion, and has never been able to prove it."

"This is fortunate for the Soviet Union," Queek replied. "We may not be able to prove it, but we believe it to be a truth nonetheless. Many of the Chinese bandits proclaim an ideology identical to yours."

"They were in China before the Race came," Molotov said. "They are indigenous, and unconnected to us." The first of those statements was true, the second tautology—of course Chinese were Chinese—and the last a resounding lie. But the Lizards hadn't caught the NKVD or the GRU in the act of supplying the Chinese People's Liberation Army with munitions to go on with the struggle. Till they did, Molotov would go right on lying.

Queek remained unconvinced. "Even that pack of bandits who have lately taken hostages from among our regional subadministrators and threatened them with death or torment if we do not return to them certain of their comrades"—the Polish interpreter, no friend to Marxist-Leninist thought, pronounced *tovarishchi* with malicious glee—"whom we are now holding imprisoned?" he demanded.

"Yes, even those freedom fighters," Molotov answered calmly. He could not prove the Lizard wasn't talking about Kuomintang reactionaries, who also carried on guerrilla warfare against the Race. And, even if Queek was talking about the patriots of the People's Liberation Army, nothing would have made Molotov admit it.

He doubted Queek was, in any case. The People's Liberation Army, he judged, would have been unlikely to threaten mere torment to whatever hostages it had taken. It would have gone straight to the most severe punishment—unless, of course, someone found some good tactical reason for the lesser threat.

"One individual's bandit, I see, is another individual's freedom fighter," Queek remarked. Molotov tried to remember whether the Lizard had been so cynical when he first became the Race's ambassador to the USSR not long after the fighting stopped. The Soviet leader didn't think so. He wondered what could have changed Queek's outlook on life.

Not to be outdone, Molotov replied, "Indeed. That, no doubt, is why even the Race can reckon itself progressive."

The chair in which Queek sat had an opening through which his short, stumpy tail protruded. That tail quivered now. Molotov watched it with an internal smile—the only kind he customarily allowed himself. He'd succeeded in angering the Lizard.

Queek said, "No matter what sort of denials you give me, I am going to reiterate a warning I have given you before: if the Chinese rebels and bandits who profess your ideology should detonate an explosive-metal bomb, the Race will hold the Soviet Union responsible, and will punish your not-empire most severely. Do you understand this warning?"

"Yes, I understand it," Molotov said, suddenly fighting to keep from showing fear rather than glee. "I have always understood it. I have also always reckoned it unjust. These days, I reckon it more unjust than ever. A disaffected German submarine officer might give his missile warheads to Chinese factionalists of any political stripe in preference to surrendering them to you. And the Japanese might furnish the Chinese such weapons to harm the Race and harm the peace-loving Soviet Union at the same time." He found the first of those far-fetched; the second struck him as only too possible. He would have done it, were he ruling in Japan.

But Queek said, "Did you not just tell me your relations with the Nipponese were correct? If they are not your enemies, why would they do such a thing to you?"

Was that naïveté, or was it a nasty desire to make Molotov squirm? Molotov suspected the latter. He replied, "Until recently, the leaders of Japan have not been in a position to embarrass the Soviet Union in this way. Do you not think it would be to their advantage to use an explosive-metal bomb against the Race and to do so in such a way as to go unpunished for it?"

To his relief, Queek had no fast, snappy comeback. After a pause, the Lizard said, "Here, for once, you have given me a justification for caution that may not be altogether self-serving. I think you may be confident that the Nipponese will receive a similar warning from our representatives to their empire. As you probably know, we do not maintain an embassy in Nippon at present, though recent developments may force us to open one there."

Good, Molotov thought. *I did distract him, then. Now to try to make him feel guilty:* "Any assistance the Race could provide us in reducing the effects on our territory from your war with the Germans would be appreciated."

"If you seek such assistance, ask the *Reich*," Queek said curtly. "Its leaders were the cause of the war."

Molotov didn't push it. He'd got the Lizard ambassador to respond to him instead of his having to react to what Queek said. Given the Race's strength, that was something of a diplomatic triumph.

A squad of little scaly devils strode through the captives' camp in central China. They stopped in front of the miserable little hut Liu Han shared with her daughter, Liu Mei. One of them spoke in bad Chinese: "You are the female Liu Han and the hatchling of the female Liu Han?"

Liu Han and Liu Mei were both sitting on the *kang*, the low clay hearth that gave the hut what little heat it had. "Yes, we are those females," Liu Han admitted.

A moment later, she wondered if she should have denied it, for the little devil gestured with his rifle and said, "You come with me. You two of you, you come with me."

"What have we done now?" Liu Mei asked. Her face stayed calm, though her eyes were anxious. As a baby, she'd been raised by the scaly devils, and she'd never learned to smile or to show much in the way of any expression.

"You two of you, you come with me," was all the little scaly devil would say, and Liu Han and Liu Mei had no choice but to do as they were told.

They didn't go to the administrative buildings in the camp, which surprised Liu Han: it wasn't some new interrogation, then. She got another surprise when the scaly devils led her and Liu Mei out through the several razor-wire gateways that walled off the camp from the rest of the world. Outside the last one stood an armored fighting vehicle. Another little devil, this one with fancier body paint, waited by it. He confirmed their names, then said, "You get in."

"Where are you taking us?" Liu Han demanded.

"You never mind that, you two of you," the scaly devil answered. "You get in."

"No," Liu Han said, and her daughter nodded behind her.

"You get in right now," the scaly devil said.

"No," Liu Han repeated, even though he swung the muzzle of his rifle in her direction. "Not till we know where we're going."

"What is wrong with this stupid Big Ugly?" one of the other scaly devils asked in their own hissing language. "Why does she refuse to go in?"

"She wants to know where they will be taken," answered the little devil who spoke Chinese. "I cannot tell her that, because of security."

"Tell her she is an idiot," the other little scaly devil said. "Does she want to stay in this camp? If she does, she must be an idiot indeed."

Maybe that conversation was set up for her benefit; the little devils knew she spoke their language. But they were not usually so devious. Liu Han had feared they were taking Liu Mei and her out to execute them. If they weren't, if they were going somewhere better than the camp, she would play along. And where, on all the face of the Earth, was there anywhere worse than the camp? Nowhere she knew.

"I have changed my mind," she said. "We will get in."

"Thank you two of you." The little devil who spoke Chinese might not be fluent, but he knew how to be sarcastic. He was even more sarcastic in his own language: "She must think she is the Emperor."

"Who cares what a Big Ugly thinks?" the other scaly devil replied. "Get her and the other one in and get them out of here."

He evidently outranked the scaly devil who spoke Chinese, for that male said, "It shall be done." He opened the rear gate on the mechanized combat vehicle and returned to Chinese: "You two of you, get in there."

Liu Han went in ahead of Liu Mei. If danger waited inside,

she would find it before her daughter did. But she found no danger, only Nieh Ho-T'ing. The People's Liberation Army officer nodded to her. "I might have known you would be coming along, too," he remarked, as calmly as if they'd met on the streets of Peking. "Is your daughter with you?" Before Liu Han could answer that, Liu Mei climbed up into the troop-carrying compartment of the combat vehicle. Nieh smiled at her. She nodded back; she couldn't smile herself. "I see you are here," he said to her.

"Where are they taking us? Do you know?" Liu Han asked.

Nieh Ho-T'ing shook his head. "I haven't the faintest idea. Wherever it is, it has to be better than where we have been."

Since Liu Han had had the identical thought, she could hardly disagree. "I was afraid they were going to liquidate us, but now I don't think they will."

"No, I don't think so, either," Nieh said. "They could do that in camp if they decided it served their interests."

Before Liu Han could answer, the scaly devils slammed the rear gate shut. She heard clatterings from outside. "What are they doing?" she asked, still anything but trusting of the little scaly devils.

"Locking us in," Nieh Ho-T'ing answered calmly. "The gates on this machine are made to open from the inside, from this compartment, to let out the little scaly devils' soldiers when they want to fight as ordinary infantry. But the little devils will want to make sure we do not go out till they take us wherever they take us."

"That makes sense," Liu Mei said.

"Yes, it does," Liu Han agreed. It went some distance toward easing her mind, too. "Maybe we are being taken to a different camp, or for a special interrogation." She assumed the little devils could hear whatever she said, so she added, "Since we are innocent and know nothing, I do not see what point there is to interrogating us any more."

Nieh Ho-T'ing chuckled at that. There were, surely, some things of which they were innocent, but carrying on the proletarian revolution against the small, scaly, imperialist oppressors was not one of them.

The mechanized combat vehicle started moving. The seats in the fighting compartment were too small for human fundaments, and the wrong shape to boot. Liu Han felt that more when the ride was jouncy, as it was here. Along with her daughter and Nieh, she braced herself as best she could. That was all she could do.

It had been cool outside. It soon became unpleasantly warm in the fighting compartment: the little scaly devils heated it to the temperature they found comfortable, the temperature of a very hot summer's day in China. Liu Han undid her quilted cotton jacket and shrugged out of it. After a while, she had a good idea: she put it on the seat and sat on it. It made things a little more comfortable. Her daughter and Nieh Ho-T'ing quickly imitated her.

"I wish I had a watch," she said as the scaly devils' vehicle rattled along. Without one, she could only use her stomach to gauge the passage of time. She didn't think they would be giving out the midday meal in camp yet, but she wasn't sure.

"We will get where we're going, wherever that is, when we get there, and nothing we can do will make that time come sooner," Nieh said.

"You sound more like a Buddhist than a Marxist-Leninist," Liu Han teased. With only him and her daughter to hear, that was safe enough to say. Had it reached anyone else's ears, it might have resulted in a denunciation. Liu Han didn't want that to happen to Nieh, who was not only an able man but also an old lover of hers.

"The revolution will proceed with me or without me," Nieh said. "I would prefer that it proceed with me, but life does not always give us what we would prefer."

Liu Han knew that only too well. When the Japanese overran her village, they'd also killed her family. Then the little scaly devils drove out the Japanese—and kidnapped her and made her part of their experiments on how and why humans mated as they did. That was why Liu Mei had wavy hair and a nose unusually large for a Chinese—her father had been an American, similarly kidnapped. But Bobby Fiore was long years dead, killed by the scaly devils, and Liu Han had been fighting them ever since.

She peered out through one of the little openings in the side wall of the combat vehicle—a viewport for the closed firing port just below. She saw rice paddies, little stands of forest, peasant villages, occasional beasts in the fields, once an ox-drawn cart that had hastily gone off to the side of the road so the combat vehicle wouldn't run it down.

"It looks a lot like the country around my home village," she said. "More rice—I liked eating it in the camp. It was an old friend, even if the place wasn't. I'd got used to noodles in Peking, but rice seemed better somehow."

"Freedom would seem better," Liu Mei said. "Liberating the countryside would seem better." She was still a young woman, and found ideology about as important as food. Liu Han shook her head, somewhere between bewilderment and pride. When she was Liu Mei's age, she'd hardly had an ideology. She'd been an ignorant, illiterate peasant. Thanks to the Party, she was neither ignorant nor illiterate any more, and her daughter never had been.

With more jounces, the mechanized combat vehicle went off the road and into a grove of willows. There, with newly green boughs screening off the outside world, it came to a stop, though the motor kept running. A rattle at the back of the vehicle was a male undoing whatever fastening had kept the rear gate closed. It swung open. In the language of the Race, the scaly devil said, "You Tosevites, you come out now."

If they didn't come out now, the little devils could shoot them while they were in the troop-carrying compartment. Liu Han saw she had no choice. Out she came, bumping her head on the roof of the vehicle.

She looked around as soon as she had her feet on the ground. The turret of the combat vehicle mounted a small cannon and a machine gun. Those bore on the Chinese men with submachine guns and rifles who advanced toward the machine. In their midst were three woebegone little scaly devils. One of the Chinese called, "You are Nieh Ho-T'ing, Liu Han, and Liu Mei?"

"That's right," Liu Han said, her agreement mixing with those of the others. She added, "Who are you?"

"That doesn't matter," the man answered. "What does matter is that you are the people for whom we are exchanging these hostages." He swung the muzzle of his submachine gun toward the unhappy little devils he and his comrades were guarding.

Negotiations between the men of the People's Liberation Army—for that was what they had to be—and the little scaly devils who made up the crew of the combat vehicle did not last long. When they were through, the little scaly devils in Chinese hands hurried into the vehicle while Liu Han and her daughter and Nieh hurried away from it. The scaly devils slammed the doors to the troop compartment shut as if they expected the Chinese to start shooting any second.

And the Chinese leader said, "Hurry. We have to get out of here. We can't be sure the little scaly devils don't have an ambush laid on."

Fleeing through the willow branches that kept throwing little leaves in her face, Liu Han said, "Thank you so much for freeing us from that camp."

"You are experienced revolutionaries," the People's Liberation Army man answered. "The movement needs you."

"We will give it everything we have," Nieh Ho-T'ing said. "The Kuomintang could not defeat us. The Japanese could not defeat us. And the little scaly devils shall not defeat us, either. The dialectic is on our side."

The little scaly devils knew nothing of the dialectic. But they, like the Party, took a long view of history. Eventually, history would show which was correct. Liu Han remained convinced the proletarian revolution would triumph, but she was much less certain than she had been that it would happen in her lifetime. *But I'm back in the struggle,* she thought, and hurried on through the willows.

Not even during the fighting after the conquest fleet landed on Tosev 3 had Gorppet seen such devastation as he found when the small unit he commanded moved into the Greater German *Reich*.

One of the males in the unit, a trooper named Yarssev, summed up his feelings when he asked, "How did the Big Uglies stay in the war so long when we did this to them? Why were they so stupid?"

"I cannot answer that," Gorppet said. "All I know is, they fought hard up till the moment they surrendered."

"Truth, superior sir," Yarssev agreed. "And now their countryside will glow in the dark for years because of their foolish courage."

He was exaggerating, but not by any tremendous amount. Every male moving into the *Reich* wore a radiation-exposure badge on a chain around his neck. Orders were to check the badges twice a day, and the troops followed those orders. Nowhere on four worlds had so many explosive-metal bombs fallen on so small an area in so short a time.

But not every area of the *Reich* had had a bomb fall on it. In between the zones where nothing was left alive, the Deutsche who had survived the war struggled to get on with their lives, to raise their crops and domestic animals, to care for refugees and demobilized soldiers, to rebuild damage from conventional weapons.

As the occupying males of the Race moved into the *Reich*, the local Tosevites would pause in what they were doing to stare at them. Some of those Tosevites would have fought against the Race in earlier conflicts. Others, though, females and young, were surely civilians. The quality of the stares was the same in either case, though.

"Nasty creatures, aren't they, superior sir?" Yarssev said.

"No doubt about it," Gorppet agreed. "I have seen stares from Big Uglies who hated us before—I have served in Basra and Baghdad. But I have never seen such hate as these Deutsche display."

"Better they should hate their own not-emperor, who was foolish enough to think he could beat us," Yarssev said.

"They never hate their own. No one ever hates his own. This is a law through all the Empire, as sure as I hatched out of my eggshell."

The detachment came to the sea not much later, came to the sea and headed west. Gorppet had seen Tosevite seas before. The one south of Basra was quite tolerably warm. The one off Cape Town was cooler, but of an interesting shade of blue. This one . . . This one was cold and gray and ugly. It splashed lethargically up onto the mud of the coastline, then rolled back.

"Why would anyone want to live in a country like this?" a male asked. "Chilly and flat and horrible . . ."

"Sometimes you live where you have to live, not where you want to live," Gorppet answered. "Maybe some other Big Uglies chased the Deutsche into this part of the world and would not let them live anywhere better."

"Maybe, superior sir," the other male said. "And maybe having to live here is what makes them so mean and tough."

"That could be," Gorppet agreed. "Something certainly has."

He wished he had a taste of ginger. He had plenty—more than plenty—stashed away in South Africa, but it might as well have been on Home for all the good it did him. He'd been very moderate all through the fighting. Males who tasted ginger thought they were stronger and faster and brighter than they really were. If they went into action against coldly pragmatic Big Uglies with the herb coursing through them, they were all too likely to do something foolish and end up dead before they could make amends.

When we stop for the evening, he thought. *I'll taste when we stop for the evening.*

They came to the vicinity of Peenemünde as light was failing. They would have gone no farther had it been early morning. Teams of the Race's engineers had already taken possession of the principal spaceport the Deutsche used. They had also set up warning lines to keep other males from venturing too far into the radioactivity without proper protection. No site in the *Reich*, Nuremberg probably included, had taken as many bombs as Peenemünde.

"Nothing will grow here for a hundred years," Yarssev predicted. "And I mean a hundred Tosevite years, twice as long as ours."

"I suppose not," Gorppet said. "And yet . . . wasn't it here that the Big Ugly who calls himself the Deutsch not-emperor these days was holed up during the fighting?"

"I think so," Yarssev replied. "Too bad the miserable creature came out alive, if you want to know how I feel."

"Truth," Gorppet said, for he agreed with all his liver. But if any Tosevite could emerge alive from the slagging the Race had given Peenemünde, that bespoke some truly formidable engineering prowess. He let out a wry hiss. The Race had seen as much in the fighting in Poland. The weapons the Deutsche used there were alarmingly close to being as good as the ones the Race owned—and the Big Uglies had had a lot more of them. If the Race hadn't pounded their not-empire too flat to let them keep supporting their army, things might have gone even worse than they had.

As usual, field rations tasted like the mud that lined the southern shore of the local sea. Gorppet fueled himself as he would have put hydrogen into a mechanized combat vehicle. Having fueled himself, he did taste ginger. He was sure he wasn't the only male in the small group who used the Tosevite herb. Penalties against it had grown harsher since females came to Tosev 3, but that hadn't stopped many males. Except for making sure his troopers didn't do anything that would get themselves and their comrades killed in combat, Gorppet didn't try to keep them from tasting. That would hardly have been fair, not when he had the ginger habit himself.

He poured some of the herb into the palm of his hand. Even before he raised palm to mouth, the heady scent of the ginger was tickling his scent receptors. He never tired of it; it always seemed fresh and new. His tongue shot out almost of its own accord.

"Ahhh," he murmured as bliss flowed through him. He felt bigger than a Big Ugly, faster than a starship, with more computing power between his hearing diaphragms than all the Race's electronic network put together. Some small part of him knew the feeling was an illusion, but he didn't care. This side of mating—maybe not even this side of mating—it was as good a feeling as a male of the Race could have.

While it lasted. Like the pleasure of mating, it didn't last long enough. And when it faded, the crushing depression that followed was as bad as it had been good. One solution was to have another taste, and then another, and . . . Gorppet chose the harder road, waiting till the depression faded, too. Over the years, he'd come to take it as part of the experience connected to the herb.

When they set out again the next morning, the road along which they were traveling west came together with another, on which were about their number of Deutsch soldiers coming home from Poland. No one had disarmed the Deutsche: they still carried all their hand weapons, and several of them wore bandoliers of bullets crisscrossed on their chests.

The males in Gorppet's unit nervously eyed the Big Uglies. The Deutsche did not have the look of defeated troops. On the contrary; they looked as if they were ready to start up the war again then and there.

They might win if they did, too, at least in this small engagement. Gorppet was uneasily aware of it. Before either side could start spraying bullets around, he stepped away from the males he commanded and strode toward the Deutsche. "I do not speak your language," he called. "Does anyone among you speak the language of the Race?" If none of them did, he was liable to be in a lot of trouble.

But, as he'd hoped, a Deutsch male came out from among the Big Uglies and said, "I speak your language. What do you want?"

"I want my small group and your small group to pass by in peace," Gorppet answered. "The war is over. Let it stay over."

"You can say that," the Tosevite replied. His face was grimy. His wrappings were filthy. He smelled powerfully of the rank odor Big Uglies soon acquired when they did not bathe. He went on, "Yes, winners can say, 'The war is over.' For losers, the war is never over. Winners can forget. Losers remember. We have much for which to remember the Race."

"I have nothing to say to that," Gorppet said. "I am not a politician. I am not a diplomat. I am only a soldier. As a soldier, I tell you this: if you attack us now, you will be sorry and your not-empire will be sorry."

With a bark of Tosevite laughter, the Deutsch soldier said, "How can you make us sorrier, after what the Race has done to the *Reich*? How can you make this not-empire sorrier, after all you have done to it?"

"If you attack us, you cannot kill us all before we radio the situation to our superiors," Gorppet replied, trying to hold his voice steady. "Helicopter gunships will punish you for fighting, and the Race will take further vengeance on the *Reich* for violating the surrender. Is this a truth, or is it not?"

"It is a truth," the Big Ugly admitted. "It is a truth about which few of my males care right now. Many of them have lost their mates and hatchlings. Do you understand what this means? It means they do not greatly care if they live or die."

"I do understand, yes," Gorppet said, though he knew he did so only in theory. Tosevite kinship ties, and Tosevites willing to kill without thought for their own lives once those ties were broken, had complicated life for the Race since the conquest fleet landed. Gorppet tried the only real direction in which he thought he could go: "What they want to do now, they may regret later. Is this a truth, or is it not? Do you command them?"

"Yes, I command them," the Deutsch soldier replied. "You make good sense. I almost wish you did not, for I am as ready as any of my males to seek revenge against the Race. But I will tell the soldiers what you have said. After that . . . we shall have to see. With the war over and lost, my hold over them is weaker than it was."

"We shall stay alert," Gorppet said. "We shall not attack you—the war is over. But if we are attacked, we shall fight back with all our strength."

"I understand." The Big Ugly walked back toward his own males, calling out in their guttural language. Some of the Deutsche shouted at him. They did not sound happy, nor anything close to it.

"Be ready for anything," Gorppet warned the males he led. "Do not open fire on them unless they fire on us, but be ready."

He was willing to let the Deutsche use the crossroads first, and held up his males so they could. The Tosevite officer led his Big

Uglies forward. They towered over the males of the Race. Some of them shouted things. Some shook their fists. But, to Gorppet's vast relief, they didn't start shooting.

"Forward," he called after the Deutsche had passed. Forward his own small group went. He kept one eye turret on the terrain, the other on the map he'd been given. Unlike the maps he'd had in the SSSR, this one seemed to know what it was talking about. When, toward evening, his males reached a town, he stopped a local and asked, "Greifswald?"

He made himself understood. The local nodded a Big Ugly affirmative and said, "Greifswald, *ja*."

Gorppet turned back to his males. "We have reached our assigned station. Dismal-looking dump, isn't it?"

☆ 3 ☆

With a curse half in Yiddish, half in Polish, Mordechai Anielewicz used the hand brake on his bicycle. "How am I supposed to get anywhere if the roads are all *kaputt*?" the Jewish fighting leader muttered.

Burnt-out trucks made the asphalt impassable. These particular vehicles were of human manufacture, but he had to look closely to see which side had used them. The Lizards had pressed plenty of human-made models into service in Poland, and most of them had been imported from Germany.

He got off the bicycle and walked it around the jam. He'd been doing that every kilometer or two on the journey down to Widawa. He'd got his family out of Lodz before the fighting started, and sent them southwest to this little town. That had kept them safe—or safer, anyhow—when the Germans hit the city with an explosive-metal bomb. But the *Wehrmacht* had overrun Widawa—and Bertha and Miriam and David and Heinrich were every bit as Jewish as he was, of course.

Even after he passed the wrecks, he couldn't get back on the road right away. Someone's airplanes had cratered it with bomblets. Anielewicz's legs ached as he brought the bicycle forward. They'd been doing that since the last round of fighting, when he'd breathed German nerve gas. Without the antidote, he would have died then. As things were, he'd got off lucky. Of the others who'd breathed the gas, Heinrich Jäger, after whom his younger son was named, had died at an early age. Ludmila Gorbunova had suffered far more from the lingering effects of the stuff than he had. Ludmila had been in Lodz. Odds were all too good—or all too bad—she wasn't suffering at all any more.

Over the years, Mordechai had come to take his aches and pains for granted. He couldn't do that now. The Nazis had used

62

poison gas again in this new round of fighting. How much of it had he breathed? How much harm was it doing? Just how much residual damage did he have? Those were all fascinating questions, and he lacked answers to any of them.

And, in a most important sense, none of them mattered much, not when measured against the one question, the overriding question. *What happened to my family?* No, there wasn't one question only. Another lay underneath it, one he would sooner not have contemplated. *Have I still got a family?*

After half a kilometer, the road stopped being too battered for a bicycle. He got back up on the bike and rode hard. The harder he worked, the worse his legs felt—till, after a while, they stopped hurting so much. He let out a sigh of relief. That had happened before. If he put in enough exercise, he could work right through the cramps. Sometimes.

No road signs warned him he was coming into Widawa. For one thing, Polish roads had never been well marked. For another, Widawa wasn't a town important enough to require much in the way of marking. And, for a third, the war had been here before him. If there had been signs, they weren't upright any more. A lot of trees in the forest just north of Widawa weren't upright any more.

When the road curved around the forest and gave him his first glimpse of the town, he saw that a lot of the houses in it weren't upright any more, either. His mouth tightened. He'd seen a lot of ruins in the first round of fighting and now in this one. Another set wouldn't have been so much out of the ordinary—except that these might hold the bodies of his wife and children.

A burnt-out German panzer and an equally burnt-out Lizard landcruiser sprawled in death a few meters apart, just outside of town. Had they killed each other, or had some different fate befallen them? Mordechai knew he would never know. He pedaled past them into Widawa.

People on the street hardly bothered to look up at him. What was one more middle-aged bicycle rider with a rifle slung on his back? They'd surely seen a surfeit of those already. He put a foot down and used a boot heel for a brake. Nodding to an old woman with a head scarf who wore a long black dress, he asked, "Granny, who knows about the refugees who came in from Lodz?"

She eyed him. He spoke Polish notable only for a Warsaw accent. He looked like a Pole, being fair-skinned and light-eyed. But the old woman said, "Well, Jew, you'd best ask Father Wladyslaw

about that. I don't know anything. I don't want to know anything."
She went on her way as if he didn't exist.

Anielewicz sighed. Some people had a radar better than anything
electronic in the Lizards' arsenal. He'd seen that before. "Thanks,"
he called after her, but she might as well not have heard.

A couple of shells had hit the church. Workmen were busy repairing it. Mordechai shrugged at that, but didn't sigh. Jews
would have fixed up a synagogue before they worried about their
houses, too. "Is the priest in?" Mordechai asked a carpenter
hammering nails into a board.

The man nodded and shifted his cigarette to the corner of his
mouth so he could talk more readily. "Yeah, he's there. What do
you want to talk to him about?"

"I'm looking for my wife and children," Anielewicz answered. "They came here out of Lodz not long before the Germans invaded."

"Ah." The cigarette twitched. "You a Jew?"

At least he asked, instead of showing he could tell. "Yes,"
Mordechai said. The other fellow had a hammer. He had a rifle.
"Don't you like that?"

"Don't care one way or the other," the carpenter answered.
"But you're right—you'd better talk to the father." He gestured
with the hammer toward the doorway. As Mordechai walked
over to it, the Pole started driving nails again.

Inside the church, Father Wladyslaw was pounding away with
a hammer, too, repairing the front row of pews. He was a young
man, and startlingly handsome in a tall, blond way. If his politics
had fit, the Nazis would have scooped him into the SS without a
second thought. With all the noise, he didn't notice Mordechai
for a bit. When he did, his smile was friendly enough. "Oh,
hello," he said, getting to his feet and brushing sawdust off his
cassock. "What can I do for you today?"

"I'm looking for my wife and children," Mordechai said
again, and gave his name.

Father Wladyslaw's eyebrows flew upward. "The famous
fighting leader!" he exclaimed. "Your kin would have been some
who came out of Lodz."

"That's right," Mordechai said. "People in town tell me you'd
know about them if anybody does. Are they alive?" There. The
question was out.

But he got no sure answer for it, for the priest replied, "I'm sorry, but I *don't* know. The Germans overran us twice, and kid-napped people each time they retreated. Some were Jews. Some were Poles who'd lived here for generations uncounted. I'm not even sure why, but who can tell with Germans?"

"They've run out of Jews in Germany," Anielewicz said bit-terly. "They need some fresh people to keep the gas chambers and the ovens busy."

"You may well be right," Father Wladyslaw said. "I wish I could give you more definite news of your loved ones, but I fear I can't. You'll have to go inquire among the refugees who are still here. I pray your family is among them."

"Thank you, Father," Mordechai said; the priest seemed a de-cent fellow. Then he added several choice comments about the Nazis. He was ashamed of himself as soon as they were out of his mouth, which was, of course, much too late. "I'm sorry."

"Don't be," Father Wladyslaw told him. "If you think I haven't called them worse than that, you're wrong."

"They're supposed to have published a list of the people they took. They're supposed to have already released those people," Anielewicz said. "And they have published it, and they have turned a few people loose. But nobody believes that list is every-body, or even close to everybody."

"Your family is not on it?" the priest asked.

"If they were, I wouldn't be here," Mordechai answered. "Thanks for your help, Father. I won't take up any more of your time. The refugee tents are on the south edge of town?"

"That's right," Father Wladyslaw said. "I wish you luck there, either in finding them or in learning of them." Nodding, Anielewicz walked out of the church. The priest started ham-mering again even before he'd left.

The tents and huts in which the refugees were staying looked even shabbier than the town of Widawa. The fighting had smashed them up, too, and they'd been less prepossessing to begin with. A sharp stink assailed Mordechai's nose. He wouldn't have let his fighting men pay sanitation so little heed.

Poles and Jews spilled out into the spaces between tents to see who the newcomer was. Anielewicz got the notion the people of Widawa would just as soon they all disappeared. But with Lodz radioactive rubble, a lot of them had nowhere to go. He stared this way and that. He didn't see his family. He did spot someone he knew. "Rabinowicz! Are Bertha and the children here?"

"Were they ever here?" the other Jew answered. "News to me if they were. But I've only been here a couple days myself."

"Wonderful," Mordechai muttered. He looked around again. He'd thought a good many Jews had come from Lodz to Widawa, but Rabinowicz's was the only face he recognized. What had happened to the Jews who were here, then? Were they dead? Were they all hauled off to the *Reich* for a fate that couldn't possibly be good? He asked some of the Poles, and got a different answer from each of them.

"Damn Nazis took 'em away," a woman said.

"Not everybody," a man disagreed. "Some got taken away, yes, but some got shot right here and some ran off."

"Nobody got shot right here," another man insisted. "The Germans said they were gonna, but they never did."

"Does anybody know if Bertha and Miriam and David and Heinrich Anielewicz got away safe, or if they got taken back to Germany?" Mordechai asked.

Nobody knew. Any which way, people were too busy arguing over what had happened to be very interested in giving details. The two men who'd disagreed went nose to nose with each other, both of them shouting at the tops of their lungs. Mordechai wanted to knock their heads together. That might have let in some sense. He couldn't think of anything else that would.

He lacked the energy to treat the two loud fools as they deserved. Instead, he turned away, sick at heart. His wife and children were either carried off to Germany or dead: a bad choice or a worse one. He would have to beard the Nazis in their den to find out. He'd need help from the Lizards there, but he thought they would give him the paperwork and help he'd require. They despised the German ruling party, too.

He tried one more thing: "My son, Heinrich, had a beffel for a pet, an animal from the Lizards' world. It would squeak when it was happy. Does anybody remember that?"

And two people did. "That damned thing," a woman said. "Yes, the Germans nabbed the people who had it. They took them away when they got run out of here." The other person, an old man, nodded.

"They *did* go into Germany, then," Mordechai breathed. "Thank you both, from the bottom of my heart." He didn't know if he ought to be thanking them. Jews who went into Germany were not in the habit of coming out again. But his family hadn't simply been slaughtered here. That was something . . . he hoped.

Nesseref was feeding Orbit, her tsiongi, when the telephone hissed for attention. The pet started eating while she hurried into the bedchamber, wondering who was calling. "I greet you," the shuttlecraft pilot said, waiting to see whose image appeared on the computer monitor.

To her surprise, it was not a male or female of the Race but a Big Ugly. "I greet you, superior female," he said in the language of the Race. "Mordechai Anielewicz here."

"Good to see you," Nesseref answered, glad he'd named himself. No matter how well she liked him, she had trouble telling Tosevites apart.

"I hope you are well," the Big Ugly said.

"On the whole, yes," Nesseref replied. "The fallout levels have been high, but my apartment building was damaged only once, and even then the filters functioned well. By now, everything has been replaced, and radioactivity levels are falling. But I hope very much that *you* are well, Mordechai Anielewicz. You have not been shielded from all the radioactivity that descended on Poland."

"I am well enough for now," Anielewicz told her. "Past that, I do not worry about myself. I worry about my mate and my hatchlings. They have been carried back into the *Reich* by retreating Deutsch armies, and they very well may be dead by now."

"Yes, they are of the Jewish superstition, as you are—is that not a truth?" Nesseref said. "I have never understood the irrational loathing of the Deutsche for Tosevites of the Jewish superstition." It struck her as no more absurd than any other Tosevite superstition. Belatedly, she realized she should say something more. She'd forgotten the strong ties of sexuality and other emotions that linked Big Uglies in family units. "For your sake, I hope you find them well."

"I thank you," Mordechai Anielewicz said. "They *were* alive, at least fairly recently. I have found Tosevites who saw and remember my youngest hatchling's beffel." He did an excellent job of imitating the squeak of the little animal from Home.

At that squeak, Orbit came racing into the bedroom, plainly furious that Nesseref might have concealed a beffel somewhere in the apartment. His tail lashed up and down, up and down. His mouth was open so his scent receptors could better pick up the hated odor of a beffel. But images on the monitor meant nothing to him. At last, with the air of someone who knew he'd been tricked but couldn't figure out how, the tsiongi went away.

Nesseref said, "There is still some hope, then. I am glad of that." She used an emphatic cough to show how glad she was.

"I thank you," Mordechai Anielewicz said again. "I want you to help me locate them, if that should prove possible."

"What can I do?" Nesseref asked in some surprise. "If it is within my ability, you may rest assured that I will do it." As the ties of family were less important among the Race than with the Big Uglies, so the ties of friendship were more important. And Mordechai Anielewicz, though a Tosevite, was unquestionably a friend.

"Once more, I thank you," he said. "As you surely know, I have some prominence with the Race because of my rank among the Jews of Poland. Still, my primary dealings these past many years have been with the Race's authorities in Lodz. Now those authorities are reporting only to the spirits of Emperors past." He didn't cast down his eyes. Other than that, his knowledge of the Race's beliefs was flawless. He finished, "I would like you to help me obtain the assistance of the authorities in Warsaw."

"Warsaw also received an explosive-metal bomb from the Deutsche," Nesseref reminded him. "The present administration for this subregion is in Pinsk."

"Ah. Pinsk. Yes. I understand. I had forgotten because of my own troubles." Anielewicz's face twisted into a grimace Nesseref believed to denote unhappiness. "The Deutsche would not have tried to bomb that city, for fear the bomb would go wrong and strike the Soviet Union, which they did not want. In any case, this new administration is made up of males and females unfamiliar to me. I would greatly appreciate your good offices in dealing with them."

"Are you planning to travel there in person?" Nesseref asked.

"If I must, but only if I must," the Big Ugly answered, and used another unhappy grimace. "I hate to travel all the way to the eastern edge of this subregion when all my concerns are here in the west. That is another reason I want your help."

"I understand. You shall have it," the shuttlecraft pilot said. She waved aside the Tosevite's further thanks. "Friends may ask favors of friends. Let me make inquiries in Pinsk." She noted the telephone code from which he was calling. It wasn't his phone, of course, but one belonging to some military detachment or bureaucratic outpost of the Race. "May I leave messages for you here?"

"You may," Mordechai Anielewicz said. "And, again, I thank you from the bottom of my heart." That was a Tosevite idiom literally translated, but Nesseref figured out what it had to mean.

After Anielewicz broke the connection, Nesseref telephoned the new authorities in Pinsk. "Yes, we have heard from this Tosevite," a female told her. "We are hesitant to grant his request for assistance in entering the *Reich* in search of those other individuals, for we know that the Deutsche are liable to make it as difficult as possible for him to carry out the aforesaid search."

"You are from the colonization fleet," Nesseref said. That was an obvious truth. No females had been part of the conquest fleet. Nesseref went on, "I think you are too inexperienced to grasp the attachment Big Uglies place on their sexual partners and hatchlings. You would not be doing this male a favor by protecting him from himself."

"You are also part of the colonization fleet," the bureaucrat in Pinsk answered sharply. "Why is your experience more valid than mine?"

"I have made a friend of this Tosevite," Nesseref replied. "Am I mistaken, or would you have recently come from a new town where you had only limited contact with Big Uglies?"

"That is a truth," the other female admitted in some surprise. "If you can note it, perhaps you do know what you are talking about. I will take what you say under advisement."

"I thank you." Nesseref made some more calls, doing all she could to get the Race's functionaries to help Mordechai Anielewicz. Two or three of the functionaries with whom she spoke said she wasn't the first person asking them to help the Big Ugly. She was miffed the first time she heard that. Then she decided she'd made a mistake—Anielewicz had the right to do whatever he could to try to recover the Tosevites who were important to him.

Orbit walked into the bedroom a couple of times while Nesseref was on the telephone. The tsiongi prowled around the room and even poked his long-snouted head into the closets a couple of times. He thought he'd heard a beffel, and it hadn't come out. That meant it should still be in there. His logic was impeccable, or would have been if he'd understood how video monitors worked. As things were, he got to be one increasingly frustrated animal.

And then Nesseref's telephone hissed again. She thought it would be one of the bureaucrats with whom she'd talked calling back for more information, or possibly Mordechai Anielewicz with a new suggestion or request. But it wasn't. It was, in fact, a Big Ugly calling on the security hookup of her apartment building. "Yes? What do you want?" she asked him.

"I have for you delivery." He spoke the language of the Race fairly well. "It is animal exercise wheel."

"Oh, yes. I thank you." Nesseref had ordered that during the fighting, but no one had been able to deliver it. More urgent concerns had all but overwhelmed the Race's supply system. "Wait one moment. I will admit you." She let him go through the building's outer door. Inside, part of the lobby had been turned into what almost amounted to an airlock system, one designed to keep as much radioactive outside air as possible from circulating in the halls and units of the building. Only after fans blew the contaminated air out onto the street did the inner door open and admit the Big Ugly.

Instead of pressing the buzzer by her doorway, as a male or female of the Race would have done, he knocked on the door. Orbit let out a growling hiss. "No!" Nesseref said sharply as she opened the door. "Stay!" The tsiongi lashed its tail, angry that it didn't get to attack this obviously dangerous intruder.

"Here." Grunting, the Tosevite delivery male lifted the crate off the dolly he'd used to move it to the elevator. The dolly was of Big Ugly manufacture, heavier and grimier than anything the Race would have used. After setting the crate in the center of the floor, the Big Ugly handed Nesseref an electronic clipboard and stylus, saying, "You sign this here, superior sir."

"Superior female," Nesseref corrected him. Before signing, she checked to make sure the crate said it contained the exercise wheel she'd ordered. As soon as her signature went into the system, her account would be debited the price of the wheel. But everything seemed to be in order. She scribbled her signature on the proper line on the clipboard.

"I thank you, superior female." The Big Ugly got it right the second time. He bent into a clumsy version of the posture of respect, then left her apartment.

"Let us see what we have here," Nesseref said. Orbit was certainly curious. His tongue lolled out so the scent receptors on it could catch all the interesting odors coming from the crate. Nesseref's eyes caught something she'd missed when ordering the exercise wheel. On the side of the crate were the dreaded words, SOME ASSEMBLY REQUIRED. She sighed. Did *some* mean a little or a lot? She'd find out.

Orbit thought he was a very helpful tsiongi. As soon as she'd opened the crate, he started jumping in and then jumping out again. He tried to kill some of the plastic bags that held fasteners. He poked his snout into every subassembly as Nesseref put it together. Long before she had the whole wheel done, she was ready to throw the animal for whom it was intended right out the window.

"Here," she said when, despite Orbit's best efforts at assistance, she finally did put the wheel together. "This says your wheel is impregnated with the odor of zisuili, to make you enthusiastic about using it." Domestic tsiongyu helped herd zisuili back on Home. Their wild cousins—and occasional unreliable or feral tsiongyu—preyed on the meat animals.

Orbit jumped into the wheel and started to run. Before long, he hopped out again. Maybe he'd worn himself out doing his best to lend Nesseref a hand. Maybe he didn't feel like running in it no matter what it smelled like. Tsiongyu had a reputation for perversity. On a smaller scale, they were something like Big Uglies.

"Miserable beast," Nesseref said, more or less fondly. As if doing her a favor, Orbit deigned to turn an eye turret in her direction for a moment. Then he curled up by the exercise wheel, slapped his tail down on the floor a couple of times, and went to sleep.

Nesseref's laugh quickly turned rueful. Orbit had no worries bigger than not being able to go outside for a good run. She wished she could say the same.

Reuven Russie came home to find his father on the telephone with Atvar. "Anything you might be able to do would be greatly appreciated, Exalted Fleetlord," Moishe Russie said. "Mordechai Anielewicz is a longtime friend, and he has also helped the Race a great deal in the fight against the Deutsche."

"I can do less than you might think," the fleetlord of the conquest fleet replied. "I can encourage our males and females in the subregion of Poland to assist him, and I shall do that. But the *Reich* retains political independence. That limits actions available to me there."

"How unfortunate," Reuven's father said, and used an emphatic cough.

"I regret not being able to do more." Atvar didn't sound regretful. He sounded, if anything, indifferent. After a moment, he went on, "And now, if you will excuse me, I have a great many things to do." His image vanished from the screen.

Moishe Russie turned away from the telephone with a sigh. He looked up in surprise. "Hello, Reuven. I didn't think you'd be back from the office so soon."

"My last two appointments canceled on me, one right after the other," Reuven answered. "You took the afternoon off; I got mine by default. The Lizards don't care what happened to Anielewicz's family?"

"Not even a little." His father made a disgusted noise, down deep in his throat. "We're good enough to do things for them. But they're too good to do things for us, especially if that would take some real work from them. I've seen it before, but never so bad as now. You don't even remember Anielewicz, do you?"

"I was just a little boy—a very little boy—when we got smuggled out of Poland," Reuven said.

"I know that. But if Anielewicz had decided to fight for the Germans against the Race when the conquest fleet landed, Poland might have stayed in Nazi hands," his father said. "That's how important he was. And now Atvar doesn't care whether his family is alive or dead."

"Lizards don't really understand about families," Reuven said.

"Emotionally, no," Moishe Russie agreed. "Emotionally, no, but intellectually, yes. They aren't stupid. They just don't want to take the trouble for someone who's done a lot for them, and I think it's a disgrace."

"What's a disgrace?" Reuven's mother asked. She glanced over to her only son. "You're home early. I hope there's nothing wrong?"

He shook his head. "Only canceled appointments, like I told Father."

"Better canceled appointments than a canceled family," Rivka Russie said. She turned a mild and speculative eye on him. "And when will you be bringing Jane by the house again?"

Was that a hint he should settle down and start having a family of his own? He was within shouting distance of thirty and still single, so it might well have been. On the other hand, Jane Archibald remained a student at the Lizards' Moishe Russie Medical College, while he'd resigned because he wouldn't go to their temple and give reverence to spirits of Emperors past. And she wasn't Jewish herself, which struck Reuven as likely to prove a bigger obstacle in his parents' eyes.

He wasn't sure how big an obstacle it was in his own eyes. It certainly hadn't been enough to keep him from becoming Jane's lover. Every male student at the medical college had wanted to be able to say that. Now that he'd actually done it, he was still trying to figure out what it meant to his life.

"You don't answer my question," his mother said.

Bringing Jane by had been simpler in the days when they were just fellow students and friends. Being lovers with her complicated everything, not necessarily because of what it meant now but because of how it might change his whole future. For the time being, he temporized: "I will, Mother, as soon as I can."

"Good." Rivka Russie nodded. "I'll be glad to see her, and you know the twins will."

Reuven snorted. His younger sisters looked on Jane as the font of everything wise and womanly. Her contours were certainly a good deal more finished than theirs, though they'd blossomed to an alarming degree the past couple of years.

Thoughtfully, Moishe Russie remarked, "I wouldn't mind seeing Jane again myself."

Rivka Russie was wearing a dish towel around her waist. She'd been back in the kitchen, cooking. She took off the towel, wadded it up in her hands, and threw it at her husband. "I'll bet you wouldn't," she said darkly—but not too darkly, for she started to laugh before Reuven's father tossed the towel back to her.

"Say something simple and you get into trouble." Moishe Russie rolled his eyes, precisely as if he hadn't expected to get into trouble by saying that particular simple thing. Jane Archibald was definitely a girl—a woman—worth seeing.

Laughing still, Reuven's mother went back to the kitchen. His father pulled a pack of cigarettes out of his breast pocket and lit one. "You shouldn't smoke those things," Reuven said, clucking like a mother hen. "You know how many nasty things the Lizards have shown they do to your lungs."

"And to my circulatory system, and to my heart." Moishe Russie nodded—nodded and took another drag. "They've shown all sorts of horrible things about tobacco."

"It's not ginger, for heaven's sake," Reuven said. "People *can* quit smoking."

"And Lizards *can* quit tasting ginger, too, for that matter," his father answered. "It just doesn't happen very often."

"You don't get the enjoyment out of tobacco that the Race gets out of ginger," Reuven said, to which his father could hardly disagree, especially when his mother might be listening. He persisted: "What *do* you get out of it, anyhow?"

"I don't know." His father eyed the glowing coal on the end of his cigarette. "It relaxes me. And one tastes very good after food."

"That doesn't sound like enough," Reuven said.

"No, I suppose not." Moishe Russie shrugged. "It's an addiction. I can hardly deny it. There are plenty of worse ones. That's about the most I can say."

"What's the most you can say about which, Father?" one of the twins asked. Reuven hadn't heard the twins come into the front room; they'd probably been helping their mother get supper ready. They sounded even more alike than they looked—Reuven couldn't be sure whether Esther or Judith had spoken.

Moishe Russie held up his cigarette. "That there are worse drugs than the ones that go into these." A thin, gray column of smoke rose into the air from the burning end of the cigarette.

"Oh." That was Esther; Reuven was sure of it. "Well, maybe." She wrinkled her nose. "It still smells nasty." Her sister nodded.

"Does it?" Their father sounded honestly surprised.

"It does." Reuven, Judith, and Esther all spoke together. Reuven added, "If you hadn't killed most of your sense of smell from years of those stinking things, you'd know it yourself."

"Would I?" Moishe Russie studied the cigarette, or what was left of it, then stubbed it out. "I don't suppose my sense of smell is really dead—more likely just dormant."

"Why don't you find out?" Reuven asked. His sisters nodded, their faces glowing. He and they often rubbed one another the wrong way, but they agreed about this.

His father ran a hand over his bald crown—a silent genetic warning that Reuven wouldn't keep his own dark hair forever. It was, in fact, already starting to retreat above his temples. Moishe Russie said, "Maybe I will . . . one of these days."

That meant never. Reuven knew it. His sisters, a lot younger and a lot more naive than he, knew it, too. Disappointment shone from them as excitement had a moment before. He was opening his mouth to let his father know what he thought when his mother preempted him by calling, "Supper!"

Supper was a leg of mutton with potatoes and carrots and onions, a dish they might have eaten back in Warsaw before the war except for the red Palestinian wine that went with it. Holding up his glass of the local vintage, Reuven said, "We've got a while to go before we catch up with France."

"You're turning into a wine *maven*?" his father asked, chuckling. Moishe Russie sipped the wine, too, and nodded. "*Maven* or not, I won't say you're wrong. On the other hand, these grapes are a lot less radioactive than the ones they use to make Burgundy or Bordeaux."

"A point," Reuven admitted. "I think we're pretty lucky the Nazis didn't try harder to land an explosive-metal bomb on Jerusalem. Then we wouldn't be able to say that about the wine." Then, odds were, they wouldn't have been able to say anything at all, but he chose not to dwell on that.

"Why didn't they try harder to bomb us?" Judith asked. At fifteen, she didn't think death was real. Reuven wished he could say the same.

His father answered, "They did send a couple of rockets our way, but the Race knocked them down. They saved most of their firepower to use against the Lizards, though." Moishe Russie's face twisted. "Either they hated the Race more than they hated us, or else they thought the Race was more dangerous. If I were a betting man, I'd put my money on the second choice."

Rivka Russie sighed. "So would I." Her eyes, like her husband's, were bleak and far away, remembering how things had been in German-held Poland before the conquest fleet landed. Reuven recalled that time only dimly, as one of hunger and fear. He was glad his memories held no more detail, too. To the twins, anything before they were born might as well have been the days of ancient Rome. *They're lucky,* he thought.

Out in the front room, the telephone hooked into the Lizards' network hissed for attention. Moishe Russie rose. "I'll get it. Maybe—*alevai*—the fleetlord has changed his mind or thought of something more he can do for poor Anielewicz." He hurried out. A moment later, though, he called, "Not Atvar at all. It's for you, Reuven."

"For me?" Reuven bounded out of his chair, even though he was only halfway through supper. The only person likely to call him on the Race's telephone system was . . . "Hello, Jane!" he said, switching from the Hebrew usual around the house to English. "How are you?"

"Couldn't be better." Jane Archibald's English had the not-quite-British accent of Australia. Blue eyes glowing, she smiled out of the screen at him. "I've passed my comprehensive exams, so I escape at the end of this term."

"Congratulations!" Reuven exclaimed. He would have been sweating out his comprehensives, too, if he hadn't left the medical college. He knew what monsters they were. Then he caught the crucial verb. "Escape?"

"That's right." She nodded. Her golden hair flipped up and down. "Canada's accepted me. You've known forever that I didn't want to start a practice anyplace the Lizards rule." Reuven nodded back at her; the Lizards had been harsh in Australia, seizing the whole continent for themselves, with humans a distinct afterthought. Jane went on, "And so, sweetheart, the time is coming—and it's coming soon—when we have to figure out where we go from here, or if we go anywhere at all from here."

"If we're going anywhere, I'm going to Canada," Reuven said slowly, and Jane nodded again. He'd known he would have to make a choice like that one day. He hadn't thought he would have to make it quite so soon. Even more slowly, he went on, "I'm going to have to think about that."

"I know you will," Jane replied. "I envy your having a family you can get along with, believe me I do. But I've got to tell you one more thing, dear: don't take too bloody long." Before he could find an answer, her image vanished from the screen.

Straha was used to fighting cravings. The ex-shiplord had started tasting ginger not long after he'd fled the conquest fleet, and had rarely been without it since. It helped make living among the American Big Uglies tolerable. Even so, now and again he wished he hadn't antagonized Atvar to the point where it was either flee or face the fleetlord's fury.

He let out a soft hiss. *If the assembled shiplords had chosen to oust Atvar and name me in his place, all of Tosev 3 might belong to the Race now,* he thought. Surely he could have led the conquest fleet better than that mediocre male. A large majority had thought he could. But the Race required three-quarters concurrence before making such a drastic change, and he hadn't got that. Atvar remained in command to this day—and Straha remained in exile to this day.

He had all the ginger he wanted. It wasn't illegal in the USA, as it was everywhere the Race ruled. Stashed away in his house—mostly of Tosevite construction, but with gadgetry from the Race—was almost enough of the precious herb to let him set up as a dealer. If he felt like a taste, he could have one. The Big Ugly who served as his driver and bodyguard wouldn't say no. If anything, he'd assume the Tosevite facial grimace connoting benevolence and get Straha more ginger still.

But turning his eye turrets away from ginger as much as he could was something Straha had long since got used to doing. Keeping the papers Sam Yeager had given him a secret was something else again. Straha didn't know exactly what. Yeager had given him those papers, only extracting a promise that he wouldn't look at them unless the Big Ugly suddenly died or disappeared. Straha had kept the promise, too, regardless of how tempted he was to see what Yeager thought so important.

What does he know? Straha wondered. *Why does he not want me to know it, too? How much trouble will come if I learn it? Not too much, surely.*

That was the voice he sometimes heard inside his head when he wanted one taste of ginger on top of another. It was an ever so persuasive voice, one that could talk him into almost everything. Almost. He counted Sam Yeager a friend in the same way that he counted friends among the Race. Yeager relied on him, trusted him. He had to be worthy of that trust . . . didn't he?

Before temptation could dig its claws into him too deeply, his driver came into the kitchen from the front room and said, "I greet you, Shiplord."

"And I greet you," Straha replied. The Big Ugly spoke his language about as well as a Tosevite could. "What do you want now?"

"Why do you think I want anything?" replied the male who served and guarded him.

Straha's mouth fell open in a laugh. "Because you are who you are. Because you are what you are."

His driver laughed, too, in the noisy Tosevite way. "All right, Shiplord. I suppose you have a point." He bent into the posture of respect, though in doing so he showed as much mockery as he did subordination. Given the security clearance and status he had to have to be allowed to work with Straha, that made a certain amount of sense.

"Very well, then," Straha said with a certain amount of asperity. He was jealous of his rank, despite the realities of the situation. "Suppose you tell me what you do want, then."

"It shall be done, Shiplord," the driver said, again mixing obedience with mockery. "You surely know that the colonization fleet has released its domestic animals in the areas the Race rules."

"I should hope so," Straha exclaimed, "considering the azwaca and zisuili in my freezer here."

"Exactly so," his driver agreed. "Are you also aware how rapidly these animals from Home are spreading in the desert regions of Tosev 3?"

"These are for the most part not deserts to us or to our beasts," Straha said. "Home is a hotter, drier world than this one. What you call desert is to us more often than not a temperate grassland."

"However you like," the Big Ugly said with a shrug very much like one a male of the Race might have used. "But that is not the point. The point is, these beasts are making themselves at home here faster than anyone could reasonably have expected. This is certainly true in northern Mexico."

"I have heard as much, in fact," Straha said.

"And you will also have heard that animals from Home respect international borders not at all. They are also establishing themselves in the American Southwest."

"Indeed: I have heard that, too," Straha said. "You still have not told me what you want, though."

"Is it not obvious?" the Tosevite returned. "How do we get rid of the miserable things? *We* do not eat them."

"Why are you asking me?" Straha said. "I am not an ecological engineer, and I do not know what resources you have available to you."

"We are willing to commit whatever resources prove necessary," his driver said. "These animals are highly unwelcome here, and they seem to be spreading very fast. Wherever the weather stays warm the year around, they appear at home."

"Unless you can hunt them into extinction, they probably will stay that way, too," Straha said.

"How nice," the Big Ugly said, his voice sour. That was an English idiom, translated literally into the language of the Race. It didn't mean what it said, but just the opposite. "I am sure my superiors will be delighted to hear that." He didn't mean what he said there, either.

Straha said, "I expect that we are also introducing the plants from Home on which our domestic animals prefer to feed. They too will take advantage of any ecological niches available to them here on Tosev 3. In fact, I am given to understand that this process has already begun in the subregion of the main continental mass called India."

"Terrific." The driver didn't bother to translate that ironic comment into the language of the Race, but left it in English. Straha had grown reasonably fluent in the language of the USA as the years went by. Gathering himself, the Tosevite switched to Straha's tongue: "How are we supposed to hunt weeds into extinction?"

"As a matter of fact, I doubt you can do it," Straha replied. "Now that we have come to Tosev 3, we are going to make this world as much like Home as we can. You would be addled to expect us to behave any differently."

"The war between the Race and us Tosevites has never really stopped, has it?" his driver said. "We are not shooting at each other as much as we used to, but we are still fighting."

"When there is shooting, you Big Uglies do not usually enjoy it," Straha said. "I offer the example of the Deutsche for your contemplation."

"Believe me, Shiplord, my superiors are contemplating it," his driver said. "But you did not answer my question, or did not answer it fully."

"I am surprised you needed to ask it," Straha replied. "Of course the struggle goes on, by whatever means appear convenient. The leaders of the Race will not be excessively concerned as to what those methods are. Results will matter far more to them. They are not in a hurry. They are never in a hurry."

"That has cost them, here on Tosev 3," the Big Ugly remarked.

"Truth," Straha admitted. "I advocated more haste myself, which led to nothing but my exile. But our usual slow pace also has its advantages. We move so slowly, our pressure is all but imperceptible. That does not mean it is not there, however."

Pursing his absurdly mobile lips, the Big Ugly let out a soft, low whistle. The sound was utterly different from anything the Race could produce. Straha had needed a long time to figure out what it meant: something on the order of resignation. At last, his driver said, "Well, we shall just have to go on exerting pressure of our own if we intend to survive—is that not also a truth?"

"Yes, I should say so," Straha answered. "The question is whether you Tosevites will be able to discover and to use effective forms of pressure."

"I think we shall manage," his driver said. "If there is one thing we Big Uglies are good at, it is making nuisances of ourselves."

Straha could hardly quarrel with that. Had the Tosevites not been good at making nuisances of themselves, their world would be firmly under the dominion of the Race today. The ex-shiplord turned an eye turret toward the driver and found a way in which to change the subject: "Are you not letting the hairs between your mouth and your snout escape from cutting?"

"I'm growing a mustache, yes," the Big Ugly replied in English.

"Why?" Straha asked. "I have seen other male Tosevites with such adornments, and I do not have a high opinion of them. When yours is complete, you will look as if you have a large, dark brown moth"—that last, necessarily, was an English word—"perched on your upper lip."

His driver laughed: loud, noisy Tosevite laughter. "*I* think it'll look good," he said, still in English. "If I decide I don't like it, I can always shave the damn thing off, you know."

"I suppose so," Straha said. "We of the Race would not be so casual about altering our appearance."

"I know that." The driver returned to the language of the Race. "It is one of the advantages we Tosevites still have over you. Ginger is another." He held up a fleshy hand to keep Straha from interrupting. "I do not mean its effect on males. I mean its effect on females. Like it or not, you are becoming more and more like us in matters pertaining to mating."

Straha's thoughtful hiss was the Race's equivalent of the driver's low whistle. The American authorities had not saddled him with a fool. Life would have been easier if they had. Slowly, the ex-shiplord said, "We are doing our best to resist these changes, and may yet succeed."

"And we *may* succeed in keeping your domestic animals out

of the United States," his driver said, "but I do not think that is the way to bet. Besides, you are not thinking in the long term here, Shiplord. How long before some enterprising male or female sends a big crate of ginger back to Home aboard a starship? What will happen then, do you suppose?"

This time, Straha's hiss was more dismayed than thoughtful. Once commerce between Tosev 3 and Home got going, half the males and females involved in it would want to smuggle ginger for the sake of the profits involved in it. Only items of enormous value and low bulk traveled between the stars: nothing else made economic sense. And, without the tiniest shred of doubt, the Tosevite herb fit the bill in every particular.

Interstellar smuggling between Home and either Rabotev 2 or Halless 1 had never amounted to much. Between Home and Tosev 3 . . . ? *Well,* Straha thought, *however large that problem may become, it is not one about which I shall have to worry.*

Winter in Edmonton had put David Goldfarb in mind of Siberia—not that he'd ever been to Siberia, of course, but he was used to the mild temperatures of the British Isles. A great many words might have described winter in Edmonton, but mild wasn't any of them.

Goldfarb had almost dreaded summer, wondering if it would rise above the subarctic. To his surprise and relief, it did. It got as warm as London ever did, and even a bit warmer. At the end of June, it soared into the eighties, and stayed there for more than a week.

"I should be wearing a pith helmet and shorts," he told his boss when he came into the Saskatchewan River Widget Works, Ltd.

Hal Walsh grinned at him. "I wouldn't lose any sleep if you did," he answered. "But you'd look like a jerk if it decided to snow while you were dressed that way."

To Goldfarb's still inexperienced ear, Walsh sounded like a Yank. An Englishman would have said something like *a right chump* in place of the widgetmaster's American slang. But that, when you got right down to it, was beside the point. "*Could* it snow?" Goldfarb asked in a small voice.

Jack Devereaux spoke before Walsh could: "It doesn't snow in summer here more than every other year."

For a horrid moment, Goldfarb thought he was serious. When Hal Walsh's grin made it plain the other engineer didn't mean it,

Goldfarb glared at Devereaux. "If you pull my leg any harder, it'll come off in your hand," he said, doing his best to seem the picture of affronted dignity.

All he accomplished was to make Walsh and Devereaux both laugh at him. His boss said, "If you can't look at the world cross-eyed, you shouldn't be working here, you know."

"Really?" Every once in a while, British reserve came in handy. "I never should have noticed."

This time, Walsh stared at him, wondering whether to believe. Jack Devereaux was quicker on the uptake. "Okay, David," he said. "Now *you* can let go of *my* leg."

"Fair enough." New boy on the block, Goldfarb often felt he had to make a stand and defend his own turf. He turned to Hal Walsh. "What's on the plate for this morning?"

"The usual," Walsh replied: "Trying to steal more secrets from the Lizards' gadgetry and turning it into things people can use."

"If you're very, very good, sometimes you're even allowed to have an idea all your own," Devereaux added. "But you're not supposed to let on that you did. Then everybody else might start having ideas, too, and where would we be if that happened?"

"About where we are, if the ideas we come up with are better than the other blokes'," Goldfarb answered.

Walsh said, "That notion you had for showing telephone numbers is a winner, David. We just got an order from the Calgary police, an order big enough that I think you've earned yourself another bonus check."

"Any time Calgary buys from Edmonton, you know we've got something good," Jack Devereaux added. "They don't love us, and we don't love them. It's like Toronto and Montreal, or Los Angeles and San Francisco down in the States."

"Glasgow and Edinburgh," Goldfarb murmured, picking an example from the British Isles. He nodded to Walsh, doing his best not to seem very pleased at the news of the bonus. The money was welcome; in this world, money was always welcome. But, as a Jew, he didn't want to seem excited about it. He cared what gentiles thought about his people, and didn't want to give them an excuse to think nasty thoughts.

After a little more chat, each of the engineers fixed a cup of tea and took it to his desk. Goldfarb had been pleasantly surprised to find tea so common in Canada; he'd assumed the Dominion, like the USA, was a land that preferred coffee. He was glad he'd been wrong.

Fortified, he studied the latest piece of hardware Hal Walsh had given him. It had, his boss assured him, come from the engine of a Lizard landcruiser. What it did in the motor was rather less certain: he just had the widget, not the engine of which it was a part. He thought it was the electronic controller for the fuel-injection system that took the place carburetors had in Earthly internal-combustion engines.

"You know what the trouble is, don't you?" he said to Jack Devereaux.

"Of course I do," his fellow engineer answered. "Our gadgets look like they do what they do. These Lizard creations are nothing but electronic components slapped together. They aren't *obvious*, the way our technology is."

"That's it!" Goldfarb nodded gratefully. "The very thing I was thinking of. We have to work hard to figure out what they're good for, and what they could be good for if we tweaked them a little."

He glowered at the control unit. It had a highly specialized job to do, and, if it was anything like most Lizard widgets, did that job extremely well. He wouldn't have been surprised to learn the Americans and Germans and Russians had copied it for their tanks—not that the Germans were allowed any panzers these days. The collapse of the *Reich* left him altogether undismayed.

Back in his days with the RAF, his work with Lizard technology had been perfectly straightforward. If it had to do with matters military, and especially with matters pertaining to radar, he'd done his best to adapt it to related human uses. If it didn't, he'd either ignored it or passed it on to someone whose bailiwick it was.

Things didn't work like that at the Saskatchewan River Widget Works. Here, the more outlandish his ideas, the better. Anybody could come up with direct conversions of Lizard gadgets to their nearest human equivalents. Sometimes that was worth doing—his system for reading phone numbers was a case in point. But thinking lefthanded was liable to pay off more in the long run.

Bloody wonderful, he thought. *How do I go about thinking lefthanded?* He couldn't force it; whenever he tried, he failed. Turning his mind away from the widget in front of him, letting his thoughts drift as they would, worked better. But that was a relative term. Sometimes inspiration simply would not strike.

He'd feared Hal Walsh would sack him if he failed to come up with something brilliant his first couple of days on the job. But Walsh, who'd been doing this sort of directed woolgathering a lot longer than he had, took dry spells in stride. And now Goldfarb had one solid achievement under his belt. Having seen that he *could* do it, his boss was less inclined to insist that he do it to order.

David spent the whole day playing with the Lizard control gadget, and by quitting time had come up with nothing in the least resembling inspiration. Walsh slapped him on the back. "Don't lose any sleep about it," he advised. "Give it another shot tomorrow. If it's still not going anywhere, we'll pull another gadget out of the bin and see what your evil, twisted imagination does with that."

"All right." At the moment, Goldfarb didn't find his imagination either evil or twisted. He had enough trouble finding it at all.

The sun still stood high in the sky when he started home. In summer, daylight lingered long here. Edmonton was farther north than London, almost as far north as Belfast, his last posting in the RAF. In winter, of course, the sun hardly appeared at all. But he didn't want to think about winter with long days to enjoy.

When he got back to his flat—they called them apartments in Edmonton, in the American style—he broke into a grin. "Roast chicken!" he exclaimed. "My favorite."

"It'll be ready in about twenty minutes," his wife called from the kitchen. "Would you like a bottle of beer first?"

"I'd love one," he answered. As far as he was concerned, Canadian taverns couldn't come close to matching proper British pubs, but Canadian beer in bottles was better than its British equivalents. He smiled at Naomi when she brought him a bottle of Moosehead. "You've got one for yourself, too, have you?"

"And why not?" she answered saucily, her accent British on top of the faint German undertone she still kept after escaping from the *Reich* in her teens, not long before no more Jews got out of Germany alive. She took a sip. "It's not bad," she said. "Not bad at all." Was she comparing it to the British brews she remembered, or to the German ones from long ago? David Goldfarb didn't have the nerve to ask.

Dinner was only a couple of minutes away when the telephone rang. Muttering under his breath, Goldfarb got up and answered it. "Hullo?" If it was some cheeky salesman, he intended to give the bugger a piece of his mind.

"Hullo, David, old chum! So good to catch up with you again!" The voice on the other end of the line was cheerful, English, educated—and familiar. Recognizing it at once, Goldfarb wished he hadn't.

"Roundbush," he said, and then, his voice harsh, "What do you want with me?"

"You're a smart lad. I daresay you can figure that out for yourself," Basil Roundbush answered cheerfully. "You didn't do as you were told, and I'm afraid you're going to have to pay for that."

Automatically, Goldfarb's eyes went to the gadget that showed the numbers of incoming calls. If he knew where the RAF officer who'd given him so much trouble was, he might be able to do something about him, or have the authorities do something about him. But the screen on the device showed no number at all. As far as it was concerned, nobody was on the other end of the call.

With a laugh, Roundbush said, "I know you've flanged up something from the Lizards' telephone switching gear. That won't help you. You know I've got plenty of chums among the Race. There are times when they need to neutralize such circuits, and they haven't any trouble doing it."

He obviously knew whereof he spoke. "Sod off and leave me alone," Goldfarb growled. "I don't want anything to do with you, and I don't want anything to do with your bleeding chums, either."

"You've made that plain enough." Roundbush still sounded happy. "But no one cares very much about your view of things, you know. You've been uncooperative, and now you're going to have to pay the price. I rather wish it were otherwise: you had promise. But such is life." He hung up.

So did Goldfarb, cursing under his breath. "Who was that?" Naomi called as she set the table.

"Basil Roundbush." Goldfarb wished he could have come up with a comforting, convincing lie.

The gentle clatter of plates and silverware stopped. His wife hurried out into the living room. "What did he want?" she asked. "I thought we were rid of him for good."

"I thought we were, too," David answered. "I wish we were, but no such luck." He sighed. "He didn't come right out and say what he wanted, but he didn't have to, not really. I already know that: he wants a piece of my hide." His right hand folded into a fist. "He'll have a devil of a time getting it, that's all I've got to say."

Glen Johnson stared into space. From the control room of the *Lewis and Clark*, in solar orbit not far from the asteroid Ceres, there was a lot of space to see. The stars blazed clear and steady against the black sky of hard vacuum. The glass that held the vacuum at bay had been coated to kill reflections; except for knowing that it kept him alive, Johnson could ignore it.

Turning to Mickey Flynn, the *Lewis and Clark*'s second pilot—the man just senior to him—he said, "I wonder how many of those stars you could see from Earth on a really clear night."

"Sixty-three percent," Flynn answered at once.

"How do you know that?" Johnson asked. He was prepared to take the figure as gospel truth. Flynn collected strange statistics the way head hunters collected heads.

"Simple," he said now, beaming as if the entire magnificent show out there beyond the window had been created for his benefit alone. "I made it up."

He had a splendid deadpan; if he'd claimed he'd read it somewhere or done some arcane calculations to prove it, Johnson would have believed him. As things were, Johnson snorted. "That'll teach me to ask you a serious question."

"No," Flynn said. "It'll teach me to give you a serious answer. If I'd been any more serious, I would have been downright morose." His face donned moroseness as he might have donned a sweater.

All it got him was another snort from Glen Johnson. Johnson peered ahead toward Jupiter, on which Ceres and the *Lewis and Clark* were slowly gaining. "I keep thinking I ought to be able to see the Galilean moons with the naked eye."

"When Jupiter's in opposition in respect to us, you will be able to," Flynn told him. "We'll only be two astronomical units away then, more or less—half as far as we would be back on Earth. But for now, we have the same sort of view we would from back home . . . minus atmosphere, of course." Before Johnson could say anything, the other pilot held up a hand, as if taking an oath. "And that, I assure you, is the truth, the whole truth, and nothing but the truth."

"So help you Hannah," Johnson said, at which Flynn assumed an expression of injured innocence. Nevertheless, Johnson believed him; the numbers felt right. Flynn and Walter Stone, the first pilot, both knew the mathematics of space travel better than he did. He'd flown fighter planes against the Lizards and then upper stages into Earth orbit—other people had done the thinking while he'd done the real piloting. If he hadn't got overly curious about what was going on aboard the American space station, he never would have been shanghaied when the space station turned out to be a spaceship. He hadn't wanted to come along, but he wasn't going back, not after two and a half years in weightlessness.

"Lieutenant Colonel Johnson! Lieutenant Colonel Glen Johnson!" His name rang out over the *Lewis and Clark*'s PA system. *Oh, Christ!* he thought. *What have I done to piss off the commandant now?* But it wasn't the commandant: the PA operator went on, "Report to scooter launching bay one immediately! Lieutenant Colonel Johnson. Lieutenant Colonel—"

"See you later," Johnson said to Flynn as he pushed off from a chair and glided out of the control room.

"And I'll be glad to be seen," Flynn called after him. Johnson was already swinging from one corridor handhold to the next: in weightlessness, imitating chimpanzees swinging through the trees was the best way to get around. Corridor intersections had mirrors mounted to cut down on collisions.

"What's going on?" Johnson asked when he got to the launch bay.

A technician was giving the scooter—a little rocket with a motor mounted at the front and another at the rear—a once-over. He said, "There's some kind of medical trouble in Dome 27, on that rock with the big black vein through it."

"Okay, I know the one you mean," Johnson said. "About twenty miles rearward of us, right?" He waited for the tech to nod, then went on, "Is it bad enough that they want me to bring a doctor over?" One of the things going out into space had done was let people find new ways to maim themselves.

But the technician said, "No. What they want you to do is bring the gal back here so the doc can look her over, see what's going on."

"Gal?" Johnson clicked his tongue between his teeth. Women made up only about a third of the *Lewis and Clark*'s crew. Losing anybody hurt. Losing a woman . . . The idea shouldn't have hurt twice as much, but somehow it seemed to. "What's wrong with her? She hurt herself?"

"No," the tech said again. "Belly pain."

"Okay. I'll go get her." The *Lewis and Clark* had a chamber that could be spun to simulate gravity—only about .25g, but that was enough for surgery. Operating in weightlessness, with blood floating everywhere, wasn't even close to practical. The chamber, so far as Johnson knew, hadn't been used yet, but there was a first time for everything.

"You're ready," the tech said. "You're fully fueled, oxygen supply is full, too, batteries are good, radio checks are all nominal."

"Let me in, then." Johnson glided past the technician and into the scooter. After he closed the gas-tight canopy, he ran his own checks. It was his neck, after all. Everything looked the way the tech said it was. Johnson would have been astonished—and furious—had that proved otherwise. As things were, he spoke into the radio mike: "Ready when you are."

"Okay." A gas-tight door slid shut behind the scooter. A moment later, another one slid open in front of it. A charge of compressed air pushed the little rocket out of its bay. Johnson waited till it had drifted far enough away from the *Lewis and Clark*, then lit up his attitude jets and his rear motor and started off toward Dome 27.

He smiled in enormous pleasure as he made the trip. Mickey Flynn and Walter Stone were both much more qualified to pilot the *Lewis and Clark* than he was. If he ever got stuck with that assignment, it would only be because something had gone drastically wrong somewhere. In a scooter, though . . .

"In a scooter, I'm the hottest damn pilot in the whole solar system," he said after making sure he wasn't transmitting. Without false modesty, he knew he was right. His years as a combat flier and in Earth-orbital missions gave him a feel for the little rocket nobody else aboard the *Lewis and Clark* came close to matching. This was spaceflight, too, spaceflight in its purest form, spaceflight by the seat of his pants.

He made only one concession to his instruments: he kept an eye on the radar screen, to make sure his Mark One eyeball didn't miss any tumbling rocks that might darken his day if they smacked into the scooter. He had to be especially watchful heading toward Dome 27, since he was going, so to speak, against the flow.

He spied one large object on the radar that he couldn't see at all, but he didn't let it worry him. He supposed it was inevitable that the Lizards should have sent out unmanned probes to keep an eye (or would it be an eye turret?) on what the Americans were doing in the asteroid belt. That made life difficult, but not impossible. And, as the Americans ran up more and more domes and spread farther and farther away from the *Lewis and Clark*, the Lizards' surveillance job got harder and harder.

Their spy ship was well off the track between the *Lewis and Clark* and Dome 27, so Johnson didn't waste more than a moment's thought on it. He fired up the radio once more: "Dome 27, this is the scooter. I say again, Dome 27, this is the scooter. I understand you have a pickup for me. Over."

"That's right, Scooter," said whoever was manning the radio at the pressure dome. "Liz Brock's hurting pretty bad. We're hoping it's her appendix—anything else would be worse. Estimate your arrive time twenty minutes."

"Sounds about right," Johnson agreed. "I'll get her back, and the doc'll figure out what's going on with her. Hope everything turns out okay. Out." Under his breath, he muttered, "Liz Brock—that's not so good." She was the ship's number-one expert on electrolyzing ice to get oxygen for breathing and fuel and hydrogen for fuel. She was also a nice-looking blonde. She'd never shown the least interest in Johnson, but he didn't believe in wasting valuable natural resources.

He used his forward rocket motor to kill his velocity relative to the little asteroid on which Dome 27 had gone up, then guided the scooter into the dome's airlock with tiny, delicate bursts from his attitude jets. Ever so slowly, the scooter settled toward the floor of the airlock: the gravity of the asteroid (which was less than a mile across) seemed almost as much rumor as reality.

As soon as the outer airlock door closed and his gauges showed there was pressure outside, Johnson unsealed the scooter's canopy. He didn't have to wait long. Two people floated into the airlock: Liz Brock and a man who was helping her. He said, "We've loaded her up with as much codeine as she can hold, and then maybe a little more for luck."

"Doesn't help," the electrolysis expert said. Her voice was slow and dragging. "Doesn't help *much*, I mean. I feel like I'm drunk. I feel like my whole head's weightless. But I still hurt." She looked like it. She had lines at the corners of her mouth that hadn't been there the last time Johnson saw her. Skin stretched tight across her cheekbones. She kept one hand on the right side of her belly, though she didn't seem to notice she was doing it.

After she got into the scooter, Johnson fastened her safety harness when she didn't do anything but fumble with it. Anxiously, he asked the fellow who'd helped her into the airlock, "She's not throwing up, is she?"

"No," the man answered, which relieved him: dealing with vomit in the scooter was the last thing he wanted to do.

He used his attitude jets to slide out of the airlock, then went back to the *Lewis and Clark* faster than he'd gone away. When he returned to the ship, Dr. Miriam Rosen was waiting at the inner airlock door to the shuttle bay. "Come on, Liz, let's get you over to the X-ray machine," she said. "We'll see if we can figure out what's going on in there."

"All right." Liz Brock sounded altogether indifferent. Maybe that was the codeine talking. Maybe, too, it was the pain talking.

Johnson wanted to tag along to find out whatever he could, but didn't have the nerve. He watched the doctor lead away the electrolysis expert. Before long, he'd get answers through the grapevine.

And he did. Things came out piecemeal, as they had a way of doing. It wasn't appendicitis. He heard that pretty soon. He didn't hear what it was for three or four days. "Liver cancer?" he exclaimed to Walter Stone, who told him. "What can they do about that?"

"Not a damn thing," the senior pilot said grimly. "Keep her from hurting too bad till she dies—that's about the size of it." He seldom showed much of what he thought, but he was visibly upset here. "Could have been you or me, too, just as easy. No rhyme or reason to this—only dumb luck."

"Yeah." Johnson felt lousy, too. He didn't mind being an ambulance driver, but he hadn't signed up to be, in essence, a hearse driver. And there were also other things to worry about. "This won't hurt the plan too much, will it?"

Now Stone looked stern and determined. "Nothing hurts the plan, Glen. Nothing."

"Good," Glen Johnson said. "We've still got a lot of work to do."

☆ 4 ☆

With a shriek of decelerating jet engines, the Japanese airliner rolled to a stop on the runway just outside of Edmonton. The pilot spoke over the intercom, first in his own language and then in English hardly more comprehensible. "What the hell is he talking about?" Penny Summers asked.

"One from column A, two from column B," Rance Auerbach guessed. Penny gave him a dirty look. He ignored it and went on, "It would have been a lot faster and a lot cheaper to fly a U.S. airliner out of Tahiti."

"And it would have made stops in the States, too," Penny pointed out. "I didn't want to take the chance."

"Well, okay," Auerbach said with a sigh. "But I'll tell you something: there aren't a hell of a lot of places left where we can go without somebody wanting to take a shot at us as soon as we get there. That gets old, you know what I mean?"

"Things ought to be pretty peaceful for the layover here." Penny sighed, too. Rance knew what that meant. Whenever she came to someplace peaceful, she got bored. When she got bored, she started turning things on their ear. He'd had enough of things' getting turned on their ear. Telling her so wouldn't do him any good. He knew as much. He didn't think she started stirring things up on purpose—which didn't mean they didn't get stirred up.

Groundcrew men wheeled a deplaning ladder up to the airliner's front door. Rance grunted even more painfully than usual as he heaved himself upright. Except for a couple of trips back to the head, he'd been trapped in a none-too-spacious seat ever since Midway Island. He hadn't been sitting here forever—he couldn't have been—but it sure as hell felt that way.

"Baggage and customs and passport control through Gate

Four," a groundcrew man bawled, again and again. "Gate Four!" He pointed toward the airport terminal, as if none of the de-planing passengers could possibly have noticed the big red 4 above the nearest gate without his help.

"Well, well, what have we here?" a Canadian customs man said, examining their documents with considerable interest. "Papers from the Race, valid for South Africa only—rather em-phatically valid for South Africa only, I might add. Then all these endorsements from Free France, a Japanese transit visa, and a transit visa for the Dominion here. Fascinating. You don't see things like this every day."

"You see anything wrong?" Rance put a little challenge in his raspy, ruined voice.

"And you, sir, do not sound like a South African," the customs man said. "You sound like an American from the South."

"Doesn't matter what I sound like," Auerbach said. "Only thing that matters is, my papers are in order."

"That's right," Penny agreed. A lot of places, they could have made things go smoothly by greasing the functionary's palm. There were parts of the USA where that would have worked like a charm. Eyeing this customs man, Auerbach thought a bribe would only get him in deeper. He kept his hand away from his billfold.

"I think we had better have a look at your baggage," the Cana-dian official said. "A good, thorough look."

He and his pals spent the next hour examining the baggage not only by eye but with a fluoroscope. A customs man patted Rance down. A police matron took Penny off into another room. When she came back, steam was coming out of her ears. But the matron shrugged to the customs men, so Penny had passed the test.

"You see?" Rance said. "We're clean." He was awfully glad neither he nor Penny had tried to sneak a gun through the Do-minion. Canadians didn't like that sort of thing at all.

The lead customs agent glared at him. "You have close to fifty pounds of ginger in your suitcases," he pointed out.

"It's not illegal." Rance and Penny spoke together.

"That's so." The customs man didn't sound happy about it, but couldn't deny it. "Still, I strongly suggest you would be very wise to keep your noses clean while you are in Edmonton. Give me those preposterous papers." With quite unnecessary force, he applied the stamps that cleared them for entry.

Because Auerbach wasn't up to carrying much, they rented a little cart to get all the luggage to the cab rank. Fortunately, the first waiting cabby drove an enormous Oldsmobile whose equally enormous trunk devoured all the suitcases with the greatest of ease.

"Four Seasons Hotel," Penny told him as he held the door open for her and Rance.

"Yes, ma'am," he answered. "Best hotel in town." His accent wasn't that far removed from her Midwestern tones. *Next best thing to being back in the States,* Auerbach thought.

He hadn't known what to expect from the hotel; choosing one from thousands of miles away couldn't be anything but a gamble. But this gamble paid off. "Not bad," Penny said as bellmen all but fought over their suitcases.

"How long do you expect to be staying, sir?" the desk clerk asked Rance.

"Only a few days," Rance answered. With luck, they'd sell their ginger here and then head on to France with a nice stash. Without luck, they'd have to try to smuggle the ginger past the noses of the Race's French chums, and probably past the Lizards' own snouts, too. Rance didn't like thinking about all the things that could happen without luck.

"Phew!" Penny said when they finally made it to their room.

"Yeah." Rance hobbled over to the bed, let his stick fall to the thickly carpeted floor, and stretched out at full length on the mattress. His back made little crackling noises. "Jesus, that feels good!" he said. "I feel like I was stuffed into a sardine can for the last month."

"I know what you mean." Penny lay down beside him. "The Japs make seats and spaces between seats that suit them, but they're too damn cramped for Americans. I'm not a great big gal, but I'm not teeny-tiny like that, either."

He reached out and let his hand rest, almost as if by accident, on her leg. One thing led to another, and then to another after that: both of them, worn out by long travel and other, happier exertions, fell asleep on that big, comfortable bed. When Rance woke up, he heard the shower going. It stopped a couple of minutes later. Penny came out, wrapped in a white hotel towel. "Oh, good," she said when she saw his eyes were open. "Now I don't have to shake you."

"You'd better not." Sitting up made Rance's ruined shoulder

yelp, but he did it anyhow. "What time is it?" Asking her was easier than looking at the clock on the nightstand.

"Half past six," she answered. "Why don't you spruce up, too? Then we can go downstairs and get ourselves some supper." As if to spur him out of bed, she let the towel drop.

"Okay," he said, groping for his stick when he would sooner have been groping her. But soap and hot water were good in their own way. After endless hours in that airplane, he felt filmed with grime. Scraping sandy, gray-streaked stubble off his chin and cheeks made him look less like a stumblebum and more like an up-and-coming ginger dealer.

Everybody in the Vintage Room, the Four Seasons' restaurant, looked like somebody, whether he was or not. Whiskies arrived with commendable speed. The steaks Rance and Penny ordered took a lot longer, though. The service was courteous and attentive, but it was slow. After Japanese food on the airliner, Auerbach's stomach seemed empty as outer space. He finally lost patience. When his waiter walked by, he growled, "What are you doing, waiting for the calf to grow up so you can butcher it?"

"I'm sorry, sir." The waiter didn't sound more than professionally sorry. "I'm sure your supper will be ready before too very long." Off he went. The restaurant wasn't crowded, but things didn't move very fast even so.

A couple of tables over, a fellow with a splendid graying handlebar mustache waved for his own waiter. "I say," he boomed in tones unmistakably upper-crust British, "has everyone in your kitchen died of old age?"

"Oh, good," Penny said with a laugh. "We're not the only ones who can't get fed."

"Not the only ones starving to death, you mean," Rance grumbled. He studied the Englishman. After a moment, he grunted softly. "God damn me to hell and throw me in a frying pan if that's not Basil Roundbush. I haven't seen him in years, but that's got to be him. Couldn't be anybody else, by Jesus."

"That ginger smuggler you have connections with?" Penny asked.

"The very same," Auerbach said. "Now what the devil is he doing here? I hadn't heard that he'd given up on England." He paused. "For that matter, with the Nazis down for the count, there's no point in giving up on England, you know?" His eyes narrowed. "Maybe he's here on business."

"Yeah." Penny's eyes lit up. "Maybe we could do some business if he is. Finding somebody like that—we wouldn't need to chase around after locals with connections. It could save us a lot of time."

"You're right. Money, too." Rance grabbed his stick and used it to get to his feet. He limped over to the table where Basil Roundbush was sitting and sketched a salute. "Long as you're not getting fed, either, want to not get fed along with my lady friend and me?"

Roundbush's gaze swung toward him. The Englishman was so handsome, Rance wondered if he ought to let him anywhere near Penny. But it was done now. And, no slower than if he'd seen Rance day before yesterday, Roundbush said, "Auerbach, as I live and breathe." He sprang to his feet and shook Rance's hand. "What are you doing in this benighted Land Without Supper?"

"This and that. We can talk about it, if you want to," Auerbach said. "And I might ask you the same question. I will ask you the same question, when you get over there."

"I hope my waiter eventually realizes where I've gone—or even that I've gone." But Roundbush grabbed his own drink and followed Rance back to his table. He bowed over Penny's hand and kissed it. She did everything but giggle like a schoolgirl. Auerbach had known she would. Sourly, he waved to his waiter for another drink. Roundbush's waiter came by the empty table and stared in blank dismay. More handwaving got that straightened out. The dinners did eventually arrive.

Over what even a Texan had to admit was pretty good beef, Rance asked, "And what *are* you doing in Canada?"

"Taking care of a nasty little spot of business," Basil Roundbush answered. "Chap named David Goldfarb—fellow wouldn't do what he was supposed to. Can't have that go on: bad for business, don't you know?"

"Goldfarb?" Rance's ears pricked up. "Not the fellow you sent down to Marseille?"

"Why, yes. How the devil could you know that?" Before Auerbach spoke, Roundbush answered his own question: "Don't tell me you were the people the Lizards had involved in that fiasco. Small world, isn't it?"

"Too damn small, sometimes," Rance said.

"It could be, it could be." Basil Roundbush waved airily. "In any case, the bloke's not wanted anything to do with us since. He knows rather more than he should, and so . . ." He shrugged. "Unfortunate, but that's how life is sometimes."

"You ask me, you ought to leave him alone," Rance said. "You asked for trouble, sending a Jew down into the *Reich*. I'd give you what-for, too, you tried that on me."

Penny kicked him under the table. He wondered why, till he remembered they might be able to sell Roundbush their ginger. Well, that was water over the dam now. The Englishman gave him a frosty stare. "I'm afraid your opinion doesn't much concern me, old man. I intend doing what suits me, not what suits you."

Rance's temper kindled. He didn't care who the limey was, or how big a wheel. Nobody brushed him off like that. Nobody. "You can goddamn well leave him alone, mister, or you'll answer to me."

Penny kicked him again, harder. He ignored that, too. He'd thought she would make trouble here, and now he was doing it. Roundbush didn't laugh in his face, but he came close. He said, "If you think your foolish words will do the slightest thing toward changing my mind, old man, I must tell you you're mistaken."

"If you think I'm just talking, *old man,* you're full of shit," Rance replied. Penny did her best to take his leg off at the ankle. The Lizards had done their best to take it off at the thigh. He wasn't afraid of anything, not any more, not even—maybe especially not—of dying. It gave him an odd sort of freedom. He intended to make the most of it.

Whenever the telephone rang these days, whether at home or at the Saskatchewan River Widget Works, David Goldfarb answered it with a certain amount of apprehension. He also answered it with pencil and paper handy, to record the phone numbers of callers. That wouldn't do him any good with Basil Roundbush, of course, but it might help with local hired muscle, if the Englishman chose to use any. Goldfarb had no way of guessing how many scrambler sets Roundbush had brought along.

"Saskatchewan River Widgets," he said now, pencil poised. "David Goldfarb speaking."

"Hello, Goldfarb. We met once upon a time, a long ways away from here. Do you remember?" It wasn't Roundbush's voice. It wasn't a British voice at all. That accent was American, with an odd twang. The fellow on the other end of the line also spoke in a harsh rasp, as if he hadn't had a cigarette out of his mouth for five minutes since the day he was born.

More than anything else, that rasp reminded David Goldfarb of who the caller had to be. "Marseille," he blurted, and then, "You're one of the Yanks the Lizards used to try to nab Pierre Dutourd."

"That's right," the American said. "Name's Rance Auerbach, in case you don't recollect. You ought to be interested in hearing I had supper with that fellow called Roundbush last night."

Goldfarb already had his number written down. He could pass it on to the police with no trouble at all. Voice tight, he said, "And I suppose you're going to tell me you're the one who plans on finishing me off." Anything more he could pass on to the police would be welcome, too.

But this Auerbach said, "Christ, no, you damn fool. I just wanted to make sure you knew old Basil was gunning for you. I told him to leave you the hell alone, and he told me to piss up a rope. So I'm on your side, son."

Nobody'd been on Goldfarb's side for a long time. Actually, that wasn't quite true. Without Jerome Jones' help, he never would have been able to emigrate from Britain at all, and without George Bagnall, he might still be languishing in bureaucratic limbo in Ottawa. But Roundbush and his chums seemed much more determined to do him harm than anybody was to do him good. He said, "I know dear Basil is in Edmonton, thanks."

"That's nice," Auerbach said. "Do you know he intends to do you in, too?"

"As a matter of fact, yes," David answered. Talking about it felt surprisingly good. "I'm taking what precautions I can." Those were pitifully few. And he could do even less for Naomi and the children than he could for himself.

"I told the son of a bitch he'd answer to me if he tried any nasty business on you," Rance Auerbach said. "He didn't cotton to hearing that, but I told him anyhow. After he sent you to France, he can damn well leave you alone now."

"*Did* you?" Goldfarb was frankly amazed, and no doubt showed it. In an absent way, he wondered what sort of name Rance was; the Yanks could come up with some strange ones.

But that didn't matter. He went on, "And what did he say to that? Nothing too kind, is my guess."

"Right the first time." Auerbach coughed, then muttered, "Damn!" He drew in a breath whose wheezing Goldfarb could hear over the telephone before continuing, "No, he wasn't too happy. But then, he doesn't think I can do much."

Remembering how physically damaged the American was, Goldfarb feared his former RAF superior was right. He didn't want to say that. What he did say was, "What can you do?"

"Less than I'd like, dammit, on account of I'm not gonna be here real long. But I've already talked to some of the cops here," Auerbach answered. "For some reason or other, Canadians take things like death threats a lot more seriously than we do down in the States."

Was that supposed to be funny? Goldfarb couldn't tell. He said, "You're *supposed* to take things like that seriously, aren't you?"

Auerbach laughed. Then he coughed again. Then he cursed again. He said, "Only goes to show you've never lived in Texas." After another round of coughs and another round of soft curses, he went on, "Listen, you know where you can get your hands on a pistol without filling out forms from here to next week?"

"No," Goldfarb answered. He'd been advised—hell, he'd been told—to leave his service weapon behind when he came to Canada. He'd done it, too, and spent the time since Basil Round-bush first called wishing he hadn't.

"Too bad," the American said. "The trouble with guys like good old Basil and his pals is, they don't play by the rules. If you do, you're liable to end up a dead duck."

"I know," David said unhappily. "But what can you do about all this? What can I do about it, for that matter?"

"Well, making sure you don't get killed would be a good start," Auerbach answered.

"I quite agree," David Goldfarb said. "I've been trying to do that myself for quite some time now. What can you do about it?"

"I don't right know. I wish I were gonna be here longer," the American said. "I've got a marker or two I may be able to call in, but God only knows if they're still worth anything. Finding out will take a little bit of doing: I haven't tried to get ahold of these people in a long time. And I won't be able to tell them everything about this business even if they aren't pushing up lilies somewhere."

David pondered that. It could add up to any number of different things, but he saw one that looked more likely than any of the others. "You know Germans?" he asked, and wondered if he really wanted to find out the answer.

For close to half a minute, he didn't. At last, Auerbach said, "Well, you're nobody's fool, are you?"

"I like to think not, anyhow," Goldfarb said. "Of course, people like to think all sorts of things that others might find unlikely."

"And isn't that the sad and sorry truth?" Rance Auerbach said. "Okay, hang in there, Goldfarb. I'll see what I can do." He hung up.

From the next desk over, Hal Walsh said, "I hope that wasn't trouble, David," as Goldfarb set his own phone back in its cradle.

"I don't . . . think so," David told his boss. Walsh nodded, not entirely convinced. Since Goldfarb wasn't entirely convinced, either, he just shrugged and went back to work. He had to look down at the drawings in front of him for a while before he could remember what the hell he'd been trying to do.

He spent the rest of the day at half speed. He couldn't keep his mind fully on the latest project Hal Walsh had sent him. His eyes kept drifting toward the telephone. When it rang half an hour later, he jumped. But it was only Naomi, asking him to stop at the grocery for a few things on the way home from work.

"I can do that," he said.

"I should hope so," his wife answered. "It's not that hard, especially now when you have sensible money to deal with." Though she'd lived in Britain for the larger part of her life, she'd never quite come to terms with pence and shillings and pounds. Canadian dollars and cents made her much happier than the traditional currency ever had.

Goldfarb left the office about half an hour later than he might have otherwise; he was doing his best to make up for being distracted. As usual when the weather was even close to decent, he walked home: his flat was less than a mile from the Widget Works. That kept the beginnings of a middle-aged potbelly from becoming too much more than a beginning.

With a choice of several grocer's shops on the way, he intended to stop at the one closest to his block of flats. Walking was all very well, but walking with a paper sack was something else again.

He was halfway across the street on whose far side stood the grocer's when he heard the roar of a racing automobile engine and a couple of shouts of, "Look out!" His head whipped around. A big Chevy—an enormous auto, for one used to British motorcars—was bearing down on him, and the driver plainly had not the slightest intention of stopping.

Had he panicked, he would have died right there. He waited as long as he thought he possibly could—perhaps a whole second—then dashed forward. The Chevy's driver couldn't react quite fast enough. The edge of his mudguard (no, they called them fenders on this side of the Atlantic) touched Goldfarb's jacket, but then he was past.

And then that driver had to slam on the brakes to keep from smashing into the cars stopped at the light at the next corner. He couldn't do that quite fast enough, either, not at the speed he was going. It had been a while since David heard the crash of crumpling metal and shattering glass, but the sound was unmistakable.

Goldfarb sprinted toward the Chevy that had come to grief. He hoped the driver had gone straight through the windscreen—it never for a moment occurred to him to doubt that the fellow had tried to run him down on purpose. And if the bastard hadn't got himself a face full of plate glass, Goldfarb wanted answers from him. Maybe the local constabulary could get them. Or maybe he'd start bouncing the bugger's head off the pavement till he sang.

But the driver hadn't gone through the windscreen (no, windshield here). He managed to get his door open and started to run. "Stop him!" Goldfarb shouted. "Stop that man!"

In Britain, a crowd would have taken off after the man. He didn't know what would happen in Canada. He found out: a crowd took off after the fellow, a crowd led by the man with whose car the driver had just collided. A younger fellow brought the fleeing driver down with a tackle that would have earned him pats on the back in a rugby scrum.

"He almost killed you, buddy," somebody said to Goldfarb. "It was like he didn't see you at all."

"Oh, he saw me, all right," David said grimly. "He's just sorry he missed." The other man stared at him and tried to laugh, thinking he'd made a joke. When he didn't laugh back, the other fellow went off shaking his head.

Goldfarb didn't care, because a police car screeched around

the corner and stopped. The men who piled out were dressed more like American cops than British bobbies, but that didn't matter much. They took efficient charge of the miscreant. "He tried to kill me," Goldfarb told one of them. "Before he smashed into that other motorcar, he almost ran me down while I was crossing the street."

"Probably drunk," the policeman said.

"No, I mean it literally," David insisted. "He did try to kill me. He swerved towards me, but I managed to dodge."

Both policemen looked at him. One of them said, "Maybe you'd better come to the station, then, sir, and give a statement."

"I'd be glad to, if you'll let me ring my wife when we get there, so she knows I'm all right and I'll be late," Goldfarb answered. The policemen nodded. He rode to the station in the front seat, the man who'd tried to run him down in the back. They didn't say a word to each other all the way there.

Sweating in his coveralls, Johannes Drucker waited for a Lizard to open the door to his cubicle aboard the starship he'd tried to destroy. At precisely the appointed moment, the door slid open. The male—Drucker presumed it was a male—who stood in the doorway said, "Come with me."

"It shall be done, superior sir," Drucker answered.

The Lizard's mouth fell open: the gesture the Race used for laughter. "I am a female," she said. "My name is Nesseref. Now come. My shuttlecraft is waiting at the rotation hub of this ship."

"It shall be done, superior *female*," Drucker said, both stressing the word and adding an emphatic cough. That made Nesseref laugh again.

When Drucker strode out into the corridor, he found two armed Lizards waiting to make sure he didn't go anywhere he wasn't supposed to. Now that they were finally releasing him, the German spaceman had no intention of doing that, but he would have mistrusted one of them were their roles reversed. He wished those roles had been reversed.

He followed Nesseref toward the hub of the starship. The guards followed him. With every deck they went inward, they got lighter. By the time they reached the rotation hub, they weighed nothing at all.

Nesseref entered her shuttlecraft first, then called, "Come in. I have an acceleration couch shaped for a Tosevite."

"I thank you," Drucker said, and obeyed. The couch looked to be of American manufacture. He strapped himself in. Nesseref wasted no time in using her maneuvering jets to get free of the starship. Drucker watched her work in silent fascination. At last, he broke the silence: "Your ship has far more in the way of computer-aided controls than the upper stage I flew."

"A good thing, too," the Lizard replied. "I think you Tosevites have to be addled to come up into space in your inadequate machines."

"We used what we had," Drucker answered with a shrug. He spoke in the past tense: the *Reich* would not be going into space again any time soon. If the Race had its way—and that was all too likely—Germans would never go into space again. He asked, "Now that I am returning to Tosev 3, where in Deutschland will you land me?"

"By the city called Nuremberg," Nesseref answered. "Such are my orders."

"Nuremberg?" Drucker sighed. He'd been warned, but still . . . "That is in the far south of the land, and my home is in the north. Could you not have picked a closer shuttlecraft port?"

"There are no closer functioning shuttlecraft ports," Nesseref answered. "In fact, I am given to understand that that is at the moment the only functioning shuttlecraft port in the subregion. Had no one told you of this?"

"Well, yes," Johannes Drucker admitted unhappily. "But it still presents great difficulties for me. How am I to travel from Nuremberg to my home? Will the railroads be working? Will folk on the ground give me money to travel?"

"I know nothing of any of this." Nesseref's voice held nothing but indifference. "My orders are to put you on the ground at the shuttlecraft port outside Nuremberg. I shall obey them."

Obey them she did, with an efficiency that outdid anything merely Teutonic. A single neat burn took the shuttlecraft out of Earth orbit. After that, she hardly even had to adjust the machine's course. Another burn halted the shuttlecraft above the tarmac of the port and let its legs kiss the ground with hardly a jar.

Nesseref opened the hatch. The mild air of German summer mingled with the hot, dry stuff the Race preferred. "Get out," she told Drucker. "I do not want any more radioactive contamination than I can help getting."

"It shall be done." Drucker scrambled down the ladder and let himself drop to the soil of the *Vaterland*.

No one, Lizard or human, came across the tarmac to greet him. Now that he was here, he was on his own. He looked toward what had been the famous skyline of Nuremberg. No more: that skyline had been truncated, abridged. Some of the massive buildings were simply gone, others were wreckage half as tall as they had been. He shook his head and let out a soft, sad whistle. No matter how harshly the *Reich* had used him and his family, it was still his country. Seeing it brought low like this tore at him.

I shouldn't have bothered attacking that starship, he thought. *The war was already lost by then. I should have landed the upper stage of my A-45 in some neutral country—the USA, maybe England—and let myself be interned.*

Too late now. Too late for everything now. He'd expected to go out in a blaze of glory when he made the attack run on the Lizard ship. No such luck. Now he had to deal with the consequences of living longer than he'd thought he would.

He glanced around the tarmac again. No, nobody cared he was here. He didn't have ten pfennigs in his pocket: what point to taking money into space? Where would he spend it? But he faced different questions here: how would he get along without it? Where would he find his next meal? If he did find a meal, how would he pay for it?

Where would he find his next meal? Somewhere to the north, that was all he knew. As the crow flew, Greifswald was about five hundred kilometers from Nuremberg. He wasn't a crow, and he didn't think he'd do much in the way of flying any time soon. He'd be walking, and likely walking a lot more than five hundred kilometers.

Who was it who'd said, *A journey of a thousand miles must begin with a single step*? Somebody Chinese, he thought. He took the first step on the way back toward Greifswald. Before long, he was off the tarmac of the shuttlecraft port. He soon discovered the Lizards had machine-gun and artillery and missile emplacements around it. None of the males—he presumed they were males, though he'd been wrong with the shuttlecraft pilot—paid him any attention. He was authorized to be there. He didn't care to think what would have happened if he hadn't been.

Before long, he came on a road leading northeast. He started tramping along it. That was the direction in which he wanted to go. Pretty soon, he'd either come to a village or farmhouse or he'd pass a stream or a pond. Any which way, he'd get himself a drink.

He wondered how much radioactivity he'd take in from the local water. For that matter, he wondered how much he was taking in every time he inhaled. However much it was, he couldn't do anything about it.

And he wondered why he saw no motor traffic on the road. He didn't need long to find the answer to that: the Lizards had cratered it with dozens of little bomblets. He remembered those weapons from the earlier round of fighting. He'd driven panzers then, and hadn't worried so much about roads. But wheeled vehicles couldn't go anywhere without them.

After a couple of kilometers, he came upon a gang filling in craters the bomblets had left behind. No bulldozers, no tractors, no powered equipment of any kind. Just men with shovels and picks and mattocks and crowbars, slowly and methodically getting rid of one hole after another. By their clothes, some were local farmers, others demobilized *Wehrmacht* men still in grimy field-gray. It was hard to tell which group seemed more weary and dejected.

A soldier picked up a bucket and raised it to his mouth. That was all Drucker needed to see. He waved and broke into a shambling trot and called, "Hey, can I have a swig out of that bucket?"

"Who the devil are you?" asked the fellow who'd just drunk. Water dribbled down his poorly shaved chin. He pointed. "And what kind of crazy getup is that?"

Drucker glanced down at his coveralls. The *Reich* had had a thousand different dress and undress uniforms, almost as many as the Race had different styles of body paint. Nobody could keep track of all of them. Drucker gave his name, adding, "Lieutenant colonel, *Reichs* Rocket Force. I was captured out in space; the Lizards just turned me loose. Tell you the truth, I'm trying to figure out what to do next."

"Rocket Force, huh?" The *Wehrmacht* man paused to wipe his sweaty forehead on his sleeve. "Fat lot of good you buggers did anybody." But he picked up the bucket and handed it to Drucker. The water was barely cool, but went down like dark beer. When Drucker set down the bucket, the fellow who'd given it to him asked, "So where are you headed, *Herr* Rocket Man?"

"Greifswald," Drucker answered. He saw that meant nothing

to anyone but him, so he made things plainer. "It's up near Peene-münde, by the Baltic."

"Ach, so." The demobilized soldier raised an eyebrow. "If it's up near Peenemünde, is anything left of it?"

"I don't know," Drucker said bleakly. "I've got—I had, anyway—a wife and three kids. I have to see if I can track them down."

"Good luck," said the fellow who'd given him water. He sounded as if he thought Drucker would need luck better than merely good. Drucker was afraid he thought the same thing. After a moment, the ex-soldier remarked, "Hell of a long way from the Baltic to here. How do you propose to get there?"

"Walk, if I have to," Drucker replied. "I'm getting an idea of what the roads are like. Are any trains running?"

"A few," the former *Wehrmacht* man said. The rest of the la-borers, who seemed happy to get a break, nodded. When he con-tinued, "Not bloody many, though," they nodded again. He waved. "And you see what the highways are like. It's not just this one, either. They're all the same. The stinking Lizards paralyzed us. We've got people starving because there's no way to get food from here to there."

"And everything you can get costs ten times too much," an-other laborer added. "The Reichsmark isn't worth the paper it's printed on any more."

"Ouch." Drucker winced. "We went through that after the First World War. Do we have to do it again?"

The ex-soldier said, "If everybody's got money and there's nothing to buy, prices are going to go through the roof. That's life." He spat. "I'll worry about all that *Scheisse* later, when I've got the time. Right now, I'm just glad I'm still breathing. A hell of a lot of people in the *Reich* aren't."

"Hey, Karl," one of the other laborers said. Several men put their heads together and talked in voices too low for Drucker to make out what they were saying. They passed something back and forth among themselves. He couldn't tell what they were doing there, either.

He was almost on the point of wondering whether he ought to turn and run like hell when they broke apart. The former *Wehrmacht* man—Karl—turned toward him and held out a moderately fat wad of banknotes. "Here you go, Colonel," he said. "This'll keep you eating for a couple-three days, anyhow."

"Thank you very much!" Drucker exclaimed. From what he could see, none of the laborers had enough to be able to spare much. But they knew he had nothing at all, and so they'd reached into their pockets. He nodded. "Thanks from the bottom of my heart."

"It's nothing," Karl said. "We all know what you're going through. We're all going through it, too—except for the ones who've been through it already. They're trying to come out the other side. Hope you make it up to Greifswald. Hope you find your family, too."

"Thanks," Drucker said again. And if he didn't find his family, he'd have to . . . to try to come out the other side, too. The phrase struck him as all too apt. With a last nod, he started walking again, heading north, heading home.

After the Nazis occupied Poland, they'd built an enormous death factory at Treblinka. They'd been building an even bigger one outside Oswiecim—Auschwitz, they'd called it in German—when the Lizards came. Mordechai Anielewicz had longed for revenge against the tormentors of the Jews for a generation. Now he had it. And now, having it, he discovered the folly of such wishes.

He could go anywhere he chose in the much-reduced Greater German *Reich*. As a leader among the Polish Jews who'd fought side by side with the Lizards against the Nazis in two wars now—and as a man who'd made sure his friends among the Lizards helped all they could—he had the backing of the Race. Before entering Germany, he'd got a document from the Race's authorities in Poland authorizing him to call on the males occupying the *Reich* for assistance. He also had documents in German, to overawe burgomeisters and other functionaries.

What hadn't occurred to him was how few German functionaries were left to overawe. The Lizards had done a truly astonishing job of pounding flat the part of Germany just west of Poland. He'd known that in the abstract. The *Wehrmacht*'s assault on Poland had petered out not least because the Germans couldn't keep their invading army supplied. As he entered Germany, he saw exactly what that pounding had done.

Kreuz, where Mordechai entered the *Reich*, had taken an explosive-metal bomb. The center of the city had simply ceased to be, except for one church spire and most of a factory chimney, which still reached toward the heavens like the skeletal fingers of a dead man. Fused, shiny glass gradually gave way to rubble outside the center of town.

This is what the Nazis did to Lodz, Anielewicz thought. *This is what they did to Warsaw, and to as many other cities as they could hit.* But they'd taken worse than they'd given: that was dreadfully clear. He asked a Lizard officer, "How many Deutsch cities did the Race bomb with explosive-metal weapons?"

"I do not know, not precisely," the male answered. "Many tens of them, without a doubt. Hundreds, very possibly. The Deutsche were stubborn. They should have yielded long before they did. They had no hope of defeating us, and merely inflicted more suffering on their own population by refusing to give up the futile fight."

Many tens. Hundreds, very possibly. The answer was horrifying enough to Mordechai when he first heard it. It became far more so when he got to the makeshift hospital on the far side of what had been Kreuz. Tents and shacks housed people maimed or blinded or horribly burned by the explosive-metal bomb. The handful of doctors and nurses and civilian volunteers were desperately overworked and had next to nothing with which to treat their patients.

Mordechai multiplied that improvised hospital by tens, hundreds very possibly. He shivered, though the day was fine, even warm. What sort of miracle was it that any Germans survived at all?

A bespectacled doctor in a long, none too clean white coat came up to him. "You are a person of some influence with the Lizards," he stated, his voice brooking no argument. "You must be, to be clean and well fed and traveling so."

"What if I am?" Mordechai asked.

"You will try to obtain for us more medical supplies," the doctor said, again as if stating a law of nature. "You see what we lack."

Humility, Anielewicz thought. Aloud, he said, "You'd ask this of me even though I'm a Jew?" He let the German he had used slide into Yiddish. If the doctor—*the Nazi doctor,* he thought—couldn't follow, too bad.

But the man only shrugged. "I would ask it if you were Satan himself," he answered. "I need these things. My patients need these things."

"You aren't the only ones who do," Anielewicz observed.

"That does not make my need any less urgent," the doctor said.

From his point of view, he might even have been right. Germans in torment suffered no less than Jews in torment. Anielewicz wished he could deny that. If he did, though, what would he be but the mirror image of a Nazi? Roughly, he said, "I'll do what I can."

By the way the doctor looked at him, the man thought he was lying. But he spoke of the matter with the first Lizard officer he encountered, a couple of kilometers farther outside of Kreuz. The male responded, "I understand the physician's difficulties, but the number of injured Deutsche far outstrips our ability to provide all physicians with all required medicaments. We shall do what we can. It may not be much and it may not be timely, but we shall make the effort."

"I thank you," Mordechai answered. *There,* he told his conscience. *Relax. I've made the effort, too.*

Every time he went into a village, he asked about soldiers bringing Jews back into Germany from Poland. Most of the time, he got only blank stares by way of reply. A few people glared at him. Nazi teachings had sunk deep. Those Germans eyed a Jew—maybe the first they'd ever seen in the flesh, surely the first they'd seen for years—as if he *were* Satan incarnate.

More Germans, though, groveled before him. He needed a little while to realize that was a residue of Nazi teachings, too. He had authority: therefore, he was to be obeyed. If he weren't obeyed, something dreadful would befall the villagers. They seemed convinced of it. At times, he wished it were true.

None of the Germans he questioned knew anything about his wife and sons and daughter. None of them had seen a beffel. He made a point of asking about Pancer; the alien pet might have stuck in people's minds where a few Jews wouldn't have registered. The logic was good, but he had no luck with it.

He pedaled into a little town called Arnswalde as the sun was setting for the brief summer night of northern Germany. With the beating the Reichsmark had taken since the Nazis surrendered, the Polish zlotys in his wallet seemed good as gold—better. He got himself an excellent roast duck, an enormous mound of red cabbage, and all the fine lager he could drink for the price of a couple of apples back in Poland.

The fellow who served him the feast was one of those who

fawned on the occupiers. "Take the leftovers with you, sir," he said. "They'll make you a fine breakfast, see if they don't."

"All right, I will. Thanks," Mordechai said. "Do you have enough for yourself here, though?"

"Ach, ja," the German answered with a chuckle that might have been jolly or might have been nervous. "When did you ever hear of a tavern keeper who starved to death?"

He didn't look as if he were in any imminent danger of starving (he looked plump, as a matter of fact), so Anielewicz took the duck and some cabbage without a qualm. He even let the tavern keeper give him an old, beat-up pot in which to carry them. Either the man was generous by nature or he was a fool or the zloty was worth even more than Mordechai had thought.

Twilight lay over Arnswalde when he came out of the tavern. He'd just climbed onto his bicycle when a young blond woman walked up to him. Pointing to the pot, she came straight to the point: "You have food in there?"

"Yes," he said, eyeing her. Not too long before, she'd probably been very pretty—*a perfect Aryan princess,* he thought. Now her hair was tangled and matted, her face and legs—she was wearing a short skirt, so he could see quite a lot of them— scrawny rather than pleasantly rounded. His nose wrinkled. She hadn't bathed in a long time.

Again, she didn't beat around the bush, saying, "Feed me and you can have me."

"Here." He gave her the pot. "Take it. I don't want you, not for that. I'm looking for my wife and children."

She snatched the pot out of his hands as if afraid he would change his mind. "Thank you," she said. "You're one of the decent ones. There are a few, but only a few, believe me." She turned her head in the direction of the tavern and spat. "Not him—he takes it all out in trade, believe me."

Mordechai sighed. Somehow, that didn't surprise him. The German girl, after all, had no zlotys to pay for roast duck.

She said, "Who are your people? Maybe I know them."

"I doubt it." His voice was dry. "They're Jews. The *Wehrmacht* would have brought them back from Widawa, in Poland. A woman my age, a girl, two boys—and a beffel, if you know what a beffel is. One of the Lizards' pets."

She shook her head. "Jews," she said in tones of wonder. "I

thought there weren't any Jews any more. I thought they were—what's the word I want?—extinct, that's it."

In Germany, in all the Greater German *Reich*, Jews were extinct, or close enough. "You're talking to one," Mordechai said, not without a certain sour pride.

"How funny." The German girl's laugh was hard. "If you had screwed me, then I'd've got in trouble for sleeping with a Jew."

"Maybe," Anielewicz said. "Maybe not, too. The rules are liable to change now, you know." He wondered if they would, if the Lizards would try to enforce tolerance on the *Reich*. He wondered if it mattered, one way or the other. The people—the peoples—the Germans would have had to learn to tolerate were dead now . . . extinct, as the girl had said.

"Who would have thought a Jew could be decent?" she murmured, more than half to herself. She'd learned what her teachers taught, all right.

"What would you say if I said, 'Who would have thought a German could be decent?' " Mordechai didn't know why he bothered. Maybe because he thought she might be reached. Maybe just because, despite dirt and hunger-induced leanness, she was a pretty girl, and part of him, the eternally optimistic male part, wouldn't have minded sleeping with her at all.

She frowned. She knew he was trying to tell her something important, but she couldn't for the life of her figure out what. "But Germans, Germans *are* decent," she said, as if stating a law of nature.

All at once, Anielewicz wanted to snatch back the pot full of duck and cabbage. The only reason he didn't was that it would have confirmed her in all the worst things she thought about Jews. Germans could always see when they were being maligned, but rarely noticed when they were maligning anyone else.

The girl could have no idea what was going through his mind. She said, "If you're looking for people, the army kept falling back to the northwest during the fighting. If they had people along with them, that's where those people would have gone."

"Thanks," Anielewicz said. She was trying to be decent, anyhow. "I guess I'll go in that direction, then."

"I hope you find them," she said. Mordechai nodded. Maybe she could be reached. Maybe she had been reached, a little. She went on, "You can sleep in my bed tonight, if you want to. I mean, do nothing but sleep."

He smiled. "I don't think I'd better. If I tried, I would want to do something besides sleeping." She smiled, too; she took it for a compliment, as he'd hoped she would. And he hadn't even been lying. With a nod, he got the bicycle rolling and started off toward the northwest, to see what he might find.

Kassquit had known this moment would come. She'd been aware of it ever since the shuttlecraft ferried Jonathan Yeager up to her starship. Sooner or later, he would go back to the surface of Tosev 3. It had turned out to be later, because the fighting that broke out with the Deutsche made it unsafe for him to go home. Now, though, the time for his return was here. Kassquit had known it would come, yes, but she'd never imagined how much it would hurt.

"If the war had not come," she said as he methodically packed his wrappings and other belongings into the satchel in which he'd brought them, "if the war had not come, I say, you would have been gone much sooner. That might have proved a good thing, for I do not think I would have missed you so much after a briefer acquaintance."

"Me?" Jonathan Yeager's expression indicated amusement or friendship or pleasure—maybe some of all three. "Superior female, I am nothing but a wild Big Ugly. How many times did you say so yourself when you were getting to know me?"

He spoke the language of the Race much more fluently than he had when he first came up to the starship. With improved fluency came an ironic slant on the world that reminded Kassquit of the electronic messages his father had posted while pretending to be a male of the Race. Could such things be inherited? Kassquit did not think so, but she knew how ignorant she was of Tosevite genetics.

In any case, such matters were far from the most urgent things on her mind. She clung to Jonathan Yeager, saying, "Do not make yourself less than you are. You are the most exciting thing that ever happened to me." She used an emphatic cough, not that she really needed one. He knew how she felt.

His arms went around her. He stroked her. She had never imagined how stimulating the touch of another could be. Of course, no male of the Race had ever touched her intending to arouse her. But she relished Jonathan Yeager's touch even when he wasn't particularly intending to arouse her.

"I cannot stay here," he said now. "You know I cannot. Your place is here; my place is down on the surface of Tosev 3. One day, if you can safely arrange it, you shall have to visit me."

Ttomalss would not approve. Kassquit knew as much. He would cite concern about disease. He would even be sincere. But he would also be afraid to let her go because he would fear the influence of wild Big Uglies on her. And he would not admit that if she subjected him to torment.

Jonathan Yeager was subjecting her to torment by going. Tears slid from her eyes and rolled down her cheeks. He turned away. That wasn't disgust, as it would have been from a male of the Race. Kassquit had learned as much. It was embarrassment. Jonathan Yeager was emotionally vulnerable to tears to a degree she found amazing.

She said, "Before you came here, I did not realize what an important part of my personality had not fully developed. Because I did not realize that, I did not know what I was missing. Now that I do, the future looks much lonelier than it did before."

"I am sorry, superior female," Jonathan Yeager answered. "I did not come up here intending to cause you pain. I came up here intending to give you pleasure, to make you happy. I hope I did that, too."

"You know you did!" Kassquit exclaimed. "But, because you made me so happy, you make me sad that you will not be making me happy any more."

That sounded convoluted even to her, but Jonathan Yeager had no trouble sorting it out. He said, "I will always remember you. I will always be fond of you. Even if a time should come that we cannot be anything more than friends, we shall always be friends."

"Why should a time come . . . ?" Kassquit answered her own half-formed question: "Tosevites contract to mate exclusively with only one partner."

"Yes, that is a truth," the wild Big Ugly agreed.

"You think you will eventually enter into one of these contracts." Kassquit knew she sounded grim, but couldn't help it.

Jonathan Yeager nodded his head, then made the Race's affirmative gesture. "It is likely. Most males and females do."

"And at that point, you will not want to mate with me?" Kassquit asked.

The wild Tosevite coughed and looked away. "It is not that I would not want to," he said. "But then I should not. If an exclusive mating arrangement proves not to be exclusive, complications soon follow. Tosevite sexuality is difficult enough without complications, I think."

As far as Kassquit could see, any sexuality was difficult. Trying to meet a partner's needs and trying to get one's own met by a partner who lacked full understanding of one's body because his was different were even more difficult than the certainties of stroking oneself. They were also much less lonely, though. She hadn't understood that, not till Jonathan Yeager came aboard the starship.

And now more loneliness loomed ahead of Kassquit. Jonathan Yeager was likely to enter one of those exclusive partnerships. Even if he didn't, mating opportunities for him would be down on the surface of Tosev 3. Kassquit wondered where she would ever find another one. She wondered if she would ever find another one. By what she knew of things, it seemed unlikely.

How much of that did Jonathan Yeager understand? He had to be intellectually aware of it; she'd explained till he was probably tired of listening. But did it mean anything to him? Sometimes Kassquit thought one thing, sometimes the other.

She got no more time to wonder now. A hiss from the door announced the presence of a visitor. And only one visitor would be coming at this time. "The shuttlecraft pilot!" Jonathan Yeager exclaimed.

"Yes, the shuttlecraft pilot," Kassquit said dully. She put on a fingerclaw to open the door.

A male of the Race stood in the corridor. "Which of you Big Uglies is the one called Jonathan Yeager?" he asked, making a botch of the name.

Jonathan Yeager barked Tosevite laughter, then said, "I am." He turned to Kassquit. "Good-bye. I hope I see you again. I know I will always remember you."

"Good-bye," she said, and embraced him.

The shuttlecraft pilot turned both his eye turrets away from them. "Disgusting," he muttered in a low voice. Kassquit didn't think she was supposed to hear it, but she did. After a moment, the shuttlecraft pilot spoke louder: "Are you ready to leave, Jonathan Yeager? The launch window will not last indefinitely, in case you are not aware of it."

"I am aware of it." Jonathan Yeager picked up the bag of belongings he'd brought up from the surface of Tosev 3. "I am ready."

"Then let us go," the shuttlecraft pilot said. And go they did. Kassquit closed the door behind them. The panel smoothly slid shut; the Race's engineers knew their business. For many years, being alone in her cubicle had seemed a refuge, a place where she was not the strange one in a starship—in effect, in a world—where no one else was like her.

Now, suddenly, the compartment seemed a prison, a trap. When she looked over at the sleeping mat, she imagined mating there with Jonathan Yeager. All she had left now were imagination and memory. The wild Big Ugly was gone. He wouldn't come back soon, if he ever came back at all.

"What am I going to do?" Kassquit whispered.

She knew what would have been expected of a female of the Race: to return to the way she had been, as if nothing had happened. When males and females of the Race weren't in season, sexuality meant nothing to them. They would assume it meant nothing to her, either. She wished it didn't. Part of her wished it didn't, anyhow. The rest longed for it.

"What am I going to do?" she said again.

Not for the first time, she wished the Deutsche had chosen some other moment to launch their attack on the Race. Her reason for that wish, though, was undoubtedly unique. Had Jonathan Yeager not been forced to stay in the starship so long, she wouldn't have developed this emotional attachment to him. Her life would have been simpler, in a sense purer.

But now you understand more of what being a Tosevite is truly like, she thought. *Now you know you are not merely a poor copy of a female of the Race.* Half of her was glad to have the knowledge. The other half would as gladly have done without it.

She sighed. She would never make a proper female of the Race. And she would never make a proper Big Ugly, either. What did that leave her? *I wonder if I could become a proper Rabotev or Hallessi.* She laughed at her own foolishness. Why not? No one else would have found it funny.

But laughter soon faded. What would she do now that she was by herself again? The question wouldn't go away. No answer suggested itself, either.

Someone outside asked for attention; the speaker by the door hissed again. "Who is it?" Kassquit asked.

"I: Ttomalss. May I come in?"

"Yes, superior sir." Kassquit opened the door for him, as she had for the shuttlecraft pilot. She bent into the posture of respect. "I greet you, superior sir."

"And I greet you, Kassquit," the psychological researcher said. "I came in to inquire about your feelings now that the wild Big Ugly named Jonathan Yeager is returning to the surface of Tosev 3."

"Yes, I thought you might." Kassquit didn't realize how sarcastic she sounded till the words were out of her mouth.

Ttomalss let out a wounded hiss. "Your well-being is a matter of considerable concern to me, you know, not only for personal reasons but also because of what I am trying to learn about successfully integrating the Race's cultural patterns with the limits imposed by Tosevite biology."

"Yes, I understand that, superior sir, and I apologize," Kassquit said, on the whole sincerely. "How do I feel?" She took a deep breath. "*Confused* may well be the best word. Too much has happened to me emotionally, and it has happened too fast, for me to be at all certain what it means. *Bereft* is another word that comes to mind."

"It was so important, then, for you to have this contact with one who was like you biologically even if so different culturally?" Ttomalss asked.

"Superior sir, at the moment I feel it was," Kassquit said. "How I will feel in several days' time, or in a year's, I cannot tell you at present, but for now I feel I have been deprived of something I never knew I needed."

Ttomalss sighed. "I feared that might be so when we began this experiment. I especially feared it might be so when Jonathan Yeager stayed longer than anticipated, solidifying your sexual and emotional bonds with him. I do take some consolation in noting that Tosevite emotions, while generally stronger than those of the Race, are also generally more transient."

That was meant to console Kassquit, too, and should have. Instead, it somehow made her furious. "So you think my emotions will go away just because I am a Big Ugly, do you?" she shouted. "I think *you* had better go away, superior sir!" She turned the honorific into a curse, and used an emphatic cough afterwards. When she took a step toward the psychological researcher, he left in a very great hurry indeed.

* * *

Jonathan Yeager descended from the shuttlecraft and let his feet thump down on the concrete runway at Los Angeles International Airport. The breeze smelled of the nearby ocean. It played on him at random, not with the gentle regularity of the starship's ventilation system. After so long, random breezes felt strange, unnatural. He laughed. Random breezes were anything but.

His teeth started to chatter. After so long aboard the Lizards' starship, the breeze that swept across the airport also felt damn cold. Because of the sea breeze, the airport was one of the coolest spots in the L.A. basin. Jonathan knew that. He'd never known it to be so downright arctic, though.

He moved away from the shuttlecraft as trucks came up to refill its hydrogen and oxygen tanks. A car came up, too, a familiar car. There was his father behind the wheel. They waved to each other. The car stopped. Jonathan's dad hopped out and gave him a hug. "Good to see you, son!" he said. "Good to have you home!"

"Good to be back, Dad," Jonathan answered. "It'd be even better if I weren't freezing to death." He tacked on an emphatic cough. It seemed the most natural thing in the world. Except for the odd word of English here and there, he'd spoken nothing but the language of the Race for a couple of months. Going back to his native tongue felt odd: English seemed sloppy and imprecise after the Lizards' language.

His father laughed. "It's a nice day, if you ask me. But you've been up in the bake oven for a while, so you wouldn't think so." He went around to the passenger side of the Buick and opened the door. "Hop in and we'll head for home. Your mom'll be just as glad to see you as I am. She's riding herd on Mickey and Donald right now."

"How are they doing?" Jonathan asked. He hadn't been able to inquire about them while he was on the starship; as far as the Race was concerned, they didn't exist.

"They're growing like weeds," his father answered. "They're only two and a half now, but they're already something like three-quarters as big as they will be. And talking quite a bit, too. If Lizard psychologists wore hats, they'd have to eat 'em, because they say that kind of thing just doesn't happen."

Jonathan slid into the car. It was warmer in there than outside. "What else has been going on while I was away?" he asked, tossing his bag onto the back seat.

His father got behind the wheel and started up the hydrogen-burning engine. "Oh, this and that," he answered. His tone was casual. Too casual? Jonathan shot him a sharp look. The elder Yeager went on, "We can talk more about that when we get home, okay?"

"Okay." Jonathan didn't know what else to say. The car glided up to a security gate in the chain-link fence that kept normal traffic off the runways. His dad showed a guard his ID. The guard nodded and handed his dad a clipboard. His father signed the paper it held and gave it back. The guard opened the gate. The car left the restricted area and went out into a parking lot. Jonathan found another question. With a certain amount of apprehension, he asked, "How's Karen doing?"

"Not . . . too bad," his father answered judiciously. "She comes over once or twice a week. She likes the hatchlings, you know."

"Yeah," Jonathan answered. "Does she . . . still like me?"

"She hasn't said much." His father paused as he left the lot and merged into traffic. "Your mother and I haven't asked her a whole lot of questions, you know. We figured it would be best if you took care of all that yourself."

"Okay," Jonathan said again, and then, after a moment, "Thanks. Uh—does she know what all I was doing up on the starship?"

"Well . . ." His father made another one of those judicious pauses. "Let me put it this way: I don't think she thinks you were playing tiddlywinks up there."

"Oh." Jonathan thought about that. He sighed. "Has she said anything about it?"

"Not much." His dad sounded admiring. On the farm and in the minor leagues and in the Army, keeping your mouth shut was praiseworthy. A phrase his father sometimes used when his mother couldn't hear was, *He wouldn't say shit if he had a mouthful.* He meant it as approval.

But what was Karen not saying? Jonathan sighed. He'd have to find out. On the other hand, Karen might not want to say anything to him ever again. But if she didn't, would she keep coming around to see Mickey and Donald? *She might, dammit,* he thought. She was wild to learn anything she could about Lizards. A lot of kids—maybe even most—her age and Jonathan's were the same way.

Getting from the airport to Jonathan's house took about half an hour. Up in the starship, he would have gone around a significant fraction of the Earth's circumference in that time. His dad pulled into the driveway. When they got out, Jonathan noticed something he hadn't before. He pointed to his father's hip. "Are you wearing that pistol all the time now, Dad?"

"Every waking minute," his father answered, dropping his right hand to the holstered .45. "And it's always where I can grab it fast when I'm sleeping, too."

"Are things really *that* bad?" Jonathan knew about the attacks on his father and the house, of course. But none of them had come to anything, so he had trouble taking them seriously.

"No." His father's voice belied the word. After a moment, the elder Yeager added, "They're worse."

Before Jonathan could respond to that, the front door opened and his mother hurried out to say hello. Between embraces and kisses, he stopped worrying about the pistol for a while. "I'm so glad to see you," his mom said over and over. "I'm so glad you're safe."

She didn't know how close that German had come to blowing the starship out of the sky. He didn't intend to tell her, either. All he said was, "It's great to be back." He wondered if he meant it. Next to where he'd been, the stucco house looked like a primitive makeshift.

"I bet you'll be glad to sleep in your own bed again," his mother said. "From what your father tells me, a Lizard sleeping mat isn't what you'd call comfortable."

"My own bed sounds great, Mom." Jonathan didn't have to work too hard to sound enthusiastic. The sleeping mat hadn't been all that great. But he'd be sleeping alone in his room. He'd had company, friendly company, up on the starship. His eyes slid to his father. By the way his dad was holding his mouth a little too tightly, he knew what Jonathan was thinking.

His mother said, "I wonder if the hatchlings will remember you. It's been a good-sized part of their lives since they've seen you."

"Let's go find out," Jonathan said. He wanted to discover if Mickey and Donald still knew who he was, too. And, if he was dealing with the hatchlings, his mom wouldn't have the chance to harass him about how he shouldn't have gone up to the starship in the first place or about how he shouldn't have spent all his time up there fooling around with Kassquit.

He missed the girl the Lizards had done their best to raise as one of theirs. He couldn't help it. He'd broken off a love affair. It never would have worked, not for life, not the way his folks' marriage had. He could see that. But it had been intense while he was up there. With him and Kassquit closed up in one little cubicle all the time, how could it have been anything else?

When he got inside the house, he dropped his bag in the middle of the living room. His mom gave him a look. His dad murmured, "It's okay this once, Barbara." His mother frowned, but nodded a second later.

Mickey and Donald were in their room. When Jonathan opened the door, he gaped at how much they'd grown. Sure as hell, they were well on their way to being full-sized Lizards. But they looked funny. He needed a moment to realize why: they wore no body paint. He wanted to speak to them in the language of the Race. That wouldn't work. They didn't know it, any more than Kassquit knew any human tongue. As she'd been raised as a Lizard, they were being brought up as people.

"Hi, guys," Jonathan said in English. "I'm Jonathan. Remember me?"

They came up to him, slowly, a little bit warily—he was bigger than either of his parents. Their eye turrets swiveled as they looked him up and down. *Did* they have any idea who he was? However much he wanted to, he couldn't tell.

Then Mickey took another step toward him and stuck out his right hand. "Hello, Jonathan," he said. His mouth couldn't make all the sounds of English, any more than Jonathan's could shape all those the Lizards' language used. He was probably talking baby talk, too. But Jonathan understood him.

"Hello, Mickey," he said gravely, and shook the little scaly hand. Then he nodded to Donald. "Hello, Donald. How are you?"

"Hello." Donald was bigger and stronger than Mickey, but Mickey talked better; he—or maybe she—had always been the more clever hatchling.

Before Jonathan and the Lizards could say anything more, the telephone rang. Jonathan jumped a bit. He'd got used to hearing hisses. But then old habit took over. "I'll get it," he said, and hurried into the kitchen. "Hello?"

"Hello, Mr. Yeager," said the voice on the other end of the line: Karen's voice. "Could I—"

"I'm not my dad," Jonathan broke in, wondering what the devil would happen next. "I'm me. I'm back. Hi."

"Oh," Karen said. Then there was silence—quite a bit of silence. At last, Karen went on, "Hello, Jonathan. Did you . . . have a good time up on the starship?" She knew what he'd been doing up there, all right. He could hear it in her voice.

"Yeah, I did." Jonathan could hardly deny it. "I didn't expect to stay up there so long, though. Who would have thought the Germans would really start that war? I'm awful glad to be home." His mother would have coughed at the colloquialism, but she'd stayed down at the other end of the house. He gave it his best shot: "I'd like to see you again, if you still want to see me."

"Well . . ." More silence. Karen finally continued, "I do want to go on seeing Mickey and Donald, and that'll mean seeing you, too, won't it? But that's not what you meant. I know it isn't. You were doing research, yeah, but . . . *that* kind of research?" Another pause. "Maybe when I come over there for the hatchlings, we can talk about the other stuff. That's about the best I can do, okay?"

"Okay," Jonathan said at once—it was as much as he'd hoped for, maybe even a little more. "Do you still want to talk to my dad?"

"No, never mind—it'll keep," Karen said. "Good-bye." She hung up. So did Jonathan.

Maybe the sound of the handset going onto the cradle told his father it was safe to come into the kitchen. He glanced at Jonathan and chuckled. "You're still in one piece, I see," he remarked.

"Yeah." Jonathan knew he sounded relieved. "Maybe we can work things out."

"I hope so. She's a nice girl." His dad pulled a couple of bottles of Lucky Lager out of the icebox and handed one to Jonathan. "Come on out to the back yard."

That wasn't an invitation he usually made, but Jonathan followed. "What's up?" he asked when they were standing on the grass.

"You asked what was new when you got into the car. I didn't want to tell you there, or in the house. Here, I think it's okay—who'd put a microphone on a lemon tree?" His father sounded as weary and cynical as Jonathan had ever heard him.

"What's up?" Jonathan asked again, swigging from the bottle of beer.

And his father told him. As he listened, his eyes got wider and wider. "That's what I'm sitting on," his father finished. "Do I need to remind you just how important it is not to repeat it?"

"No, sir," Jonathan said at once, still shocked—maybe more shocked than he'd ever been in his life. "Besides, who'd believe me?"

☆ 5 ☆

Everything Kassquit and Jonathan Yeager had done together on the starship—everything from mating to cleaning their teeth—was recorded. Ttomalss studied the video and audio records with great attention: how better to learn about the interactions between a civilized Tosevite and one of the wild Big Uglies from the surface of Tosev 3?

What he found distressed him in a number of ways. He had spent Kassquit's entire lifetime shaping her as he thought she should go. When she was with him even now, she behaved as a civilized being ought to behave. But when she was with Jonathan Yeager . . .

When Kassquit was with Jonathan Yeager, she behaved much as a wild Big Ugly did. She learned to imitate him far more quickly than she had learned to imitate Ttomalss—and she'd startled Ttomalss with how fast she'd learned to imitate him while she was a hatchling.

Also infuriating to the senior researcher was how quickly and accurately Jonathan Yeager could divine what was in Kassquit's mind. *Blood will tell,* the male thought unhappily. That was not the conclusion he would have wanted as a culmination of his long-running experimental project.

He was so distressed about what he found, he called Felless to talk about it. "I greet you, Senior Researcher," she said when she saw his image in the video screen. "I am glad to speak with you."

"And I greet you, superior female." Ttomalss wondered if his hearing diaphragms were working as they should. Felless only rarely admitted to being glad to speak with anyone, and most especially not with him.

A moment later, she explained why she was: "After so much

123

time spent dealing with the Français, it is good to talk shop with a member of my own species."

"Ah," Ttomalss said. "Yes, I can certainly understand that."

"And why are you interested in speaking with me?" Felless asked.

"For your insights, of course," Ttomalss answered, which was even more or less true. He told her of the disturbing data about Kassquit.

"Why does this surprise you?" she asked, sounding surprised herself. "A common law of psychological development states that hatchlings are more influenced by their peers than by the previous generation. This holds for the Race, it holds for the Rabotevs, and it holds for the Hallessi, too. Why should it not also hold for the Big Uglies?"

"I had assumed it would be different as a result of the prolonged parental care they receive, which makes them unlike the species—the other species, I should say—of the Empire," Ttomalss replied. "I might also note that the leading Tosevite psychological theories stress the primacy of the relationship between parents and hatchlings."

Felless' mouth opened wide in hearty, unabashed laughter. "Why in the name of the Emperor do you take Tosevite psychological theories seriously?" she asked. "I have examined a few of them. For one thing, they strike me as preposterous. For another, they contradict one another in any number of ways, demonstrating that they cannot all be true and that, very likely, none of them is true."

"I do understand that," Ttomalss said stiffly. "I have been examining Tosevite psychological theories a good deal longer than you have, I might add. And one point where they are in unanimity is on the vital importance of this bond."

"But it makes no logical sense!" Felless exclaimed. "Even in Tosevite terms, it makes no logical sense."

"There I might well disagree with you, superior female," Ttomalss said. "Some of the Big Uglies appear to have very persuasive arguments for the nurturing influence of parents upon hatchlings. Given their biological patterns, I have no trouble finding these arguments plausible."

"Plausibility and truth hatch from different eggs," Felless said, something Ttomalss could hardly deny. The female from the colonization fleet went on, "Consider, Senior Researcher. Where will even a Big Ugly end up spending most of his time? With his parents and their other hatchlings, or with his peers? With his peers, of course. Whom will he have to work harder to accommodate, his parents and their other hatchlings, or his peers? Again, his peers, of course. His parents and close kin are biologically programmed to be accommodating to him. If they were not, they probably could not stand him at all, Big Uglies being what they are. If, however, he acts as if he has his head up his cloaca among his peers, are they not likely to inform him of this in no uncertain terms? No male or female of the Race with whom I am familiar has ever composed songs of praise for the Tosevites' kindness or gentle manners."

The pungent irony there forced a laugh from Ttomalss, who also could hardly deny Felless' words held some truth. "No, no songs of praise," he agreed, laughing still. And, after some thought, he continued, "That may well be a cogent analysis, superior female. It may indeed. As always, experimental data would be desirable, but the superstructure of your thought certainly appears logical."

"For which I thank you," Felless replied. She sounded more cordial toward him than she had for some time. On the other fork of the tongue, he hadn't praised her much lately, either. She was a female who took praise seriously.

In musing tones, Ttomalss said, "You might provoke some interesting responses if you were to publish that thesis in a Tosevite psychological journal."

"For which I do *not* thank you." Felless used an emphatic cough. "I have enough difficulties with Big Uglies as is to want to avoid more, not to provoke them."

"Very well." Ttomalss shrugged. "I thought you might find it amusing to watch the allegedly learned Tosevites banding together to destroy you with overheated rhetoric."

"Again, no," Felless said. "The trouble with Big Uglies is, they might not stop with overheated rhetoric. If I upset them badly enough, they might try to destroy me with explosives. Is it not a truth that the followers of the male called Khomeini still raise a rebellion against us despite his capture and imprisonment?"

"Yes, that is a truth," Ttomalss admitted. "But they remain imprisoned in the grip of superstition. Contributors to psychological journals, even Tosevite psychological journals, have a more rational outlook."

"I do not care to test this experimentally," Felless said. "And here is my suggestion for you, Senior Researcher: since Kassquit *will* be influenced by her peers, you would do well to persuade her that her true peers are males and females of the Race, not the barbaric Big Uglies on the surface of Tosev 3. And now, if you will excuse me . . ." She disappeared from the video screen.

Even so, Ttomalss protested, "But I have always done my best to persuade her of that." And it had worked. It still worked, to a point. Ttomalss couldn't imagine Kassquit betraying the Race in any truly important matter. But the sexual bond she'd so quickly established with Jonathan Yeager formed the basis of a social intimacy with him different from the sort she'd established with the Race.

I wonder if I ought to arrange a new sexual partner for her, he thought. That might lessen her despondence over the departure of the wild Big Ugly. But it might also present new and more serious problems. Solving one difficulty with Tosevites all too often did produce another worse one. The whole world of Tosev 3 was a large, unexpected difficulty, or rather a multitude of them.

He dictated a note to himself so he would not forget the possibility, then returned to analyzing the recordings of Kassquit's conversations with Jonathan Yeager. At one point, she'd asked him, "Would you not like to spend all your time living and working among the Race?" Ttomalss suspected she meant, *Would you not like to spend all your time staying with me?*

"If I could do it in the service of my not-empire, then maybe," the wild Tosevite male had answered. "But I would like to have some of my species around for the sake of company. We are too different from the Race to be very comfortable with its members all the time."

Was that U.S. propaganda, countering the Race's propaganda that formed the only indoctrination Kassquit had had till Jonathan Yeager's arrival? Or was it simply his view of where the truth lay? If so, was he right?

Ttomalss feared he was. No wild Rabotev or Hallessi would ever have said such a thing. The other two species in the Empire had been on the same road as the Race; they just hadn't gone so far along it when the conquest fleets got to their planets. The Big Uglies had been going in another direction altogether when the Race arrived.

That so many of them were still going in a different direction told how strong their impetus had been. And yet the direction was not so different as it had been before the conquest fleet came; it was the resultant of their former course and that which the Race tried to impose on them. Which component of the vector would prove stronger in the end remained to be seen.

The telephone hissed for attention. "Senior Researcher Ttomalss speaking," Ttomalss said. "I greet you."

"I greet you, superior sir." Kassquit's image appeared in the screen.

"Hello, Kassquit." Ttomalss did his best to disguise his concern. "How may I help you?" How was he supposed to analyze her behavior if she kept subjecting him to it?

"I do not know. I doubt anyone knows."

"If you do not know how I can help you, why did you call me?" Ttomalss asked in some irritation. He didn't expect a rational answer. He'd had several similar conversations with Kassquit since Jonathan Yeager departed for the surface of Tosev 3.

"I am sorry, superior sir," she said, something he'd heard a great many times before. "But I have no one else with whom I might speak."

That, unfortunately, was a truth. And it was a truth of Ttomalss' own creation. He sighed. He recognized the obligation under which it placed him. "Very well," he answered. "Say what you will."

"I do not know what to say," Kassquit wailed. "I feel as if my place in this society is not what I thought it was before I made the acquaintance of the wild Big Ugly."

"That is *not* a truth." Ttomalss appended an emphatic cough. "Your place here has not changed in the slightest."

"Then I have changed, for I do not feel as if I fit that place any more," Kassquit said.

"Ah." That, for once, was something Ttomalss could get his teeth into. "Many males from the conquest fleet have similar feelings in trying to reintegrate with the more numerous members of the colonization fleet. Their time on Tosev 3 and their dealings with Tosevites have changed them so much, they no longer find the old ways of our society congenial. Something like this seems to have happened to you."

"Yes!" Now his Tosevite ward used an emphatic cough of her own. "How is this syndrome cured?"

By all appearances, it wasn't always curable. Ttomalss had no intention of admitting that. He said, "The chief anodyne is the passage of time." He had also heard this was true of the aftermath of brief Tosevite sexual relationships, another point he carefully did not bring up.

Kassquit's shoulders slumped. "I shall try to be patient, superior sir."

"That is all you can do, I fear," Ttomalss said. He would have to try to be patient, too.

After a brief tour of duty at Greifswald, Gorppet's small unit had returned to the Deutsch center with the preposterous name of Peenemünde. The move made sense; the place was plainly the largest and most important center in the area. Or rather, it had been: it had taken a worse pounding than any he'd imagined, let alone any he'd seen. He and the males he commanded were constantly checking their radiation badges to make sure they were not picking up dangerous levels of radioactivity.

Despite the explosive-metal bombs that had fallen on the site, the wreckage remained impressive. Gorppet spoke to one of his troopers: "This was on its way to becoming a spaceport as large as any back on Home."

"That would seem to be a truth, superior sir," the male called Yarssev agreed.

"When we first came to Tosev 3, the Deutsche had not even begun launching rockets from this site," Gorppet said.

Yarssev made the affirmative hand gesture. "That is also a truth, superior sir."

"How long did the Race take to move from the first launch of a rocket to a spaceport?" Gorppet asked.

"I have no idea, superior sir," Yarssev answered. "It has been a long time since they tried to make me learn history, and I have long since forgotten most of what they taught me."

"So have I," Gorppet said. "But this I will tell you: we did not go from rocket to spaceport in a fraction of an individual's lifetime."

"Well, of course not, superior sir," Yarssev said. "If you ask me, there is something unnatural about the way the Big Uglies change so fast."

"I would have a hard time arguing with you there, because I think that is also a truth," Gorppet said. "And I will tell you something else: I think there is something unnatural about the way the Deutsche are surrendering their armaments."

"Do you?" Yarssev gestured. The broad, low, damp plain was full of the implements of war: landcruisers, mechanized fighting vehicles, artillery pieces, rocket launchers, machine guns, stacked infantrymales' weapons.

But Gorppet made the negative gesture. "Not enough. Remember what these Big Uglies threw at us in Poland? They had more than this—and better than this, too. They do not love us. They have no reason to love us. I think they are trying to hold out, to conceal, as much as they can."

"What will you do, superior sir?" Yarssev asked.

And Gorppet had to hiss in dismay. That was an unfortunate question. He wished with every lobe of his liver that the trooper had not asked it. He answered, "There is not much I *can* do, you know. I am only a small-unit group leader. I have no tremendous authority, certainly not enough to compel the Deutsche to do anything. All I have is a lot of combat experience, and it tells me something is wrong here."

Yarssev found another unfortunate question: "Have you given your views to the company commander?"

Gorppet let out another dismayed hiss. "Yes, as a matter of fact, I have. His opinion of the situation differs from mine."

That was all he would say to Yarssev. The company commander was smugly convinced the Deutsche were obeying all treaty requirements. Gorppet hissed once more. Back in the days when he was an ordinary trooper, he'd seen that officers all too often didn't want to listen to him. It wasn't so much that they were smarter or more experienced than he was. But they had rank, and so they didn't have to listen. He'd been sure things were different among officers, that they paid attention to their fellows if not to their inferiors. To his company commander, though, he remained an inferior.

Deutsch males moved among the weaponry they were turning over to the Race. Deutsch civilians were properly submissive to the Race. They knew their not-empire had taken a beating. These were not civilians. They wore the gray wrappings and steel helmets of soldiers. They also wore an almost palpable air of resentment and regret that the fighting had ended.

"Look at them." Gorppet pointed with his tongue. "Do they

have the look of males who will contentedly return to civilian life?"

"Does it matter if they are contented or not?" Yarssev asked in return. "So long as they are demobilized and have no weapons with which they can wage war against us, why should we care if they hate us?"

"Because, if they hate us, they will seek to hide and to regain weapons," Gorppet answered patiently. "At the moment, they are merely submitting because they have no choice. I would sooner see them truly conquered."

Yarssev didn't argue with him any more. *Of course not,* Gorppet thought. *I am an officer. He sees no point to arguing with officers, because he will not convince them even if he is right.*

Gorppet laughed. When he'd been a trooper himself, most officers had looked like addled eggs to him, too. Now, though, he was sure he was right and Yarssev wrong. Perspective counted for a great deal.

Perspective . . . Gorppet made the affirmative hand gesture, although no one had asked him anything. Even if his company commander wasn't interested in what he had to say, he could think of some males who might be. He found his top-ranking underofficer and told him not to let the Deutsche steal any troopers while he was gone, then went over to the tents marking brigade headquarters not far away. The brigade commander's tent, of course, was bigger and more impressive than any of the others. Gorppet ignored it. The tent he had in mind was the least obtrusive one in the whole compound.

When he walked in, a male of a rank not much higher than his turned one eye turret away from a computer terminal and toward him. "Yes? What do you want?" the fellow asked, his tone implying that it had better be something interesting and important.

"Superior sir, does brigade Intelligence believe the Deutsche are in fact turning over all weapons required under the terms of their surrender?" Gorppet asked.

Now both the male's eye turrets swung his way. "What makes you think they are not, Small-Unit Group Leader?" he asked sharply.

"What I see delivered here, superior sir," Gorppet answered. "It does not seem to be matériel of the quality my unit faced when we fought the Deutsche in Poland. If it is not, where has that matériel gone?"

"Where has it gone?" the officer from Intelligence repeated. "The Deutsche say the Race destroyed most of it in combat. There is, without a doubt, some truth to that: would you not agree?"

"Certainly, superior sir," Gorppet said. Then, brash as if he'd just had a big taste of ginger—which he hadn't—he went on, "But would you not agree that it also gives the Deutsche a very handy excuse for hiding whatever they think they can get away with?"

"Give me your name." The male from Intelligence rapped out the order. Liver in turmoil, Gorppet obeyed. How much trouble had he found for himself? The other male spoke into the computer, then to Gorppet again: "And your pay number?" Gorppet gave him that, too. He wondered if anything would be left of him by the time this male was through. But then, after a hiss of surprise, the fellow asked, "You are the male who captured the agitator Khomeini?"

"Yes, superior sir," Gorppet admitted with what he hoped was becoming modesty.

"Have you spoken of this matter to your company commander?" the male from Intelligence asked.

"I have. He is of the opinion that the Deutsche are honoring their obligations," Gorppet said.

"I am of the opinion that he is a fool," the male from Intelligence said. "He could not see a sunrise if he were out in space." He paused. "What made you come here, Small-Unit Group Leader, if your superior officer told you this matter that concerned you was unimportant?"

"What made me come here?" Gorppet echoed. "Superior sir, I did not like fighting the Deutsche once. You may believe me when I say I never want to have to fight them again." He added an emphatic cough.

"No one wants to fight the Deutsche again—no one with sense," the male said. "No one wants to fight any of the independent Tosevite not-empires again. The *Reich* caused us altogether too much damage. Another war would only be worse."

"Truth!" Gorppet said with another emphatic cough.

"And you do not know everything the Deutsche are doing," the other male said, "or rather, everything they are not doing.

Their delivery of missile components and their surrender of poison gas have been well behind schedule. Their excuses, I might add, challenge credulity."

"More blame on battle damage?" Gorppet asked.

"Why, yes, as a matter of fact. You have encountered similar claims?" the other male returned. Gorppet made the affirmative gesture. The other male eyed him appraisingly, then said, "Small-Unit Group Leader Gorppet, you show wit and initiative. Have you ever wondered if you were wasted as an infantrymale?"

"What do you mean, superior sir?" Gorppet asked.

"My name is Hozzanet," the male from Intelligence said—a sign he was interested in Gorppet, sure enough. And he went on, "It might be possible to arrange a transfer to my service, if you are interested. Then you would be able to devote your full energies to tracking down Tosevite deceit."

"That *is* tempting," Gorppet admitted. "But I am not sure I would want to pursue it." He did not think males from Intelligence would be encouraged to taste ginger. The reverse: he was sure they would be more closely monitored than ordinary infantrymales. And if they ever connected him with the ginger deal in South Africa that had involved males of the Race shooting at one another . . .

But if they ever connected him with that deal, he was in endless trouble no matter which service he belonged to. Still . . .

Hozzanet said, "Speaking off the record and hypothetically— I ask no questions, note—sticking your tongue in the ginger vial every once in a while would not disqualify you. If you are in the habit of doing things like feeding females ginger to get them to mate with you, you would be well advised not to consider such a position."

"I . . . see," Gorppet said slowly. "No, I am not in the habit of doing any such thing with females. I have mated with females who have tasted ginger, but such tasting has always been at their initiative."

"I understand," Hozzanet said. "Many males have done that here on Tosev 3, I among them. Whether we like it or not, the herb is changing our sexual patterns here, and will continue to do so. But that, at the moment, is a patch of scales shed from one's back. I ask again: are you interested in serving in Intelligence?"

"I . . . may be, superior sir," Gorppet said. "May I have a day to think on it?" Hozzanet made the affirmative gesture. Gorppet assumed the posture of respect and left the tent. He didn't know what he'd expected on visiting brigade Intelligence, but he was sure he hadn't expected an invitation to join it.

He was on his way back to his small group when a beffel trotted across the path in front of him. It turned one eye turret his way, gave him a friendly beep, and went on about its business.

"And hello to you, too, little fellow," Gorppet said: a beffel was a welcome reminder of Home. He'd walked on for several paces before he paused to wonder what in the Emperor's name a beffel was doing in the midst of the wreckage of the Greater German *Reich*.

DOWN BUT NOT OUT. Monique Dutourd had seen those signs so many times in Marseille, she was sick of them. She was, by late summer, sick of everything that had anything to do with her home town. She was sick of wreckage. She was sick of high prices everywhere she looked. She was especially sick of the tent city in which she had to live, and of being crammed into a tent with her brother and his lover.

French officials had promised things would be back to normal by now. She hadn't believed the promises, and her skepticism was proving justified. The French hadn't done anything but what the Germans told them to do for a solid generation. Now the Germans were gone. The French bureaucrats were on their own. With no one to tell them what to do, they didn't do much of anything.

Monique picked her way through one of the market squares. Everybody who had peaches and apricots wanted an arm and a leg for them. She scowled. Shipping hadn't come back the way the bureaucrats promised it would, either.

She almost ran into a Lizard. *"Pardonnez-moi, monsieur,"* the creature said in hissing French. Monique wanted to laugh in its pointed, scaly face, but she didn't. In a way, dealing with some-one who couldn't tell whether she was male or female was re-freshing. She wished a good many of her crude countrymen had the same problem. She wished even more that Dieter Kuhn had had it.

For once, thinking of the SS *Sturmbannführer* made her smile. Odds were, he'd died when the Lizards detonated their explosive-metal bomb on Marseille. If he hadn't, he'd gone back to the *Reich* once France regained her freedom. Any which way, he was out of her life for good.

Thinking of his being out of her life for good made her a lot more cheerful than she would have been otherwise. That, in turn, made her more inclined to spend her money—well, actually, her brother's money—on the fruit she wanted than she would have been otherwise.

Stringbag full of apricots in a wire basket behind her, she rode a battered bicycle back to the tent city. She'd had a far better machine before the bomb fell. Now she was glad to have any bicycle at all. The chain she'd used to secure it while she shopped weighed more than it did.

Commotion rocked the tent city when she reached it. A squad of hard-faced men in uniform were trundling a man and woman into a waiting motorcar. A crowd followed, yelling and cursing and throwing things. Monique couldn't tell if they were pelting and reviling the captives or their captors.

"What's going on?" she asked a man who was just standing there watching. With luck, that made him something close to neutral.

"Purification squad," he answered, and jerked a thumb toward the captives. "They say those two were in bed with the *Boches*."

"Oh, are they finally down here?" Monique said, and the man nodded. Now that France was free again, everyone who'd collaborated with the Nazis in any way was all at once fair game. Since the country had been under German rule for a quarter of a century, the new government could make an example of almost anyone it chose. No one said a word in protest, though. To complain was to appear unpatriotic, un-French, and probably pro-German: and therefore a fitting target for the purification squads.

They'd been in the news for weeks, fanning out through northern France to get rid of people described as "traitors to the Republic." But everything reached Marseille more slowly than almost anywhere else. Till now, traitors here had been allowed to go on about their business like anybody else.

One of the men from the purification squad drew his pistol and fired it into the air. That gave the angry crowd pause. It let the men get the couple they'd captured into the automobile. Some of them got into it, too. Others piled into another motorcar behind it. Both cars drove away in a hurry.

"Are they really collaborators?" Monique asked.

"Ferdinand and Marie? Not that I ever heard of, and I've known them for years." With a shrug, the man went on, "It could be that I did not know everything there is to know about what they did. But it could also be that someone who does not care for them for whatever reason—or for no reason at all—wrote out a denunciation."

He said no more. Had he said any more, he might have got into trouble himself. Twenty-five years under the Nazis had taught wariness. They'd also taught Frenchmen, once lovers of freedom, to write denunciations against their neighbors for any reason or, as the man had said, for none.

"Do the purification squads ever let people go once they seize them?" Monique asked.

She got only another shrug by way of answer. The man with whom she'd been talking had evidently decided he'd said everything he was going to say. Monique shrugged, too. She couldn't blame him for that. Under the Germans, talking to strangers had been a good way to land in trouble. Things didn't look to have changed too much with the coming of the new regime.

With the motorcars gone, the crowd that had followed the purification squad out to them began to break up. Monique walked her bicycle to the tent she shared with Pierre and Lucie. She brought the bicycle into the tent, too. The folk of Marseille were notoriously light-fingered even at the best of times. In times like these, a bicycle left outside for the evening was an open invitation to theft.

"Hello," Monique said as she ducked her way through the tent flap and came inside. She wondered if her brother would be dickering with Keffesh or some other Lizard, and would have to explain her presence. What infuriated her most was that he always sounded so apologetic.

But he and Lucie were alone in the tent this evening. Lucie was cooking something that smelled good on a little aluminum stove. Pointing to it, Monique asked, "Is that *Wehrmacht* issue?"

"Probably," Lucie answered. She went on, "If it is, what difference does it make?"

"I don't know for certain that it makes any difference," Monique said. "But I wouldn't let the purification squads know you've got a German stove."

Patiently, Pierre Dutourd said, "Monique, probably seven-eighths of the people in this camp are cooking off *Wehrmacht*-issue stoves. There are a lot more of them in France than there are French-made stoves these days."

"Without doubt, you have reason," Monique said. "But will the purification squads care even the least little bit about reason?"

"Oh." Pierre nodded. His jowls wobbled a little. Monique was glad she was slimmer than her older brother. "I don't think we need to worry about the purification squads. We have enough friends among the Race to make it very likely indeed that they'll leave us alone."

"I hope you're right." Monique was willing to admit he might well be. The Lizards didn't formally occupy France, as the Germans had. But the French were still too weak, still too unused to ruling themselves, to have an easy time standing on their own two feet. If they weren't going to lean on the Nazis, the Race was their other logical prop.

That savory odor Monique smelled turned out to come from a rabbit stew full of wild mushrooms. With a tolerable rosé, with some cheese and afterwards the fruit Monique had bought, it made a good supper.

Monique and Lucie washed the dishes in a bucket of water. Then Lucie and Pierre settled down, as they usually did of evenings, to hard-fought games of backgammon. Backgammon held no interest for Monique. She wished she had her reference books. She never had finished that article on the cult of Isis in Gallia Narbonensis. Her books, like the apartment from which her brother had spirited her, were bound to be radioactive dust these days.

She sighed, wondering if she would be able to find a teaching position in the new France. She was sick of living with her brother and Lucie. But the Reichsmarks the Race had given her not so long ago were worth hardly anything at the moment. New French francs were coming into circulation, and German money was shrinking in value almost as fast as it had after the First World War. It seemed most unfair.

Her brother didn't think so. "There!" he exclaimed in triumph after winning the game. "If we'd been playing for money, I'd own you now, Lucie."

For all practical purposes, he did own Lucie. Monique was almost angry enough to say so, which wouldn't have made the tent a more enjoyable place to live. Pierre and Lucie started another game. That didn't make the tent any more enjoyable, either, not as far as Monique was concerned. Her brother and his lover, unfortunately, had other ideas, and they outnumbered her. *The tyranny of democracy,* she thought.

She heard footsteps outside: not the soft, skittering strides of Lizards, but the solid steps of men, and men wearing heavy shoes at that. One of them said, "Here, this is the place," right outside the tent flap. He spoke clear, Parisian French. That should have warned Monique what would happen next, but she was taken by surprise when the men with pistols burst into the tent. The man who'd spoken outside now spoke again: "Which of you women is Monique Dutourd?"

"I am," Monique answered automatically. "What do you want with me?"

"You were a Nazi's whore," the man snapped. "France needs to be cleansed of the likes of you. Come along, or you'll be sorry." He gestured with his pistol.

"Now see here, my friends," Pierre Dutourd said, making what sounded to Monique like a dangerously unwarranted assumption. "You are making a mistake. If you will but wait a moment—"

"Shut up, you fat tub of goo," the leader of the purification squad said coldly. "I tell you this only once. After that . . ." Now the muzzle of the pistol pointed right at the bridge of Pierre's nose. Monique's brother sat silent as a stone. "Good," the other man said. "Come along with me, whore."

"I'm not a whore," Monique insisted, trying to fight down a nasty stab of fear. How could she make these hard-eyed purifiers understand? How could she make them believe?

"You are to be interrogated," their leader said, as if she hadn't spoken. "After the interrogation, your punishment will be set." He sounded as if there weren't the slightest doubt she would be punished. In his mind, there probably wasn't.

"The Nazis interrogated me, too, at the Palais de Justice," Monique said. "I hope you will be gentler than they were." Terror at the thought of another such interrogation was what had made her let Dieter Kuhn do what he wanted with her.

But the leader of the purification squad said, "We shall do everything that is necessary." The fire of righteousness burned in his eyes, as it had burned in the eyes of the Germans who'd questioned and tormented her.

She'd had no choice with the Germans. She had no choice now. With such dignity as she could muster, she said, "Be it noted that I come with you under protest."

"Be it noted that no one cares," the zealot answered. "Get moving." Under the cover of his comrades' automatics, Monique left the tent and stepped out into the warm night. Somewhere close by, a cricket chirped. *You can afford to make noise,* Monique thought bitterly. *No one is going to interrogate you.* The purification squad hustled her through the camp toward a waiting motorcar.

As she had on her previous tour of duty in Marseille, Felless found that she liked the place better than Nuremberg. Since she'd hated Nuremberg with a deep and abiding loathing, that wasn't saying much, but it was something. The weather here, though not up to the standards of Home or even of the new town in the Arabian Peninsula where she'd been a refugee, was certainly an improvement on Nuremberg's. At this season of the year, it was more than tolerable.

She soon discovered she liked Marseille better now than she had on her first visit, too, even though the Race's explosive-metal bomb had torn out its liver. Then the Deutsche had been in charge of the city, and their arrogance, their automatic assumption that they were not just equal but superior to the Race, had gone a long way toward making her despise them and the place both.

The Français, now, the Français were easier to deal with. Technically, this subregion called France still wasn't part of the territory the Race ruled from Cairo. It functioned as an independent not-empire. But the Français Big Uglies listened to what the Race had to say to them. The alternative was listening to the Deutsche, and the Français had done that for too many years to want to do it any more.

Felless did wish Ambassador Veffani wouldn't keep turning an eye turret her way, but she couldn't do anything about that. "I greet you, superior sir," she said, polite as always when he telephoned.

"And I greet you, Senior Researcher," Veffani said, sounding more friendly than he usually did. "I seek your opinion in an area that falls within your field of professional expertise."

"Go ahead, superior sir." Felless vastly preferred a technical question to his hectoring her over her ginger habit, the reason he usually called.

"I shall," he said. "Here is my question: do you believe that, by leaving Tosevite not-empires formally independent but in fact dependent on the Race, we can lay the foundations for fully incorporating them into the Empire?"

It was an interesting question. Felless had no doubt she was far from the only one contemplating it. At last, she said, "On the two other planets the Race conquered, half measures were unnecessary. Here, they may well be expedient. We have the chance to experiment, both with France and with the *Reich*."

"Ruling Big Uglies should not be a matter for experiment." Veffani laughed a wry laugh. "Too often, though, it is."

"You would know better than I, superior sir." Felless didn't like flattering him, especially not in view of all the grief he'd caused her, but his question might prove important for the Race, and so she was willing to put aside her own feelings. And it wasn't as if she were speaking an untruth; as a male from the conquest fleet, Veffani *did* have more experience with Tosevites than she. She went on, "Perhaps such an approach could aid in the ultimate assimilation of Tosev 3."

"Perhaps it could," Veffani said. "Perhaps we should find out. If you can draft a memorandum outlining your views, I will forward it to Cairo with a recommendation for serious consideration—and with your name noted, of course."

"I thank you, superior sir," Felless said. "It shall be done."

"Excellent," Veffani answered. "I have long known you are capable of excellent work. I am glad to see you realizing your potential. Good-bye." His image vanished from her monitor.

He hadn't even taken her to task for her ginger habit, not directly. Maybe he thought she'd given up tasting. If so, he was wrong. She still used the Tosevite herb whenever she got the chance. But she did try to be careful about giving her pheromones a chance to subside before appearing in public; she didn't want to lay yet another clutch of eggs. She'd mated once since coming to France, but, to her relief, hadn't become gravid as a result.

She'd got involved in the memorandum when the speaker by the door hissed for attention. Felless hissed, too, in annoyance. "Who is it?" she asked.

"I: Business Administrator Keffesh," came the reply. "I would like to ask your assistance on a matter of some delicacy."

Now what is that supposed to mean? Felless wondered irritably. She realized she'd have to find out. She could open the door without fear of embarrassment; she hadn't tasted in several days. With a sigh, she rose from her desk and poked a fingerclaw into the door's control panel. As it slid open, she said, "I greet you, Business Administrator."

"And I greet you, superior female." Keffesh assumed the posture of respect. That was polite, but not altogether necessary, not with his rank close to hers. It likely meant he wanted something from her, and so wanted her in a good mood. Well, he'd already come out and said he was after something.

"What is this delicate matter?" Felless asked.

Keffesh approached it obliquely. "Do I correctly understand that, in a psychological experiment before this latest round of fighting with the Deutsche, you awarded a Tosevite female named Monique Dutourd a large sum of money?"

"Before I answer, let me consult my records." Felless did, then made the affirmative gesture. "Yes, that appears to be correct. Is it germane?"

"It is, superior female," Keffesh answered. "You see, Monique Dutourd has the same mother and father as Pierre Dutourd, a Big Ugly with whom I have done a substantial amount of business. You surely know how, among the Tosevites, these connections count for a good deal."

"Indeed I do." Felless made the affirmative gesture again. "You do well to note their importance, I might add. But I do not quite see . . ."

"Let me explain," Keffesh said. "Monique Dutourd is at the moment in a certain amount of difficulty with the Français authorities, for she is accused of having had a sexual relationship with a Deutsch officer while the Deutsche occupied this subregion. The Français, as you must also know, are seeking to destroy memories of the Deutsch occupation and to punish those who aided and comforted the occupiers."

"Yes, I know that, too," Felless said. "The Race encourages it, as it makes the Français more likely to be dependent on us."

"In principle, I approve of this," Keffesh said. "In practice, Monique Dutourd's difficulties make it harder for Pierre Dutourd to carry on his business."

"That is unfortunate, perhaps, but . . ." Felless shrugged. "Why should it matter to me, or to the Race as a whole?" Before Keffesh could answer, she swung both eye turrets toward him. "Wait. What sort of business is this Big Ugly in?"

Now Keffesh hesitated. "Superior female, I told you this was a matter of some delicacy. I hope I may rely on your discretion." He brought his hand up near his mouth and shot out his tongue, as if he were tasting ginger.

Had Felless not been in the habit of tasting, too, she probably wouldn't have known what that meant. As things were, she said, "I believe I understand."

"Ahh." Relief filled Keffesh's hiss. "I hoped you would. I had been given to understand that you would." By that he no doubt meant he'd heard of Felless' ginger-induced disgrace. He went on, "If you could arrange leniency from the Français, superior female, you would not find me ungrateful. You would not find Pierre Dutourd ungrateful, either."

What exactly was he offering? All the ginger she could taste? Something like that, surely. Her tailstump quivered in excitement. She tried to make it hold still. Doing her best to sound casual, she said, "I make no promises—who can make promises where Big Uglies are involved?—but I will see what I can do."

"I thank you, superior female." Keffesh went into the posture of respect again. "I could ask for nothing more. And now I shall not disturb you any further." He left the chamber.

Felless returned to the memorandum. *First things first,* she told herself. But she couldn't concentrate. Her mind kept going back to ginger.

At last, sighing, she saved the memorandum and started trying to telephone the Français authorities. That didn't prove easy; the links between the Race's phone system and that of France were as yet tenuous. At last, though, she reached an official with the formidable title of Minister of Purification. "Do you speak the language of the Race?" she asked, wondering where she could find an interpreter if he didn't.

But Joseph Darnand did, after a fashion. "I speak it but a little bit," he replied, his accent thick but comprehensible. "Speak you slowly, if it please you. What is it that you want?"

"I want you to release a certain prisoner here in Marseille, a female named Monique Dutourd," Felless told him.

She waited for the Big Ugly to say, *It shall be done.* But Darnand acted for all the world as if France were as much an independent not-empire as the *Reich* had been before the fighting. "One moment, if it please you," he said. "I shall consult my records."

"Very well." Felless could hardly say no to that.

It took a lot longer than the promised moment. Felless reminded herself that Tosevite data-retrieval systems were much less efficient than those of the Race. She had to remind herself of that several times before Joseph Darnand finally returned to the line. He said, "I regret, Senior Researcher, that this will be difficult. Without doubt, this female carried on a sexual relationship with a Deutsch officer—and not just any Deutsch officer, but one from their secret police. Such betrayal must be punished, unless there is some vitally important reason to forgive."

At first, Felless thought he was flat-out refusing. Such disobedience from a Big Ugly supposed to be dependent on the Race would have infuriated her. But then she saw a possible loophole in his words. "Is it not true that this particular female was forced into this sexual relationship against her will?" That counted for a great deal among Tosevites, she knew. Thanks to ginger and ingenious males, it was also beginning to matter to the Race on Tosev 3.

"She claims this," Joseph Darnand said scornfully. "But what female in such circumstances would not claim it? Our interrogators do not believe it to be true, not at all."

"But I—and the Race, speaking through me—do believe it to be true in this case." Felless knew how far she was stretching things. She personally knew next to nothing about the case, and speaking through her was not the fleetlord or an ambassador but a ginger dealer. With a small hiss of annoyance at herself and her role here, she went on, "And this female has cooperated with us. We would strongly appreciate her release." She added an emphatic cough for good measure.

After another long silence on the other end of the line, the Français minister of purification sighed. "Oh, very well," he said. "I shall give the appropriate orders. At least you, unlike the Deutsche, are polite enough to disguise your commands as requests." He knew he was supposed to be subservient, then. Felless had wondered.

Having got what she wanted, she could afford to be gracious. "I thank you very much," she said, wondering how much ginger Keffesh would pay her for her services.

"It is nothing." By Joseph Darnand's tone, it was much more than that. He growled something in his own language as he broke the connection. Felless didn't mind annoying him. In fact, she rather enjoyed it.

"Comrade General Secretary, the ambassador from Finland is here," Vyacheslav Molotov's secretary said.

"Good. Very good," Molotov said. "By all means show him into the office. I have looked forward to this interview for many years. At last, I am in the position to bring it off."

"Good morning, Comrade General Secretary," Urho Kekkonen said in fluent Russian. He took tea from the samovar in the corner of the room and helped himself to smoked salmon on rye bread.

"Good morning," Molotov replied: enough socializing. "Now—has your government come to a decision about the contents of the note you received from the foreign commissariat of the Soviet Union?"

Kekkonen slowly and deliberately chewed and swallowed. He was a big, broad-shouldered man who wore glasses thicker than Molotov's. "We have, Comrade General Secretary," he answered. "Finland rejects your demands in all particulars."

"What?" Molotov was astonished, and had to work hard not to show it. "I would strongly suggest that you reconsider. I would very strongly suggest that you reconsider."

"Nyet." Kekkonen spoke one of Molotov's favorite words with almost offensive relish.

"Are you mad?" Molotov demanded. "Is your government mad? For a generation, you have sheltered under the wing of the *Reich*. But the *Reich*, these days, is a dead bird. Where will you shelter now from the just wrath of the workers and peasants of the Soviet Union at your aggression?"

"You were unjust when you invaded us in 1939," Urho Kekkonen answered, "and you have not improved since. We have no intention of reconsidering. If you invade us again, we shall fight again."

"We defeated you then," Molotov said coldly. "We can do it again, you know. And, as I said, Germany is in no position to aid you."

"I understand that," the Finn said. "I understand it most thoroughly. That is why my government has entered into consultations with the Race. We were not eager to do this, you must understand, but the Soviet Union's attitude left us no choice."

For Molotov, the words were like a blow in the belly. He hadn't made a worse miscalculation since the pact with the Nazis. "You would betray mankind?" he barked, his voice harsh.

"Nyet," Kekkonen repeated. "Our government would—and will—protect our country from aggression. Dealing with the Lizards is the only choice available to us at the moment. Because it is our only choice, we have taken it."

It was not the choice Molotov had expected the Finns to take. They'd jealously protected their independence against the USSR. They'd also protected it, as much as they could, against the Germans. They'd been the *Reich's* allies, but not, unlike Hungary and Romania, its subject allies. Molotov tried the best arrow left in his quiver: "How will your people take the news that you have surrendered to the Race?"

Kekkonen's smile was almost as cold as any Molotov might have produced. "You misunderstand, Comrade General Secretary. In no way have we surrendered to the Race."

"What?" Molotov was so furious, and so alarmed, he had trouble sounding dry. "Did you not just tell me that you are allowing the Race to occupy Finland?"

"Yes, the Race will have a military presence in my country," Urho Kekkonen replied. "But the Lizards will not occupy us, any more than the Germans occupied us. We remain independent. The males of the Race in Finland will remain in their bases unless we are attacked, in which case they will cooperate with us in our defense. An attack on Finland will be construed as an attack on the Race."

"I . . . see," Molotov said. "This . . . agreement does not infringe on your sovereignty?"

Kekkonen shook his big head. "We do not care to have *anyone* infringe on our sovereignty. The Soviet Union has had some small trouble grasping this over the years. It includes you, it includes the *Reich*, and it also includes the Race."

"I . . . see," Molotov said again. "I had not believed the Lizards would enter into such an agreement." *If I had, I never would have issued that ultimatum.*

"Perhaps no one had proposed such an arrangement to them before," the Finnish ambassador answered. "Perhaps no one was in a position to propose such an agreement to them before. But we did, and they wasted no time in accepting."

"Of course they accepted," Molotov snapped. "You've let them put their foot in the door."

"We judged it better to let them put their foot in the door than for you to force your foot in," Kekkonen said.

Molotov didn't answer right away. He was thinking furiously. The Lizards never would have agreed to such a bargain before the latest round of fighting with the Germans. (That the Finns wouldn't have needed to ask for such an arrangement then was for the moment beside the point.) But they'd left the *Reich* independent but weak. They'd re-created an independent but weak France. And now they were fostering an independent Finland that could never be anything but weak.

They have hit upon something new, he thought. *Now they are seeing what they can do with it.* The Lizards still weren't skilled diplomats, not by Earthly standards. Odds were, they never would be. But they played the game better than they had on first coming to Earth: then, they'd hardly realized there was a game to be played. They could learn. He wished they hadn't started learning here.

Kekkonen said, "I presume we may now consider your ultimatum withdrawn?"

I ought to tell him no, Molotov thought. *I ought to tell him we would be happy to go to war with the Finns and the Lizards both. That would jolt him out of his smug bourgeois complacency.*

But it would also result in disaster for the Soviet Union. Molotov knew that only too well. Had he not known it, the recent horrid example of the Greater German *Reich* would have rubbed his nose in it. Fighting the Lizards was a tactic of last resort. And so, staring hatefully at Kekkonen through his spectacles, he bit off one word: *"Da."*

He took a certain amount of satisfaction in noting how relieved the Finn looked. Kekkonen hadn't been sure he wouldn't throw his country onto the funeral pyre for the sake of pride. The Nazis had, after all. But the Nazis weren't rational, and never had been. The USSR was and would remain in the struggle against imperialism indefinitely. If he had to retreat today, he would advance tomorrow.

After Urho Kekkonen had left, Molotov summoned Andrei Gromyko and Marshal Zhukov. He told them what the Finns had done. Zhukov cursed. Gromyko came to the point: "What did you tell him, Vyacheslav Mikhailovich?"

"That we withdraw the ultimatum." The words were sour as vomit in Molotov's mouth, but he brought them out even so. Turning to Zhukov, he asked, "Or do you think I made a mistake?"

"No," Zhukov said at once. "When the devil's grandmother starts fooling with your plans, you have to change them."

Molotov was relieved there. Unlike Kekkonen, he didn't show it. Had Zhukov been bound and determined to fight the Lizards, he would have brushed Molotov aside and done it. But he'd fought them a generation before and wasn't eager to repeat the experience, any more than Molotov was.

Gromyko's shaggy eyebrows twitched. "Just when you think the Race too stupid to survive, you get a surprise like this."

"What do you suggest to avoid similar unfortunate surprises, Andrei Andreyevich?" Molotov asked.

"Well, if we were going to present Romania with an ultimatum, this would be a good time to put it back on the shelf," Gromyko answered. "Of course, we had no such plan in mind."

"Of course," Molotov said in a hollow voice. All three men looked at one another. Romania still held Bessarabia and northern Bukovina, lands the USSR had reclaimed under the 1940 Vienna Award, only to lose them again in the aftermath of the Hitlerite invasion. Now that the *Reich* could no longer come to the aid of its friends, the Romanian government would have been next on the list after Finland. But if the Romanians screamed for help and the Lizards answered, that would just give the Race a longer frontier with the USSR.

"Dammit, why wasn't this anticipated?" Zhukov glared at Molotov. "We could have ended up with our dicks in the sausage machine."

As he had with Kekkonen, Molotov had to fight for calm. If Zhukov got angry enough, the Red Army would start running the Soviet Union the very next day. But Molotov knew that acting as if he was afraid of that only made it more likely to happen. After a deep breath, he asked, "Georgi Konstantinovich, did *you* expect the Finns to seek support from the Lizards?"

"Me? No way in hell," Zhukov answered. "But I'm a soldier. I don't pretend to be a diplomat. I leave that kind of worrying to people who do pretend to be diplomats." Now he glowered at Andrei Gromyko. *Better at Gromyko than at me,* Molotov thought.

Gromyko's equanimity was almost as formidable as Molotov's. The foreign commissar said, "We tried something. It didn't work. The world will not end. No one reasonable could have imagined that the Finns would prefer the Race to their fellow humans."

Zhukov grunted. "They preferred the Nazis to their fellow humans, back in '41. They don't much like us, for some reason or other."

That would do as an understatement till a better one came along. As Zhukov said, the Finns had become Hitler's cobelligerents as soon as they got the chance. Now they were teaching the Lizards to play balance-of-power politics? All that to avoid the influence of the peace-loving workers and peasants of the USSR? Molotov shook his head. "The Finns," he said, "are an inherently unreliable people."

"That's true enough," Marshal Zhukov agreed. In musing tones, he went on, "We could probably win a war in Finland, even against the Race. The Lizards' logistics are very bad."

"We could probably win a war against the Race *in Finland,*" Gromyko said acidly. "The Nazis more or less won a war against the Race *in Poland.* But they didn't win their war against the Race. Could we?"

"Of course not," Zhukov answered at once.

"Of course not. I agree," Molotov said. "That is why, when Kekkonen presented me with a *fait accompli,* I saw no choice but to withdraw our note. We cannot anticipate everything, Georgi Konstantinovich. Even the dialectic shows only trends, not details. We shall have other chances."

"Oh, very well." Zhukov sounded like a sulky child.

"It is not as if our own sovereignty were weakened," Gromyko said, and the marshal nodded. That satisfied him, at least for the moment. It salved Molotov, but it didn't satisfy him. The Soviet Union's sovereignty survived; its prestige, as he knew too well, had taken a beating.

Something would have to be done about that. Not in Europe, barring desperate times he didn't foresee. The Lizards' eye turrets were looking that way. But the USSR had the longest land frontier of any nation—any human nation—on Earth. "Persia," Molotov murmured. "Afghanistan. China, of course. Always China."

With considerable pleasure, Atvar studied the reports he had received from Helsinki and Moscow. Swinging one eye turret toward Pshing, he said, "Here is something that, for once, appears to have worked very well indeed. The Soviet Union has retreated from its threats against Finland, and our influence over that small not-empire is increased." His mouth fell open in a laugh. "Since we had essentially no influence over Finland up until this time, any influence is an increase."

"Truth, Exalted Fleetlord," his adjutant agreed. After a moment, though, he added, "A pity we could not arrange to incorporate the not-empire into the territory we administer directly."

"I too would have liked that," Atvar said. "But when our representative broached the idea to the leaders of the Finnish not-empire, they flatly refused. We have taken what we could get—not everything we wanted, but much better than nothing."

Pshing sighed. "On this world, Exalted Fleetlord, we have never been able to get everything we wanted. Too often, we have had to count ourselves lucky to get any of what we wanted."

"That, unfortunately, is also truth," the fleetlord said. "It is why I agreed to this half measure—in fact, something less than a half measure. But it did succeed in making the SSSR pull back."

"What would you have done had the SSSR chosen to invade this small not-empire in spite of our presence there?" Pshing asked.

"Let me put it this way: I am glad we did not have to put it to the test." Atvar felt like adding an emphatic cough to that, but didn't; he didn't care to have his adjutant know just how glad he was. "One thing we have done since coming to Tosev 3 is show the Big Uglies that they can—indeed, that they must—rely on our word. Because of that, the Russkis were convinced we would honor our commitment to Finland, and so did not presume to test it. If you think this makes me unhappy, you are mistaken."

"What can we do to increase our influence over the Finns now that we have established this presence?" Pshing asked.

"I do not yet know that," Atvar answered. "We have had little to do with that subgroup of Big Uglies up till now, not least because of the truly horrendous climate of their not-empire. Reports from both the Russkis and the Deutsche indicate that they are first-rate fighters. Our own experts indicate that the Deutsche have not stinted in keeping them supplied with the most sophisticated Tosevite weaponry."

"Not explosive-metal bombs, I hope," his adjutant exclaimed.

"Not to my knowledge, for which I praise the spirits of Emperors past." Atvar cast down his eye turrets for a moment. "No, we are nearly certain the Finns do not possess weapons of that type."

"Then, in case of emergency, we can use the threat of employing such weapons against them to bring them toward meeting our requirements," Pshing said.

But Atvar made the negative hand gesture. "That has been considered. It has also been rejected. Analysis indicates that the Finnish Tosevites would be more likely either to resist on their own or to call on the Russkis for aid against us."

"How could they do that?" Pshing asked. "They are presently calling on us for aid against the SSSR."

"Tosevite diplomatists have a phrase: balance of power," Atvar said. "What this means is, using your less annoying neighbor to protect you from your more annoying neighbor. If the annoyance level changes, the direction of the alliance can also change, and change very quickly."

"I see," Pshing said. "Yes, that is the sort of system Big Uglies would be likely to devise."

"You speak sarcastically, but your words hold an egg of truth," the fleetlord said. "Because the Big Uglies have always been divided up into so many competing factions, they have naturally needed to develop means for improving their particular group's chance for short-term success—the only kind they consider—and reducing the chances of their opponents. And now that we are a part of this competitive system, we have had to adopt or adapt these techniques ourselves. Without them, we would be at a severe disadvantage."

"Back in the days of ancientest history, I am certain that our ancestors were more virtuous," Pshing said.

"You would probably be surprised," Atvar answered. "In preparing for this mission, I had to study a good deal more ancientest history than is commonly taught in schools. I can understand why so much of it is suppressed, as a matter of fact. Back in the days before the Empire unified Home, our ancestors were a cantankerous lot. They would likely have been better equipped to deal with the Big Uglies than we are, because they seem to have spent a good deal of their time cheating one another."

"Exalted Fleetlord, you shock me," Pshing said.

"Well, I was shocked myself," Atvar admitted. "The trouble is, our early ancestors actually did these things and were experienced in diplomacy and duplicity. Since the Empire unified Home a hundred thousand years ago, we have forgotten such techniques. We did not really need them when we conquered the Rabotevs and Hallessi, though the fleetlords of those conquest fleets studied them, too. And, of course, our so-called experts aboard the colonization fleet studied our earlier conquests on the assumption that this one would be analogous. That is why they have been of so little use to us: false assumptions always lead to bad policy."

"Experts aboard the colonization fleet," Pshing echoed. "That reminds me, Exalted Fleetlord—you will surely recall Senior Researcher Felless?"

"Oh, yes." Atvar made the affirmative gesture. "The alleged expert on Big Ugly psychology who decided to imitate or exceed the Tosevites' sexual excesses. Why should I recall her, Pshing? What has she done now to draw my eye turrets in her direction? Another disgrace with ginger?"

"I am not precisely sure, Exalted Fleetlord," his adjutant answered. "No one appears to be precisely sure. She used her influence in France to obtain the release of a certain prisoner charged with previous collaboration—sexual collaboration— with the Deutsche. As I understand things, it does appear that the prisoner was in fact coerced into this sexual collaboration, a Tosevite crime that ginger has allowed us to discover as well."

"Indeed," the fleetlord said. "What is the difficulty if Felless was acting in the interest of justice, as appears to be the case?"

"The difficulty, Exalted Fleetlord, is that the prisoner in question also has a family connection to one of the leading Tosevite ginger smugglers in Marseille," Pshing replied.

"Oh. I see." Atvar's voice was heavy with meaning. "Did Senior Researcher Felless come to the Big Ugly's aid from a sense of justice or from a longing for a limitless supply of the Tosevite herb, then?"

"No one knows," Pshing answered. "Ambassador Veffani notes that her work has been excellent of late, but he also suspects that she still tastes ginger. Judging motivation is not always simple."

"One could hardly disagree with that," Atvar said. "Veffani is a more than competent male. I presume he is continuing to monitor developments in France?"

"He is, Exalted Fleetlord," Pshing said. "If ambiguity diminishes, he will notify us, and will take the actions he deems justified."

"Very well." It wasn't very well, but Atvar couldn't do anything about it save wait. "What other tidbits of news have we?"

"We have received another protest from the not-empire of the United States concerning incursions of our domestic animals into their territory," Pshing said. "They have also begun complaining that the seeds of certain of our domestic plants have spread north of the border between our territory and theirs."

"If those are the worst complaints the American Big Uglies have, they should count themselves lucky," Atvar said with a scornful laugh. "They *are* fortunate. They seem not to realize how fortunate they are. I shall not personally respond to this protest. You may tell them to compare their situation to that of the Deutsche and, having done so, to decide if their sniveling— use that word—has merit."

"It shall be done, Exalted Fleetlord," Pshing replied. "In fact, I shall take considerable pleasure in doing it. The American Tosevites complain because they have lost a fingerclaw, not because they have lost fingers."

"Exactly so," Atvar said. "You may also tell them that, and you need not soften it very much. And you may tell them that they are welcome to slay any of our domestic animals they find on their side of the border, and to enjoy the meat once they have slain them. Furthermore, tell them they may pull up any plants of ours they find in their land. We shall have no complaints if they do. But if they labor under the delusion that we can stop animals from wandering and plants from propagating and spreading, my opinion is and shall remain that they are deluded indeed."

"May I tell them *that*?" Pshing asked eagerly.

"Why not?" the fleetlord said. "The Americans have self-righteousness as a common failing, as the Deutsche have arrogance and the Russkis have obfuscation. Tell Ambassador Lodge what he needs to hear, not just what he might want to hear."

"Again, Exalted Fleetlord, it shall be done," his adjutant said. "And, again, I will enjoy doing it."

Atvar called up some maps of the northern part of the lesser continental mass. He checked climatological data, then hissed in derision. "It appears unlikely that our plants will be able to flourish in most of the regions where the American Big Uglies raise most of their food crops—their harsh winters will kill plants used to decent weather. They have not lost even a finger-claw; they may perhaps have chipped one. The farmers in the subregion of the greater continental mass called India have a genuine grievance against us: there, our plants compete successfully against those they are used to growing."

"As you say, the Americans have nothing large that exercises them, so they have to get exercised over small things," Pshing answered. "The next Tosevite we discover who cannot complain at any excuse or none will be the first."

"Truth!" Atvar used an emphatic cough. "I truly believe that their constant carping was what finally pushed the Deutsche into war against us. They complained so often and over so many different things, they finally persuaded themselves they were doing what was good and true and right. And so they attacked, and so they failed. I doubt it will teach them much of a lesson, but we shall do our best to make sure they lack the strength to try adventurism again."

"Unlike Tosevites, we have the patience for such a course," Pshing observed.

"Yes." The fleetlord's thought went down another road. "Fortunate that the SSSR, unlike the *Reich*, chose to see reason. Had the Russkis been determined to try to annex Finland in spite of our prohibition, life would have become more difficult."

"We would have beaten them," Pshing said.

"Of course we would have beaten them," Atvar replied. "But beating them would have been the same as beating the Deutsche:

difficult, annoying, and much more trouble than the cause of the quarrel was worth." He paused. "And if that is not a summary of our experience on Tosev 3, I do not know what is."

☆ 6 ☆

Sam Yeager swung up onto his horse with a certain amount—a certain large amount—of trepidation. "I haven't done any riding since Hector was a pup," he said. "Hell, I haven't done any riding since *I* was a pup: not since I got off the farm, anyhow. That's more than forty years ago now."

His companion, a sun-blasted sheriff named Victor Watkins, let out a chuckle around a cigarette. "It's like riding a bicycle, Lieutenant Colonel—once you figure out how to do it, you don't forget. We could go farther and faster in a jeep, but four legs'll take us where four wheels couldn't, even if the wheels are on a jeep. And I know where the critters are, and the stuff they're grazing on."

"Okay." Yeager couldn't remember the last time he'd heard anybody actually say *critters*. Maybe Mutt Daniels, his manager when the Lizards came to earth, had—Mutt was from Mississippi, and had a drawl thick as the mud there. Sam went on, "Seeing them is what I came here for, so let's do it."

"Right." Sheriff Watkins urged his horse forward with knees and reins. Awkwardly, Sam followed suit. The horse didn't give him a horse laugh, but it could have. It wasn't like riding a bicycle. He wished he were riding a bicycle.

At a slow walk, they went south out of Desert Center, California, toward the Chuckwalla Mountains. Desert Center lived up to its name: it was a tiny town, no more than a couple of hundred people, on U.S. 70, a place for folks on the way to somewhere else to stop and buy gas and take a leak. Yeager couldn't imagine living there; it was ever so much more isolated than the farm where he'd grown up.

He wiped sweat from his face before putting back on the broad-brimmed Stetson Watkins had lent him. "I can see how

154

Desert Center got its name," he said. "Weather only a Lizard could love."

"Oh, I don't know," the sheriff said. "I like it pretty well myself—I've lived in these parts more than thirty years. Of course, I was born up in St. Paul, so I got sick and tired of snow in a big fat hurry."

"I can see that." Sam let out a small sigh. He'd never played in St. Paul; it belonged to the American Association, only one jump down from the majors, and one jump up from any league where he had played. If he hadn't broken his ankle on that slide into second down in Birmingham . . . He sighed again. Plenty of ballplayers might have made the big leagues if they hadn't got hurt. It was more than twenty years too late to worry about that now.

He yanked his mind back to the business at hand. Something— a small "l" lizard?—scurried away from his horse's hooves and disappeared into the shade under a cactus. When he looked up, he saw a few buzzards wheeling optimistically through the sky. Other than that, the land might have been dead: nothing but sagebrush and cacti scattered not too thickly over the pale yellow dirt. Their sharp-edged shadows seemed to etch themselves into the ground.

Somehow, the landscape didn't look quite the way Sam had thought it would. After a couple of minutes, he put his finger on why. "None of those tall cactuses," he said. "You know the kind I mean: the ones that look like a man standing there with his hands up."

Victor Watkins nodded. "Saguaros. Yeah, you don't see that many of 'em this side of the Colorado River. Over in Arizona, now, they're all over the damn place."

"Are they?" Yeager said, and the local nodded again. Sam went on, "Hardly seems as if anything much *could* live here."

"Well, it's after ten in the morning," Sheriff Watkins said. "Pretty much all the critters are laying in burrows or under rocks or anywhere they can go to get out of the sun. Come here around sunup or sundown and you'll see a lot more: jackrabbits and kangaroo rats and snakes and skunks and I don't know what all. And there are owls and bobcats and coyotes"—he pronounced it *keye-oats*—"at night, and sometimes deer down from the mountains. In spring, after we get a little rain, it's real pretty country."

"Yeah?" Yeager knew he sounded dubious. Thinking of this

country as pretty any time struck him as being on the order of thinking Frankenstein handsome because he'd put on a new suit.

But Watkins said, "Hell, yes. Flowers and butterflies all over the place. You even get toads breeding in the mud puddles and croaking away like mad."

"If you say so." Sam couldn't really argue; he hadn't been in these parts just after some rain. From what he could see, they didn't get rain any too often. Something large enough to be startling buzzed past his nose. "What was that?" he asked as it zipped away. "June bug?"

"Nope. Hummingbird." Watkins glanced over at Yeager. "Listen, remember to drink plenty of water. That's what we've got it along for. Heat like this, it just pours out of you." He swigged from one of his canteens.

Sam dutifully drank. The water had been cold back in Desert Center. It wasn't cold any more. He pointed to a small cloud of dust a couple of miles ahead. "What's that, if everything takes it easy in the middle of the day?"

"Lizard critters don't," the sheriff said. "Far as they're concerned, this is like a day in the park. They like it fine—better'n fine. Mad dogs and Englishmen and these funny-lookin' things." They rode on a little while longer, heading toward the dust. Then Watkins pointed, too, at a plant Sam might not have noticed. "There. These started growing about the same time the critters showed up."

Now that his attention was drawn to it, Yeager saw it was different from the others past which his horse had taken him. It wasn't quite the right shade of green; it put him in mind of tarnished copper. He'd never seen any leaves that looked like these: they might almost have been blades of grass growing along its branches. It didn't have flowers, but those red disks with black centers at the ends of some of the branches might have done the same job. Sam reined in. "Can I get a closer look at it?"

"That's what we're here for," Watkins said.

Sam dismounted as clumsily as he'd boarded his horse. He walked over to the plant from the Lizards' world, scuffing up dust at every step. When he reached out to touch it, he yelped and jerked his hand back in a hurry. "It's like a nettle," he said. "It's got little sharp doohickeys"—a fine scientific term, that—"in between the leaves."

"Found that out, did you?" Sheriff Watkins' voice was dry.

Rubbing his hand, Yeager asked, "You ever see anything eating these plants?"

"Nope," the sheriff answered. "Not unless you mean the Lizards' animals. Nothin' that oughta live here'll touch 'em. Haven't seen any bees go to those red things, either."

"All right." That had been Sam's next question. He took a notebook from his pocket and scribbled in it. If bees wouldn't visit these things, how did they get pollinated? Could they get pollinated—or whatever they used as an equivalent—here on Earth? Evidently, or this one wouldn't be here.

Watkins said, "You put on leather gloves and try and yank that thing out, you'll find out it's got roots that go clear to China."

"Why am I not surprised?" Yeager wrote another note. Back on Home, plants would have to suck up all the water they possibly could. It made sense for them to have roots like that. A lot of Earthly plants did, too. Sam suspected these would prove very efficient indeed.

Sheriff Watkins said, "Come on. These things are just the sideshow. You really want to see the animals, right?"

"I don't know," Sam said thoughtfully. "Do I? If these things start crowding out the stuff that used to grow here, what'll the bugs and the kangaroo rats and the jackrabbits eat? If they don't eat anything, what'll the lizards and the bobcats eat? The more you look at things like this, the more complicated they get." Remounting his horse proved pretty complicated, too, but he managed not to fall off the other side.

"Supposing you're right," Watkins said as they rode on toward the animals from Home. "Isn't that reason enough to give the Lizards hell for what they're doing to us? What they're doing to Earth, I mean, not just to the USA."

"They don't want to listen," Yeager answered. "They say we've got cows and sheep and dogs and cats and wheat and corn, and that's what these things are to them: only natural they've brought 'em along."

"Natural, my ass." Watkins spat. "These critters are about the most *un*natural-looking things I've seen in all my born days." He pointed ahead. "Look for yourself. We're close enough now."

Sure enough, Sam could peer through the dust now and see what raised it. The Lizards' domestic animals made him feel he'd been yanked back through seventy million years and was staring at a herd of dinosaurs. They weren't as big as dinosaurs, and they had the Lizards' turreted eyes, but that was the general impression. They were low-slung, went on all fours, and had, instead of horns, bony clubs on the ends of their tails. One of them whacked another in the side. The one that had been whacked bawled and trotted away.

"Those are zisuili," Sam said. "The Lizards use them for meat and for their hides. Zisuili leather is top of the line, as far as they're concerned."

"Hot damn," Watkins said sourly. "What do we do about 'em? Look how they eat everything right down to the ground. Worse'n goats, for Christ's sake. There's nothing but bare dirt left once they've gone through somewhere, and this land won't take a whole hell of a lot of that."

"I see what you're saying," Yeager answered. "It's probably why they kick up so much dust." He clicked his tongue between his teeth. "You were right, Sheriff—this is what I came to find out about, sure enough."

"I've already found out more than I want," Victor Watkins said. "Question is, like I said, what do we do about the goddamn things?"

The two men had no trouble getting close to the zisuili, though their horses didn't much care for the alien animals' smell. Neither odors nor sight of Earthly creatures and people bothered the beasts from Home. Noting that, Yeager said, "We shoot 'em whenever we see 'em. They aren't shy of us, are they?"

"No, but when the shooting starts they run like hell," Watkins replied. "A guy with a machine gun would get a lot more done than a guy with a rifle. Desert Center's a rugged kind of place, but machine guns don't exactly grow on trees around here."

"Some machine guns can probably be arranged," Sam said, but he wondered how many machine guns the USA would need from the Pacific to the Gulf of Mexico, and for how many miles north of the border. And machine guns couldn't do anything about plants from Home. What could? Nothing he saw, short of an army of people pulling them up by the roots.

The Lizards were making themselves at home on Earth. Sam had read plenty of science-fiction stories about people reshaping other planets to suit themselves, but never one about aliens reshaping Earth for their convenience. He didn't need to read a story about that. By all the signs, he was living it.

Neither he nor Watkins had much to say as they rode back to Desert Center. They passed another couple of plants from Home. However the things propagated, they'd sure as hell got here.

"We'll do everything we can," Sam promised as he got down from his horse and, with more than a little relief, headed for his car.

"You'd better," the sheriff said. He walked off toward his office, not looking back.

Another car was parked by the Buick. It hadn't been there before. A couple of men in business suits came out of the little café across the street and walked briskly toward Sam. "Lieutenant Colonel Yeager?" one of them called. When Sam nodded, both men produced revolvers and pointed them at him. "You'd better come along with us, sir," the first one said. "Orders. Sorry, pal, but that's how it is."

Walter Stone stared out through the window of the *Lewis and Clark*'s control room in considerable satisfaction. "Amazing what you can do with aluminized plastic, isn't it?" he said.

"Not so bad," Glen Johnson agreed. "You put out a big enough mirror, you pick up plenty of sunshine for power and for heat and for I don't know what all else."

Stone looked sly. "Are you sure you don't?"

Johnson looked sly, too. "Who, me?" They both grinned. A mirror that focused a lot of light down to one small point was a splendid tool. It was also a weapon. If that point of light ever suddenly swung across a Lizard spy ship . . .

With a sigh, Stone said, "The only trouble is, that would mean war back home, which we can't afford."

"I know." Johnson grimaced. "It's not just that we can't afford it, either. We'd damn well lose."

"Are you sure?" the senior pilot asked.

"You bet your ass I am," Johnson said, and tacked on an emphatic cough. "Don't forget, I'm the guy who flew all those orbital missions. I know what the Race has got out there; hell, I know half that hardware by its first name. Push comes to shove, we get shoved."

"Okay, okay." Half to Glen's relief, half to his disappointment, Stone didn't want to argue with him. He liked arguments he wouldn't have any trouble winning. Stone waved at the mirror again. "One of the reasons we're out here is to complicate the

Lizards' lives in all sorts of ways they haven't even thought about yet. Having plenty of power and energy available is a long step in that direction."

"Did I say you were wrong?" Johnson asked, and then, "Say, what's this I hear about another ship heading this way before too long?"

Walter Stone suddenly looked a lot less like a buddy and a lot more like a pissed-off colonel. "Goddamn radio room here leaks like a goddamn sieve," he growled. "They open their mouths any wider, they'll fall right in."

"Yeah, well, probably," answered Johnson, who hadn't heard the rumor from any of the radio operators. "But come on. Now that I've got some of the word, give me the rest of it. It's not like I'm going to send the Race a postcard or anything."

"Bad security," Stone said. Johnson gave him a look. It must have been an effective look, because the senior pilot turned red and muttered under his breath. At last, with very poor grace, he went on, "Yeah, it's true. They're building it out in orbit now. Next opposition, or somewhere fairly close to then, it'll head out here, and we'll see some new faces."

"Good," Johnson said. "I'm sick of seeing your old face." That earned him a glare from Stone's old face. Grinning, he probed some more: "How many people will they be sending out?"

"All I know is, the complement is supposed to be larger than the crew of the *Lewis and Clark*," Stone answered. Johnson nodded, glad of the news; that was more than he'd known. Stone went on, "Two reasons. First, they won't have as long a trip, so they can bring more people with the same resources. And second, they'll have improved the design of the new ship."

"How?" Johnson asked eagerly. This was the stuff he wanted to hear, all right.

But Stone said, "How? How the devil should I know? Matter of fact, I don't know that for a fact." He paused, listened to himself, and shook his head in annoyance before continuing, "I'm just assuming there will be. We're not Lizards, after all; we don't think our designs are set in cement."

"Neither do they, not exactly," Johnson said. "It's just that we've been refining our designs for fifty years—a hundred, tops—and they've been doing it for fifty thousand. After that long, they don't find the need to make a whole lot of changes."

"Don't teach your grandma to suck eggs," Stone said irritably. "I know all that as well as you do, and you know I know it, too."

"Yeah, but you're cute when you're angry," Johnson said, which won him another glare from the senior pilot. He grinned again and went on, "With more people, we'll be able to spread out a lot farther. The Lizards won't be able to keep an eye on us so easy."

"Which is the point of the exercise," Stone said, as if to an idiot.

"No kidding." Johnson grinned once more, refusing to let the other man get his goat. Then he let his imagination run away with him. "One of these days, maybe, we'll have a regular fleet of ships going back and forth between Earth and the asteroid belt." His eyes and voice went far away. "Maybe, one of these days, we *will* be able to go home again."

But Walter Stone shook his head again, this time in flat negation. "Forget about it." His tone brooked no contradiction. "If a ship comes out here, it'll stay out here for good. We haven't got enough to let us afford to send anything back, especially not a big ship. Nice to dream about, yeah, but it won't happen."

Johnson thought it over and discovered he had to nod. "Might have done poor Liz Brock some good, though," he said.

"No." Again, Stone wasn't taking any arguments. "For one thing, you die with cancer of the liver back on Earth, too. And for another, the point is to make it so we don't need to go back to Earth for anything. We're supposed to be figuring out how to do everything we need here without going back to Earth. That's the plan, and we're going to make it work."

"It's only part of the plan," Johnson said.

"Well, of course." Stone sounded surprised he had to mention that.

A chime from the ship's PA system announced the hour. Johnson said, "I'm off." His shift was done. Stone's still had two hours to go. Adding, "Don't let anybody steal the chairs while I'm gone," Johnson glided out of the control room.

Since the chairs, like all the furniture, were bolted down, that didn't seem likely. As a parting shot, though, it could have been worse. Johnson brachiated to the galley. He ate strawberries, beans, potatoes—plants from the ever-growing hydroponics section. He also gulped vitamin pills. Not a whole lot of food that had come up from Earth was left; it was mostly reserved for celebrations. He missed meat, but less than he'd thought he would when it disappeared from the menu.

Some people were still complaining about that. The dietitian fixed one of them with a fishy stare and said, "It's healthy. It'll help you lose weight."

"I'm already weightless," the irate technician answered. "If I lose any more, I'll invent antigravity."

"There, you see?" said the dietitian, who didn't realize her leg was being pulled. "That would be worthwhile, wouldn't it?"

"That would be impossible, is what it would be," the technician snarled. "Christ, I'd eat a lab rat by now, but we haven't got any more of those left, either." He took his food and glided off in high dudgeon.

Johnson was dutifully chewing his beans and wondering if the methane they made people generate was put to good use—he supposed he could ask somebody from the life-support staff about that—when Lucy Vegetti came floating into the galley. When the geologist saw Glen, she smiled and waved. So did he. He would have flown over and given her a big hug, but men didn't make moves like that, not by the rules that had sprung up, for the most part informally, aboard the *Lewis and Clark*. Since men outnumbered women about two to one, women had all the choice. Johnson didn't necessarily like it, but he knew better than to fight city hall.

After Lucy got her food, she came over to him and gave him a hug. That was in the rules. "How you doing?" he asked. "I didn't know you'd gotten back from Ceres."

"They don't need me down there, not for a while," she answered. She was short and stocky and very definitely looked Italian. On Earth, she might have been dumpy, but nobody sagged in space. She ate some potato and sighed. "God, I miss butter. But anyhow, I'm here for a while. The ice miners are a going concern on the asteroid, so pretty soon they'll send me out prospecting somewhere else. Meanwhile, I get to come back to the big city and look at the bright lights for a while." Her wave encompassed the *Lewis and Clark*.

"God help you," Johnson said. "All that time away has softened your brain." They both laughed. But he knew what she meant. There were more people aboard the *Lewis and Clark* than anywhere else for millions of miles. Seeing faces she hadn't set eyes on for a while—*not* seeing the faces she'd been cooped up with for weeks—had to feel pretty good. Glen added, "You need somebody to drive your hot rod for you, just let me know."

"I'd do better to let Brigadier General Healey know," she said, and he nodded with regret altogether unfeigned. His opinion of the spaceship's commandant was not high; the commandant's opinion of him was, if anything, even lower. Had Healey had his druthers, he would have flung Johnson out the air lock when he came aboard the *Lewis and Clark*. Unlike the others here, Johnson hadn't intended to come out to the asteroid belt in the first place. He'd just been curious about what was going on at the orbital space station. He'd found out, all right. Lucy's smile changed. She lowered her voice and went on, "I like riding with you."

His ears heated. So did certain other relevant parts. He and Lucy had been lovers before the water-mining project took her away. Now that she was back, he hadn't known whether she would be interested again. All a guy on the *Lewis and Clark* could do was wait and hope and look cute. He snorted when that crossed his mind. He'd never been real good at cute.

But Lucy had made the first move, so he could make the next one: "Any time, babe. More fun than the exercise bike—I sure as hell hope."

She laughed again. "Now that you mention it, yes. Not that it's the highest praise in the world, you know."

Later, in the privacy of his tiny cubicle, she gave him praise of a more substantial nature. Weightlessness wasn't bad for such things, except that the people involved had to hang on to each other to keep from coming apart: no gravity assist there. Johnson found nothing at all wrong with holding Lucy tightly.

When he peeled off his rubber afterwards, though, he had a thought foolish and serious at the same time. "What the devil will we do when we run out of these things?" he asked.

Lucy gave him a practical answer: "Anything but the real thing. We can't afford to have any pregnancies till we build a spinning station to simulate gravity, and we can't stand the drain on our medical supplies that a lot of abortions would cause."

"I hear they've already had one or two," he said, not much liking the idea. But none of the animal research suggested that getting pregnant while weightless was a good idea for people.

"I've heard the same thing," Lucy said, nodding. "But nobody's named names, which is probably just as well."

"Yeah." Johnson reached out and caressed her. Sure as hell, in the absence of gravity nothing sagged. Pretty soon, Lucy was caressing him, too. He wasn't so young as he had been, but he wasn't so old as he would be, either. He rose to the occasion, and he and Lucy spent the next little while trying not to get her pregnant again.

Straha woke one morning to find the weather exasperatingly chilly. "It is going to be autumn again before long," he said to his driver at breakfast, as if the Big Ugly could do something about that. "I shall have to endure the worst of this planet's weather."

"In Los Angeles? No such thing, Shiplord," the driver replied, shaking his head. As an afterthought, he used the Race's negative gesture, too. "If you wanted to go to Siberia, now . . ."

"I thank you, but no," Straha said with dignity. "This is quite bad enough; I do not require worse."

"And remember," his driver went on after another forkful of scrambled eggs, "winter here only comes half as often as it does on Home."

"That is a truth," Straha admitted. "The inverse truths are that it lasts twice as long and is more than twice as bad, even here."

His driver let out several yips of Tosevite laughter. "We would call this weather perfect, or close enough. You really need to go to someplace like Arabia to make you happy. That is one place the Race is welcome to."

"Although the Race may be welcome to Arabia, I am not welcome *in* Arabia," Straha said. "That will be true for as long as Atvar lives, and our medical care is quite good."

"Then go out to the desert here," his driver said. "It will be cooler than it was in high summer, but not so cool as it is here."

"Now that," Straha said, "that is almost tempting. And have I heard that certain of our animals and plants have begun making homes for themselves in that area?"

"That is a truth, Shiplord," the Big Ugly agreed. "It is not a truth we are very happy about, but I do not know what we can do about it."

"Is not Sam Yeager investigating this truth you find so unfortunate?" Straha enjoyed mentioning Yeager's name every now and again, for no better reason than to make his driver jumpy.

Today it worked as well as it ever did. "How do you know that?" the driver demanded, his voice sharp.

"Because he told me," Straha answered. "I did not and do not think that was any great secret. Azwaca and zisuili are not beasts easily confused for anything Tosevite. Your newspapers and your television shows have been full of reported sightings and speculations—some clever, some anything but—about what their effect on the landscape will be."

"Speculations about the beasts from your planet are one thing," his driver answered. "Speculations about Sam Yeager are something else again, something a good deal more sensitive."

Straha started to ask why, then checked himself. He knew why. His driver had spelled it out for him before: Yeager was the sort of Tosevite who kept sticking his snout where it didn't belong. Hidden in a safe place in the house were papers Yeager had entrusted to him, the results of that snout-sticking. Straha had fairly itched to learn what those papers contained ever since the Big Ugly gave them to him. But Yeager was his friend, and had asked him not to look at them except in case of his death or sudden disappearance. He would have obeyed such a request from a friend who was a member of the Race, and he had obeyed it for the Tosevite, too. That didn't mean he wasn't curious.

His driver went on, "One of these days, I fear that Yeager will go too far for his superiors, if indeed he has not gone too far already. When that happens, saying you are his friend will do you no good. Saying you are his friend may end up doing you a good deal of harm."

"Is it as bad as that?" If it was as bad as that, maybe he would have to arrange to warn Yeager again.

"It is not as bad as that, Shiplord," his driver answered, now in tones of somber relish. "It is a great deal worse than that. He has done quite a lot to upset those superior to him."

"Really?" Straha said, as if he couldn't imagine such a thing. "How did matters come to such a pass?"

"Because he would not leave well enough alone," the Big Ugly answered. "If you fail to listen to warnings for long enough, no more warnings come. Things start happening to you instead. Unfortunate things. Very unfortunate things." He spoke the proper words, but he did not sound as if he thought such things were unfortunate—to the contrary, in fact.

"What could he have learned that was so dreadful?" Straha asked, now seriously alarmed.

His driver's mobile Tosevite face twisted into an expression

Straha recognized as annoyance. "I do not know," the Big Ugly said, adding, "I do not want to learn. It is none of my affair." Now pride filled his voice. "I am not like Yeager—I obey my orders. If my superiors were to order me to put my hand in the fire, I would do it." To show he meant what he said, he took out a cigarette lighter and flicked the wheel to produce a flame.

"Put that thing away," Straha exclaimed. "I believe you. You do not need to demonstrate." He was speaking the truth, too. Big Uglies, far more than the Race, reveled in such displays of fanaticism.

Another click closed the lighter. "You see, Shiplord? You are my superior, and I obey you, too." The driver laughed again.

"I thank you." Straha tried to hold irony out of his voice. Which of them was the superior varied from day to day, sometimes from moment to moment. Straha's rank meant little here; his utility to the American government counted for more, and his driver, these days, was much more consistently useful than he was.

The Big Ugly dropped into English: "I'm going outside to fiddle with the car for a while. I can't get the timing quite the way I like it. These hydrogen engines are a lot harder to monkey with than the ones that use gasoline."

"I hope you enjoy yourself, Gordon," Straha answered, also in English. Some males and females of the Race had the same fondness for tinkering with machinery. Straha had never understood it himself. Tinkering with the way males and females worked had always been more interesting to him.

He went to the computer and turned it on. Using the Race's network to send and receive electronic messages was risky. He was only illicitly present on the network; the more he did anything but passively read, the more likely he was to draw the system's notice and to be expelled from it. But this was the one safe way he had to communicate with Sam Yeager. Sometimes risks had to be calculated. His telephone might be monitored, and so might the Big Ugly's. The same went for the mail.

As I have warned you before, he wrote, *I am once more given to understand that the authorities from your not-empire are seriously concerned with your putting your snout where they wish it would not go. I trust you will do nothing so rash as to cause them to have to punish you.* He studied the message, made the affirmative gesture, and sent it. When he walked out to the front room once more, he saw his driver still bent over the engine of his motorcar.

Sam Yeager usually responded very promptly to his electronic messages. Here, though, a couple of days went by with no answer. That puzzled Straha, but he could hardly ask anyone what it meant.

When a reply did come, he knew at once that Yeager had not written it. His friend had some odd turns of phrase, but handled the language of the Race about as well as any male. This message was formal and tentative, and had a couple of errors in it that Sam Yeager wouldn't have made. *My father has not come to home for several days now,* it read. *We have a message that new duties call him away, but we have not heared from him. We are worried. Jonathan Yeager.*

Straha stared at that. He stared at it most unhappily, wondering how much trouble Sam Yeager was in and whether his Tosevite friend still remained alive to be in trouble. His driver had known what he was talking about. But if he had intended Straha to deliver another message, it came too late.

And Yeager had delivered a message to Straha. If the Big Ugly disappeared, the ex-shiplord was to read the papers with which he'd been entrusted. He'd wanted to do that ever since he got them. Now that he could, his eagerness felt oddly diminished. Some things, he discovered, were more desirable before they were attained than afterwards.

And, now that he felt free to look at those papers, he had to wait for the chance. His driver stuck annoyingly close to home for the next several days, as if he knew something was going on under his snout but couldn't put a fingerclaw on what.

Eventually, though, the Tosevite discovered errands he had to run. When he drove off, Straha hurried to his bookshelves and pulled out a fat volume full of pictures of the Fessekk Pass region of Home, one of the most scenic spots on the whole planet. The volume was a gift from a male of the colonization fleet who'd visited Straha; he'd glanced at it once and set it aside. But its size made it perfect for concealing the papers Yeager had given him. His driver, who cared nothing for the Fessekk Pass, had walked by it hundreds of times without paying it the least attention. So, for that matter, had Straha.

He sighed as he opened the envelope. The papers inside were liable to be the only memorial his Tosevite friend would ever have. He took them out and began to read.

They were, of course, in English. Straha understood the spoken language well enough. He read it only haltingly. Its spelling drove him mad. Why did this set of Big Uglies need several different characters to symbolize the same sound, and why did they let the same character represent several different sounds? *Because they are egg-addled idiots,* Straha thought resentfully.

But, after a little while, as he realized just what Sam Yeager had given him, he stopped fretting about the vagaries of English spelling. He stopped fretting about anything at all. He read on, spellbound, to the last page.

That last page was a note from Yeager. *If you are reading this, I am dead or in deep trouble,* the Tosevite wrote in Straha's language. *If you can get this to the Race, I expect it will be plenty for them to let you back into their territory in spite of everything you have done. I know you have often been unhappy here in the United States. Everyone deserves as much happiness as he can get. Grab with both hands.* The signature below was written twice, once in English, once in the characters of the Race.

"He is right," Straha whispered in slow astonishment. "With this, I truly could restore my good name." He had not the tiniest bit of doubt about it.

He'd dreamt of returning to the eggshell of the Race since very shortly after defecting to the United States. He had known it would take a miracle as long as Atvar remained fleetlord. Now, here in his hands, he held a miracle.

The next question was, did he want to use it? He had never imagined that question might arise with a miracle, but here it was. He could take this to the Race's consulate in Los Angeles and be assured of reconciliation, forgiveness, acceptance. He could see the new towns. He could live in one of them, in the society of his own kind.

But what else would happen if he did?

After the little scaly devils' prison camp, Liu Han didn't mind living in a peasant village, not in the least. She'd hated the idea after living in Peking for a good many years. Nieh Ho-T'ing laughed at her when she said that out loud. He answered, "It proves everything is in the yardstick you use to measure it."

"You're probably right," she answered. "What yardstick do we use to measure the little scaly devils' imperialism?"

That got his attention, and also his thought. Slowly, he said, "In China, they are worse than the Japanese and worse than the round-eyed devils from Europe. What other yardstick is there?"

"None, I suppose," Liu Han admitted, not much liking the thought. "And how do we measure our struggle against the little devils?"

To her surprise, Nieh brightened. He said, "There I have good news."

"Tell me," Liu Han said eagerly. "We could use some good news."

"Truth," he said in the little devils' language. Liu Han made a face at him, almost as if they were still lovers. Laughing, Nieh Ho-T'ing returned to Chinese. "Our fraternal socialist comrades in the Soviet Union have seen fit to increase their arms shipments to the People's Liberation Army. They have seen fit to increase them by quite a bit, in fact."

Liu Han clapped her hands. "That *is* good news! Why, when the Russians have kept us half starved for so long?"

"Well, I don't know for certain. I don't think anyone knows for certain what goes through Molotov's beady little mind," Nieh said, which made Liu Han laugh in turn. The People's Liberation Army officer went on, "I meant that seriously. Mao understood Stalin; he could think along with him. But Molotov?" He shook his head. "Molotov is inscrutable. I'll tell you what I think, though."

"Please." Liu Han nodded.

"Remember not long ago the Soviet Union gave Finland an ultimatum? And the Finns, instead of knuckling under to the Russians, ran under the wing of the scaly devils like a duckling running to its mother?"

Finland, as far as Liu Han was concerned, was so far away, it might as well have been on the world the little scaly devils came from. She wasn't sure she'd even heard of it till the Soviet Union pressured it. Even so . . . She nodded again. "I understand. This is the Russians' revenge. If they cannot get what they want from Finland"—she had to pronounce the unfamiliar name with care—"they will do what they can do to make the little devils sorry elsewhere—and we happen to be the elsewhere."

"Exactly so." Nieh eyed her with respect. "The Party was lucky when you joined us and got an education. You see very clearly; you would have wasted your life as an oppressed peasant woman."

But Liu Han laughed at him this time. "This has nothing to do with education. If a strong peasant loses a quarrel with a stronger one, what does he do? Not fight him again—he would lose again, and lose face doing it. No: he sows hatred against his enemy in the other people in the village, so the other man will have trouble wherever he goes."

"*Eee!*" Nieh said, a high-pitched sound of glee. "You are right. You are so very right. That's just what the Russians are doing. So Comrade Molotov thinks like a peasant, does he? I'm sure he would be offended to hear it."

"What kind of weapons are we getting?" Liu Han was sure that would be answered at the next Central Committee meeting, but she didn't want to wait. She had one particular question: "Will the Russians send us anything that we can use to wreck the scaly devils' landcruisers?" That last was a word Chinese had adapted from the language of the Race; the Japanese had had only a few of the fearsome vehicles, while those of the scaly devils roamed everywhere, deadly and all but unstoppable.

Nieh Ho-T'ing was smiling again. "Yes. For once, the Red Army truly is opening its storehouse to us. The Russians are sending us plenty of their mines with the wooden casings, the ones even the little devils have trouble detecting. Bury those on roadways and in fields, and the landcruisers will be most unhappy."

"Good," Liu Han said. "They deserve to be unhappy. But mines are not enough. What about rockets, so we can take the fight to the little devils instead of waiting for them to come to us?"

"You know what the Russians always say about those things," Nieh answered. "That has not changed while we were imprisoned."

Liu Han made another face, a sour one this time. "They say they cannot send us anything like that, because it would let the little scaly devils know where the weapons came from. But I thought you said they truly opened their storehouse to us."

"They did." Nieh was grinning again. "After the fighting in Europe, they somehow got hold of a lot of German antilandcruiser rockets. I don't know how—maybe these were rockets the Germans gave them instead of surrendering them to the little devils, or maybe they got them from one of the German puppet regimes. However they got them, they have them—and they are sending them to us."

"Ahhh." Liu Han bowed to Nieh as if he'd been responsible for getting the rockets rather than just for giving her the news about them. "Are these weapons only promised, or are they really on the way?"

"The first caravan has already crossed the Mongolian desert," he answered. "The weapons, or some of them, are in our hands."

Liu Han did not have sharp teeth like a tiger's, but her smile would have sent any tiger with a drop of sense scurrying back into the undergrowth. She'd been fighting the little scaly devils most of her adult life, fighting them with a hatred not only ideological and nationalistic but personal. If the People's Liberation Army had the chance to strike them a heavy blow, that delighted her on every one of those levels.

Before she could say as much, a woman's cry of anger and, a moment later, a man's cry of pain burst from a peasant hut not far away. She whirled in surprise. So did Nieh Ho-T'ing. A heartbeat later, the man himself burst from the hut, running for all he was worth. He might have run faster had he not been yanking up his trousers with one hand.

"Ten million little devils!" Liu Han exclaimed. "Who has Hsia Shou-Tao tried to outrage now?"

No sooner had she spoken than her own daughter came out of that hut. Liu Mei was carrying a chamber pot. Her expressionless face was even more frightening than it would have been had fury filled it. She flung the pot with both hands, as a man might fling a heavy stone. The pot flew through the air and smashed against the back of Hsia's head. He fell forward onto his face and lay motionless, as if shot. Blood poured from his scalp. So did urine and night soil; the chamber pot had been full.

.Eyes blazing in her dead-calm countenance, Liu Mei said, "He tried to take what I did not want to give him. First I stamped on his foot, then I kicked him, then I did this, and now I'm going to kill him."

"Wait!" Nieh Ho-T'ing got between Hsia Shou-Tao and Liu Mei, who plainly meant exactly what she'd said: she'd drawn a knife and was advancing on the officer and Communist Party dignitary she'd felled.

Hsia groaned and tried to roll over. Liu Han had wondered if the flying chamber pot smashed in the back of his skull. Evidently not. *Too bad,* she thought. "You know how he is with women," she said to Nieh. "You know he's always been that way with women. He tried to outrage me, too, you know, back in Peking not long after the little devils came. I'm not pretty enough for him any more, so now what does he do? He tries to molest my daughter. If you ask me, he deserves whatever Liu Mei gives him."

A crowd had gathered, drawn by the commotion. Several women laughed and jeered to see Hsia Shou-Tao bleeding and filthy on the ground. If that didn't mean Liu Mei was far from the only one he'd tried to molest, Liu Han would have been astonished.

But Nieh still held up a hand, ordering Liu Mei to stop. "You have punished him as he deserves," the People's Liberation Army general said. "He is a good officer. He is a bold officer. He is fierce against the little scaly devils."

Liu Mei did stop, but she didn't put away the knife. "He is a man. You are a man," she said. "He is an officer. You are an officer. He is your friend. He has been your aide. No wonder you take his side."

The women, most of them peasants but some lesser Party functionaries, yelled raucous agreement. One of them threw a stone at Hsia. It thudded into his ribs. He writhed and grunted; he still wasn't more than half conscious.

"No!" Now Nieh spoke sharply, and set a hand on the pistol in his belt. "I say enough. Hsia may be subject to self-criticism and revolutionary justice, but he will not be mobbed. The revolutionary struggle needs him."

His words probably wouldn't have stopped the angry women. The pistol did. Liu Han wondered if the struggle between men and women would end before the struggle against the little scaly devils. She doubted it; she wasn't sure even the coming of perfect Communism would make men and women get along.

"Mother!" Rage still filled Liu Mei's voice. "Will you let this, this *man* protect his friend so?"

No, the struggle between the sexes surely had a long way to go. With great reluctance, Liu Han nodded. "I will. I do not like it, but I will. Let revolutionary justice see to him from here on out. We will remember him smeared with blood and night soil. We will all remember him like that. He won't trouble you again—I'm sure of it."

"No, but he will touch someone else," Liu Mei said grimly. "I didn't knock out enough of his brains to keep him from doing that."

She was bound to be right. Liu Han wouldn't have minded seeing Hsia dead, not personally, not even a little bit. But Nieh said, "He will also trouble the scaly devils again, and that is more important."

"Not to me," Liu Mei said. "He didn't put his filthy hands inside your trousers." She didn't advance on Hsia any more, though, and she did put the knife away. A couple of people drifted back toward their huts. The worst was over. Hsia Shou-Tao wouldn't get all of what was coming to him, but Liu Mei had already given him a good piece of it.

Hsia groaned again. This time, he managed to sit up. Something like reason was in his eyes. His hand went to the back of his head. When he found it was wet, he jerked it away. When he found what the moisture was, he frantically rubbed his hand in the dirt beside him.

"I should have cut it off you when I had the chance," Liu Han told him. "If I had, this wouldn't have happened to you."

"I'm sorry," Hsia said vaguely, as if he couldn't quite recall why he should be apologizing.

"Sorry you got hurt. Sorry you got caught," Liu Han said. "Sorry for what you did? Don't make me laugh. Don't make us all laugh. We know better." The women who were still watching Hsia wallow in filth and blood clapped their hands and cried agreement. Liu Han found a smile stretching wide across her face. Russian arms for the People's Liberation Army, Hsia Shou-Tao humiliated—it was a very good day indeed.

Reuven Russie walked slowly and glumly to the office he shared with his father. The sun shone hot and warm in Jerusalem even in early autumn, making the yellow limestone from which so much of the city was built gleam and sparkle like gold. The beauty was wasted on him. So was the sunshine.

His father had to keep slowing down so as not to get ahead. About halfway there, Moishe Russie remarked, "You could have gone to Canada."

"No, I couldn't, not really." Reuven had already wrestled with himself a great many times. "Emigrating would have been too easy. And if I had, my children probably would have ended up not being Jewish. I didn't want that, not after we've been through so much to hold on to what we are."

His father walked on a few paces before reaching out to set a hand on his shoulder for a moment. "That's a fine thing to say, a fine thing to do," he observed, "especially when you think about the woman you were giving up."

Don't remind me, was the first thing that went through Reuven's mind. He'd miss Jane's lush warmth for . . . he didn't know how long, but it would be a while. After a few silent steps of his own, he said, "I'm going to be thirty before too long. If I'd had to decide the same thing six or eight years ago, who knows how I would have chosen?"

"Maybe that has something to do with it," Moishe Russie admitted. "On the other hand, maybe it doesn't, too. Plenty of men your age, plenty of men my age—*gevalt,* plenty of men my father's age, if he were still alive—would think with their crotch first and worry about everything else later."

That was probably true. That was, in fact, undoubtedly true. And, as far as Reuven was concerned, anyone who didn't think with his crotch around Jane Archibald had something wrong with him. After a bit, he said, "Too easy," again.

His father understood him, as his father generally did. "Being a Jew in Canada, you mean?" he said. "Well, maybe. But, once more, maybe not. It *is* possible to be a Jew in a country where they don't persecute you for it. Up until just a little while ago, remember, the Race didn't charge us anything for the privilege of worshiping in our own synagogues."

Reuven nodded. "I know. But people take it more seriously now, don't they? Because they see it's endangered."

"Some do," his father said. "Maybe even most do. But some don't take anything seriously—for a while, when you were a little younger, I was afraid you might be one of those, but I think every young man makes his father worry about that." He let out a wry chuckle, then sighed. "And some—a few—go to this temple the Lizards put up and give reverence to the spirits of Emperors past."

"Jane went," Reuven said. "She had to, if she wanted to stay in the medical college. She always said it wasn't anything bad— said the atmosphere put her in mind of a church, as a matter of fact."

"I never said it was bad—for the Race," Moishe Russie

replied. "Or even for people, necessarily. But it's not a place for Jews. A church isn't bad. A mosque isn't bad. But they're not *ours*." He paused. "You know the word *apikoros*?"

"I've heard it," Reuven answered. "It's as much Yiddish as Hebrew, isn't it? Means somebody who doesn't believe or doesn't practice, doesn't it?"

His father nodded. "Usually a particular kind of person who doesn't believe or practice: the kind who thinks it's unscientific to believe in God, if you know what I mean. Comes from the name of the Greek philosopher Epicurus. Now, I happen to think Epicurus was a good man, not a bad one, though I know plenty of rabbis who'd have a stroke if they heard me say that. But he wasn't *ours*, either. Back in the days of the Maccabees, ideas like his led too many people away from being Jews. These shrines to the spirits of Emperors past are another verse of the same song."

"I suppose so," Reuven said after some thought. "A good education will make you an *apikoros* sometimes, too, won't it?"

"It can," Moishe Russie agreed. "It doesn't have to. If it did, you'd be in . . . where in Canada did Jane end up?"

"Somewhere called Edmonton," Reuven answered. She'd sent a couple of enthusiastic letters. He'd written back, but she'd been a while replying now. As she'd said she would, she was busy making a new life for herself in a land where the Lizards didn't rule.

"Canada," his father said in musing tones. "I wonder how she'll like the winters there. They aren't like the ones in Jerusalem, or like the ones in Australia, either, I don't think. More like Warsaw, unless I miss my guess." He shuddered. "The weather is one more thing I don't miss about Poland."

Almost all of Reuven's childhood memories of the land where he'd been born were of hunger and fear and cold. He asked, "Is there anything you *do* miss about Poland?"

His father started to shake his head, but checked himself. Quietly, he answered, "All the people the Nazi *mamzrim* murdered."

Reuven didn't know what to say to that. In the end, he didn't say anything directly, but asked, "Has Anielewicz had any luck finding his family?"

"Not the last I heard," his father answered. "And that doesn't look good, either. The fighting's been over for a while. Of course"—he did his best to sound optimistic—"a country's a big place, and I doubt even the *verkakte* Germans could keep proper records while the Lizards were pounding them to pieces."

"*Alevai* you're right, and *alevai* they'll turn up." Reuven walked around the last corner before their office. "And now we've turned up, too."

After the grim talk, Moishe Russie put on a smile. "Bad pennies have a way of doing that. I wonder what we have waiting for us today."

"Something interesting, maybe?" Reuven suggested, holding the door open for his father. "When I started practice, I didn't think so much of it would be just . . . routine."

"That's not always bad," his father said. "The interesting cases are usually the hard ones, too, the ones that don't always turn out so well."

"Did you become a doctor so you could sew up cut legs and give babies shots and tell people with strep throats to take penicillin?" Reuven asked. "Or did you want to see things you'd never seen before, maybe things nobody else had seen, either?"

"I became a doctor for two reasons: to make sick people better, and to make a living," Moishe Russie answered. "If I see a patient who's got something I've never seen before, I always worry, because that means I haven't got any knowledge to fall back on. I have to start guessing, and it's easier to guess wrong than it is to guess right."

"You'd better be careful, Father," Reuven said. "You sound like you're in danger of turning into a conservative."

"Some ways, maybe," Moishe Russie said. "That's what general practice does—it makes you glad for routine. Consider yourself warned. If you wanted to stay radical your whole life long, you should have gone in for surgery. Surgeons always think they can do anything. That's because they get to play God in the operating room, and they have trouble remembering the difference between the One Who made bodies and the ones who try to repair them."

They went into the office. "Good morning, Dr. Russie," Yetta the receptionist said, and then, "Good morning, Dr. Russie." She smiled and laughed at her own wit. Reuven smiled, too, but it wasn't easy. He'd heard the same joke every third morning since starting in practice with his father, and he was bloody sick of it.

His father managed a smile that looked something like sincere. "Good morning," he said, a good deal more heartily than Reuven could have done. "What appointments have we got today?"

Yetta ran down the list: a woman with a skin fungus they'd been fighting for weeks, another woman bringing in her baby for a booster shot, a man with a cough, another man—a diabetic—with an abscess on his leg, a woman with belly pain, a man with belly pain . . . "Maybe we can do both of those at once," Reuven suggested. "Two for the price of one." His father snorted. Yetta looked disapproving. She liked her own jokes fine, no matter how often she repeated them. A doctor making jokes about medicine was almost as bad as a rabbi making jokes about religion.

"All right, we'll have enough to do today, even without the people who just drop in," his father said. "We'll have some of those, too, I expect; we always do." Some people, of course, got sick unexpectedly. Others didn't believe in appointments, any more than Reuven believed in Muhammad as a prophet.

He got to see the woman with the stubborn skin fungus, a Mrs. Kratz. Yetta stayed in the room to make sure nothing improper occurred, as she did with all female patients. Custom aside, she could have stayed out. Reuven had no lecherous interest in Mrs. Kratz, and would have had none even without the fungus on her leg. She was plump and gray and older than his father.

"Here," he said, and handed her a little plastic tube. "This is a new cream. It's a sample, about four days' worth. Use it twice a day, then call and let us know how it's doing. If it helps, I'll write you a prescription for more."

"All right, Doctor." She sighed. "I hope one of these creams works one of these days."

"This one is supposed to be very strong," Reuven said solemnly. The active ingredient, one new to human medicine, was closely related to the chemical the Lizards used to fight what they called the purple itch. He didn't tell that to Mrs. Kratz. He judged her more likely to take offense than to be delighted.

After she left, the man with a cough came in. Reuven's nose wrinkled. "How much do you smoke, Mr. Sadorowicz?" he asked; the aroma that clung to the fellow's clothes gave him a head start on etiology here.

"I don't know," Mr. Sadorowicz answered, coughing. "Whenever I feel like it. What's that got to do with anything?"

Reuven delivered his standard lecture on the evils of tobacco. Mr. Sadorowicz plainly didn't believe a word of it. He didn't want to get an X ray when Reuven recommended one, either. He didn't want to do anything Reuven suggested. Reuven wondered why the devil he'd bothered coming in. Mr. Sadorowicz departed, still coughing.

Yetta came in again. "Here's Mrs. Radofsky and her daughter, Miriam. She's here for Miriam's tetanus booster."

"All right," Reuven answered. Then he brightened: Mrs. Radofsky was a nice-looking brunette not far from his own age, while Miriam, who was about two, gave him a high-wattage little-girl smile. "Hello," Reuven said to her mother. "I'm afraid I'm going to make her unhappy for a little while. Her arm may swell up and be tender for a couple of days, and she may run a bit of a fever. If it's anything more than that, bring her back and we'll see what we can do." It wouldn't be much, but he didn't say that.

He rubbed Miriam's arm with an an alcohol-soaked cotton swab. She giggled at the sensation of cold, then shrieked when he injected her. He sighed. He'd known she would. He taped a square of gauze over the injection site.

Mrs. Radofsky cuddled and comforted her daughter till she forgot about the horrific indignity she'd just suffered. "Thank you, Doctor," she said. "I appreciate that, even if Miriam doesn't. I want to do everything I can to keep her well. She's all I've got to remember her father by."

"Oh?" Reuven said.

"He got . . . caught in the rioting last year," Mrs. Radofsky— the widow Radofsky—said. As Reuven expressed sympathies, she asked Yetta, "And what do I owe you?" Reuven hoped the receptionist would give her a break on the bill, but she didn't.

The Polish Tosevite named Casimir pointed proudly to the shuttlecraft port. He bowed to Nesseref: not the Race's posture of respect but, she'd learned, an equivalent the Big Uglies often used. "You sees, superior female?" he said, speaking the language of the Race badly but understandably. "Field is ready for usings."

"I see." Nesseref tried to sound happier than she felt. Then she made the affirmative gesture. "Yes, it is ready for use. That is a truth, and I am very glad to see it."

During the fighting, the Deutsche had done their best to render the shuttlecraft port unusable. By what the males from the conquest fleet said, their best was far better than it had been during the earlier round of combat. They'd plastered it with bomblets from the air, just as the Race might have done. Some of the bomblets were concrete-busters; others were antipersonnel weapons, and had had to be disposed of with great care—they could blow the foot off a male or female of the Race, or, for that matter, off a Big Ugly. Despite the Race's best efforts, a couple of them had done exactly that. They lurked in the weeds off the edges of the port's concrete landing area. Nesseref wasn't altogether sure every single one of them had been disposed of even yet.

And, with resources so scarce after the fighting ended, Casimir's construction crew had had to repair the landing field with hand tools rather than power machines. Nesseref had never imagined Big Uglies slapping hot asphalt into holes and smacking it down flat with shovels. That gave the shuttlecraft port a curiously mottled appearance, and contributed to her feelings of unease about it.

She had other reasons for feeling uneasy, too. Pointing, she said, "Your patches are not as strong as the concrete they replace—is that not also a truth?"

"It are, superior female," Casimir admitted ungrammatically. "But the patchings will do well enough. One of this days, make all pretties again. Pretty not importants. Neat not importants. Working are importants."

"There is some truth in what you say," Nesseref admitted.

"Are much truthings in what I say," Casimir answered.

Nesseref didn't want to admit that. The locals' whole way of doing things struck her as slipshod. They had a habit of fixing things just well enough to get by for a while: that well and no better. As a result, they were always mending, tinkering, repairing, where the Race would have done things right the first time and saved itself a lot of trouble.

Sometimes, work that was fast and sloppy, work that would last for a while but not too long, was good enough. Nesseref suspected that was the case here. Better repairs would come, but they could wait. For now, the shuttlecraft port was usable.

A male of the Race waved to Nesseref from the control building, off to one side of the patched concrete. She skittered off toward him without so much as turning an eye turret back toward Casimir. She wouldn't have been so rude to a member of the Race, but that thought didn't cross her mind till she'd gone a long way from the Big Ugly. She shrugged as she trotted along. It wasn't as if he were a particular friend, as Mordechai Anielewicz was.

"Well, Shuttlecraft Pilot, are we operational?" the male asked. "Does everything meet with your approval?"

"Senior Port Technician, I believe we are," Nesseref answered. "The field is not all it could be, but it can be used for operations."

"Good," the technician said. "This was also my opinion, but I am glad to have it confirmed by one who will actually fly a shuttlecraft."

"It will be good to have shuttlecraft coming in and going out again, too," Nesseref said. "This subregion has been cut off from direct contact with our space fleet for too long now. Air transport is all very well, but we did not come to Tosev 3 in aircraft."

"Indeed," the shuttlecraft technician said. "Unlimited access to space and its resources and the mobility it gives us are our principal remaining advantages over the Big Uglies."

"I suppose you are right, but, if you are, that is a genuinely depressing thought," Nesseref said. The technician only shrugged. Maybe that meant he didn't find it depressing. More likely, it meant he did, but didn't know what the Race could do about it. Nesseref shrugged. She didn't know what the Race could do about it, either.

The first shuttlecraft that had come into western Poland since the fighting stopped landed the next day. It disgorged a new regional subadministrator to replace Bunim, who was now only radioactive dust. The female, whose name was Orssev, looked around in disapproval verging on horror. "What a miserable place to find oneself," she said. "Is it always so cold here?"

Listening to her carp, Nesseref began to understand why males from the conquest fleet complained about males and females from the colonization fleet. Nesseref was a female from the colonization fleet herself, of course, but even she could see that Orssev was not inclined to give Poland a fair chance.

And she knew things Orssev didn't. "Superior female," she said, "this is the end of the period of relatively *good* weather in this area. We shall have most of a year of truly bad, truly freezing weather on the way—a year of Home's, I mean."

"Tell me you are joking," Orssev said. "Please tell me so. What did I do to deserve such a fate?"

Nesseref didn't know the answer to that question, either, and wasn't much interested in finding out. Orssev was plainly a prominent female, or she wouldn't have had the rank of regional subadministrator. But she might well have got her post here because she'd offended someone even more prominent; Poland's weather was not of the sort to which administrators were drawn. And Nesseref could not tell a lie about that. "I am sorry, but I spoke the truth," she said. "Winter in this subregion is unpleasant in the extreme."

"I shall protest to Fleetlord Reffet," the new regional subadministrator said. "I am being used with undeserved cruelty."

"I wish you good fortune," Nesseref said, as neutrally as she could. She didn't want to come right out and call Orssev an idiot addled in her eggshell; offending the prominent was rarely a good idea. But, however prominent she was, Orssev wasn't very bright. The males of the conquest fleet, not those from the colonization fleet, kept administrative appointments firmly in their fingerclaws. That made sense; they knew the Big Uglies better than the colonists did. Nesseref didn't think the fleetlord of the colonization fleet would be able to get Orssev's assignment changed, even if he were inclined to do so.

Orssev went into the control building, presumably to start pulling whatever wires she could to try to leave Poland. The shuttlecraft pilot who'd brought her down also went into the control building, which meant the shuttlecraft wasn't scheduled to fly out again right away. Nesseref hoped it also meant she would be assigned to take it wherever it did need to go next.

Technicians swarmed over the shuttlecraft, inspecting and adjusting. Lorries rolled out and topped up its hydrogen and oxygen tanks. No one shouted Nesseref's name and told her to be prepared at short notice. She concluded she could go back to her apartment and get ready before she was summoned to duty once more.

Getting ready consisted largely of making sure Orbit had enough food and water to keep him happy while she was gone. The tsiongi ran in his wheel. He'd run in it enough to give it a squeak. Nesseref thought that reprehensible; it seemed more like the slipshod manufacturing Big Uglies might do than anything she would have expected from the Race. She sprayed the hub of the exercise wheel with a lubricant. Orbit didn't care for the odor, and hopped out and lashed his tail till it diminished.

No sooner had Nesseref put away the container of lubricant than the telephone hissed. "I greet you," she said.

"And I greet you, Shuttlecraft Pilot," a male from the shuttle-craft port replied. "Your first assignment has come in."

"I am prepared," she answered—the only possible response from a pilot. "Where am I to go?"

"This continental mass, the eastern subregion known as China," the male said. "Burn parameters and time are already in the shuttlecraft's computer. Anticipated launch time is—" He named the moment.

"I shall be there," Nesseref said. "Do I have a passenger, or will I fly this mission by myself?"

"You have a passenger," the male at the port answered. "She is a physician named Selana. Her specialty is skin fungi: Tosevite bacteria and viruses do not trouble us, but some of these organisms find us tasty. This problem appears to be more severe in China than elsewhere."

"Very well," said Nesseref, who thanked the spirits of Emperors past that such fungi had never troubled her. She snatched up the small bag she always took on shuttlecraft flights—since she didn't use cloth wrappings, her needs while on a journey were less than those a Big Ugly would have had in similar circumstances.

The jolt of acceleration, the weightlessness that followed, felt like old friends that had been away too long. Once weightlessness began, she had a chance to make small talk with Selana. "Why are these skin fungi so common in China, Senior Physician?" she asked.

"I believe it is the astonishing amount of excrement in everyday use there," the other female answered. "The local Big Uglies use it for manure and fuel and sometimes, mixed with mud, as a building material as well. Facilities for disinfecting bodily waste, as you may imagine from that, are for all practical purposes nonexistent."

"I am sorry I asked," Nesseref said. Weightlessness did not nauseate members of the Race, as it sometimes did Tosevites, but disgust could do the job. Another thought occurred to her. "How do any Tosevites raised in such an environment survive? Their burden of disease must be far worse than ours."

"It is, and a great many of them do not survive," Selana said. "This takes me back to the most primitive days of the Race, at the very dawn of ancientest history. We once lived something like this, though the greater abundance of water in China creates a more unsanitary situation than we ever knew over such a wide area."

Nesseref did not want to believe that the Race had ever lived in such close conjunction to filth. Such a thought would damage the sense of superiority she felt toward the Big Uglies. She said, "Spirits of Emperors past be praised that we do not live in such appalling conditions any more."

"Truth," Selana said, and added an emphatic cough. "But, here on Tosev 3, we are forced to do so because the natives do so. This creates difficulties of its own."

"Senior Physician," Nesseref said, "the Big Uglies do nothing but create difficulties." Selana did not argue with her.

☆ **7** ☆

Having got to Greifswald, Johannes Drucker rather wished he hadn't. The town where he and his family had lived hadn't taken an explosive-metal bomb, but it had been heavily fought over. And nearby Peenemünde and Stralsund and Rostock had taken any number of hits from explosive-metal weapons, so the radioactivity level remained high.

Few people still dwelt among the ruins. The ones who did might have slipped back in time several hundred years. Instead of coal or gas, they burned wood from the wrecked buildings all around them. They had no running water. They stank, and so did the city.

The neighborhood where the Druckers had lived was even more ruinous than the rest of the town. No one seemed to live there these days; gangs of scavengers prowled through the wreckage, after whatever they could find. Nobody admitted to hearing of Drucker or his family.

"Try the Red Cross shelters, pal," one heavily armed forager told him. "Maybe you'll have some luck there."

"Try the graveyards," the forager's sidekick added. "Plenty of new people staying there these days." He laughed. So did his comrade.

Drucker wanted to kill them both. He had a pistol, too, a comforting weight on his right hip. But the ruffians looked very alert. He gave a curt nod and walked off through the rubble-strewn streets.

Checking the Red Cross shelters was actually a good idea. Drucker had done that every time he passed one on the long road up from Nuremberg. But, even having done so, he knew too well that he might have missed his family. He couldn't go through the endless tents and huts one by one looking for Käthe and Heinrich and Claudia and Adolf. He had to rely on the records in each camp headquarters, and the records were in a most shocking state of disarray—anyone who expected the usual German efficiency, as he had, was out of luck.

It's the war, he thought. At last—and for the first time since Bismarck and Kaiser Wilhelm I unified Germany—the *Reich* had run into a catastrophe too large for it to cope with. Surviving from day to day took precedence over keeping the files that would have made administering the state over the long haul so much easier. Drucker understood that without liking it. It made his life too difficult for him to like it, even a little.

Checking the graveyards also wasn't the worst idea in the world, he realized glumly. Or it wouldn't have been, if so many bodies hadn't been bulldozed or just flung into mass graves without headstones of any sort—and if so many others didn't still lie under rubble, and if so many hadn't simply been vaporized.

Someone rode past on a bicycle—the way things were now, a sign of prosperity. The man knew how valuable that bicycle was, too; he had an assault rifle slung on his back, and looked extremely ready to use it. Drucker called out to him: "Excuse me, but where is the Red Cross shelter closest to town?"

"North," the man answered. "On the road to Stralsund, not quite halfway there, not far from the damned Lizards' camp." He started to pedal on, but then grudged a few more words: "I hope you find whoever you're looking for."

"Thanks," Drucker said. "So do I."

He trudged up the road. To his right, the gray, ugly Baltic rolled up the flat, muddy beach and then sullenly retreated again. He smelled salt water and stale seaweed and dead fish: the odors of home. And, when he got to the shelter in the late afternoon, he smelled ordure and unwashed humanity, the same stinks he'd known in every camp and in every town on his way up from Bavaria.

More Lizard troopers prowled around this Red Cross shelter than he'd seen at most of the others. They looked jumpier and more alert than the males he'd seen elsewhere, too. He came up to one of them and said, "I greet you," in the language of the Race.

"And I greet you," the Lizard answered. It wasn't much of a greeting; the male looked ready to shoot first and ask questions later, if at all. "What do you want?" His hissing voice was hard with suspicion.

"I am looking for my mate and hatchlings, from whom I am long separated," Drucker said. The answer, and the fluency with which he used the Race's language, made the Lizard relax a little. He went on, "And I am also curious why you watch the refugees in this particular camp so closely."

"Why? I will tell you why," the male said. "Because there are many Deutsch soldiers here, males against whom we fought in Poland. We do not trust them. We have no great reason to trust them."

"I see," Drucker said slowly. He nodded. He'd been running into occupation troops up till now: Lizards who'd come into the *Reich* after the surrender, and who hadn't done any fighting beforehand. But the males here had been combat soldiers. No wonder they didn't trust anything or anybody. Drucker risked one more question: "Where is the administrative center for this camp?"

"That way, where the flag flies," the Lizard answered, pointing with the muzzle of his weapon. "You may proceed."

"I thank you," Johannes Drucker said. The Lizard didn't wish him any sort of luck finding his family. Some of that, no doubt, was because Lizards didn't think in terms of families. And the rest? He was an enemy. Why should a male of the Race waste any sympathy on him?

He was just coming up to the large tent above which the Red Cross flag flew when a man not far from his own age rode up on a bicycle. The fellow carried an impressive collection of lethal hardware. He swung down from the bicycle, grunted and stretched, and started to walk it into the tent.

A woman standing in the entranceway exclaimed, "You can't do that! It is forbidden!"

"Too bad," the man answered in German flavored by Polish and something else. "I'm not going to have it stolen. If you don't like it, that's rough."

"He's right," Drucker said. "There's no place to chain it up out here, and it'll disappear without a trace if he just leaves it."

"Most irregular," the woman sniffed. She didn't seem to see that things were different in the *Reich* nowadays. But, after another glance at the weaponry festooning the other fellow, she stopped arguing.

"Thanks, pal," the stranger said to Drucker. "Appreciate it. Some people have trouble getting the idea that times have changed through their thick heads."

After a moment, Drucker placed the man's secondary accent. He'd heard it before, thicker, in Poland and the Soviet Union before the Lizards landed. Yiddish, that was it. "You're a Jew," he blurted.

With an ironic bow, the other man nodded. "And you're a German. I love you, too," he said. "Mordechai Anielewicz, at your service. I'm trying to find my family after some of you Nazi bastards hauled them out of Poland."

All Drucker said was, "I'm trying to find my family, too. They were in Greifswald, but they aren't any more, and not much of the town is left." He paused, staring at the other man. "Mordechai Anielewicz? Jesus: I know you. A million years ago"— actually, back in the first round of fighting against the Race—"I was Colonel Heinrich Jäger's panzer driver." He gave his own name.

"*Were* you?" Anielewicz's eyes narrowed. "*Gottenyu,* maybe you were. And if you were, maybe you're not quite a Nazi bastard after all. Maybe. My younger son is named for Heinrich Jäger."

"My older son is," Drucker said. "What happened to him after that Russian pilot took him off to Poland?" He didn't mention how he and his fellow tank crewmen had killed several SS men to make Jäger's escape possible.

"He married her," the Jew answered. "He's dead now. You know the explosive-metal bomb Skorzeny tried to set off inside Lodz? We stopped that, he and Ludmila and I. We all breathed in some nerve gas doing it, too. It hit him hardest; he was never quite right afterwards, and he died twelve, thirteen years ago."

"I'm sorry to hear it," Drucker said, "but thanks for telling me. He was a good man—one of the best officers I ever served under—and I always wondered what happened to him once he got away."

"He was one of the best." Mordechai Anielewicz eyed Drucker. "You drove a panzer then. What have you been doing since?"

"I stayed in the *Wehrmacht*," Drucker replied. "I ended up in the upper stage of an A-45. The Lizards captured me after I shot two missiles at one of their starships. If they hadn't knocked both of them down, I don't suppose they would have bothered taking me alive, but they did. Eventually, they set me down in Nuremberg. I had a devil of a time getting here, but I managed. Now if I could manage to find my wife and kids . . ."

Anielewicz looked at him as if he'd failed a test. "You served under Heinrich Jäger, and you stayed in the *Wehrmacht*? He had the sense to get away."

"Don't get high and mighty with me," Drucker snapped. "I know something about what the *Reich* was doing to Jews. I didn't do any of that. I had it done to me, in fact."

"You had it done to you?" Anielewicz snarled. "You son of a bitch, you"—he cursed in Yiddish and Polish—"what do you know about it?" He looked ready to grab one of his weapons and start shooting. Drucker had thought him a dangerous man a generation before, and saw no reason to change his mind now. He slid his legs into a position from which he could better open fire, too.

But, instead of grabbing for his pistol, he answered Anielewicz in a low, urgent voice: "I'll tell you what I know about it. The SS grabbed my wife because they got wind she had a Jewish grandmother, that's what." He'd never thought he would tell that to anyone, but who in the *Reich* ever imagined talking with a Jew?

And it worked. Mordechai Anielewicz relaxed, suddenly and completely. "All right, then," he said. "You *do* know something." He cocked his head to one side. "From what you've said, you got her back. How'd you manage that? I know a thing or two about the SS."

"How?" Drucker chuckled mirthlessly. "I told you—I was an A-45 pilot. I had connections. My CO was General Dornberger—he's *Führer* now, wherever the devil he is. I had enough pull to bring it off. Officially, Käthe got a clean pedigree."

"If you have pull, you should use it," Anielewicz agreed. His face clouded again. "Back in the 1940s, there were an awful lot of Jews who didn't have any."

Drucker didn't know how to reply to that. All he could do was nod. He hadn't thought much about Jews, or had much use for them, before Käthe got in trouble with the blackshirts. At last, he said, "The only thing I want to do now is find out if my family is alive, and get them back if they are."

"Fair enough. We're in the same boat there, no matter how we got dropped into it." Anielewicz pointed at Drucker. "If you know the *Führer*, why aren't you using your pull now to have him help you look for your kin?"

"Two main reasons, I suppose," Drucker answered after a little thought. "I wanted to do it myself, and . . . I'm not sure there's anyone to find."

"Yes, knowing they're dead would be pretty final, wouldn't it?" Anielewicz's voice was grim. "Still and all, if you've got a card left to play, don't you think it's time to play it?"

Drucker considered, then slowly nodded. He raised an eyebrow. "And if I try to find out for myself, maybe I should try to find out for you, too?"

"That thought did cross my mind," Mordechai Anielewicz allowed. "*I've* got pull with the Lizards, myself. Shall we trade?" Drucker considered again, but not for long. He stuck out his hand. Anielewicz shook it.

Sam Yeager had never imagined that a jail could be so comfortable. His place of confinement didn't look like a jail. It looked like, and was, a farmhouse somewhere in . . . nobody had told him exactly where he was, but it had to be Colorado or New Mexico. He could watch television, though no station came in real well. He could read Denver and Albuquerque papers. He could do almost anything he wanted—except go outside or write a letter or use a computer. His guards were very polite but very firm.

"Why are you keeping me here?" he demanded of them one morning, for about the five hundredth time.

"Orders," replied the one who answered to Fred.

Yeager had heard that about five hundred times, too. "You can't keep me forever," he said, though he had no evidence that that was true. "What will you do with me?"

"Whatever we get told to do," answered the one called John. "So far, nobody's told us to do anything except keep you on ice." He raised an eyebrow. "Maybe you ought to count your blessings about that, Lieutenant Colonel."

By which he no doubt meant they could have buried Yeager in the yard behind the house without anyone's being the wiser. That was probably—no, that was certainly—true. "But I haven't done anything," Sam said, knowing full well he was lying. "And you haven't even tried to find out whether I've done anything," which was the God's truth.

Fred looked at John. John looked at the one named Charlie, who hardly ever said anything. He didn't say anything now, either—he only shrugged. John, who seemed to be the boss, answered, "We haven't had any orders to interrogate you, either. Maybe they don't want us knowing whatever you know. I don't ask questions. I just do what I'm told."

"But I don't know anything," Sam protested, another great, thumping lie.

Fred chuckled. "Maybe they don't want us catching igno-rance, then." Of the three there that day, and of the other three who spelled them in weekly shifts, he was the only one with even a vestigial sense of humor. He pointed at Sam's empty cup. "You want some more coffee there?"

"Sure," Yeager answered, and the—agent?—poured the cup full again. After a couple of sips, Sam tried a question he hadn't asked before: "By whose orders are you keeping me here? I'm an officer in the U.S. Army, after all."

He didn't really expect to get an answer. Charlie just sat there looking sour. Fred shrugged, as if to say he was pretending he hadn't heard the question. But John said, "Whose orders? I'll tell you. Why the hell not? You're here on the orders of the president of the United States, Mister Officer in the U.S. Army."

"The president?" Sam yelped. "What the dickens does Presi-dent Warren care about me? I haven't done anything."

"He must think you did," John said. "And if the president thinks you did something, buddy, you did it."

That, unfortunately, was likely to be correct. And Sam knew only too well what Earl Warren was liable to think he'd done. He'd done it, too, even if these goons didn't know, or want to know, that. He had to keep up a bold front, though. If he didn't, he was ruined. And so he said, "Tell the president that I want to talk to him about it, man to man. Tell him it's important that I do. Not just for me. For the country." He remembered the papers he'd given Straha and the things he'd told Barbara and Jonathan. It was important, all right.

"Crap," Charlie said—from him, an oration.

John said the same thing in a different way: "President Warren's a busy man. Why should he want to talk to one not par-ticularly important lieutenant colonel?"

"Why should he want to make one not particularly important lieutenant colonel disappear?" Sam returned.

"That's not for us to worry about," John answered. "We got told to put you on ice and keep you on ice, and that's what we're doing."

Yeager didn't say anything. He just sat there and smiled his most unpleasant smile.

Charlie didn't get it. Yeager hadn't expected anything else. John didn't get it, either. That disappointed Yeager. After a few seconds' silence, Fred said, "Uh, John, I think he's saying the big boss might want to see him for the same reason he had him put on ice, whatever the hell that is."

"Bingo," Sam said happily.

John didn't sound or look happy. "Like I care what he's saying." He sent Sam an unpleasant look of his own. "Other thing he's been saying all along is that he doesn't know why he got nabbed. If he's lying about that, who knows what else he's been lying about?"

What that translated to was, *Who knows what we're liable to have to try to squeeze out of him?* Back in his baseball days, Sam had known a fair number of small-time, small-town hoodlums, men who thought of themselves as tough guys. It had been a good many years, but the breed didn't seem to have changed much, even if these fellows got their money from a much more important boss.

At this point, Sam had two choices of his own. He could say something like, *Anything happens to me, you'll be sorry.* Or he could just sit tight. He decided to sit tight. These guys struck him as the sort who would take a warning as a sign of weakness, not as a sign of strength.

He wondered if Straha had yet decided he was really missing, and whether the ex-shiplord had looked at the papers he'd given him. Sam had his doubts. If Straha had seen those papers, wouldn't he have got them to the Lizards in Cairo just as fast as he could? Yeager's bet was that he would have. And if he had, the fur would have started flying by now. Sam was sure of that.

Maybe his captors had been expecting him to speak up and warn them. When he sat tight, they didn't seem to know what to make of it. Were they unused to people who could bargain from a position of strength? Or were they just too dumb—and too far down on the totem pole—to realize he had some strength in this bargaining match?

Fred was the one who looked to have a clue. He gathered up the other two by eye and said, "I think we need to talk about this."

They couldn't go off into another room and leave Sam unattended. If they did, he was liable to be out the door like a shot. He didn't know where the next closest house was—he'd come here at night, and had no idea how big a farm this was—but he might well make life difficult for these guys. Of course, they might shoot him if they caught up with him. It would be too bad if they did, too bad for him and, very possibly, too bad for the USA and the whole world.

He wondered if he could slide out of here while they talked among themselves. No sooner had the idea crossed his mind than John said, "Don't even think about it, buddy." Yeager wondered how he'd given himself away. Had his eyes slid longingly toward the door? Whatever the answer, he sat where he was.

After a couple of minutes, his guards broke apart. "Tell you what we're going to do," Fred said, his voice so full of sweet reason, Sam instantly grew suspicious. "We're going to do just like you say, Lieutenant Colonel. We'll pass your request along, and we'll see what comes of it. If it gets turned down, it's not our fault. Is that fair?" He beamed at Yeager.

"I don't think kidnapping me in the first place was exactly fair," Sam answered. "Besides, how do I know I can believe you? You can say you'll pass it along and then just forget about it. How would I know you're telling the truth?"

"What do you want us to do?" John asked. "Put it in writing?"

"That'd be nice," Yeager said dryly.

Everybody laughed, as if they were good buddies sitting around shooting the breeze somewhere. Nobody was going to put anything in writing. If some people hadn't put this, that, and the other thing in writing, Sam wouldn't have been where he was now. In a lot of different ways, he wished he weren't.

He decided to press just a little: "When you do pass the word along, you might want to let people know it's already liable to be later than they think."

"Crap," Charlie said again.

"If you say so," Sam answered. "But I think it's important for the president to know everything that's going on."

"Now you listen up, Lieutenant Colonel," John said. "You aren't in a real good place to start telling people what to do. Nothing's happened to your family—yet. You want to make real sure nothing does, you know what I mean?"

"Why, you son of a—" Sam surged to his feet.

He took half a step forward, but only half a step. All three of his watchdogs packed Army .45s. All three of them had the pistols out and pointed at his brisket in less time than he would have imagined possible. The difference between these guys and the small-town muscle he'd known in his younger days suddenly became obvious. The small-town punks had been minor leaguers, same as he'd been in those days. These fellows could have played in Yankee Stadium, and made the all-star team every year, too. Yeah, they were bastards, but they were awfully damn good at what they did.

Very slowly, Yeager sat down again. John nodded. "Smart boy," he said. His .45 disappeared again. So did Fred's. Charlie held on to his. He looked disappointed that Sam hadn't given him the chance to use it. John went on, "You really don't want to get your ass in an uproar, Lieutenant Colonel, honest to God you don't. We said we'd pass things along, and we will."

Sam studied him. "Saying things is easy. Really doing them— that's something different. I'm telling you, President Warren needs to talk to me. He doesn't know how much trouble he may end up in if he doesn't."

"Talk is cheap," John said.

"That's what I just told you," Yeager answered. "But how many laws are you guys breaking by holding me here like this, not letting me see my lawyer, not letting me know what the charges against me are, or even if there are any charges against me?"

"National security," Charlie intoned, as if reciting Holy Writ.

Yeager might have guessed he would say that. Yeager had, in fact, guessed he would say that. And he had a comeback ready: "If it turns out you're right and everything works out okay, you guys are heroes. But if things go wrong, who's going to end up with egg on his face? You guys will, because whoever's over you sure as hell isn't going to sit still and take the blame."

"That's not for you to worry about, Lieutenant Colonel," Fred said. "That's for us to worry about—and do we look worried?"

"No," Sam admitted. "But the point is, maybe you ought to."

"Crap," Charlie said: a man of strong opinions and limited vocabulary. John and Fred didn't contradict him—and, dammit, they *didn't* look worried. Sam had to hope he'd planted some seeds of doubt . . . and that planting seeds of doubt mattered.

* * *

Because of the time he'd spent in space, Jonathan Yeager was going to graduate from UCLA a couple of quarters later than he would have otherwise. That had been the biggest thing on his mind when he got back to Gardena—till his father disappeared. He and his mother both knew, or thought they knew, why his father had disappeared. If they went to the papers, they might raise enough of a stink to get his dad released. They hadn't done it, not yet. The stink they would raise might turn out to be a lot bigger and messier than that.

And so, now that classes had started again, Jonathan drove up to Westwood every day feeling as if he were in limbo. He didn't know where his dad was, or when—or if—he might return. The police were supposed to be looking for Sam Yeager. So was the Army. So was the FBI. Nobody'd had any luck. Jonathan feared nobody was likely to have any luck, either.

He felt in limbo at UCLA, too. Because he'd dropped a couple of quarters behind, he wasn't in so many classes with his friends— they'd gone on, and he hadn't. What he'd learned from Kassquit and from the Race was and would be immensely valuable to him, but it wasn't the sort of thing that fit into the university curriculum.

That was on his mind as he left his modern political science class—*modern,* of course, meaning *since the coming of the Lizards*—and headed out to the grass between Royce Hall and Powell Library to eat the ham sandwich and orange and cookies he'd brought from home. Brown-bagging it was cheaper than buying lunch from any of the campus greasy spoons, and his mom had started watching every penny since his dad hadn't come home from Desert Center. "After all," she'd said once, "you never know, I might disappear next."

He was just sitting down when Karen walked by. Before he quite knew what he was doing, he waved. "Hi!" he said. "You got a few minutes?"

She paused, obviously thinking it over. They'd been an item— they'd been more than an item; they'd been drifting toward getting married—till he went up to the starship to instruct Kassquit about Tosevite sexual customs. Since then . . . since then, things had been tense, no two ways about it. He'd known they would be when he rode the shuttlecraft into space. He hadn't known the war between the *Reich* and the Race would strand him up there for so long—which only made things between Karen and him that much tenser.

At last, though frowning, she nodded. "How are you?" she asked, leaving the walkway to sit down beside him. "Any word about your father?" She sounded genuinely worried there. They'd known each other since high school, and she'd always got on well with his folks.

"Nothing," Jonathan answered with a grimace. "Zero. Zip. Zilch. I wish to God there were."

"I'm sorry," she said, and brushed a lock of red hair back from her face. Freckles dusted her nose and cheeks and shoulders; she sunburned if you looked at her sideways. Despite that, she wore a flesh-colored halter top to show off the body paint that alleged she was a military communications specialist: like a lot of people of their generation, she was as passionately interested in the Lizards as was Jonathan. After a moment, she found another safe question to ask: "How are Mickey and Donald?"

She'd been there when they hatched from their eggs. Jonathan supposed that was a breach of security, but he hadn't cared at the time, and his father had let him get away with it. "They're fine," he answered. "Growing like weeds, and learning new words all the time." He hesitated, then plunged: "You know they always think it's hot when you come over to see them."

"Do they?" Karen's voice wasn't hot; it was colder than winter in Los Angeles ever got. "I like seeing them. I like seeing your mom, too. You . . . that hasn't worked out so well since you got back, and you know it hasn't."

Jonathan's sack lunch lay by him, forgotten. "Go easy," he said. "I've told you and told you—what happened up there wasn't what I thought it was going to be when I left."

"I know," she said. "It lasted longer, so you had more fun than you figured you would when you left. But you went up there intending to have fun. That's the long and short of things, isn't it, Jonathan?"

He admitted what he could scarcely deny: "That's some of it, yeah. But it's not all. It was almost like what fooling around with a real Lizard would be. We both learned a lot from it."

"I'll bet you did," Karen said.

"I didn't mean it like that, darn it," Jonathan said. "Now she's thinking about coming down here to see what life among the Big Uglies is like, and all she ever wanted to do before was stay on the starship and pretend she was a Lizard."

"And what would she do if she did come down here?" Karen demanded. "Whatever it was, would she do it with you?"

Jonathan's ears heated. That had nothing to do with the weather, even though the day, like a lot of allegedly early-autumn days in Los Angeles, was well up into the eighties. "I don't know," he muttered. "It's research, is what it is."

"Is that what you call it?" Karen said. "How would you like it if I were doing *research* like that?" She laced the word with scorn.

And Jonathan knew he wouldn't like it for hell. He took a deep breath. "There's one way that wouldn't happen, even if Kassquit did come down to Earth," he said.

"Sure there is—if she landed in Moscow," Karen said.

"That's not what I meant," Jonathan said. "Not even close. She knows about marriage—I don't think she really understands it, but she knows what it means. That's why"—he blushed again—"that's why my dad wasn't up there being experimental, if you know what I mean."

"And so?" Karen said.

"And so . . ." Jonathan plunged: "And so, if I were engaged to you, it wouldn't be the same as married, but it would be on the way to the same thing, and she'd see that it meant she and I couldn't do, uh, anything any more." He brought the words out in a quick, almost desperate rush.

Karen's eyes widened—widened more, in fact, than Jonathan had ever seen them do. Ever so slowly, she said, "Are you asking me to marry you?"

"Yeah." Jonathan nodded, feeling very much as if he'd just gone off the high board without bothering to see if there was any water in the pool. "I guess that kind of is what I'm doing. Will you?"

"I don't know. I don't know what to tell you." Karen shook her head, not in rejection but in bemusement. "If you'd asked me before you went up to the starship the last time, I'd've said yes in a minute. Now . . . ? Now it sounds more like you're asking me to marry you to give you an excuse not to fool around with Kassquit than for any other reason, and I don't think I like that very much."

"That isn't why," Jonathan protested, though it had sounded like why to him, too. He did his best to make it sound like something else: "It was the only way I could think of to tell you I'm sorry about what happened up there and that there isn't anybody but you I want to spend my life with." His mother wouldn't have approved of his ending a sentence with a preposition. Right this minute, he didn't care whether his mother would have approved or not.

And this time he'd said the right thing, or something close to it. Karen's expression softened. "That's . . . very sweet, Jonathan," she said. "I've thought for a long time that we might one day. Like I say, I used to like the idea—but things changed when you went up there. I'm going to have to sort that out."

"We weren't engaged or anything." Jonathan thought about adding that he'd used some of the things Karen had taught him with Kassquit. But, not being of a suicidal bent, he didn't.

"No, not really," Karen said, "but we were as close as makes no difference—*I* thought so, anyway."

That had teeth, sharp ones. Jonathan considered explaining again how he'd done everything he'd done with Kassquit purely in the spirit of scientific inquiry. Again, he thought better of it. What he did say was just as inflammatory, though he didn't realize it at the time: "Come to think of it, maybe you'd better not marry me. It might not be safe for you."

"What do you mean, not safe?" Karen asked. "I know you're crazy, but I never thought you were especially dangerous."

"Thanks—I think." He wished he'd kept his mouth shut. He hadn't told her about this when he found out about it after he got back from the starship. He hadn't told anybody. The son of an officer, he knew secrets could leak if you started running your mouth. But he was afraid his father had disappeared because of what he knew. Didn't that mean he, Jonathan, had an obligation to make sure the secret couldn't be wiped out? And Karen could be counted on. After all, she knew about the hatchlings, didn't she?

The more you looked at things, the more complicated they got. His father had insisted on that for as long as he could remember. Here as other places, his old man looked to have a point.

"You still haven't told me what you meant," Karen reminded him.

"Well . . ." Jonathan did his best to temporize. "I've got some idea of why my dad disappeared, and it has to do with something he knew and something he told me."

"Something he knew?" Karen echoed, while people worrying about nothing but classes and lunch walked back and forth only a few feet away. "Something he knew that he wasn't supposed to, you mean? Sounds like something out of a spy story."

"I know it does. I'm sorry," Jonathan answered. "You're liable to be in trouble just because you know me. I'm sorry." He realized he was repeating himself. He also wondered how the devil the conversation had got so far away from his proposal so fast.

Karen said, "You know something?" That was just an ordinary question; she waited for him to shake his head before going on, "You're going to have to tell me now. If you want me to marry you, I mean. You can't have that kind of great big secret from somebody you're married to."

"Hey! That's not fair. You don't even know what you're asking for," Jonathan protested. "You don't know how much trouble you might get into, either. Remember the guy who tried to fire-bomb our house? As far as we could find out, nothing ever happened to him."

Karen only folded her arms across her chest—across that ridiculously unconcealing halter top—and waited. She said one word; "Talk."

And Jonathan saw that, having come this far, he couldn't do anything but talk. He leaned close to her so none of the happy, unconcerned students going by would hear anything out of the ordinary. Telling what he knew didn't take long. When he was done, he said, "There. Are you satisfied?"

"My God," Karen said quietly. "Oh, my God." She looked around the bright, sun-splashed UCLA campus as if she'd never seen it before. "What do we do now?"

"That's what I've been trying to work out," Jonathan replied. "I still don't have any answers I like. And speaking of answers, you still owe me one for the question I asked you a little while ago."

"What? Oh, that." Karen's voice remained far away. "I'll worry about that later, Jonathan. This is more important."

Jonathan wondered if he ought to be insulted. He wondered if he ought to get angry. He discovered he couldn't do either. The trouble was, he agreed with her.

Mordechai Anielewicz had imagined any number of things in his search for his family. Having a German along, though, a German who was interested in helping him, had never once crossed his mind. But Johannes Drucker had a missing family, too. Anielewicz had always had trouble imagining Germans as human beings. How could they be human and have done what they'd done? But if a man desperately searching for his wife and sons and daughter wasn't a human being, what was he?

What was funny, in a horrid, macabre sort of way, was that what Drucker had thought about Jews pretty much mirrored what he himself had thought about Nazis. "I never worried my head about the enemies of the *Reich*," he told Mordechai one evening. "If my leaders said they were enemies, I went out and dealt with them. That was my job. I never cared about rights or wrongs till Käthe got in trouble."

"Nothing like the personal touch." Anielewicz's voice was dry.

"You think you're joking," the German spaceman said.

"No, dammit, I'm not joking." Now Mordechai couldn't help letting some of his anger show. "If every other German had a Jewish grandmother or grandfather, none of that murderous nonsense would have happened."

Drucker sighed and looked around the little tavern in which they were drinking beer and eating a rather nasty stew. There wasn't much to see; only the fireplace gave light and heat. "Hard to say you're wrong," he admitted, and then laughed without much humor. "Hard to imagine I'm sitting here talking with a Jew. I can't remember the last time I did that."

"Oh? What about your wife?" Anielewicz asked acidly. He watched the German flush. But maybe that wasn't altogether fair; again, he had the feeling that one of them was looking out of a mirror at the other.

Drucker said, "I didn't mean it like that, dammit. I meant with somebody who really believes."

"What difference does that make?" Mordechai said. "The taint is in the blood, not in the belief, right? Otherwise they wouldn't have cared about your wife. They wouldn't have cared about converts. They wouldn't have—*ahhh!*" He made a disgusted noise. "Why do I waste my time?"

He took another pull at the pilsner in his stein. It was thin and sour, a telling measure of the *Reich*'s troubles. Across the table from him, Johannes Drucker bit his lip. "You don't make this easy, do you?"

"Should I?" Mordechai returned. "How easy was it for us when you held Poland? How easy was it for us when you invaded

Poland again this spring? Explosive-metal bombs, poison gas, panzers—what did we do to deserve that?"

"You sided with the Lizards instead of mankind," Drucker answered.

There was just enough truth in that to sting. But it wasn't the whole truth, nor anything close to it. "Oh, of course we did," Anielewicz said. "That's why I came looking for your Colonel Jäger, because I sided with the Lizards all the time."

Drucker sighed again. "All right. Things weren't simple. Things are never simple. Just getting here, or trying to, taught me that."

Jews, Anielewicz thought, were born knowing that. He didn't say as much to the German—what point to it? What he did say was, "We've both been through the mill. If we start fighting with each other now, it won't do us any good, and it won't make it any easier for us to find our families."

"If they're there," Drucker said. "What are the odds?" He poured down his remaining beer in a couple of long, dispirited gulps.

"I've pulled the wires I know how to pull looking for my family," Mordechai said. "I didn't have any luck, but I'll pull them again for yours. And I'll help you get in touch with your *Führer*"—*am I really saying this?* he wondered—"so you can pull your wires for your family."

"And for yours," Drucker said.

"Yes. And for mine." Anielewicz wondered whether the *Reich* would have bothered keeping records of Jews kidnapped in the fighting in Poland. With anyone but the Germans, he would have had his doubts. As a matter of fact, he still did have his doubts, big ones. But the possibility remained. He'd seen German efficiency and German bureaucracy in action in the Warsaw ghetto. If any battered, beaten, retreating army would have kept track of the prisoners with whom it was falling back, the *Wehrmacht* was that force.

The next morning, after a breakfast about as unpleasant as supper had been, Anielewicz led Drucker to the little garrison the Race used to watch the refugee camp. There he ran into Lizard bureaucracy, which turned out to be every bit as inflexible as the German variety. "No," said the male to whom he addressed his request. "I have not the authority to take any such action. I am sorry." In the best tradition of bureaucrats regardless of species, he sounded not in the least sorry.

Trying to conceal his exasperation, Mordechai demanded, "Well, who does have the authority, and where do I find him?"

"No one here," the Lizard replied. Again, like any good bureaucrat, he seemed to take pleasure in thwarting those who came before him.

Johannes Drucker proved fluent in the language of the Race: "You did not fully answer the Jewish fighting leader's question. Where can we find someone with that authority?" He didn't use Anielewicz's religion as a slur but as a goad, reminding the Lizard he wasn't helping an ally.

It got through, too. With a resentful hiss, the male said, "The closest officers with the authority to treat with the upper echelons of the *Reich* are based near the place called Greifswald." He made a hash of the pronunciation, but it wasn't a name easy to mistake for any other.

Anielewicz turned to Drucker. "Back where we started from. I've got a seat on the rear of my bicycle."

"Must be close to twenty kilometers," Drucker answered. "We can split the pedaling."

"I won't argue," Mordechai said. Drucker wasn't far from his own age, and very likely had stronger legs. Odds were he'd never breathed in nerve gas, anyhow.

They returned to Greifswald in the early afternoon, after going back through some of the flattest, dullest terrain Mordechai had ever seen. Bomb craters gave it most of the relief it had. None of them was from an explosive-metal bomb, but he still wondered how much radioactivity he was picking up. He'd wondered that ever since he came into Germany. For that matter, he'd wondered back in Poland. He tried to make himself stop wondering. He couldn't do anything about it.

Drucker was pedaling as they rode into the Lizard encampment. Over his shoulder, he said, "Do you suppose these males will give us the runaround, too?"

"I hope not," was all Anielewicz could say. If the Lizards chose to be difficult, he couldn't do much about that, either.

But they didn't. One of the males in their communications section turned out to have fought alongside some of the Jewish fighters Mordechai had commanded. "Your males helped save my unit several times," he said, folding into the posture of respect. "Anything you require, you have but to ask."

"I thank you," Mordechai answered, a little taken aback at

such wholehearted cooperation. He introduced Drucker and explained why the German spaceman needed to be connected to the leader of what was left of the *Reich*.

"It shall be done," the Lizard said. "I do not fully understand this business of intimate kinship, but I know of its importance to you Tosevites. Come with me. I shall arrange this call."

Drucker stared at Anielewicz in something close to amazement. "This is too easy," he said in German. "Something will go wrong."

"You'd better be careful," Mordechai answered in the same language. "You keep saying things like that and people will start thinking you're a Jew yourself." Drucker laughed, though Anielewicz again hadn't been joking.

But nothing went wrong. Inside of a couple of minutes, the Lizard was talking with a male of the Race in Flensburg, a not too radioactive town near the Danish border from which General Dornberger was administering the broken *Reich*. A couple of minutes after that, Dornberger's image appeared on the screen. He was older than Anielewicz had expected he would be: old and bald and, by all appearances, tired unto death.

"Ah, Drucker," he said. "I'm glad to see you're alive. Not many who went up into orbit came down again."

"Sir, I was lucky, if you want to call it that," the spaceman answered. "If I'd killed my starship instead of failing, I'm sure the Lizards would have killed me, too."

"We need every man we have to rebuild," Walter Dornberger said, a sentiment that struck Anielewicz as almost too sensible to come from the mouth of a German *Führer*. Dornberger went on, "Who's that with you, Hans?"

Anielewicz spoke for himself: "I'm Mordechai Anielewicz, of Lodz." He waited to see what reaction that brought.

All Dornberger said was, "I've heard of you." Hitler would have pitched a fit at the idea of talking to a Jew. Himmler, no doubt, would have been quietly furious. Dornberger just asked, "And what can I do for the two of you?"

"We're looking for our families," Anielewicz answered. "Drucker's is missing from Greifswald, and mine was kidnapped from Widawa by retreating German troops." He'd said it so many times, it hurt less than it had before. "If anyone can order German records examined to help us find them, you're the man." He startled himself; he'd almost added *sir*.

Dornberger's hand disappeared from the screen for a moment. It came back with a cigar, which he puffed. "How is it that the two of you have become friends?"

"Friends?" Mordechai shrugged. "That may go too far," he said, to which Drucker nodded. The Jewish fighting leader went on, "But we both knew, and we both liked, a panzer officer named Heinrich Jäger."

"You knew and liked . . ." Walter Dornberger's expressions sharpened. "Jäger. The deserter. The traitor."

"Sir"—now Anielewicz did say it—"he saved Germany from getting in 1944 what you got in 1965. He also saved my life, but you'd probably think that was a detail."

"That may be true," Dornberger replied. "It doesn't make him any less a deserter or a traitor."

"Sir, he was a deserter," Drucker said, "but a traitor, never."

"Et tu, Brute?" the German *Führer* murmured. His eyes swung back to Mordechai. "And if I don't help you, I suppose you'll tell your friends the Lizards on me."

"Sir, it's my family," Anielewicz said tightly. "I'll do whatever I can, whatever I have to, to get them back. Wouldn't you?"

Dornberger sighed. "Without a doubt. Very well, gentlemen, I will do what I can. I do not know how much that will be. Things being as they are, our records are in no small degree of chaos. Good-bye." His image vanished.

"Hope," Mordechai said as he and Drucker left the tent from which they'd spoken with the new *Führer*.

"I know," Drucker said. "Is it a blessing or a curse?" He cocked his head to one side. "What's that funny noise?"

Had he not asked, Anielewicz might not even have noticed the small, whistling beep. But when it came again, the hair prickled upright on his arms and at the nape of his neck. "My God," he whispered. "That's a beffel."

"What's a beffel?" Drucker asked. But Mordechai didn't answer. He'd already started running.

Straha watched his driver take the motorcar off on an errand that would keep him gone for at least an hour. The ex-shiplord let out a hiss of satisfaction. He hurried into the bathroom and scrubbed off his body paint with rubbing alcohol, as he would have if he were going to redo it.

But instead of repainting himself as the male of third-highest rank in the conquest fleet, he chose the much simpler pattern of a shuttlecraft pilot. The job he did wasn't of the best, but it would serve. Neither the Big Uglies nor his own kind would be likely to recognize him at once.

As he carried an attaché case of Tosevite manufacture out the front door of his house, he turned one eye turret back toward the building, wondering if he would ever see it again, and if it would still be standing in a few days' time. A considerable portion of him wished Sam Yeager had never entrusted him with this burden.

But Yeager had, and the Big Ugly must have known the likely consequences of that. Sighing, Straha walked down to the end of the block, turned right, and walked two more blocks. In front of a small grocery store stood a public telephone in a booth of glass and aluminum.

Straha had never used a Tosevite public phone before. He read the instructions and followed them, letting out a relieved hiss when he was rewarded with a dial tone after inserting a small coin. He dialed the number he had memorized back at the house. The phone rang three times before someone answered it. "Yellow Cab Company."

"Yes. Thank you." Straha spoke the best English he could: "I am at the corner of Rayen and Zelzah. I wish to go to downtown, to the consulate of the Race."

He waited, wondering if he'd have to repeat himself. But the female on the other end of the line just echoed him: "Rayen and Zelzah. Yes, sir. About five minutes."

"I thank you," Straha said, and hung up.

The cab took about twice as long as the predicted time to arrive, but not so long as to make Straha much more nervous than he was already. The driver hopped out and opened a rear door for him. "Hello!" the Big Ugly said. "Don't pick up a male of the Race every day." When he spoke again, it was in Straha's language: "I greet you, superior sir."

"And I greet you," Straha replied in the same tongue. "How much of my language do you speak?"

"Not much. Not well," the Tosevite answered. "I like to try. Where you want to go?" His accent was indeed thick, but comprehensible.

"To the consulate." Straha repeated it in English, to make sure he was not misunderstood, and gave the address in English, too.

"It shall be done," the driver said, and proceeded to do it. Straha had judged his regular driver a Tosevite who cared less for safety on the road than he might have. Next to this fellow, the other male Big Ugly was a paragon of virtue. How the cab driver arrived at the consulate with his motorcar uncrumpled baffled Straha, but it was a fact. "Here we are," he remarked cheerfully as he pulled up in front of the building.

"I thank you," Straha answered, though he was feeling anything but thankful. He gave the Big Ugly a twenty-dollar bill, which more than covered journey and gratuity. American money had never felt quite real to him, and odds were good—one way or another—he would never have to worry about it again.

A couple of Tosevites who reminded Straha of his regular driver stood outside the consulate. They glanced at him as he walked inside, but did nothing more. He wondered if his driver had yet discovered him missing. If so, the Big Uglies would be looking for a shiplord, not a shuttlecraft pilot. Straha hurried up to the reception desk.

"Yes?" asked the male at that desk, swinging an eye turret his way. "How may I help you, Shuttlecraft Pilot?" He too saw only what he expected to see, what Straha wanted him to see.

Now, with more than a little pleasure, Straha threw off the disguise. "I am not a shuttlecraft pilot," he replied. "I am a shiplord: Shiplord Straha, commanding—well, formerly commanding—the *206th Emperor Yower* of the conquest fleet."

His mouth flew open in a laugh at the receptionist's startled jerk. The other male recovered fairly quickly, saying, "If you are who you claim to be, you must know there is and has been an order for your arrest."

"I am who I say I am," Straha answered. "I am certain you have a database with the scale patterns of my snout and palm included in it. You are welcome to take those patterns from me and compare them."

"To verify such an incendiary claim, we would of course have to do that," the receptionist said. "But if you are who you say you are, why would you subject yourself to arrest and certain punishment after so many years of treason?"

Straha hefted the attaché case. "What I have in here will protect me from punishment. Once he sees it, once he understands what it means, even Atvar will recognize as much." *He had better,* Straha thought. *Not even his malice against me could withstand this . . . could it?* Half of him wanted to flee the consulate. But he'd already come too far for that. Now he was in trouble with the Americans as well as the Race.

"I do not know anything about that." The receptionist would not give him his proper title, but was talking into a telephone attachment to the computer. After a moment, he swung his eye turrets toward Straha. "Please go to the Security office on the second floor. Your identity will be ascertained there."

"It shall be done," Straha said.

When he got to the Security office, he found the males and females there almost jumping out of their hides. Their tailstumps quivered with excitement. Most of them hadn't been anywhere near Tosev 3 when he staged his spectacular defection, but they all knew of it. "This will not take long," the senior Security officer said, advancing on him with a couple of trays full of waxy greenish plastic. "I have to take the impressions and then scan the patterns into the computer."

"I am familiar with the procedure, I assure you," Straha replied. He let the officer press the plastic to his snout and left palm, then waited for him to finish the scanning and comparison. By the way the officer stiffened when the data came up on the monitor, Straha knew he'd proved he was himself. He said, "You will now please be so kind as to take me to the consul here. I believe his name is Tsaitsanx—is that not correct?"

Absently, the Security officer made the affirmative gesture. "It shall be done." He sounded dazed. "Although perhaps I should formally place you under arrest first."

"No. Not while I have this." Straha waved the attaché case. "If Tsaitsanx is not fluent in written English, it would be wise to have a male or female—I suppose a male from the conquest fleet—who is fluent with us."

"The consul does read the local language, yes," the Security male said. He ordered a couple of his subordinates to escort Straha to Tsaitsanx's office, as if afraid the former shiplord would do something nefarious if allowed to walk the corridors unattended.

Tsaitsanx proved to have come with the conquest fleet, though Straha had not known him. The consul said, "I always knew you lived in my area: indeed, I have spoken with males and females who met you at functions given by, ah, more legitimate expatriates. But I never expected to make your acquaintance here, and I do not know whether to greet you or not."

"You had better greet me." Straha opened the attaché case and pulled out the papers Sam Yeager had given him. "Examine these, if you would be so kind. I assure you, they are genuine. I would not be here if they were not. They were given to me by one of those rare creatures, a Tosevite with a conscience."

"Examine them I shall," Tsaitsanx replied. "What have we here . . . ?" He read with great attention for a little while. Then, as if of their own accord, his eye turrets lifted from the papers in front of him and focused intently on Straha. "By the Emperor, Shiplord, do you know what these papers mean?"

"I know exactly what they mean, Consul. Exactly," Straha said. "I would not be here if I did not."

"I believe that." Tsaitsanx returned to his reading, but not for long. "Have I your permission to scan these documents and transmit them to Cairo?"

"You have." Straha was sure the consul would have done so without his permission had he withheld it, but he did appreciate being asked.

After sending the papers on their electronic way, Tsaitsanx said, "That brings me to the next question: what to do about you, Shiplord. I cannot scan you and transmit you to Cairo."

"It would be convenient if you could," Straha said. "Before long, the Big Uglies will realize I have gone missing. They may not know why. On the other fork of the tongue, they may. And this is bound to be one of the first places they search."

"Truth," Tsaitsanx agreed. "Not only a truth, but one that presents a certain difficulty: under Tosevite usages, a consulate, unlike an embassy, is not considered part of the territory of the group the consul represents. Of course, while you wear that body paint, Big Uglies will have a difficult time knowing who you are."

"Big Uglies will, yes," Straha said. "But an expatriate will know me regardless of my body paint, just as one Big Ugly has little difficulty recognizing another regardless of wrappings."

"That is also a truth," the consul said with a sigh. Before he could say anything more, the telephone attachment on his computer hissed. After so long listening to ringing bells, Straha was startled by what he should have taken for granted. Then Tsaitsanx said, "Yes, Exalted Fleetlord, he sits before me even as I speak. Do you want to talk to him?"

"I do indeed," Atvar said.

Tsaitsanx gestured. Straha came around behind the consul's desk. Staring out of the monitor at him was the fleetlord of the conquest fleet. "I greet you, Atvar," Straha said. "It has been a long time."

"Yes," the fleetlord agreed. "A very long time. Do you think these documents will buy your forgiveness?"

"Frankly, yes," Straha answered.

"However much I hate to say it, you may even be correct," Atvar said. "Are you aware, though, that you may have hatched another war here?"

"Painfully so," Straha told him.

"In all this time, you have not lost your knack for being impossible," Atvar said. "Why did you give me these documents at this moment?"

"Not for your sake, I assure you," Straha replied. "A Tosevite friend gave them to me to read if anything happened to him. Something did. Having read them, I passed them to you. Now they are your worry. That is what you get for being fleetlord." *I could have been sitting there these many years,* he thought, *with Atvar the hapless exile. I could have.*

Tsaitsanx broke in: "Exalted Fleetlord, will you not want to arrange transportation out of the United States for Shiplord— uh, ex-Shiplord—Straha? I cannot guarantee his safety here."

Atvar stayed silent for quite a while. Straha knew how much trouble the fleetlord could cause him simply by saying no. But at last, with a grudging affirmative gesture, Atvar replied, "I suppose so." Straha still didn't think much of his old rival. But Atvar did have a sense of justice—of sorts.

Having spent so long in Basra and Baghdad, Gorppet was used to excitable Big Uglies. He'd seen enough of them thereabouts to last him a lifetime. Even though the weather in Poland and the *Reich* was abominable, he hadn't minded coming here all that much because the local Tosevites were generally calmer. Some of the Poles and Jews had actually been friendly to him, something he hadn't imagined possible from Big Uglies. And even the Deutsche—not the males on the battlefield, of course, but the civilians in their not-empire—were resigned and polite toward the males of the Race who had defeated them.

But now, here in this camp near Greifswald where he'd thought he could get used to his new duties as an intelligence officer, Gorppet found himself confronted by perhaps the most excited Big Ugly he'd ever seen. And the reason the Big Ugly was excited struck him as utterly incomprehensible.

"That beffel!" the Tosevite said, pointing to the little beast from Home that was sharing Gorppet's tent with him. "Where did you get that beffel?"

"Beep!" said the beffel, and trotted over to the Tosevite, who had another male Big Ugly with him.

"Why do you care?" Gorppet asked. "For that matter, how do you know the animal is a beffel? Not many Tosevites would."

When the Big Ugly spoke, it wasn't to him but to the beffel: "Hello, Pancer! Do you remember me?" He switched from the language of the Race—which he spoke quite well—to his own tongue, and bent down and patted and scratched the beffel in a way that showed he was indeed familiar with its kind.

"Beep!" the beffel said again. It wiggled happily; by all appearances, it was a lot more familiar with Tosevites—and maybe even with this Tosevite in particular—than Gorppet would have thought it could be.

Gorppet wished he had a taste of ginger. It would have made him think faster and more clearly. He would have thought he was thinking faster and more clearly, anyhow. As things were, he could only repeat his earlier questions: "Why do you care about this beffel? And how do you know about befflem in the first place?"

"I am Mordechai Anielewicz," the Tosevite said, as if the name ought to mean something to Gorppet. After a moment, it did: this Big Ugly was a leader of the fighters of the Jewish superstition in Poland, and so an ally, and a fairly important one, of the Race. Anielewicz went on, "I am searching for my mate and hatchlings, who were taken from Poland to the *Reich*."

"I understand your words," Gorppet said carefully, "but I do not understand what they have to do with this beffel here."

"My youngest hatchling—the younger of my two male hatchlings—had a beffel for a pet," Mordechai Anielewicz answered. "He found it on the streets of Lodz and brought it home with him."

"And named it for a landcruiser, I notice," the other Big Ugly said, also using the language of the Race. He barked Tosevite laughter. "I see the resemblance."

"Who are you?" Gorppet demanded. This whole business was getting very confusing very fast.

And it got more confusing still, for the second Tosevite answered, "I am Johannes Drucker, formerly of the *Wehrmacht* Rocket Force. I was a pilot in space. I almost killed one of your starships."

"Wait!" Gorppet's head started to ache. "What are the two of you doing here together, then? Jews and Deutsche are enemies. I know that for a fact." It was one of the few facts about this area that he did know, and he clung to it.

Both Big Uglies laughed. "We have a friend in common," the one called Drucker answered. "And we have something else in common: my mate and hatchlings are also missing."

That mattered much more to Tosevites than to members of the Race. Ties of kinship, and ties of vengeance because of them, had kept on marring the Race's efforts to control the Muslim fanatics around Baghdad and Basra. But to Gorppet, all that was a distraction. "Back to the beffel," he said, and swung his eye turrets in the direction of Mordechai Anielewicz. "Very well. Your hatchling had a beffel. Why do you think it was this beffel?"

"It looks like the same beffel," Anielewicz said. "It has the same markings—I think it has, anyhow. It seems to know me. At the very least, it is familiar with Tosevites, and how many befflem are? And I have learned that the Deutsch military unit that kidnapped my mate and hatchlings withdrew in this direction."

"I mean no offense, but you are a Tosevite," Gorppet said. "Would you not have trouble telling one beffel from another, just as your kind has trouble telling one male of the Race from another, and even males from females?"

"You have the same trouble with us," Anielewicz answered, and Gorppet, even though he'd recognized and captured the infamous Khomeini, could hardly deny it. The Big Ugly went on, "I have had reason to examine my hatchling's beffel very closely. There was a fire, a bad fire, in my block of flats. It might have killed all of us, but the beffel woke my hatchling, and he woke the rest of us."

"I . . . see," Gorppet said slowly. He knew Tosevite buildings were firetraps; he'd seen frequent blazes in his duties all over the planet. The Big Uglies didn't come close to the standards of safety the Race had taken for granted for millennia.

"And you still have not answered my question," Mordechai

Anielewicz said. "Where did you find this beffel?" He added an emphatic cough to the interrogative cough at the end of the sentence—a barbarous usage to Gorppet's hearing diaphragms, but one that got across his urgency.

"I found it near here, as a matter of fact," Gorppet answered. "I heard it calling, and it came out of some bushes. It was going somewhere; I had to coax it back. It has made a pleasant pet."

"Near here," Anielewicz said, and Gorppet wondered if the Tosevite had heard anything else he said. "If this is Pancer, that means my mate and hatchlings are somewhere close by."

"There are a lot of refugee centers close by," Johannes Drucker said. "There are a lot of them all over the *Reich*."

"I know that," Anielewicz said, and even Gorppet could sense his impatience. The Jewish Big Ugly turned his head back toward Gorppet. "From what direction did the beffel come?"

"I was not paying much attention, you must understand," Gorppet replied. "I had no idea this would be important. I am still not altogether convinced it is important, either. Let me think . . ." He tried to remember where he'd been when the beffel first trotted past him. "It was that direction, I believe." He pointed southeast.

"I thank you," Anielewicz exclaimed, and trotted off in that direction. The beffel trotted after him as if he were a male of the Race. Maybe that said it had belonged to his hatchling. Maybe it said nothing of the sort. Gorppet called to the creature, but it kept going. That irritated him; he'd enjoyed having it around. He shrugged. It might be back soon, after the excitement of doing something new wore off.

Johannes Drucker sighed. "I wish I had even so much luck in finding any trace of my mate and hatchlings."

"Who knows? Maybe you will," Gorppet said. "And now, if you will excuse me . . ." He probably wouldn't have been quite so rude to a male of the Race, but he might have. He didn't like commotions. He'd seen altogether too many of them, and too many of the ones he'd seen had proved dangerous.

"Oh, yes." Drucker's words were polite, his tone anything but. "You have everything you need. You have your tent and your rifle and your beffel and maybe your ginger, and this is all you need. We Tosevites, we are not like that. We are different. We need one another." Without waiting for a reply, he turned and went after

Mordechai Anielewicz and the beffel that might or might not have been named for a landcruiser.

Gorppet answered as if Drucker had stayed around to listen to him: "You need not boast of your own weaknesses."

And, regardless of whether Drucker was listening, the Big Ugly had been right about one thing—Gorppet did have everything he needed, right there in his tent. He had less ginger than he might have wanted, but he did have enough for a taste. He took a little plastic vial out of his kit, poured some of the powdered herb into the palm of his hand, and brought it up to his mouth. Almost of its own accord, as if it had somehow become independent of the rest of him, his tongue shot out and lapped up the ginger.

"Ahh," he said softly. As the herb took effect, he stopped caring about the Big Uglies and their preposterous kinship groupings. He stopped caring about much of anything. He felt above care, above concern, above everything. With a snout full of ginger, his being in a miserable tent in a miserable camp in a miserable (to say nothing of radioactive) part of Tosev 3 stopped mattering. With so much pleasure coursing through him, he might have been the Emperor himself, in his palace back on Home.

He made the negative hand gesture. He was better off than the Emperor. The Emperor, poor fellow, had never tasted ginger.

No starship had yet flown from Tosev 3 back to Home. It would be a while before any did. When interstellar traffic between this new world and the rest of the Empire started up, though, Gorppet would have bet that some enterprising male, or perhaps even female, would find a way to smuggle the herb past the inspectors who would surely try to block its importation.

Gorppet wished he could be part of *that* smuggling operation. He would eventually get rich off the ginger he had waiting for him down in South Africa. But there was rich, and then there was *rich*. The first members of the Race who took ginger to Home would be *rich*.

His mouth fell open in amusement. Wouldn't it cause a fuss when females who tasted the herb started coming into season all around the calendar rather than just at the proper time? It had certainly caused a fuss here on Tosev 3.

And then the ginger ebbed out of his system, and his laughter went with it. He knew how the herb had made life difficult here on Tosev 3, knew from the inside out. Would it bring chaos to

Home? At bottom, the Race viewed—and had reason to view—
any change with suspicion.

"Poor Home," he murmured, post-tasting depression crashing
down on him. "Poor, poor Home. It will never be the same, not
after ginger gets there." Thinking of Home's not being the same
saddened him. Of course, in the gloom that followed ginger's exhilaration, everything saddened him.

He thought about tasting again, but refrained. He was a veteran at ginger, as he was at combat. If he dipped his tongue a
second time, the enjoyment would be shorter, the depression
afterwards longer and deeper.

The beffel he'd found didn't come back. He wondered what
that meant, and wondered if he'd ever find out.

☆ 8 ☆

By now, Nesseref had flown into Los Angeles several times. It was, in her view, one of the better Tosevite facilities for receiving shuttlecraft. For that matter, she would rather have landed there than at Cairo. No one had ever shot at her when she descended toward the Los Angeles airport that also did duty as a shuttlecraft port.

"Shuttlecraft, your descent is nominal in all respects," a Big Ugly at the local control center radioed to her. "Continue on trajectory and land in the usual area."

"It shall be done," Nesseref answered. "I hope the ambulance is waiting to bring the sick male directly to the shuttlecraft." Had she been dealing with her own kind, she would have assumed that to be the case. With Big Uglies, you never could tell.

But the Tosevite on the other end of the radio link said, "Shuttlecraft Pilot, that ambulance is waiting at the terminal here. So are the hydrogen and oxygen for your next burn. As soon as you are refueled, you are cleared for launch, so you can get that male to proper medical facilities for your kind. I hope he makes a full recovery."

"I thank you," Nesseref said, "both for your kind wishes and for the well-organized preparations you have made to assist one of my species."

Braking rockets fired. Deceleration pressed Nesseref into her seat. She eyed the radar and her velocity. The Race's engineering was good, very good. Most shuttlecraft pilots—almost all, in fact—went through their whole careers without ever coming close to using a manual override. But the pilot who wasn't alert to the possibility was the one who might come to grief.

Not this time. Electronics and rocket motor functioned with their usual perfection. Landing legs deployed. The shuttlecraft gently touched down on the concrete of the Los Angeles airport. Three vehicles immediately rolled toward it: the hydrogen and oxygen trucks, and another one with flashing lights and with red crosses painted on it in several places. Nesseref had seen vehicles with such symbols in Poland, and recognized this one as a Tosevite ambulance.

"Will the male require aid to board the shuttlecraft?" she asked, releasing the landing ladder so that its extensible segment reached the concrete.

"I am given to understand that he will not," replied the Tosevite in the control tower. "He is said to be weak but capable of moving on his own."

"Very well," Nesseref said. "I await him." She didn't have to wait long. Her external camera showed the male leaving the ambulance by the rear doors and moving toward the landing ladder at a startlingly brisk clip. Noting his body paint, she let out a small hiss of surprise as he scrambled up toward the cabin— nobody had bothered to tell her he was a shuttlecraft pilot, too.

"I greet you," he said as he slid down into the compartment with her. He got into his seat and fastened the safety harness with a practiced ease that showed he was indeed familiar with shuttlecraft.

"And I greet you, comrade," Nesseref answered. "Are you in pain? I have analgesics in the first-aid kit, and will be happy to give you whatever you may need."

"I thank you, but I am not suffering in the least, except from anxiety," the male said. "When this shuttlecraft lifts off, I shall be the happiest male on—or rather, above—the surface of Tosev 3."

He certainly didn't seem infirm. Nesseref wondered why she'd been summoned halfway around the planet to take him to Cairo. For that matter, she wondered why she wasn't taking him to the nearby city of Jerusalem, which boasted more specialized medical facilities. What sort of pull did he have? She was astonished to discover a shuttlecraft pilot with any pull at all.

She said, "We cannot go anywhere till the Big Uglies give us hydrogen and oxygen."

"I understand that," he said, a touch of asperity in his voice.

Who do you think you are? Nesseref thought in some annoyance. Before she could call him on it, the Tosevite in the tower radioed, "Please open the port to your hydrogen tank. I say again, to your hydrogen tank."

"It shall be done," Nesseref said. "I am opening the port to my hydrogen tank. I repeat, to my hydrogen tank." The Tosevites had sensibly adopted the Race's refueling procedures, which minimized the possibility of error. Nesseref's fingerclaws entered the proper control slot. The hydrogen tank rolled forward and delivered its liquefied contents. As soon as Nesseref said, "I am full," the hose uncoupled and the truck withdrew.

"Now open the port to your oxygen tank. I say again, to your oxygen tank," the Big Ugly in the control tower told her.

"It shall be done," Nesseref repeated. She went through the ritual once more. The control activating that port was nowhere near the one for the hydrogen port, again to make sure the two were not mistaken for each other. After the oxygen truck finished refilling her tank, it also disengaged and drove away from the shuttlecraft.

"Am I now cleared for takeoff?" Nesseref asked. "I want to get this male to treatment as quickly as possible."

"I understand, Shuttlecraft Pilot," replied the Big Ugly in the control tower. "There will be a five-minute delay. Do you understand five minutes, or shall I convert it to your time system?"

"I understand," Nesseref said, as the male beside her let out a loud hiss of dismay. "What is the difficulty?"

"We have an airliner coming in for a landing a little low on fuel," the Tosevite answered. "Due to the short notice given for your arrival, we could not divert it to another airport. As soon as it is down, you will be cleared."

"Very well. I understand." Nesseref didn't see what else she could say. The other shuttlecraft pilot, the male, was twisting and wriggling as if he had the purple itch. Nesseref turned an anxious eye turret toward him. She hoped he didn't. The purple itch was highly infectious; she didn't want to have to have the cabin here sterilized.

"Hurry," the male kept muttering under his breath. "Please hurry."

After what wasn't a very long delay for Nesseref—but one that must have seemed an eternity to that male—the Big Ugly in the control tower radioed, "Shuttlecraft, you are cleared for takeoff. Again, apologies for the delay, and I hope your patient makes a full recovery."

"I thank you, Los Angeles Control." Nesseref's eye turrets swiveled as she gave the instruments one last check. After satisfying herself that everything read as it should, she said, "Control, I am beginning my countdown from one hundred. I shall launch at zero."

The countdown, of course, was electronic. As it neared the zero mark, her fingerclaw hovered over the ignition control. If the computer didn't trigger the shuttlecraft's motor, she would. But, again, everything went as it should. Ignition began precisely on schedule. Acceleration squashed her.

It squashed the other shuttlecraft pilot, too. Even so, he let out an exultant shout through the roar of the rocket: "Praise the Emperor and spirits of Emperors past, I am finally free!"

Nesseref asked him no questions till acceleration cut off and left them weightless and the shuttlecraft quiet. Then she said, "Can you tell me how you can sound so delighted in spite of an illness?"

"Shuttlecraft Pilot, I have no illness," the male answered, which, by then, wasn't the greatest surprise Nesseref had ever had. He went on, "Changes in my appearance are from makeup, which makes me look infirm and also disguises me. Nor, I must confess, do I share your rank. My name is Straha. Perhaps you will have heard of me."

Had Nesseref not kept her harness on, her startled jerk would have sent her floating around the cabin. "Straha the traitor?" she blurted.

"So they call me," the male replied. No, he was no shuttlecraft pilot; he'd been a shiplord, and a high-ranking one, before going over to the Big Uglies. He continued, "No—so, they called me. I have redeemed myself now."

"How?" Nesseref asked in genuine astonishment, wondering what could have made the Race welcome Straha once more. Something must have, or she wouldn't have been ordered to Los Angeles, and no one there would have helped him disguise himself to get to the shuttlecraft.

He answered, "I am sorry, but I had better not tell you that. Until the authorities decide what to do with this information, it should not be widely spread about."

"Is it as sensitive as that?" Nesseref asked, and Straha made the affirmative gesture. Once more, she wasn't very surprised. If he hadn't learned something important, the Race *wouldn't* have done anything for him.

Cairo Control came on the radio then, to report that the shuttlecraft's trajectory accorded with calculations. "But your departure was late," the control officer said in some annoyance. "We have had to put two aircraft in a holding pattern to accommodate your landing."

"My apologies," Nesseref said. "The Big Uglies held me up, because one of their aircraft was landing at the facility and lacked the fuel to go into a holding pattern."

"Inefficiency," the control officer said. "It is the Tosevites' besetting flaw. The only thing in which they are efficient is addling us."

"Truth," Nesseref said, while Straha's mouth opened wide in amusement.

Even though it hadn't been her fault, Nesseref felt bad about inconveniencing the aircraft her landing was delaying. Since she couldn't do anything about it, though, she put it out of her mind and concentrated on making sure the landing went perfectly. On her radar, she spotted not only those two aircraft but also helicopter gunships on patrol around the landing area.

Straha saw them, too, and understood what they meant. "I should be honored," he said. "Atvar does not want this shuttlecraft shot out of the sky."

"I too am thoroughly glad the fleetlord feels that way," Nesseref replied. "I have taken gunfire from the Big Uglies a couple of times while landing here, and I do not wish to do it again. There are too many parts of this planet where our rule is far less secure than it should be."

"If *I* had succeeded in overturning Atvar during the first round of fighting—" Straha began, but then he checked himself and laughed again, this time with a waggle in the lower jaw that showed wry amusement. He finished, "It is entirely possible that things might look no different, save that you would be flying Atvar here to see me and not the other way round. I like to think that would not be so, but I have no guarantee that what I like to think would be a truth."

Braking rockets roared. The shuttlecraft approached the concrete landing area. To Nesseref's vast relief, no fanatical Big Uglies opened fire on it: It settled to the surface of Tosev 3 as smoothly as it might have on a training video.

No mere mechanized combat vehicle came out to meet the shuttlecraft, but a clanking, slab-sided landcruiser. "The fleetlord takes your safety very seriously," Nesseref said to Straha. "I have not been met by a landcruiser here since my first descent to this city."

"Perhaps he worries about my security," Straha replied, "and perhaps he just wants to secure me." He sighed. "I have no choice but to find out. You, at least, Shuttlecraft Pilot, are sure to remain free." Nesseref pondered that as she and the renegade shiplord left the shuttlecraft and headed for the massive armored vehicle awaiting them.

Inside the Race's administrative center in what had once been known as Shepheard's Hotel, Atvar awaited the arrival of the landcruiser coming through Cairo from the shuttlecraft with all the delighted anticipation with which he would have faced a trip to the hospital for major surgery. "I hoped Straha would stay in the United States forever," he said to Kirel and Pshing. "As long as he remained out of my jurisdiction, I could pretend he did not exist. Believe me, such pretense left me not in the least unhappy."

"That is understandable, Exalted Fleetlord," Pshing answered. "Straha's defection, his treason, hurt us far more than any of the mutinies ordinary soldiers raised during the first round of fighting against the Big Uglies."

"Truth." Atvar sent his adjutant a grateful look. "And now, with what he has given us, I am not altogether sure I can punish him at all, let alone as he deserves for that treachery."

"What he has given us," Kirel said, "is, in a word, trouble. I would not have been altogether dismayed had that knowledge, like Straha himself, stayed far, far away. We shall have to calculate our response most carefully."

"We have always had to calculate our responses to Straha and everything that has to do with him most carefully," Atvar replied, to which Kirel returned the affirmative gesture. The two of them had been the only males in the conquest fleet who outranked Straha. What would Straha's rank be now? That, at the moment, was the least of Atvar's worries. But it would not be shiplord again—so he vowed.

He peered out the window toward the west, the direction from which the landcruiser would come. And there it was, like a bad dream brought to life. The outer armored gate of the compound slid back to admit it. As soon as it had gone through, the outer gate closed and the inner gate opened. The two gates were never open at the same time; that would have invited the Big Uglies to fire a gun or launch a rocket through them. *As if they need an invitation to make trouble,* Atvar thought.

A voice came from the intercom: "Exalted Fleetlord, the passenger has entered the compound."

"I thank you," Atvar replied, one of the larger lies he'd ever hatched. No one felt easy about speaking Straha's name in public. He'd been an object of reproach among the males of the conquest fleet since fleeing to the Americans, while males and females of the colonization fleet had trouble believing such a defection could have taken place; to them, it seemed like a melodrama set in the ancientest history of Home, back in the days before the Empire unified the planet. For a hundred thousand years, treason had been unimaginable—except to Straha.

"Exalted Fleetlord, ah, what shall we do with him now that he is here?" asked one of the males at the gate.

Shoot him as soon as he comes out of the landcruiser, Atvar thought. But, however much he was tempted to imitate the savage and barbarous Big Uglies, he refrained. "Send him here, to my office," he said. "No—escort him here. He will not know the way. The last time he had anything to do with the business of the conquest fleet, our headquarters were in space."

"It shall be done, Exalted Fleetlord," came the reply. The male down there was properly obedient, properly subordinate. Atvar wished he hadn't been.

Kirel spoke in musing tones: "I wonder what he will have to say for himself. Something clever, something sneaky—of that I have no doubt."

"Straha knows everything," Atvar said. "If you do not believe me, you have but to ask him."

Both Kirel and Pshing laughed. Then, as the door to the fleetlord's office opened, their mouths snapped shut. In strode Straha, two armed infantrymales flanking him. The first thing Atvar noticed was that he wouldn't have recognized Straha in a crowd. The next thing he noticed was that Straha's body paint was not as it should have been. Irony in his voice, the fleetlord said, "I greet you, Shuttlecraft Pilot."

Straha shrugged. "I needed the makeup and the false body paint to get away from the American Big Uglies. They worked." Only then did he bend into the posture of respect. "And I greet you, Exalted Fleetlord, even if neither of us much wants to see the other."

"Well, that is a truth, and I will not try to deny it," Atvar said. "You relieve me in one way, Straha: you are not claiming friendship, or even comradeship, as I feared you might."

"Not likely," Straha said, and appended an emphatic cough. "As I told you, I did not do what I did for your sake. I did it for the sake of my friend, the Big Ugly. Having done it, though, I thought I might get a warmer reception here than among the American Tosevites." He waggled an eye turret at Atvar. "Or was I wrong?"

"As a matter of fact, I truly am not sure," Atvar replied. "You know the harm you did the Race when you defected."

Straha made the affirmative gesture. "And I also know the service I just did the Race with those documents I sent you."

"Is it a service? I wonder." Straha spoke in musing tones.

"Fleetlord Reffet would reckon it one," Straha said slyly.

"Fleetlord Reffet's opinion . . ." Atvar checked himself. He did not care to advertise his long-running feud with the head of the colonization fleet. Picking his words with some care, he went on, "Fleetlord Reffet has had a bit of difficulty adapting to the unanticipated conditions existing on Tosev 3."

Straha laughed at that. "You think he is as stodgy as I always thought you were."

Atvar sighed. Evidently, he didn't need to advertise the feud. "There is some truth to that," he admitted. "But we have just fought one war that was harder and far more expensive than anyone thought it would be. There was, I am told, a Big Ugly who exclaimed, 'One more such victory and I am ruined,' after a fight of that sort. I understand the sentiment. I not only understand it, I agree with it. And so I am something less than delighted to receive these documents, though I cannot and do not deny their importance."

"Tosev 3 has changed you, too," Straha said in surprised tones. "It took longer to change you than it did me, but it managed."

"Perhaps," Atvar answered, knowing the renegade shiplord was right. "Tosev 3 changes everyone and everything it touches."

Straha made the affirmative gesture. "We discovered that even before we made planetfall," he said. "Now, if this were up to me, what I would do is—"

Atvar let out an angry hiss. Before he could turn that hiss into coherent speech, Kirel said, "I see there is one way in which

Tosev 3 has not changed you at all, Straha: you still want to give orders, even when you are not entitled to do so."

"Truth," Pshing put in.

Straha ignored Pshing. He did not ignore Kirel. "You have not changed, either: you hatched out of Atvar's eggshell right behind him."

"And something else has not changed," Atvar said: "We are taking up the quarrels that preoccupied us before your defection as if you had never left. It is, if you like, a tribute to the power of your personality."

"For which I thank you." Yes, Straha sounded smug. Atvar had been sure he would.

The fleetlord went on, "But Shiplord Kirel is correct. You do continue to seek to take command where you have no authority. It is possible"—the words tasted bad on Atvar's tongue—"it is possible, I say, that by providing these documents to the Race you have made it unnecessary for us to punish you for defecting."

Straha's hissing sigh held nothing but relief. "You *are* stodgy, Atvar, even yet. But you do have integrity. I thought you would. I counted on it, in fact."

"Do not waste praise too soon," Atvar warned. "You may perhaps be allowed to live once more in lands the Race rules, to rejoin the society of your kind. But, Straha, I am going to tell you something that is not only possible but certain: you will live here as an ordinary citizen, as a civilian. If you think for an instant that your past rank will be restored to you, you are completely and utterly addled. Do you understand me?"

He watched the male who had come so close to overthrowing him, watched with the greatest and closest attention. Ever so slowly, ever so reluctantly, Straha made the affirmative gesture. But then, still full of self-importance, the ex-shiplord said, "A civilian, yes, but not, I hope, an ordinary one. When I went over to the Americans, they interrogated me most thoroughly on matters pertaining to the Race. Now that I have lived so long in the United States, do you not believe I will know things about these Big Uglies you could not learn elsewhere?"

"Well, that is undoubtedly a truth," Atvar agreed. "We will indeed debrief you, and no doubt you will provide us with some valuable insights. Perhaps we will even use you as a consultant, should the need arise." He gave his old rival such salve for his pride as he could before going on, "But I repeat: under no circumstances will you ever return to the chain of command."

"Count yourself lucky that you enjoy the fleetlord's mercy," Kirel added. "Were his body paint on my torso, you would not be so fortunate."

"Were the fleetlord's body paint on your torso, Kirel, the Big Uglies would be ruling all of Tosev 3," Straha said.

Unadulterated fury filled Kirel's hiss. "Enough!" Atvar said loudly, and tacked on an emphatic cough. "Too much, in fact. Straha, you would do well to remember that your continued well-being depends on our goodwill. For example, you are known to be a ginger addict. Perhaps, in gratitude for the services you have performed, a supply of the herb will quietly be granted you. On the other fork of the tongue, perhaps it will not."

Straha shot him a baleful glare. "Maybe I spoke too soon when I praised your integrity."

"Maybe you did." Atvar gestured to the guards who had accompanied the returned renegade into his office. "Take him to Security. Let his interrogation begin now. Tell the staff there that I will want him questioned by particular experts in Tosevite affairs. I do not wish to lose any possible information we might gain from him."

"It shall be done, Exalted Fleetlord," the more senior of the two guards said. He and his comrades led Straha away.

The door had hardly closed behind them before Kirel said, "As far as I am concerned, the Americans were welcome to him."

"I agree," Atvar said. "But he *is* here, and he *has* given us valuable information." He paused for a moment. "And oh, by the Emperor and by the spirits of Emperors past, how I wish he had not!"

"Exalted Fleetlord, we have sought this information for years," Pshing said.

"Yes, and now, having obtained it, we are going to have to act upon it, one way or another," Atvar said. "I was not lying when I told Straha this war would be harder than the one we fought against the *Reich*. The American Big Uglies have a larger land mass, more industrial capacity, a larger presence in space, and, if reports are correct, more missile-carrying submarines full of explosive-metal bombs. I do not relish the prospect of fighting them."

"Given all this, how can we possibly avoid fighting them?" Kirel asked.

"I do not know the answer to that, either," Atvar said unhappily. "And I blame Straha for putting me in this predicament." As long as the renegade had returned, Atvar intended to blame him for everything he could.

Ttomalss had not wanted to go down to the surface of Tosev 3 again. His visit to China had found him a prisoner of the Big Uglies. His visit to the Greater German *Reich* hadn't involved him in any physical danger, but had been acutely frustrating, leaving him wondering whether the Deutsche truly were rational beings. The hopeless war they'd launched against the Race had shown him he'd had good reason to wonder, too.

But, when the fleetlord of the conquest fleet personally commanded him to report to the Race's administrative center in Cairo, what choice had he? None whatever, and he knew it. And, he had to admit, the prospect of talking about the Big Uglies with a returned expatriate was intriguing.

Traveling from the shuttlecraft port to Shepheard's Hotel—for some reason, the Tosevite name had stuck—was almost enough to give him a panic attack. Cairo reminded him too much of Peking, where he'd been kidnapped, in its astonishing crowding and equally astonishing medley of stinks. Oh, the Big Uglies here wore different kinds of wrappings and spoke a different language—the bits of Chinese he remembered did him no good at all—but those, he thought, were incidentals. The essences of the two places struck him as being all too similar.

When he got his first look at the administrative center, he exclaimed, "This was once a place where Big Uglies came for pleasure? I know Tosevites are addled, but the notion strikes me as improbable even so."

With a laugh, the male who was driving him replied, "We have somewhat improved the defensive perimeter, superior sir."

"Somewhat, yes," Ttomalss replied with what he thought of as commendable understatement. "I note a double wall, machine-gun emplacements, and rocket emplacements. I am sure there are also many other things I do not note."

"That would be an accurate assumption, yes, superior sir," the driver said as the first armored gate opened for his vehicle.

When the second gate closed behind it, Ttomalss said, "I must

admit, I feel a good deal more secure now. This may be an illusion—
I know such things often are on Tosev 3—but the feeling is not to be
despised anyhow."

The chamber to which he was assigned had plainly been built
with Big Uglies in mind. Its proportions—especially the high
ceiling—and the plumbing fixtures proclaimed as much. But the
sleeping mat, the furniture, the computer in its little alcove, and
the heating system that made sure Tosevite chill did not creep into
the room made it tolerable, perhaps even better than tolerable.

As soon as Ttomalss had stowed his effects (which didn't take
long; he wasn't a Tosevite, to have to worry about endless suitcases full of wrappings), he telephoned Straha. The computer in
the ex-shiplord's chamber said he was out and could not be immediately reached, which annoyed Ttomalss till he realized he
couldn't be the only member of the Race questioning Straha. He
recorded a message and settled down at the computer to find out
what had happened in space and around Tosev 3 while he was
traveling down from the starship and making his way through
Cairo.

None of the news channels mentioned Straha's return to the
eggshell of the Race or the inflammatory information that had
made the return possible. That struck Ttomalss as wise; things
would only be worse if a public clamor made coming to a wise
decision more difficult. The lead story was consolidation of the
Race's informal control over the subregion called France.
Ttomalss heartily approved of that. Informal control did not
seem to raise the Big Uglies' ire, and had a good chance of
leading to formal control some time in the future.

Ttomalss was still getting the details of the story about France
when the computer's telephone attachment hissed. "I greet you,"
he said.

"And I greet you, Senior Researcher." The male a screen
window showed was wearing the body paint of a shuttlecraft
pilot, not a shiplord.

That presented Ttomalss with a problem. After giving his own
name, he asked, "How shall I address you?"

"Superior Nuisance seems to fit," Straha answered, and
Ttomalss' mouth fell open in startled laughter. The renegade
went on, "The Big Ugly named Sam Yeager respects your work,
Senior Researcher, for whatever that may be worth to you."

"Praise from one who does good work himself is praise indeed," Ttomalss said. "I have met Sam Yeager only briefly, but I know his hatchling, Jonathan Yeager, a good deal better. He shows considerable promise. And I am familiar with the older Tosevite's work. He is perceptive."

"He is more than perceptive. There are times when I wonder if he somehow had the spirit of a male of the Race hatched by mistake into a Big Ugly's body," Straha said. "When I was in exile, he was the best friend I had, regardless of species."

"I see." Ttomalss wondered what that said about Straha and about the expatriates from the Race in the United States.

"Do you?" Straha said. "I doubt it. Did anyone tell you that I did what I did not for the sake of the Race but for the sake of Sam Yeager, to try to save him from the difficulties into which he seems to have fallen with officials of the government of his own not-empire?"

"Yes, I was informed of that," Ttomalss said. "It does not particularly surprise me. Ties of kinship are stronger among the Big Uglies than they are among us. Ties of friendship are stronger among us than among them. This bespeaks our higher degree of civilization: an individual chooses his friends, but has no control over who his kinsfolk are. Still, a friendship across species lines is somewhat out of the ordinary."

"Sam Yeager is no ordinary Big Ugly, as you have already admitted," Straha said. "I hope he is safe and unharmed; the Tosevites play political games more violently than we do." The renegade paused. "The other thing I will note, Senior Researcher, is that I am no ordinary male of the Race."

"You could not have made yourself so difficult if you were," Ttomalss replied.

"Truth." Straha used an emphatic cough. Fortunately, he took the comment as praise rather than the reverse. "And I am proud to note that I have proved as difficult for the Tosevites as I have for the Race." He waggled one eye turret at Ttomalss. "And now, I have no doubt, you will want to put me under the microscope, the way all these other snoops have done."

"It is my duty." But Ttomalss wondered how much Straha cared about duty. He had abandoned first the Race and then the American Big Uglies when expedience seemed to dictate such a course. That sort of untrammeled individualism was more typical of Tosevites than of his kind.

"Well, go ahead, then." Straha suddenly sounded amiable—so amiable, it made Ttomalss suspicious.

But he had the invitation, and would do his best to make the most of it. "Very well. How is it that you put the Tosevite Yeager's welfare above that of any male of the Race?"

"Why should I not?" When Straha returned a question for a question, Ttomalss' certainty that he was in for a difficult time hardened. But then the ex-shiplord condescended to explain: "I have become more intimately acquainted with him than with any male of the Race on Tosev 3. I like him better, too. He is both intelligent and reliable. And he obtained the information I sent on to Atvar at considerable risk to himself. I do not even know if he is presently living. If he is not, I am more certain the spirits of Emperors past will cherish his spirit than those of a good many males of the Race I could name."

That was a more detailed answer than Ttomalss had expected. Straha showed a good deal of hostility toward the Race, but a defector could hardly be expected to show anything else. Ttomalss tried a related question: "Do you believe Yeager's virtues, as you describe them, reflect him as an individual or the not-empire from which he comes?"

"Now that is an *interesting* question," Straha said. "One can tell you are a true psychological researcher and not one of those males from Security, whose vision is so narrowly focused, they might as well have no eye turrets at all."

"I thank you," Ttomalss said, his voice dry. "Now, instead of praising the question, would you be so kind as to answer it?"

Straha laughed. "If I happen to feel like it," he said. "Do you enjoy this chance to be rude to a male whose proper rank is so much higher than your own?"

That was a well-aimed claw. Ttomalss had to look inside himself before replying, "Yes, perhaps I do." After a heartbeat's pause, he added, "And you still have not answered the question."

"Since you show a certain basic honesty, perhaps I will." Straha still sounded amused. "I fear the answer will be more ambiguous than you might prefer, however."

"Life is full of ambiguities," Ttomalss said.

"Well, well. My congratulations," Straha told him. "You are not a hatchling any more. You have become an adult."

More than half mockingly, Ttomalss bent into the posture of

respect. "Once more, I thank you," he said. "And, once more, you have not answered."

He wondered if Straha would keep on playing word games with him, but the ex-shiplord just said, "Oh, very well. Part of it is Yeager as Yeager, and part is Yeager as an American. That not-empire stresses individualism to a degree the Race finds incomprehensible. Good Big Uglies can be very fine indeed under that system, and Yeager is. Bad Big Uglies have full scope for their evil, inept ones for their incompetence. There are many great successes in the United States, and as many dreadful failures."

"Yes, I have heard something of this," Ttomalss said. "In my view, it is freedom turned to license."

"I think the same thing," Straha said. "Do you know that, not long after the ships of the colonization fleet were attacked, I told an American reporter I believed his not-empire had made the assault? He was fully prepared to print the story in a leading periodical until I explained I was merely yanking his tailstump."

"The government of the United States would never have permitted such a story to appear," Ttomalss said.

"So I thought as well, Senior Researcher, but he assured me I was wrong. Other American Big Uglies have told me the same thing," Straha said. "The Americans insist that an altogether untrammeled flow of information produces the most rapid progress—their preferred word for change. If progress is seen as desirable, one would be hard pressed to disagree with them."

"Amazing," Ttomalss said. Even he was unsure whether he meant the American Tosevites' preposterous lack of concern for security or their astonishing pace of technological change.

"There is, I trust you will agree, a certain irony to my present situation," Straha said.

"Oh, indeed," Ttomalss replied. "But then, your situation in the United States was full of irony almost from the beginning, was it not? Most of what has changed lately is the scope of things."

"I like the way you put that: the scope of things," Straha said. "Before, the Big Uglies used me without much trusting me because I had betrayed the Race. Now the Race will use me without much trusting me because I am betraying the Americans. This leaves me nowhere to go, no one to turn to."

Ttomalss had wondered if Straha fully understood his own

situation. Hearing that, the psychological researcher decided he had one less thing to worry about.

Because of whom she knew, Kassquit found herself sitting on several secrets that, when they hatched from their eggs, might go up like explosive-metal bombs. The first electronic message from Jonathan Yeager asking for the Race's help in locating his father had come some days before.

I shall do what I can, she'd written back. *I do not know how much that will be.*

She had liked Sam Yeager well enough in their couple of meetings, and rather better than well enough in their electronic correspondence. But her feelings for Jonathan Yeager were the main factor in her seeking to help his father.

She had telephoned Reffet's office first of all. Because she'd discovered that Sam Yeager, wild Tosevite, was roaming the Race's electronic network, she thought she might get prompt attention from the fleetlord. And, in fact, she did; he returned her call quite quickly. When she explained what she wanted and why, he said, "As a matter of fact, that matter is already under investigation. No decision has yet been made as to whether to raise it with the relevant Tosevite authorities."

"I . . . see," Kassquit said, not seeing at all. "There is some concern for this Big Ugly's safety."

"I understand that," Reffet said. "There is concern for more than the safety of this one Big Ugly, I assure you."

That was all he would say. Kassquit tried calling Fleetlord Atvar, but his adjutant would not forward her call. She reported the curious and not altogether satisfactory conversations to Jonathan Yeager.

And then, almost without warning, Ttomalss departed for the surface of Tosev 3. "I must aid in the interrogation of a returned defector, a shiplord who has spent almost all of his time on Tosev 3 in the not-empire of the United States," he said.

"The infamous Straha?" Kassquit asked, and Ttomalss made the affirmative gesture. Kassquit's mind leaped. "Does his arrival have anything to do with the disappearance of the Big Ugly called Sam Yeager?"

She succeeded in astonishing her mentor. "How could you possibly know that?" Ttomalss demanded.

"I am, you will remember, still in touch with Jonathan

Yeager," Kassquit replied, "and I know that Sam Yeager and Straha are acquaintances. The connection struck me as logical."

"I . . . see," Ttomalss said, much as Kassquit had to Reffet. "That is very perceptive of you. My data indicate that Sam Yeager and Straha are not merely acquaintances but friends. I hope to confirm this in discussion with Straha." He paused. "That remark, in fact, was perceptive enough to make me believe you deserve to wear your junior researcher's body paint not merely to show you are my ward and my apprentice, but with all appropriate rights and privileges. Would you like me to initiate the approval process when I find the time?"

"I thank you, superior sir," Kassquit exclaimed. "That would be very generous of you." It would also give her a secure place of her own in the Race's hierarchy, which was not to be despised. And . . . "How your colleagues who disliked you for undertaking to raise a Big Ugly hatchling will be discomfited to see that hatchling taking a place in their profession."

"I have not even the faintest notion of what you are talking about," Ttomalss said, so matter-of-factly that Kassquit almost failed to notice the irony.

Then he'd gone down to the surface of Tosev 3. He kept in touch with Kassquit through electronic messages and telephone calls. Jonathan Yeager also kept in touch with her through electronic messages. The wild Big Ugly, she gradually realized, was frantic with concern over his father's safety. Kassquit wondered if anyone would ever feel that much concern for her. She doubted it; such things were not in the style of the Race. Noting his intensity made her wish they were.

Do you know why your father has disappeared? she wrote him.

Of course I do, he wrote back. *He disappeared because he knew too much.* He added the Race's conventional symbol for an emphatic cough.

Too much about what? Kassquit asked.

About things it was dangerous to know about, Jonathan Yeager replied.

"Well, of course," Kassquit said with a snort when she saw that. She wrote, *What sorts of things?*

I told you: the sorts of things that are dangerous to know, the wild Big Ugly answered.

That made Kassquit hiss in annoyance. Jonathan Yeager was

being deliberately obscure. His father had played the same sorts of games with electronic messages. After a moment, though, her annoyance subsided. *Are you not being more specific for reasons related to security?* she inquired.

Exactly so, he replied. *I am sorry, but that is how things are. If you knew everything, it might put you in danger, and it might put me in more danger than I am already in, too.*

Kassquit hadn't thought about danger to Jonathan Yeager. Once she did think about it, though, it made sense. If Sam Yeager had disappeared because of something he knew, and if Jonathan Yeager knew the same thing, logic dictated that he too might disappear. Kassquit did make one attempt to learn more, writing, *If this knowledge is dangerous, perhaps you should pass it on so that it is not lost if something unfortunate happens to you.*

I thank you, but I think I had better not, wrote the wild Big Ugly who had been her lover—an English word he used to describe a relationship with which the Race was not familiar. *I also think my father took care of this matter, to make sure the data would not disappear with him.*

Puzzle pieces that hadn't quite fit together now suddenly did. *He passed the data on to the Shiplord Straha, who brought them to Cairo with him,* Kassquit wrote. She did not include the conventional symbol for an interrogative cough.

Jonathan Yeager waited longer before replying this time, as if thinking through just what his response ought to be. When it finally came, it was cautious: *I believe that to be a truth, yes.* He broke off the electronic conversation a little later, perhaps from concern that he might reveal too much.

What he'd already said was enough—much more than enough—to stimulate Kassquit's always active curiosity. Straha had been a stench in the scent receptors of the Race ever since his spectacular defection. He had been favorably received on his return to Cairo. Kassquit knew that from Ttomalss. He had to have learned something important to get a favorable reception from Atvar. That reinforced the notion that Sam Yeager had known something vital and passed it on to the renegade shiplord.

The next time she spoke with Ttomalss, she asked him, "What spectacular piece of information did Straha learn from Sam Yeager?"

She was pleased when Ttomalss did not bother pretending he had no idea of what she was talking about. What he did say was,

"I had better not tell you. The information is inflammatory enough that I am lucky—if that is the word I want, which I doubt—to have been entrusted with it myself."

"Whom would I tell?" Kassquit asked. "Who among the Race would want to learn anything from me? Please remember, superior sir, I am nothing but a Big Ugly from an orphaned clutch." The metaphor fit imperfectly, but it was the only one the Race had. "Few take me seriously. What you tell me would stay safe and secure."

Ttomalss laughed. "You are ingenious. I cannot deny that. In fact, I applaud it. Few in the Race would have thought to use outcast status as a justification for receiving sensitive data. Even so, I am afraid I must tell you no. The secrecy classification for this data is too red for me to have any other choice."

"By the Emperor!" Kassquit exclaimed, irked that her ploy had failed. "By the way you make things sound, we might be at war with another Tosevite not-empire by this time tomorrow."

"Truth," Ttomalss said. "We might be." And then, as Jonathan Yeager had before him, he ended his conversation with Kassquit as fast as he could.

"By the Emperor!" she said again, and again looked down at the floor of her cubicle to show reverence for a male she'd never seen and never would see. "Is it as bad as that?" It almost surely was; Ttomalss, as she knew from a lifetime of experience, was not the sort to panic over nothing.

What could Straha know? The question tormented her, like an itch under the scales. She laughed when the simile crossed her mind, laughed and ran a hand along her smooth, scaleless skin. No, the language of the Race and its images did not always fit her well. That she could laugh instead of mourning said she was in a better mood than usual.

But laughing brought her no closer to the truth, whatever that was, wherever it lay. What could Straha know? What could Sam Yeager have known? How was she supposed to figure that out when she'd never set foot on the surface of Tosev 3? Whatever it was, though, it had to be something that had to do with the Race. Maybe her not setting foot on Tosev 3 didn't matter after all.

I should not be guessing, she thought. *I should know. The data are all in front of me.* Some of the Race's games, played either in groups or against a computer, involved solving elaborate puzzles where all the relevant pieces and many that were not were displayed together. This was like one of those games, except she wasn't sure she could see all the pieces.

As in those games, she could pause and review the evidence. She didn't have access to the conversations she and Sam Yeager had had when he visited the starship; Ttomalss and other psychological researchers endlessly studied those recordings for what they revealed about how Big Uglies thought. But she could go over all the electronic conversations she'd had with the wild Tosevite—those where he admitted his species and also those in which he appeared as Regeya and Maargyees—fictitious members of the Race under whose names he'd managed to sneak onto the electronic network.

Kassquit discovered she enjoyed reviewing those messages. Sam Yeager had an odd and interesting slant on the world. Part of that, of course, was because he wasn't really a male of the Race. His perspectives were alien. But part, she'd gathered from meeting Jonathan Yeager and the Deutsch pilot Johannes Drucker, was Sam Yeager himself. He had an odd and interesting slant on the world even compared to other Big Uglies.

He also had wide-ranging interests, wide-ranging curiosity. That, Kassquit knew, was more common among Tosevites than among the Race. But, even for a Tosevite, Sam Yeager had a sense of what was interesting that swooped and darted and landed in unpredictable places.

Among them . . . Kassquit paused and reread a few of the things Sam Yeager had said in the guise of Regeya. She let out a soft, speculative hiss, very much as if she were in truth the female of the Race she wished herself to be. She didn't know. She couldn't know, not without asking some questions to which she wouldn't get answers: Ttomalss had already told her that those answers, whatever they were, were too secret for her to be allowed to learn them.

No, she didn't, couldn't, know. But she had what she thought was a pretty good idea. She almost wished she didn't. The Deutsche had come much too close to destroying this starship, and had destroyed too much that was the Race's. Now, she feared, the Americans might get their chance.

Glen Johnson was sleeping when alarms inside the *Lewis and Clark* started screaming. He jerked and thrashed and tried to get out of his sleep sack without undoing the straps that secured him in it. That didn't work. He had to wait till his brain fully engaged before his hands could reach for and open the fastening.

"Screw you, Brigadier General Healey," he muttered as the sirens howled insistently. He understood the need for periodic drills. He just resented having this one wake him up. Anything he resented, he blamed on the spaceship's short-tempered commandant. That seemed fair. Whenever Healey found something he didn't like, he blamed Johnson.

The number-three pilot had just pushed off toward the doorway to his cubicle when he realized what sort of drill it was. The ones the *Lewis and Clark* ran most often were pressure-loss drills, because that was the sort of misfortune likeliest to strike. Not this time. This set of sirens was summoning the spaceship's crew to battle stations.

"Jesus!" Johnson muttered as he swung hand over hand to the control room. He couldn't remember the last time the ship had run a battle-stations drill. He couldn't remember any battle-stations drills. That made him wonder if it was a drill.

If it's not, we go down swinging, he thought. That wasn't a good thought to have, not when they wouldn't even take out any Lizards while they fought. The Race's machines would do the dirty work.

He almost bumped into Mickey Flynn at the entrance to the control room. They did an Alphonse and Gaston act—after you; no, after *you*—before Flynn preceded him into the *Lewis and Clark*'s nerve center. Walter Stone was already there; it was his shift.

"Well?" Flynn asked. "Are we radioactive dust?"

"Gas," Stone answered. "Radioactive gas."

"I am wounded," Flynn declared. Wounded or not, he strapped himself into his chair.

Johnson got into the seat behind those of the two men senior to him. "What the hell's going on?" he asked. "This *is* a drill, isn't it?" *Please, God, tell me it's a drill.*

"We're not under attack," Stone said. "All the Lizard spy ships we've identified are sitting there quietly. If there are any we haven't identified, they're sitting there quietly, too."

Even before Johnson had finished his sigh of relief, Flynn said, "The assumption here, of course, is that they may not necessarily keep on sitting there quietly. I've heard assumptions I liked better."

"Now that you mention it, so have I," Johnson said. "They haven't shown hostility since we first spotted them. Why are we worried all of a sudden?"

From behind him, a rough voice said, "You always were a nosy son of a bitch, weren't you, Johnson?"

"Yes, sir, General Healey," Johnson answered. As far as he was concerned, Brigadier General Charles Healey won the SOB prize hands down. He turned around and smiled into the commandant's hard, blunt-featured face. "It's made me what I am today, sir."

Healey didn't like taking sarcasm; he preferred dishing it out. After muttering under his breath, he said, "You're plainly supernumerary here. Perhaps your station ought to be out in the scooter, engaging targets from the flank."

"If you say so, sir." Johnson shrugged. It wasn't even a bad idea. He didn't think it would help much—he didn't think anything would help much against a determined Lizard attack—but it wouldn't hurt, either. Of course, if things went wrong, as they were bound to do, he'd have the loneliest death in the solar system. "Tell me where to go, and I'll go there."

He knew Healey would rise to the line like a trout rising to a fly. But before Healey could say anything, Walter Stone asked, "Sir, what the devil *is* going on?"

Stone could get away with questions like that; the commandant approved of him. Brigadier General Healey scowled and sighed and answered, "Things are heating up between Cairo and Little Rock. I don't know why, exactly"—the scowl got deeper; he didn't like not knowing—"but they are. We need to be ready for whatever happens."

"I've heard news I liked better," Mickey Flynn observed.

"Me, too," Stone agreed. "What touched this off, sir? President Warren's not crazy, the way the Nazis were. He couldn't be threatening the Lizards."

"He's not," Healey said. "They're angry at us, and I don't know just why. I told you that." He shook his head, annoyed at having to repeat himself.

"If they want to bad enough, they can wipe us right out of the asteroid belt, and that's with the ship full of johnny-come-latelies," Johnson said. Healey gave him another venomous look, presumably for seeing the truth and presuming to tell it.

"If they want to bad enough, they can wipe us off the face of the Earth," Flynn said.

"We'd hurt 'em if they tried it." Healey's voice was savage. "We'd hurt 'em a lot worse than the Germans did. We're stronger to begin with, and the Nazis already gave their defenses one good pounding."

Johnson nodded at that. Every word the commandant said was true. And yet . . . He didn't have to put *and yet* into words. Walter Stone did it for him: "Mickey's right, sir. I'm not saying you're wrong. We'd hurt 'em. We'd hurt 'em plenty. But if they wanted to, they could smash us back to the Stone Age."

"They'd really have to want to," Johnson said. "That's the point of all the bombs and rockets and submarines. They'd know they were in a fight."

"Another few years," Healey muttered. "Maybe just another couple of years. Another couple of years and the goddamn Lizards would have been talking out of the other side of their snouts. You boys all know it. That's why we're here."

"One of the reasons, anyhow," Flynn said.

"The A-number-one reason, and you know it as well as I do," Healey ground out. He scowled at Mickey Flynn, challenging him to disagree. The *Lewis and Clark*'s number-two pilot maintained a discreet silence.

"There are a few other things going on," Johnson said. "The mining, the colonies on every rock where we can run up a dome—we haven't just come out here to fight a war. We're here to stay, if we can do a little more spreading out before the Lizards try and drop the hammer on us."

"All sorts of good things here," Stone agreed. "The Race doesn't have any real notion of how many goodies there are, either. From what they say, the solar systems in their Empire are tidier places than ours."

"Smaller suns," Mickey Flynn said. "Fewer leftover chunks of rock after their planets formed." An eyebrow quirked. "They don't know what they're missing."

"If they give us the time we need, it won't be missing them," Johnson said.

Brigadier General Healey gave him a nasty look. "Don't violate security," he snapped.

And that did it. Johnson lost his temper. "Christ on a crutch, sir, give it a rest," he said. "I'm not on the radio to the Race, and we all know what's going on."

"You're insubordinate," Healey said.

"Maybe I am—and maybe it's about time, too," Johnson retorted. "Somebody's needed to tell you to go piss up a rope ever since before we left Earth orbit. If I'm the one stuck belling the cat, okay, I am, that's all."

"You have been nothing but trouble since you came aboard this spacecraft," Healey said. "I should have put you out the air lock then."

"Oh, he has his uses, sir," Flynn said. "After all, whose money would we take in card games if he weren't here?"

That was slander; Johnson more than held his own. But it distracted the commandant—and Johnson, too. Stone continued the work of changing the subject: "If the Lizards are angry enough at us now, what we might be able to do in a few years doesn't matter. Remember the *Hermann Göring*." The *Reich*'s imitation of the *Lewis and Clark* had been blown to atoms during the last round of fighting. Stone went on, "So why the devil *are* the Lizards ticked at us?"

Brigadier General Healey shook his head. "I do not have that information. I already told you I don't have it. I wish to God I did." Every inch of him screamed that he thought he was entitled to the information, and that he blamed people back on Earth for withholding it from him. "The Lizards are playing it close to their scales, too, dammit. You'd think they'd be screaming from the housetops if they caught us doing something we weren't supposed to, but they aren't."

Thoughtfully, Stone said, "Sounds like they will fight if they're pushed, but they don't want to do it unless they decide they have to."

"But they're pushing us," Healey said. "That's what makes this such a confusing mess."

"Have they given us any demands?" Flynn asked.

"Nothing I've heard." The commandant sounded all the more frustrated. "And I should hear, God damn it to hell. How am I supposed to do my job if I don't know what the devil is going on?"

"What it sounds like is, if anybody admitted what the fuss was about, everything would go up in smoke right then and there," Johnson said.

Brigadier General Healey nodded as if he and Johnson hadn't had words a few minutes before. The riddle facing him was a bigger source of irritation than even his number-three pilot. "You're right—and that doesn't make any sense, either."

"Nothing makes sense if you don't know the answers," Mickey Flynn observed. "The people who do know the answers must have, or think they have, good reason to make sure nobody else finds out. We call them senseless. They call us ignorant. Odds are, we and they are both right."

"They'd better not be senseless, or all of us—and an awful lot of people and Lizards back on Earth—are in a ton of trouble," Johnson said.

"This is true," Flynn agreed. "On the other hand, I could refer you to the late Doctor Ernst Kaltenbrunner—if he weren't late, of course. He was senseless, and now he is and will remain permanently senseless."

Johnson grimaced and protested, "Yeah, but the Nazis have been off the deep end ever since Hitler started slaughtering Jews. We aren't like that. We've always played straight." He hesitated. "We played straight with everything I know about except the *Lewis and Clark*, as a matter of fact."

"It's not us," Healey said. "I have been assured of that. Had it been us, the Race has had plenty of chances to take us off the board."

And that was also true. Then Johnson said, "What if we haven't played straight with things nobody up here knows anything about?"

"Like what?" Walter Stone asked.

"How should I know?" Johnson answered. "If I did know, it wouldn't be something nobody knew about."

"Elementary, my dear Watson," Flynn murmured.

"What if, what if, what if," Brigadier General Healey snarled. "What we need are facts. The only fact we've got is that the Race is leaning on the United States. If it leans too hard, we've got to fight back or knuckle under. We're not about to knuckle under."

"Well, there's one other fact, too," Johnson said. "If the USA goes to war with the Lizards now, we lose. And no matter how many drills we hold, the *Lewis and Clark* is lunch." He waited—he hoped for—Healey to argue with him. The commandant didn't.

* * *

"Why on earth are the Lizards gearing up for war against the United States?" Reuven Russie asked his father over the supper table. "Has everybody in the whole world gone *meshuggeh*?"

Moishe Russie said, "I wouldn't be surprised. It's the only explanation that makes much sense."

"Have you talked with the fleetlord?" Reuven's sister Judith asked.

"I've called him several times," Reuven's father answered. "Most of them, he hasn't wanted to talk to me. When he has been willing to talk on the phone, he hasn't had anything much to say."

"But what could the United States have done to get the Race so angry?" Reuven asked. "With the Germans, everybody else had plenty of good reasons to hate them. But the USA has just sat there and minded its own business. What's wrong with that?"

"I don't know," his father said. "Since he won't really talk to me, I'm having a devil of a time finding out, too. But I can tell you this—Straha is back in the Race's territory, and that's not anything I thought I'd see while I was alive."

It was also something that meant very little to Reuven. "Straha?" He put the name into a question half a beat before his sisters could.

Moishe Russie's smile was half amused, half wistful. "You were only a little boy when he defected to the Americans, Reuven," he said. "Esther and Judith, you weren't even imagined yet, let alone here. He was something like the third- or fourth-highest ranking male in the conquest fleet. He tried some sort of coup against Atvar, and it didn't work, and he fled."

"I don't suppose you're going to ask the fleetlord about the details now," Reuven said.

His mother laughed. "See what your fancy education does for you?"

"Mother!" he said indignantly. His father made cracks like that all the time. His sisters made them whenever they thought they could get away with them. For Rivka Russie to make one, too, felt like a betrayal.

"But the point," his father said, "the point is that he's left the United States and come to Cairo—I think he's in Cairo. He had to know something important, or else he'd be imprisoned some-where, and he's not."

"And it's probably something that has to do with the United States, since he lived there so long," Reuven said.

"Very good, Sherlock." That was Esther, who'd been reading a lot of Arthur Conan Doyle in Hebrew translation. "Now all you have to do is figure out what he knows."

Reuven looked at his father. Moishe Russie shrugged and said, "I already told you, I don't know. Maybe we'll all find out one day before too long. I'm hoping we never find out, because that will mean the trouble's gone away."

"I hadn't thought of it like that." Reuven took another bite of beefsteak. He raised his wineglass. "Here's to ignorance!"

Everyone drank the toast. Amid laughter, Reuven's father said, "That's probably the first time anyone has ever made that toast inside a Jewish house. *Alevai,* it'll be the last time, too." His face clouded. "*Alevai,* we won't need to make that kind of toast again."

"*Omayn.*" Reuven and his mother spoke together.

After supper, Reuven asked his father, "If the United States and the Lizards go to war, what do we do?"

"We here in Palestine, you mean?" Moishe Russie asked, and Reuven nodded. His father sighed. "About the same thing we did when the Race fought the Germans: sit tight and hope the Americans don't manage to land a missile on Jerusalem. I think that would be less likely in this fight than in the war with the Nazis. The Americans don't particularly hate Jews, so they don't have any big reason for aiming a missile here—and most of their missiles are farther away than the ones the Germans fired at us."

"How do you know that?" Reuven asked. "They may have three submarines sitting right off the coast. How would we know?"

"We wouldn't, not until something either happened or didn't," his father said. "I told you what I thought was likely. If you don't like that, come up with your own answers."

"I like it fine. I hope you're right," Reuven said. "Actually, I hope we're all worrying over nothing, and that there won't be a war."

This time, his father said, *"Omayn!"*

When they walked to work the next morning, someone had painted new black swastikas on several walls, and the phrase *Al-*

lahu akbar! by them. Reuven laughed to keep from cursing. "Haven't the Arabs noticed that that firm's gone out of business?"

"Who can say?" Moishe Russie answered. "Maybe they wish it were still operating. Or maybe it is still operating, but being quiet about it. That wouldn't surprise me. Once some things get loose, they're hard to kill."

"I thought Dornberger was supposed to be a relatively civilized man," Reuven said.

"Compared to Hitler, compared to Himmler, compared to Kaltenbrunner—how much praise is that?" his father asked. "He's still a German. He's still a Nazi. If he can find some way to make the Lizards unhappy, don't you think he'll use it? Getting the Arabs to erupt is one easy way to do it."

"And if he incites them against us, too, all the better," Reuven said. His father didn't contradict him. He wished Moishe Russie had.

Once they got to the office, Yetta showed them their appointments. Reuven sighed. When he'd been studying at the Moishe Russie Medical College, human physiology and biochemistry had looked like important subjects. And they'd looked like fascinating subjects. Seeing them exemplified in the persons of his patients was much less exciting. A lot of the answers he got were ambiguous. Sometimes he couldn't find any answers at all. And even a lot of the ones that were perfectly clear weren't very interesting. Yes, sir, that boil will respond to antibiotics. Yes, ma'am, that toe is broken. No, it doesn't matter if we put a cast on it or not. It'll do the same either way, and yes, it will hurt for a few weeks.

He gave a tetanus shot. He removed a splinter of metal that had got lodged in a construction worker's leg. He took the cast off a broken wrist his father had set a few weeks before. He swabbed a four-year-old's throat to see if the girl was coming down with a streptococcus infection. He injected local anesthetic and stitched up a cut arm. Every bit of that needed doing. He did it well. But it wasn't what he'd imagined a physician's career was like.

He was putting a clean dressing on the cut arm when Yetta stuck her head into the room and said, "Mrs. Radofsky just telephoned. Her daughter is screaming her head off—she thinks it's an earache. Can you fit her in?"

A screaming toddler—just what I need, Reuven thought. But he nodded. "One way or another, I'll manage."

"That's good," the receptionist said. "I asked your father, but he said he was too busy and told me to go to you instead." Yetta was plain to the point of frumpishness, but at the moment she looked almost comically amused. "I'll tell her she can bring Miriam in to you in an hour, if that's all right."

"Fine," Reuven said. He almost asked her what was so funny, but held off at the last minute because he saw a possible answer. *She thinks my father is trying to fix me up with a pretty widow,* he realized. That almost started him laughing. Then he wondered what was so laughable about it. With Jane gone to Canada, he wouldn't have minded getting fixed up with anybody.

As if Mrs. Radofsky cares about you for anything but whether you can make her little girl feel better, he thought. That didn't bother him. That was the way things were supposed to be.

Even back in his examination room, he could tell when the widow Radofsky brought her daughter into the office. The racket Miriam was making left no possible doubt. Reuven was looking at another widow, a little old lady named Goldblatt whose varicose veins were troubling her. *"Gevalt!"* she said. "That one's not very happy."

"No, she's not," Reuven agreed. "I'm going to recommend an elastic bandage on that leg to help keep those veins under control for you. I don't think they're bad enough to need surgery now. If they bother you more, though, come back in and we'll have another look at them."

"All right, Doctor, thank you," Mrs. Goldblatt said. Reuven hid his smile. *I'm learning,* he thought. If he'd told her straight out that she was fussing over very little, she'd have left in a huff. As things were, she seemed well enough pleased, even though all he'd done was sugarcoat essentially the same message.

"Can you see Mrs. Radofsky and Miriam now?" Yetta asked.

"Why not?" Reuven raised an eyebrow. "I've been hearing them—or Miriam, anyhow—for a while now." The receptionist sniffed. No, she didn't care for anyone's jokes but her own.

A moment later, the young widow carried her daughter into

the examination room. Miriam was still howling at the top of her lungs, and was tugging at the lobe of her left ear and trying to stick her finger into it. That would have been diagnostic all by itself. Mrs. Radofsky gave Reuven a wan smile and tried to talk through the din: "Thank you for seeing me on such short notice. She woke up like this at four in the morning." No wonder her smile was wan.

Reuven grabbed his otoscope. "We'll see what we can do."

Miriam didn't want to let him examine her, not for beans she didn't. She screeched, "No!"—a two-year-old's favorite word anyway, as Reuven remembered from his sisters—and tried to grab the otoscope and keep it away from her ear.

"Can you hold her, please?" Reuven asked her mother.

"All right," the widow Radofsky said. Even in his brief time in practice, Reuven had discovered that almost no mother would hold her precious darling tight enough to do a doctor one damn bit of good. He'd thought about investing in pediatric straitjackets, or even manufacturing them and making his fortune from grateful physicians the world around. He expected to do half the holding himself this time, too.

But he got a surprise. Mrs. Radofsky battled Miriam to a standstill. Reuven got a good look inside a red, swollen ear canal. "She's got it, sure enough," he said. "I'm going to give her a shot of penicillin, and I'm going to prescribe a liquid for her. You have an icebox to keep it cold?" Most people did, but not everybody.

To his relief, Miriam's mother nodded. She rolled her daughter onto her stomach on the examining table so Reuven could give her the shot in the right cheek. That produced a new set of screams, almost supersonically shrill. When they subsided, the widow Radofsky said, "Thank you very much."

"You're welcome." Reuven felt like sticking a finger in his ear, too. "She should start getting relief in twenty-four hours. If she doesn't, bring her back. Make sure she takes all the liquid. It's nasty, but she needs it."

"I understand." Mrs. Radofsky didn't have to shout, for Miriam, finally exhausted, hiccuped a couple of times and fell asleep. Her mother sighed and said, "Life is never as simple as we wish it would be, is it?" She brushed back a lock of dark hair that had come loose.

"No," Reuven said. "All you can do is your best." Miriam's

mother nodded again, then sent him a sharp look. *Is she noticing me and not just the man in the white coat?* he wondered, and hoped she was.

☆ **9** ☆

"Queek and his interpreter are here, Comrade General Secretary," Molotov's secretary told him.

"Very well, Pyotr Maksimovich. I am coming." It wasn't very well, and Molotov knew it. He'd hated the *Reich*, but he missed it now that it was reduced to a battered shadow of itself. And the United States was in trouble. If the Race found an excuse for smashing the USA, how long could the USSR last after that? No matter what the dialectic said about inevitable socialist victory, Molotov didn't want to have to find out for himself.

He hurried into the office reserved for visits from the Race's ambassador. A couple of minutes later, his secretary led in Queek and the Pole who translated his words into Russian. "Good day," Molotov told the human. "Please convey my warm greetings to your principal." His words were as warm as a Murmansk blizzard, but he'd observed the forms.

The Pole spoke to the Lizard. The Lizard hissed and popped back at him. "He conveys similar greetings to you, Comrade General Secretary."

Queek's greetings were probably as friendly as Molotov's, but the Soviet leader couldn't do anything about that. He said, "I thank you for agreeing to see me on such short notice."

"That is my duty," Queek replied. "Now that I am here, I will ask why you have summoned me." His interpreter made it sound as if Molotov would find himself in trouble if he didn't have a good reason.

He thought he did. "If at all possible, I want to use my good offices to help the Race and the United States come to a peaceful resolution of the dispute that has arisen between them." He didn't know why the dispute had arisen, which frustrated him no end, but that didn't matter.

Queek gestured. The interpreter said, "That means he rejects your offer."

Molotov hadn't expected anything so blunt. "Why?" he asked, fighting to keep astonishment from his voice.

"Because this dispute is between the Race and the United States," Queek replied. "Do you truly wish to include your not-empire and suffer the consequences of doing so?"

"That depends on the circumstances," Molotov said. "If the Soviet Union were to include itself on the side of the United States, do you doubt that the Race would also suffer certain consequences?"

When the interpreter translated that, Queek made the boiling and bubbling noises he used to show he was an unhappy Lizard. The interpreter didn't translate them, which might have been just as well. After half a minute or so, the Race's ambassador started spluttering less. Now the Pole turned his words into Russian: "You would destroy yourselves if you were mad enough to attempt such a thing."

"Possibly." Even for Molotov, sounding dispassionate while speaking of his country's ruin didn't come easy, but he managed. "If, however, the Race attacked first the United States and then the peace-loving peasants and workers of the Soviet Union, our destruction would be even more certain. If you think the Germans hurt you, you had better think very hard on what the United States and the Soviet Union could do together."

"Do you threaten me, Comrade General Secretary?" Queek asked.

"By no means, Ambassador," Molotov replied. "I warn you. If you leave the Soviet Union out of your calculations, you make a serious mistake. This government cannot be, is not, and will not be blind to the danger the Race poses to the other chief independent human power, and thus to all of mankind."

"I assure you that, whatever the danger in which the United States finds itself, it is a danger that that not-empire has abundantly earned," Queek said. "I also assure you that it is none of your business."

"If you assure me it is none of my business, I have no way to examine your other assurances," Molotov said. "Therefore, I must assume them to be worthless."

"Assume whatever you please," Queek said. "We are not interested in your efforts to mediate. If we ever do seek mediation, we shall inquire of you. And as for your threats, you will find that you cannot intimidate us."

"I have no intention of intimidating you," Molotov said, glad he had the knack of lying with a straight face. "You will follow your interests, and we shall follow ours. But I did want to make sure you understood what the Soviet Union considers to be in its interest."

"The Soviet Union does not understand what is in its interest, not if it courts destruction like—" The interpreter broke off and went back and forth with Queek in the Lizards' language. Then he returned to Russian: "The expression people would use is 'like a moth flying into a flame.'"

"It is possible that we might be defeated." Molotov knew it was as near certain as made no difference that the Soviet Union would be defeated. Sometimes, though, a demonstrated willingness to fight made fighting unnecessary. Switzerland had never become a part of the Greater German *Reich*. "Think carefully, Ambassador, on whether you and the Race care to pay the price."

"I assure you, Comrade General Secretary, that our discussions shall revolve around that very subject," Queek replied. "I think we have now said everything that needs saying, one of us to the other. Is that not a truth?"

"It is," Molotov said.

Queek rose. So did the interpreter—*like a well-trained hound,* Molotov thought scornfully. "Perhaps I shall see you again," the ambassador said. "Then again, perhaps not. Perhaps this ugly building will cease to exist in the not too distant future. It would be no enormous loss if that came to pass."

"I care nothing for your views on architecture," Molotov said. "And if this building should cease to exist, if many buildings throughout the Soviet Union should cease to exist, the Race and the buildings it cherishes would not come through unscathed."

The Lizard's tailstump quivered, a sign of anger. But Queek left without making any more cracks, which was probably just as well.

As soon as the door closed behind the Race's envoy and his interpreter, Molotov rose from his chair and went into a chamber off to the side of the office. There he changed his clothes, including socks, shoes, and underwear. The Race could make extraordinarily tiny mobile surveillance devices; he did not want to take the chance of carrying them through the Kremlin.

Marshal Zhukov waited in Molotov's own office. "You heard, Georgi Konstantinovich?" Molotov asked.

"Oh, yes." Zhukov patted the intercom speaker that had relayed the conversation to him. "I heard. You did about as well as anyone could have, Comrade General Secretary. Now we wait and see what happens."

"Is everything in readiness to defend the *rodina*?" Molotov asked.

Zhukov nodded. "Strategic Rocket Forces are ready to defend the motherland. Admiral Gorshkov tells me our submarines are ready. Our ground forces are dispersed; the Lizards will not find it easy to smash large armies with single weapons. Our forces in space will do everything they can."

"And our antimissiles?" Molotov suppressed hope from his voice as efficiently as he had suppressed fear.

With a big peasant shrug, Zhukov answered, "They will also do everything they can. How much that is likely to be, I've got no idea. We may knock some down. We will not knock down enough to make any serious difference in the fighting."

"How many of ours will they knock down?" Molotov asked.

"More," Zhukov said. "You spoke accurately. We can hurt them. Together with the United States, we can hurt them badly. They can do to us what they did to the *Reich*. I wish you could have learned how this trouble with the USA blew up so fast."

"So do I." Molotov's smile was Moscow winter. "Do you suppose President Warren would tell me?"

"You never can tell with Americans, but I wouldn't hold my breath," the leader of the Red Army replied. Molotov nodded; that was also his assessment. Zhukov cursed. "I don't want to fight the damned Lizards blind. I don't want to fight them at all, with or without the Americans on my side."

"Would you rather they came and fought us after beating the Americans? That looks to be our other choice," Molotov said.

"You were right. That's worse," Zhukov said. "But this is not good. I wish the Lizards would have let you mediate."

"Queek did not want mediation," Molotov said gloomily. "Queek, unless I am very much mistaken, wanted the Americans' blood."

"That is not good, not good at all." Zhukov slammed his fist down onto Molotov's desk. "Again, I think you were right."

The telephone rang. Molotov quickly picked it up, not least to make sure Zhukov wouldn't. Andrei Gromyko was on the other end of the line. "Well?" the foreign commissar asked, one word that said everything necessary.

Molotov gave back one word: "Bad."

"What are we going to do, Comrade General Secretary?" Gromyko sounded worried. When Gromyko sounded like anything, matters were serious if not worse. "The threat the Lizards present makes that of the Hitlerites in 1941 seem as nothing beside it."

"I am painfully aware of that, Andrei Andreyevich," Molotov answered. "I judge that the threat from the Race will not decrease if the Lizards are allowed to ride roughshod over the United States and then come after us. Marshal Zhukov, who is here with me, concurs. Do you disagree?"

"No, I do not. I wish I could," Gromyko said. "All our choices are bad. Some may be worse than others."

"Our best hope, I believe, is persuading the Race that another war of aggression would cost them more than they could hope to gain in return," Molotov said. "Since that is obviously true, I had no trouble making my position, the Soviet Union's position, very plain to Queek."

He spoke with more assurance than he felt. The phone lines to his office were supposed to be the most secure in the Soviet Union. But the Lizards were better at electronics than their Soviet counterparts. He had no guarantee they were not listening. If they were, they weren't going to hear anything secret different from what he'd said to their ambassador's scaly face.

Gromyko understood that. "Of course, Vyacheslav Mikhailovich," the foreign commissar said. He was good. No one, human or Lizard, would have said that he was using a public voice, an overly fulsome voice, to put undue stress on his words.

"Have you any further suggestions?" Molotov asked.

"No," Gromyko replied. "I am content to leave everything in your capable hands." Had Molotov been unsure Gromyko was content to do that, someone else would have held the foreign commissar's job. Gromyko added, "Good-bye," and hung up.

"Does he agree with you?" Zhukov asked.

Molotov nodded. "*Da.* And you?" He wanted it out in the open. If Zhukov didn't agree, somebody else would start holding the general secretary's job.

But the marshal, however reluctantly, nodded. "As you say, our best hope. But it is not a good one."

"I wish I thought it were," Molotov said. "Now we can only wait."

Rance Auerbach spoke French slowly and with a Southern accent nothing like the one the people in the south of France used. But he read the language pretty well. Everything he saw in the Marseille newspapers made him wish he were back on the other side of the Atlantic. "Christ, I wonder if they'd let me back in the Army if I asked 'em nice."

Penny Summers looked at him from across their room at La Résidence Bompard. The hotel lay well to the west of the city center, and so had survived the explosive-metal bomb without much damage. Penny said, "What the hell were you drinking last night, and how much of it did you have? The Army wouldn't take you back to fight off an invasion of chipmunks, let alone Lizards."

"Never can tell," he said. "Back when the Race first hit us, they took anybody who was breathing, and they didn't check that real hard, either."

"*You* aren't hardly breathing right now," Penny retorted, which was cruel but not altogether inaccurate. "I can hear you wheezing all the way over here."

Like her previous comment, that one held an unfortunate amount of truth. Auerbach glared just the same. "You want to be over here if the Lizards try and kick the crap out of the country?"

"I'd sooner be here than there, on account of they can kick our ass from here to Sunday, and you know it as well as I do," Penny said.

One more home truth he could have done without. Putting the best face on it he could, he said, "We'll go down swinging."

"That won't do us a hell of a lot of good." Penny walked past him to the window and looked north toward the blue, blue waters of the Mediterranean. The hotel sat on the headland west of the inlet that had prompted Greek colonists to land at Marseille what seemed a very long time ago by Earthly standards. Turning back, Penny went on, "You want to go back, go ahead. It's no skin off my nose. You won't see me doing it, though."

Rance grunted. He was just gassing, and he knew it. If he'd thought the Army would take his ruined carcass, he would have

gone back if he had to swim the Atlantic to do it. As things were . . .
As things were, he wanted a drink and he wanted a cigarette. The
cigarettes hereabouts were nasty items; they tasted like a blend
of tobacco, hemp, and horse manure. He lit one anyway, as much
an act of defiance as anything else.

He looked at his watch. "It's half past ten," he said. "We're
supposed to see Pierre the Turd at noon. We'd better get moving."

"One of these days, you're gonna call him that to his face, and
you'll be sorry," Penny predicted.

"I still say that's what his name sounds like." Rance took another quick drag on his cigarette, then stubbed it out. He'd sated
his craving for nicotine, and he didn't like the taste for hell.

By writing out what he wanted, Auerbach got the concierge to
call him a cab. It showed up a few minutes later: a battered Volkswagen. "Where to?" the cabby asked. He was smoking a cigarette like the one Rance had had, but he'd worked it down to a
tiny little butt.

"I would like . . . to go . . . to the refugee center . . . to the
north . . . of the city." Auerbach spoke slowly, and as carefully as
he could. Sometimes the locals would understand him, sometimes not.

This time, the driver nodded. *"Oui, monsieur,"* he said, and
opened the door so Penny and Rance could get into the back
seat. Auerbach grunted and grimaced as he squeezed himself
into the narrow space. He ended up knee to knee with Penny,
which was pleasant, but not so pleasant as to keep him from
wishing he had more room.

The road north skirted the Vieux Port, the inlet at the heart of
the city. It also skirted the worst of the wreckage from the bomb.
Rance eyed the ruins with fascination. He'd seen plenty of pictures of the kind of damage explosive-metal bombs produced,
but never the real thing till now. Everything looked to have been
blasted out from a central point, which, he supposed, was exactly
what had happened. It happened with ordinary bombs, too, but
not on such a scale. He wondered how many had died when the
bomb went off. Then he wondered if anybody knew, even to the
nearest ten thousand.

But a lot of people remained very much alive, too. The tent
city north of town was enormous. Penny wrinkled her nose.
"Smells like the septic tank just backed up," she said.

"It's a wonder they don't have disease." Rance spoke with the authority of a former officer. "They will before too long, if they don't do something about their sanitation pretty damn quick."

"Dix-huit francs, monsieur," the driver said as he brought the Volkswagen to a halt. Eighteen francs was about three bucks—it would have been high for the trip back in the States, but not outrageously so. Auerbach dug in his pocket and found two shiny ten-franc coins. They didn't weigh anything to speak of; they were stamped from aluminum, which struck him as money for cheapskates. The driver seemed glad enough to get them, though. *"Merci beaucoup,"* he told Rance.

Then Auerbach had to tell him the same thing, because the fellow and Penny had to work together to extract him from the back seat of the VW. Rance normally hated standing up, which made his ruined leg hold more weight than it really felt like bearing. Compared to being crammed into that miserable back seat, standing up wasn't half bad. He took as much of his weight as he could on his stick and his good leg.

A dumpy little woman a few years younger than Penny came up to them. "You are the Americans?" she asked. Rance's eyes snapped toward her the minute she started to speak: if she didn't have a bedroom voice, he'd never heard one. Not much to look at, but she'd be something between the sheets in the dark.

He had to remind himself he needed to answer. "Yes, we are the Americans," he said in his slow, Texas-flavored Parisian French. "And you?"

"I'm Lucie," she told him. "I'm Pierre's friend. Come with me."

They came. Even without running water, the tent city had better order than Rance would have guessed from the smell on his arrival. There were latrine trenches off in the distance. *Just too many people, and they've been here too long,* he thought. He knew about that; he and Penny had been stuck in a refugee camp for a while after the first round of fighting ended. Kids in short pants ran by, making a godawful racket. Rance almost tripped over a yappy little dog.

The tent in which Lucie and Pierre lived was a good-sized affair whose canvas had been bleached by sun and rain. Ducking through the tent flap wasn't easy for Rance, either, but he managed, leaning on the stick. When he straightened up again, he said, "Oh, hello," rather foolishly, in English, because another woman was in the tent with Pierre and Lucie. She was younger than the ginger dealer, but they had a family look to them—

though she was better looking than old Pierre the Turd ever dreamt of being.

She surprised him by answering in English: "Hello. I am Monique Dutourd, Pierre's *soeur*—his sister."

He went back to his own bad French: "How is it that you speak English?"

"I am a professor of Roman history," she said, and then, with a flash of bitterness, "A professor too long without a position. I read English and German much better than I speak them." Her mouth narrowed into a thin line. "I hope never to speak German again."

"Any language can be useful," Pierre Dutourd said, first in English and then in the language of the Race. He went on in the latter tongue: "Is that not a truth?"

Rance and Penny had spent too much time in the company of Lizards over the past few years. They both made the Race's affirmative hand gesture at the same time. Lucie laughed, which raised a couple of goosebumps on Rance's arms. Penny gave him a sour look; she must have known what the Frenchwoman's voice was doing to him.

Lucie hefted a green glass bottle. "Wine?" she asked.

"Merci," Auerbach said, and Penny nodded. Rance would have preferred either real booze or beer, but this was France, so what could you do?

Pierre Dutourd raised his glass in salute. "This is a better meeting than our last one," he said.

"Amen!" Rance exclaimed, and drank. He fumbled for words. "No Nazis with rifles, no trouble, no fear."

"Less fear, anyhow," the ginger dealer said. "Less trouble. The Lizards—the Lizards in authority—still do not love us. With France as she is today, this causes certain difficulties."

"But you're getting around them," Penny said after Auerbach translated for her. He started to turn that back into French, but Pierre's sister did the job faster and better than he could have.

"Yes, we are." This time, Pierre Dutourd spoke the language of the Race. "Do we all understand this speech?" Everyone did but Monique, and she seemed not particularly unhappy at being excluded. "Good," Pierre said. "Now—I am given to understand you have some of the herb you are interested in selling me?"

"Truth," Penny said.

"Congratulations on getting it into this not-empire," Dutourd said. "That is more difficult these days. Officials are altogether too friendly with the Race. Some of my former suppliers are having troubles, which is a pity: there are many males and females hereabouts who are longing for a taste."

"I hope Basil Roundbush is one of those suppliers," Rance said.

"As a matter of fact, he is," Pierre said. "You know him?" He waited for Rance to nod, then went on, "He is, I believe, fixing his troubles now."

"I hope he does not," Auerbach said, and used an emphatic cough.

"Ah?" Dutourd raised an eyebrow, scenting scandal.

"Dealing with Penny and me will mean you have less need to deal with him," Rance said. "I aim to hurt his business if I can." He didn't wait for the French ginger dealer to ask why, but went on to explain his run-in with Roundbush in Edmonton and the way the Englishman was hounding David Goldfarb.

Pierre Dutourd listened, but didn't seem much impressed. *Business is business to him, the son of a bitch,* Auerbach thought. But when he mentioned Goldfarb's name, Monique Dutourd perked up. She and her brother went back and forth in rapid-fire French, most of it too fast for Rance to keep up with. He gathered Pierre was filling her in on what he'd said.

Then she seemed to slow down deliberately, to give Auerbach a chance to understand her next words: "I think that, if it is possible for you to do without the Englishman and his ginger, you should. Anyone who would send a Jew—and a Jew who did not speak even so much as a word of French—in among the Nazis is not a man who deserves to be trusted. If he has the chance to betray you, he will take it."

"I have been guarding my back for many years, Monique," Pierre said with amused affection. "I do not need you to tell me how to do it."

His sister glared at him. Auerbach was sure he'd lost the play. But then Lucie said, "It could be Monique has reason. I have never trusted this Roundbush, either. He is too friendly. He is too handsome. He thinks too much of himself. Such men are not to be relied upon—and now we have another choice."

Rance had been trying to keep up with a translation for Penny, but he caught that. With a nod to good old Pierre the Turd, he said, "*C'est vrai.* Now you have another choice."

"It could be," Dutourd said. Auerbach carefully didn't smile. He knew a nibble on the hook when he felt one.

Monique Dutourd looked up from the letter she was writing. She wondered how many applications she'd sent out to universities all over France. She also wondered how many of those universities still existed at the moment, and how many had vanished off the face of the earth in an instant of explosive-metal fire.

And she wondered how many letters she'd sent to universities still extant had got where they were addressed. The situation with the mail in newly independent France remained shockingly bad. The Nazis would never have tolerated such inefficiency. Of course, the Nazis would have read a lot of the letters in the mailstream along with delivering them. Monique dared hope the officials of the *République Française* weren't doing the same.

She also dared hope department chairmen *were* reading the letters she sent them. She had very little on which to base that hope. Only three or four letters had come back to the tent city outside Marseille. None of them showed the least interest in acquiring the services of a new Romanist.

Because nobody cared about her academic specialty, she remained stuck with her brother and Lucie. She wished she could get away, but they were the ones who had the money—they had plenty of it. They were generous about sharing it with her: more generous, probably, than she would have been were roles reversed. But being dependent on a couple of ginger dealers rankled.

Not for the first time, Monique wished she'd studied something useful instead of Latin and Greek. Then she could have struck out on her own, got work for herself. As things were, she had to stay here unless she wanted to spend the rest of her days as a shopgirl or a maid of all work.

Pierre glanced over to her and said, "Do you really think I ought to tell the Englishman to go peddle his papers? He and I have done business for a long time, and who can be sure if these Americans are reliable?"

"You're asking me about your business?" Monique said, more than a little astonished. "You've never asked me about business before, except when it had to do with that *cochon* from the *Gestapo.*"

"I knew plenty about him without asking you, too," her

brother said. "But he did make a nuisance of himself when he connected the two of us."

"A nuisance of himself!" Now Monique had to fight to keep from exploding. Dieter Kuhn might have hounded Pierre, but he'd not only hounded Monique but also subjected her to a full-scale Nazi-style interrogation and then forced his way into her bed. As far as she was concerned, the one good thing about the explosive-metal bomb that had burst on Marseille was that it turned Kuhn to radioactive dust.

"A nuisance," Pierre repeated placidly. Monique glared at him. He ignored the glare. His thoughts were fixed firmly on himself, on his own affairs. "You did not answer what I asked about the Americans."

"Yes, I think you should work with them," Monique answered. "If you have a choice between someone with a conscience and someone without, would you not rather work with the side that has one?"

"You're probably right," Pierre said. "If I have none myself, people with a conscience are easier to take advantage of."

"Impossible man!" Monique exclaimed. "What would our mother and father say if they knew what you'd turned into?"

"What would they say? I like to think they'd say, 'Congratulations, Pierre. We never expected that anyone in the family would get rich, and now you've gone and done it.' " Monique's brother raised an eyebrow. "Getting rich does not seem to be anything you're in severe danger of doing. When you were teaching, you weren't getting much, and now you can't even find a job."

"I was doing what I wanted to do," Monique said. "If I weren't your sister, I'd still be doing what I wanted to do."

"If you weren't my sister, you'd be dead," Pierre said coldly. "You'd have been living back at your old flat, and it was a lot closer to where the bomb went off than my place in the Porte d'Aix was. Next time you feel like calling me nasty names or asking about our parents, kindly bear that in mind."

He was, infuriatingly, bound to be right. That didn't make Monique resent him any less—on the contrary. But it would make her more careful about saying what was on her mind. "All right." Even she could hear how grudging she sounded. "But I have spent a lot of time learning to be a historian. I've never spent any time learning the ginger business."

"It's all common sense," her brother told her. "Common sense and a good ear for what's true and what's a lie—and the nerve not to let anyone cheat you. People—and Lizards—have to know you'll never let anybody cheat you."

A historian needed the first two traits. The third . . . Monique wondered how many people Pierre and his henchmen had killed. He'd been willing enough—more than willing enough—to use his Lizard friends to try to arrange Dieter Kuhn's untimely demise. It hadn't worked; the Lizard assassin, unable to tell one human from another, had gunned down a fish merchant by mistake. Of course, that effort had been in Pierre's interest as well as Monique's. She wondered if he ever did anything not in his own interest.

And she didn't like the way he was eyeing her now. In musing tones, he said, "If I go with the Americans, little sister, you could be useful to me—you know English, after all. Even if I find the Americans don't work out, I'll go back to the Englishman—and you could be useful with him, too."

"Suppose I don't want to be . . . useful?" Monique had never—well, never this side of Dieter Kuhn—heard a word whose sound she liked less.

Her brother, as she'd already seen, was a relentless pragmatist. With a shrug, he answered, "I've carried you for a while now, Monique. Don't you think it's time you started earning your keep, one way or another?"

"I'm trying to do just that." She held up the letter she was working on. "I haven't had any luck, that's all."

"One way or another, I said." Pierre sighed. "I admire you for trying to go on doing what you had done, truly I do. You can even go on trying to do it. I have no objection whatsoever, and I will congratulate you if you get a position. But if you don't . . ." His smile was sad and oddly charming. "If you don't, you can work for me."

"I was just thinking you hadn't been cruel enough to say anything like that to me," Monique replied, her voice bitter. She snapped her fingers. "So much for that."

"You don't have to make up your mind right away," Pierre said. "But do remember, I pulled wires to get you away from the purification police. I hoped you might want to show you were grateful."

Monique scornfully tossed her head. "If you weren't my brother, you'd be using that line to get me to go to bed with you."

All of a sudden, the prospect of being a maid of all work didn't look so bad.

"Thank you, but no. I would not be interested even then—I've never had much use for women who argue and talk back all the time," Pierre replied with wounding dignity. Monique wondered how well he knew himself. Lucie was anything but a shrinking violet.

But that thought flickered in her mind and then was gone. She wanted to hit back, to wound. "I believe you there," she said. "The only time you'd want them to open their mouths would be to swallow something—just like that damned SS man. I'm surprised you didn't jump to put on your own black shirt. They'd have paid you well, after all, and what else is there?"

Pierre surprised her with an immediate, emphatic answer: "Not being told what to do, of course. I had a bellyful of orders in the Army. I've done my best not to have to take them ever since."

"You don't care to take them, that could be," Monique snarled. "But you don't mind giving them, do you? No, you don't mind that a bit."

Her brother spread his hands in a startlingly philosophical gesture. "If one does not take orders, it is because he can give them, n'est ce-pas? Do you see any other arrangement?"

"I *had* another arrangement, till being your sister turned my life upside down," Monique said. "I taught my classes, and outside of that I studied what I wanted, what interested me. No one made me do it. No one would have been interested in making me do anything. People *let me alone*. Do you understand what that means? Do you have any idea what that means?"

"It means you were very lucky," Pierre said. "If you get another position, you will be lucky again. But if you are not so lucky, what then? Why, then you have to work for a living, just like everyone else."

"There is a difference between working for a living and playing the whore," Monique said. "Maybe you can't understand that, but the Germans already made me play the whore. I'll be damned if I let my brother do the same."

She threw down the letter—why not? it was bound to be useless, anyhow—and stormed out of the tent. She fled not just the tent but the whole tent city as if it were accursed. It might as well have been, as far as she was concerned. If she'd had a little lead tablet and thought inscribing a curse in the name of the gods would have wiped the miserable place from the face of the earth, she would have done it in a heartbeat. As things were, all she could do was storm away.

Marseille was a great racket of bulldozers and jackhammers and saws and ordinary hammers and tools for which she didn't even have names. Wrecked buildings were coming down. New buildings were going up. Most of those new buildings were supposed to be blocks of flats. Monique didn't see the tent city shrinking, though. She had a pretty good idea what that meant: somebody's pockets were getting lined.

She didn't want to look at the buildings. Looking at them reminded her she wasn't living in one of them, that she wouldn't be able to afford to live in one of them. They had things she could buy—unless Pierre cut off all her money. *What would I do then?* she wondered. *Could I stand his business?* She doubted it. And yet . . .

A man smoking a pipe called out a lewd proposition. Monique rounded on him and, in a voice that could be heard all over the square, suggested that he ask his mother for the same service. He turned very red. He turned even redder when people jeered him and cheered her. Puffing furiously at the pipe, he withdrew in disorder.

"Nicely done, Professor Dutourd," someone behind Monique said. "A boor like that deserves whatever happens to him."

She whirled. The world whirled around her. There stood *Sturmbannführer* Dieter Kuhn. In civilian clothes, he looked like a Frenchman, but his accent declared who and what he was. "In that case, you deserved to be blown to the devil," she snapped. "I thought you were. I *prayed* you were."

He smiled the smile he no doubt thought so charming. "No such luck, I'm afraid. I was sent back to the *Vaterland* two days before the bomb fell here. They were going to put me in a panzer unit, but the *Reich* surrendered before they could." He shrugged. *"C'est la vie."*

"What are you doing *here* again?" Monique asked.

"Why, I am a tourist, of course. I have a passport and visa to prove it," the SS man replied with another of those not quite charming smiles.

"And what are you here to see?" Monique's wave took in ruin and reconstruction. "There isn't much left *to* see."

"Oh, but Marseille is still the home of so many wonderful herbs," Kuhn said blandly. *Christ,* Monique thought. *He's still in the ginger business. The Reich is still in the ginger business. He'll be looking for Pierre. And if I start working for Pierre, he'll be looking for me, too.*

Every time David Goldfarb crossed a street, he didn't just look both ways. He made careful calculations. If a car suddenly sped up, could it get him? Or could he scramble up onto the sidewalk and something close to safety? Nothing like almost getting killed to make one consider such things.

Of course, that fellow who'd tried to run him down wasn't the first driver in Edmonton who'd almost killed him—just the first one who'd meant to. David had a lifetime of looking left first before stepping off the curb. But Canadians, like their American cousins, drove on the right. That was a recipe for attempted suicide. Goldfarb didn't try to do himself in quite so often as he had after first crossing the Atlantic, but it still happened in moments of absentmindedness.

This morning, he got to the Saskatchewan River Widget Works unscathed by either would-be murderers or drivers he didn't notice till too late. "Hello, there," Hal Walsh said. As usual, the boss was there before any of the people who worked for him. He pointed to a Russian-style samovar he'd recently installed. "Make yourself some tea, get your brains lubricated, and go to town."

As usual, Goldfarb complained about the samovar: "Why couldn't you leave the honest kettle? That damn thing is a heathen invention."

"You're a fine one to talk about heathens, pal," Walsh retorted. Every now and again, he would make cracks about David's Judaism. Things being as they were in Britain, that had made Goldfarb nervous. But Hal Walsh, unlike Sir Oswald Mosley and his ilk, didn't mean anything nasty by it. He gave Jack Devereaux a hard time about being French-Canadian, and also derided his own Anglo-Saxon and Celtic ancestors. Goldfarb had decided he could live with that.

He did get himself a cup of tea. "Bloody miracle you set out milk for it," he said. "With this contraption, I'd think you'd want us to drink it Russian-style, with just sugar. My parents do that. Not me, though."

"You're acculturated," Walsh said. Goldfarb must have looked blank, because his boss explained: "England was your mother country, so you got used to doing things the way Englishmen do."

"Too right I did," Goldfarb said, and explained how he was in danger of doing himself an injury every time he tried to cross the street.

Walsh laughed, then stopped abruptly. "My brother went to London a couple of years ago, and I remember him complaining because he kept looking the wrong way. I hadn't thought about your being in the same boat here."

"What boat's that?" asked Jack Devereaux. He made straight for the samovar and got himself a cup of tea. He didn't worry that the gleaming gadget was un-British; he wasn't British himself, not by blood, though he spoke English far more fluently than French. "David, did you take the *Titanic*?"

"Of course, and you're daft if you think I didn't have fun rigging a sail on the iceberg afterwards so I could finish getting over here," Goldfarb retorted.

Devereaux gave him a quizzical look. "What all have you got in that teacup?" he asked, and then, before David could answer, "Can I have some, too?"

"We don't need spirits to lift our spirits," Walsh said; "or we'd damn well better not, anyhow." He didn't mind people drinking beer with lunch—he'd drink beer with lunch himself—but frowned on anything more than that. He led by example, too. Since he worked himself like a slave driver, the people who worked for him could hardly complain when he expected a lot from them. He tilted back his cup to drain it, then said, "What's on the plate for today?"

"I'm still trying to work the bugs out of that *skelkwank*-light reader," Devereaux answered. "If I can do it, we'll have a faster, cheaper gadget than the one the Lizards have been using since time out of mind. If I can't . . ." He shrugged. "You don't win every time you bet."

"That's true, however much you wish you did," Walsh said. "What about you, David?"

"I've got a couple of notions to improve the phone-number reader," Goldfarb said, "but they're just notions, if you know what I mean. If I get a chance, I'll do some drawings and play with the hardware, but odds are I'll spend a lot of my time giving

Jack a hand. I think he's pretty close to getting where he wants to go."

"As opposed to getting where you want me to go," Devereaux said with a grin.

"The climate's better there in winter than it is here, but probably not in summer," Goldfarb said.

"That would be funny, if only it were funny," Walsh said. "It's not by accident we call our football team the Eskimos."

Goldfarb didn't call what the Canadians played football at all. It was, to him, one of the most peculiar games imaginable. Of course, the Canadians didn't call the game he was used to football, either. To them, it was soccer, and they looked down their noses at it. He didn't care. More of the world agreed with him than with them.

Walsh fixed himself a second cup of tea, then said, "Let's get going."

There were times when David was reminded he was a jumped-up technician, not a properly trained engineer. This morning gave every sign of being one of those times. He got only so far looking at drawings of the phone-number reader he'd devised. Then, muttering, he went back to the hardware and started fiddling with it. Cut-and-try often took him further faster than study. He knew that could also be true for real engineers, but it seemed more emphatically so for him.

He wasn't altogether sorry when Jack Devereaux looked up and said, "David, what about that hand you promised?" Goldfarb applauded him. Devereaux groaned. "I suppose I asked for that. Doesn't mean I had to get it, though."

"Of course it does," Goldfarb said, but he made a point of hurrying over to see what he could do for—rather than to—the other engineer.

The motors that turned the Lizards' silvery *skelkwank*-light disks—a technology mankind had copied widely—all operated at the same speed. As far as anyone human knew, they'd been operating at that same speed for as long as the Race had been using them. It worked. It was fast enough. Why change? That was the Lizards' attitude in a nutshell, or an eggshell.

People, now, people weren't so patient. If you could make the disks turn faster, you could get the information off them faster, too. Seeing that was obvious. Getting a motor anywhere near as compact and reliable as the ones the Lizards used was a different question, though. Expectations for quality had gone up since the Race came to Earth. People didn't come so close to insisting on perfection as the Lizards did, but breakdowns they would have taken for granted a generation earlier were unacceptable nowadays.

"It runs fine," Devereaux said, "but it's too goddamn noisy." He glared at the motor, which was indeed buzzing like an angry hive.

"Hmm." Goldfarb eyed the motor, too. "Maybe you could just leave it the way it is and soundproof the case." He knew that was a technician's solution, not an engineer's, but he threw it out to see what Devereaux would make of it.

And Devereaux beamed. "Out of the mouths of babes," he said reverently. "Let's do it. Let's see if we can do it, anyhow."

"What measurements will we need for the case?" David asked, and answered his own question by measuring the motor. "Let me cut some sheet metal. We ought to have some sort of insulation around here, too. That'll give us an idea of whether this'll be practical."

He'd got used to flanging up this, that, or the other thing in the RAF. Cutting sheet metal to size was as routine as sharpening a pencil. But when he was carrying the metal back to the motor, his hand slipped. He let out a yelp.

"What did you do?" Devereaux asked.

"Tried to cut my bloody finger off," Goldfarb said. It was indeed bloody; he added, "I'm bleeding on the carpet," and grabbed for his handkerchief.

Hal Walsh hurried over. "Let's have a look at that, David," he said in commanding tones. Goldfarb didn't want to take off the handkerchief. The blood soaking through told its own story, though. Walsh clicked his tongue between his teeth. "You're going to need stitches with that. There's a new doctor's office that's opened up in the building next door, and a good thing right now. Come along with me."

David didn't argue. He couldn't remember the last time he'd been so clumsy. He didn't want to look at his hand. Whenever he did, he felt woozy and wobbly. Blood was supposed to stay on the inside, not go leaking out all over the place.

JANE ARCHIBALD, M.D., read the sign on the door. "A lady doctor?" Goldfarb said.

"I hear she studied under the Lizards," Walsh answered. "She ought to be able to patch you up, wouldn't you say?"

"What happened here?" the receptionist asked when Walsh brought David into the office. Then she said, "Never mind. Come into the examining room with me, sir. The doctor will be with you right away."

"Thanks," David said vaguely. Hardly noticing he'd done so, he sat down on the chair there. He was cursing softly to himself in Yiddish when the doctor hurried into the room. He stopped in embarrassment all the worse because he hadn't expected the female physician to be so decorative. More slowly than he should have, he realized this tall, blond, obviously Anglo-Saxon woman was unlikely to have understood his pungent remarks.

But her laughter said she did, which embarrassed him all the more. A moment later, she was all business. "Let's have a look at it," she said, her accent lower-class British or perhaps Australian. David undid the makeshift bandage. Dr. Archibald examined the wound and nodded briskly. "Yes, that'll take a few stitches. Hold the edges together while I give you a bit of novocaine so you won't feel the other needle so much."

"All right," he said, and did. As she injected him, he asked, "Do you really know Yiddish? How did that happen?"

"Just bits and pieces, Mister—?" Dr. Archibald said, threading catgut or whatever they used for sutures these days onto a needle.

"Goldfarb." David looked away. He didn't care to see what would happen next. "David Goldfarb."

She stared at him, blue eyes going wide. "Not the David Goldfarb who's related to Moishe and Reuven Russie?" She was so astonished, she almost—but not quite—forgot to start stitching him up.

And he was so astonished, he almost—but not quite—forgot to notice it stung despite the novocaine. "My cousins," he answered automatically. "How do you know them?"

"I was at the Russie Medical College with Reuven," she answered. "Hold still there, please. I want to put in a couple of more stitches." That was spoken in physician's tones. Then she went back to talking as if to a person: "I might have married Reuven, but he wanted to stay in Palestine and I couldn't stomach living under the Race any more, not after what they did to Australia." Her tone changed again: "There. That's done. Let me bandage you."

As she wrapped the finger with gauze and adhesive tape,

Goldfarb said, "I didn't meet you when I was in Jerusalem. I would have remembered." That was probably more than he should have said. He realized it too late. Well, Naomi didn't need to know about it.

Dr. Archibald didn't get angry. She'd probably heard such things from the age of fourteen up. "It's very good to meet you now," she said. "I heard about your troubles in France, and getting out of England. That you'd wound up here in Edmonton had slipped my mind. You'll need to come back in about ten days to have the sutures removed. See Myrtle out front for an appointment." She stuck her head out the door and called to the receptionist: "No charge for this one, Myrtle. Old family friend."

As David went back to the Widget Works, Hal Walsh turned to him and said, "I saw the doctor. Old family friend? You lucky dog." David smiled, doing his best to look like the ladykiller he didn't come close to being.

Felless hadn't had a holiday in much too long. She hadn't done much work after fleeing Marseille for the new town in the Arabian Peninsula, but life as a refugee was vastly different from life as a vacationer. Here in Australia, too, the Race had claimed the land for its own, even more emphatically than it had in Arabia. And, unlike in Arabia, here no fanatical Big Uglies willing, even eager, to die for their superstitions prowled the landscape and had to be warded against.

The landscape in the central part of the continent reminded Felless eerily of Home. The rocks and sand and soil were all but identical. The plants were similar in type though different in detail. Many of the crawling creatures reminded members of the Race of those of Home, though a rather distressing number of them were venomous.

Only the furry animals that dominated land life on Tosev 3 really told Felless she remained on an alien world. Even those were different from the large beasts on the rest of the planet; Australia, by all indications, had long been ecologically isolated. The bipedal hopping animals filling the large-herbivore ecological niche hereabouts were so preposterous, Felless' mouth fell open in astonished laughter the first time she turned an eye turret toward one. But the creatures were very well adapted to their environment.

She saw less of that environment than she might have otherwise. Business Administrator Keffesh had been even more generous than she'd hoped after she arranged the release of the imprisoned Big Ugly, Monique Dutourd. She'd brought a lot of ginger to Australia, and she was enjoying it.

That required care. Felless would spend one day in an orgy of tasting, the next in her hostel room waiting for her pheromones to subside so she could go out in public without exciting all the males who smelled them into a mating frenzy. Getting meals sent to the room rather than eating in the refectory cost extra. Felless authorized the charge without the slightest hesitation.

All the individuals who brought meals to her were females. Once she noticed the pattern, she found that very interesting. Were the males and females who ran the hostels quietly adapting to the unavoidable presence of ginger on Tosev 3? She couldn't have proved it. She didn't dare ask about it. But the assumption certainly looked reasonable.

On the days when she was out and about, she noticed that ginger did indeed make its presence known in these new towns. She couldn't smell the pheromones she emitted in her season; they were for males. But she saw a couple of matings on the sidewalks, and she saw more than a few males hurrying along in unusually erect posture and with the scales of their crests upraised. That meant they smelled female pheromones and were looking for a chance to mate.

How foolish they look, she thought. Back on Home, she wouldn't have seen males interested in mating unless she was in her season herself. Then she would have found them attractive, not absurd. As things were, she viewed them with a cool detachment unlike anything she'd known on Home.

I wonder if this is the attitude Tosevite females have toward their males. That struck her as an interesting notion. It might repay further research when she got back to France. *I might even ask this Monique Dutourd,* she thought. *She owes me favors, and I know she was involved in at least one sexual relationship.*

The idea didn't occur to her on a day when she'd been tasting ginger, but on one when she hadn't, and when she was feeling the gloomy aftereffects of overindulgence in the herb. She wondered what that meant. Ginger was supposed to make a female clever. Maybe it only made a female think she was clever.

Such reflections disappeared when she got a telephone call

from Ambassador Veffani. Without preamble, he said, "Senior Researcher, I strongly recommend that you return to France at once."

"Why, superior sir?" Felless asked, doing her best to disguise dismay.

"Why? I shall tell you why." Veffani sounded thoroughly grim. "Because there is serious danger of war between the Race and the not-empire known as the United States."

"By the Emperor!" Felless was so upset, she barely remembered to cast down her eyes after naming her sovereign. "Have all these Tosevite not-empires gone addled at the same time?"

"It could be so," Veffani answered. "There are threats that, if we fight the United States, the not-empire called the Soviet Union will join in on the side of their fellow Big Uglies."

"That might almost be for the best," Felless said. "Once we have smashed them both, Tosev 3 will be ours without possibility of dispute."

"Truth," the ambassador to France said. "Truth to a point, at any rate. The question remaining is, how much damage can the Big Uglies do us while we are smashing them? Estimates are that each of these not-empires could by itself hurt us at least as badly as the Deutsche did. If they fight us together, they may be able to do a good deal more than that, because we would not be able to concentrate all our military strength against either one of them."

"Oh." Felless stretched out the word. However much she wished it didn't, that made good logical sense. But a new question occurred to her: "Why should I cut short my holiday to return to France? Will I not be in at least as much danger there as I am here?"

Veffani made the negative gesture. "I do not think so, Senior Researcher. Australia is part of the territory the Race rules, and so is a legitimate target for both the USA and the SSSR, as it was for the *Reich*. But France is an independent Tosevite not-empire. By the rules of war on Tosev 3, it is not a fair target for them unless it declares itself to be at war against them. The government of the Français shows no willingness to do this."

"They are ungrateful after we regained for them the independence they had lost to the Deutsche?" Felless asked indignantly.

"They are the most cynical beings I have ever known," Veffani replied. "They know we did not free them from the Deutsche for their benefit, but for our own. And our efforts to use Big Uglies as soldiers against other Big Uglies have been far less successful than we would have wished. Let them be independent. Let them be neutral. Let their not-empire be a safe haven. It was not during the fight against the Deutsche."

"Well, that is a truth," Felless said, and then, "Tell me, superior sir, what is the cause of the latest crisis with the not-empire of the United States? I thought that, except for such peculiarities as snoutcounting, it was relatively civilized."

"I know the answer to your question, Senior Researcher, but security forbids me from telling you," Veffani replied. "Negotiations with the USA are still in progress; there is some hope that this war may be prevented. That will be more difficult if reasons for the crisis become too widely known. Even we are not immune from being forced to actions we might otherwise not take."

"But will the Big Uglies of the USA not bellow these reasons to the sky?" Felless asked. "That not-empire is notorious for telling everything that should stay secret."

"Not always," Veffani said. "The American Big Uglies concealed the launch of their spaceship to the belt of minor planets in this solar system very well. And they have more reason to conceal this—believe me, they do." He used an emphatic cough. "They would not bellow unless they wanted a war with us in the next instant."

"I am not sure I understand, superior sir," Felless said—an understatement, because she was annoyed Veffani wouldn't trust her with whatever secret he knew, "but I shall obey, and shall arrange to return to Marseille as soon as I can."

"You are wise to do so," Veffani told her. "Now you colonists are beginning to get some notion of the delights we of the conquest fleet faced when we first came to Tosev 3. For you, though, these delights are less a surprise."

He broke the connection before Felless could tell him how utterly mistaken he was. Everything about Tosev 3 had been a horrible surprise to the males and females of the colonization fleet. Felless remembered waking from cold sleep weightless, in orbit around what she'd thought would be the new world of the Empire, to be informed that nothing she'd believed on setting out from Home was true.

I will go back to Marseille, she thought. *I will go back to Marseille—after I enjoy myself one more time here.* She still had more ginger in her luggage than she knew what to do with. No, that wasn't true—she knew exactly what to do with it. She set out to taste as much as she could in one day.

Normally, a ginger-taster rode from exhilaration to depression and back again. Intent on tasting all she could, Felless didn't wait for one taste to wear off before enjoying another. She stayed strung as tight as the herb would make her.

When a female she telephoned to arrange an early return to France pointed out a couple of difficulties in her revised schedule, Felless screamed insults. The other female said, "There is no reason to snap my snout off."

"But—" Felless began. She seemed to have the Race's entire aircraft schedule at the tips of her fingerclaws. But, when she tried to access the information with the thinking part of her mind, she discovered she couldn't.

Yes, ginger makes you believe you are smart, she reminded herself. *It does not really make you smarter, or not very much.* It also made her far more vulnerable to frustration than she would have been otherwise.

"Here." The female proposed another schedule. "Will this do?"

Felless examined it. "Yes," she said, and the other female, with every sign of relief, vanished from her screen. Felless took another taste. She wasn't sure the departure time would be late enough to let her stop producing pheromones by then. With so much ginger coursing through her, she didn't care.

She cared the following day. For one thing, the depression that followed her binge was the worst she'd ever known. For another, she *hadn't* stopped pumping out pheromones. She mated in the hotel lobby, in the motorcar that took her to the airfield, and in the terminal waiting to board the aircraft.

"A good holiday," the last male said, with an emphatic cough.

And Felless answered, "Truth." The pleasure of mating was different from that of the herb, but it was enough to lift her partway out of the shadows in which she'd walked since taking her tongue out of the ginger vial.

She wondered if she would lay a clutch of eggs. *If I do, I do,* she thought, and then, *But if I do, Veffani had better not find out about it.* The ambassador would not be pleased. He might even be angry enough to send her back to the *Reich*.

Fortunately, she was able to board the aircraft without stirring up a commotion. That could have been dangerous, especially if the flight crew had males in it. But her fellow passengers paid her no special heed. She settled down for the long, dull flight to Cairo, where she would board another aircraft for the return to Marseille.

Not so bad, she thought. She wished the holiday had been longer. That would have let her taste more. But she'd made up for a lot of lost time even so. Maybe she really was ready to get back to work.

Liu Han and Liu Mei sat side by side in an insanely crowded second-class car as the train of which it was a part rattled north. Children squealed. Babies screamed. Chickens squawked. Ducks quacked. Dogs—likelier headed for the stew pot than for the easy life of a pet—yelped. Several young porkers made noises even more appalling than those that came from the human infants. The smells were as bad as the racket.

"Can we get any fresh air?" Liu Mei asked her mother.

"I don't know," Liu Han answered. "I'll try." She was sitting by the window. She had to use all her strength to get it to rise even a little. When it did, she wasn't sure she was glad it had. The engine was an ancient coal-burner, and soot started pouring in as the stinks poured out.

Liu Mei got a cinder in the eye, and rubbed frantically. Once she'd managed to get rid of it, she said, "Maybe you ought to close that again."

"I'll try," Liu Han repeated. She had no luck this time. What had gone up refused to come down. She sighed. "We knew this trip wouldn't be any fun when we set out on it."

"We were right, too." Liu Mei coughed. Several people had lit up cigarettes and pipes so they wouldn't have to pay quite so much attention to the pungent atmosphere they were breathing. Their smoke made the air that much thicker for everyone else.

One of the babies in the car—or possibly one of the dogs—had an unfortunate accident. Liu Han sighed. "I wouldn't have enjoyed walking back to Peking, but I'm not enjoying this, either. You, at least, you're going home."

Liu Mei leaned toward Liu Han so she could speak into her ear: "We're going back to begin the revolutionary struggle again. The struggle is our home."

"Well, so it is." Liu Han glanced over at her daughter. Liu Mei could think of the struggle as home. She was young. Liu Han was getting close to fifty. Trapped in this hot, smelly, packed car, she felt every one of her years. There were times when she wished she could settle down somewhere quiet and forget about the revolution. She generally got over that once she'd had a chance to rest for a while, but she found it happening more and more often these days.

The dialectic said the proletarian revolution *would* succeed. For many years, that had kept Liu Han and her comrades working to overthrow the imperialist little scaly devils despite all the defeats they'd suffered. It had kept them confident of victory, too. But now the dialectic made Liu Han thoughtful in a different way. If the revolution would inevitably succeed, wouldn't it succeed just as inevitably without her?

She didn't say anything like that to Liu Mei. She knew it would have horrified her daughter. And she supposed that, once she got to Peking, the fire of revolutionary fervor would begin to burn in her own bosom once more. It always had. Still, there were times when she felt very tired.

I'm getting old, she thought. Her skin was still firm and her hair had only a few threads of silver in it, but Chinese showed their age less readily than round-eyed devils did. She'd seen that on her visit to the United States. But whether she showed her age or not, she felt it. This miserable car made everyone feel her age, and twenty years older besides.

Brakes squealing, the train stopped in a small town. A few people left her car. More tried to crowd on. Nobody wanted to make room for anybody else. Men and women pushed and shouted and cursed. Liu Han had ridden enough trains to know things were always like that.

Hawkers elbowed their ways through the cars, selling rice and vegetables and fruit juice and tea. They didn't do a whole lot of business; most people had the sense to bring their own supplies with them. Liu Han and Liu Mei certainly had. Only the naive few riding a train for the first time gave the hawkers any trade.

A conductor came through, too, screaming for the hawkers to get off or buy a ticket—they were going to get moving. The hawkers laughed and jeered; they knew to the second when the train would really set out, and they also knew the conductors always tried to get rid of them early. The last one leaped off just as the train started to roll. He stuck out his tongue in derision.

"That'll cost him extra squeeze the next time this train crew comes through here," Liu Han predicted.

"You're probably right," her daughter replied. "But he asserted his freedom even so. In his small way, he is a revolutionary."

He was more likely to be a bad-tempered fool, but Liu Han didn't argue with Liu Mei. Instead, she wrestled with the window again. She had no luck; it was stuck, and looked as if it would stay stuck. The smoke that poured in was thick and black, because the train wasn't going fast enough to dissipate it. Liu Han coughed and cursed. People nearby were coughing, too, and cursing her.

Things got better as the train picked up speed, but they never got very good. As far as Liu Han could tell, *not very good* was about as good as rail travel ever got in China.

And then, less then half an hour later, the train slowed to a stop again, not at a station but in the middle of the countryside. "Now what?" a woman behind Liu Han demanded indignantly.

"Have we broken down?" Three or four people asked the same question at the same time.

"Of course we've broken down," Liu Han murmured to Liu Mei. "The little scaly devils don't care whether trains work well, or even if they work at all, so they don't bother keeping them up."

But, for once, this wasn't something she could blame on the scaly devils. A conductor poked his head into the car and shouted, "We can't go on because bandits have blown up the tracks ahead of us. We are going to be here for a while. We may have to go back and find a way around the damage."

That set people yelling and screaming at him and at one another. He just kept repeating what he'd said the first time. Most of the unhappy passengers cursed the bandits up one side and down the other. People would curse anything that made them late.

Liu Mei asked, "Do you suppose the People's Liberation Army sabotaged the track?"

"It could be," Liu Han said. "Not everyone will have known we were on this train. But it could have been the Kuomintang, too. No way to tell."

The sun beat down on the car. Because it was standing still, it got hotter and hotter. People started opening more windows. Some wouldn't open at all. People started breaking them. That brought in an angry conductor, but he had to flee in the face of the passengers' wrath.

"Whoever it was probably wanted to make the train derail," Liu Han said. "That would really have done damage."

It would have done damage to us, she thought. Derailing trains was a favorite game of the People's Liberation Army, and of the Kuomintang as well. It taught people that the rule of the little scaly devils remained insecure. It also caused a lot of casualties. She and Liu Mei could have been among them as easily as not.

And, of course, a machine-gun crew might have been waiting to shoot up the train once it derailed, Liu Han thought. That was another game both the People's Liberation Army and the Kuomintang played. So did independent bandit outfits, who kept themselves in business by robbery. But no one started shooting here.

After what seemed like forever, the train began to inch backwards. Because it was going in reverse, the smoke from the engine's stack blew away from the passenger cars, not into them. The breeze the slow motion stirred up wasn't very strong, but it was ever so much better than nothing. Sweat began to dry on Liu Han's face. She took off her conical straw hat and fanned herself with it. People all over the car were doing the same thing. They started smiling at one another. A couple of babies and a couple of dogs stopped howling. It was as pleasant a time on a train as Liu Han had ever known.

The train rolled back over a switch. Then it stopped, presumably so a couple of men from the engine could get down and use crowbars to shift the switch and let the train go down the other track. After that, the train started going forward again, and swung onto the route it hadn't used before.

With the exhaust now blowing back once more, the car filled with coal smoke. Since the passengers had broken a good many windows, they couldn't do anything about it. The conductor laughed at them. "You see, you stupid turtles? It's your own fault," he said. Somebody threw a squishy plum at him, and hit him right in the face. Juice dribbled down the brass-buttoned front of his uniform. He let out a horrified squawk and retreated in disorder. Everyone cheered.

But then somebody not far from Liu Han said, "Since we're going up a track we're not supposed to, I hope there's no train coming down it toward us."

That produced exclamations of horror. *"Eee!"* Liu Han said. "May ten thousand little demons dance in your drawers for even thinking such a thing."

No train slammed head-on into theirs. No stretch of tracks on the new line had been blown up. Thoroughgoing guerrillas often did such things, which caused more than double the delay and aggravation of a single strike. On the receiving end for once, Liu Han was glad these raiders hadn't been thorough.

Her train was scheduled to get into Peking in the early evening. Even at the best of times, even under the little devils, railroad schedules in China were more optimistic guesses than statements of fact. When things went wrong . . . Trying to sleep sitting up on a hard seat, with the air full of smoke and other stinks and noise, was a daunting prospect. Liu Han thought she dozed a little, but she wasn't sure.

She was sure she watched the sun rise over the farmlands to the east a couple of hours before the train did at last roll into the railroad yard in the southwestern part of Peking. It took more time crawling up to the station itself. Liu Han minded that less. It let her look around the city.

Liu Mei was doing the same thing. "We fought them hard. We fought them with everything we had," she said, and pride rang in her voice.

"So we did," Liu Han agreed. Wrecked buildings outnumbered those still intact. Laborers carrying buckets on shoulder poles were everywhere, hauling away rubble. Liu Han sighed. "Fighting hard is important, but only up to a point. More important, ever so much more important, is winning."

The little scaly devils had won this fight, and taken Peking back for their own. Liu Han found fresh proof of that at the station. Along with the other passengers, she and her daughter had to walk through a machine that could tell if they were carrying weapons. They weren't, and had no trouble. Someone else in the car was. Chinese police, running dogs to the imperialist scaly devils, hustled him away. Liu Han and Liu Mei walked out of the station and into the city. "Home," Liu Mei said, and Liu Han had to nod.

☆ **10** ☆

Though Atvar had promised him his freedom, Straha found himself more nearly a prisoner in Cairo than he had been in Los Angeles. "Is this how you reward me?" he asked one of his interrogators, a female named Zeshpass. "I hoped to return to the society of the Race, not to be closed off from it forever."

"And so you will, superior sir," Zeshpass said soothingly. But Straha was not soothed. Back in the USA, even the Big Uglies who exploited him had called him *Shiplord*. Whatever he was here, he wasn't a shiplord, and he never would be again. Zeshpass went on, "As soon as the crisis is resolved, a final disposition of your situation will be made."

That sounded soothing, too—till Straha turned an eye turret toward it. "What did you just say?" he demanded. "Whatever it was, it did not mean anything."

"Of course it did." Zeshpass sounded irate. Like any interrogator, she took her own omniscience for granted, and resented it when others failed to do likewise.

"All right, then," Straha said. "Suppose you explain to me why my case cannot be disposed of now."

Most reluctantly, the female said, "I do not have that information."

Straha laughed at her. "I do. Atvar has not yet figured out what to do with me because he has not yet decided whether I am a hero or a nuisance or both at once. My opinion is that I am both at once, which is bound to make me more annoying to the exalted fleetlord." As he was in the habit of doing, he laced Atvar's title with as much scorn as he could.

Her voice stiff with disapproval, Zeshpass said, "It is not for me to judge the exalted fleetlord's reasons. It is not for you, either."

"And if no one judges him, how will anyone know when he

276

makes a mistake?" Straha inquired. "He has made enough of them already, in my not so humble opinion. How is he to be held accountable for them?"

"Held accountable? He is the fleetlord." Zeshpass sounded as if Straha had suddenly started speaking English rather than the language of the Race. Plainly, the idea that the fleetlord, like any other mortal, needed to be questioned and criticized when he made a mistake had never crossed her mind.

Do you know what has happened to you? Straha asked himself. And he did know. *You have become a snoutcounter, at least in part. Living among the American Big Uglies for so long has rubbed off on you.*

Of course, he'd had a low opinion of Atvar's abilities even before fleeing to the United States. If he hadn't had a low opinion of Atvar's ability, if he hadn't tried to take command himself, he wouldn't have had to flee to the USA. But years spent in a land that institutionalized snoutcounting and made it work had left him even less respectful of the Race's institutions than he'd expected. *We* are *a stodgy lot*, he thought discontentedly.

"He may be the fleetlord," Straha said aloud, "but he is not the Emperor."

"That is a truth," Zeshpass admitted, casting down her eye turrets. Straha had to remind himself to do the same thing. He hadn't realized how far his habits had slipped in exile till he returned to the society of the Race. Zeshpass continued, "In fact, Reffet, the fleetlord of the colonization fleet, has had frequent disagreements with Fleetlord Atvar."

"I believe that." Straha's voice was dry. As far as he was concerned, anyone who didn't disagree with Atvar had to have something wrong with him. "What sort of things have they disagreed about? Do you happen to know?"

Given the chance to gossip, Zeshpass didn't notice she'd gone from interrogator to interrogated. "I certainly do," she said. "If you can imagine it, Atvar has proposed to levy soldiers from among the males and females of the colonization fleet, to create what would be in effect a permanent Soldiers' Time on Tosev 3."

"Has he?" Straha said. That struck him as only common sense. Even Atvar, however much the returned renegade hated to admit it, wasn't stupid all the time. He sounded even more thoughtful as he asked, "And Reffet disapproves of this?"

"Of course he does," Zeshpass answered. "We came here to colonize this world, not to fight over it."

"I understand that," Straha said. "But if the Big Uglies continue to be ready to fight against us, what shall we do once the males of the conquest fleet begin to grow old and die?"

That plainly hadn't occurred to Zeshpass. After some thought, she said, "I suppose we shall have to finish the conquest before that happens. This hatching conflict with the United States gives us the opportunity to take a long stride in that direction."

"Truth—but only to a point," Straha said. "Even in lands we have supposedly conquered, rebellion continues. That must be one of the reasons you refuse to allow me to go out into Cairo and see for myself what sort of society the Race is building."

"You have also spoken truth, superior sir—but only to a point," Zeshpass replied. "The Big Uglies under our rule get arms and encouragement from the independent Tosevite not-empires. If there were no more independent not-empires, how could they continue the struggle against us?"

It was a good question. Straha could not answer it, not at once. After some thought of his own, he replied, "That is a possibility, I suppose. But, given what we of the conquest fleet have seen of Tosevite stubbornness and perversity, I believe it is folly to assume all resistance will die within a generation."

"We shall consider your opinions, of course," Zeshpass said. "But we are under no obligation to do anything more than consider them."

"I understand that." Straha sighed. "By my own actions, I made certain I would never again help form the Race's policy here on Tosev 3." He sounded resigned, even humble. He didn't feel humble, or anything close to it. He remained convinced he could have done a better job with the conquest fleet than Atvar had. And if Reffet couldn't see the need for soldiers from the colonization fleet, he was just another male with fancy body paint and with sand between his eye turrets.

Straha crossed the first and second fingers of his right hand, a gesture American Big Uglies sometimes used when they said something they didn't mean. That gesture meant nothing to Zeshpass, of course. To Zeshpass, Big Uglies were nuisances, annoyances, no more. Despite the war with the Deutsche, she didn't fully seem to grasp how dangerous they could be and, therefore, how important they were to study.

That gesture also summarized Straha's feelings about his return to the Race. The meeker and milder he seemed, the sooner his interrogators and those who did lead the Race these days would let him get on with his life. So he hoped, anyhow.

But Zeshpass, though naive about Tosevites, was by no means foolish about matters that had to do with the Race. She said, "When you delivered your information, superior sir, that act helped form our policy."

"I suppose it did," Straha admitted, "but that was not why I did it. As I have said before, I did it because my friend, Sam Yeager, had asked me to do it."

"Friendship with a Big Ugly counting for more than policy concerns of the Race?" Zeshpass said. "Surely your priorities became distorted during your long years of exile."

"I disagree." Straha used the negative gesture and added an emphatic cough. "Sam Yeager did a great deal for me while I was in exile. The actions of the leadership of the Race were what drove me into exile. Naturally, Yeager's wishes and his wellbeing were and are important to me."

"I shall make a note of that," Zeshpass said, with the air of a magistrate passing sentence on a criminal. Straha realized he'd been too vehement, too outspoken, too opinionated. *So much for meek and mild,* he thought. Now more like a hunting beast than a confidante, Zeshpass returned to the questioning: "So you believe it was legitimate for you to hatch friendships among the Big Uglies?"

"Yes, I do," Straha answered. *Of course I do, you addled egg.* "After all, I believed I would live among them the rest of my life." Maybe he could steer his way back toward meek and mild after all.

Zeshpass wasn't about to make things easy for him. Voice sharp as filed fingerclaws, she demanded, "It was for this reason, then, that you put your individual concerns and the concerns of this Big Ugly friend of yours above those of the Race as a whole?"

"The species of my friend is not relevant," Straha said, pushing her away from the major accusation and toward something smaller. "Rabotevs and Hallessi are citizens of the Empire, no less than males and females of the Race. If the conquest here succeeds in the end, the same will be true of Big Uglies."

"That may well be a truth." Zeshpass admitted what she

plainly would sooner have denied. She had to admit it; equality of species under the law and in the afterlife was a cornerstone of the Empire. She tried to rally: "You said nothing, I notice, about your rampant and unwarranted individualism."

There was the dangerous charge, especially from the viewpoint of members of the colonization fleet. Straha said, "Have you noticed that the males of the conquest fleet show more individualism than would have been common back on Home?"

"I have," Zeshpass answered. "Everyone from the colonization fleet has noticed this. No one from the colonization fleet approves. Our view is that the males of the colonization fleet have been contaminated by the bizarre ideologies of the Tosevites."

"We have done what we needed to do to survive and flourish on a world of individualism run wild," Straha said. "That is the Race's view, of course. To the Big Uglies, we are hopeless reactionaries."

"I do not see why the views of the local barbarians should carry any special weight," Zeshpass said primly.

"Do you not?" Straha said. "I would think the answer fairly obvious, and shown by the recent war with the Deutsche if it was not adequately obvious without that demonstration. What the Big Uglies think about us matters because they can hurt us. They can hurt us badly. Why do you have so much trouble believing that?"

Zeshpass said, "This is not the way things were to be when we got to Tosev 3. This is not the way we were told things would be when we got to Tosev 3."

"But this is the way things are," Straha said. "If you cannot see that, if you cannot adapt to that, the colonization effort will face severe difficulties."

"We are the Race," Zeshpass said. "We shall prevail. We have always prevailed. We can do it again."

"We can, certainly," Straha agreed. "Whether or not we shall . . . that is a different question. If we act as if our triumph is guaranteed, that only makes it more difficult. The Tosevites present the most severe challenge we have ever faced. Turning our eye turrets away from that challenge, acting as if it does not exist, will make things worse, not better. You may be sure the American Big Uglies, whom I know best, do not believe their triumph is guaranteed. As a result, they work unceasingly to subvert us."

"Working is one thing. Succeeding is another," Zeshpass said. "I submit to you, superior sir, that your view of these matters is colored by your having lived among the American Tosevites for so long."

"And I submit to you that your view is colored by not having lived among any Big Uglies, and by your ignorance of them," Straha retorted.

They glared at each other in perfect mutual loathing. "Time will tell which of us is correct," Zeshpass said, and Straha made the affirmative gesture.

It was some time after midnight when the guard named Fred shook Sam Yeager awake. "Come on, pal," he said when Yeager showed signs of returning to the real world. "You sleep like a rock. Shows you've got a clean conscience. I wish to God I did, believe me."

Sam yawned and rubbed his eyes. Around the yawn, he asked, "What's going on that won't keep till morning?" He sounded mushy without his false teeth.

"Somebody wants to see you," Fred answered. "Come on."

"Yeah?" Yeager tensed, wishing he hadn't made that sound quite so dubious. Who'd want to see him in the middle of the night? Were the guards waking him up so they could dispose of him more conveniently?

Fred might have read his mind. "Don't do anything stupid, Yeager," he said, and his .45 appeared as if by magic in his right hand. "If I wanted to ice you, I could blow your brains out without bothering to wake you up, right? No fuss, no muss, no bother. But I wasn't blowing smoke up your ass. Somebody wants to see you, and he's waiting in the living room."

Yeager sniffed. The odor of fresh-perked coffee wafted in from the kitchen. As much as Fred's words, that convinced him the guard was telling the truth. He put in his dentures and slid out of bed, asking, "Who is it? And can I get out of my pajamas first?"

"Don't bother about the PJ's," Fred answered. "As for who, come on out front and see for yourself."

"Okay." Sam sighed. Whoever was out there would be in a uniform, or maybe a business suit. Facing him in blue-and-white striped cotton pajamas would only put Yeager at a disadvantage.

Well, he was at a big enough disadvantage already. His feet slid into slippers. "Let's go."

"Attaboy." Fred made the pistol vanish as smoothly as he'd brought it out.

Up the hall Yeager went. When he walked into the living room, he wasn't surprised to see John and Charlie already there. With them stood another couple of men he hadn't seen before. They wore nearly identical off-the-rack suits, and they both looked jumpy and alert despite the hour. Sam noticed that much about them, but nothing more, for his eyes went to the man in the rocking chair by the far wall. Despite pajamas, he wanted to come to attention. He didn't, not quite. Instead, he nodded and spoke as casually as he could: "Hello, Mr. President."

Earl Warren returned the nod. "Hello, Lieutenant Colonel Yeager," he replied. "Officially, I'll have you know, this conversation is not taking place. Officially, I'm somewhere else—you don't need to know where—and sound asleep. I wish I were." He glanced over to one of the strangers in a suit. "Elliott, why don't you get Yeager here a cup of coffee? I expect he could use one. I know I'm glad to have mine."

"Sure," said the Secret Service man—or so Sam assumed him to be. "You take cream and sugar, Lieutenant Colonel?"

"Both, please. About a teaspoon of sugar," Yeager answered, for all the world as if this were an utterly normal conversation. Elliott went off to the kitchen.

"Sit down, Lieutenant Colonel, if you please," President Warren said, and Sam saw that all the guards had left the armchair across the room from the rocker for him. The only reason they were there was to make sure he didn't strangle the president. He'd asked to see Warren not really expecting anyone would pay any attention to him, but now Warren was here.

Elliott brought him the coffee. Not a drop had slopped from cup into saucer; the Secret Service man had steady hands. "Thanks," Sam told him, and got a curt nod in return. He sipped the coffee. It was hot and strong and good.

President Warren let him drink about a third of the cup, then said, "Shall we get down to brass tacks?"

"Okay by me." Yeager pointed to Fred and Charlie and John. "But these fellows have said they don't want to know why they've been keeping me here. Should they listen in?"

His guards and the Secret Service men put their heads together. Then, to his surprise, the fellows who'd ridden herd on him trooped out of the living room and out of the house; he heard the door close behind them. President Warren said, "I think Jim and Elliott should be able to keep me safe." Yeager nodded; they were bound to be armed. Even if they weren't, either one of them could have broken him in half. With a sigh, the president asked, "Well, Lieutenant Colonel, what's on your mind?"

Sam took another sip of coffee before answering. He took a deep breath, too. Now that he had to bring them out, the words wanted to stick in his throat. He wished the coffee were fortified with something stronger than cream and sugar. But he said what he had to say: "Sir, why did you order the attack on the colonization fleet?"

Both Secret Service men started. Elliott muttered something under his breath. He and the one named Jim stared at the president. Earl Warren sighed again. "The classic answer is, it seemed like a good idea at the time. And it *did* seem like a good idea. It was the hardest blow humans have ever struck against the Race, and the Lizards never really suspected the United States. No one did—except you, Lieutenant Colonel. Are you happy to realize that, by being right, you may have brought your country down in flames?"

That made Sam take another deep, anything but happy breath. "Mr. President, I decided a long time ago that whoever launched missiles at the colonization fleet was a murderer," he answered. "I swear to God, I thought it was the Nazis or the Reds. I never imagined the trail would lead back to us."

"But you kept looking, didn't you?" President Warren said. "You couldn't take a hint. You just kept poking your nose where it didn't belong."

"A hint, sir?" Yeager said in real puzzlement. "What kind of hint?"

Warren sighed again. "Wouldn't you say that the unfortunate things that kept almost happening to you and your family—that would have happened if you'd been less on your guard—were a hint that you were digging in places you shouldn't be? We even tried to pass that message to you, first through General LeMay and then through Straha's driver."

"General LeMay was only talking about the *Lewis and Clark*," Sam said, "and I didn't know just what Straha's driver was talking about—not till I found out what had happened to the colonization fleet, anyway. And by then it was too late."

"It may be too late for all of us," the president said heavily. "What on earth possessed you to give Straha a printout of what you'd found?"

"When I did find it, Mr. President, all of a sudden I understood why I'd been having all the trouble I'd been having," Yeager answered. "I thought of Straha as a life-insurance policy—if anything happened to me or to my kin, the word would still get out. I guess it has?"

"Oh, it has, all right." Earl Warren glared at him. "That damned Lizard sneaked out of the USA and into Cairo, and by every sign those documents got there ahead of him. And Atvar has been threatening war against the United States ever since. That is a war you must know we would lose."

"Yes, sir, I do know that," Sam said. "I've known it all along. I thought you did, too. The Lizards have always said they'd do something dreadful if they ever found out who hit the colonization fleet. I figured Germany or Russia would deserve it. I have trouble thinking we don't. I'm sorry, sir, but that's how it looks to me."

"Do you know what one of the Race's principal demands has been?" the president asked with an angry toss of the head.

"No, sir. I have no idea," Sam replied. "I haven't seen much in the way of news lately. Is my family all right?" They could have held him and done God knows what to Barbara and Jonathan. The guards had said they hadn't, but still . . . Doing that would screw up the experiment with Mickey and Donald, but they probably wouldn't care. They'd figure keeping a secret was more important.

But now President Warren nodded. "Your wife and son are fine. You have my word on it." Yeager had always thought his word good. Now he knew it wasn't, or wasn't necessarily. Before he could do more than realize that, Warren went on, "The Lizards are insisting that you be released unharmed, and that no harm befall your kin. It is a condition we intend to meet."

God bless Straha, Sam thought. *He lived among Big Uglies so long, he got some notion of how important family members are to us. And thank heaven he managed to get that across to the Lizards in Cairo.* Aloud, he made his voice harsh: "Is that the reason I'm still breathing? And my wife and son?"

"It is . . . one of the reasons," Warren answered. Yeager gave the president reluctant credit for not flinching from the question. "It is also the only condition we find easy to meet. The Race is demanding that we either let them incinerate one of our cities with an explosive-metal bomb or make concessions to them that would permanently weaken us—not quite to the degree the *Reich* has been diminished, but something not far from that."

Yeager winced. Sure enough, the Lizards hadn't been kidding. "And if you tell them no on both those counts, it's war?"

"That is about the size of it, Lieutenant Colonel Yeager," the president said. "We have you to thank for it."

But Yeager shook his head. "No, sir. You were the one who ordered the launch. The Race would have found out sooner or later, and they'd have been just as furious a hundred years from now as they are right this minute."

"We would be in a stronger position to fight back a hundred years from now," Warren said.

"Maybe," Sam said, "but maybe not, too. Who knows what'll be heading this way from Home now that the Lizards know we're not pushovers?"

"At any rate, we have to deal with what is happening now," the president said, "which is to say, with what you've wrought. The Russians may stand with us. The thought that they might has given the Lizards pause."

"Would they?" Sam knew he sounded surprised. After a little thought, though, it seemed less implausible. "If we go down, they know they're next, and they haven't got a prayer of fighting off the Lizards by themselves." He didn't think the USA and the USSR together could beat the Race, but they'd sure as hell let the Lizards know they'd been in a fight.

President Warren's big head soberly went up and down. "I believe that is Molotov's reasoning, yes, although you never can tell with Russians."

In all his days, Sam Yeager had never imagined he would sit in judgment on a president of the United States. His voice hardly more than a whisper, he asked, "What will you do, sir?"

"What I have to do," Earl Warren answered. "What seems best for the United States and for all of humanity. That's what I've been doing all along." What was intended as a smile lifted only one corner of his mouth. "Thanks to you, it didn't work out quite the way I expected."

Sam let out a long sigh. "No, sir, I guess not." He started to add, *I'm sorry,* but that didn't pass his lips. Part of him was, but a much bigger part wasn't.

President Warren said, "I shall of course arrange for your release. I would be grateful for your public silence and that of any loved ones you may have informed until the present crisis ends. I am not going to order it, but I would be grateful for it."

"How will I know when that is?" Sam asked.

The president looked at him—looked through him. "Believe me, Lieutenant Colonel, you will not be left in any doubt."

Pshing came up to Atvar and said, "Exalted Fleetlord, the ambassador from the not-empire of the United States is here to see you."

Atvar made the affirmative gesture. "I will see him. Show him in. No—wait. First bring in a chair suitable for a Tosevite's hindquarters. I do not intend to insult him in any trivial way."

"It shall be done, Exalted Fleetlord." Pshing hurried off. He brought in first the chair and then the Big Ugly named Henry Cabot Lodge.

"I greet you, Exalted Fleetlord," the ambassador said.

"And I greet you," Atvar replied. "You may sit." As far as he was concerned, the wild Tosevite didn't really deserve the privilege, but the fleetlord had grown used to diplomatic niceties since the first round of fighting stopped. The USA and the Race were theoretically equals and were not at war—not yet. Not offering Lodge a chair would have been an insult: a small one, but an insult nonetheless. No, Atvar did not intend to offer the United States any small insults.

"I am here, Exalted Fleetlord, among other reasons, to bring you the apology of the government of the United States for the unfortunate incident involving the colonization fleet," Lodge said.

"I am here to tell you, Ambassador, that no apology is adequate," Atvar replied. "No apology can be adequate. I am here to tell you that the Race will have compensation for what the United States did."

Henry Cabot Lodge's gray-maned head bobbed up and down, the Tosevite equivalent of the affirmative gesture. "I am prepared to negotiate such compensation if you truly require it."

"If we truly require it?" Atvar sprang to his feet. His mouth opened, not in a laugh but in a way that suggested his ancestors

had been carnivores. He held out his hand so his fingerclaws
were ready to tear. Had he been standing erect instead of leaning
forward, had his crest risen, he would have looked ready to fight
a mating battle. "We have said from the moment this outrage occurred that we would require it, once we learned who the guilty
party was. You may be grateful that we have not already embarked on war without limits."

In the abstract, he had to admire the American ambassador.
The Big Ugly sat there as calmly as if he hadn't embarked on his
tirade. When he finished, Lodge said, "One reason you have not,
of course, is that we could hurt you badly if you did. If the Russians join us—and we are no more certain about that than you—
the damage to the Race and the lands it rules will be even
greater."

He was all the more infuriating partly because he stayed calm,
partly because he was without a doubt correct. But Atvar would
not admit that no matter how obvious it was. He said, "Regardless of what you can do to us, we can do far more to you." That
was also a manifest truth. "And we shall, to avenge the murder of
males and females in cold sleep, before they ever had the chance
to come down to the surface of Tosev 3."

"Unless I can negotiate some other solution that would satisfy
you and my government at the same time," Lodge said.

"You know what our demands are." Atvar made his voice hard
as stone, hoping the Big Ugly would grasp his tone. "Return of the
Lewis and Clark and the new ship from their present location
among the minor planets. No further expeditions to those planets.
American orbital forts to have their explosive-metal weapons
removed to prevent further unprovoked attacks. American ground-
based missiles to be reduced in number. American submersible-
ship-based missiles to be eliminated. The Race's inspectors to go
where they please when they please in the United States to make
certain these terms are carried out."

"No," Henry Cabot Lodge said. "My instructions are specific
on that point. These terms are unacceptable to the United States.
President Warren has not given me permission to deal with them
even hypothetically."

"You also know the other alternative," Atvar said. "To let one
of your cities be incinerated, as our colonists were incinerated."

"No," the American ambassador said again. "That is also
unacceptable."

"When the weak propose something, the strong may say it is unacceptable," Atvar told him. "When the strong propose something, the weak may say only, 'It shall be done.' Who here is strong? Who is weak? I suggest you think carefully on this, Ambassador. If you reject both these demands, we shall have war. Regardless of the damage it may do us, it will destroy you. Do you understand?"

"I understand, Exalted Fleetlord," Lodge said, still calmly.

"Then I dismiss you," Atvar said. "You had better make sure that your not-emperor understands. Unless he complies with the Race's just demands—and they *are* just demands, without the tiniest fragment of doubt—we shall visit ruination on his not-empire."

Henry Cabot Lodge rose and bent at the waist—not the posture of respect, but about as close to it as wild Big Uglies came. "I shall convey your words to President Warren. Shall we meet again in two days' time?"

Atvar glared at him. "You are using this delay to increase your armed forces' readiness to resist us."

"No, Exalted Fleetlord." Lodge shook his head. "We have been at maximum readiness for some time. The only way we could be more ready would be to start the fight ourselves. That, I assure you, we do not intend to do."

"Of course not," Atvar snarled. "We would be ready if you did. You could not strike a stealthy blow this time."

Lodge bowed again and departed without another word. That left the fleetlord feeling vaguely punctured. As soon as the Tosevite had left, Pshing came into the office. "Any progress, Exalted Fleetlord?" he asked.

"None." Atvar made the negative gesture. "None whatsoever." He sighed. "We shall be fortunate to avoid another war, and this one far worse than that which we fought against the Deutsche. The American Big Uglies refuse to give up their clawhold on space, and they also naturally refuse to yield up a city to our wrath."

"Did you expect them to yield one?" Pshing asked.

"No," Atvar answered. "I intended to use that threat to get them out of space and to reduce their weaponry, which would let us dominate them henceforward even if they stay nominally independent. But they plainly perceive the long-term danger in that course of events. If they refuse us, however, the danger is not long-term but short-term."

His telephone hissed. Pshing hurried out to answer it in the antechamber. A moment later, he called, "Exalted Fleetlord, it is Fleetlord Reffet."

Atvar wanted to speak to the leader of the colonization fleet about as much as he wanted to have an ingrown toeclaw cut free without local anesthetic, but realized he had no choice. With another sigh, he said, "Put him through."

Reffet looked angry. That was Atvar's first thought when he saw his opposite number from the colonization fleet. Reffet sounded angry, too: "Well, has that cursed Big Ugly caved in to our demands yet?"

"Unfortunately, no," Atvar answered.

"All right, then," Reffet said. "We just have to blow his stinking not-empire—stupid name for a piece of land, if anybody wants to know what *I* think—clean off the surface of Tosev 3. Those Tosevites deserve whatever happens to them, after what they did to us. A bite in the back, that is what it was. Nothing but a miserable, treacherous bite in the back."

"Truth," Atvar agreed. "If we fight them now, however, they will without a doubt bite us in the front several times. Their not-empire is far larger and is also more populous than that of the Deutsche. Their military preparedness is not to be despised. And, if we get heavily involved in fighting them, the Russkis may indeed bite us in the back."

"And whose fault is that?" The question from the fleetlord of the colonization fleet was rhetorical. He was convinced he knew whose fault it was: Atvar's, and no one else's.

With a sigh—how many times had he sighed on or in orbit around Tosev 3?—Atvar answered, "If you must blame anyone, blame the planners who sent a probe to this miserable world sixteen hundred years ago and assumed it would not change in the meanwhile. A probe a hundred years before we set out would have warned us and saved us much grief. I have already recommended that this be made standard practice in planning any future conquest fleets."

"Wonderful," Reffet said. "This does us exactly no good now, of course."

"I agree," Atvar said. "Have you any constructive suggestions to make, or did you call just to complain at everything I am doing?"

The fleetlord of the colonization fleet glared at him. "I have already made my suggestion: punish these Big Uglies with every means at our disposal."

"I asked you for constructive suggestions," Atvar replied. "That is a destructive suggestion. How destructive it turns out to be, we will know only after the fighting ends." He held up a hand before Reffet could speak. "You will tell me it is more destructive to the Big Uglies. Again, I agree. It had better be, anyway. But it will hurt us, too. However much you may wish to scratch sand over it, that also remains a truth."

Reffet hissed in frustrated fury. "Will you let these Tosevites get off without punishment for their crime, then?"

"By no means." Atvar used an emphatic cough. "I am trying to arrange a punishment for them that will not involve damage to the Race. If I can do that, well and good. If I cannot . . . I will take whatever other steps I deem necessary."

"You had better," Reffet said. "If you fail here, the effort to depose you that Straha led will look like a hatchlings' game."

Atvar supposed he shouldn't have been surprised at a threat like that. Somehow, he still was. Having gone through such humiliation once, did he really want to face it a second time? Did he have any choice? If he did botch this negotiation with the Americans, wouldn't he deserve to be overthrown? He said, "I hear you, Reffet. Since you admit you have nothing constructive to contribute, I bid you good day."

"I admit nothing of the—" Reffet began. Atvar took savage pleasure in breaking the connection and cutting him off in mid-squawk.

After that, he had to deal with minutiae: the eternal rebellion in China, the equally eternal rebellion in India, a new outbreak in the subregion of the southern part of the lesser continental mass called Argentina. All of those would eventually be solved, and none of them, even unsolved, was more than a nuisance to the Race. Atvar issued directives confident that, regardless of whether they were right or wrong, the world would go on. He had margin for error.

He had none with the American Big Uglies, and he knew it. He had to keep the pressure on them, and had to do so in such a way that he resisted the pressure from his own extremists. Two days later, as promised, Henry Cabot Lodge returned to his office. "I have a proposal for you from President Warren," Lodge said, and set it forth.

When he'd finished, Atvar said, "Are you certain you understood him correctly? Is he certain of what he is doing?"

"Yes and yes, respectively," Lodge replied. "He requests one additional item: personal foreknowledge—not much, but a little—of the precise timing. Your intelligence resources will be able to make sure that the United States does not use this for any untoward purpose."

"I had not expected—" Atvar began.

Lodge cut him off: "Does this proposal meet with your approval or not? If not, I see no way to avoid war."

Atvar had never imagined that a Big Ugly could squeeze him. But he felt squeezed now. He stared at Lodge. The Tosevite kept his face very still. His impression after pondering was the same as it had been at first scent: he would never get a better offer from the Americans. His left hand shaped the affirmative gesture. "I accept," he said.

Jonathan Yeager had never been so glad to sit on the couch in his own front room watching a baseball game. Having his father sitting there beside him made all the difference in the world. Sam Yeager had his legs crossed. He took a swig from a bottle of Lucky Lager, then returned it to its resting place on top of his upper knee. It stayed there quite happily; the hollow in the bottom of the bottle fit the curve of his knee very well. Whenever Jonathan tried such things, he spilled beer or soda on his pants.

The Kansas City batter lashed a double to the gap in left-center. Two runners scored. "That makes the score 5–4 Blues, as the Yankees' bullpen lets them down again," Buddy Blattner shouted from the set.

"They overthrew the cutoff man," Jonathan's dad said. "If they hadn't, the Yankees might have nailed Mantle as he rounded second—he was thinking triple, but he had to put on the brakes."

Barbara Yeager said, "You pick apart ballgames the way I was trained to analyze literature."

"Why not?" Jonathan's dad said. "*I* was trained to hit the cutoff man on a throw from the outfield, no matter what. I didn't have the talent to make the big leagues—especially after I tore up my ankle—but I always knew what I was doing out there."

Before anybody could say anything more, the baseball game

disappeared from the TV screen, to be replaced by a slide with the words URGENT NEWS BULLETIN. "What's this?" Jonathan said.

Chet Huntley's long, somber face replaced the slide. It looked even longer and more somber than usual. "In an assault apparently launched without any warning to U.S. authorities, the Race has detonated a large explosive-metal bomb above Indianapolis, Indiana," he said. "Casualties, obviously, are as yet unknown, but they must be in the tens, if not in the hundreds, of thousands."

As the picture cut away from Huntley to show a toadstool cloud rising above some city or other—it might have been Indianapolis, or it might have been stock footage—Jonathan and his parents all said the same thing at the same time: "Oh, Jesus Christ!"

"They've paid us back," Sam Yeager added. "It was this or get out of space forever and turn over most of our weapons. Those were the terms Atvar set. I didn't think we'd do it this way, though." He emptied his beer in a couple of long, convulsive gulps.

Chet Huntley reappeared, but only to say, "Now we're going to Eric Sevareid in Little Rock for the administration's response to this unprovoked attack."

It wasn't unprovoked, as Jonathan knew only too well. And when Sevareid came onto the screen, his face, normally as dead a pan as any newsman's, was wet with tears. He said, "Ladies and gentlemen, President Earl Warren has just been found dead in a Gray House bedroom. He appears to have died by his own hand."

Again, Jonathan and his father and mother said the same thing at the same time: "Oh, my God!"

Eric Sevareid said, "The presidential press secretary has before him a statement that he will read to the nation. We will also be hearing from Vice President—excuse me, from President—Harold Stassen as soon as he can be found and informed of the dual tragedies of the day. The vice president—excuse me again, the president; that *will* take some getting used to—is on a fishing trip in his home state of Minnesota. And now, Mr. Hagerty."

The camera cut away from Sevareid and over to the briefing room of the Gray House. James Hagerty blinked under the bright lights. He licked his lips a couple of times, then said, "As what seems to have been his final living act, President Warren wrote by hand the statement I have before me. He set it where it would surely be found when he was sought after the destruction of Indianapolis. He was, by that time, unfortunately deceased. These are, then, the last words of the president of the United States."

"I never thought he'd do this," Sam Yeager said. Jonathan and his mother both hissed for him to be quiet.

" 'My fellow citizens, by the time you hear these words, I will be dead,' " James Hagerty read. " 'The demands the Race has made upon the United States of America have left me in a position where I could not in good conscience accept either of them, but where rejecting them would have resulted in the destruction of our great nation.' "

Hagerty blinked and licked his lips again. *He's getting all this for the first time, too,* Jonathan realized. *Poor bastard.* The press secretary went on, " 'And yet, there was justice in the Race's demands upon us, for it was at my order that rocket forces of the United States launched explosive-metal-tipped missiles against twelve ships of the colonization fleet not long after it took up Earth orbit. I and no one else am responsible for that order. I still believe it was in the best interest of mankind as a whole. But now my role has been discovered, and my country and I must pay the price.' "

Jonathan's father cursed and grimaced. Jonathan's mother patted him on the shoulder. Jonathan himself hardly noticed. He was staring, transfixed, at the television screen.

" 'Fleetlord Atvar presented us with a dreadful choice,' " Earl Warren's press secretary read. " 'Either withdrawal of our weapons and installations from space and the great reduction of our ground- and sea-based weapons systems—essentially, the loss of our independence—or the destruction of a great American city. "Eye for eye, tooth for tooth, hand for hand, foot for foot." If neither of those, then war, war we could not hope to win.' "

Hagerty paused to wipe his eyes on the sleeve of his jacket. "Excuse me," he said to the millions watching. Then he resumed: " 'I could not, I would not, sacrifice our future by reducing our installations as the Race demanded. And I could not lead us into a war where, however much we might hurt the foe, the United States would surely suffer the fate of the Greater German *Reich*. That left me with no choice but to sacrifice Indianapolis to the vengeance of the Race.' "

"Jesus," Jonathan muttered. He wondered what he would have done in Warren's shoes. The devil and the deep blue sea . . .

" 'Having made that decision,' " the press secretary continued, " 'I also decided that I . . . could not live when the men, women, and children I had sacrificed were dead. I hope I may find forgiveness in the hearts of the living and in the sight of God. Farewell, and may God bless the United States of America.' "

James Hagerty looked up from the podium, as if about to add a few words of his own. Then he shook his head. His eyes overflowed with tears again. Fighting back a sob, he hurried away. The camera lingered on the empty podium, as if unsure where else to go.

"Are you all right, dear?" Jonathan's mother asked his father. For a moment, Jonathan had no idea what she meant. But then he saw that, if the blood of the people of Indianapolis was on Earl Warren's hands, it was also on the hands of his dad. If the Lizards hadn't found out who'd attacked the colonization fleet, they wouldn't have destroyed the city. He too looked anxiously toward his father.

"Yeah, I'm okay, or pretty much so, anyhow." Sam Yeager's voice was harsh. "Warren couldn't live after he had to throw Indianapolis into the fire. Okay, but what about all the Lizards he killed? He didn't lose a night's sleep over them, and they hadn't done anything to anybody, either. They couldn't have—they were in cold sleep themselves. If Lizards aren't people worth thinking about, what are they?"

Slowly, Jonathan nodded. "Truth," he said—in the Lizards' language.

At last, the TV screen cut away from the podium with nobody behind it. But when it did, Jonathan wished it hadn't, for what it showed were the ruins of Indianapolis. Chet Huntley's voice provided commentary: "These are the outskirts of the city. We cannot get closer to the center. We are not altogether sure it is safe to come even so close."

A man walked into the camera's line of sight. The right side of his face looked normal. The left, and his left arm, had been dreadfully burned. "Sir," called a newsman behind the camera, "what happened, sir?"

"I was watering my lawn," the man with half a normal face said. "Watering my lawn," he repeated. "I was watering my lawn, and the whole goddamn world blew up." He swayed like a tree in a high breeze, then slowly toppled.

"Flash must have got him," Jonathan's dad said. "If he'd been turned the other way, it would have been the other side of his face. Or if he'd been looking right at it . . ." His voice trailed away. Jonathan had no trouble figuring out what would have happened then. His stomach lurched. The camera panned across devastation.

The telephone rang. He sprang up and ran to answer it, as much to escape the images on the TV screen as for any other reason. "Hello?"

"Jonathan?" It was Karen. "My God, Jonathan . . ." She sounded as ravaged, stunned, disbelieving as he was.

"Yeah," he said, for want of anything better. "This is what we were sitting on."

"I know," she answered. "I never imagined it would turn out like . . . this."

"I didn't, either. I'm just glad they turned Dad loose and he got home okay." Looking at some tiny private good in the midst of general disaster was a very human trait. Maybe that thought impelled what came next: "Karen, *will* you marry me, dammit?" She hadn't said yes and she hadn't said no.

It was the wrong time. It couldn't have been a worse time. Maybe it couldn't have been a better time, either, though, for she answered, "Yes, I think we should do that." And then, before he could say anything else, she hung up.

Dazed, he walked back into the living room. He still didn't get a chance to say anything, because his mother told him, "They've caught up with Vice President—*President*—Stassen."

Sure enough, there was Harold Stassen, with the words THIEF LAKE, MINNESOTA superimposed on his image. He wore a fisherman's vest that was allover pockets, a floppy hat, and an expression as sandbagged as everybody else's. Jonathan thought it was cruel for a reporter to thrust a microphone in his face and bark, "In light of the present situation, Mr. President, what do you intend to do?"

Stassen gave what Jonathan thought was about the best answer he could: "I'm going to go back to Little Rock and find out exactly what happened. After that, with God's help, I'll try to take this country forward again. I have nothing else to say right now."

In spite of that last sentence, the reporter asked, "Mr. President, were you aware that the United States launched the attack on the colonization fleet?"

"No," Stassen said. "I was not aware of that, not until you told me a moment ago. Some officers will have some things to answer for. I expect to find out which ones."

"You can start with Lieutenant General Curtis LeMay," Jonathan's father said, and then, thoughtfully rather than in anger, "I wonder if he'll have the decency to kill himself. Too much to hope for, unless I'm wrong. And I wonder just how many know. Not a lot, or the secret wouldn't have stayed secret this long."

"Dad, Mom," Jonathan said, "Karen just said she'd marry me."

"That's good, son," his father said.

"Congratulations," his mother added. But neither one of them heard him with more than half an ear. Almost all of their attention was on the TV screen, which cut away from the most unpresidential images of the new president to new scenes of the ruin that had without warning overtaken Indianapolis. Jonathan would have been angrier at them if his own eyes hadn't been drawn as by a magnet to the television set.

"I was in orbital patrol when that satellite launched on the ships of the colonization fleet," Glen Johnson said in the galley of the *Lewis and Clark*. "I figured it had to be the Nazis or the Reds. I never imagined the United States would do such a thing."

"Now that you know better," Dr. Miriam Rosen said, "what do you think of what President Warren did?"

"Falling on his sword, you mean?" Johnson said. "The country would have strung him up if he hadn't."

But the doctor shook her head, which made her dark, curly hair flip back and forth in a way that would have been impossible under gravity. "No, that's not what I meant. What do you think of his sacrificing a city instead of everything we've done in space?"

Before Johnson could answer, Mickey Flynn said, "If the United States survives as an independent power, he'll go down in history as a tragic hero of sorts. If we don't, he'll be a villain, of course."

Johnson ate another mouthful of beans and diced peppers. The peppers provided essential vitamins. They were also hot enough to make his eyes cross. In a way, that was a welcome change from the blandness of most of what he ate aboard the spaceship. In another, more immediate, way, though, it made him drink from his plastic bottle of water before he could speak. When he did, he said, "Winners write history, sure enough."

Flynn had another question: "What do you think of the fellow who let the Lizards know what we'd done?"

"That's a funny thing," Johnson said. "I watched those ships blow up. I don't know how many thousands or hundreds of thousands of Lizards were in them. They never had a chance. They never even knew they died, because they never woke up out of cold sleep. If I'd known whether the Germans or the Russians launched on them, I'd've told the Race in a red-hot minute. I wouldn't have felt bad about it. I'd have figured the bad guys were getting what they deserved."

"It's different when the shoe is on your own foot," Dr. Rosen observed.

"Ain't it the truth!" Johnson's agreement was wholehearted if ungrammatical.

"If I had to guess—" Flynn began.

Johnson cut him off: "If I know you, Mickey, that means you've analyzed it seventeen ways from Sunday."

"Not this time," the second pilot said with dignity. "Not enough data. As I was saying before I was so rudely interrupted, if I had to guess, I'd say Warren took the Race by surprise when he gave them Indianapolis instead of everything out here and everything in Earth orbit."

"Congratulations," Miriam Rosen said. "Second-guessing a dead man from a couple of hundred million miles away isn't just a world record. If it's not a solar system record, it's got to be in the running."

Flynn gravely inclined his head, which, since he floated perpendicular to the doctor, made him look absurd. "Thank you kindly. I'm honored to have such a distinguished judge. Now I shall elucidate."

"That means explain, right?" Johnson asked—more harassing fire.

But Flynn gave better than he got, remarking, "Only a Marine would need an explanation of an explanation. Now if I may go on?" When Johnson, licking his wounds, didn't rise to that, the second pilot did continue: "On the surface, giving up the installations is the easy, obvious choice. It costs no lives, it costs no

money—in the short term, it looks better. And the Race is con
vinced we Tosevites live in the short term."

"But in the long term, it would ruin the United States,"
Johnson said. "It would put us at the Lizards' mercy."

"Exactly." Flynn nodded again. "Whereas losing Indianapoli
does us very little harm in the long run—unless, of course, one i
unfortunate enough to live in Indianapolis. The fleetlor
probably threw in the destruction of a city as a goad to make u
do what he really wanted. But when President Warren took hir
up on it, he had no choice this side of war but to accept, and th
United States is and will be a going concern for some time t
come. That's why I say President Warren has a decent chance o
being remembered kindly."

"All that makes a good deal of sense," Dr. Rosen said. "Wha
do you think, Glen?"

"The last time you asked me that, Mickey got up on hi
soapbox," Johnson replied, at which Flynn sent him an injure
stare. Ignoring it, Johnson found himself nodding. "But I think i
makes sense, too. Warren took a big chance, he got caught, an
he paid the price that hurt the country least. Going on living afte
that . . . I guess I can see how he wouldn't have wanted to."

"He'd have been impeached and convicted as soon as the story
broke," Dr. Rosen said. "I wonder if we would have handed hir
over to the Lizards after that. Maybe it's just as well we don'
have to find out."

"Probably," Flynn said.

Johnson couldn't quarrel with that, either. He said, "When w
did give him to the Lizards, he'd have been covered with tar an
feathers. He almost screwed up everything he'd been building—
everything we've been building—for years and years."

"And yet . . ." Flynn said in the thoughtful tones he use
whenever he was going to go against conventional wisdom
"And yet, I wonder whether that one blow he got in against th
colonization fleet before the Lizards were expecting anythin
hurt them more than losing Indianapolis hurt us. Five hundre
years from now, historians will be arguing about that—but wil
they be our historians or males and females of the Race?"

"To be or not to be, that *is* the question," Dr. Rosen said.

"I wasn't joking, Miriam," Mickey Flynn said.

"Neither was I," she answered.

Slowly, Johnson said, "By doing what he did, Warren made

sure the *Lewis and Clark* and now the *Columbus* would stay out here. He made sure we wouldn't lose whatever space stations we build in Earth orbit and the weapons we've already got there. The Race still has to take us seriously. That's not the smallest thing in the world. Twenty years from now, fifty years from now, it's liable to be the biggest thing in the world. Five hundred years from now, it's liable to say who's writing the history books." He raised his water bottle in salute. "Here's to Earl Warren—I think."

Flynn and Dr. Rosen also drank, with much the same hesitation he'd shown in proposing the toast. The PA system chimed the hour. As if he couldn't believe it, Johnson's eyes went to his wristwatch. It said the same thing the chime did.

He said something, too: "I'm late. Walt's not going to be very happy with me."

"An understatement I would be proud to claim," Flynn said. "I am also late—for my rest period. To sleep, perchance to dream . . ."

"Perchance to soak your head," Johnson said over his shoulder as he pushed off to deposit his dishes in their boxes before heading for the control room. He thought he saw Flynn and the doctor leaving together by another exit, but was in too much of a hurry to escape the chief pilot's wrath to be sure.

"So good of you to join me, Lieutenant Colonel," Stone said in frigid tones when Glen did fly into the control room. "It would have been even better, of course, had you joined me four minutes and, ah, twenty-seven seconds ago."

"I'm sorry, sir," Johnson said. Then he broke a cardinal military rule: never offer an excuse to atone for a failure. "Mickey and Miriam and I were trying to figure out what the devil's going on back on Earth, and I just didn't pay any attention to the time."

And, for a wonder, it worked. Walter Stone leaned forward in his seat and asked, "Any conclusions?"

"Either Earl Warren is a hero or a bum, but nobody's going to know for sure for the next five hundred years," Johnson answered; that seemed to sum up a lunch's worth of conversation in a sentence. He added a comment of his own: "Only God or the spirits of Emperors past can tell now, anyhow."

Stone grunted laughter and said, "Truth," in the Lizards' language, tacking on an emphatic cough for good measure. After a couple of seconds of silence, he fell back into English: "He may be a hero for what he did, if you look at things that way. He *may* be.

But I'll tell you one thing, Glen—he's the biggest bum since Benedict Arnold for letting himself get caught. If he was going to give those orders, every one of them should have been oral. If anybody did write anything down, he should have burned it the second the launch happened. Then there wouldn't have been anything for Nosy Parkers later on. Am I right, or am I wrong?"

"Oh, you're right, sir. No doubt about it. Nosy Parkers . . ." Johnson's voice faded.

Stone thought he knew why, and laughed at the junior pilot. "You don't think that's so funny, because you were a Nosy Parker yourself, and look what it got you."

"Yeah." But Johnson remained abstracted. He'd known another Nosy Parker, a fellow named Yeager out in California who'd been as curious about what the hell was going on with the space station that became the *Lewis and Clark* as he was himself. And Yeager was a hotshot expert on the Race, too. If he'd been snooping, and if he'd found stuff that would have been better off gone, who was more likely to run and tell stories to the Lizards? Johnson almost spoke up, but he didn't know anything, not for sure, and so he kept quiet about that. Instead, he said, "There's almost always a paper trail in that kind of business. There shouldn't be, but there is."

"Well, I won't say you're wrong, because you're not," Stone said. "Even so, you'd think they'd be more careful with something that important. We're goddamn lucky we didn't have to pay anything more than Indianapolis."

"Yeah," Johnson said again. "It's not like we lost an important town." The two men eyed each other in perfect understanding. They were both from Ohio, where Indianapolis was often known as Indian-no-place.

Stone said, "The one thing I do give Warren high marks for is keeping us in space. You know the concept of a fleet in being?"

"Sure." Johnson nodded. "We've got enough stuff that they have to pay attention to us whether we do anything or not."

"That's it," Stone agreed. "If we'd had to give up everything, what would we be? An oversized New Zealand, that's what."

"But now we get to go on," Johnson said. "It cost us. It cost us like hell. But we're still in business. And one of these days . . ." He looked out through the glare-resistant glass at the seemingly countless stars.

"One of these days." Like him, Walter Stone spoke the words as if they were a complete sentence.

"I wonder what kind of funeral they've got planned for Warren," Johnson said. "A big fancy one, or just toss him in a trash can with his feet sticking out?"

"Me, I'd take the second one, and some hobo could steal his shoes," Stone said. "But he was the president, so odds are they'll do it up brown." He paused. "Dammit."

The last place on Earth Vyacheslav Molotov wanted to be was in Little Rock, Arkansas, for a state funeral. He hated flying, but Earl Warren wasn't going to keep till he could cross the Atlantic by ship. He'd had a measure of revenge by ordering Andrei Gromyko to come with him.

To his annoyance, the foreign commissar was reacting philosophically rather than with annoyance of his own. "Things could be worse," he said as he and Molotov met in the Soviet embassy before heading for the gathering procession.

"How?" Molotov was irritable enough to let his irritation show. He hadn't slept at all on the airplane that brought him to America, and even a long night in bed at the embassy left his body uncertain of what time it was supposed to be.

"If this had happened a couple of months ago, it would be forty degrees centigrade outside, with humidity fit to swim in," the foreign commissar answered. "Washington was bad in the summertime. Little Rock is worse."

"Bozhemoi!" Molotov said. Good Communists weren't supposed to mention God, but old habits were hard to break. The general secretary went on, "I am given to understand Dornberger came in person to represent the *Reich*, and Eden from England. Is Tojo here also?"

"Yes," Gromyko answered. "If the Lizards wanted to hurt all the leading human states, they could throw a missile at Little Rock."

"Heh," Molotov said. "Losing Eden would probably help England. And Doriot, I notice, is conspicuous by his absence. He collaborated with the Germans so long and so well, he had no trouble collaborating with the Lizards when they became the leading foreigners in France."

Gromyko clucked. "Such cynicism, Vyacheslav Mikhailovich. Officially, the government of the Race has sent its condolences to the government of the United States, so everything is correct on that score."

"Correct!" Molotov turned and twisted, trying to help his back recover from sitting in the airliner seat for what felt like a month. He wasn't a young man any more. He seldom felt his three-quarters of a century back in Moscow; thanks to iron routine, one day usually went by much like another. But when he was jerked out of his routine, he took much longer recovering than he would have twenty years before. He had to pause and remember what he'd just said before continuing, "Relations are at their most correct just before the shooting starts."

"Warren seems to have avoided that," Gromyko said. In a lower voice, he added, "For which we may all be thankful."

"Yes." Molotov nodded emphatically. "That would have been a pretty choice, wouldn't it? We could have joined the United States in a losing war against the Race, or we could have waited for the Race to finish devouring the USA, and then faced a losing war against the Lizards."

"By putting things off, and by keeping the USA in the game, humanity has gained a chance." By Gromyko's tone, he didn't think it a very good chance.

Molotov's private opinion was much the same, but he wouldn't have told himself his private opinion if he could have avoided it. He kept up a bold front to Gromyko: "Moscow seemed on the point of falling first to the Germans and then to the Lizards. But the hammer and sickle still fly above it."

Since that was nothing but the truth, the foreign commissar couldn't very well disagree with it. Before he had the chance, the protocol officer came in and said, "Comrades, the limousine is waiting to take you to the Gray House."

"Thank you, Mikhail Sergeyevich." Molotov had made a point of learning the young man's name and patronymic; by all reports, he was able, even if inclined to put form ahead of substance. Well, if ever there was a protocol officer's failing, that was it.

The limousine was a Cadillac. Seeing as much, Molotov raised an eyebrow. Gromyko said, "Impossibly expensive to import our own motorcars to all our embassies. In the *Reich*, we use—used—a Mercedes. I don't know what we're doing there now."

"Did we?" Molotov hadn't concerned himself with the point

before. He shrugged as he got inside. If he was going to worry about it, he'd worry after he got back to Moscow. For the time being, he would simply relax. The automobile *was* comfortable. But he wouldn't let it lull him into a false sense of security. To Gromyko, he said, "No substantive conversations here. Who can tell who might be listening?"

"Well, of course, Comrade General Secretary." The foreign commissar sounded offended. "I am not a blushing virgin, you know."

"All right, Andrei Andreyevich." Molotov spoke soothingly. "Better to speak and not need than to need and not speak."

Before Gromyko could reply, the limousine started to roll. The Soviet embassy was only a few blocks from the Gray House. One thing that struck Molotov was how small a city Little Rock really was, and how new all the important buildings were. Before the Lizard invasion, before it succeeded Washington as a national capital, it had been nothing to speak of, a sleepy provincial town like Kaluga or Kuibishev.

Well, had the Nazis or the Lizards broken through, Kuibishev would have had greatness thrust on it, too. "This place seems pleasant enough," Molotov said: about as much praise as he would give any town.

"Oh, indeed—pleasant enough, barring summer," Gromyko said. "And with air conditioning, even that is a smaller problem than it would have been twenty years ago." Almost silently, the car pulled to a stop. The foreign commissar pointed. "There is Stassen—President Stassen, now—speaking with General Dornberger."

"Thank you for pointing him out," Molotov answered. "If you hadn't, I wouldn't have recognized him." Like Dornberger, Stassen was bald. But the American was a younger man—probably still on the sunny side of sixty—and looked to have been formed in a softer school. He might not have had any trouble in his life from the end of the first round of fighting to Earl Warren's suicide. Well, he would have troubles now.

The driver opened the door to let out the Russian leaders. "Shall I introduce you?" Gromyko asked. "I speak enough English for that."

His English was actually quite good, though he preferred not to show it off. Molotov nodded. "If you would. I have never met Dornberger, either. Does he speak English?"

"I don't know," Gromyko said. "I've never had to deal with him. But we can find out."

He and Molotov approached the American and German leaders. Stassen turned away from Dornberger and toward them. He spoke in English. "Purely conventional," Gromyko said. "He thanks you for your presence and says it is a pleasure to meet you."

"Tell him the same," Molotov answered. "Express my condolences and the condolences of the Soviet people." As Gromyko spoke in English, Molotov extended his hand. The new president of the United States shook it. His grip, firm but brief, said nothing about him save that he'd shaken a lot of hands before.

Stassen spoke in English. Gromyko translated again: "He hopes we can live in peace among ourselves and with the Race. He says staying strong will help in this."

"Good. He is not altogether a fool, then," Molotov said. "Translate that last into something friendly and agreeable."

As the foreign commissar did so, the new German *Führer* came up and waited to be noticed. He was a poor man waiting for rich men to deign to see him: not a familiar position for a German leader these past ninety-five years. When Dornberger spoke, it was in English. "He says he is pleased to meet you," Gromyko reported.

"Tell him the same." Molotov shook hands with the Germans, too. "Tell him I am happier to meet him now that the *Reich* no longer has missiles aimed at the USSR."

Through Gromyko, Dornberger replied, "We had those, yes, but we had more aimed at the Race."

"Much good they did you," Molotov said. After the *Reich*'s misfortunes, he didn't have to worry so much about diplomacy.

Dornberger shrugged. "I did not make the war. All I did was fight it as well as I could once the people set above me made it. When no people set above me were left alive, I ended it as fast as I could."

"That was wise. Not starting it would have been wiser." Molotov wished more Russian generals showed the disinclination of their German counterparts to meddle in politics. Zhukov came close. But even Zhukov, though he didn't want the title, wanted at least some of the power that went with it.

"Now I have to pick up the pieces and gather my nation's

strength as best I can," Dornberger said. "Maybe the Soviet Union can help there, as it did after the First World War."

"Maybe," Molotov said. "I can offer no promises, even if the idea is worth exploring. The Race has espionage far better than the Entente powers did after that war." He turned away from the German *Führer*, who no longer led a great power, and back to the American president, who still did. "President Stassen, I want to be sure you understand how brave President Warren was not to leave you at the mercy of the Lizards for the sake of a temporary political advantage."

"I do," Stassen replied. "I also understand that he has left me at the mercy of the Democrats because he gave the Lizards Indianapolis. I do not expect to be reelected in 1968." He smiled. "Just for the moment, and just a little, I envy your system."

Had he thought of it, Molotov would have envied the American tradition of peaceful succession when Beria mounted his coup against him. He would not have admitted that no matter what. Before he could say anything at all, an American started calling to the assembled dignitaries. "Their protocol officer," Gromyko said. "He is telling us how to line up."

The ceremony was not so grand as it would have been in the Soviet Union—as it had been when Stalin died—but it had a spare impressiveness of its own. Six white horses drew the wagon on which lay the flag-draped casket that held Earl Warren's remains. Behind it, a nice touch, a soldier led a riderless black horse with empty boots reversed in the stirrups.

President Warren's widow, his children, and their spouses and children walked behind the horse. Then came the new U.S. president and his family, and then the assembled foreign dignitaries, with Molotov in the first rank. Behind them marched military bands and units from the American armed forces, some on foot, some mounted.

At a slow march, the procession went east on Capitol Street—Embassy Row—for more than a mile, then turned south toward a large church. Molotov cared little for any of that, except when his feet began to hurt. He took sardonic pleasure in the certainty that Walter Dornberger, who wore Nazi jackboots, was suffering worse than he.

What really interested him were the people who crowded the sidewalks to watch the coffin as it rolled by. Some were silent and respectful. Others called out, as they would not have done in the USSR. Gromyko murmured in Molotov's ear: "Some of them say he should have hit the Lizards harder. Others curse him for striking them at all."

"Someone will take the names of those people." Molotov spoke with great certainty. The United States might boast of the freedom of speech it granted its citizens. When they criticized the government, though, he was convinced they would be fair game.

He endured a religious service in a language he did not understand. Gromyko didn't bother translating. Molotov knew what the preacher would be saying: Warren had been important and was dead. One day, Party functionaries would say the same of Molotov. Not soon, he hoped.

Felless was about to taste ginger when the telephone hissed. She hissed, too, in frustration and annoyance. After scraping the herb off her palm and back into the vial, she touched the *accept* control and said, "I greet you."

Ambassador Veffani's image appeared in the screen. "And I greet you, Senior Researcher," he replied. "I hope you are well?"

"Yes, superior sir; I thank you." Felless was glad she hadn't tasted before answering. Who could guess in what kind of trouble she might have found herself? Actually, the kind was easy enough to guess; the degree was a different question altogether. "And you?"

"I am well," Veffani said. "I am calling to inform you that you are being placed on detached duty and transferred from Marseille to Cairo."

"I . . . am being transferred to Cairo?" Felless had trouble believing her hearing diaphragms. "After the unfortunate incident with the males from the staff of the fleetlord of the conquest fleet?"

"After they all mated with you, yes, as did I." Veffani was at pains to spell out the details Felless would sooner have avoided. "I trust you will not go there full of ginger. It would be unfortunate if you did." He used an emphatic cough.

"That will not be a difficulty, superior sir," Felless said, though it would have been had Veffani called a little later. "I would like to know the reason why I am being summoned to Cairo, especially in light of the impression the unfortunate incident must have created." She wouldn't call it anything else.

"The reason is simple," Veffani answered. "Fleetlord Atvar is forming a commission to examine the reason the American Big Uglies sacrificed one of their cities to us."

"I should think it would be obvious," Felless said: "to keep us from devastating their land with warfare, as we devastated the *Reich*."

Veffani made an impatient noise. "Why did they choose to sacrifice a city rather than weaken such space installations as they possess? Superficially, that was the easier choice, and the Tosevites are nothing if not superficial. It was the choice we expected them to make. We offered the other primarily at Fleetlord Reffet's urging. Now that they have accepted it, they remain a major power—and a major danger to us."

"I see." Felless made the affirmative gesture to show she did. "Yes, that is a worthwhile subject for consideration. Who will my colleagues be?"

"I know of Senior Researcher Ttomalss and Security Chief Diffal, both from the conquest fleet," Veffani answered. "Your inclusion with them and with whoever else will be present is a distinct compliment, as you are so recently come to Tosev 3."

"Very well," Felless said; for once, she could not argue with the ambassador. "When is the next flight from Marseille to Cairo?"

"Check your computer," he told her. "Bill the administrative system; when you give your own identification number as well, it will accept the charges."

"It shall be done," she said. "I thank you for not holding the past against me."

"I had nothing to do with it," Veffani replied. "Atvar asked for you by name, and I was in no position to refuse the fleetlord. Neither are you." His image vanished.

Felless discovered a flight was leaving that afternoon. She checked; it had seats available. As Veffani had said, she could charge her reservation to the administrative system. She was on the aircraft. No one shot at it when it landed. On any other world of the Empire, that would have been a given. On Tosev 3, Felless was willing to accept it as something of a triumph.

No one shot at her armored vehicle as it traveled to Shepheard's Hotel, either. "The Big Uglies seem to be more accepting of our rule," she remarked to the female sitting beside her as the second armored gate closed behind the vehicle.

"So they do," the female replied, "at least until something else gets them bouncing like drops of oil in a hot pan." Felless didn't answer. By everything she could see, cynicism that had been unique to the males of the conquest fleet was now infecting the colonists, too. Maybe that would make it easier for the males of the conquest fleet to fit in. Maybe it just meant the colonists would have a harder time in their efforts to form a stable society on this world.

Ttomalss was waiting for Felless when she came into the lobby of the Race's administrative center. "I greet you, superior female," he said. "You could get a room number and a map from the computer terminal there, but this place is like a maze. Your room is across the corridor from mine. If you like, I will escort you there."

"I thank you, Senior Researcher. That would be kind of you," Felless answered. As they walked through the hallways—hallways that struck her as too wide and too tall—she asked, "Who besides Diffal will be on the commission with us?"

"The only other member who has yet been chosen is Superior Nuisance Straha," Ttomalss said. Before Felless could remark on that, he continued, "That is his own suggested title for himself these days. From my experience in working with him, I must say it is a good one."

"Working with a defector?" Felless started to get angry. Then she checked herself. "It may not be such a bad move after all. He has lived longer and more intimately with the Big Uglies than we have."

"Your reaction mirrors mine," Ttomalss said. "I have been interrogating him, as you may know. When I heard he would be a part of this commission, I was at first horrified, but then realized, as you did, that his insights would prove valuable. And so they have. He has an empirical knowledge of Tosevites few of us could match."

"Good enough," Felless said. "The next obvious question is, can we trust his insights? Or is he still in some degree loyal to the Big Uglies who sheltered him for so long?"

Ttomalss made the negative gesture. "He has been interrogated under truth-revealing drugs. His comments about the authorities in the United States, though less coherent than when he is undrugged, are of the same sardonic tenor. The only loyalty to a Tosevite that he does exhibit is a personal one to Sam Yeager, whom he truly reckons a friend."

"All right. We may discount that, then," Felless agreed. "A pity we do not have such drugs to use on the Big Uglies."

"We tried some during the first round of fighting," Ttomalss said. "They worked imperfectly when they worked at all. And, because males relied too much on the false results they got with them, they turned out to be worse than interrogation with no drugs at all."

"That is unfortunate," Felless said.

"It often turned out to be very unfortunate for the males involved," Ttomalss said. "Most of them can explain their misfortune only to spirits of Emperors past, however." He stopped. "Here is your room. Mine, as I told you, is across the hall. By all means let me know if you need anything. I suspect we will be meeting too often to let you taste ginger without complicating your life and everyone else's. I do not mean that as criticism, merely as a statement of fact."

"And as a warning," Felless said. Ttomalss made the affirmative gesture. Felless sighed. "I thank you. The habit is hard to break." It was especially hard to break when she didn't want to break it. She asked, "When will the first meeting be?"

"After breakfast tomorrow morning," Ttomalss answered. "That will give you a chance to relax and recover from your flight."

"Good enough," Felless said again. "I thank you for your help." She went into the room and closed the door behind her. Her eye turrets swiveled. Like the hall, the room had been built for Tosevites, and so struck her as outsized. Some of the plumbing fixtures were also left over from the days when Big Uglies had come here. But the rest had been modernized, and the appointments suited her well enough.

When she made her way to the refectory, she found the food quite good. Then she noticed the fleetlord of the conquest fleet at a table in one corner of the room, in animated discussion with a shiplord whose body paint was almost as complex as his. If the fleetlord ate here, the food *would* be good, or someone would hear about it in short order.

Breakfast the next morning was good, too. She used a map of the complex to find the meeting room. Diffal and Ttomalss were already there. A male with the body paint of a shuttlecraft pilot came in right behind her. Ttomalss said, "Senior Researcher, I present to you the returned defector and former shiplord, Straha."

"I greet you," Felless said.

"And I greet you, Senior Researcher," Straha said easily. "The paint is the pattern I used to escape the United States. I have been ordered not to wear that of my former rank. It would upset too many males and females, Atvar chief among them. Call me whatever you please. A lot of males have called me a lot of things over the years." He seemed perversely proud of that.

"Let us get down to business," Ttomalss said. "We have been assembled here to analyze why an apparently successful leader like Earl Warren, after being discovered in his treachery, would sacrifice a city rather than the weaponry we expected him to give up."

"His actions do not show any failure of intelligence on our part," Diffal said. The male from Security went on, "He made the decision on his own, consulting no one. He offered us no trail of signals to intercept."

"No one here is criticizing you," Felless said.

"My opinion is simple," Straha said. "He never expected to be caught for the attack on the colonization fleet. When he was, he chose the option that hurt the United States least. End of story."

"It cannot be so simple," Diffal said.

"Why not?" Straha asked. "That is not something Drefsab, your predecessor, would have said."

"Drefsab had a gift for thinking like a Big Ugly. I lack it. I admit as much," Diffal said. "But what did his gift get him? It got him killed in a worthless skirmish, and nothing more. I am still here to do the best I can."

"You are a Security male, so you see complications everywhere," Straha jeered.

"Complications *are* everywhere," Diffal said.

"You said as much to me, Superior Nuisance." Ttomalss seemed to enjoy using the title Straha had given himself.

"I said ambiguities are everywhere," Straha said. "There is a difference."

"Perhaps," Ttomalss said.

Felless would not have yielded the point so readily. She said, "Let us return to the issue we are supposed to grasp with our fingerclaws. Was Warren a male with a complex personality, or was he one who could be relied upon to do the obvious thing?"

"Having met him several times, I can state without fear of contradiction that he was one of the most obvious males ever hatched," Straha said.

But Diffal made the negative gesture. "He wished to be seen as obvious: that is a truth. But no male who truly was obvious could have ordered the attack on the colonization fleet and successfully concealed it for so long. No male who was obvious could have refused our demand to weaken his not-empire and sacrificed a city instead. We seek the subtleties under his scales."

"Any male who is able to keep a secret, to keep his mouth shut, always seems a prodigy to someone from Security," Straha said.

"Any male who is able to keep a secret should certainly seem a prodigy to you," Diffal retorted. "You have value only when your mouth is open."

Straha hissed in fury. "Enough, both of you!" Felless shouted. "Too much, in fact. The only thing this commission is showing is our own foibles, not those of the Tosevite we are supposed to be investigating." She thought she was speaking an obvious truth, but the others stared at her as if she'd just hatched a miracle of wisdom. The way things were going, maybe she had.

By the time the Warren commission had been meeting for a few days, Ttomalss had learned more about the foibles of his colleagues than he'd ever wanted to know. Straha thought he knew everything about everything. Diffal was convinced nobody knew anything about anything. And Felless was convinced she could reconcile the other two males no matter how ferociously they disagreed.

What were they learning about him? If anything, he inclined toward Diffal. "To imagine that we are going to be certain of the reasons for any Big Ugly's behavior is an exercise in presumption," he said one morning when they were more rancorous than usual.

"Then what are we doing here?" Straha demanded.

"Looking for probabilities," Felless answered. "Even those are better than complete ignorance and wild speculation."

"Security's speculation is never wild," Diffal said. "We are, however, forced to analyze wildly conflicting data, which—"

"Gives you an excuse when you go wrong, as you do so often," Straha broke in.

Ttomalss felt like biting both of them. Instead, he tried to change the subject: "Let us examine why Warren ended his life at the same time as he chose to allow the destruction of the American city."

"My opinion is that this was an impulse reaction, one taken on the spur of the moment," Diffal said. "Big Uglies seldom have the foresight for anything more complex."

"Here, I would agree," Felless said.

Ttomalss would have agreed, too. Before he could state his agreement out loud, Straha laughed a tremendous, jaw-gaping laugh, the laugh of a male coming from the countryside to the city for the first time. With enormous relish, he said, "I happen to know—to *know*, I tell you—that you are both mistaken."

"And how do you *know* that?" Diffal did his best to match the ex-shiplord's sarcasm.

But Straha had a crushing rejoinder: "Because I have been in electronic communication with Sam Yeager, who was in personal communication with Warren before he killed himself. Yeager makes it quite plain that Warren knew what he was doing, knew its cost, and was not prepared to live after inflicting that cost on his not-empire."

"That is not fair!" Felless said. "You knew the answer to the question before it was asked."

"I said so." Straha's voice was complacent. "Which would you rather do, learn the actual truth or sit around debating endlessly till you decide upon what you imagine the truth ought to be?"

By the indignant forward slant of their bodies, both Felless and Diffal would sooner have spent more time in debate. A veteran of endless committee meetings, and of committee meetings that only seemed endless, Ttomalss had some sympathy for their point of view, but only some. He said, "The truth does seem to be established in this particular interest. I suggest that we adjourn for the day so we can approach other questions with our minds refreshed."

No one objected. The commission dissolved itself for the day. Diffal and Felless both left in a hurry. Straha stayed to gloat: "Facts? Facts are ugly things, Senior Researcher. They pierce the boldest theory through the liver and send it crashing to the ground."

"In some ways, Superior Nuisance, you have become very much like an American Big Ugly," Ttomalss said. "I suppose this was inevitable, but it does seem to have happened."

Straha made the affirmative gesture. "I am not particularly surprised. I have been observing the Americans for a long time, and it is a truism that observer and observed affect each other. I suppose I have affected them, too, but rather less: they are many, and I only one."

"You are not the only expatriate male of the Race there, though," Ttomalss said. "We have examined the expatriates' effect on pushing American technology forward. But we have not really considered their effect on the society of the not-empire as a whole. They must have some."

"So they must." Now Straha sounded thoughtful rather than vainglorious. "As I told you while you were interrogating me, you ask interesting questions. You could even answer that one, I think, were you interested in doing so. Most expatriates—unlike me—can freely come and go between the USA and territory the Race rules."

But Ttomalss said, "That is not what I want, or not most of what I want. I would like to grasp the Americans' view of the influence of the expatriates—it strikes me as being more important. And it could be that the expatriates are influencing the Americans in ways of which neither group is aware."

"Those are all truths, every one of them," Straha agreed. "They are all worth investigating, too, I am sure. I am not sure the Americans are doing anything similar themselves."

That the Americans might be doing something similar hadn't crossed Ttomalss' mind. He said, "You have considerable respect for those Big Uglies—is that not another truth? And for Warren, their leader?"

"Yes to both," Straha said. "Warren was a very great leader. Unlike the Deutsche, he found a way to hurt us at relatively low cost to his not-empire. Had his luck been a little better—had he not had males in his not-empire already influenced by the Race—he might have hurt us at no cost at all."

"You sound as if you wish he had succeeded," Ttomalss remarked.

To his horror, Straha thought that over before answering, "On the whole, no. His failure, after all, is what allowed me to return to the society of the Race, and I must admit I have longed to do so since shortly after my defection, and especially since the arrival of the colonization fleet."

"That is the most self-centered attitude I have ever heard,"

Ttomalss said. "What about the males and females aboard the ships that were destroyed?"

"They were in cold sleep, and so had no idea whatever that they had died," Straha said. "All things considered, it is an end to be envied—a better one than you or I can expect."

"Sophistry. Nothing but sophistry." Ttomalss was furious, and didn't try to hide it. "What about the Big Uglies in and around Indianapolis, many of whom are still in torment as a result of the strike?"

"They are only Big Uglies," Straha said with chilling indifference. But then he checked himself. "No, Senior Researcher, you have a point there, and I have to admit it. Do you know what the Tosevites are apt to say about the males and females who died in the attack on the colonization fleet? 'They are only Lizards.' " The last word was in English. Straha explained it: "That is the slang term the Tosevites use for us, just as we call them Big Uglies when they are not around to hear."

"Sometimes looking at them is like looking into a mirror—we see ourselves, only backwards," Ttomalss said, and Straha made the affirmative gesture. Ttomalss went on, "Other times, though, we see ourselves in a distorting mirror—the case of their sexuality comes to mind."

Straha laughed. "That may be true of how things were back on Home. With ginger, it is not true of how things are here, as you know very well."

"Prohibitions against the herb—" Ttomalss began.

"Are useless," Straha interrupted. "In his infinite generosity, the exalted fleetlord hinted he might let me continue to use the herb in gratitude for the service I had rendered the Race, but he would not if I were not a properly obedient male. The threat alarmed me at first, but I needed about a day and a half to find my own supplier, and I am far from the only one in this complex who tastes. Have you never caught the scent of a female's pheromones?"

"I have," Ttomalss admitted. "I wish I could say I had not, but I have."

"Whenever a female tastes where males can smell her, odds are she will mate," Straha said. "Whenever a female mates out of season, whenever females incite males to mating, our sexuality becomes more like the Big Uglies'. Is that a truth, or am I lying and deceiving you?"

"That is a truth," Ttomalss said. "Without a doubt, it is also the worst social problem the Race is facing on Tosev 3."

"It is only a problem if we insist on calling it one," Straha said. "If we do not, it becomes interesting, even enjoyable."

"That is disgusting," Ttomalss said with considerable dignity. Straha laughed at him. He didn't care. He got to his feet and walked out of the conference chamber. As he opened the door, he turned an eye turret back toward the ex-shiplord and added, "When we talk again, I hope we can do so without such revolting comments." Straha didn't say a word, but he kept on laughing.

Ttomalss fumed as he went down the corridor and toward his own chamber—a safe haven from Straha's depravity. He had to bank the fire of his anger to find his way through the winding maze of corridors that made up Shepheard's Hotel. It had been a confusing place when the Big Uglies ran it, and the Race's additions, thanks to security concerns, often made things worse rather than better.

When a certain odor reached Ttomalss' scent receptors, he let out a soft hiss and started walking faster . . . and a little more nearly erect. He hardly noticed he was doing it till he'd reached his own corridor. By then, the scales of the crest atop his head were standing erect, too—the sure sign of a male ready to mate, and also ready to fight about mating if he had to. He wouldn't have called Straha's words disgusting then. Part of his mind realized that, but only a small part.

The door across the hallway from his own stood open. The delicious pheromones wafted out from in there. Ttomalss hurried inside. He almost bumped into another male who was leaving. "Go on," the other fellow said happily. "You get no quarrel from me. I have already mated."

Felless stood in the middle of the floor. She'd started to straighten up from the mating posture, but the sight of Ttomalss' erect stance and crest—his mating display—sent her back down into it. Even as her tailstump twitched out of the way so his cloaca could join hers, she mumbled, "I did not intend for this to happen."

"What you intended does not matter," Ttomalss answered. The hiss he let out as pleasure shot through him was anything but soft. He could have mated with her again, but the drive to do so felt less urgent now. Instead, he turned away and went to his own room. Even as he left Felless' chamber, another excited male was hurrying toward it.

In his room, the door closed behind him, he could scarcely smell the pheromones. Rational thought returned. He'd never tasted ginger, not even once. But the herb reached out and touched his life all the same. Maybe Straha hadn't been so far wrong, no matter how crudely he put things.

Ttomalss sighed. He'd wanted to talk with the ex-shiplord about the dead leader of the United States. Somehow, the conversation had got round to sexuality. By way of ginger, he remembered. Straha seemed not at all unhappy about being addicted to it. Ttomalss would have been ashamed. Maybe Straha had been ashamed, once upon a time. But Tosev 3 eroded shame as it eroded everything else that made the Race what it was. Ttomalss reminded himself not to tell Kassquit he'd mated with Felless again.

Mordechai Anielewicz studied the farm from a low rise. He might have been an officer working out the best plan of attack. In fact, that was exactly what he was. He turned to the squad of Lizards behind him and spoke in their language: "I thank you for your help in this matter."

Their leader, an underofficer named Oteisho, shrugged an amazingly humanlike shrug. "We are ordered to assist you. You have assisted the Race. We pay our debts."

So you do, Mordechai thought. *You're better about it than most people.* Aloud, he said, "We had best advance in open order. I do not think this Gustav Kluge will open fire on us, but I might be wrong."

"He will be one very sorry Deutsch male if he tries," Oteisho remarked: half professional appraisal, half anticipation. The males of the Race who'd fought the Germans in Poland had no love for them. Oteisho turned and gave orders to the infantry-males in his squad. They spread out, weapons at the ready. Oteisho gestured to Anielewicz. "Lead us."

"I shall." He couldn't say, *It shall be done,* not when he was in charge. He hoped he wasn't leading them on a wild-goose chase. Briefly, he wondered what Lizards chased on Home instead of wild geese. But then he swung his rifle down off his shoulder and started toward Kluge's farm.

People were working in the fields. That was to be expected,

with harvest time on the way. What wasn't to be expected was that other people—men, all of them—were standing guard in the fields to make sure none of the workers escaped. The guards were armed and looked alert. How many farms in Germany had used slave labor before this latest round of fighting? How many had kept right on doing it even after the *Reich* got smashed into the dust? Quite a few, evidently. From the farmers' point of view, why not? Germany remained independent of the Lizards; who was going to tell them they couldn't do that any more?

"I am, by God," Mordechai muttered. Oteisho turned one eye turret his way. When he said nothing more, the Lizard under-officer relaxed and kept his attention on his males. They were veterans; Anielewicz could see as much by the way they handled themselves. Even so, he wondered if he'd brought as much fire-power with him as Gustav Kluge had on the farm. Kluge's men were liable to be veterans, too: demobilized soldiers looking for work that would keep them fed.

One of the guards, in a civilian shirt and, sure enough, field-gray *Wehrmacht* trousers, strolled toward Anielewicz and the Lizards. He had a cigarette in a corner of his mouth and an assault rifle slung on his back. Keeping his hands well away from the weapon, he asked the inevitable question: *"Was ist los?"*

"We're looking for some people," Anielewicz answered. He was careful to speak German, not Yiddish. Kluge's men wouldn't love him anyhow; they'd love him even less if—no, when—they found out he was a Jew.

"Lots of people are, these days." The guard leaned forward a little bit, the picture of insolence. "Why should we let 'em go, even if you find 'em? If they've got labor contracts, buddy, they're here for the duration, and if you don't like that, you can take it to court."

"They're my wife and children," Anielewicz said tightly. "Bertha, Miriam, David, and Heinrich are the names." He didn't give his surname; it would have told too much.

"And who the devil are *you?*" the guard asked. The question didn't come out so nastily as it might have. The next sentence explained why: "You must be somebody, if you've brought tame Lizards along."

One of the infantrymales turned out to speak some German. "We are not tame," he said. "Move wrong. You will see how not tame we are." He sounded as if he hoped the guard would make a false move.

Up from the farmhouse came a burly, gray-haired man who walked with a cane and a peculiar, rolling gait that meant he'd lost a leg above the knee. The guard turned back to him with something like relief. "Here's Herr Kluge, the boss. You can tell him your story." He stepped aside and let the farmer do his own talking.

Kluge had some of the coldest gray eyes Anielewicz had ever seen. "Who are you, and what are you doing coming onto my land with Lizard soldiers at your back?"

"I'm looking for my wife and children," Mordechai replied, and gave their names as he had to the guard.

"I don't have any workers by those names." Kluge spoke with complete confidence—but then, as a slavemaster, he would.

"I'm going to look," Anielewicz said. "If I find them after you tell me they're not here, I'm going to kill you. No one will say a word about it. You can take that to the bank—or to the Pearly Gates. Do you understand me? Do you believe me?"

A German is either at your throat or at your feet. So the saying went. Mordechai watched the farmer crumble before his eyes. Kluge had been on top for a generation—probably ever since he recovered from the wound that had cost him his leg. He wasn't on top any more, and he didn't need long to figure it out. In a voice gone suddenly hoarse, he said, "Who are you, anyhow?"

Now was the time to drop the mask. Mordechai smiled a smile that was all pointed teeth. "Who am I?" he echoed, letting himself slide out of German and into Yiddish. "I'm Mordechai Anielewicz of Lodz, that's who I am. And if you think I wouldn't shoot you as soon as look at you, you're out of your goddamn mind."

"A kike!" the guard exclaimed, which almost got him killed on the spot.

Instead, Anielewicz just smiled again. "Yes, I'm a kike. And how much do you think I owe the Third *Reich* after all this time? I can take back a little piece of it right now. Talk, Kluge, if you ever want to see your *Frau* again."

If his wife and children weren't here, that thunderous bluster would do Mordechai no good. Even if Kluge had nerve, it might not do him any good. But the farmer pointed past the big house where his wife and children no doubt lived in comfort despite the disaster that had overwhelmed their nation. "There, in that field of rye. Putting families together helps me get the most out of them, I've found."

"Have you?" Mordechai said tonelessly. "What a swell fellow you are. Lead me to them. If you're lying, somebody else will have to swing the whip for you from here on out. Now get moving, and tell your pals with the rifles not to get cute, or they'll have themselves one overventilated boss."

Kluge turned and started shouting at the top of his lungs. After that, Anielewicz's one big worry was that a guard would try to take out a few Lizards and wouldn't give a damn about what happened to the fellow who paid his salary. But it didn't happen. At Kluge's slow, ponderous pace, they headed down a path toward that field of rye.

Mordechai's heart thudded faster and faster. Before they'd gone very far, he started shouting his wife's name and those of his children. He didn't have lungs to match those of the German farmer. But he didn't have to shout more than a couple of times before heads came up in the field. And then four figures, three pretty much of a size and one smaller, were running through the field toward him.

"The grain . . ." Kluge said in pained tones. He could have died right there; Anielewicz started to swing the muzzle of his rifle toward him. But the Jewish fighting leader checked the motion, and the German went on, "You will see they have not been mistreated."

"I'd better," Mordechai growled. Then he started running, too.

His first thought was that his wife and sons and daughter were painfully thin. His next was that they were wearing rags. After that, he stopped thinking for a while. He hugged them and kissed them and said as many foolish things as needed saying and listened with delight while they said foolish things, too. The watching Lizards undoubtedly didn't understand at all.

And then, as bits of rationality returned, he asked, "Are you all right?"

"It could have been worse," his wife answered. Bertha Anielewicz nodded to David and Heinrich. "He knew we were Jews, of course. But he still fed us—he needed work from us."

"He *bought* us," David said indignantly. "He bought us for a big pile of bread from the soldiers who had us. He looked at

Mother's teeth first. I swear he did. She might have been a horse, for all he cared."

Gustav Kluge came up to them. "It is as I told you," he said to Anielewicz, as near a direct challenge as made no difference. "They are here. They are well. They have not been mistreated. I have treated them the same as all the others who work for me."

Even though they're Jews. It hung in the air, though he hadn't said it. Mordechai couldn't resist a dig of his own: "I'm not sure those last two things are the same—I'm not sure at all." But the German farmer—*plantation owner*, Anielewicz thought, remembering *Gone with the Wind*—hadn't lied too extravagantly.

"Take them. If they are your kin, take them." Kluge made pushing motions with the hand not gripping his cane, as if to say he wanted Mordechai's family off his farm as fast as they could go.

Oteisho and the other Lizards came up, too. They still kept their weapons aimed at Gustav Kluge. The underofficer asked Anielewicz, "Is it well? Have you found your mate and hatchlings?"

"It is very well. I thank you." Mordechai folded himself into the posture of respect. "Yes, this is my mate. These are my hatchlings."

Heinrich Anielewicz had been studying the Lizards' language in school in Lodz, back when there was a school, back when there was a Lodz. He too bent into the posture of respect. "And I thank you, superior sir," he said.

That seemed to amuse and please the infantrymales. The mouths of three or four of them dropped open in laughter. Gravely, Oteisho answered, "Tosevite hatchling, you are welcome."

Heinrich returned to Polish, asking, "Father, do you know anything about Pancer? Is he all right?" To the Lizards, he explained, "I have a beffel. I named him for a landcruiser in my language." That set the troopers laughing again.

Miriam said, "Don't bother your father about that silly animal now."

But Mordechai said, "It's no bother. Pancer's back at my tent, as a matter of fact. An officer of the Race had him. I heard him beeping and started asking questions about where the male had got him, and that helped lead me here."

Heinrich let out a whoop of triumph that proved nothing was seriously wrong with him. "You see? Pancer helped save us again, even when he got lost."

David said, "Where will we live? What will we do? Lodz is gone."

"I don't know," Mordechai answered. "I've been in the field since before the fighting started, and I've been looking for you since it ended." He shook his head. He felt dizzy, drunk, though he'd had nothing stronger than water. "And do you know what else? I don't much care. We're together again. That's all that really matters."

"Can we go someplace now where there's real food?" David asked.

That spoke volumes about what things were like on the farm. Anielewicz shot Gustav Kluge another venomous glance. But he had to say, "There's not a whole lot of real food anywhere in Germany right this minute. We'll do the best we can."

"We're free again," his wife said, which also spoke volumes. She went on, "Next to that, nothing else really matters."

Mordechai put one arm around her, the other around Miriam. His sons embraced them. "Truth!" he said. They all added emphatic coughs.

Not for the first time, Kassquit was feeling neglected and left out of things. She knew she'd been on the edge of great events, but she hadn't been able to get any closer than the edge. Only belatedly had she learned that Jonathan Yeager's father was the wild Big Ugly who'd given the Race the information it needed to show that his not-empire had been responsible for the attack on the colonization fleet.

She sent Sam Yeager an electronic message, saying, *Congratulations. Because of you, the Race was able to take the vengeance it required.*

That is a truth, he wrote back, *but it is a truth with a high price. A male who was a fine leader except for his attack on the colonization fleet—which was wrong—killed himself, and a large city in my not-empire was destroyed. Look at the vengeance before you gloat over it.*

Calling up video images of the ruins of Indianapolis was easy enough. The Race had broadcast them widely, to show males from the conquest fleet and males and females from the colonization fleet that the Big Uglies' attack had indeed been avenged. Smashed buildings were smashed buildings; motorcars half melted into the asphalt on which they'd been driving testified to the power of the explosive-metal bomb that had burst above the town.

Those were the images the Race had shown again and again. But there were others, of Tosevites charred dead or half charred and wishing for death, that hadn't been broadcast so much. Kassquit understood why: they were sickening, even when of another species. And, of course, for her they were not of another species. Had she been hatched—no, born—there, the same thing could have happened to her. One moment contented, the next with a new sun in the sky . . . It did not repay thinking about in any great detail.

The males and females in cold sleep had not known what hit them. Many of the Big Uglies, the ones near the city center, couldn't have known, either. But many had. That was a side of revenge the Race didn't publicize so widely. Kassquit, observing it, could understand why.

She needed a while before she wrote to Sam Yeager again. *Did you know such a thing would happen to your not-empire?* she asked.

When I began searching for answers, I thought it would happen to another not-empire, he answered. *I was convinced the* Reich *or the* SSSR *would deserve it. How, then, could I say my own not-empire did not?*

That makes perfect logical sense, Kassquit wrote. *Am I correct in guessing you are not happy with it even so?*

Yes, he wrote back. *A not-empire is an extension of one's mate and hatchlings. When dreadful things happen to the members of one's own not-empire, one is more unhappy than he would be if those dreadful things happened in a different not-empire.* He used the conventional symbol for an emphatic cough.

That made Kassquit wonder just how strong an emotion he was feeling. The not-emperor of the USA had killed himself after permitting the destruction of that city. She hoped Sam Yeager would not feel similarly obliged. Asking him about it, though, might touch off the urge, and so she refrained.

And then Jonathan Yeager wrote to her: *I have to let you know that I am going to enter into a permanent mating arrangement with the female named Karen Culpepper whom I mentioned from time to time while I was aboard the starship. I told you that this might happen. I am glad it finally has. I hope very much that you will be glad for me, too.*

Kassquit stared at that for what seemed a very long time. At last, her fingers moving more on their own than under the guidance of her will, she wrote, *I congratulate you.* She stared at the words, wondering how they had got up on the screen. At least they replaced the ones Jonathan Yeager had sent her. Still not thinking very much—still trying not to think very much—she sent her message.

She had read that soldiers could be hurt in the heat of battle, sometimes badly hurt, and not notice it till later. She'd always supposed that a reaction unique to the Race, one Big Uglies didn't share; whenever she'd been hurt, she'd always known about it. Now she began to understand. She knew she'd been wounded here, wounded to the core. Somehow, though, she felt nothing. It was as if her entire body had been dipped in refrigerant.

No, not quite her entire body. A tear slid from each eye and rolled down her cheeks. She hadn't known the tears were there till they fell. When those first two did, it was as if they released the floodgates. Tears streamed down her face. Mucus began flowing from her small, blunt snout; she'd always hated that.

She stumbled to a tissue dispenser, grabbed one, and tried drying her face and wiping away the slimy mucus. The more she dabbed at herself, the more tears fell and the more mucus flowed. At last, she gave up and let her body do what it would till it finally decided it had had enough.

That took an amazingly long time. When the spasms finally quit wracking her, she stooped a little to look at herself in the mirror. She gasped in horrified dismay. She hadn't really known her soft, scaleless skin could become so swollen and discolored around the eyes, or that the white part of those eyes could turn so red. She'd always been ugly compared to males and females of the Race, but now she looked extraordinarily hideous.

But Jonathan Yeager said I was not ugly, she thought. *He said I was sexually attractive to wild Tosevites, and he proved it by being attracted to me.*

Thinking about Jonathan Yeager set off a new paroxysm of tears and nasal mucus. By the time she was through, she looked even uglier than she had before, and she wouldn't have believed that possible.

At last, the second spasm ended. Kassquit recoiled from the mirror in disgust. She used water to wash her face again and again. That did something to reduce the swelling, but not enough. She supposed her skin would eventually return to normal. But how long would it take?

Before I have to go to the refectory again, please, she thought, directing the prayer to spirits of Emperors past. With Ttomalss down on the surface of Tosev 3, she was unlikely to have to see anyone till then. Who sought out a junior, a very junior, psychologist different from every other citizen of the Empire on or around Tosev 3?

She wished she had someplace to hide even from herself. Even more, she wished she had someplace to hide from Jonathan Yeager's electronic message. It wasn't as if he told any lies in it. He didn't. He had mentioned that he would probably enter into a permanent mating arrangement once he returned to the surface of Tosev 3. Kassquit hadn't expected him to do it anywhere near so soon, though.

"It is not fair," she said aloud. Jonathan Yeager would go on to indulge a normal Tosevite sexuality. He would mate with this Karen Culpepper female whenever he wanted, for years and years to come. He would forget all about her, Kassquit, or, if he did remember her, it would be only for brief moments of pleasure.

Fury filled her in place of despair. What did she have to look forward to in years to come? This cubicle. Her own fingers. Memories of a brief, too brief, contact with another of her own kind. How long, how often, could she replay those memories in her mind before they started to wear out or wear thin?

"It is not fair," she repeated, this time in an altogether different tone of voice. Anger burned in her. She added an emphatic cough.

Had she had Jonathan Yeager there before her, she would have given him a piece of her mind—a large, jagged-edged piece. He'd come up here, taken his sexual pleasure with her, and then gone down to the surface of Tosev 3 to resume his ordinary life? How dared he?

She wondered if any female Big Ugly had ever been betrayed in the way she was since the species evolved such intelligence as it had. She doubted it. Jonathan Yeager had surely devised a unique way to play on the affections of one who was, one who could not help being, naive.

She hurried to the computer to let him know exactly what she thought of him, but refrained at the last minute. For one thing, she didn't want to give him the satisfaction of knowing he'd succeeded in wounding her. For another, she still esteemed his father. She didn't want Sam Yeager reading a nasty message intended for his hatchling. What his hatchling did was not his fault. He surely never would have done such a thing with—or to—a female.

But what did that leave her? Nothing but sullen acceptance. Nothing but living on memories. That wasn't good enough.

Kassquit snapped her fingers. Jonathan Yeager had taught her to do it. She ignored that for now, enjoying the small sound for its own sake. "I can have another male brought up from the surface of Tosev 3. I can have my own pleasure."

I shall have to talk with Ttomalss about that, she thought. *He had better not tell me no, either.*

Even so, she wondered if it would be the same. Because Jonathan Yeager was the first, he was the one against whom she would measure all later comers. And she had given him her affection without reservation; she hadn't known to do anything else. Would she do that again? Of itself, her hand shaped the negative gesture. *I would not be so foolish twice.*

She kicked at the metal floor to her cubicle. If she brought a male up for sexual pleasure alone, if no affection was involved, what could he give her that her fingers could not? What except betrayal?

"I have had enough betrayal," she said. Would other male Big Uglies prove as treacherous, as devious, as Jonathan Yeager? It wasn't impossible.

That brought her back to where she'd begun: alone, with only her own hand for company. She hadn't minded that—too much—before meeting Jonathan Yeager. He'd shown her something of the spectrum of Tosevite sexually related emotions . . . and now he was lavishing them on this Karen Culpepper female.

Kassquit looked in the mirror again. To her relief, the blotches and swelling were fading. Soon, they would be gone. No one would be able to note any outward signs of distress on her. But the distress was there, whether visible or not.

"What am I going to do?" she asked the metal walls. She got no more answer there than anywhere else.

I might have done better never to have met wild Big Uglies in the flesh at all, she thought. *I certainly might have done better never to have started a sexual relationship with one of them. I could have gone on doing my best to emulate a female of the*

*Race. I would not have known about some of the emotions acces-
sible to Big Uglies, emotions for which the Race has no real
equivalents. I had no real equivalents, only a dim awareness
that I felt things Ttomalss did not. Now I understand much more,
now these areas have opened up in my mind—and I cannot use
them. Would it not have been better that they stayed closed?*

She had no real answer for that. She could not go back into the
eggshell that had held her before. But she could not use the new
areas, enjoy the new areas, as long as she was alone. Even if a
new Big Ugly male came up to the starship, even if he was
everything Jonathan Yeager had been and more . . . sooner or
later, he would go back down to Tosev 3, and she would be alone,
cut off, once more.

"What am I going to do?" she repeated. Again, no answer.

"Congratulations," Johannes Drucker told Mordechai Anielewicz. "Congratulations," he repeated to Anielewicz's family. A
wife, two boys, a girl—achingly like his own family, though
Anielewicz's girl was the eldest, where his Claudia was sand-
wiched between Heinrich and Adolf.

They didn't particularly look like Jews, or what he imagined
Jews looking like. He suspected German propaganda of exaggerating noses and lips and chins. They just looked like . . .
people. Bertha Anielewicz, Mordechai's wife, was plain till she
smiled. When she did, though, she turned very pretty. When she
was younger, she'd probably been gorgeous when she smiled.

"I hope you find your wife and children, too," she told him.
She spoke Yiddish, not German. The gutturals were harsh and
the vowel sounds strange, but he understood well enough.

"Thanks," he said. Hearing Yiddish reminded him how strange
it was to be standing outside a Red Cross shelter—another Red
Cross shelter—near Greifswald talking with five Jews. Before this
last war, it wouldn't have been strange; it would have been impossible, unimaginable. A lot of things that would have been unimaginable a few months before now seemed commonplace. "What
will you do?" he asked the Anielewiczes, trying his best not to be
jealous of their good fortune. "Go home?"

Mordechai laughed. "Home? We haven't got one, not with
Lodz blown off the map. We'll find something back in Poland, I
expect. Right this minute, I have no idea what. Something."

"I'm sure you will," Drucker agreed. No, staying away from jealousy wasn't easy. "You'll help pick up the pieces back there. And I'll help pick up the pieces here . . . one way or another." He didn't want to dwell on that. Holding on to hope came hard.

Anielewicz set a hand on his shoulder. Part of him wanted to shake it off, but he let it stay. The Jewish fighting leader said, "Don't quit, that's all. Never quit."

He could afford to say that. He could quit now—he'd found his needle in a haystack. But he wasn't wrong, either. If he hadn't scoured this corner of Prussia, he never would have come up with his wife and sons and daughter. "I know," Drucker said. "I'll go on. I have to. What else can I do? Kill myself like the American president? Not likely."

He tried to imagine Adolf Hitler killing himself if faced by some disaster. *Not likely* rang again in his mind. The first *Führer* would surely have grabbed some soldier's Mauser and kept firing at his foes till he finally fell. Suicide was the coward's way out.

Heinrich Anielewicz—like Drucker's own Heinrich, named for the Heinrich Jäger they'd both admired—was holding his pet beffel. The little animal from Home swiveled one eye turret toward Drucker. It opened its mouth. "Beep!" Pancer said, almost as if it were a squeeze toy. The corners of Drucker's mouth couldn't help twitching up a few millimeters. That really was one of the most preposterously friendly sounds he'd ever heard.

Heinrich Anielewicz scratched the beffel between the eye turrets and under the chin. Pancer liked that, and said, "Beep!" again. The boy spoke to it in Polish. Drucker had no idea what he said; he'd never known more than a handful of words in the language, and he'd long since forgotten those. Then Heinrich Anielewicz switched to Yiddish and spoke to him: "If it hadn't been for Pancer, you know, we might never have been found."

"Yes, I do know that. I was with your father when he heard him," Drucker answered. "I didn't know what the noise was. But he did."

"You could have knocked me over with a feather," Mordechai Anielewicz said. "It was luck, nothing else. But sometimes, when you haven't got anything else, you'll take luck."

"You don't just take it. If you get it, you grab it with both hands," Drucker said, the soldier in him speaking. Had Bertha and Miriam Anielewicz not been there, he might have put it more earthily.

"Listen," Mordechai Anielewicz said. "I've talked to that male named Gorppet, the one who had Pancer. He knows I'm a Big Ugly"—he used the language of the Race to say that—"the Lizards want to keep happy. I've asked him to give you whatever help he can. He's an intelligence officer, too, so whatever they hear, he can get his hands on it. I hope that does you some good."

"Thanks." Drucker nodded. "That's—damned good of you, all things considered."

"All things considered." Anielewicz savored the phrase. "There's a lot to consider, all right, *Herr Oberst*. There's the *Reich* you fought for. But then there's your wife and your children. And you got Jäger loose from the SS, you tell me, and if you hadn't done that, Lodz would have gone up in 1944 instead of this spring. Bertha and I would be dead, and the first round of fighting might have gone on and ended up wrecking the whole world. So I didn't spend a lot of sleepless nights worrying about this one."

"Thanks," Drucker said again. That didn't seem to be enough. He stuck out his hand. Anielewicz shook it. Bertha Anielewicz hugged him, which took him by surprise. No woman had done that since . . . since the last time he'd seen Käthe, before the fighting started up. Too long. God, too long. Roughly, he said, "I'm going into the camp now."

"Good luck," they chorused behind him.

He'd seen too many refugee camps by now for this one to hold any surprises. Tents. People in shabby clothes. More shabby clothes hanging out as laundry. The smell of latrines and unwashed bodies. The dull, apathetic look of men and women who didn't think things would or could ever get better again.

In the middle of the camp, as in the middle of all these camps, stood a tent with a Red Cross flag flying above it. The men and women—they'd be mostly women—in it would be clean. They'd have clean clothes, fresh clothes, clothes they could change. They'd mislike anyone entering their realm who didn't give them their full due.

As he ducked through the tent flap, he heard rhythmic tapping. Someone in there had a typewriter. It wasn't a computer, but it was still a surefire sign of superiority in the middle of a refugee camp. Several women—sure enough, all of them scrubbed till they gleamed—looked up from whatever important things they were doing to give him the once-over. By their expressions, he didn't pass muster. They probably took him for one of the people they were there to help.

"Yes?" one of them said. "What is it?" By her tone, it couldn't possibly have been as urgent as the forms she was filling out. Yes, she must have taken him for an inmate here.

"I am here to look for my family. My wife. My sons. My daughter. Drucker. Katherina—Käthe. Heinrich. Adolf. Claudia." Drucker stayed polite and businesslike.

"Oh. One of those." The woman nodded. Now she knew in which pigeonhole he belonged. She pulled out a form from a box on the table behind her and said, "Fill this out. Fill it out very carefully. We will search. If we find them in our records, you will be notified."

"When will you search? When will I be notified?" Drucker asked. "Why don't you search now? I'm here now." By all the signs, she needed reminding of that.

A slow flush darkened her cheeks. It wasn't embarrassment; it was anger. "We have many important duties to perform here, sir," she said in a voice like winter on the Russian front. "When we have the opportunity, we shall search the records for you." That might be twenty years from now. It might, on the other hand, be never. "Please fill out the form." The form was important. The family it represented? That might matter, but more likely it wouldn't.

Drucker had seen that attitude before. He had a weapon to combat it. He took from his wallet a telegram and passed the woman the yellow sheet. "Here. I suggest you read this."

For a moment, he thought she'd try to crumple it instead. He would have prevented that—by force, if necessary. But she did read. And her eyes, the dull blue and white of cheap china, grew bigger and bigger as she read. "But this is from Flensburg," she said, and all the other Red Cross women exclaimed when she mentioned the new capital. Even the typist stopped typing. In an awed whisper, the woman went on, "This is from the *Führer*, from the *Führer* himself. We are to help this man, he says."

They all crowded around to examine, and to exclaim over, the special telegraph form with the eagle with the swastika in its claws. After that, Johannes Drucker found things going much more smoothly. Instead of being a client and hence an obvious inferior, he was a man known to the *Führer*—*the* Führer *himself*, Drucker thought sourly—and hence an obvious superior.

"Helga!" the blue-eyed woman barked. "Check the records at once for the *Herr Oberstleutnant*. Drucker. Käthe. Heinrich. Adolf. Claudia. At once!" Drucker's eyebrows rose. She'd been listening. She just hadn't wanted to do anything about it. To him, that made things worse, not better—lazy, sour bitch.

Helga said, *"Jawohl!"* and went for the file boxes at the run—so fast that a lock of her blond hair escaped the pins with which she imprisoned it. She grabbed the right one without even looking and riffled through the forms in it. Then, on the off chance something had gone wrong, she went through the boxes to either side. Having done that, she looked up at Drucker and said, "I'm sorry, sir, but we have here no record of them." Since he was known to the *Führer*, she actually sounded sorry, not bored as she might well have otherwise.

It wasn't as if Drucker hadn't heard it before, too many times. Lately, though, he'd added a new string to his bow. "See if you have anyone who was living on Pfordtenstrasse in Greifswald." Maybe a neighbor would know something. Maybe.

"Helga!" the woman holding the telegram thundered again. While Helga went to a different set of file boxes, Drucker got the precious sheet of yellow paper back. He'd need it to overawe people somewhere else.

Sorting through those boxes took longer. After fifteen minutes or so, Helga looked up. "I have an Andreas Bauriedl, at 27 Pfordtenstrasse."

"By God!" Drucker exclaimed. "Andreas the hatter! He lives—lived—only three doors down from me. Can you have him fetched here?"

They could. They did. Half an hour later, there was skinny little Andreas, ten years older than Drucker, hurrying in to shake his hand. "Good to see you, Hans!" he exclaimed. "Didn't know you'd made it."

"I'm here," Drucker answered. "What about my family? Do you know anything?"

"They gave Heinrich a rifle, same as they did me, and put him in a *Volkssturm* battalion," Bauriedl answered. "That was when the Lizards were getting close to Greifswald, you know. If you were a man and you were breathing, they gave you a rifle and hoped for the best. It was pretty bad."

Boys and old men, Drucker thought. Everybody else would have already gone into the *Wehrmacht.* He asked the question he had to ask: "Do you know what happened to him?"

Bauriedl shook his head. "I couldn't tell you, Hans. He got called in a couple of days before I did, and into a different unit. I'm sorry. I wish I could tell you more."

Drucker sighed. He'd learned a little something, anyhow. "What about Käthe and the other children?"

"They left town right after Heinrich went in. Piled into the VW and took off." Bauriedl frowned. "Something about Uncle Lothar? Uncle Ludwig? I was coming up the street when she drove by. She called out to me, in case I saw you. I'd tell you more, but they bombed the block a few minutes later. They got Effi, damn them. We were in different rooms, and . . ." He grimaced. "I went into the *Volkssturm* hoping I'd get killed too. No such luck."

"I'm sorry." Drucker hoped *he* sounded sincere. He'd heard so many stories like that. But excitement burned in him, too. "Käthe has"—he made himself use the present tense—"an uncle down in Neu Strelitz. I think his name starts with an L. I'll tell you one thing—I'm going to find out." Neu Strelitz wasn't so far away, not when he'd already walked from Nuremberg. But maybe he wouldn't have to walk. He had connections now, and he intended to use them.

Gorppet was discovering he liked intelligence work. It was for males of a mistrustful cast of mind. It was also for males who wanted more than just to be given orders. He got to think for himself without becoming an object of suspicion.

He was writing a report on what he suspected to be underground activity among the Deutsche when a Big Ugly came into the tent and said, "I greet you, superior sir. I am Johannes Drucker, the friend of Mordechai Anielewicz."

"And I greet you." The Tosevite had named himself, which Gorppet found considerate. Even after so long on Tosev 3, even after his spectacular capture of that maniac of a Khomeini, he still found that most Big Uglies looked alike. Since this Drucker had announced who he was, Gorppet could proceed to the next obvious question: "And what do you want with me today?"

"Superior sir, does the Race have a garrison in the town of Neu Strelitz?"

"I have no idea," Gorppet answered. "Say the name again, so that I can enter it into our computer and find out." Drucker did. As best Gorppet could, he turned the odd sounds of the Deutsch language into the Race's familiar characters. The screen displayed a map of the *Reich*, with a town south of Greifswald blinking on it. That the displayed town was blinking meant the computer system wasn't sure of the identification. Gorppet pointed at the town with his tongue. "Is this the place you mean?"

Johannes Drucker leaned forward to get a better look at the monitor. His head went up and down in the Big Uglies' affirmative gesture. "Yes, superior sir, that is the right place."

"Very well." Gorppet spoke to the computer. The light indicating Neu Strelitz stopped blinking. Gorppet interrogated the data system, then turned back to the Tosevite. "No, at present we have no males in that town. We cannot be everywhere, you know." That was a truth that worried him. The Deutsche might well be hatching trouble under the Race's snout—there just weren't enough males to watch everything at once. But he said nothing of that to Drucker: no point in giving a former Deutsch officer ideas. He probably had too many already. Gorppet did ask, "Why do you wish to know that?"

"My mate and two of my hatchlings may be there," Drucker replied. "I was hoping that, if the Race did have males in that place, I could there in one of your vehicles travel." Every so often, he would forget about the verb till the end of a sentence. A lot of Deutsche did that when speaking the language of the Race. The Big Ugly's sigh was amazingly like that of a·male of the Race. "Now must I walk."

"Wait." Gorppet thought hard. Mordechai Anielewicz was a Tosevite the Race needed to keep happy. That meant keeping his friend happy, too—especially where kin were concerned. Anielewicz himself had been almost insane with joy after recovering his own hatchlings and mate. And having a former Deutsch officer owing the Race a debt of gratitude might not be the worst thing in the world, either. It might, in fact, prove very useful. Gorppet said, "Let me make a telephone call or two and I will see what I can do."

"I thank you," Drucker said. "Do you mind if I on the ground sit? I do not fit well inside this tent."

Sure enough, he had to bend his head forward a little to keep from bumping the fabric of the roof, an unnatural and uncomfortable posture for a Big Ugly. "Go ahead," Gorppet said, and made the affirmative gesture. As Drucker sat, Gorppet spoke on the telephone. Had he still been an ordinary infantry officer, he was sure the quartermaster he called would have laughed in his face. The fellow took an officer from Security more seriously. Gorppet hardly had to raise his voice. When the quartermaster broke the connection, Gorppet turned an eye turret back toward the Big Ugly. "There. I have arranged it."

"Have you?" Drucker asked eagerly. "So thought I, but when you speak rapidly, I have trouble following."

"I have indeed." Gorppet sounded smug. He'd earned a little smugness. "Go three tents over and one tent up"—he gestured to show directions within the Race's encampment—"and you will find a motorcar waiting for you. The driver will take you to this Neu Strelitz place."

"I thank you," the Big Ugly said again, this time with an emphatic cough to show how much. "You are generous to a male who was your enemy."

"I am not altogether disinterested," Gorppet said. Drucker, he judged, was smart enough to figure that out for himself. Sure enough, the Tosevite nodded once more. Gorppet went on, "You Deutsche and we of the Race should try to live together as smoothly as we can now that the war is over."

"That is always easier for the winner than for the loser to say," Johannes Drucker answered. "Still, I also think it is a truth. And the Race fights with honor—I cannot deny it. I almost killed a starship of yours, but your pilot accepted my surrender and did not kill me. And now this. It is very kind."

"Go on. You will not want to keep the driver waiting, or he will be annoyed," Gorppet said. The driver would undoubtedly be annoyed anyhow at having to take a Big Ugly somewhere, but Gorppet didn't mention that. He did say, "I hope you find your mate and your hatchlings."

"So do I," Drucker said. "You have no idea how much I do." That was bound to be literally true, given the different emotional and sexual patterns of Tosevites and members of the Race.

Drucker got to his feet. He bent into an awkward version of the posture of respect, then hurried out of the tent.

Hozzanet, the male who'd recruited Gorppet into Security, came into the tent just after Drucker had left. "Making friends with the Big Uglies?" he asked, his voice dry—but then, his voice was usually dry.

"As a matter of fact, yes, superior sir." Gorppet explained what he'd done, and why. He waited to find out if Hozzanet would think he'd overstepped.

But the other male said, "That is good. That is very good, in fact. The more links we have with the Tosevites, the better off we are and the easier this occupation will be."

"My thought exactly," Gorppet said. "By all the signs, the only thing that keeps the Deutsche from rising against us is the certainty that they will lose."

"I agree," Hozzanet said. "Our superiors also agree. They take the idea of trouble from the Deutsche very seriously indeed. You were right, and I was right—these Big Uglies are caching weapons against a day of rebellion. We recently discovered a double ten of landcruisers, along with supplies, hidden in the galleries of an abandoned coal mine."

"A good thing we *did* discover them," Gorppet exclaimed. "I missed that report. The other interesting question is, what have we failed to discover? And will we find out only when it is too late?"

"Yes, that is always the interesting question." Hozzanet shrugged. "We made this place radioactive once. We can always make it radioactive again. I do not think the Deutsche have managed to conceal any great number of explosive-metal weapons, anyhow."

"And they surely have no long-range delivery systems left," Gorppet said. "Whatever they have, they can only use it against us here inside the territory of the *Reich*." He laughed a wry laugh. "How reassuring."

"Reassuring for the Race," Hozzanet said. "Not so reassuring for the males here—that I can hardly deny." He swung an eye turret toward Gorppet. "Things could have been worse, you know, if you had stayed in the infantry. Then you could have been trying to fight your way up into the not-empire called the United States."

"I am just as well pleased we avoided that fight, thank you very much," Gorppet said. "I do not think we would have had a pleasant time trying to force our way up from the south on a front that got wider the farther we went—you see, I have been examining the maps."

"That is what you should do. That is why they go into the data-bases," Hozzanet said. "But I do not think there would have been so much ground combat on the lesser continental mass as there was here. Here, the Deutsche invaded our territory, so we had to fight them on the ground. Against the USA, we probably would have used missiles to batter the not-empire into submission, then picked up the pieces with infantrymales."

Gorppet considered. "Yes, that sounds reasonable. But they would have used missiles against us, too, as the Deutsche did. That would have been . . . unpleasant. Just as well the war did not happen."

He expected Hozzanet to say, *Truth!* But the other male hesitated. "I wonder," he said. "What was hoped, of course, was that the American Big Uglies would surrender their space installations. When they gave up a city instead, that left their capacity for mischief undiminished. Sooner or later, we *will* have to deal with them."

"I suppose so." Gorppet sighed. "This world is doing horrible things to all of us. When I went into one of the new towns the colonists ran up, I did not fit there at all, even though it hatched out of an egg from Home. I am sick of being a soldier, but I have no idea what else I might do with my life. And if we of the conquest fleet stop being soldiers, what will the colonists do against the Big Uglies?"

Hozzanet sighed, too. "That, I am given to understand, is under discussion at levels more exalted than our own. As I see it, the colonists have two choices: they can learn to be soldiers, or they can learn to live under the rule of the Big Uglies."

"Oh, good," Gorppet said. "I see no other choices, either. I was wondering if you did." He stood up from the computer monitor. "Shall we head over to the refectory tent? My insides are empty."

"Mine, too," Hozzanet agreed.

The refectory was serving azwaca ribs. Gorppet fell to with a will. He'd got used to eating Tosevite foods before the colonization fleet came. He'd come to like some of them, especially pork. But the meats of Home were better, without a doubt.

After eating, he went back to work. The day was drawing to a close when the telephone attachment hissed. When he answered it, the quartermaster's face appeared in the monitor. He said, "The motorcar I sent out with the Big Ugly has not come back."

"It should have," Gorppet answered. "That Neu Strelitz place is not very far away."

"Well, it cursed well has not," the quartermaster answered. "I am worried about my driver. Chinnoss is a good male. What have you got to say for yourself?"

"Something has gone wrong." That was all Gorppet could think of to say. Had Drucker betrayed him, or had someone betrayed Drucker? "We had better find out what."

☆ **12** ☆

David Goldfarb looked up from his work as Hal Walsh sauntered back into the Saskatchewan River Widget Works after going out for lunch. Goldfarb scratched his head. His boss was a high-pressure type if ever there was one. Up till the past couple of weeks, David had never seen him saunter; he'd moved everywhere as if he needed to get there day before yesterday. That dreamy look on his face was new, too.

Seeing it made a lightbulb come on above Goldfarb's head. "You went out to lunch with my doctor again."

To his amazement, Walsh blushed like a schoolgirl. "Well, yes, as a matter of fact, I did," he said. "Jane's . . . quite something."

"Can't argue with you there," Goldfarb said, most sincerely. "If I were ten, fifteen years younger and single, I'd give you a run for your money. Maybe even if I weren't ten, fifteen years younger."

"Next time I see Naomi, I'll tell her you said that," Walsh said.

"I'm allowed to look," Goldfarb answered. "I'm allowed to think. I'm also allowed to keep my hands to myself if I want to keep them on the ends of my arms."

"Sounds like a sensible arrangement," his boss said. "Oh, and speaking of your hands, Jane asked me to ask you how your finger's doing since she took out the stitches."

After flexing the digit in question, David said, "It's not half bad. Still a little sore, but not half bad." He eyed Hal Walsh. "I gather she thinks you'll have the chance to pass this on to her some time fairly soon?"

Sure as the devil, Walsh blushed again. "That's right." He coughed a couple of times, then went on, "You know, cutting that finger may have been the best thing you ever did for me."

"I like that!" Goldfarb said in mock high dudgeon. "I like that quite a lot. Here I give you the phone-number reader, and what do I get credit for?" He grinned. "For working my finger to the bone, that's what." He held it up again.

Walsh groaned and held up a different finger. They both laughed. Jack Devereaux came into the office just then. He saw his boss's upraised digit. "Same to you, Hal," he said, and used the same gesture.

"You don't even know why you did that," Walsh said.

"Any excuse in a storm," Devereaux answered.

"The RAF was never like this," Goldfarb said. The only time he'd known anything even close to such informality in the RAF had been in the days when he was working under Group Captain Fred Hipple, desperately trying to learn all he could about Lizard radars and jet engines. He'd looked back fondly on those days—till Basil Roundbush, who'd worked with him then, came back into his life.

He hadn't heard anything from Roundbush lately, or from any of Roundbush's Canadian associates, either. Nor had anybody tried to kill him lately. He approved of that. He would have been hard pressed to think of anything he approved of more than not getting killed, in fact. He would have been happier still had he known Roundbush had given up for good. Unfortunately, he knew nothing of the sort. And Roundbush was not the sort to give up easily.

But every day without trouble was one more day won. He'd thought that way during the war, first during the Battle of Britain when nobody'd known if the Nazis would invade, and then after the Lizards came till they did invade. With the return of peacetime, he'd been able to look further ahead again. But trouble brought him back to counting the days one at a time.

Walsh said, "Shall we see if we can get something more useful than the odd obscene gesture done today?"

"Mine wasn't odd," Devereaux said. "I did it right."

"By dint of long practice, I have no doubt," his boss replied. Goldfarb expected the French-Canadian engineer to demonstrate the gesture again, but Devereaux refrained. Walsh looked faintly disappointed. Devereaux caught David's eye and winked. Goldfarb grinned, then coughed to give himself an excuse to put a hand in front of his face so Hal Walsh wouldn't notice.

Eventually, they did get down to work. David had the feeling it was going to be one of those afternoons where nothing much got accomplished. He turned out to be right, too. He'd had a lot of those afternoons in the RAF, far fewer since coming to Canada. The reason for that wasn't hard to figure out: the British government could afford them a lot more easily than the Saskatchewan River Widget Works could. But they did happen now and again.

He was, as always these days, wary when he walked home. *Nothing like almost getting killed to make you pay attention to the maniacs on the highway,* he thought. But nobody tried to run him down. All the maniacs in the big American cars were maniacal because of their native stupidity, not because they wanted to rub out one David Goldfarb.

"Something smells good," he said when he opened the door.

From the kitchen, Naomi answered, "It's a roasting chicken. It'll be ready in about half an hour. Do you feel like a bottle of beer first?"

"Can't think of anything I'd like more," he answered. She popped the tops off a couple of Mooseheads and brought them out to the front room. "Thanks," Goldfarb said, and kissed her. The kiss went on for a while. When it broke, he said, "Well, maybe I can think of something I'd like more. What are the children doing right now?"

"Homework." Naomi gave him a sidelong look and doled out another word: "Optimist."

"We made it here to Edmonton, didn't we?" David said, and then, in what wasn't quite a non sequitur, "The children are bound to go to bed sooner or later." As big as they were getting, that marked him as an optimist, too.

He sat down on the sofa and sipped the beer. "That's not bad," he said. "It doesn't match what a proper pub would give you, right from the barrel, but it's not bad. You can drink it." He took another sip, as if to prove as much.

"What's new?" his wife asked.

"I'll tell you what: my boss is seeing the doctor who sewed up my finger," he said. "She's worth seeing, too, I will say." Smiling sweetly, Naomi put an elbow in his ribs. "Careful, there," he exclaimed. "You almost made me spill my beer. Now I have to figure out whether to say anything about it the next time I write to Moishe in Jerusalem."

"Why wouldn't you say—? Oh," Naomi said. "This is the doctor who was going with Reuven Russie, isn't it?"

David nodded. "That's right. She didn't want to stay in a country the Lizards ruled, and he didn't feel like emigrating, and so . . ." He shrugged. He suspected that, had he been close to marrying Jane Archibald and she told him she wanted to move to Siam, he would have started learning Siamese. Having already got one elbow in the ribs, he didn't tell that to Naomi.

Instead of another elbow, he got a raised eyebrow. They'd been married twenty years. Sometimes he could get in trouble without saying a word. This looked to be one of those times.

"I'm going to check the chicken," she said. He'd never heard that sound like a threat before, but it did now.

She'd just opened the oven door when the telephone rang. "I'll get it," David said. "Whoever it is, he's messed it up—he was bound to be trying to call us at suppertime." He picked up the handset. "Hullo?"

"Hello, Goldfarb." Ice and fire ran up David's back: it was Basil Roundbush. Goldfarb looked to the phone-number reader. It showed the call's origin as the United Kingdom, but no more than that: Roundbush's blocking device was still on the job.

"What the devil do you want?" Goldfarb snarled.

"I rang to tell you that you can call off your dogs, that's what," Roundbush answered. He sounded ten years older than he had the last time he'd blithely threatened Goldfarb's destruction, or maybe it was just that, for once, his voice had lost its jauntiness.

"What the hell are you talking about?" David asked. He kept his voice low so as not to alarm Naomi. That, of course, was plenty to bring her out of the kitchen to find out what was going on. He mouthed Roundbush's name. Her eyes widened.

"I told you—call off your dogs," the RAF officer and ginger dealer said. "I've got the message, believe you me I do. I shan't be troubling you any more, so you need no longer be concerned on that score."

"How do I know I can believe a word of that?" Goldfarb still hadn't the faintest idea what Basil Roundbush was talking about, but he liked the way it sounded. Letting on that he was ignorant didn't strike him as a good idea.

"Because I bloody well don't want to get my sodding head blown off, that's how," Roundbush burst out. "Your little friends have come too close twice, and I know they'll manage it properly sooner or later. Enough is enough. In my book, we're quits."

If he wasn't telling the truth, he should have been a cinema actor. Goldfarb knew he was good, but hadn't thought he was that good. "We'll see," he said, in what he hoped were suitably menacing tones.

"I've said everything I'm going to say," Roundbush told him. "As far as I'm concerned, the quarrel is over."

"Don't like it so well when the shoe is on the other foot, eh?" Goldfarb asked, still trying to find out what the devil was going on. A conciliatory Basil Roundbush was as unlikely an item as a giggling polar bear.

"Bloody Nazis haven't got enough to do now that the *Reich* has gone down the loo," Roundbush said bitterly. "I really hadn't thought you of all people would be able to pull those wires, but one never can tell these days, can one?" He hung up before David could find another word to say.

"Nu?" Naomi demanded as Goldfarb slowly hung up the phone, too.

"I don't know," he answered. "I really don't know. He said he was going to leave me alone, and that I should call my dogs off him. He said they'd almost killed him twice. He said they were Nazis, too."

"He's *meshuggeh*," Naomi exclaimed. She added one of the Lizards' emphatic coughs for good measure.

"I think so, too," David said. "He must have fallen foul of the Germans somehow, and he thinks I'm behind it. And do you know what? If he wants to think so, it's fine by me."

"But what happens if these people, whoever they are, keep going after Roundbush?" Naomi asked. "Won't he blame you and get his friends over here to come after you again?"

"He might," Goldfarb admitted. "I don't know what I can do about it, though. Whoever's going after that *mamzer*, I haven't got anything to do with it." He rolled his eyes. "Nazis. The only Nazis I ever knew were the ones I saw with radar during the fighting."

"What do you think we ought to do?" Naomi asked.

Goldfarb shrugged. "I don't know what we can do, except go on the way we've been going. As long as we're careful, dear Basil's goons won't have an easy time getting us, anyhow." One eyebrow climbed toward his hairline. "And who knows. Maybe those blokes, whoever they are, will put paid to him after all. I wouldn't shed a tear, I'll tell you that."

"Neither would I," Naomi said.

* * *

Warm Mediterranean sunshine poured down from a brilliant blue sky. The water was every bit as blue, only two shades darker. Gulls and terns wheeled overhead. Every so often, one of them would plunge into the sea. Sometimes it would come out with a fish in its beak. Sometimes—more often, Rance Auerbach thought—it wouldn't.

He lit a cigarette. It was a French brand, and pretty vile, but American tobacco, even when you could get it, was impossibly expensive over here. Of course, American tobacco would have set him coughing, too, so he couldn't blame that on the frogs. He sipped some wine. He'd never been much for the stuff, but French beer tasted like mule piss. Raising the glass, he grinned at Penny Summers. "Mud in your eye." Then he turned to *Sturmbannführer* Dieter Kuhn, who was sharing the table at the seaside café with them. *"Prost!"*

They all drank. The SS man spoke much better French than either Rance or Penny. In that good French, he said, "I regret that Group Captain Roundbush unfortunately survived another encounter with my friends."

"Quel dommage," Rance said, though he didn't really think it was a pity. "It will be necessary to try again." For *again*, he said *wieder*, because he could come up with the German word but not its French equivalent. He'd taken French and German both at West Point. Because he'd been using his French here in Marseille, it had less rust on it than his German did, but neither was what anybody would call fluent.

"Life is strange." Penny's French, like Auerbach's, relied on clichés. She went on, "In Canada, we tried to deal with Roundbush. Now we try to kill him."

"Strange indeed," Kuhn said with a smile he probably thought was a real ladykiller. "The last time we were all in Marseille, it was part of the *Reich*, and it was my duty to arrest the two of you. Now the *République Française* is reborn, and we are all here as simple tourists."

Nobody laughed too loudly. That might have drawn more notice than they wanted. Penny said, "Now we are on the same side."

"We have the same enemies, anyhow," Rance said. He didn't want to think of the SS man as being on his side, even if that was how things stood.

"The same enemies, yes, but different reasons," Dieter Kuhn said. Maybe he wasn't happy about lining up with a couple of Americans, either. "We want to make Pierre Dutourd want to work with us and not with Roundbush and his associates, while you want to help your friend in Canada."

"Reasons are not important," Penny said. "Results are important."

"Truth." Auerbach and Kuhn said it at the same time, both in the Lizards' language. They gave each other suspicious looks. Neither of them used an emphatic cough. Auerbach drank some more wine, then asked the German, "Will you tell your superiors in Flensburg you work with us to help a Jew?"

"Of course not," Kuhn answered at once. "But I do not think they would care much, not as things are now. I break no secrets in saying that. To rebuild, the *Reich* needs money. We can get money through selling ginger to the Lizards. If Dutourd works with us, works through us, that helps bring in money. And so, for now, I do not much care about Jews. Getting rid of the Englishman and bringing Dutourd to heel is more important for the time being."

As things are now. For the time being. Rance eyed the *Sturmbannführer* as he would have eyed a rattlesnake. Kuhn—and, presumably, Kuhn's bosses—hadn't given up. Taking it on the chin—hell, getting knocked out of the ring—had made them change their priorities, but Auerbach didn't think it had made them change their minds.

He asked, "How goes the rebuilding? How closely do the Lizards watch you?"

"Merde alors!" Kuhn exclaimed in fine pseudo-Gallic disgust. "Their eye turrets are everywhere. Their snouts are everywhere. A man cannot go into a *pissoir* and unbutton his fly without having a Lizard see how he is hung."

"Too bad," Rance said. About half of him meant it. The balance of power between the Lizards and mankind had swung toward the Race when Germany went down in flames. The other half of Auerbach, the part that remembered the days before the Lizards came, the days when Hitler's goons were the worst enemies around, hoped the Nazis would never get back on their feet.

Maybe a little of that showed on his face. Or maybe Dieter Kuhn was a pretty fair needler in his own right. Deadpan, he asked, "And how is it with Indianapolis these days?"

Auerbach shrugged. "All I know is what I read in the newspapers. Newspapers here say what the Lizards want."

"The French are whores." Kuhn didn't bother keeping his voice down. "They gave to the *Reich*. Now they give to the Race." He rose, threw down enough jingly aluminum coins to cover the tab, and strode away.

Penny went back to English: "That's one unhappy fellow, even if he hides it pretty good."

"You bet," Rance agreed. "I'll tell you, I like him a hell of a lot better by his lonesome than in front of a bunch of soldiers toting submachine guns."

"Amen!" Penny said fervently. "You know something, Rance? I'm goddamn tired of having people point guns at me, is what I am."

After lighting another foul-smelling French cigarette, Auerbach eyed her through the smoke he puffed out. "You know, kid, you might have picked the wrong line of work in that case."

She laughed. "Now why the hell didn't I think of that?"

"We're not doing too bad here this time around," Rance said. "Better than I expected we would, I'll say that."

Instead of laughing again, Penny pretended to faint. That made Auerbach laugh, which made him start coughing, which made him feel as if his chest were coming to pieces. Penny thumped him on the back. It didn't help much. She said, "Don't tell me things like that. My heart won't stand it."

"Don't worry. I'm not going to make a habit of it." Auerbach filled his glass from the carafe of red wine that sat on the table. "This is a complicated deal, you know? We've got to stay on Dutourd's good side on account of we're doing business with him, and we've got to stay on Kuhn's good side on account of we're doing business with him, too, and they don't like each other for beans."

"It'd be a lot easier if you didn't have anything to do with that damn Nazi," Penny said. "We don't need to, not as far as money's concerned."

"Oh, I know," Rance answered. "But I told that Roundbush son of a bitch that I was going to tie a tin can to his tail, and I damn well meant it. He laughed at me. Nobody laughs at me and gets away with it. Nobody, you hear?"

Penny didn't say anything right away. She lit a cigarette of her own, took a puff, made a face, and took a sip of wine to help get rid of the taste. She studied him through her smoke screen. At last, words did come from her: "Anybody took a look at you or listened to you for just a little while, he'd figure you were a wreck."

"He'd be right, too," Rance said at once, with a certain perverse pride.

But Penny shook her head. She drew on the cigarette again. "Goddamn, I don't know why I smoke these things, except I get so jumpy when I don't." She paused. "Where was I? Oh, yeah. You're like an old crowbar all covered with rust. Anybody looks at it, he figures he can break it over his knee. But it's solid iron in the middle. You can smash somebody's head in with it as easy as not."

Auerbach grunted. He wasn't used to praise—even ambiguous praise like that—from her. And he enjoyed feeling decrepit; whenever he failed at something, he had a built-in excuse. He said, "Hell, my own crowbar doesn't work the way it's supposed to half the time these days."

Penny snorted. Then she said, "You're sandbagging," which held an uncomfortable amount of truth. "You want to head back to the hotel, or you want to come shopping with me?"

"I'll head back to the hotel," he said without the least hesitation. "You go shopping the way a big-game hunter goes on safari." That was also a compliment of sorts.

Penny headed off to pit her bad French and her air of Midwestern naïveté against the merchants of Marseille. Rance took a taxi over to La Résidence Bompard. He hadn't been there long before somebody knocked on the door. The Luger he'd acquired wasn't legal, but a lot of the things he'd been doing in France weren't legal. "Who is it?" he asked, his raspy voice sharp with suspicion—he wasn't expecting company.

To his surprise, the answer came back in English: "It is I—Monique Dutourd."

"Oh." He slid the pistol into a pocket before opening the door. "Hello," he said, also in English. "Come in. Make yourself at home."

"Thank you." She looked around the room, then slowly nodded. "Yes. This is what it is like to be civilized. I remember. It has been a while."

"Sit down," Auerbach said. "Can I get you some wine?" She shook her head. He asked, "What can I do for you, then?"

"I wish to know"—her English was slow and precise; she had to think between words, as he did for French, though she spoke a little better—"why it is that you are friendly with that SS man, that Dieter Kuhn." She said several words after that in incandescent French, French nothing like what he'd studied at West Point. He didn't know exactly what they meant, but the tone was unmistakable.

"Why?" he said. "Because he and I have an enemy who is the same. Do you remember Goldfarb, the Jew that English ginger dealer sent here when this was still part of the *Reich*?" He waited for her to nod, then went on, "I am using the Nazi to take revenge on the Englishman."

"I see," she said. "If it were me, I would use the Englishman to take revenge on the Nazi, who made me into his harlot. Is that a proper English word, harlot?"

"I understand it, yes," Rance said uncomfortably. "I'm sorry, Miss Dutourd, but what it looks like to me is, a lot of the people in the ginger business are bastards, and you have to pick the one who will help you the most at any one time. For me right now, that's Kuhn. Like I say, I'm sorry."

"You are . . ." She groped for a word again. "Forthright." Rance smiled. He couldn't help himself. He'd never heard anybody actually say *forthright* before. He waved for her to go on, and she did: "In this, you are like my brother. He makes no apology for what it is that he does, either."

"I'm not sorry to do the Lizards a bad turn any way I can," Rance said. "Turning them into ginger addicts isn't as good as shooting them, but it will do."

"I do not love the Lizards, but I feel about the *Boches* as you feel about they—about *them*." Monique Dutourd corrected herself.

"And how does your brother feel?" Auerbach wasn't about to waste a chance to gather information on the people with whom he was dealing.

He got more than he bargained for. "Pierre?" Monique Dutourd's lip curled in fine contempt. "As long as he can get his money, he does not care whence it comes." Auerbach hadn't heard *whence* very often, either. He got the idea she'd learned English from books. She added, "And if he does not get his money when he should, then unfortunate things, it could be, would happen."

Sure as hell, that was worth knowing. All the same, Rance might have been happier not hearing it. He and Penny remained small fish in a tank full of sharks.

Peking *was* home. Liu Han hadn't been sure, not when she first came back to the city, but it was. To her real astonishment, she even found herself glad to be eating noodles more often than rice.

"This is very strange," she said to Liu Mei, using her chopsticks to grab a mouthful of buckwheat noodles from their bowl of broth and slurping them up. "Noodles felt like foreign food to me when I first came here."

"They're good." Liu Mei took noodles for granted. Why not? She'd been eating them all her life.

Talking about noodles was safe. This little eatery wasn't one where Party members gathered. The scrawny man at the next table might have been a Kuomintang operative. The fat fellow on the other side, the one who looked as if he'd bring in a good sum if rendered into grease, might have worked for the little scaly devils. That was, in fact, pretty likely. Men who worked for the scaly devils made enough to let them eat well.

"Hard times," Liu Han said with a sigh.

Her daughter nodded. "But better days are coming. I'm sure of it." Saying that was safe, too. All sides—even the little devils—thought their triumph meant better times ahead for China. Liu Han raised the bowl of noodles to her face and took another mouthful. She hoped that would cover the outrage she might show when thinking of what a triumph by the little scaly devils would mean.

They finished eating and got up to go. They'd already paid—this wasn't the sort of place where the proprietor would trust people to leave money on the counter. As they went out onto the *hutung*—the alley—in front of the little food shop, Liu Han said, "We finally have enough tea in the city."

"Do we?" Liu Mei said as men and women, all intent on their own affairs, hurried past. The *hutung* was in shadow; it was so narrow that the sun had to be at just the right angle to slide down into it. A man leading a donkey loaded with sacks of millet had people flattening themselves against the walls to either side to let him by. Liu Mei didn't smile—she couldn't—but her eyes brightened at what her mother said. "That's good. It took us long enough."

Before Liu Han could answer, a fly lit on the end of her nose. Looking at it cross-eyed, she fanned her hand in front of her face. The fly flew off. It was, of course, only one of thousands, millions, billions. They flourished in Peking as they did in peasant villages. Another would probably land on her somewhere in a minute.

She said, "Well, this is special tea, you know, not just the ordinary sort. It took a long time to pick the very best and bring it up from the south."

"Too long." Liu Mei was in one of those moods where she disapproved of everything. Liu Han understood that. Staying patient wasn't easy, not when every day saw the little scaly devils sinking their claws ever deeper into the flesh of China. Liu Mei went on, "We'll have to boil the fire up really hot."

"Can't make good tea any other way," Liu Han agreed.

They came out of the alley onto *Hsia Hsieh Chieh*, Lower Slanting Street, in the western part of the Chinese City, not far from the Temple of Everlasting Spring. Bicycles, rickshaws, wagons, foot traffic, motorcars, buses, trucks—Lower Slanting Street was wide enough for all of them. Because it was, and because everyone used it, traffic moved at the speed of the slowest.

More often than not, that was an annoyance. The little scaly devils in a mechanized fighting vehicle must have thought so; they had to crawl along with everyone else. Scaly devils were impatient creatures. They hated having to wait. They ran their own lives so waiting was only rarely necessary. Moving along jammed Chinese streets, though, what choice did they have?

When Liu Han said that aloud, Liu Mei said, "They could just drive over people or start shooting. Who would stop them? Who could stop them? They are the imperialist occupiers. They can do as they please."

"They can, yes, but they would touch off riots if they did," Liu Han said. "They are, most of them, smart enough to know that. They don't want us to get stirred up. They just want us to be good and to be quiet and to let them rule us and not to cause them any trouble. And so they'll sit in traffic just as if they were people."

"But they have the power to start running people over or to start shooting," Liu Mei said. "They think they have the right to do those things, whether they choose to do them or not. There's the evil: that they think they have the right."

"Of course it is," Liu Han agreed. "I don't suppose people can do anything about having the little scaly devils here on Earth with us—it's too late for that. But having them think they have the right to rule us—that's a different business. We should be free. If they can't see that, they need reeducating." She smiled. "Maybe we could all sit down together over tea."

No, her daughter couldn't smile: one more score to lay at the feet of the little devils. But Liu Mei nodded and said, "I think that would be very good."

The little scaly devils' machine tried to slide into a space just ahead. But a man on an oxcart squeezed in first. He had to lash the ox to make it move fast enough to get ahead of the armored vehicle. As soon as he found himself in front of it, he set down the whip and let the ox amble along at its own plodding pace. That did infuriate the scaly devils. Their machine let out a loud, horrible hiss, as if to cry, *Get out of the way!* The man on the ox-cart might have been deaf, for all the good that did them.

People—Liu Han among them—laughed and cheered. The fellow on the oxcart took off his broad straw hat and waved it, acknowledging the applause. If the little scaly devils understood that, it probably made them angrier than ever. Unless they chose to get violent, they could do nothing about it.

Then more laughter rose. It started a couple of blocks up Lower Slanting Street and quickly spread toward Liu Han and Liu Mei. Liu Han stood on tiptoe, but couldn't see over the heads of the people around her. "What is it?" she asked her daughter, who was several inches taller.

Liu Mei said, "It's a troop of devil-boys, cutting up capers and acting like fools." Disapproval filled her voice. The young men and—sometimes—young women who imitated the little scaly devils and adopted their ways were anathema to the Communist Party. They learned the little devils' language; they wore tight clothes decorated with markings that looked like body paint; some of them even shaved their heads so as to look more like the alien imperialists. There were such young people in the United States, too, but the United States was still free. Perhaps people there could afford the luxury of fascination with the scaly devils and their ways. China couldn't.

But then Liu Mei gasped in surprise. "Oh!" she said. "These are not ordinary devil-boys."

"What are they doing?" Liu Han asked irritably. "I still can't see." She stood on tiptoe again. It still didn't help.

Annoying her further, all her daughter said was, "Wait a bit. They're coming this way. You'll be able to see for yourself in a minute."

Luckily for Liu Mei, she was right. And, by the time Liu Han could see, shouts and cheers from the crowd had given her some idea of what was going on. Then, peering over her daughter's shoulder and through a gap in the crowd in front of them, she did indeed see—and, like everyone around her, she started laughing and cheering herself.

Liu Mei had also been right in saying this was no ordinary troop of devil-boys. Instead of slavishly imitating the little scaly devils, they burlesqued them. They pretended to be a mixed group of males and females, all taking ginger and all mating frenetically.

"Throw water on them!" shouted one would-be wit near Liu Han.

"No! Give them more ginger!" someone else yelled. That got a bigger laugh.

And then Liu Han started shouting, too: "Tao Sheng-Ming! You come here this instant!"

One of the devil-boys looked up in surprise at hearing his name called. Liu Han waved to him. She wondered how well he could see her. She also wondered whether he'd recognize her even if he could see her. They hadn't met in more than three years, and she didn't think he knew her name.

Whether he knew it or not, he hurried over when she called. And he did recognize her; she could see that in his eyes. Or maybe he just recognized Liu Mei, who, being much closer to his own age and much prettier, was likelier to have stuck in his mind. No—when he spoke, it was to Liu Han: "Hello, lady. I greet you." The last three words were in the language of the Race.

"And I greet you," she answered in the same tongue. Then she returned to Chinese: "I am glad to see you came through safe, after all the troubles Peking has seen since the last time we ran into each other."

"I managed." From his tone, he was used to managing such

things. His grin was wry, amused, older than his years. "And I'm glad to see you're all right, too, you and your pretty daughter." Yes, he remembered Liu Mei, all right. He sent that grin her way.

She looked back as if he were something nasty she'd found on the sole of her shoe. That only made his grin wider, which annoyed Liu Mei and amused Liu Han. She asked the question that needed asking: "Did you ever go and visit Old Lin at Ma's brocade shop?"

If Tao Sheng-Ming had visited Old Lin, he'd have been recruited into the Communist Party. If he hadn't, it was just as well that he didn't know Liu Han's name. But he nodded. His eyes glowed. "Oh, yes, I did that," he said. "I know more about comradeship now than I ever did before. Shall I tell you what"—he lowered his voice—"Mao says about the four characteristics of China's revolutionary war?"

"Never mind," Liu Han said. "So long as you know them." He wouldn't, unless he was a Communist himself. *Or unless he's bait for a trap,* Liu Han thought. But she shook her head. Had the little scaly devils known she was coming into Peking, they would have seized her. They wouldn't have bothered with traps.

Tao's grin came back. "Oh, yes. I know them. I know all sorts of things I never thought I would know. I have many things to blame you for—I mean, to thank you for."

He might be a Communist. But he was still a devil-boy, too. He enjoyed being outrageous. The foolish skit that he and his fellows had been performing proved that. "Did you have fun there, making the little devils look ridiculous to the masses?" Liu Han asked him.

He nodded. "Of course I did. That was the point of the antics. Good propaganda, don't you think?"

"Very good," Liu Han agreed. "I will have to do some talking with the Central Committee"—that made Tao Sheng-Ming's eyes widen, as she'd hoped it would—"but I think you and your devil-boys may prove even more useful in the continuing revolutionary struggle."

"How?" Tao was pantingly eager.

Liu Han smiled at Liu Mei. "Why, in the matter of the special tea that's come up from the south, of course." Liu Han laughed. Liu Mei didn't, but she nodded. Tao Sheng-Ming looked most intrigued. Liu Han laughed again. Sure enough, she knew how to get devil-boy wildness to serve the Party.

* * *

"There is no justice." Monique Dutourd spoke with great assurance and equally great bitterness.

Her brother was shaving with a straight razor, a little soap, and a handheld mirror. Pierre paused with the right side of his face scraped clean and the left still full of lather and whiskers. All he said was, "Now tell me something I did not know."

"Oh, shut up," she snarled. "You don't mind working with that Nazi again, no matter what he did to me."

Pierre Dutourd sighed and raised his chin so he could shave under it. Some small part of Monique hoped he'd cut his throat. He didn't, of course. He guided the razor with effortless, practiced skill. He didn't talk while shaving around his larynx. But when he started on his left cheek, he said, "Nobody in this business is a saint, little sister. The Nazi was screwing you. The Englishmen were screwing somebody else—that Jew, the American said."

"Nobody is a saint?" Monique rolled her eyes. "Well, if I didn't already know that, you would prove it."

"Merci beaucoup." Pierre was hard to infuriate, which was one of the most infuriating things about him. He finished shaving, rinsed and dried his razor, then washed his face with the water left in the enameled basin. He toweled himself dry and examined himself in the mirror. Only after a self-satisfied nod did he continue, "You know that, if you grow too unhappy here, you are always free to go elsewhere. There are times when I would say you were welcome to go elsewhere."

Ha! Monique thought. *I did hit a nerve there, even if he doesn't want to let it show.* But Pierre had hit a nerve, too, and painfully. Monique still had nowhere else to go, and she knew it. She had received a couple of more letters from universities that had survived the fighting. Nobody seemed to need a Roman historian whose university was now nothing but rubble that made a Geiger counter click.

She said, "You may be sure that, when the chance comes, I will take it." Each word might have been chipped from ice.

"Meanwhile, though, you would be wise not to bite the hand that feeds you," her brother went on, almost as if she hadn't spoken. "You would also be wise to become useful to someone in some way."

"Useful!" Monique made it a swear word. "Aren't you glad you're *useful* to the Lizards?"

"Of course I am," he answered. "If I weren't, I would have had to work much harder for most of my life. People I don't like would have told me what to do much more than they do now. Things could have been better, yes, but they also could have been much worse."

He was impervious. Monique stormed out of the tent. She'd been doing that more and more often these days. This time, she almost ran into a Lizard who was about to come in. *"Excusez-moi,"* he said in hissing French. Monique strode past him without a word.

She'd just got to the edge of the tent city when a double handful of Lizards hurried past her. They were all carrying weapons. She was no great expert on the many patterns of body paint the Race used, but she thought theirs—which were all similar to one another—had to do with law enforcement.

Uh-oh, she thought. She turned and looked back. Sure enough, they too were heading for the tent she'd just left. And she couldn't do anything about it. They were moving faster than she could. She was too far away to scream out a warning to her brother. And, after this latest blowup, she wasn't much inclined to scream out a warning anyway.

She waited. Sure enough, the Lizards emerged with not only the one who'd gone before them but also with her brother in custody. They marched their prisoners out of the camp—marched them right past Monique, though Pierre didn't notice her—hustled them into a waiting motorcar with flashing orange lights, and drove them away.

Well, Monique thought, *what do I do now?* She hadn't wanted to look for work in a shop. That would have been as much as admitting that she'd never find another academic position. As long as she could live with Pierre and Lucie, she'd been able to indulge those hopes. When you couldn't indulge your hopes any more, what did you do? If you had any sense, you buckled down and got on with your life.

With her brother a captive of the Race, she was going to have to get on with her life if she wanted to keep eating. Shop girl, scullery maid . . . anything this side of selling herself on the street. Dieter Kuhn had made her do something all too close to that. *Never again,* she vowed to herself. Better to jump off a cliff and hope she landed on her head. Everything would be over in a hurry then.

Hitting bottom here, realizing she'd have to look for work that had nothing to do with her degree, might have felt like that. It might have, but it didn't. Instead, it was oddly liberating. All right, she couldn't be a professor—or, at least, she couldn't be a professor right now. She'd be something else, then.

She started out of the camp and toward the rebuilding city of Marseille. She hadn't gone very far before she ran into Lucie coming back from the city. Unlike her own brother, Lucie recognized her. Of course, the Lizards hadn't just seized Lucie, either.

Monique was tempted to let her go back to the tent. Maybe the Lizards had left some sort of alarm behind so they could swoop down again when she did return. But Pierre's mistress hadn't given Monique a bad time. Lucie had, in fact, been easier to get along with than her own brother.

And so she said, "Be careful. The Lizards just grabbed Pierre."

"Oh, for the love of God!" Lucie said. "Was that the car I saw going downhill toward town?"

"That's right." Monique nodded. "Pierre and I had another fight. I'd just gone out when a Lizard—a customer, I mean—went in. And I hadn't gone a whole lot farther before a whole squad of Lizard *flics* came in and grabbed Pierre and the Lizard customer, too."

Lucie said something considerably more pungent than, *Oh, for the love of God!* She went on, "Keffesh was afraid they were shadowing him. Pierre was a fool to let him come to the tent."

"What are you going to do?" Monique asked.

Lucie grimaced. "I'll need to find somewhere to stay. I'd be an idiot to go back there now. Then I'll have to make some phone calls. I need to warn some people and some Lizards, and I have to ask a few questions. If I like the answers I get, I'll set up in business for myself. I've been Pierre's right hand and a couple of fingers of his left for a long time. My connections are as good as his, and I daresay I'm a lot better at being careful than he ever was."

All that took Monique by surprise. She didn't know why it should have. She knew Roman history. What did Lucie know? Selling ginger. Ruefully, Monique admitted to herself that the demand for ginger dealers seemed to be stronger than that for Romanists.

Her brother's mistress might have been thinking along with her. "What about you, Monique?" she asked. "What will you do?"

"Look for work," Monique answered. "I mean any kind of work, not a university position. I have to eat. And"—she sighed— "I suppose I'll see what I can do about getting Pierre out of jail." She noticed Lucie hadn't said anything about that.

Pierre's mistress also sighed. "Yes, I guess we will have to see about that, won't we? But it won't be easy. The Lizards' officials are death on ginger. You need connections to be able to get anywhere with them. Have you got any?"

"I may," Monique answered, which seemed to take Lucie by surprise. "And I'm sure that you do."

"Maybe." Yes, Lucie sounded grudging. If Pierre got out of jail, she would have more trouble going into business for herself.

Bleakly, Monique said, "One of the connections we both may have is Dieter Kuhn. If we decide we need to use him, you'll have to be the one who makes the approach. I can't do it, not even for my brother."

"I don't think we'll have to worry about that," Lucie said. "When the Lizards question Pierre, he'll sing. He'll sing like a nightingale. That's about the only thing I can think of that might make them go easy on him. Don't you think they'd be pleased if he could hand them a nice, juicy Nazi? That might let them squeeze some fresh concessions out of the Germans."

Monique eyed her with sudden respect. Lucie wasn't a fool. No, she wasn't a fool at all. And ginger smuggling was a network that tied the whole world together. No wonder Pierre's mistress was so quick to think in terms of geopolitics.

"If Pierre sings," Monique said slowly, "he'll sing about the Americans, too."

"But of course," Lucie said. "And so what? I never did see the point of dealing with them. Americans." Her lip curled. "They deserved to have a city blown up. Up till now, they've had it easy. Most of them still do."

"They're people," Monique said. "I don't want to give them to the Lizards."

"I'm sure I don't know why not." Lucie shrugged. "Have it your way. I'm not going to lose any sleep about them, I tell you that, or lift a finger for them, either. They wouldn't do it for me." However wide her world view could be, Lucie still came first in her own eyes.

Monique went on into Marseille. She didn't dare go back to the tent even to get her bicycle. The Lizards might return for her, too. Keffesh had seen her with Pierre and Lucie, and she'd interpreted for Pierre when he talked with the Americans. In the eyes of the Race, that was probably more than enough to convict her.

When she got to the edge of the city, she found a public telephone and fed a couple of francs into it. She called the hotel where Rance Auerbach and Penny Summers were staying. The phone rang several times. She was on the point of giving up when a man answered: *"Allô?"*

Auerbach's accent was ludicrously bad. Monique chose English to make sure he wouldn't misunderstand her: "The Lizards have Pierre. Do you know what that means?"

"You bet I do," he answered, which she took for an affirmative. "It means I'm in a hell of a lot of trouble. *Merci.*" He hung up.

For good measure, Monique wiped the telephone clean of fingerprints with her sleeve after she hung up, too. She assumed the Lizards would be listening to Auerbach's phone, and that they could trace the call back to this one. But let them try proving she'd been the one who made it.

And, having done one of the things she'd needed to do, she could get on with taking care of the rest. She walked into a dress shop, strode up to a man who looked like the manager, and asked, "Excuse me, but could you use another salesgirl?"

Nesseref was glad she could finally take Orbit for walks again without worrying much about residual radioactivity. The tsiongi was glad, too. He'd used the exercise wheel in her apartment, but it hadn't been the same. Now he could go out, see new sights, smell new smells, and get frustrated all over again when Tosevite birds flew away just as he was on the point of catching them.

He still looked absurdly indignant every time the feathered creatures eluded him. He seemed to think they were cheating by fluttering off. This world had a much larger variety of flying beasts than Home did. Local predators probably took such escapes for granted. As far as Orbit was concerned, they broke the rules.

Befflem running around without leashes broke the rules, too. As on Home, there were regulations in the new towns on Tosev 3 against letting befflem run free. As on Home, those regulations weren't worth much here. Befflem were much more inclined to do what they wanted than what the Race wanted them to do. If they'd had more brains, they might have served as models for Big Uglies.

Had Orbit been able to get his mouth and claws on a beffel, he would have made short work of it. But the befflem seemed smart enough to understand he was on a leash and they weren't. They would squeak as infuriatingly as they could, inviting him to chase them. And he would, just as he went after birds. The leash in Nesseref's hand brought him up short every time.

"No," she told him for the third time on the walk. Inside the apartment, he knew what the word meant. He obeyed it most of the time. Out in the fresh air, he did his best to forget.

"Beep!" said a beffel half a block away. Once more, Orbit tried to charge after it. Once more, Nesseref wouldn't let him. Orbit turned an eye turret toward her in what had to be reproach. The other turret he kept fixed on the beffel, which sat there scratching itself and then said, "Beep!" again.

"No!" Nesseref repeated as the tsiongi again tried to go after it. She used an emphatic cough. That meant nothing to Orbit, even if it gave her some small satisfaction.

Still beeping, the beffel trotted off long before Orbit got close enough to be dangerous. By then, Nesseref was starting to wonder whether her pet had pulled her arm out of its socket. *Who is getting the exercise here?* she thought, glaring at the tsiongi.

Shortly thereafter, neither of them got any exercise. Orbit sat down on the sidewalk and refused to move. His attitude seemed to be, *If I am not allowed to do what I want, I have no intention of doing what you want.* Tsiongyu were proud beasts. Offend their dignity and you had trouble.

But Nesseref knew tsiongyu, and knew how to coax them out of their sulks. She reached into a pouch she wore on a belt around her middle and pulled out a treat. She tossed it a little in front of Orbit. Sure enough, he forgot he was sulking. He trotted over and grabbed it. After that, he was walking again. Nesseref gave him another treat to keep him moving.

Some tsiongyu eventually figured out that staging sulks every so often would get them more than their share of treats. Orbit was still young, and hadn't acquired such duplicity. As tsiongyu went, he was a good-tempered beast, too, and not in the habit of sitting down on the job.

He tried to catch a couple of birds on the way back to the apartment, but no more befflem appeared to torment him, for which small favor Nesseref cast down her eye turrets and muttered a few words of thanks to spirits of Emperors past. As it always did, the elevator that took her and Orbit up to the story on which her apartment stood fascinated the tsiongi. Orbit's eye turrets went every which way before settling on Nesseref once more. She wondered what was going through his mind—perhaps that she'd just performed a particularly good conjuring trick.

Once inside the apartment, Orbit jumped into his wheel and started running as if a beffel as big as a bus were hot on his heels. "You are a very foolish beast," Nesseref said severely. Orbit paid no attention whatever. Nesseref hadn't expected him to, and so wasn't disappointed.

She went into her bedchamber and checked to see if she had any electronic messages. She found none that needed answering right away, and a couple that she immediately deleted. Why males and females she'd never met thought she would shift credit to their account for services she didn't want and they seemed unlikely to perform was beyond her. She supposed they found customers here and there on the electronic network; to her, that only proved that a hundred thousand years of civilization weren't long enough to produce sophistication.

Into the electronic garbage heap those messages went. Nesseref had just seen them vanish when the telephone hissed. "Shuttlecraft Pilot Nesseref—I greet you," she said crisply, wondering if it were a new assignment.

But the image that appeared on the screen was not a superior with orders, but a Big Ugly. "I greet you, Shuttlecraft Pilot," he said. "I know males and females of the Race have trouble telling one Tosevite from another, so I will tell you that I am Mordechai Anielewicz."

"And I greet you, my friend," Nesseref replied. "I will tell you that you are the only Tosevite likely to call me at my home. How are you? Was your search for your mate and hatchlings successful?"

Too late, she wished she hadn't said that. The answer was too likely to be no. If it were no, she would have saddened the Big Ugly. Friends had no business saddening friends.

But Anielewicz answered, "Yes!" and used an emphatic cough. He went on, "And do you know what? Pancer the beffel, my hatchling Heinrich's pet, helped lead me to them."

"Did he?" Nesseref exclaimed. "Tell me how—and I promise not to tell my tsiongi." By the concise way Anielewicz gave her the story, she guessed he'd already told it several times. When he'd finished, she said, "You were very fortunate."

"Truth," he agreed. "I will thank God"—a word not in the language of the Race—"for the rest of my life." He paused. "You would call this my superstition, and thank the spirits of Emperors past instead."

"I understand." Nesseref paused, too, then offered a cautious comment: "You Tosevites take your superstitions very seriously. When we opened shrines to the spirits of Emperors past here in Poland, hardly any Tosevites—either of your superstition or that of the Poles—entered them." After the latest round of fighting, few of those shrines still stood. She suspected they would be rebuilt one day, but more urgent concerns preoccupied the Race.

Mordechai Anielewicz laughed loud Tosevite laughter. "How many males and females of the Race give reverence to God at Tosevite shrines?"

"Why, none, of course," Nesseref said. A moment later, she added, "Oh. I see." Big Uglies kept thinking of themselves as equal and equivalent to members of the Race. Such thought patterns didn't come naturally to Nesseref. She might reckon Mordechai Anielewicz a friend, but most Big Uglies were to her nothing but barbarians—dangerous barbarians, but barbarians even so.

"Maybe you do," Anielewicz said, laughing again. "But I did not call you to discuss superstition. I hope I am not troubling you, but I called to ask another favor, if you would be so kind."

"Friends may ask favors of friends," Nesseref said. "That is one of the things that defines friendship. Ask. If it is in my power, you shall have it."

"I thank you." Anielewicz added another emphatic cough. "Friends are all I have now. Except for my mate and hatchlings, I believe all my relations died in the bombings of Lodz and Warsaw."

"I am sorry to hear it," Nesseref said. "I understand that, among Tosevites, relations take the place good friends hold among the Race." She understood that in her mind, not her liver, but she assumed Anielewicz realized as much. "As I said before, ask. If I can help you, I will."

"Very well." Anielewicz paused, then said, "We are, for now, staying in a refugee center. We lived in Lodz, and Lodz, of course, is no longer a city. Can you suggest some officials in Pinsk with whom we might talk to help arrange housing, real housing, for us?"

"Of course. Please wait while I check to see who would be most likely to help you quickly." She used the computer's keyboard to access the Race's table of organization in Pinsk. After giving Anielewicz three or four names, she said, "If you like, wait a day or two before calling them. I will speak to them first and let them know who you are and what you need."

"That would be wonderful," the Tosevite told her. "Many of your administrators are also new in Poland, replacing males and females who perished in the fighting and who were more familiar with me."

"Exactly why I made the suggestion," Nesseref said. "Let me do that now, then."

"Fine." Anielewicz even understood she meant the conversation was over. A good many members of the Race would have gone right on chattering after such a hint, but he broke the connection.

The first call Nesseref made to Pinsk was to the officer in charge of liaison between the Race's military forces and those of the Big Uglies in Poland. Nowhere else on Tosev 3 would the Race have had such a liaison officer. That it had one here still struck Nesseref as unnatural, but she made use of the male.

And he, to her relief, knew who Mordechai Anielewicz was. "Yes," he said. "I have received reports of his search for his blood kin from a male in Security in the *Reich*. Everyone seems to be astonished that he succeeded in finding them, especially with the Deutsche so inimical to those of his superstition."

"I certainly was, when he telephoned me just now," Nesseref said. "I was also surprised to learn that a male who has done the Race so many important services should have to inhabit a refugee center because he is unable to find housing for himself, his mate, and his hatchlings."

"That *is* unfortunate," the liaison officer agreed. "I thank you for bringing it to my attention. Perhaps I should speak to someone in the housing authority."

"I wish you would," Nesseref said. "I intended to do the same thing myself, but they are likelier to listen to a male from the conquest fleet than to a shuttlecraft pilot without any great connections."

"Sometimes I think the bureaucrats, especially the ones from the colonization fleet, pay no attention to anyone except themselves," the liaison officer said. "But what I can do, I shall do: I assure you of that."

"I thank you," Nesseref said. "I think I will also make those phone calls myself. Perhaps I can reinforce you. I count Mordechai Anielewicz as a friend, and I am pleased to do whatever I can for him."

"Well, of course, if he is a friend," replied the male from the conquest fleet. "I have Tosevite friends myself, so I understand how you feel."

"Oh, good. I am very glad to hear that," Nesseref said. "It gives me hope that, in spite of everything, we may yet be able to live alongside the Big Uglies on a long-term basis." She hesitated. Rather defensively, she added, "We may." The liaison officer didn't laugh at her. She feared that was more likely to mean he was polite, though, than that he agreed with her.

"Reuven!" Moishe Russie called from the Lizards' computer-and-telephone unit. "Come here for a minute, would you? You may be able to give me some help. I hope you can, anyway—I could use some."

"I'm coming, Father." Reuven hurried into the front room. "What's up?" he asked, and then stopped in surprise when he saw Shpaaka, one of the leading Lizard physicians at the Russie Medical College, looking out of the monitor screen at him. He shifted into the language of the Race: "I greet you, superior sir."

"And I greet you, Reuven Russie," Shpaaka answered. "It is good to see you again, even if you decided that your superstition precluded you from finishing your studies with us."

"I thank you. It is good to see you, too." Seeing Shpaaka reminded Reuven how much he missed the medical college, something he tried not to think about most of the time. Trying not to think about it now, he asked, "How can I help?"

His father coughed a couple of times. "I think I will let Shpaaka explain it to you, as he had begun to explain it to me."

"Very well," Shpaaka said, though by his tone it was anything but very well. He looked about as uncomfortable as Reuven had ever seen a male of the Race. *It's something to do with sex,* he thought. *It has to be.* And, sure enough, the Lizard physician said, "I called your father, Reuven Russie, to discuss a case of perversion."

That made Moishe Russie speak up: "It would be better, Doctor, if you discussed the case itself and let us draw the value judgments, if any."

"Very well, though I find it difficult to be dispassionate here," Shpaaka said. "The problem concerns a pair from the colonization fleet, a female named Ppurrin and a male called Waxxa. They were best friends back on Home, and they resumed that close friendship after coming to Tosev 3. Unfortunately, after coming to Tosev 3, both of them also became addicted to ginger, that most pernicious of all herbs."

"Uh-oh," Reuven said to his father. "Do I know what's coming next?"

"Half of it, maybe," Moishe Russie answered. "That's about how much I guessed."

Shpaaka said, "May I continue?" as if they'd talked out of turn during one of his lectures. When they looked back toward the monitor, he went on, "As you might imagine, the two of them began to mate with each other when Ppurrin tasted ginger. And, due to these repeated matings, they have conceived a passion for each other altogether inappropriate for members of the Race. After all, during a proper mating season, how is one partner much different from another?"

"You understand, superior sir, that we Tosevites feel rather differently about such things." Reuven did his best not to sound anything but dispassionate himself. He didn't use an emphatic cough. He didn't burst into laughter, either.

"I said the same thing," his father remarked.

"Of course I understand that," Shpaaka said impatiently. "It is exactly why I am consulting with you. You see, Ppurrin and Waxxa are so blatant in their perverse behavior that they seek a formal, exclusive mating arrangement, such as is the custom among your species."

"They want to get married?" Reuven exclaimed. He said it first in Hebrew, which Shpaaka didn't follow. Then he translated it into English, a tongue the Lizard physician did know fairly well.

And, sure enough, Shpaaka made the affirmative gesture.

"That is exactly what they want to do. Can you imagine anything more disgusting?"

Before answering him, Reuven spoke quickly to his father: "Well, you were right. I didn't think of *that*." Then he returned to the language of the Race and said, "Superior sir, I gather you are not simply punishing them because they use ginger."

"We could do that," Shpaaka admitted, "but both of them, aside from this sexual perversion, perform their jobs very well. Still, sanctioning permanent unions of this sort would surely prove destructive of good order. Why, next thing you know, they would probably want to rear their hatchlings themselves and teach them the same sort of revolting behavior."

This time, Reuven did laugh. He couldn't help it. He made himself grow serious again, saying, "We Tosevites do not consider any of the behavior you have mentioned to be disgusting, you know."

"I would agree. It is not disgusting—for Tosevites," Shpaaka said. "We of the Race found it disgusting in you when we first learned of it, but that was some time ago now. We have come to see that it is normal for your kind. But we do not want our males and females imitating it, any more than you would want your males and females imitating our normal practices."

"Some of our males might enjoy your mating seasons, while their stamina lasted," Moishe Russie said. "Most of our females, I agree, would not approve."

"You are being irrelevant," Shpaaka said severely. "I had hoped for assistance, not mockery and sarcasm. Except for their drug addiction and perverse attraction to each other, Ppurrin and Waxxa, as I say, are excellent members of the Race."

"Why not just ignore what they do in private, then?" Reuven asked.

"Because they refuse to keep it private," Shpaaka answered. "As I told you, they have requested formal recognition of their status. They are proud of what they do, and predict that, on account of ginger, most males and females of the Race on Tosev 3 will eventually find permanent, exclusive sexual partners."

"Missionaries for monogamy," Moishe Russie murmured.

Reuven nodded. "What if they are right?" he asked Shpaaka.

His former mentor recoiled in horror. "In that case, the colonists on Tosev 3 will become the pariahs of the Empire when the truth is learned back on Home," he answered. "I think it altogether likely that the spirits of Emperors past would turn their backs on this whole world as a result."

He means it, Reuven realized. The Lizards dismissed his religion as a superstition. He sometimes did the same with theirs. Here, that would be a mistake.

He said, "If you do not wish to punish them and you do wish to silence them, why not suggest that they emigrate to one of the independent not-empires?—to the United States, perhaps. Ginger is legal there and"—of necessity, he dropped into English—"they could get married, too."

"That is a *good* idea." Moishe Russie used an emphatic cough. "That is a very good idea. It would get this couple out from under your scales, too, Shpaaka, so they cannot agitate among the colonists any more."

"Perhaps." Shpaaka turned an eye turret toward Reuven. "I thank you, Reuven Russie. It is, at any rate, an idea we had not thought of for ourselves. We shall consider it. Farewell." His image disappeared from the screen.

"Lizards who want to get married!" Reuven turned to his father. Now he could laugh as much as he wanted to, and he did. "I never would have believed that."

"They've made people change a lot since they got to Earth," Moishe Russie said. "They're just starting to find out how much they've changed, too. As far as they're concerned, changing us is fine. But they don't like it so well when the shoe is on the other foot. Nobody does."

"If they could stamp out ginger, they'd do it in a minute," Reuven said.

"If we could stamp out alcohol and opium and a lot of other things, a lot of us would do it, too," his father said. "We've never managed it. I don't think they'll have an easy time getting rid of ginger, either."

"You're probably right, especially since we use it so much in food," Reuven answered. "One of these days, though, they may try—try seriously, I mean. That will be interesting."

"There's one word for it." Moishe Russie winked. "If these Lizards do get married, who'd give the bride away?"

Before Reuven could reply, the ordinary telephone rang. He went over and picked it up. "Hello?"

"Dr. Russie?" A woman's voice, one with pain in it. "This is

Deborah Radofsky. I'm sorry to bother you, but I just kicked the wall by accident, and I'm afraid I've broken my toe."

Reuven started to tell her that a doctor couldn't do much for a broken toe no matter what—news that always delighted his patients. He started to tell her to come to the office in the morning if she really wanted to get it examined. Instead, he heard himself saying, "Remind me of your address, and I'll come over and have a look at it." His father blinked.

"Are you sure?" the widow Radofsky asked. Reuven nodded, a useless thing to do over a phone without a video attachment. After he gave her assurances she could hear, she gave him an address. It wasn't more than fifteen minutes' walk away; Jerusalem was an important city, but not on account of its size.

"A house call?" Moishe Russie asked when Reuven hung up. "I admire your energy, but you don't do that very often."

"It's Mrs. Radofsky," Reuven answered. "She thinks she's broken her toe."

"Even if she has, you won't be able to give her much help, and you know it perfectly well," his father said. "I don't see why you didn't just tell her to come to the office tomorrow morn . . ." His voice trailed off as he made the pieces fit together. "Oh. Mrs. Radofsky. The widow Radofsky. Well, go on, then."

After grabbing his doctor's bag, Reuven was glad to get out of the house. His father didn't mind his paying a professional call on a nice-looking widow. His mother probably wouldn't mind when his father told her, either. What the twins would say—no, he didn't want to contemplate that. At romantic fifteen, they thought he was a fool for not having gone to Canada with Jane Archibald. About three days a week, he thought he was a fool, too.

He had no trouble finding the widow Radofsky's little house. When he knocked on the door, he had to wait a bit before she opened it. The way she limped after he came inside showed why. "Sit down," he told her. "Let me have a look at that."

She did, in an overstuffed chair under a lamp, and held up her right foot. She winced when he slid the slipper off it. Her fourth toe was swollen up to twice its size, and purple from base to tip. She hissed when he touched it, and hissed again and shook her head when he asked her if she could move it. "I have broken it, haven't I?" she said.

"I'm afraid so," Reuven answered. "I can put a splint on it, or I can leave it alone. It'll heal the same either way."

"Oh," she said unhappily. "It's like that, is it?"

"I'm afraid so," he repeated, and tried to make her think about something besides his inability to help: "What's your daughter doing?"

"She's gone to sleep," the widow Radofsky answered. She wasn't easily distracted. "Why did you bother coming here, if you knew you wouldn't be able to do much? You could have told me to wait till morning."

"It's all right—it might have been just a nasty bruise. It's not, but it might have been." Reuven hesitated, then added, "And—I hope you don't mind my saying so—I was glad for the chance to see you, too."

"Were you?" After a pause of her own, she said, "No, I don't mind."

☆ **13** ☆

"Scooter calling *Columbus*. Scooter calling *Columbus*," Glen Johnson radioed as he approached the second American constant-acceleration spaceship to reach the asteroid belt. "Come in, *Columbus*."

"Go ahead, Scooter," the radio operator aboard *Columbus* said. "We have you on our radar. You're cleared to approach airlock number two. The lights will guide you."

"Thanks, *Columbus*. Will do. Out." The lights aboard the spaceship had been guiding him for a little while now. He'd hardly needed the chatter. But the *Columbus'* radio operator on duty was a woman with a nice, friendly voice. He enjoyed listening to her, and so talked more than he might have otherwise.

He had no idea whether he would enjoy looking at her; they'd never met in person. He knew he enjoyed looking at the *Columbus*. *That's doing things right,* he thought. The *Lewis and Clark* had started out as a space station, and had had to be expanded and revised before leaving Earth orbit. It had reached the vicinity of Ceres, yes, and done what it was supposed to do once it got here, but that didn't mean it wasn't the spacegoing equivalent of a garbage scow.

By contrast, the *Columbus* had been designed and built as an interplanetary spacecraft from the inside out. It wasn't quite so elegant a piece of engineering as a Lizard starship, but it was on the right track. It was a series of spheres: one for the crew, then a boom, another sphere for the reaction mass, then a second boom, and finally, in lonely splendor, the nuclear engine that heated and discharged the mass. It was a better job in just about every way than the *Lewis and Clark*. And the spaceship that came after the *Columbus* would be better still. Human technology wasn't static, the way the Race's was.

368

Using eyeballs and the scooter's radar, Johnson killed almost all of his velocity relative to the *Columbus* and drifted forward at a rate better measured in inches per second than in feet. He made further minute adjustments with his little maneuvering rockets as he slid into airlock number two, which was big enough to accommodate the scooter. "*Columbus*, I'm all the way inside," he reported. "Velocity . . . zero."

"Roger that." It wasn't the radio operator who answered, but the airlock officer, a man. The outer door slid shut behind the scooter. Once it had securely closed, the inner door slid open. The airlock officer said, "We have pressure for you, Lieutenant Colonel Johnson. You can open the top and come out for a bit."

"Thanks," Glen said. "Don't mind if I do." He had to equalize pressure before the canopy would come off; the *Columbus* kept its internal pressure a little higher than either the *Lewis and Clark* or the scooter. When Johnson did emerge, he was wearing a grin. "Always good to see an unfamiliar face."

"I believe that," the airlock officer said. "Hell, it's good for me to see you, and I've only been stuck aboard this madhouse for a few months."

"You don't know what a madhouse is," Johnson said, loyally slandering his own shipmates.

"Well, maybe you're right," the other fellow admitted. "You folks even had a stowaway, didn't you? Somebody who wasn't supposed to be aboard, I mean."

"We sure did." Glen Johnson would have drawn himself up in pride, but didn't see much point in weightlessness. "As a matter of fact, you're looking at him."

"Oh," the airlock officer said. "I'm sorry. No offense."

"Don't worry about it," Johnson said easily. "After all the different things Brigadier General Healey has called me over the past couple of years, you'd have a hard time getting me mad." He pushed off against the scooter and grabbed the nearest handhold. The corridors of the *Columbus*, like those of the *Lewis and Clark*, were designed so that people could impersonate chimpanzees.

"Doctor Harper should be along any minute now," the airlock officer said.

"It's all right. I'm not in any big hurry," Johnson answered. "We don't have scheduled flights yet—that'll have to wait for a while. Not enough traffic that we have to worry about it, either. As soon as he gets here, I'll take him where he needs to go."

"She. Her," the fellow from the *Columbus* said. "Doctor Chris Harper is definitely of the female persuasion."

"Okay. Better than okay, in fact," Johnson said. "I figured anybody who's a doctor of electrical engineering was odds-on to be a guy, even if Chris is one of those names that can go either way. Not sorry to find out I'm wrong, though."

"We brought along as even a mix as we could, same as the *Lewis and Clark* did," the airlock officer replied. "It's not fifty-fifty—more like sixty-forty."

"That's better than our blend—we're closer to two to one," Johnson said. He wondered if the larger number of newly arrived women would change the social rules that had developed aboard the *Lewis and Clark. Time will tell,* he thought with profound unoriginality.

From what the airlock officer had said, he'd expected Dr. Chris Harper to be a beautiful blonde who might have gone into the movies instead of electrical engineering. She wasn't; she had light brown hair, chopped off pretty short, and wasn't anywhere near beautiful. *Cute* was the word that sprang to Johnson's mind: again, something less than original. "Pleased to meet you," he said, and stuck out the hand he wasn't using to hold on.

"Same to you, I'm sure," she said. "You're supposed to take me to Dome 22, isn't that right?"

"Uh-huh," he said. "They're just about ready for you there. They probably could have gotten things going by themselves, but we'll be able to get twice as much done—maybe more than twice as much done—with more people doing it."

"That's the idea," Dr. Harper said. She pointed toward the scooter. "And what am I supposed to do here?"

"Get in, sit in the back seat, and fasten your belt," Johnson answered. "Fare is seventy-five cents, fare box is on the right-hand side. Because of company policy, your driver's not allowed to accept tips."

She snorted and grinned. "They kept telling us the people who came out on the *Lewis and Clark* were a little strange. I see they were right."

Before Johnson got the chance to deny everything with as much mock indignation as he could, the airlock officer pointed at him and said, "He's the stowaway."

Dr. Harper's eyes widened. "You mean there really was one?

When we heard about that, I thought it was like a lefthanded monkey wrench or striped paint—something they pulled on the new people." She swung her attention back to Glen Johnson. "Why did you stow away? *How* did you stow away?"

"I didn't quite," he said, "I was flying orbital patrol, and I came aboard the *Lewis and Clark*—the space station, it still was then—when my main engine wouldn't ignite." He'd arranged the engine trouble himself, but he'd never told that to anybody, and didn't intend to start here. "I got there just before the ship was going to leave Earth orbit, and the commandant didn't want anybody who wasn't in on the secret going back down and saying something he shouldn't, letting the Lizards know what was up. So he kept me aboard, and I came along for the ride."

"Oh," she said. "That's not as exciting as hiding in a washroom or something, is it?"

"Afraid not," Johnson answered. Now he pointed to the scooter. "Shall we get going?" He pushed off from the wall and glided toward the little cockpit. Dr. Harper did the same. She was good in weightlessness, but she still didn't take it quite so much for granted as did the crewfolk of the *Lewis and Clark*. She scrambled in behind him and strapped herself down.

He sealed the canopy, double-checked to make sure it *was* sealed, and waved to the airlock officer to show he was ready to go. The officer nodded and touched a button. The inner door to the lock closed. Pumps pulled most of the air back into the *Columbus*. The outer door opened. Using tiny burns with his maneuvering jets, Johnson eased the scooter out of the airlock. The outer door closed behind him.

"You're good at this," Chris Harper remarked.

"I'd better be," Johnson answered, swinging the scooter's nose in the direction of Dome 22. Once he'd done that, he decided he ought to elaborate a little more: "I was a fighter pilot when the Lizards got here, and then, like I said, I did a lot of orbital patrolling. And I've been out here a while now, too. So I've had more practice at this kind of thing than just about anybody."

"I always enjoy watching somebody who knows what he's doing, no matter what it is," she said. "You do. It shows."

"Glad you think so," he said. "Now I have to make extra sure not to let any little rocks bounce off us, or anything stupid like that."

Dome 22 had been set up on an asteroid about half a mile across at its thickest point. "This is the one they're going to use as a test, isn't that right?" Chris Harper asked as they drew near the drifting chunk of rock and metal.

"Yeah, I think so," he answered. "That's why you've come, isn't it? For a last look to make sure everything goes the way it should?"

"That's about the size of it," Dr. Harper agreed. "Do you suppose the Lizards will notice when we do test?"

"Everyone's assuming they will, or at least that they'll notice the beginning," he said. "Of course, they may stop paying any attention to this asteroid once we shut down the dome and take everybody off. We're hoping that's what they do, but don't bet anything you can't afford to lose on it."

"Fair enough," she said briskly, and then, to his surprise, tapped him on the shoulder. "I know you said it was against the rules to tip the driver, but I've got something for you, if you want it."

He wondered what she had in mind. The cockpit of a scooter wasn't the ideal place for some of the things that leaped into *his* mind, especially not when they'd come so close to the dome. "Well, sure," he said in tones as neutral as he could make them. He might have been wrong, after all.

And he was. She said, "Here, then," and handed him a couple of things.

They were small enough for both of them to fit in the palm of his hand: a roll of Lifesavers and a pack of Wrigley's Spearmint gum. They weren't her reasonably fair white body, but he exclaimed, "Thank you!" just the same.

"You're welcome," Dr. Harper answered. "My guess was that you people had probably run out of things like that a while ago."

"And you're right, too," he said. "As far as teeth and such go, we're probably better off on account of it, but that doesn't mean I won't enjoy the hell out of these. Cherry Lifesavers . . . Jesus."

He was close enough to the asteroid now to let him see all the construction that had gone on alongside of Dome 22. He clenched the candy and gum. In a way, that was what the construction was all about: so the USA could go right on making such frivolous things. He laughed at himself. *If you don't sound like something out of a recruiting film, what does?*

"Hydrogen, oxygen—who needs anything else?" he said, and

then, as a concession to his passenger, "A little alien engineering doesn't hurt, either."

"Thank you so much," Chris Harper said. They both laughed.

Stargard was one of the towns of northeastern Germany that the *Wehrmacht* and the *Volkssturm* had defended to the last man and the last bullet. The Lizards hadn't expended an explosive-metal bomb on it; they'd smashed it with armor and with strikes from the air, and then gone on to larger, more important centers of resistance. Once the *Reich* yielded, they hadn't bothered putting a garrison in the town between Greifswald and Neu Strelitz.

Johannes Drucker didn't blame the Lizards for that. In their shoes, he wouldn't have garrisoned Stargard, either. What point to it? Before war rolled through the little city, it might have held forty or fifty thousand people—about as many as Greifswald. These days? These days, he would have been astonished if even a quarter of that number tried to scratch out a living here. He knew for a fact that ruins and empty houses far outnumbered inhabited ones.

All that made Stargard a perfect place for holdouts. Drucker wondered how many other smashed-up towns throughout the *Reich* held company- to battalion-sized units of *Wehrmacht* men or brigands—sometimes the line between them wasn't easy to draw—who would sometimes sneak out and do what they could against the occupiers of the *Reich*.

He doubted he'd ever find out the answer to that. He did know Stargard held such a unit. And, at the moment, the holdouts were holding him. The Lizard who'd been driving him down to Neu Strelitz was no longer among the living. Had a couple of bullets from the machine-gun burst that wrecked the motorcar and killed the driver gone a few centimeters to the left or right of their actual courses, Drucker wouldn't have been among the living any more, either.

As things were, he remained unsure how long he'd stay among the living. The holdouts kept him in the cellar whose second story had taken a couple of direct hits from a landcruiser's cannon. It hadn't burned, but nobody would want to live up there, either.

With a screech of rusty hinges, the cellar door opened. Two guards came down the stairs. One carried a kerosene lamp to shed more light than the candles the holdouts gave Drucker. The other had an assault rifle. He pointed it at Drucker's midriff. "Come with us," he said.

"All right." Drucker got off the cot where he'd been lying. The alternative, plainly, was being shot on the spot. "Where are we going?" he asked. They'd taken him out for questioning a couple of times, which had let him see a little of Stargard, not that there was much worth seeing.

But the fellow with the lamp had a different answer today: "To the People's Court, that's where. They'll give you what you deserve, you lousy traitor."

"I'm not a traitor." Drucker had been saying the same thing ever since they captured him. Had the holdouts believed him, they would have let him go. Had they thoroughly disbelieved him, they would have shot him when they killed his driver. They almost had. "What do you mean, People's Court?" he asked as he approached the stairs.

The guards both backed up. They weren't about to let him get close enough to grab either the rifle or the lantern. The one holding the rifle said, "The People's Court, to give out justice for the *Volk*."

"To give collaborators what they deserve," the other fellow added.

Wearily, Drucker said, "I'm not a collaborator, either." He'd been saying that over and over, too. Had he just been saying it, it would have done him no good. But he'd also had in his wallet the telegram from Walter Dornberger. A personal message from the *Führer* had given even the holdouts pause.

When Drucker came out onto the street, he was surprised to see it was early morning. Down in the windowless cellar, he'd lost track of day and night. He'd lost track of which day it was, too. He thought he'd been a prisoner for a couple of weeks, but he could have been off by several days either way.

Only a few people were out and about so early. None of them seemed to find the sight of a man marched along at gunpoint in any way remarkable. Drucker wondered what would happen if he shouted for help. Actually, he didn't wonder; he had a pretty good idea. Nobody would do anything for him, and the youngster with the assault rifle would fill him full of holes. He kept quiet.

"In here," said the fellow with the lantern. In daylight, even the murky, cloudy daylight of Stargard, it was useless.

Here had been a tobacconist's. The plate-glass window at the front of the shop had been smashed. Drucker was morally certain not a gram of tobacco remained inside. He'd lost the craving up on the Lizards' starship, and had never had it too strongly— smoking in the upper stage of an A-45 while in Earth orbit was severely impractical. But for the shattered window, though, the tobacconist's looked pretty much intact.

The back room had probably kept the stock that wasn't on display. Now it held a table and eight or ten chairs that didn't match one another. Three men sat along one side of the table. Drucker had seen two of them before. They'd interrogated him. The third, who sat in the middle, wore a *Wehrmacht* major's tunic. He was young, but had a face like a steel trap: all sharp edges and angles, without humor, without mercy. Drucker wondered why he hadn't served in the SS rather than the Army. Whatever the reason, he feared he wouldn't get much of a fair trial here.

"We, the *Volk* of the *Reich*, bring the accused traitor, Johannes Drucker, before the bar of justice here," the major said.

Drucker wasn't invited to sit down. He sat anyway. The guards growled. The major glowered, but didn't say anything. Drucker did: "All I've ever wanted to do was find my family. That's not treason. I haven't done anything that is treason, either."

One of his interrogators said, "A Lizard was doing you a favor. Why would the Lizards do you a favor if you weren't a traitor?"

"We've been over this before," Drucker said, as patiently as he could. "They knew who I am because I flew the upper stage of an A-45. They captured me in space, and held me till the fighting was over. I suppose they were helping me because the *Führer* was my old commandant at Peenemünde. He was generous enough to send me that wire. I heard some of my family might be down in Neu Strelitz, so I asked the Lizards for a lift. I'd walked from Nuremberg to Greifswald. If I didn't have to walk again, I didn't want to. That's all. It's simple, really."

It wasn't so simple. He said not a word about Mordechai Anielewicz. If the holdouts learned he'd consorted with a Jew, he *was* a dead man.

By the hard-faced young major's eyes, he was liable to be a dead man any which way. The officer—evidently the leader of this band of holdouts—said, "You were consorting with the enemy. No proper citizen of the *Reich* should have anything to do with the Lizards under any circumstances."

Drucker glared at him. "Oh, for Christ's sake," he said, not so patiently any more. Maybe losing his temper was a mistake, but he couldn't help it. "I started out in the *Wehrmacht* when you were in short pants. I was a panzer driver. If I hadn't been shooting up Lizard landcruisers then, you wouldn't be here to call me a traitor now."

"What you did in the past is gone." The major snapped his fingers. "Gone like that. What you do now, with the *Reich* in peril— that is what matters. And you have not denied that you were captured in the company of a Lizard."

"How could I deny it?" Drucker said. "I was sitting next to him when your men shot him. What I do deny is that my sitting next to him makes me disloyal to the *Reich*. I'm as loyal to the *Führer* as any man here. Where's *your* telegram from General Dornberger, *Herr* Major?"

That should have been a corker. Unfortunately, Drucker saw that it didn't do as much corking as he'd hoped it would. Sure enough, the young major's eyes might have come off an SS recruiting poster: they were gray-blue like ice, and every bit as cold. He said, "It is by no means certain that the *Führer* is not a traitor to the *Reich*. He yielded to the Race too soon, and he yielded far too much in the terms for what he calls peace but is in fact only appeasement."

More royal than the king, Drucker thought. Aloud, he said, "If he hadn't yielded, every square millimeter of Germany would be covered with radioactive glass right now. You wouldn't be alive to tell me this nonsense. I might still be alive, because I was out in space. But I wouldn't have gone for a ride with that Lizard, because I would have known everybody in my family was dead."

"If you support the *Führer*'s spinelessness, you condemn yourself out of your own mouth," the holdouts' leader replied in a voice as frigid as his eyes.

Drucker felt like pounding his head against the table. "If you don't follow the policies of your own *Führer*, of the *Reich*'s *Führer*, how can you call yourself soldiers of the *Reich* any more? You're not soldiers. You're just bandits."

"We are soldiers of the true *Reich*, the pure *Reich*, the *Reich* we struggle to bring back into being, the *Reich* that will have a *Führer* worthy of it, not a collaborationist." By a slight change in tone, the major suggested the *Reich* might not have to look too far to find such a *Führer*. And, by the faces of the two men who'd grilled Drucker before, they agreed with him.

As far as Drucker was concerned, they were all out of their minds. Of course, nine hundred ninety-nine people out of a thousand in Munich in 1921 would have said the same thing about Hitler and his handful of followers, too. But how many would-be Hitlers had there been in Germany then? Hundreds, surely. Thousands, more likely. What were the odds this fellow was the genuine article? Slim. Very, very slim.

Genuine article or not, he had the whip hand here. And he plainly intended to use it. "By the power vested in me as an officer of the *Reich*—the true *Reich*, the uncorrupted *Reich*—I now pass sentence on you for treason against that *Reich*," he said. "The sentence will be—"

Before he could tell Drucker what it would be, one of his young bully boys strode into the tobacconist's back room with a package in his hand. The major paused. Drucker wondered why he bothered. He wondered why the major bothered with the whole rigmarole in the first place, when he'd plainly decided to execute Drucker in the name of what he called people's justice.

His bully boy sent Drucker a curious glance. The fellow was seventeen or eighteen, with the fuzzy beginnings of a beard. Drucker's hand started to go to his own chin; in however long he'd been in captivity, he'd raised a thicker growth than that kid owned.

The hand froze halfway to his face. The kid was staring at him, too. "Heinrich?" Drucker whispered, at the same time as the bully boy was saying, "Father?" Drucker sprang out of his chair, the hard-faced major and his own impending death sentence utterly forgotten. He and his son jumped into each other's arms.

"What's going on here?" the major demanded.

"What's going on here, sir?" Heinrich Drucker demanded in return. "I knew we'd taken a prisoner, but I didn't know who." By the look on *his* face, he was ready to fight his commander and everyone else in the world. Drucker had been the same way at the same age. Danger in his voice, Heinrich went on, "Was this a treason trial?"

"Now that you mention it, yes," Drucker said. He had to grab his son to keep him from going for the major's throat.

"Perhaps," the holdout leader said, "in the light of this new evidence—"

"Evidence, am I?" Heinrich growled.

"In the light of this new evidence," the major repeated, "perhaps we can justify suspending sentence for the time being. Perhaps." Considering what had been about to happen to him, Drucker didn't even mind the qualifier.

Felless was glad to escape Cairo and return to Marseille. She'd never imagined she would think such a thing, but it remained a truth nonetheless. She'd seen for herself that she couldn't get rid of her ginger habit. Creating another scandal right under the eye turrets of the fleetlord of the conquest fleet would undoubtedly have got her sent to a worse place than Marseille. That not-empire called Finland, newly under the Race's influence, was supposed to have weather abominable even by Tosevite standards.

She let out a hiss of relief that she'd touched off only one small mating frenzy in Cairo, and that word of it hadn't got back to Atvar. She had Ttomalss to thank for that. She didn't like being indebted to the other psychological researcher, but knew full well that she was. If he wanted something from her one of these days, she didn't see how she could keep from giving it to him.

At least she wasn't gravid—or she didn't think she was. That took away one worry pertaining to ginger-induced sexuality, anyhow. And so she peered out of the small windows of her aircraft at the blue water below—such a lot of water on this world—and waited to land at the field outside Marseille.

Once the aircraft had rolled to a halt, she got out and arranged transportation to the new consulate building. Formalities were minimal; the Français, unlike the Deutsche, didn't go out of their way to make things difficult for the Race.

They had better not, she thought. *They owe us a great deal more than I owe Ttomalss.* Of course, by all indications, the Big Uglies worried a great deal less than the Race did about their debts.

All the motorcars outside the terminal building were of Tosevite manufacture and had Big Uglies driving them. She got into one and said, "To the consulate." She spoke in her language, since she knew no other.

"It shall be done," the driver said. He opened and closed his hands four times. "Twenty francs." Francs, she knew, were what the local Big Uglies used for money. She had some of the little metal disks. They differed in value, depending on their size and design. Somewhere on them, no doubt, were Tosevite numerals. Felless had never bothered learning those, but she did know which size was worth ten francs. She gave the driver two of those. He made the Race's affirmative gesture. "I thank you."

By the time he got her to the consulate, Felless was by no means sure she thanked him. She had seen that many Tosevites drove as if they did not care whether they lived or died. This Français male seemed to be actively courting death. He drove as if his motorcar were a missile, and guided it into tiny openings, even into imaginary openings, defying everyone around him. Back on Home, males of some animal species used such challenges to establish territories during the mating season. What purpose they served here was beyond Felless' comprehension.

She escaped from the motorcar as if escaping prison—though she had trouble imagining a prison as dangerous as the trip from the airfield—and fled into the consulate. After exchanging greetings with some of the males and females there, she went back to her own room. The chamber she'd had at Shepheard's Hotel had been adequate, but this was home.

She felt like having a taste of ginger to celebrate surviving her encounter with the maniacal Big Ugly, but refrained. Suppertime was coming, and she knew she would want to go down to the refectory: through some tradition probably older than the unification of Home under the Empire, aircraft never served adequate meals. *The time for the herb will come,* she told herself. Sooner or later, she always found a chance to taste.

When she did go to the refectory, she had trouble getting time to eat. She was too busy greeting friends and acquaintances and giving them gossip from Cairo and about her work with Straha. Everyone paid attention when she talked about that; the ex-shiplord fascinated veterans from the conquest fleet and also males and females from among the colonists. He'd fascinated Felless, too; his tale of disobedience and defection was far outside the Race's normal pattern of behavior.

Because Felless spent so much time talking, she took a while to notice that the food wasn't up to the quality of what she'd been eating in Cairo. She shrugged—what could one expect in a provincial place like France? She also took a while to notice that one familiar face was missing. "Where is Business Administrator Keffesh?" she asked the female sitting beside her.

"Had you not heard?" the other female exclaimed in surprise. "But no, you could not have—you were in Cairo. How foolish of me. Well, Business Administrator Keffesh is now Prisoner Keffesh, I am afraid. He was caught dealing ginger with a notorious Tosevite. The herb is such a nuisance." She spoke with the smug superiority of one who had never tasted.

"Truth: the herb is indeed a nuisance," Felless said in a hollow voice. If Keffesh was a prisoner, he'd presumably been interrogated and had presumably confessed and told all he knew in the hope of gaining leniency. Felless wondered if he'd reckoned his dealings with her important enough to mention to the authorities.

One way or the other, she would find out before long. Either nothing would happen or she would get yet another unpleasant telephone call from Ambassador Veffani. Or perhaps Veffani wouldn't bother telephoning. Perhaps he would simply send law-enforcement officials to search her chamber and arrest her if they found any illicit ginger—a redundancy if ever there was one.

But then she made the negative gesture under the table. Veffani could have ordered her chamber searched while she was in Cairo. Had he done so, he would without a doubt have radioed an order for her arrest to the Race's administrative center. Since he hadn't, maybe Keffesh hadn't implicated her after all. She could hope he hadn't, anyhow.

She sipped at the fermented fruit juice that accompanied her meal. Alcohol was a pleasure familiar from Home, and she didn't mind the taste of this particular Tosevite variation on the theme. Next to ginger, though, alcohol seemed pretty pallid stuff. *I will taste again,* she thought fiercely. *I will, by the Emperor.*

As she cast down her eye turrets, the irony of swearing by her sovereign when contemplating the illegal herb struck her. She shrugged. The Emperor didn't know what he was missing. It would be many years before he found out, if he ever did.

After learning the news about Keffesh, getting out of the refectory and back to her chamber felt like escape, almost as much as getting out of the wild Big Ugly's motorcar had. But that Français male couldn't have pursued her here. The telephone, that dangerous instrument, could—and did. She flinched when it hissed. "Senior Researcher Felless," she said. "I greet you."

As she'd feared, Veffani's image was the one that appeared on her monitor. "And I greet you, Senior Researcher," he replied. "Welcome home. I trust your journey from Cairo went well?"

"I thank you, superior sir. Yes, it went well enough." Felless was delighted to stick to polite commonplaces. "It went well enough till I landed here at Marseille, at any rate." She had no trouble working up indignation while recounting the antics of her driver.

And Veffani was sympathetic there, when he'd proved much less so elsewhere. "This is a problem here, and it is a problem in many parts of Tosev 3 where we rule directly," he said. "Before we came to Tosev 3, the Big Uglies did not even build their motorcars with safety belts. They kill one another by the tens of thousands, and seem utterly indifferent to the carnage."

"I count myself lucky that I was not among the slain earlier today," Felless said.

"I am glad you were not," Veffani said. "I have had nothing but fine reports of your work in Cairo, and I take no small pleasure in telling you so."

"That is very good news, superior sir," Felless replied. *You have no idea how good it is. If you did have any such idea, you would be telling me something altogether different. And you would take no small pleasure in that, either.* "It was a very interesting experience, and one where I learned a good deal."

"Do I understand that your commission concluded the Tosevite Warren acted as he did from reasons of policy rather than on a whim or out of despair after being discovered in his efforts against us?" Veffani asked.

"That is the consensus, yes," Felless answered. "Thanks to data Straha obtained from private Tosevite sources, no other conclusion seemed possible."

"Too bad," Veffani said. "I would rather have been able to reckon him a fool, but he served his not-empire well."

"He was a murderous barbarian, and I am glad to know that he is dead and no longer a danger to the Race," Felless said.

"I agree with every word of what you have said," Veffani answered. "None of that, however, in any way contradicts what I said."

"No, I suppose not." Felless paused and thought about the ambassador's tone of voice. "You *admire* him, superior sir. Is that not a truth?" She knew she sounded accusing. She enjoyed sounding accusing, as a matter of fact. She'd spent a lot of time listening to Veffani's accusations, which were usually all too well justified. Now she could get some of her own back.

"Maybe I do," Veffani admitted. "Have you never admired some particularly skillful opponent in a game?"

"Of course I have." Felless made her voice stiff with disapproval. "But I would hardly call our continuing struggle against the Big Uglies a game."

"No? Would you not, Senior Researcher?" Veffani said. "Then what else is it? To me, it is the largest, most complex game ever played, and also the game with the highest stakes. One can hardly help respecting the Big Uglies who played it well."

"They play it with our lives," Felless said angrily.

"Well, so they do," Veffani said. "We play it with their lives, too. And if you are going to look at methods, they have done few things to us that we have not also done to them. They save their worst horrors for their own kind."

"And I suppose you will be excusing those next," Felless said.

The ambassador made the negative gesture. "I excuse nothing. But neither do I diminish the Tosevites and their accomplishments. That is a failing too much encountered among the males and females of the colonization fleet. The Big Uglies are barbarians, yes. They are *not* fools." He used an emphatic cough. "Treat them as fools and you will regret it." That rated another emphatic cough.

"I understand, superior sir," Felless said, which was a long way from saying that she agreed.

With maddening patience, Veffani said, "Experience will eventually teach you the same thing, Senior Researcher." Felless thought he would say farewell then. Instead, he added, "Experience should also teach you to be wary of which males you choose as your acquaintances. Good day." His image did disappear then.

Felless stared at the monitor even after Veffani was gone. *He knows.* She shuddered. *He may not know quite enough to charge me, but he knows. What do I do now?*

Penny Summers set hands on hips and glared at Rance Auerbach across their hotel room. She was wearing a beige dress with a flowery print. That almost made her disappear into the wallpaper, which was also beige and floral. She said, "I didn't know we were setting ourselves up as a charity. I reckoned we got into this business to make money, not to save the poor and the downtrodden."

"Oh, we might make some money off this," Rance answered. He'd known Penny would be angry. He hadn't thought she'd be quite so angry as she was.

"That's not why you're doing it, though," she snapped. "You're doing it because you think that little French gal is cute."

Oho, he thought. *So that's it.* As a matter of fact, he did think Monique Dutourd was cute, but letting Penny know that didn't strike him as the smartest idea he'd ever had. He said, "Yeah, and I gave David Goldfarb a hand on account of he was just the prettiest thing I ever did see." He rolled his eyes and sighed as if he meant it.

Penny did her best to stay mad, but she couldn't quite manage. "God damn you," she said affectionately. "You are a piece of work, aren't you?"

"Have to be, to keep up with you," he said. That was flattery, but flattery with a good deal of underlying truth. He went on, "Besides, with Pierre the Turd in the Lizard hoosegow, doing our regular sort of business isn't as easy as it used to be. We ought to thank God he hasn't ratted on us. So we'll try something different for a while, okay? And his sister did warn us the Lizards caught him."

Penny still didn't look happy. "I know when I'm being sweet-talked, Rance Auerbach. I know when I'm being conned, too. And if this ain't one of those times . . ."

"Then it's something else," Auerbach said. "That's what I've been trying to tell you, if you'd only listen to me."

"You've been trying to tell me all kinds of things," Penny said sourly. "I haven't heard a whole lot of what I'd call truth. But you're bound and determined to try this, aren't you?" She waited for Rance to nod, then nodded herself. "Okay. If it works out, great. If it doesn't, or if you start fooling around behind my back, there's not going to be any place far enough away for you to hide."

Rance nodded again. "I like lost causes. I must. I took you in a while ago, didn't I? Or did you manage to forget about that?"

Astonishment spread over her face as she raised a hand to her cheek. "Now you've gone and made me blush, and I don't know when the hell the last time I did that was. Okay, Rance, go do it, and we'll see what happens. But you better remember what I said about that French gal, too."

"I'm not likely to forget," he said. "You want to come along and hold my hand?"

"I oughta say yes," Penny answered. "But you're the one who speaks French, and I'm the one Pierre's likelier to have fingered to the Lizards, if he went and fingered anybody. Go on. Just be careful, that's all."

"I will." Auerbach wondered how much help he'd get from Penny if something did go wrong. *One more thing I don't want to have to find out,* he thought.

He met Monique Dutourd in a little café not far from the dress shop where she'd found work after her brother was arrested. *"Bonjour,"* he said, and then, in English, "Are you ready?"

"I think so," she said. "I hope so." She rose, draining the wineglass in front of her.

"Then let's go," he said. *"Allons-y.* I have the taxi waiting outside."

The taxi, inevitably, was a Volkswagen. Rance hated getting into and out of the buggy little holdovers from the *Reich*. Being knee to knee with Monique in the back seat made up for some of that, as it had with Penny, but not enough. Monique was the one who spoke to the driver: "The consulate of the Race, if you please."

"It shall be done," he said in the Lizards' language, and got the VW going with a horrible clash of gears.

Getting out of the taxi, as usual, was even harder for Auerbach than getting into it had been. He paid off the driver; from what he'd seen, Monique wasn't rolling in loot. They went into the consulate together. A Lizard looked up from whatever he—or maybe she—had been doing and spoke in hissing French: *"Oui? Qu'est-ce que vous désirez?"*

"We want to see the female named Felless," Rance answered in the language of the Race. He didn't speak it well, but judged it would be useful here.

It got the receptionist's attention, at any rate. "I will ask," the Lizard said. "Give me your names."

"It shall be done," Rance said, as the taxi driver had before him. Once he'd named himself and Monique, he added, "I thank you." When dealing with Lizard officialdom, he made a point of being polite.

"You are welcome," this Lizard said, so it must have done some good. "Now please wait." After talking on the telephone, the Lizard swung an eye turret back toward Auerbach and Monique. "Senior Researcher Felless will be here shortly."

"I thank you," Rance said again. Monique nodded. He switched to French for her: "It could be that this will work."

"It could be," she echoed. Then, just for a moment, she set a hand on his arm. "Thank you very much for trying. No one else has cared at all."

"We'll see what we can do, that's all," he said in English. "If you don't bet, you can't win." He wasn't sure he could have put that into French. She nodded again to show she understood.

Auerbach started to say something more, but a Lizard came up the hallway from the back part of the consulate. The receptionist pointed with his—her?—tongue. The newly arrived Lizard walked over to him and Monique and said, "I greet you. I am Felless. Which of you is which?"

"I am Auerbach," Rance said in the Lizards' language. Then he introduced Monique, adding, "And we greet you." He wanted to laugh about Felless' inability to tell them apart at a glance, but he didn't. If Monique hadn't told him, he wouldn't have known Felless was a female, so why wouldn't it work the other way?

"What is it that you want with me?" Felless asked. Did she recognize Monique's name? Rance couldn't tell. He didn't think she would have heard his before. That was probably just as well.

He said, "Can we find some private space to speak?" That was probably a warning—it was certainly a warning if she had any brains—but he didn't see what else he could do. He sure didn't want to talk business out here in the foyer.

Felless drew back and hesitated before she spoke. She had brains, all right; she knew something was fishy, even if she didn't know what. After that momentary hesitation, she said, "Very well. Come with me." Brusquely, she turned away and went down the hallway from which she'd come. Rance and Monique followed.

He didn't know what he'd expected: that she would take the two humans back to her own quarters, perhaps. She didn't. The room into which she led them was the obvious Lizard equivalent of an Earthly conference room. Rance didn't much like the Lizards' chairs, which were too small and shaped for beings without much in the way of buttocks. With his bad leg, though, he liked standing even less. He sat. So did Monique.

Felless, for her part, paced back and forth. When she spoke, he thought he heard bitterness in her voice: "Now you will tell me what you want. It will be something to do with ginger, I do not doubt."

"Not directly," Auerbach said. "My friend here is a scholar. She is grateful that you saved her from the prison of the Français." He delivered a running translation for Monique, mostly in English, some in French.

"She is welcome," Felless said. "What is the point of this? It is not directly connected to ginger, you said. How is it indirectly connected?"

"When the explosive-metal bomb destroyed much of Marseille, it destroyed Monique's university, too," Rance answered. "Now she has no position. She wants work in what she knows about, not in selling wrappings to other Tosevites."

"How nice," Felless said with polite insincerity. "But I do not see how that has anything to do with me."

"We hoped you could use your connections and your high rank as a female of the Race to help her gain a position somewhere in France," Auerbach said. "When a female of the Race, especially a high-ranking female of the Race, speaks, Tosevites have to pay attention."

"Tosevites, from all I have seen, do not 'have to' do anything," Felless answered. "And why should I help her again in any case?"

Before answering her, Rance spoke in English to Monique: "Now we see what we see." He went back to the language of the Race: "Because you helped her before because of Business Administrator Keffesh."

Felless flinched. Auerbach hid his smile. The female said, "What do you know of Business Administrator Keffesh?"

"I know he is in trouble for ginger," Rance said. "I know you do not want authorities of the Race to know you did favors for him."

"That is—" Felless used a word he didn't know. He assumed it meant *blackmail*. She went on, "Why should I do anything like that, and how do I know you will not betray me even if I do?"

Now Rance did smile. When she put it like that, he knew he had her. He said, "I do not ask for money." *Yet,* he thought. "I ask help for a friend, nothing more. She deserves help. She is a good scholar. She should have the chance to work at what she was trained to work at."

"And what were *you* trained to work at, Rance Auerbach?" Felless demanded.

He smiled again, even if she might not understand exactly what the expression meant. "War," he said.

"Were you?" Felless said. "Why am I not surprised? And if I refuse you, you will inform my superiors of my unfortunate connections."

"We do not want to do that," Rance said. "We want you to help us."

"But if I do not help you, you will do this," Felless said.

Rance shrugged. "I hope it is not needed. You are a scholar. Do you not want to help another scholar?"

"What sort of scholar is this Tosevite female?" Felless asked.

When Auerbach asked Monique just how she wanted to answer that, she said, "Tell her I studied—and want to go on studying—the history of the Roman Empire." He translated her words into the language of the Race.

Felless sniffed. "I find it strange that you Tosevites should speak of empires. You do not really know the meaning of the word. There is only one true Empire, that of the Race."

"Very interesting," Rance said, "but it has nothing to do with what we are talking about here. Will you help my friend, or is it necessary for us to embarrass you?"

" 'Embarrass' is not the word." Felless sighed. "Very well. I will help. As you say, this is a relatively small matter." She sounded as if she was trying to convince herself of that.

After Auerbach translated that for Monique, he said, "What do you think?"

"I think it is wonderful, if it is true," she answered in English. "I will believe it is true when I see it, however."

"If it's not true, we'll just have to talk to the Lizards' authorities," Rance said, also in English. Then he translated that into the language of the Race for Felless' benefit. By the way she winced, she didn't think she was particularly benefited. Rance's smile got bigger. That wasn't his worry. It was all hers.

* * *

To her astonishment, Monique Dutourd found that she enjoyed selling dresses. In her academic days, she'd learned how to deal with people without panicking. That served her in good stead now. She'd also learned to dress reasonably well without spending an arm and a leg: on a professor's salary, she could barely afford to spend fingernail clippings. And so she could help other women look as good as they could without helping them to go broke doing it.

Her boss was a fellow named Charles Boileau. After she'd been working at the dress shop for a couple of weeks, he said, "I had my doubts about hiring you, *Mademoiselle* Dutourd. I thought you would either be too educated to work with the customers, or that you wouldn't be able to learn the business. I was wrong both ways, and I'm not too proud to admit it."

"Thank you very much." Monique was pleased and, again, surprised to admit it to herself. "I'm glad you think I fit in."

Boileau nodded. "I knew you knew what you were doing when you talked *Madame* du Cange out of that green dress without insulting her or making her ashamed of her own judgment."

"I had to, sir, even though the sale we got was for a little less," Monique said. "*Madame* du Cange is a woman of . . . formidable contours." Her gesture said what she wouldn't: that the customer in question was grossly fat. "If she'd bought that dress, she would have looked like nothing so much as an enormous lime with legs."

Her boss was a sobersided man. He fought—and lost—a battle against laughter. "I wouldn't have put it that way," he said, "but I won't tell you that you're wrong."

"And if she did that," Monique said earnestly, "it would have reflected badly on her, and it would have reflected badly on us. People would have said, 'Where did you get that dress?' She would have told them, too—she would have thought it a compliment. And none of the people she told would have come here ever again."

"It wouldn't have been quite so bad as that, I don't think," Boileau said, "but your attitude does you credit."

Her attitude turned out to do rather more than that. When she got her paycheck at the end of the week, it had an extra fifty francs in it. That wasn't enough to make her rich. It wasn't even enough to make her anything but very dubiously middle-class. But every one of those francs was welcome and more than welcome.

She'd found herself a tiny walk-up furnished room a couple of blocks from the dress shop. It had a hot plate and a sink. No stove, no toilet, no bathtub, no telephone. The toilet and tub were down at the end of the hall. In the whole building, only the landlady had a phone and a stove.

After cooking in the tent, Monique had no trouble cooking on a hot plate. And she discovered she didn't miss a telephone. Dieter Kuhn couldn't call her, assuming he was still in Marseille. Lucie couldn't get hold of her, either. Neither could Rance Auerbach, but she could always reach him on a public telephone whenever she needed to.

She kept waiting for news that Felless had managed to persuade a university to give her a position. The news didn't come. Once when she telephoned, Auerbach asked, "Shall we turn her in now?"

But Monique, not without regret, said, "No. She helped me out of prison. I do not wish to betray her unless it is very plain she is betraying us."

"Okay," Auerbach said—they were speaking English. "I still think you're too damn nice for your own good, but okay."

Monique had to work out exactly what that meant in French. When she did, she decided it was a compliment. "Things could be worse," she said. Remembering Dieter Kuhn, she shivered a little. "Yes, things could be much worse. Believe me, I know."

"Okay," Rance Auerbach said again. "You know best what you want. I'm just trying to help."

"I know. I thank you." Monique hung up then, scratching her head. She'd seen that Auerbach was partial to such gestures. He'd given David Goldfarb a hand, even if that meant going to the Nazis to put pressure on the Englishman who was giving Goldfarb a hard time. So no wonder the American would squeeze a vulnerable Lizard to help her.

Did he have an ulterior motive? With most men, that added up to, did he want to go to bed with her? She wouldn't have been surprised, but he wasn't obnoxious about it if he did. He wasn't making it a *quid pro quo*, as so many men would have. Kuhn certainly had, damn him—if she gave him her body, he kept his fellow SS goons from interrogating her. The worst of that was, she still felt she'd made the best possible bargain there, no matter how she loathed the *Sturmbannführer*.

Maybe she shouldn't have thought of Kuhn on the way back to her roominghouse. Maybe if she hadn't, he wouldn't have been sitting on the front steps waiting for her. Monique stopped so short, she might have seen a poisonous snake there. As far as she was concerned, she had.

"Hello, sweetheart," he said in his German-accented French. "How are you today?"

"Go away," she snarled. "Get out. I never want to see you again. If you don't leave right now, I'm going to scream for the police."

"Go ahead," Kuhn answered. "I'm just a tourist, and I've got the papers to prove it."

"You're a damned SS man, no matter what your papers say," Monique retorted. Her mouth twisted in a bitter quirk that was not a smile. "You've got the little tattoo to prove it. I ought to know. I've seen it too often."

His smile was a long way from charming. "Go ahead. Tell them you were fucking an SS man. If you don't, I will—and then see how much fun you have."

Laughing in his face gave Monique almost as much pleasure as she'd ever had in bed—certainly far more than she'd ever had with him. "Go ahead. See how much good it does you. I've already been to jail for that, and I got out again, too. I proved you made me do it. Go away right now and don't come back, or I *will* yell for the police."

"You'd sooner screw that American, the cripple," Kuhn said scornfully.

"Any day," she answered at once. "Twice on Sundays. Go away." She took a deep breath. She really did intend to scream her head off.

Dieter Kuhn must have seen that, for he got to his feet with the smooth grace of an athlete. "All right," he said. "I'll go. Sleep with the American. Sleep with the Lizards, for all I care. But I tell you this: the *Reich* isn't done. The Lizards haven't heard the last of us. Neither have you." Off he went, arrogant as ever.

Monique took hold of the iron banister and sagged against it with relief. Up till this second round of fighting, she'd lived her whole adult life in a country under the Nazis' thumb, a country where the *Gestapo* could do whatever it pleased. She'd lived that way so long, she'd come to take it for granted. Now, for the first time, she saw what living in her own country, an independent country, meant. If she yelled for the police, they could arrest Kuhn instead of having to knuckle under to him.

She went up the stairs and into the roominghouse. As she walked up to her own room, she realized things weren't quite so simple. The purification squad from her own independent country had arrested her and thrown her into prison, too. Her brother hadn't got her out because her case was good or her cause just. He'd got her out because he'd pulled wires with the Lizards. France was almost as much obliged to do what they wanted as it had been to do what the Germans wanted.

"Almost," Monique murmured. The difference was enormous, as far as she was concerned. For one thing, the Lizards did formally respect French freedom. And, for another, they weren't Nazis. That alone made all the difference in the world.

She was sautéeing liver and onions on the hot plate when she realized she ought to be doing more to help get Pierre out of the Lizards' jail. He'd pulled wires for her, after all. But she didn't have any wires to pull, not really. Rance Auerbach might, but he was already pulling them on her behalf. How could she ask him to do more? The answer, unfortunately, was plain: she couldn't.

If she bribed him with her body, would he help her with Pierre? Angrily, she flipped the liver over with a spatula and slammed it down into the pan. She never would have started thinking like that if it hadn't been for Dieter Kuhn. And she never would have had to worry about Kuhn if she hadn't been Pierre's sister. That struck her as a good reason to let her brother stay right where he was.

A couple of evenings later, she was writing yet another letter of application—who could guess whether or not Felless would come through?—when someone knocked on the door. She didn't hesitate about answering it, as she would have before the Nazis had to leave France. The only thing she worried about was robbers, and robbers, she reasoned, had to know there were more lucrative targets than an upper-floor room in a cheap boardinghouse.

When she opened the door, she stared in astonishment. Her brother nodded to her. "Aren't you going to ask me if I want to come in?" Pierre Dutourd asked.

"Come in," Monique said automatically. As automatically, she shut the door behind him. Then, a little at a time, her wits started to work. She asked the first question that popped into them: "What are you doing here?"

"I came to say thank you," Pierre answered, as seriously as she'd ever heard him speak. "I'm not going to ask you what you had to do to get Dieter Kuhn to help me get out of that damned cell. I probably don't want to know. You probably don't want to tell me. I'm sure it wasn't anything you wanted to do—I know what Kuhn is. But you did it anyway, even though you've got to think I'm more a nuisance than a brother. So thank you, from the bottom of my heart." His nod was almost a bow.

And now Monique's stare was one of complete bewilderment. "But I didn't do anything," she blurted. "He came around here the other day—sniffing after me, nothing to do with you—and I told him to go to hell."

"He has connections, even now," Pierre said. "He used them. I thought it was on account of you. If I'm wrong . . ." He shrugged, his face a frozen mask now. "If I'm wrong, I won't trouble you any more. That would probably suit you best anyhow. *Au revoir.*" Before Monique could find anything to say, he went out the door. He didn't even bother slamming it after him.

Monique sank into one of the two ratty chairs in the room. She couldn't believe Dieter Kuhn had done that to gain her favor. He had to have some motive of his own, and what it might be seemed pretty obvious. The more trouble the Lizards had with ginger, the less trouble they would be able to give the *Reich.* Even so, she wondered if the *Sturmbannführer* would come around seeking the hero's reward. *If he does,* she thought, *he isn't going to get it.*

But the one who came around, a few days later, was Rance Auerbach. He was waiting outside her dress shop when she left for home. Monique's heart started to pound. She couldn't help it. "Well?" she demanded.

He grinned. He knew she was impatient. He wasn't angry, either. "How does the University of Tours sound?" he asked.

"Tours?" she said. It was in the north, southwest of Paris but still unquestionably the north—more an Atlantic than a Mediterranean town. She'd sent a letter there—she'd sent letters everywhere. She'd got no answer. Now she had one. "They want me?" she whispered.

"They'll take you," he answered.

That wasn't quite the same thing, but it would do. "Thank you!" she said. "Oh, thank you!" She kissed him. If he'd wanted something more, she probably would have gone up to her room with him right that minute. But all he did was grin wider than ever. *Dear God in heaven,* she thought. *I have my life back again. Now what do I do with it?*

Atvar was studying the daily news reports when he came upon something of a new and different sort. He called in his adjutant for a look. "Here is something you will not see every day, Pshing," he said.

"What is it, Exalted Fleetlord?" Pshing asked.

"Turn an eye turret this way," Atvar answered. "Photographs—necessarily, long-distance, highly magnified photographs—of a major meteoric impact on the worthless fourth planet."

"It looks as if a large explosive-metal bomb had hit there," Pshing said.

"From what the astronomers say, the impact was a good deal more energetic than that," Atvar said.

"Tosev's solar system is an untidy place, especially compared to the one in which Home orbits," Pshing said. "Imagine if such a rock had struck Tosev 3 instead of the worthless Tosev 4. It would have been most unfortunate, especially in or near a populated area."

"Such bombardment is a fact of life in this solar system," Atvar said. "Look at any of the bodies here. The only one without immediately obvious evidence of these impacts is Tosev 3, and that because it is so geologically active."

"The atmosphere must protect this world to some degree," Pshing said.

"No doubt. But one that size would have got through," the fleetlord said. "And, as you remarked, the results would have been unfortunate."

"Indeed." Pshing made the affirmative gesture. "And now, Exalted Fleetlord, if you will excuse me . . ." He went back to his own desk.

After one last look at the new crater on Tosev 4, Atvar went on to other matters his staff thought worthy of his notice. Northern India was facing more and more riots as plants from Home spread through the fields there. That subregion's climate was ideal for their propagation, and they were cutting into the Big Uglies' food supplies—which, in that part of Tosev 3, were no better than marginal at the best of times.

It is of course necessary to make Tosev 3 as Homelike as possible, an ecologist wrote. *In doing so, however, we may cause as many casualties among the Big Uglies from environmental change as we did in the course of the fighting. This is unfortunate, but appears unavoidable.*

Atvar sighed. If the conquest did finally succeed, he feared historians would not look kindly upon him. If he didn't get a sobriquet like Atvar the Brutal, he would be surprised. But he didn't know what to do about the Tosevites in India, past suppressing their riots. He couldn't get rid of the plants from Home now even if he wanted to. They *would* flourish in that subregion; it was reasonably warm and reasonably dry, and they had no natural enemies there. The local ecosystem *would* be transformed, and not to the Tosevites' advantage.

He wondered if he could move some of the Big Uglies from the affected areas to those where Tosevite ecologies remained more or less intact. But no sooner had the thought crossed his mind than certain difficulties became obvious. The Tosevites of northern India might not want to be moved; Big Uglies were reactionary that way. Wherever he moved them, the current inhabitants were all too likely to prove less than welcoming. They might not have excess food, either; Tosevite agriculture was at best imperfectly efficient. And ecological change would come to many more areas of the planet, even if it hadn't yet.

He sighed again. Some problems simply had no neat, tidy solutions. That would have been an unacceptable notion back on Home. A hundred thousand years of unified imperial history argued that the Race could solve anything. But the Big Uglies and their world presented challenges different from, and worse than, any the Race had known since the days of its ancientest history—and maybe worse than any it had known then, too.

The fleetlord went on to the next item in the daily briefing. It made him hiss in alarm. Superstitious fanatics from the main continental mass had traveled to the lesser continental mass and mounted an attack on the fortress where that maniac of a Khomeini was imprisoned.

"By the Emperor!" Atvar exclaimed, and let out yet another sigh, this one of relief, when he discovered the attack had failed. "Would that not have been a disaster—Khomeini on the loose again!" There would surely have been uprisings throughout the areas where the Muslim superstition predominated . . . including Cairo itself. Atvar had seen enough such disturbances—too many, in fact.

I commend the males who prevented Khomeini's escape, he wrote. *I also commend the Tosevite constabulary officials who fought side by side with our males. And I particularly commend the individual who thought to incarcerate Khomeini in a region inhabited by Big Uglies of a superstition different from his. That helped to insure the loyalty of local protective officials.*

Next on the agenda was a note that, with two spaceships in the belt of minor planets, the American Tosevites were spreading rapidly and were busy at so many sites that the Race's surveillance probes could not keep track of everything they were doing. *Shall we let them continue unobserved, being more or less sure they can find no way to harm us from such a distance?* the head of the surveillance effort asked. *Or shall we expend the resources to continue keeping an eye turret turned in their direction?*

Atvar did not hesitate. *If we need more probes, we must send more probes,* he wrote. *The Americans sacrificed a city in preference to withdrawing from space. It follows that they expect to reap some benefit from their continued presence among these minor planets. Perhaps that benefit will be only economic. Perhaps it will be military, or they think it will. We dare not take the chance that they will prove mistaken.*

His tailstump quivered with agitation he could not hide. The commission he'd appointed to study Earl Warren's motivation had concluded that the Big Ugly had known exactly what he was doing, and had just had the misfortune—from his point of view, though not from the Race's—to get caught. That was what Atvar had least wanted to hear. He would much rather have believed the Tosevite leader addled. That would have made Warren less dangerous. But the evidence, Atvar had to admit, was on the commission's side.

He read on, and found more complaints from occupation officials in the *Reich* that the Deutsche were not turning in their surviving weapons, but were doing their best to conceal arms against a possible future uprising. That made his tailstump quiver again, this time from raw fury.

Still in the grip of that fury, he wrote, *Convey to their not-emperor that their cities remain hostage to their good behavior. If they refuse to turn over weapons as they promised on their*

*surrender, one of those cities shall cease to be as abruptly as did
Indianapolis. If that fails to gain their attention, another city
shall vanish. They have already hit us too hard and too often.
They shall get no further chances.*

An order like that would get him remembered as Atvar the
Brutal, too. Back on Home, it would have been impossible.
Anyone who tried to issue such an order there would be reck-
oned a bloodthirsty barbarian, and immediately sacked. Here on
Tosev 3 . . . Atvar didn't even feel guilty, not after everything the
Deutsche had done to the Race. Here on Tosev 3, the order was
simply common sense.

Only a couple of items remained. He hoped they'd prove inconsequential. A forlorn hope, he knew. Inconsequential items
were dealt with at levels far lower than his. For the most part, he
never found out about them. What reached him was what his
subordinates, for whatever reason, felt they couldn't handle
themselves.

Sure enough, the next report had to do with China. Not
least because of its long border with the SSSR and the zealots
who shared the independent not-empire's political doctrines,
that subregion refused to stay pacified. The latest rumors had
those zealots plotting another uprising. Whenever they tried
to rise, the Race crushed them. They did not seem to believe
they couldn't win. Every so often, they would have another go
at it.

Atvar was tempted to order the use of explosive-metal weapons there, too. With a certain amount of reluctance, he refrained.
That would anger the SSSR, and he'd had enough trouble with
the Tosevite not-empire lately. And now the Nipponese Empire
had explosive-metal weapons, too, and had to be treated more
circumspectly. Conventional means had sufficed to hold the lid
on China thus far. They would probably keep doing so a while
longer.

Before he could check the last item in the day's briefing,
Pshing called, "Exalted Fleetlord, I have Fleetlord Reffet on the
telephone."

"Tell him I am shedding my skin and cannot be disturbed,"
Atvar said, but then, having mercy on his adjutant, he relented:
"Put him through." When the fleetlord of the colonization fleet

appeared on the monitor, he did his best to be polite. "I greet you, Reffet. What can I do for you today?"

Politeness proved wasted. Without preamble, Reffet said, "You are surely the most arrogant, high-handed male in the history of the Race. How dare you—how *dare* you—unilaterally order a Soldiers' Time and commence preparations for conscripting members of the colonization fleet into the military?"

"As usual, you ask the wrong question," Atvar answered. "The right question is, how could I have waited so long? With the fighting against the Deutsche, with the near conflict against the Americans, it becomes ever more plain that we are going to have to have the ability to fight for generations to come. Would you sooner rely on Tosevite hirelings to resist the independent not-empires?"

"Well, no," Reffet said, "but—"

"If the answer is no, but me no buts," Atvar said. "You have delayed and resisted every time I proposed this course. We have no more time for delay and resistance. We need colonists able to defend themselves. That being so, I have begun taking the steps necessary to insure that we have them."

"Do you have any idea how this will disrupt the economy of the Race on Tosev 3?" Reffet demanded. "Fighting is not profitable. Fighting is the opposite of profitable."

"Survival is profitable," Atvar answered. "As for the economy, no, I do not know how badly this will disrupt it. Losing a war with the Big Uglies would disrupt it worse. I do know that. And I know that we can get from our subject Tosevites much of what the members of the Race who become soldiers would have produced."

"We already get from our subject Tosevites and from the wild Big Uglies too much of what we should be making for ourselves," Reffet said. "This has also been destabilizing and demoralizing. We did not anticipate industrial competition, you know."

"In that case, the members of the Race who should be producing but are not will now have the chance to give a different kind of service." Atvar forced good cheer into his voice: "You see? Benefits on every side."

"I see a male who has exceeded his authority," Reffet snarled.

"You see a male doing what needs doing," Atvar replied. "I realize this may be a spectacle new to you. Nevertheless, I shall go forward. I aim to preserve the Race on Tosev 3 no matter how much you want to return the whole planet to the Big Uglies." As he'd hoped, that made Reffet break the connection. With silence in the office, Atvar got back to work.

☆ **14** ☆

Gorppet turned an eye turret toward Hozzanet. "Excuse me, superior sir, but exactly how much of the Greater German *Reich* does the Race in fact control?"

"Ah." Hozzanet waggled an eye turret of his own: ironic approval. "You are beginning to understand, I see. How much of the *Reich* do *you* think we control?"

"As much as we can see," Gorppet answered at once. "Not the thickness of a scale more. Wherever our eyes or our reconnaissance photographs do not reach, I am convinced the Deutsche do as they please. And what they please is anything that can harm us."

"I should bring more infantrymales into Security," Hozzanet remarked. "You have no trouble seeing that which appears invisible to many whose body paint is a great deal more complex than yours."

"Why am I not surprised?" Gorppet said. "Males of high rank never get out to see for themselves. They rely on reports from others, and the reports commonly tell them everything is fine. And everything usually *is* fine . . . where we are known to be looking. Elsewhere—I will not answer for elsewhere."

"I think you are wise not to," Hozzanet replied. "Here is another question for you: what is the only thing that keeps the Deutsche from rising against us?"

"The certainty that we will smash them flat if they try," Gorppet said. "Smash them flatter, I mean. I almost wish they *would* rebel, to give us the excuse to do it."

"In this, you are not alone," Hozzanet said. "In fact, for your hearing diaphragms only, I will say that there has been some discussion of touching off a Deutsch rebellion, to give us an excuse to punish these Big Uglies again and take fuller control over the area."

"But for one difficulty, I would like to see us do that," Gorppet said.

"I know what you are going to say," Hozzanet told him. "You are going to say something like, 'Where will we get the males to garrison the *Reich*?' Am I right, or am I wrong? Was that what you were going to say, or not?"

"As a matter of fact, it was, superior sir," Gorppet admitted. "We have enough trouble finding the males to garrison this not-empire now. Where would we come up with more, no matter how much we need them?"

To his surprise, Hozzanet said, "I may have an answer for you. I am given to understand that we may actually start training members of the colonization fleet to fight. That would give us the extra soldiers we need."

"So it would," Gorppet agreed. "I will, however, believe it when I see it, and not a moment before. We should have done it as soon as the colonization fleet got here. When we did not do it then, my guess was that we never would, that the colonists had done such a good job of fussing and complaining that they would never have to start earning their own keep."

"You *are* a cynical fellow." Hozzanet spoke with considerable admiration. "Here again, I admit you have had some reason to be. But I think you are wrong this time. After all, however much we wish we would, we are not going to stay around forever. Sooner or later, the colonists will have to protect themselves against the Big Uglies. If they do not, who will do it for them?"

"They have not worried about that so far," Gorppet said. "Why should they worry now?" Something else occurred to him; he started to laugh. "I wish I were an underofficer training them. I would enjoy that, I think."

"Yes, plenty of males will be looking for the chance to show the colonists just how ignorant they are of the way things work on Tosev 3," Hozzanet agreed. "We shall have no shortage of volunteers for that duty."

Gorppet made the affirmative gesture. Then another new thought struck him. "Do they intend to teach males and females to be soldiers, or just males? Before, it would have mattered only during mating season. With ginger, though, it matters all the time. Has anyone bothered to think about that?"

"I do not know," Hozzanet said. "It would not surprise me if our leaders did their best to forget about the herb."

"They would be fools if they did," Gorppet said. "Of course, that may not stop them. But I am far from sure that military discipline and mating behavior can stand side by side. Someone ought to point that out to them."

"Truth," Hozzanet said. "Go ahead."

"Me?" Now Gorppet made the negative gesture. "No one would pay any attention to me. I am lucky to be an officer at all."

"Your skill made you an officer. Luck had nothing to do with it," Hozzanet said. "Draft a memorandum. I will endorse it and pass it up the line."

"It shall be done, superior sir." Gorppet could say nothing else. What he thought was, *Look what your big mouth got you into this time.* After a moment, he did add, "Some members of the Race are likely to say that this makes us like the Big Uglies, who also usually exclude their females from combat."

"Some members of the Race are fools," Hozzanet replied. "You will, I suspect, have observed this for yourself. The Big Uglies are sexually dimorphic to a greater degree than we are, and have practiced mechanized warfare only a short time. Up till recently, raw strength was necessary for their combat, so it is no wonder their females were commonly excluded. That is not an issue for us, but control of our sexuality is. Can you imagine what the Deutsche would have done to us after spraying ginger over a battlefield with both males and females on it?"

"I can, but I would rather not." Gorppet shuddered at the thought. "Very well, superior sir. I will emphasize that point when I write."

He didn't enjoy drafting the memorandum. He hadn't had to do such things very often as an infantrymale and then an underofficer. The risks of combat were familiar: pain, mutilation, death. The risks here were subtler, but real nevertheless: embarrassment, mockery, humiliation. He was no writer, and was painfully aware of his own deficiencies. He feared everyone else who saw the memorandum would be painfully aware of them, too.

With some—more than some—trepidation, he showed Hozzanet the document once he'd finished it. The other officer read through the piece without a word. Gorppet was sure he'd produced nothing but a broken egg. At last, when Hozzanet turned one eye turret away from the monitor and toward him, he managed to ask, "Well, superior sir?" He sounded miserable. Fair enough—he felt miserable.

"I shall do what I said," Hozzanet answered. "I shall endorse it and send it on to our superiors in the hope that it will do some good. I think it is very effective—very clear, very straightforward. You make a good case. You certainly have convinced me. Some of the officers set above us, of course, have trouble seeing past the ends of their own snouts. Maybe they will ignore this. But maybe, on the other fork of the tongue, it will help them see farther. We can but hope, eh?"

"Yes, superior sir." Now Gorppet sounded dazed. Delight coursed through him, almost as if he'd had a taste of ginger. "Clear? Straightforward? My work? I thank you, superior sir!"

"You are welcome," Hozzanet said. "You are very welcome indeed. You did the work. I am merely approving its quality, which should be—and, I think, will be—obvious to everyone."

"I thank you," Gorppet repeated, more dazed still. This was better than ginger, for the pleasure lingered. It didn't steal away to be replaced by gloom at least as strong.

"As I said, you have earned the praise," Hozzanet told him. "I would not be surprised if I were calling you 'superior sir' one of these days."

That, as far as Gorppet could see, was a preposterous extravagance. He didn't say so; contradicting Hozzanet would have been rude. But he didn't take the notion seriously, either. His longtime service below officer's rank had convinced him that surviving was more important than advancing, anyhow.

Work went on while he waited for his superiors to respond to the memorandum. Longtime service below officer's rank had convinced him that they would take their own sweet time about it, too. One afternoon, he let out a surprised hiss. Hozzanet swung an eye turret his way and asked, "Something interesting?"

"Yes, superior sir," Gorppet answered. "Remember that Tosevite male named Drucker, who was going down to Neu Strelitz to search for his mate and hatchlings?"

Hozzanet made the affirmative gesture. "I am not likely to ～him. That trip cost us a good male and a motorcar. Cursed ～ndits. Why? What about him now?"

～～ positively identified in Neu Strelitz," Gorppet

said. "Up till now, the assumption was that he too perished in the attack, even if his body was not found."

"Assumptions are commonly worth their weight in ginger," Hozzanet said, which made Gorppet laugh. The other male went on, "Do you suppose he might tell you the truth about what happened if you went down to Neu Strelitz and asked him?"

"Superior sir, I do not know," Gorppet answered. "Some of that, I suppose, will depend on what *did* happen and how close his ties to the bandits are. Even if he owes me certain debts, Big Uglies reckon kinship more important and friendship less so than we do."

"I understand that," Hozzanet said. "I ought to, on this miserable ball of mud. Go on. Do your best."

"It shall be done," Gorppet said—again, what other choice had he?

When he got to Neu Strelitz, he found it to be another small city that had taken considerable damage during the fighting. The Deutsche were doing their best to put things to rights again. They were energetic and hardworking, almost alarmingly so.

"There!" said the informant whose tip had got back to him—a yellow-haired Tosevite female who went by the name of Friedli. She spoke the language of the Race badly but understandably. "See you him, walking there?"

"Yes." Gorppet found one question to ask before going after Drucker: "Why do you give him away to us?"

"He my mate threatened and betrayed," she answered. "Now get him!"

Kinship, not friendship, Gorppet thought. He skittered down the street after Johannes Drucker. When he caught up, he said, "I greet you."

The Deutsch male stopped and stared down at him. "Gorppet?" he said, and Gorppet used the affirmative gesture. "What are you doing here?"

"I came to ask you the same question," Gorppet said. "How did you escape the ambush that killed Chinnoss? Have you found your mate and your hatchlings?"

Drucker hesitated before answering. In that moment of hesitation, Gorppet became convinced he wouldn't learn anything. And he was right. The Big Ugly replied, "I am sorry, but I really cannot tell you what happened that day. I was knocked unconscious when the motorcar rolled over, so I know nothing."

"I do not believe you," Gorppet said bluntly.

"I am sorry," Drucker repeated. "I was lucky not to be killed."

"That was not luck," Gorppet said. "You were not killed because you are not a male of the Race."

Johannes Drucker shrugged. "I must go. Will you excuse me?"

"Suppose I arrest you instead?" Gorppet demanded, his temper kindling.

"You may try." The Big Ugly shrugged again. "I doubt you will succeed, not here in a town without a garrison."

He was, unfortunately, almost sure to be correct. Gorppet sent him a reproachful stare, not that any Tosevite was likely to recognize it as such. He said, "I thought we were friends, you and I."

Drucker surprised him by using the Race's negative hand gesture. "You and I are not enemies. That is a truth. But your folk and mine are not friends, and that is also a truth. Now I must say farewell." He walked on down the street.

Gorppet could have gone after him. Gorppet could have raised his weapon and started shooting. Instead, with a sigh, he returned to his vehicle. No, keeping the Deutsche suppressed wouldn't be easy, or anything close to it. *As if I hadn't known as much already,* he thought bitterly.

Sam Yeager wondered why he'd been summoned to Little Rock. He hadn't wanted to come to the capital. His wife and son hadn't wanted him to go, either; *sticking your head in the lion's mouth* was the phrase Barbara had used. But he remained an officer of the U.S. Army. Unless he wanted to resign his commission, he had to follow orders. And he didn't want to resign it; he'd worked too hard to get where he was. Resigning would have been like admitting that everything he'd been through was something he'd somehow deserved. He was damned if he'd do that.

Don't rub. He'd learned that code in the bush leagues. *Don't let the bastards know they hurt you.* A pitcher who'd just stuck a fastball in your ribs might suspect you weren't too happy about it. But not rubbing was all about not letting the other guys know what you were feeling, or that you were feeling anything.

And so, outwardly calm, he sat in a waiting room in the Gray House, reading a *Newsweek* and pretending everything was just routine. After a while, a flunky came up to him and said, "The president will see you now, Lieutenant Colonel."

"Okay." Yeager put down the magazine and got to his feet. The Gray House dignitary led him into the president's office. Seeing Harold Stassen behind the big desk there was a jolt. Yeager didn't want to show that, either. He stiffened to attention and saluted. "Reporting as ordered, sir."

"Sit down, Lieutenant Colonel," President Stassen said. His voice didn't carry nearly the weight of authority Earl Warren's had. But Warren was gone, dead and buried. *The king is dead; long live the king.* Stassen asked, "Would you care for coffee, or anything else?"

"No, thank you, sir," Sam answered.

"All right." The president looked down at what were probably notes. "I understand you and your family are responsible for raising a couple of Lizard hatchlings as though they were human beings."

"That's right, Mr. President." Hope blossomed in Yeager. Maybe Stassen had called him here to talk about Mickey and Donald. They were important, no doubt about it. If he were here on account of that, maybe Warren hadn't said anything to anybody about his role in bringing down a presidency and wiping a city off the face of the earth. *Maybe I'm the only one who knows the whole story,* Sam thought. *Christ, I hope I am.*

President Stassen said, "And how are the hatchlings now?"

"They're fine, sir," Sam said. "They're toddlers right now, you know: growing like weeds and learning something new every day. They talk a lot more than regular Lizard hatchlings the same age would."

Stassen shuffled papers—notes, sure enough. "I understand the Lizards have a long head start on us in this sort of research."

"That's true, but there's nothing we could do about it," Yeager said. "They got a hatchling—uh, a human baby—right after the first round of fighting ended. We couldn't even think of trying the same sort of experiment till the colonization fleet brought females of the Race here."

"Of course." The president nodded. "Now, you've met the girl the Lizards are raising as one of their own." He waited for Sam to nod, too, then asked, "What do you think of her?"

"Sir, Kassquit's . . . pretty screwy, I'm afraid," Yeager answered. "I don't know how else to put it. Considering the way she was brought up, I don't suppose that's any big surprise. It's probably God's own miracle that she's not even crazier than she is."

"Does that mean . . ." Stassen glanced down again. "Does that mean Mickey and Donald are liable to end up disturbed, too?"

"From the point of view of the Race, do you mean, sir?" Sam sighed. "I'm afraid it does. I don't know what to do about that. I don't think there's anything to be done about it. I feel bad sometimes, but it's important for us to know just how much like people they can become." He sighed again. "Ttomalss, the Lizard who's raised Kassquit, probably feels the same way in reverse."

"I see." Stassen scribbled something on a scratch pad. "To turn to another matter, how seriously do you view the spread of plants and animals from the Lizards' home planet here on Earth?"

Did Stassen know Yeager had been seized while investigating that very thing? If he did, he didn't show it. Sam decided to assume he didn't, and answered, "It's going to be a problem, yes, Mr. President. It may not be too big a problem here in the States, because I didn't think too many creatures from Home will be able to stand the winters in most of the country. But in the tropics, especially the deserts, I'd bet there'll be wholesale replacements. The Lizards are going to try to make Earth over to suit themselves. We'd probably do the same thing if the shoe were on the other foot."

"I wouldn't be surprised." Stassen wrote himself another note, "Your opinion closely matches the views of other experts I've consulted."

"I'm glad to hear it, sir." Sam breathed a little easier. This was just business. With any luck at all, he'd be able to get back home and go on raising the Lizard hatchlings—and, rather more than incidentally, getting ready for Jonathan's wedding. He shifted in his chair, getting ready to stand up. "Is there anything else?"

"Just one thing more, Lieutenant Colonel." The president switched gears: "How do you feel about your part in everything that's happened over the past few months?"

Yeager grunted, but did his best to pull his face straight. *Don't rub.* "Sir, I did what I thought I had to do," he said. "I don't know what else to tell you."

"And you have no trouble living with the loss of Indianapolis?" Stassen asked.

"No trouble?" Sam shook his head. "I wouldn't say that, Mr. President. I wouldn't say that at all. A day doesn't go by that I don't think about it. But the scales balance, as far as I'm concerned. Do you think President Warren lost any sleep over the Lizards in the colonization fleet?"

"I honestly don't know," Stassen said. "Until the recent tragic events, I had no idea he'd had anything to do with them." His chuckle was mirthless. "As you may know, the vice president mostly has about as much use as the vermiform appendix."

"If you don't mind my saying so, sir, you should have known what he'd done," Yeager said. "The way things are these days, a vice president needs to be able to hit the ground running if he finds out he's president all of a sudden. And that's happened a couple of times lately—well, Cordell Hull wasn't vice president when he took over, but you know what I mean."

"I know what you mean," the president agreed. "Hull probably had an easier time taking over than I did, because he was more involved in making decisions than I was. President Warren did as he thought best. Now I have to do the same."

He started to say something more, but checked himself. Sam had a pretty good idea of what it would have been, though. *Everything would have been fine if only you hadn't stuck your big nose into the middle of things.* It was even true, for those who didn't think of the Lizards as people. Earl Warren hadn't, not down deep where it counted.

"Is there anything else?" Sam asked again.

This time, Harold Stassen shook his head. "That will be all, Lieutenant Colonel. I did want to meet you, though. I think you understand the reasons for my curiosity."

"Yes, sir, I think so." Now Yeager was the one who didn't say everything he was thinking. *If it weren't for me, you wouldn't be president right now.* He'd never dreamt of having that kind of influence on events. He'd never wanted it, either. But what you wanted and what you got were two different things. He'd turned fifty-eight this year. For a while there, in that house somewhere near the Four Corners, he'd wondered if he would ever see another birthday.

"All right, then," Stassen told him. "You may go."

"Thank you, Mr. President." But before he left the office, Sam said, "May I ask you something, sir?"

"Go ahead," the president said. "But I don't promise to answer. I think you understand the reasons for that, too."

Nobody will ever trust you with anything truly important again, not as long as you live. That was what the president meant, even if he was too polite to say so. Sam held his face steady. *Don't rub, no matter how much it hurts.* He tried to speak casually, too: "Wasn't that an awfully big meteor that slammed into Mars? The Race's computer network had some pretty spectacular pictures from their space-based telescopes."

"Yes, I've seen a few of them," Harold Stassen said. "The astronomers will have a new crater to name, from what I understand. Mars, fortunately, is pretty much worthless real estate."

"A good thing a rock that size didn't hit Earth," Sam agreed. "It would have been worse than an explosive-metal bomb, from what the Lizards say."

"You're probably right—or my briefing officers tell me the same thing, anyhow," Stassen said. "Now, what was this question you wanted to ask?"

"Never mind, sir," Sam said. "You'd probably just tell me I was sticking my nose in again where it didn't belong, and I don't see much point to that. I'll keep my mouth shut from the beginning this time."

"That is probably a very good idea," the president said. "Good day, Lieutenant Colonel, and a safe flight back to Los Angeles."

"Thank you, Mr. President." Yeager wished Stassen hadn't said that. Now he was going to worry till the airplane's landing gear hit the runway at L.A. International Airport. The president, or people close to him, wouldn't make an airliner crash to get rid of one gadfly . . . would they? Sam didn't want to think so, but he knew there were people who wanted to see him dead.

If something like that happened, the Lizards would have a lot of sharp questions to ask American authorities. If they didn't like the answers they got, they were liable to take a spectacular revenge. Sam didn't care too much about that—he wouldn't be around to see it. But the thought of such revenge might give second thoughts to anybody who wanted his family to cash his life-insurance policy.

When Yeager got back out onto the street, he noticed that some of the trees were going from green to yellow and red. He'd been too worried about the meeting to pay any attention to that when he came to the Gray House. Now the sight made him smile. Living in California as he did these days, he seldom got such strong reminders of the passage from one season to the next.

He took a deep breath, then let it out. *I made it,* he thought. *If my plane home doesn't crash, I made it, anyhow.* He didn't really believe that would happen. Had Stassen wanted to get rid of him, his flight coming into Little Rock could have crashed, too. *Everything's going to be okay.* Sometimes he could make himself believe that for as long as two or three minutes at a time.

"I shall soon be returning to the starship," Ttomalss said from the monitor. Kassquit watched him with something less than delight. He was, as happened all too often these days, oblivious to that. Sounding more cheerful than he had any reasonable business being, he went on, "And then, I hope, your life can return to something approaching normal after the stressful time you have endured."

"How do you define 'normal,' superior sir?" Kassquit asked.

"Why, as things were before you became involved with Big Uglies, of course," Ttomalss answered. "That is your default setting, so to speak. Would not a return to such conditions prove welcome?"

He does not understand, Kassquit thought. *And he has no idea how much of my interior life he either misunderstands or misses altogether.* He was, after all, a male of the Race. And she ... wasn't a female of the Race, no matter how much of a duplicate of a female of the Race he'd tried to make her into.

Speaking carefully, she replied, "If I could forget the memories of the time when Jonathan Yeager was here, that might perhaps be possible, superior sir. As things are, however, I have learned what it means to be part of a species with a continuously active sexuality. This knowledge goes some way toward redefining normality for me."

And the inside of a fusion reaction is rather warm, and walking from Tosev 3 to Home would take a long time. Kassquit felt in her belly the size of the understatement she'd just given her mentor.

Ttomalss, however, took it as literal truth without understatement. He said, "I suspect time will create a certain distancing effect. Your emotions will no longer seem so urgent as they do now."

That did it. Kassquit snapped, "Do you not see—can you not see—that I do not want these emotions to fade? I want to preserve them. I want to feel others like them. They come closer to making life worth living than anything I have ever known aboard this starship."

"Oh," Ttomalss said tonelessly.

Kassquit knew she'd wounded him. Part of her was too angry to care. The rest of her remembered the time when he'd been far and away the most important individual in her universe. It hadn't been very long before. It only seemed like forever. Her hands folded into fists. She was at war within herself. She feared she would stay that way as long as she lived.

Gathering himself, Ttomalss said, "Obliging you in this regard will not be easy, you know. I must tell you that, even among Tosevites, regular sexual relations do not necessarily guarantee happiness. The literature and music and moving pictures the Tosevites produce demonstrate as much without the shed skin of a doubt."

"I believe it," Kassquit said. "Please understand that I am not seeking only sexual pleasure. I can, to some degree, supply that for myself. But the companionship I enjoyed with Jonathan Yeager along with the sexual pleasure ... I miss that very much." She sighed. "However much I might wish to be one, I am not and cannot be a female of the Race. I am, to some degree, irrevocably a Big Ugly."

She'd had that thought before she'd ever met any wild Tosevites, too. It had horrified and disgusted her then. It still did, to some degree. But she could not deny that she wanted to know more of the feelings she'd had when Jonathan Yeager was aboard the starship with her.

Ttomalss said, "Several Tosevite languages have a word for the emotional state you describe. Jonathan Yeager used the tongue called English, is that not a truth? In English, the term is . . ." He paused to consult the computer, then made the affirmative gesture to show he'd found what he wanted. "The term is *love*."

By the nature of things, he could have only an intellectual understanding of the emotion he named. But he was not a fool; he had indeed identified the feeling Kassquit craved. She made the affirmative gesture, too. "Jonathan Yeager taught me the word," she agreed. "And, as you must know, he has informed me that he is entering into a permanent mating arrangement with a wild female Big Ugly—that, in effect, he loves someone else. This has been difficult for me to accept with equanimity."

There. She'd topped her own earlier understatement. She hadn't thought she could.

"You knew when Jonathan Yeager came to the starship that his relation with you would be only temporary," Ttomalss reminded her. "It was as much an experiment from his perspective as from yours—an experiment prolonged because of the fighting that broke out against the Deutsche. Perhaps it would have been better had the experiment not been prolonged."

"Yes, perhaps it would have," Kassquit said. "But I cannot do anything about that except try to adjust as well as I can to the consequences of what did happen. Learning to experience this intensely pleasurable emotion and then having it taken away has been difficult." Another fine understatement.

"I have asked you before if you wanted me to find you another Tosevite male," Ttomalss said. "If you wish me to do so, I will do my best to provide you with one who will be pleasing."

"I thank you, superior sir, but that is still not what I want," Kassquit said. "For one thing, I have no certainty of matching the pleasure I received from Jonathan Yeager, pleasure both sexual and emotional. For another, suppose I should. That liaison would also necessarily be temporary, and I would go into another fit of depression after it ended. From what I am given to understand, this is rather like the emotional cycle ginger tasters experience."

"Perhaps it is. I cannot speak there from personal experience, and I am glad I cannot," Ttomalss said. "I can say that some ginger tasters appear to enjoy the cycle between pleasure and gloom, while others wish they could escape it and escape from their use of the herb."

"But what am *I* to do?" Kassquit asked, though Ttomalss was hardly in a position to be able to tell her.

He pointed that out: "Your two choices are to remain as you are and to regret the one sexual and emotional relationship you had or to embark on another and then come to regret that, too. I would be the first to admit that neither of these strikes me as ideal."

"They both strike me as disastrous." Kassquit's fingerclaws were short and wide and blunt. They bit into the soft flesh of her palms even so. "And yet, superior sir, I see no others, either."

"We shall do what we can for you, Kassquit. On that you have my word," Ttomalss said. Kassquit wondered how much his word would be worth, and whether it would be worth anything. But she did believe he would try. He went on, "Soon I shall see you in person. I look forward to it. For now, farewell."

"Farewell," Kassquit echoed, and Ttomalss' image vanished from the monitor.

She looked around her cubicle and sighed again. For most of her life, this little space had been her refuge against the males—and, later, the females—of the Race who'd scorned her. Now it seemed much more like a trap. What could she do here by herself? What could she do anywhere here by herself? And how, among the males and females of the Race, could she ever feel as if she weren't by herself? Her hand shaped the negative gesture. It was impossible.

After shaping that gesture, she scratched her head. It felt rough and a little itchy. She should have shaved it the day before, but she hadn't felt like taking the trouble. The next time she washed, though, she would have to do it.

Why bother? she wondered. The answer leaped into her mind as soon as the thought formed: *to look more as if I were a member of the Race.*

Kassquit walked over to the built-in mirror in the cubicle. As always, she had to stoop a little to see herself in it; it was made for a member of the Race, not a Big Ugly. She looked at her flat, vertical, short-snouted, soft-skinned, eye-turretless face with the fleshy sound receptors to either side.

"What difference would hair make?" she said aloud. Try as she would, she'd never look like a member of the Race. Then a new thought occurred to her. "Rabotevs and Hallessi do not look like members of the Race, either, but they are citizens of the Empire. I am a Tosevite citizen of the Empire. If I want, I can look like a Tosevite."

Wild Big Uglies—except the ones like Jonathan Yeager, who also imitated the Race—let their hair grow. Even Jonathan Yeager had shaved only the hair on his scalp and face, not that on the rest of his body. And, from what he had said, most females, even among those who imitated the Race, let the hair on their scalps grow.

That female with whom he will be mating, that Karen Culpepper, probably has hair, Kassquit thought. At first, that struck her as a good argument for shaving. But then she hesitated. Perhaps hair increased sexual attractiveness, in the same way that, among the Race, a male's upraised scaly crest helped prompt a female to mate with him.

I am a Big Ugly. I cannot help being a Big Ugly. Even after this world becomes part of the Empire, Tosevite citizens of the Empire will probably go right on letting their hair grow. Why should I not do the same? I cannot be a female of the Race, but I can be a Tosevite female who is a citizen of the Empire. In fact, I cannot be anything else.

She ran a hand over her scalp, wondering how long the hair would take to grow to a respectable length. Then she let that hand slide down between her legs. She would grow hair there, too, and under her arms as well. She wondered whether she ought to keep shaving those areas even if she left her scalp alone. Then she shrugged. Jonathan Yeager hadn't shaved around his private parts, or under his arms, either. She decided to let the hair grow. If she decided she didn't like it, she could always get rid of it later.

The hair on her scalp quickly became noticeable. After she'd ignored the razor only a few days, the researcher named Tessrek spoke to her in the refectory: "Are you trying to look like a wild Big Ugly? If so, you are succeeding."

He'd never liked her, not even when she was a hatchling. She didn't like him, either, not even a little. She answered, "Why should I not look like a Tosevite, superior sir? As you never tire of pointing out, it is what I am."

"High time you admit as much, too, instead of trying to act like a photocopy of a member of the Race," he said, but warily— she'd already proved she could hold her own in a war of wits.

"Civilization does not depend on shape or appearance," she said now. "Civilization depends on culture. You certainly prove that."

"I thank you," he said, before realizing she didn't mean it as a compliment. A couple of males at the table with him were quicker on the uptake. Their laughter told Tessrek he'd made a fool of himself. He sprang to his feet and angrily skittered away. Kassquit ran her hand over her now fuzzy scalp. It itched a little. So did her underarms and private parts. Even so, she thought she might learn to enjoy having hair.

* * *

When Jonathan Yeager's father got off the telephone, he was laughing fit to burst. "What's funny, Dad?" Jonathan asked.

"We've got ourselves something brand new, that's what," his father answered. "We're going to accept a couple of Lizards—and I do mean a couple, in every sense of the word—who aren't just political refugees. They're sexual refugees, too. Sexual outlaws, you might even say."

"Outlaws?" That intrigued Jonathan, as his dad must have known it would. "Why? What have they done?" He tried to imagine what sort of sex crime a Lizard—no, two Lizards—could commit. Imagination, unfortunately, failed him.

Grinning, Sam Yeager said, "They've fallen in love, and they want to get married. And so the Lizards are throwing them right out of their territory and letting us worry about 'em. They'd tar 'em and feather 'em and ride 'em out of town on a rail, too, except they think feathers are just about as strange and unnatural as falling in love."

Jonathan didn't think falling in love was unnatural. He enjoyed it. But it hadn't occurred to him that Lizards might do the same. "How on earth did that happen?" he asked. Before his father could answer, he held up a hand. "It's got something to do with ginger, doesn't it? It would have to."

"Sure enough." His father nodded. "The female Lizard and her male friend would mate whenever she tasted ginger, and she tasted a lot. After a while—from what I heard over the phone just now, they were best friends before she got the habit—they decided they wanted to stay together all the time. And boy, did they get in trouble when they told their local mayor or whomever it was they told what they wanted."

"I bet they would," Jonathan exclaimed. He tried to look at things from the point of view of a Lizard official. Having done so, he whistled softly. "It's a wonder they didn't lock 'em in jail and throw away the key."

"Truth," his father said in the language of the Race, and added an emphatic cough. "Maybe they figured this pair would be a bad influence even in jail. I don't know anything about that. What I do know is, the Race let 'em ask for asylum here in the United States, and we've granted it. They expect to settle in California, as a matter of fact."

"We've probably got the biggest expatriate community in the country—either Los Angeles or Phoenix," Jonathan said.

His father laughed again. "Not a whole lot of them move to Boston or Minneapolis," he agreed. "They don't much fancy the weather in places like those. I grew up not all that far from Minneapolis. I don't much fancy the weather there, either."

Having lived most of his life in Los Angeles, Jonathan had trouble imagining the sort of weather Minneapolis got. He didn't waste his time trying. Instead, he asked, "May I tell Karen about this? She'll think it's funny, too."

"Sure, go ahead," his dad answered. He walked across the kitchen and set a hand on Jonathan's shoulder. "And thanks for asking before you talked with her, too. This one isn't classified, but it could've been."

"I know better than to run my mouth, Dad," Jonathan said righteously. After a moment, though, he admitted, "I did tell her about what you'd found out—but only after those goons grabbed you. Looking back, I don't suppose I was doing her any big favor."

"No, I don't think you were, either," his father said. "But you were trying to make sure people didn't get away with what they'd done to the Race. And, incidentally, you were trying to save my neck, so I guess I'll forgive you."

"Okay." Jonathan walked over to the phone. "I'm going to call her now, if that's okay with you. The people she works with'll think that's funny, too."

Because of his time up on the space station, he still had a couple of quarters left at UCLA. After Karen graduated, she'd landed a job at a firm that adapted Lizard technology to human uses. Jonathan dialed her work number. When she answered, she didn't go, *Borogove Engineering—Karen Culpepper speaking,* the way she had the day before. What she did say was, "Hello, Jonathan. How are you today?"

"I'm fine," he answered automatically. Then he blinked. "How'd you know it was me? I didn't say anything."

"We've just got a new gadget—we're sublicensing it from a company up in Canada," she answered. "It reads phone numbers for calls you get and displays them on a screen."

"That's hot," Jonathan said. "Somebody had a real good idea there. Anyway, the reason I called . . ." He repeated the story he'd heard from his father.

When he finished, Karen gurgled laughter. "Oh, I do like that," she said. "That's *funny*, Jonathan. I wonder what the Race will think of us from now on. The United States of America, the place where they can dump their perverts."

"Yeah." Jonathan laughed, too, but not for long. "You know, that might not be so good. If they start looking at us that way, it's liable to make them start looking down their snouts at us, too."

"Maybe you ought to say something about that to your dad," Karen said.

"I think I will," he answered. "You still want to go to Helen Yu's for dinner tonight?"

"Sure," Karen said. "It's Friday, so we can do something afterwards, too—we don't have to get up in the morning. Come get me around half past six, okay? That'll let me hop in the shower after I get home."

"Okay. See you at six-thirty. 'Bye." He hung up and turned to his father. "Dad . . ."

"I know what you're going to want from me." Sam Yeager pulled his wallet out of his hip pocket. "Twenty bucks do the job?"

"Thanks. That'd be great." Jonathan took the bill and stuck it in his own pocket. "But that wasn't the only thing I had in mind."

His father laughed at him. "That's a line you're supposed to use with Karen, not with me." Jonathan's ears burned. Sometimes his dad could be very crude. Sam Yeager went on, "I'll bite. What's so important besides money?"

"Something Karen said," Jonathan answered, and explained her reaction to what the Race might think about America sheltering the two Lizards who wanted to get married.

"That *is* interesting," his father said. "But we're a free country, and we keep getting freer a little bit at a time. If we can start giving our own Negroes a fair shake, I expect we'll be able to find room for a few Lizards who do strange things. The Race already thinks we're too free for our own good."

"All right," Jonathan said. "If you're not going to worry about it, I won't, either."

"I expect you've got other things on your mind right now, anyway," his dad said. Jonathan did his best to look innocent. His father laughed some more, so his best probably wasn't very good.

He pulled up in front of Karen's house at six-thirty on the dot. Since they were engaged, he could even give her a quick kiss in front of her parents. When they got to Helen Yu's, on Rosecrans

near Western, only a couple of spaces in the lot were empty.
Jonathan grabbed one. Yu's was one of the oldest and most
popular Chinese restaurants in Gardena—actually, just outside
the city limits.

They ate egg-flower soup and sweet-and-sour pork ribs and
chow mein and crunchy noodles and drank tea, something neither of them did outside a Chinese restaurant. After a while,
Karen said, "I wonder what Liu Mei would think of the food
here."

"She'd probably say it was good," Jonathan replied. "I don't
know how Chinese she'd think it was." That question had occurred to him before. He'd sensibly kept his mouth shut about it.
When Liu Mei visited the States with her mother, he'd had something of a crush on her. Karen had known it, too, and hadn't been
very happy about it. But now that she'd asked the question, he
could safely answer it.

After fortune cookies and almond cookies, Jonathan paid for
dinner. They went out to the car. His arm slipped around Karen's
waist. She leaned against him. "What time is it?" she asked.

Jonathan looked at his watch. "A little past eight," he answered. "Next show at the drive-in starts at 8:45. We can do that,
if you feel like it."

"Sure," Karen said, so Jonathan drove east on Rosecrans to
Vermont and then south past Artesia to the drive-in. It wasn't
very crowded. The movie—a thriller about the ginger trade set in
Marseille before it had gone up in radioactive fire—had been
there for a couple of weeks, and would be closing soon. Jonathan
didn't mind. He found a spot well away from most of the other
cars, under a light pole with a dead lamp.

Karen snickered. "How much of the movie are we going to
watch?" she asked.

"I don't know," he answered. "We'll find out. Shall I go get
some Cokes?"

"Sure," she said. "Don't bother with candy or popcorn,
though—not for me, anyway. I'm pretty full."

"Okay. Me, too. Be right back." Jonathan got out of the car
and went over to the concession stand. When he returned to the
car with the sodas, he found Karen sitting in the back seat. His
hopes rose. They probably wouldn't see a whole lot of the film.
He slid in beside her. "Here." He handed her one of the Cokes.
"We'd better be careful not to spill these later."

She looked at him. "I don't know what you're talking about," she said, which made both of them laugh so hard, they almost spilled the Cokes then.

They did pay some attention to the first few minutes of the movie, but even then they were paying a lot more attention to each other. Jonathan put his arm around Karen. She snuggled against him. He never did figure out which of them started the first kiss. Whichever one it was, the kiss went on and on. Karen put a hand on the back of his neck to pull him to her.

He rubbed her breasts through the fabric of her blouse. She made a noise deep in her throat—almost a growl. Thus encouraged, he undid two buttons of the blouse and reached inside the cup of her bra. Her flesh was soft and smooth and warm.

Before very long, her blouse and bra were off. Now that they were engaged, there didn't seem to be much point to the stop-and-start games they'd played while they were dating. She rubbed him, too, through his chinos. He hoped he wouldn't explode.

He slid his hand under her skirt to the joining of her legs. "Oh, God, Jonathan," she whispered as he stroked her.

"I've got a rubber in my wallet," he said. She hesitated. They still hadn't gone all the way. But then she lay back on the seat. Jonathan tried to get her panties off, get his trousers down far enough, and put on the rubber, all at the same time. At last, he managed all three. "I love you," he gasped as he clumsily poised himself over her.

The rubber helped. Without it, he was sure he would have come as soon as he started. As he had with Kassquit, he discovered this was Karen's first time. Since it wasn't his, he had a better notion of what to do than he'd had up in the starship. Karen still winced when he pierced her.

Even with the rubber, he didn't last long. After gasping his way to delight, he asked, "Are you okay? Was it okay?"

"It hurt," she answered. "I know it's supposed to get better. Right now, I like your hand and your mouth more. Is that all right?" She sounded anxious.

"I guess so," Jonathan answered. He liked her hand and especially her mouth at least as well, too. But this had a finality to it that nothing else could match. He kissed her. "I love you."

"I love you, too," Karen said. "Give me my top back, will you?" Inside a couple of minutes, they were fully dressed again—just in time for the big car chase. Jonathan couldn't think of a movie he'd enjoyed more.

Ttomalss wondered whether all the time he'd spent raising Kassquit had been for nothing. Every time he looked at her, his liver twinged inside him. Her hair grew longer every day, making her resemble a wild Big Ugly more and more. Her spirit seemed more like a wild Big Ugly's every day, too.

In something close to despair, he railed at her: "Will you also wash off your body paint and put on wrappings?"

"No, I see no need for that," Kassquit answered with maddening calm. "But if I am a Tosevite citizen of the Empire, should I not follow Tosevite usages where they do no harm? I do not think a head of hair is very harmful."

"In any direct sense, probably not," Ttomalss admitted. "But your growing it seems a slap in the snout at the Race, which has spent so much effort to nurture you and to acculturate you."

"You have made me a creature, a tool, a thing to be used," Kassquit said. "It has taken me a long time, probably too long, to realize I can be more than that. If I am a citizen of the Empire, I should have as much freedom as any other citizen. If I choose to be eccentric, I may." She ran a hand over her dark, hairy scalp.

"If you choose to make yourself ugly, you mean," Ttomalss said.

But Kassquit made the negative gesture. "For Tosevites, and especially for Tosevite females, hair seems to contribute to attractiveness. I should prefer to be judged by the standards of my own biological species there. I have had enough of being thought a repulsively ugly imitation of a female of the Race. Believe me, superior sir, I have had more than enough of that." She used an emphatic cough.

Ttomalss flinched. He knew some of the things Tessrek and other males had said while he was rearing Kassquit. He'd never really thought about the effect that hearing such things might have on a young individual isolated from everyone around her because of her appearance and biology. There were probably a lot of things he'd never thought about while rearing Kassquit. Some of them were coming up out of the shadows to bite him now.

Slowly, he said, "Punishing me for errors I made in the past serves no useful purpose I can see."

"I am not punishing you. That is not my intention at all,"
Kassquit said. "I am, however, asserting my own individuality.
Any citizen of the Empire may do as much."

"That is a truth," Ttomalss said. "Another truth, however, is
that most citizens of the Empire suppress a good deal of their individuality, the better to fit into the society of which they are but
small parts."

Kassquit ran a hand over her hair again, and then along her
smooth, scaleless, upright body. Even as she bent into the posture of respect, she spoke with poisonous politeness: "Exactly
how, superior sir, am I supposed to suppress my individuality?
You cannot change me into a female of the Race. You do not
know how many times I have wished you could. Since I cannot
be a female of the Race, how can I do better than to be the best
Tosevite female I can possibly be?"

Her argument was painfully cogent. But Ttomalss had an argument of his own: "You are not culturally prepared to be a Tosevite female."

"Of course I am not," Kassquit said. "You were the one who
told me I was the first Tosevite citizen of the Empire. Do you
now disavow those words because I have learned to see that I am
truly a Tosevite and cannot imitate the Race in every imaginable
way?"

"At the moment, you seem to be doing your best not to imitate
the Race in any imaginable way." Ttomalss didn't try to hide his
bitterness.

"I have spent my whole life imitating the Race," Kassquit
said. "Am I not entitled to spend some little while discovering
what the biological part of my individuality means, and how I
can best adjust to its demands?"

"Of course you are," Ttomalss answered, wishing he could say
no. "But I do wish you would not throw yourself into this voyage
of discovery with such painful intensity. It will do you no good."

"No doubt you were the proper judge of such things when I
was a hatchling," Kassquit said. "Now that I am an adult, however, I will plot my course as I think best, not in accordance with
anyone else's views."

"Even if that course proves a disastrous mistake?" Ttomalss
asked.

Kassquit made the affirmative gesture. "Even if that course
proves a disastrous mistake. You, of course, superior sir, have

never made a single mistake in all the days since you broke out of your eggshell."

At the moment, Ttomalss was thinking the most disastrous mistake he'd ever made was deciding to rear a Tosevite hatchling. He'd thought that before, when the terrifying Chinese female named Liu Han kidnapped him as vengeance for his trying to raise her hatchling as he'd succeeded in raising Kassquit. But even his success here was proving full of thorns he'd never expected.

"Every male, every female makes mistakes," he said. "Wise ones, however, do not make unnecessary mistakes."

"Which are which is for me to judge, superior sir," Kassquit said. "And now, if you will excuse me . . ." She didn't wait to find out if he would excuse her. She just turned and strode out of his chamber. Had the door been the type common on Tosev 3, she would have slammed it. As things were, she could only leave in a huff.

With a sigh, Ttomalss got down to the rest of his work, to everything that had accumulated while he was down in Cairo working with the other members of the commission on Earl Warren. He studied a report of Tosevite attendance at shrines dedicated to the spirits of Emperors past. Since establishing those shrines had been his idea, reports naturally came to him.

He would have liked to see the numbers larger than they were. Few Big Uglies in the regions where their native superstitions were particularly powerful sought to modify those superstitions. That was unfortunate, because those were the areas where Ttomalss had most hoped to change Tosevite behavior and beliefs.

"Patience," Ttomalss said to himself. Patience was the foundation upon which the Race had built its success. But it seemed to be more a virtue on Home than here on Tosev 3.

Ttomalss hissed in surprise on noticing that the shrines with the highest attendance were not on territory the Race ruled at all, but in the not-empire of the United States. He wondered what that meant, and wondered all the more so because the Americans had gone to the extreme of immolating their own city to keep the Race from gaining influence over them.

Further investigation of this apparent paradox may well prove worthwhile, he wrote. Then he noticed that Atvar had arranged to send the two perverts who had caused so much scandal to the United States. The Americans would apparently put up with anything, no matter how bizarre.

The telephone hissed. "Senior Researcher Ttomalss," he said. "I greet you."

"And I greet you." The image that appeared on the monitor belonged to Tessrek, who'd been an itch under Ttomalss' scales ever since he started trying to raise Tosevite hatchlings. *With him, I have to put up with anything, too,* Ttomalss thought. Tessrek went on, "Are you aware of the latest disgusting behavior on the part of your pet Big Ugly?"

"She is not my pet," Ttomalss said. However much Kassquit disheartened him, Tessrek was the last male before whom he would show that. "She is a citizen of the Empire, as I am and as you are."

"She certainly boasts of being one," Tessrek said, "but her behavior hardly makes the boast anything in which she or the Empire can take pride."

"By which I suppose you mean that you tried baiting her again and found yourself unhappy at the outcome," Ttomalss said. "You really should learn, Tessrek. This has happened before, and it will keep right on happening as long as you refuse to recognize that she is an adult and an intelligent being." He himself was none too eager to recognize Kassquit as an adult, but he wouldn't admit that to Tessrek, either.

Tessrek hissed scornfully. "I am not referring to the Big Ugly's usual rudeness. I am resigned to that." He was lying, as Ttomalss knew, for the sake of moral advantage. Before Ttomalss could call him on it, he continued, "I am referring to the disgusting growth of hair she is cultivating on top of her head. It truly does sicken me. I want to turn my eye turrets away every time I see her."

"You have never complained about the hair wild Big Uglies grow," Ttomalss replied, "so I think you are singling her out for undue, unfair attention."

"But those other Big Uglies are, as you point out, wild," Tessrek said. "Both you and Kassquit have been prating that she is a proper citizen of the Empire. Proper citizens of the Empire do not grow hair."

"I know of no law or regulation forbidding citizens of the Empire from growing hair." Ttomalss swung both eye turrets toward

Tessrek and spoke in judicious tones: "As a matter of fact, you might try it yourself. It could do wonders for your appearance."

Tessrek hissed again, this time in real fury. Ttomalss broke the connection in the middle of the hiss. With any luck, Tessrek wouldn't bother him for some time. Ttomalss' mouth fell open in a laugh. He hadn't enjoyed himself so much since . . . *Since mating with Felless,* he thought. But then he made the negative gesture. The pleasures of mating were altogether distinct from other sorts.

He went back to work with a lighter liver. A moment later, though, he too hissed, in chagrin and dismay. He'd bounced Kassquit's arguments off Tessrek's snout. They made a surprisingly good case when he used them against a male he'd long disliked.

Of course, when Kassquit used those arguments against him, he'd thought them absurd. What did that mean? He was scientist enough to see one possibility he'd rejected out of hand before. *By the Emperor,* he thought, and cast down his eye turrets. *What if she is right?*

Once conquered, the Rabotevs and the Hallessi had soon abandoned almost all of their own cultural baggage and been assimilated into the larger, more complex, more sophisticated culture that was the Empire. And their cases had always been the Race's models for what would happen on Tosev 3.

But what if the model was wrong? In terms of biology, the Big Uglies were far more different from the Race than either the Rabotevs or the Hallessi. And in terms of culture, they were far closer to the Race than the Rabotevs or the Hallessi had been. Both those factors argued that they would acculturate more slowly and to a lesser degree than either of the other species the Race had conquered.

Even if Tosev 3 was finally conquered in full, Tosevites might go right on letting their hair grow and wearing wrappings. They might keep speaking their own languages and practicing their own superstitions. That would make life—to say nothing of administration—more difficult for the Race.

Ttomalss wondered if in their own history the Big Uglies had known any situations analogous to this one. He knew less than he should have about Tosevite history. So did the Race as a whole. It hadn't seemed germane. But maybe it was. *I wonder how I can get in touch with a Tosevite historian,* he thought.

Maybe Felless will know a way, down there on the surface of Tosev 3.

"No," Pshing told Straha when he tried to call Atvar. "The fleetlord is busy with important matters, and has given orders that he cannot be disturbed."

"Am I no longer an important matter, then?" Straha demanded angrily. "Were it not for me, you would still have no idea which Tosevite not-empire struck at the colonization fleet."

"I am sorry, sup—" Atvar's adjutant checked himself. Straha's rank remained a point of ambiguity. He wasn't a shiplord any more, not to anyone but himself. What *was* he? Nobody quite knew. Not enough for Pshing to call him *superior sir,* evidently. "I am sorry," Pshing repeated. "The fleetlord has given me explicit orders, and I cannot disobey them."

Straha wondered if he were the only male of the Race on Tosev 3 who'd ever imagined disobeying orders. After a moment's thought, he realized he wasn't. There had been mutinies during the first round of fighting—only a handful, but they did happen. By all he'd been able to find out, few of them had had happy aftermaths for the mutineers.

Had his own defection had a happy aftermath for him? He was still trying to figure that out. It could have been worse. He did know that. He could have defected to the SSSR, for instance. He shuddered at the thought. He might have done it. He hadn't known any better then.

"And now, if you will excuse me . . ." Pshing said, and broke the connection.

Straha wondered what would happen if he tried to walk into Atvar's office despite being unwelcome. By far the most likely result would be his expulsion. He sighed. Much as he enjoyed irritating the fleetlord, here he would get more irritation than he gave out.

I was freer in the United States, he thought. For a moment, the idea of redefecting crossed his mind. But he made the negative gesture. After the destruction of Indianapolis, the Americans would not welcome him.

On the other fork of the tongue, the Race didn't welcome him, either. He was still Straha the traitor as far as males and females here in Cairo were concerned. What he knew was useful. He himself? They wished they could take his knowledge and leave him alone. They might as well have been Americans.

He made the negative gesture again. In that regard, the Race was worse than the Americans, because his own kind were more self-righteous and sanctimonious. And, he realized, he had more of a taste for freedom, for doing what he wanted to do when he wanted to do it, than had been true before he defected to the United States.

Who would have believed it? he thought. *The Big Uglies' ideology has painted itself on me.* That wasn't true to any enormous extent—he still thought the American reporter who would have printed his opinion that the United States had been responsible for attacking the colonization fleet was addled. The male had had no business doing any such thing.

And then the ex-shiplord's mouth fell open in a startled laugh. When he'd offered the reporter that opinion, he'd thought of it as nothing but a joke, a way to get under the Tosevite's scales—no, *under his skin* was the English idiom, because Big Uglies had no scales. But he'd told the fellow the truth after all.

So what? he thought. *Even if it was the truth, it had no business appearing in a newspaper. Maybe I am not so enamored of freedom as I thought.* But he made the negative gesture once more. Compared to the Americans, he was a reactionary. Compared to his own kind, he was a radical, and a worse radical than he'd been before fleeing to the USA.

And there were plenty of males—and, by now, very likely some females, too—who were a good deal more radical than he. The expatriate community in the United States was flourishing. Some males were even prepared to look kindly on snout-counting, and to propose institutionalizing it for the Race as well. That still struck Straha as laughable.

That members of the Race could hold such ideas, though, was bemusing. Everyone talked about the ways in which the Race was influencing Tosev 3 and the Tosevites. And with good reason: the Race's influence on the planet and its folk was profound. And the Race's influence on the Tosevites had been envisioned since the first probe sent to this world found it habitable.

No one—at least, no one among the Race—seemed much interested in talking about ways in which Tosev 3 and the Tosevites were exerting influence in the other direction. Nobody had expected the Big Uglies to own any ideas worth investigating.

The probe sent to this world hadn't shown everything worth showing—or rather, Tosev 3 and the Tosevites had changed far faster than anyone back on Home had imagined possible. The leading civilizations here were formidable intellectually as well as technologically.

And Tosev 3 itself was influencing the Race. A good-sized jar of ginger sat on the floor by Straha's sleeping mat. He went over and had a taste. How many males, how many females, indulged themselves so whenever they found the chance? He could freely do so—a small mercy from Atvar, who did not seem inclined to grant any large ones.

For the Race as a whole, though, and especially for females, ginger remained illegal, with harsh penalties levied against those caught using it. But males and females kept right on tasting. Mating season as a brief, separate time was a thing of the past. The colonists were still new to Tosev 3. They hadn't fully adjusted to the change yet; a lot of them kept trying to pretend it hadn't happened. But how would things look in a couple of generations?

Straha had heard the scandalous story of the two perverts who'd become as sexually addicted to each other as they were physically addicted to the herb. All things considered, Straha supposed Atvar had been wise to exile them to the USA, where the Big Uglies reckoned such infatuations normal.

"But Atvar has all the imagination of a mud puddle," Straha said. He was sure his chamber was monitored, but didn't care; his opinion of the fleetlord was about as far removed from secret as it could be. Atvar no doubt believed the two perverts an aberration. Maybe they were. Straha wouldn't have bet on it. To him, they seemed far more likely to be the shape of things to come.

The telephone hissed. "Former shiplord and current nuisance Straha speaking," Straha said. "I greet you."

"And I greet you." Atvar's image appeared in the monitor. "You have named yourself well."

"For which I more or less thank you." With ginger making every nerve twang, Straha didn't much care what he said.

"Pshing tells me you tried to call," Atvar said. "I was occupied. I am no longer. What do you want? If it is anything reasonable, I will try to get it for you."

"That is more than you have said for some time," Straha replied. "What I chiefly want to know is whether you have finally extracted all the yolk from my egg. If you have, I would like to live somewhere other than Shepheard's Hotel."

"Your debriefing appears to be complete, yes," Atvar answered. "But what will you do if you are turned loose on the members of the Race here on Tosev 3? How will you support yourself? The position of shiplord came with pay. The position of nuisance, while otherwise eminent, does not."

In genuine curiosity, Straha asked, "Where did you learn such sarcasm? You did not speak so when I was a shiplord."

"Dealing with Fleetlord Reffet may have something to do with it," Atvar told him. "Dealing with Big Uglies may have something to do with it, too. In different ways, they drive a sensible male mad."

That assumed he was sensible. Straha made no such assumption. But he kept quiet about the assumptions he did make. Atvar held his fate in his fingerclaws. All he said was, "You are not quite the male you were."

"No one who comes to Tosev 3 escapes unchanged," Atvar said. "But you have not answered my question. Have you any plans for making a living if you are allowed entry into the greater society of the Race?"

"As a matter of fact, I have," Straha said. "I was thinking of drafting my memoirs and living off the proceeds of publication. I am, I gather, notorious. I ought to be able to exploit that for the sake of profit."

"No one who comes to Tosev 3 escapes unchanged," Atvar repeated. "When you were a shiplord, you would never have debased yourself so."

"Perhaps not," Straha said. "But then again, who knows? I have had unique experiences. Why should others not be interested in learning of them?"

"Because they were illegal?" Atvar suggested. "Because they were shameful? Because your descriptions of them may be libelous?"

"All those things should attract interest to my story," Straha said cheerfully. "No one would care to read the memoirs of a clerk who did nothing but sit in front of a monitor his whole life long."

"No one will read your memoirs if they are libelous," Atvar said. "You are not in the United States any more, you know."

"Exalted Fleetlord, I do not need to be libelous to be interesting," Straha said.

"I will be the judge of that, when my aides and I see the manuscript you produce," Atvar said.

Had Straha been a Big Ugly, he would have smiled. "You and your aides will not be the only ones judging it. I am sure Fleetlord Reffet and many of the colonists would be fascinated to learn *all* the details of what happened before they got here. And, as I say, I doubt I would need to distort the truth in any way to keep them entertained and their tongues wagging."

He waited to see how Atvar would take that. He despised Reffet almost as much as Atvar did, but if he could use the fleetlord of the colonization fleet as a lever against the fleetlord of the conquest fleet, he would not only do it, he would enjoy doing it. And, sure enough, Atvar said, "You mean you will go out of your way to embarrass me and hope Reffet will like the result enough to let you go ahead and publish it."

"That is not at all what I said, Exalted Fleetlord," Straha protested, although it was exactly what he'd meant.

"Suppose I let you get away with that," Atvar said. "Suppose I pretend not to notice whatever you may have to say about me. Will you include in your memoirs passages indicating the need for a long-term Soldiers' Time here on Tosev 3, to help stop the endless grumbling from the colonists? The Race, after all, is more important than either one of us."

Straha hadn't expected that, either. Yes, Atvar had changed over the years. To some degree, that made him harder to dislike, but only to some degree. Straha made the affirmative gesture. "I think we have a bargain."

"Imagine my delight." Atvar broke the connection. No, he wasn't so hard to dislike after all.

☆ **15** ☆

As Reuven and Moishe Russie were walking from their home to the office they now shared, Reuven's father asked him, "And how is Mrs. Radofsky's toe these days?"

His tone was a little too elaborately casual to be quite convincing. "It seems to be coming along very well," Reuven answered. Listening to himself, he found he also sounded a little too elaborately casual to be quite convincing.

"I'm glad to hear it," Moishe Russie said. "And what is your opinion of those parts of Mrs. Radofsky located north of her fractured toe?"

"My medical opinion is that the rest of Mrs. Radofsky is quite healthy," Reuven replied.

His father smiled. "I don't believe I asked for your medical opinion."

"Well, it's what you're going to get," Reuven said, which made Moishe Russie laugh out loud. After a few more paces, Reuven added, "I think she's a very nice person. Her daughter is a sweet little girl."

"Yes, that's always a good sign," Moishe Russie agreed.

"A good sign of what?" Reuven asked.

"That someone is a nice person," his father said. "Nice people commonly have nice children." He gave his own son a sidelong glance. "There are exceptions every now and then, of course."

"Yes, I suppose an obnoxious father could have a nice son," Reuven said blandly. His father laughed again, and thumped him on the back.

They were both still chuckling as they went into the office. Yetta, the receptionist, had got there ahead of both of them. She sent them disapproving looks. "What's waiting for us today, Yetta?" Moishe Russie asked. He and Reuven already had a pretty good idea of their scheduled appointments, but Yetta got fussy if they didn't respect what she saw as her prerogative.

Sometimes, as now, she got fussy anyhow. "Neither one of you has enough to keep you busy," she complained. "I don't know how you expect to pay the bills if you don't have more patients."

"We're doing all right," Reuven said, which was true and more than true.

"Well, you won't keep doing all right unless more people come down sick," Yetta snapped. Reuven looked at his father. His father was looking at him. That made it harder for both of them to keep from laughing. Somehow, they managed. They went past the disapproving Yetta and into their own offices. Neither of them had an appointment scheduled till ten o'clock, an hour and a half away. Reuven caught up on paperwork—a never-ending struggle—and was working his way through a Lizard medical journal when his father called him.

"What's up?" Reuven asked.

"I hear Ppurrin and Waxxa really have gone to the United States," Moishe Russie answered.

"Have they?" Reuven said. "Well, that's one problem solved for old Atvar, then, and some credit for us because we came up with the idea for him."

"Credit for us, yes," his father said. "A problem solved? I don't know. I wouldn't bet on it, though for the time being I think Atvar thinks he won't have to worry about it any more."

"What do you mean?" Reuven said. "The Americans will let those Lizards stay. They may be perverts to the Race, but not to us."

"I'm sure the Americans will let them stay, yes." His father nodded. "That's not the problem, or not as I see it, anyhow."

Reuven scratched his head. "What is, then? I'm sorry, Father, but I'm not following you at all."

"No?" Moishe Russie grinned. "All right. Let's put it like this: do you think Ppurrin and Waxxa will be the only pair of what the Lizards call perverts that they'll have? A lot of Lizards taste ginger."

"Oh," Reuven said, and then, in an altogether different tone of voice, *"Oh."* He gave his father an admiring look. "You think those two are just the tip of the iceberg, don't you?"

"Don't you?" his father returned. "The colonists haven't been here very long, after all, and this is already starting to happen. What will things be like when you're my age? What will things be like when your children are my age?"

Most times, Reuven would have pointed out with some heat that he had no children at present. Today, though, he nodded thoughtfully. "They'll have to change a lot of things to adjust to that, won't they? I mean, if they really do start forming permanent mated pairs."

"Start falling in love and getting married," Moishe Russie said, and Reuven nodded, accepting the correction. His father went on, "It will be as hard for them to get used to the idea of pairs settling down together as it would be for us to get used to the idea of being promiscuous all the time." He wagged a finger at his son. "And wipe that dirty grin off your face."

"Who, me?" Reuven said, as innocently as he could. "I don't know what you're talking about."

"That's pretty funny," Moishe Russie said. "Now tell me another one."

"No." Reuven shook his head. He cautiously looked out the door, then lowered his voice anyhow: "Who do you think I am, Yetta or somebody?"

His father rolled his eyes. "She does her work well. As for the rest . . ." He shrugged and then, in a near whisper, went on, "We might get somebody who's a pain in the neck and doesn't do her job well. I can put up with bad jokes."

"I suppose so." Reuven pulled his mind back to the business at hand. "Do you really think we'll see a day when the Lizards start pairing off by the thousands instead of just one couple at a time? That would make this world different from all the others in the Empire in some very important ways."

"I know," Moishe Russie said. "I'm not sure the Race has really figured all of that out yet. And it will be years before the other planets in the Empire find out what ginger is doing here, even if it does what I think it will. It's always going to be years between stars as far as radio goes, and even more years between them as far as travel. The Race is more patient than we are. I don't think we could have built an empire that would hang together in spite of all the delays in giving orders and getting things done."

"You're bound to be right about that," Reuven said. "Somebody who was governor on one planet would decide he wanted to be king or president or whatever he called himself, and he'd stop taking orders and set up his own government or else start a civil war."

"That's how we are," his father agreed. "The Lizards here know it, too. I wonder what they think of us back on Home."

"So do I," Reuven said. "Whatever it is, it's bound to be ten years out of date."

"I know." Moishe Russie laughed. "And by the time Home answers, it's twenty years out of date. Atvar is just now finding out what the Emperor thinks of the truce he made with us Big Uglies."

"And what does the Emperor think?" Reuven asked. "Has Atvar said?" He was going to use his father's connections with the Race for all they were worth.

"He hasn't said much," his father answered. "I gather the Emperor knows Atvar's the man, uh, the Lizard on the spot, and so he has to do what he thinks best. It's a good thing the Emperor didn't order him to go back to war with all of us, and you had best believe that's a truth." He'd been speaking Hebrew, but threw in an emphatic cough even so.

"Do you really think he would have done it if the Emperor had told him to?" Reuven asked. That unpleasant possibility hadn't crossed his mind.

But his father nodded. "If the Emperor told Atvar to stick a skewer through Earth and throw it on the fire, he'd do it. I don't think we can even imagine how well the Lizards obey the Emperor."

"I suppose not." Reuven knew the males of the Race with whom he'd dealt over the years didn't understand what made him tick. He was willing to believe it worked both ways.

The front door opened. "Hello, Mr. Krause," Yetta said. She raised her voice: "Dr. Russie, Mr. Krause is here."

"He's mine," Reuven's father said. In a soft aside, he added, "If he'd lose twenty kilos and stop drinking and smoking, he'd add twenty years to his life."

Reuven said, "He probably thinks they'd be twenty boring years." He got up and went back to his own office while his father was still scratching his head over that. If Mr. Krause was here, his own first patient would come through the door pretty soon, too.

Before Yetta announced that first patient's arrival, Reuven picked up the telephone and made a call. After the phone rang a couple of times, somebody on the other end of the line, a woman, picked it up. "Hello?"

"Mrs. Radofsky?" Reuven said.

"No, she's at work. This is her sister," the woman answered. "Who's calling, please?" In the background, Miriam prattled something—the sister was undoubtedly looking after her.

"This is Dr. Russie," Reuven answered. "I'm calling to find out how her broken toe is doing."

He wondered if the sister would simply tell him and hang up. Instead, she said, "Oh, thank you very much, Dr. Russie. Let me give you her number."

She did. Reuven wrote it down. After he said his good-byes, he called it. "Gold Lion Furniture," a woman said.

This time, Reuven recognized Mrs. Radofsky's voice. He named himself, and then asked, "How's your toe doing these days?"

"It's still sore," the widow Radofsky answered, "but it's getting better. It's not as swollen as it was, and it doesn't hurt as much as it did, either."

"I'm glad to hear it," he said, for all the world as if he, as opposed to the passage of time, had had something to do with her recovery.

"Thank you very much for calling," she said. "I'm sure most doctors wouldn't have done it for their patients."

Reuven was sure he wouldn't have done it for most of his patients, too. He also had a pretty good notion the widow Radofsky was sure of that. Even so, he nervously drummed his fingers on his desk before asking, "Would you, ah, like to go out to supper with me one of these evenings to celebrate feeling better?"

Silence on the other end of the line. He braced himself for rejection. If she said no, if she still had her dead husband and nobody else in her heart, how could he blame her? He couldn't. For that matter, if she just wasn't interested in him for a multitude of other reasons, how could he blame her? Again, he couldn't.

But, at last, she said, "Thank you. I think I would like that. Call me at home, why don't you, and we'll make the arrangements."

"All right," he said. Yetta chose that moment to bawl out his name. His first patient had made an appearance after all. Reuven said his good-byes and hung up. He was smiling. The patient had waited just long enough.

* * *

Marshal Zhukov had, or could have, more power than Vyach-eslav Molotov. Molotov knew it, too. But, because of his Party office, he exercised a certain moral authority over the marshal—as long as Zhukov chose to acknowledge it, which he did.

Molotov took advantage of that now. He said, "I assume our support for the People's Liberation Army will be altogether clan-destine, Georgi Konstantinovich. It had better be, at any rate."

"If it isn't, Comrade General Secretary, it will be at least as big a surprise to me as it is to you," Zhukov answered.

That was, no doubt, intended for a joke. As usual, Molotov disapproved of jokes. All they were good for, in his jaundiced opinion, was clouding the issue. He did not want this issue clouded. He wanted no ambiguity whatsoever here. "If we are detected, Comrade Marshal, very unfortunate things will spring from it. Consider the *Reich*. Consider the United States."

"I do consider them. I consider them every day," Zhukov said. "As far as the People's Liberation Army knows, our aid has not been detected. As far as the GRU knows, it has not been detected. As far as the NKVD knows, it has not been detected. We are as secure as we can possibly be."

His lip curled when he condescended to name the NKVD at all. The Party's espionage and security service, as opposed to the Red Army's (which it frequently was), had fallen on hard times since Beria's botched coup. That was partly at Molotov's insistence, partly at Zhukov's—the NKVD spied on the Red Army as well as the rest of the world. It had needed purging of Beria's henchmen, and had got it.

Even so, Molotov wished he had the NKVD running at a higher level of efficiency than it possessed right now. The GRU was a good service, but its first loyalty lay with the Army, not with the Party: with Zhukov, not with him. And he wanted more than one perspective on his course of action. Having to rely on the GRU alone left him feeling like a one-eyed man.

He said nothing of that to Zhukov, of course. It would have roused the marshal's suspicions, and Zhukov had plenty even when they weren't roused. He would have thought Molotov was trying to rebuild an independent political position. He would have been right, too.

Aloud Molotov was mild, as he had to be: "Let us hope the assessments are correct, then. Given the German arms we have been able to supply to the People's Liberation Army, do you think they stand any serious chance of throwing off the Race's yoke in China?"

"Probably not, but they can make enormous nuisances of themselves, and when was Mao ever good for any more than that?" Zhukov answered, proving Molotov did not have the exclusive franchise for cynicism among the Soviet leaders. "Besides, even if the Chinese do seem on the brink of expelling the Lizards, the Race has explosive-metal bombs, and the People's Liberation Army doesn't."

"Not from us, anyhow," Molotov agreed. "But life gets more difficult and more complicated now that the Japanese do have them."

Zhukov nodded. "They had imperialist designs on China before the Lizards showed up. They haven't forgotten, either. They still think of it as their rightful sphere of influence."

"That is part of it, Georgi Konstantinovich, but only part." Molotov was glad the marshal did leave him control over foreign policy. Zhukov was a long way from stupid, but he didn't always see the subtleties. "The rest is, the Race may also hesitate longer before using explosive-metal weapons now that they have to take the Japanese more seriously."

"Maybe." Zhukov didn't sound convinced. "The Lizards didn't give a fart about what we thought when they pounded the Nazis flat. We're going to be worrying about fallout in the Baltics and Byelorussia and the western Ukraine for years to come."

"Not all of that fallout is from the Lizards' bombs," Molotov said. "Some of it comes from the ones the Germans used on Poland."

"Doesn't matter," Marshal Zhukov insisted. "The point is the same either way: they'll do what they think needs doing, and they'll worry about everything else later. If the rebels in China look like winning, their cities will start going up in smoke." He waved his hand. "*Do svidanya,* Mao."

Molotov considered. Maybe he'd looked for subtleties and missed a piece of the big picture. "It could be," he admitted.

"There are times I wouldn't miss him, believe you me there are," Zhukov said. "He's as arrogant as Stalin ever was, but Stalin did plenty to earn the right. Mao's nothing but a jumped-up bandit chief, and a lot of the jumping up is only in his own mind."

More than the foolish joke earlier, that did tempt Molotov to smile. It also made him look nervously around the office. He noticed Zhukov doing the same thing. "We're both afraid Iosef Vissarrionovich is listening," he said.

"He's been dead twelve years and more," Zhukov said. "But if anybody could still be listening after all that time, he's the one."

"That is the truth," Molotov agreed. "Very well, then. Do your best to get still more weapons to the Chinese. If they are going to annoy the Lizards, we want them to do it on a grand scale. The more attention the Race pays to China, the less it will be able to pay to anything else—including us."

"And the less attention the Race pays to us, the better we shall like it." Zhukov nodded; he saw the desirability of that as plainly as Molotov did. After another nod, he got to his feet. "All right, Comrade General Secretary. We'll continue on the course we've set." A grin spread over his broad peasant features. "And with any luck at all, the Nazis will get the blame."

"Yes, that would break my heart," Molotov said, which made Zhukov laugh out loud. The marshal's salute was unusually sincere. He did a smart about-turn and left the general secretary's office.

Molotov scratched his chin. Little by little, he was, or thought he was, regaining some of the authority he'd had to yield to Marshal Zhukov after the Red Army crushed Beria's abortive coup. He hadn't really tried to exert it; he could have been wrong. One of these days, though, he might have to try. He wouldn't live forever. He didn't want his successor as beholden to the Army as he was. Of course, what he wanted might end up having nothing to do with the way things turned out.

His secretary stuck his head into the office. "Your next appointment is here, Comrade General Secretary," he said. "It's—"

"I know who it is, Pyotr Maksimovich," Molotov snapped. "I do keep track of these things, you know. Send him in."

"Yes, Comrade General Secretary." His secretary retreated in a hurry, which was what Molotov had in mind.

David Nussboym came into the office. "Good day, Comrade General Secretary."

"Good day, David Aronovich," Molotov answered automatically. Then even his legendary impassivity cracked. "Sit down. Take it easy. Here, I will get you some tea." As he rose to do that, he added, "How are you feeling?"

"I have been better," Nussboym allowed. He sounded as battered as he looked. The last time Molotov had seen him—when he'd given Nussboym permission to go into Poland—the Jewish NKVD man had been thin and bald and nondescript. He was thinner now: skeletally lean. And he was balder: he had not a hair on his head, not even an eyebrow or an eyelash. No Lizard could have had less hair than he did. And he was no longer nondescript, either: with his skin a pasty yellowish white, anyone who saw him would remember him for a long time, though possibly wishing he wouldn't.

"Here." Molotov gave him the tea, into which he'd dumped a lot of sugar. "Would you care for a sweet roll, too?"

"No, thank you, Vyacheslav Mikhailovich." Nussboym shook his head. Even so small a motion seemed to take all his strength. "I'm afraid I still haven't got much in the way of an appetite." His rhythmic Polish accent gave his Russian the appearance of a vitality lacking in truth.

"I had heard you were suffering from radiation sickness," Molotov said, returning to his desk after the unusual show of solicitude, "but I had no idea . . ."

Nussboym's shrug looked effortful, too. "By everything the doctors tell me, I ought to be dead from the dose of radiation I took." He shrugged again. "I'm still here. I intend to be here a while longer. They say I'm a lot likelier now to get cancer later on, but I can't do anything about that, either. Who knows? Maybe I'll beat the odds one more time."

"I hope so," Molotov said, on the whole sincerely. Nussboym hadn't had to get him out of the cell where Beria had imprisoned him, but he'd done it. Afterwards, the NKVD man had been reasonable in the rewards he'd requested. And so Molotov did wish him well. He was useful, after all.

"Thank you," Nussboym said. "In the meantime, I serve the Soviet Union."

"Good." Molotov nodded approval. "Spoken like an Old Bolshevik." Stalin, of course, had purged most of the Old Bolsheviks, the men who'd made the Russian Revolution. At need, Molotov could always purge Nussboym. Knowing that was reassuring. The general secretary went on, "Speak to me of the situation in Poland."

"You will—or you had better—have more up-to-date information than I can give," Nussboym replied. "I've spent most of the past few months on my back with needles and tubes sticking into me."

Molotov had always been a scrawny, even a weedy, little man—which might well have helped keep him safe during Stalin's tenure, for Iosef Vissarionovich hadn't been any too big, either. Despite looking anything but robust, though, he'd always been healthy. The idea of going into a hospital—of entrusting his physical wellbeing to a physician he could not fully control—gave him the cold chills. Doing his best not to think about that, he said, "You were on the spot for some time, and you survived the fighting, which a good many of our operatives did not. And, of course, you are a native of Poland. Your impressions of what is going on there, then, will be of particular value to me."

"You are too kind, Comrade General Secretary," David Nussboym murmured, seeming genuinely moved. "From what I saw, the Jews are solidly behind the Race, which understands that and exploits it. A good many Poles favor independence, but they too—all except for a few fascist madmen or progressive Communists—prefer the Lizards to either the *Reich* or the Soviet Union."

That accorded well with everything Molotov had already heard. He asked, "How much do you think the extensive damage Poland suffered as a result of the fighting will make Poles and Jews resent the Race?"

"There I fear I cannot tell you much." Nussboym gave the Soviet leader a bony grin. "I suffered my own extensive damage too early in the fighting to have an opinion. If you like, though, I will go back to investigate."

"I will think about that," Molotov said. "First, though, you plainly need more recovery time." Had the NKVD man argued with him, he would have sent Nussboym back to Poland right away—no tool was better than one that actively wanted to be used. But David Nussboym didn't argue. That left Molotov a trifle disappointed, though he showed it no more than he showed anything else.

Mordechai Anielewicz lifted a glass of plum brandy in salute. *"L'chaim,"* he said, and then added, "And to life as a whole family."

"Omayn," his wife said. His sons and daughter raised their glasses—even Heinrich had a shot glass' worth of *slivovitz* tonight. Mordechai drank. So did Bertha and their children.

Heinrich hadn't drunk plum brandy more than once or twice before. Then, he'd taken tiny sips. Tonight, imitating his father, he knocked back the whole shot at once. He spluttered and choked a little and turned very red. "Am I poisoned?" he wheezed.

"No." Mordechai did his best not to laugh. "Believe me, you have to drink a lot more *slivovitz* than that to get properly poisoned."

"Mordechai!" Bertha Anielewicz said reprovingly.

But Anielewicz only grinned at his wife—and at Heinrich, whose color was returning to normal. "Besides, if you do drink too much, you don't usually know how poisoned you are till the next morning. You haven't had nearly enough to need to worry about that."

His wife sent him another reproachful look. He pretended not to see it. They'd been married long enough that he could get away with such things every now and then. The look his wife sent him for ignoring the first one warned him he couldn't get away with such things any too often.

His daughter Miriam was old enough to make the more regular acquaintance of *slivovitz*, but she'd had the good sense not to get greedy with what he'd given her. Now she raised her glass, which still held a good deal of the plum brandy. "And here's to Przemysl, for taking us in."

Everybody drank to that—everybody except Heinrich, who had nothing left to drink. The town in southern Poland, not far from the Slovakian border, hadn't been hit too hard in the fighting. And it kept its good-sized Jewish community. Back in 1942, the SS had been on the point of shipping the Jews to an extermination camp, but local *Wehrmacht* officials hadn't let it happen—the Jews were doing important labor for them. And then the Lizards had driven the Nazis out of Poland, and Przemysl's Jews survived.

Thinking of *Wehrmacht* men who'd been, if not decent, then at least pragmatic, made Mordechai also think of Johannes Drucker. He said, "I wonder if the German space pilot ever found his kin."

"I hope so," his wife said. "After all, his wife and children are part Jewish, too."

"No matter how little they like it." That was David, Mordechai's older son.

"He wasn't the worst of fellows," Anielewicz said. "I've

known plenty of Germans worse, believe me." He used an emphatic cough.

"His own family helped remind him what being a human being meant." David was, at fifteen, convinced everything came in one of two colors: black or white. What he said here, though, probably held a lot of truth.

Bertha Anielewicz said, "He'll go his way, we'll go ours, and with any luck at all we'll never have anything to do with each other again. Odds are good, anyhow." That also probably held a lot of truth.

Before Mordechai could say so, Pancer walked up to him and said, "Beep!" The beffel stretched up toward him, extending its forelegs as far as they would go. That, he'd learned, meant it wanted to be scratched. He obliged. The beffel might have been hatched on Home, but it got on better with humans than the Lizards did.

"We should have drunk a toast to Pancer," Heinrich said. "If it weren't for him, we wouldn't all be here now."

Mordechai lifted the bottle of *slivovitz*. "Here, son. Do you want another drink? You can have one." Heinrich hastily shook his head. Anielewicz's grin covered his relief. He would have given the boy one more shot of brandy, but he was just as well pleased that Heinrich didn't want it.

"I'll tell you what I'd drink a toast to," Miriam said with a toss of the head, "and that's a bigger flat."

"This isn't so bad," Mordechai said. "Next to what things were like in Warsaw before the Lizards came, this is paradise."

"And in Lodz," his wife agreed. Their children didn't know how things had been back in the Nazi-created ghettos. That also was all to the good.

Miriam didn't see the benefits of ignorance. "I'm tired of sleeping on a cot here in the front room," she said, and tossed her head again.

"We're all sleeping on cots," Mordechai pointed out. "Your brothers are in one bedroom, your mother and I in the other, and you have this room here. The only other places for you to sleep are under the shower or on the kitchen table."

"I know that," Miriam said impatiently. "It's why we need a bigger flat."

"It doesn't matter so much," Bertha Anielewicz said. "Everything we used to have went up in smoke. I wish it hadn't—I'd be lying if I said anything different—but we'll get by as long as we've got each other."

Miriam started to say something, then visibly thought better of it. Anielewicz wondered what it would have been. Maybe he was better off not knowing.

But his wife didn't need to wonder. She knew. She wagged a finger at her daughter. "You were going to say we've got altogether too much of each other, weren't you? But that's not so, either. Just remember what things were like in the barracks at that Nazi's farm. Next to that, this is paradise, too."

"We didn't have any choice there, though," Miriam said.

"We don't have any choice here, either, not now," Bertha Anielewicz said. "But be patient for a little while, and we will. If your father hadn't tracked us down, we never would have had any choices there."

"And if Pancer hadn't beeped when he did, so Father heard him, he might never have tracked us down." Heinrich scratched his pet. The scaly little animal wiggled sinuously.

Miriam rolled her eyes. "If you were a *goy*, you'd say that beffel ought to be canonized."

"Pancer deserves it more than some saints I can think of," Heinrich retorted.

"Enough of that," Mordechai Anielewicz said sharply. "The *goyim* can afford to make jokes about us—they outnumber us ten to one. We can't afford to make jokes about them. Even with the Lizards to lean on, it's too dangerous."

His children looked ready to argue about that, too. They were less aware of how dangerous being a small minority could prove than he was. But before the argument could get going, the telephone rang. Bertha was closest to it. "I'll get it," she said, and did. A moment later, she held the handset out to Anielewicz. "For you. A member of the Race."

"Nesseref?" he asked, and his wife shrugged. He took the telephone. "I greet you," he said in the Lizards' language.

"And I greet you," the Lizard replied. "I am Odottoss, liaison officer between the Race's military and your Tosevite forces here in Poland. We have spoken before."

"Truth," Anielewicz agreed. "Shuttlecraft Pilot Nesseref was kind enough to give me your name. I thank you for the assistance you were able to give my mate and my hatchlings and me."

"You are welcome," Odottoss replied. "You and your fighters

have served the Race well. It is only fair that you should have some recompense for that service."

"Again, I thank you. And now, superior sir, what can I do for you?" He did not for a moment believe the male of the Race had called merely to throw bouquets at him.

And he was right, for Odottoss inquired, "Do you know the whereabouts of the explosive-metal bomb you Jews have claimed to have since the end of the first round of fighting?"

"At the moment, I do not know that, no," Mordechai admitted. "Since the recent fighting against the *Reich*, I have been concerned with other things. Till now, no one has mentioned any problems with this explosive-metal bomb."

"I do not know that there are any," Odottoss said. "But I do not know that there are none, either. As best the Race has been able to determine, the bomb is not where we formerly thought it was. Have you ordered its transfer?"

"Have I personally? No," Anielewicz said. "But that does not mean other Jewish fighters may not have given such an order. For that matter, we never wanted the Race to know where we keep it."

"I understand your reasons for that," Odottoss said. "You will understand, I hope, our reasons for seeking this knowledge."

"I suppose so." Anielewicz tried not to sound grudging, but it wasn't easy.

"Very well, then," the Lizard said. "If this bomb has been moved clandestinely, you will also understand our concern about where it is now and to what use it may be put." Clandestinely moving the explosive-metal bomb wasn't easy. Mordechai wondered how well Odottoss understood that. The device weighed about ten tonnes. The Germans had just been learning how to make such bombs in 1944. They'd got better since.

But even that old, primitive weapon would be devastating if it went off. Anielewicz wasn't sure it could detonate. He also wasn't sure it couldn't. He realized there were too many things about which he wasn't sure. "I shall do my best to find out what is going on here, superior sir," he said.

"And then you will report to me?" Odottoss asked.

"I may not give you much detail," Mordechai said. "If I find nothing much has gone wrong, but that the bomb was moved for security reasons during the fighting, I would just as soon have its whereabouts stay secret from the Race."

"I understand," Odottoss replied. "I do not approve, mind you, but I understand. Arrangements in Poland have been so irregular for so long, one more irregularity probably will not hurt much. But I would appreciate learning that the bomb is safe and is in responsible hands."

"That is a bargain," Anielewicz said. "If I learn that, I will tell you. Farewell."

After he hung up, Bertha asked, "What was that all about? You speak the Lizards' language a lot better than I do." Once Mordechai had explained, she said, "You don't know where the bomb is, either? It's not a good thing to lose."

"I know." Mordechai started to reach for the phone, then checked himself. "I'd better not call from here. If the Lizards know where I am, I have to assume they're tapping the line. Why make things easy for them?"

He needed several days before he could get hold of Yitzkhak, one of the Jews up in Glowno who'd had charge of the bomb, on a line he reckoned secure. They spent a couple of minutes congratulating each other on being alive. Then Yitzkhak said, "I suppose you're calling about the package." Even on a secure line, he didn't want to come right out and talk about an explosive-metal bomb.

Mordechai didn't blame him. "Yes, as a matter of fact, I am," he answered. "Somebody's worried that it might get delivered to the wrong address. The post's gone to pot lately, and everybody knows it."

"Well, that's true. Actually, I'm afraid it could happen." Yitzkhak was precise to the point of fussiness. If he said he was afraid, he meant it. "The people who took charge of it during the confusion are pretty careless, and they may try to deliver it themselves."

"Oy!" That was about the worst news Moishe could imagine. Who had got hold of the bomb during the fighting? Had some of David Nussboym's NKVD henchmen spirited it off toward Russia, or would some Jewish hotheads try to give the Greater German *Reich* one last kick while it was down? Mordechai phrased the question somewhat differently: "Has it headed east or west?"

"West, I think," Yitzkhak answered.

"Oy!" Anielewicz repeated. If a bomb went off in Germany now, would the Nazis reckon themselves betrayed and try to

retaliate? Did they have anything left with which they *could* retaliate? He suspected they would and could. With a sigh, he said, "I suppose we have to try to get it back." He paused. "Dammit."

Tao Sheng-Ming came up to Liu Han and Liu Mei with his shaved head gleaming and with an impudent grin on his face. "I greet you, superior female," the devil-boy said in the language of the little scaly devils. "Give me an order. Whatsoever you may request, it shall be done."

Liu Han stuck to Chinese: "Suppose I order you not to be so absurd?" But she shook her head. "No. That would be foolish. No good officer gives an order knowing it will be disobeyed."

Tao bowed as if she'd paid him a great compliment. "You give me too much credit," he said, still in the scaly devils' tongue. "All I aim to be is the biggest nuisance possible."

"Do you mean to the little devils or to the People's Liberation Army?" Liu Han's voice was dry.

"Why, both, of course," Tao Sheng-Ming answered. "Life would be boring if we all did exactly what we were supposed to all the time."

"That is a truth," Liu Mei said. "A little unpredictability is an asset." She also used the little devils' language, as if to show solidarity with Tao Sheng-Ming.

Liu Han thought her daughter's response entirely predictable. Liu Mei was fond of the devil-boy. Liu Han wondered what, if anything, would come of that. Nothing at all would come of it if Tao didn't pay more attention to what came out of his mouth before he opened it. "If you do not precisely obey the orders of your superiors, you will find yourself purged as an unreliable," she warned him. "That would be unfortunate."

"I would certainly think so," Tao Sheng-Ming said. He had trouble taking anything seriously, even the Chinese Communist Party.

Liu Mei might have been fond of him, but she was a dedicated revolutionary. "You must obey the dictates of the Party, Tao," she said seriously. "It is our only hope against the unbridled imperialism of the little scaly devils."

He drew himself up, as if affronted. "I did not come to your roominghouse to argue politics," he said. "I came to find out how things were going, and what I could do to help them go."

"Do you think no one will tell you when the time comes?" Liu

Han demanded. "Do you think you will be left on the sidewalk standing around when the revolutionary struggle begins anew?"

"Well, no," he admitted, using Chinese for the first time— perhaps out of embarrassment. "But I am not a mah-jongg tile, to be played by somebody else. I am my own person, and I want to know what I am doing, and why."

Liu Mei spoke to her mother: "He sounds more like an American than a proper Chinese."

That held some truth. Liu Han chose not to acknowledge it. She said, "He sounds like a foolish young man who thinks he is more important than he is." She didn't want to anger Tao Sheng-Ming too much, so she tempered that by adding, "He is important to a degree, though, and he will—I assure you, he *will*—learn what he's supposed to know when he's supposed to know it."

Unabashed, Tao said, "But I want to know more, and I want to know sooner."

"I will tell you what you need to know, not what you want to know," Liu Han said. "What you need to know is, soon we will rise against the little scaly devils. When we do, you and your fellow devil-boys will help lure them to destruction. They will trust you more than they would trust other human beings. You will make them pay for their mistake."

"Yes!" Tao Sheng-Ming said, and used an emphatic cough. His eyes glowed with anticipation.

Liu Han anticipated that most of the devil-boys assigned to mislead the little scaly devils would pay the price for their deception. She said nothing about that. If Tao Sheng-Ming didn't see it for himself, he would perform better as a result of his ignorance.

When she thought about such tactics, she sometimes knew brief shame. But it was only brief, because she remained convinced the struggle against the imperialist little devils was more important than any individual's fate.

"I need to tell you one other thing," Tao said. "Some of the scaly devils are beginning to suspect that something may be going on. They are talking about making moves of some kind. My fellow devil-boys and I do not know as much about that as we would like, because they quiet down around us. They know a lot of us speak their language, and they do not want us overhearing."

"That is not good," Liu Mei said.

"No, it's not," Liu Han agreed. "The knife has two edges. The little devils trust the devil-boys because they know the devil-boys imitate their ways. But they also know the devil-boys understand what they say. We need to send out more ordinary Chinese who know their language and hope the scaly devils will be indiscreet around them."

"You will know the people who can arrange that. I hope you will know those people, anyway," Tao Sheng-Ming said. "I've tried to tell some people with higher rank than mine, but they don't take me seriously. After all, I'm only a devil-boy. I'm funny-looking, and I have strange ideas—and if you don't be-lieve me, just ask anybody from the People's Liberation Army." He didn't try to hide his bitterness. What he did do, a moment later, was swagger around like a pompous general who was round in the belly and empty in the head.

Liu Mei laughed and clapped her hands. Liu Han laughed, too; she couldn't help herself. She tried to put reproof in her voice as she said, "I am from the People's Liberation Army, Tao, and so are you." She tried to put reproof in her voice, yes, but she heard herself failing.

"We're with the People's Liberation Army, yes, but we're not old men who haven't had a new thought since the last emperor ruled China," Tao answered with the ready scorn of the young. Liu Mei nodded emphatically. Why not? She was young, too.

Liu Han wasn't so young any more, as her body and some-times her spirit kept reminding her. But she knew the kind of people Tao Sheng-Ming meant. She hoped she wasn't one of those people. "I'm on the Central Committee," she said. "I can make people listen to me." She lowered her voice: "Besides, things *will* start to happen before very long." Tao's face lit up. That was the kind of news he wanted to hear.

Liu Han did have the rank to get Tao's message noted. She hoped that would do the cause some good. One thing it did was get the date for the start of the operation moved forward again. That made Liu Mei clap her hands once more. She wanted ac-tion. Liu Han wanted action, too, but not at the cost of striking before the People's Liberation Army was ready. Success was a long shot even if they struck when the People's Liberation Army was ready. Everyone on the Central Committee understood that. No one seemed willing to admit it, not out loud.

When the Second World War started in Europe, back in the

dim dark days before the little scaly devils came, the Germans had staged a border incident to give themselves an excuse to go to war against Poland. The Germans were fascists, of course, but Mao admired the stratagem: it turned the *Wehrmacht* loose exactly when its leaders wanted it to move.

Borrowing from the Germans' book, Mao arranged for an incident in the railroad yards in the southwestern part of Peking. Liu Han wasn't far away. When she heard the first gunshots ring out after sudden provocation from the devil-boys turned unbearable, she spoke one word into a radio: "Now." Then she shut it off and took herself elsewhere, lest the little devils trace the transmission. That one word was the signal for riots to break out around the railroad yards, too, in carefully chosen places.

As the planners in the People's Liberation Army had been sure they would, Chinese policemen—tools of the imperialist scaly devils—came rushing from all over Peking to quell those secondary riots. And they rushed straight into withering machine-gun fire: those emplacements had been sited and manned for a couple of days, and covered the likely routes of approach.

The Chinese police reeled back in dismay. Watching from a third-story window, Liu Han hugged herself with glee. The scaly devils' running dogs weren't soldiers, and couldn't hope to hold their own in a fight against soldiers. Now that they'd discovered they couldn't hope to put down the rioters, what would they do? *Call in the little devils themselves, of course,* Liu Han thought, and hugged herself again.

As usual, the little scaly devils wasted no time in responding. They *were* soldiers, and formidable soldiers at that. Three of their mechanized fighting vehicles, machines identical to the one in which Liu Han, her daughter, and Nieh Ho-T'ing had left the prison camp, rattled past her, guided toward the trouble—and toward ruination—by a couple of devil-boys. But they didn't rattle very far. Barricades had already started going up. When the machines tried to bull them aside, the obstacles proved to have surprisingly solid cores.

Chinese rushed out from houses and storefronts to heave bottles of burning gasoline at the mechanized fighting vehicles. Liu Han had never learned why those were called Molotov cocktails, but they were. Two of the vehicles quickly caught fire. The third one sprayed death all around with its light cannon and with the scaly devils shooting from the firing ports set into the sides of the machine. Fighters fell one after another. At last, though, the third vehicle started burning, too, and the little devils inside had to bail out or be roasted. They lasted only moments outside their armored shell.

Columns of smoke began rising into the sky all over Peking. Liu Han nodded in sober satisfaction as she watched them sprout. Now the little scaly devils would really know they had an insurrection on their hands. What would they do next, now that their mechanized fighting vehicles were having trouble? *Send in the landcruisers, of course,* Liu Han thought. Landcruisers were the bludgeon they'd used to retake Peking after the last progressive uprising.

Sure enough, here came a pair of them, with infantrymales skittering along beside them spraying gunfire to keep would-be flingers of Molotov cocktails from getting close enough to harm them. Some of the little devils fighting on foot went down. The rest stayed with the landcruisers. They were brave. Liu Han wished she could have denied them that virtue—and many others.

But the landcruisers got a surprise not long after they rolled past the burnt-out hulks of the mechanized fighting vehicles and shouldered aside the barricades that had stalled the lesser machines. Spewing tails of fire, antilandcruiser missiles manufactured by the *Reich* slammed into their relatively thin side armor. They brewed up, flame belching from their turrets.

"See how you like that!" Liu Han shouted. The Russians wouldn't give rockets they made themselves, but they were willing to supply plenty of these.

And, when a helicopter thuttered by overhead, another missile swatted it out of the sky. Liu Han whooped again. If the little scaly devils thought they were going to keep China forever, if they thought they could get away with ruling over a people who yearned to rule themselves, some reeducation for them was in order. The People's Liberation Army would provide it.

"I give you the option of declining this flight, Shuttlecraft Pilot," the female in the monitor told Nesseref. "Missiles have been fired at shuttlecraft attempting to land in the subregion known as China. Shuttlecraft have been damaged. Two, I am sorry to report, have been destroyed."

Nesseref wondered how much truth that held. If the dispatcher admitted two shuttlecraft destroyed, how many more had gone down in flaming ruin? Nevertheless, she said, "Superior female, I will accept the mission. I have seen the aftermath of fighting here in Poland. We must maintain control of the areas of Tosev 3 where we presently rule."

"I thank you for your display of public spirit," the dispatcher said. "Many from the colonization fleet in particular have seemed reluctant to accept any personal risk in maintaining our position on Tosev 3."

"I find that unfortunate," Nesseref said. "It lends truth to the disparaging comments certain males of the conquest fleet have been known to make about us colonists. Tosev 3 is now our world, too."

"Exactly so." The other female made the affirmative gesture, then turned one eye turret toward a monitor other than the one in which she was speaking with Nesseref. "Report to your shuttlecraft port at once. The male you are transporting to China will be waiting there for you."

"It shall be done," Nesseref said, and broke the connection. She didn't leave her apartment quite *at once*. First, she made sure Orbit had enough food and water to last him till her expected return, and for some little while after that, too. "Behave yourself while I am gone," she told the tsiongi. He yawned in lordly disdain, as if to say she had no business telling him what to do.

She couldn't wait for the regularly scheduled transport to the shuttlecraft port. That meant she had to hire a Big Ugly to drive her there. In her experience, Tosevites in motorcars were more dangerous than members of the Race in shuttlecraft, but she survived the journey and gave her driver enough of the metal disks the locals used as currency to keep him happy.

One of the males in charge of maintaining shuttlecraft hurried up to her. He pointed to the machine waiting on the concrete. "You are fully fueled, and your oxygen supply is also full. We have thoroughly checked the shuttlecraft. I assure you, everything is as it should be."

"I thank you for your care." As always, Nesseref would make her own checks before she let her fingerclaw press the launch control. She asked, "Is my passenger ready? He had better be, seeing how urgently I was sent here."

"Here he comes now," the technician answered, pointing with

his tongue toward the blockhouse by the broad concrete expanse of the landing area. And, sure enough, another male hurried up to the technician and Nesseref.

"I greet you, superior sir," Nesseref told him, for his body paint was a good deal more ornate than hers.

"And I greet you, Shuttlecraft Pilot," he answered. "I am Relhost. I have considerable experience in fighting Big Uglies, both in full-scale combat against organized forces and in battle against irregulars. I am given to understand the situation in China combines elements of both combat modes."

"All right, superior sir." Nesseref didn't need to know anything about Relhost's expertise. She assumed he had it; if not, he wouldn't have been sent to China. She started for the shuttlecraft. Relhost followed. She climbed the mounting ladder and took her place in the pilot's seat. Relhost strapped himself into the passenger's seat with a familiarity that showed he'd flown in a shuttlecraft a good many times before.

"Must we give the SSSR notice that we will be flying over its territory?" Relhost asked.

"I am afraid so, superior sir," Nesseref answered. "Permission is routine, but the Big Uglies are touchy about being informed of our flights. And we are required to treat their independent not-empires as if they were our equals."

"I understand," Relhost said with a sigh. "But the SSSR shares an ideology with the Chinese Big Uglies. The rebels will thus learn of our flight as soon as we launch, if they do not already know of it. They may well be waiting for us on our arrival."

"Nothing to be done about that, superior sir," Nesseref said. She radioed the blockhouse: "Are we cleared for launch?"

"You are, Shuttlecraft Pilot," came the reply. Nesseref's eye turrets swiveled, checking all the gauges one last time. Everything was as it should have been. She would have been astonished were it otherwise, but she did not want astonishment of that sort. Her fingerclaw stabbed at the launch control. The motor roared to life beneath her. Acceleration shoved her back in her seat.

It was, of course, only a suborbital hop, perhaps a quarter of the way around Tosev 3. After the motor cut off—precisely on schedule—they had a brief stretch of weightlessness before Nesseref would have to begin preparations for landing.

Relhost sighed. "Now to see what new horrible tricks the Big

Uglies have devised to drive us mad. I commanded the attack on Chicago, over on the lesser continental mass, back during the first winter of the fighting. The conditions were terrible, and the American Big Uglies struck hard at our flanks. They threw us back. It was then that we really knew what a desperate struggle we would have before we could make this world our own."

"We still have not made it our own." Nesseref was perhaps less diplomatic than she might have been.

"No, we have not," Relhost agreed. "But whatever else we do, we cannot allow a rebellious area to break away from our control. That would be an open invitation to Tosevites all over the planet to try to break away from us."

"That is probably a truth." Nesseref corrected herself before her high-ranking passenger could correct her: "No, that is certainly a truth."

A Tosevite voice came from the radio receiver: "Shuttlecraft of the Race, this is Akmolinsk Control. Your trajectory is acceptable. You are warned not to maneuver over the territory of the peace-loving workers and peasants of the Soviet Union, or we shall be forced to respond vigorously to your aggression."

"Acknowledged, Akmolinsk Control," Nesseref said, and then turned off the transmitter with quite unnecessary violence. To Relhost, she added, "I grow very tired of the arrogance the Big Uglies display."

"As do we all, Shuttlecraft Pilot," the officer answered. "And they display less than they feel—in Akmolinsk, our name is cursed, as it is over much of the planet. They truly do believe they are our equals, as you said. Reeducating them will require generations: like their preposterous superstitions, their political ideologies have taken deep root among them. Sooner or later, though, we shall succeed."

"May it be so," Nesseref said. "And now, superior sir, if you will excuse me . . ." She examined the plot of the actual trajectory as measured against the planned one, and authorized the computer to make the small burns necessary to bring the one into conformity with the other. "We should be landing soon."

As if to confirm that, a member of the Race came on the radio: "Shuttlecraft, we have you on radar. Trajectory for the shuttlecraft port outside Peking is acceptable."

"How nice," Nesseref said, acid in her voice. "The Big Uglies in the SSSR told me exactly the same thing."

"Be glad they did," answered the controller at the shuttlecraft port. "They can be most difficult, even dangerous, if your trajectory varies in any way from that which is planned. You will no doubt know this for yourself. But, speaking of dangerous, I will tell you something the Big Uglies in the SSSR did not: be extremely alert in your descent. Tosevite rebels are active in the area, and are equipped with missiles homing on radar and on the heat emissions of your engine as you brake for landing."

"And what do I do if they launch one of these missiles at me?" Nesseref asked.

"You do the best you can, Shuttlecraft Pilot," the controller answered. "In that case, you discover how good a pilot you truly are, and how well you have studied and practiced the manual overrides. Shuttlecraft computers are not programmed to operate on the assumption that something is trying to shoot them down."

"Here on Tosev 3, they should be," Nesseref said indignantly.

"As may be, Shuttlecraft Pilot," the controller said. "Perhaps they will be, at some time in the future. For the present, good luck. Out."

Relhost waggled an eye turret in an ironic way. "Good luck, Shuttlecraft Pilot."

"I thank you so very much, superior sir," Nesseref said.

Her own eye turrets went to the manual controls. Of course she'd put in endless simulator practice with them. But how seriously had she taken it? How well could she fly the shuttlecraft on her own? And, if something happened to her, who would take care of Orbit? Mordechai Anielewicz, perhaps? No. He had a beffel. The two animals wouldn't get along. Nesseref hoped she wouldn't have to find out the answers to any of her questions.

But, even as the computer activated the braking rocket for final descent into the shuttlecraft port, she kept an anxious eye turret on the radar screen. And so the controller's shout of alarm in the radio was not a warning, only a distraction. "I can see it," she snarled. "Now shut up."

Her fingerclaw stabbed the manual override control. She didn't adjust the burn right away, but eyed the radar and the displays around it for data on the missile's performance. That was alarmingly good. Whatever she was going to do, she didn't have long to do it.

Relhost said, "I suggest, Shuttlecraft Pilot, that you do not waste time."

"You shut up, too," Nesseref hissed, a moment later absently adding, "superior sir."

She would have only one chance. She saw as much. If she maneuvered too soon, that cursed missile would follow and knock her down. If she maneuvered too late, she wouldn't get the chance to maneuver at all. She checked her fuel gauge. She would worry about that later, too. Now . . .

Now her fingerclaw hit the motor control, giving her maximum thrust and, in effect, relaunching her. The missile had only begun to pull up when it burst a little below the shuttlecraft. Shrapnel fragments pattered off her ship. Some of them didn't patter off—some pierced it. Alarm lights came on.

Nesseref gave control back to the computer. She hoped she had enough fuel to brake again. If she didn't, the Big Uglies who'd launched the missile would win even if they hadn't disabled her. She also hoped with all her liver that they had no more missiles to launch. She'd been lucky once—she thought she'd been lucky. She doubted she could manage it twice.

"Well done," Relhost said.

"I hope so," Nesseref answered. Fuel alarms weren't hissing at top volume, so maybe she would be able to get down in one piece. She went on, "You had better help suppress these rebels, superior sir. Otherwise, I will be very disappointed in you." She granted herself the luxury of an emphatic cough.

When David Goldfarb came into the office of the Saskatchewan River Widget Works, Ltd., he found Hal Walsh there before him. That was nothing out of the ordinary; he often thought Walsh lived at the office. The music blaring out of a *skelkwank*-disk player was a different matter. It was a song by a quartet of shaven-headed young Englishmen who called themselves, perhaps from their appearance, the Beetles.

As far as David was concerned, they made noise, not music. His boss, most of a generation younger, loved it. So did a lot of people Walsh's age; the Beetles were, in Goldfarb's biased opinion, much more popular than they had any business being. Walsh was singing along at the top of his lungs when Goldfarb walked in.

Since Walsh couldn't carry a tune in a pail, he didn't improve the music, if that was what it was. He did have the grace to stop, and even to look a little shamefaced. Better yet, at least from David's point of view, he turned down the player.

"Good morning," he said in the relative quiet thus obtained.

"Good morning," Goldfarb answered. If Walsh wanted to play Beetles music at top volume, Goldfarb knew he couldn't do much about it except look for another job. He didn't care to do that, and his boss didn't usually go out of his way to make the office miserable for him.

"I just wanted you to know, I'm the happiest fellow in the world right now," Hal Walsh said. "I asked Jane to marry me last night, and she said she would."

"Congratulations! No wonder you're singing—if that's what you want to call it." David stuck out his hand. Walsh pumped it. Goldfarb went on, "That's wonderful news—really terrific."

"*I* think so," his boss said, tacking on a Lizard-style emphatic cough. "And just think—if you hadn't cut your finger, I probably never would have met her."

"Life's funny that way," Goldfarb agreed. "You never can tell how something that seems little will end up changing everything. If you'd missed a phone call you ended up getting, or hadn't got out of your motorcar five minutes before a drunk smashed it to scrap metal . . ."

"I know." Walsh nodded vigorously. "It almost tempts you to wonder if bigger things work the same way. What if the French had won on the Plains of Abraham? Or if the Lizards hadn't come? Or any of a dozen more things that occur to me in the blink of an eye?"

"I hadn't thought about it like that," David said. The mere idea made him open his eyes very wide. Thinking about changes in your life was one thing. You could see where, if things had happened differently or if you'd chosen differently, what happened next wouldn't have stayed the same, either. But trying to imagine the same phenomenon on a larger level, trying to imagine the whole world changing because something had happened differently . . . He shook his head. "Too big an idea for me to get my brain around so early in the morning."

"You should read more science fiction," Hal Walsh said. "Actually, that's not the worst thing for somebody in our line of work to do anyhow. It goes a long way toward helping people think lefthanded, if you know what I mean. The more adaptable your mind is, the better the chance you have of coming up with something new and strange while you're working with Lizard electronics."

"I suppose there's something to that," Goldfarb admitted. "I used to read the American magazine called *Astounding*, back before the Lizards came. But it stopped getting across the Atlantic then, and I lost the habit."

"They still print it," Walsh said. "You can find it in the magazine counter at any drugstore here." That was an Americanism David had taken a while to get used to; because he was so accustomed to *chemist's*, the new word struck him as faintly sinister. His boss went on, "The issues from back before the war would be worth a pretty penny, if you've still got any of them."

"Not likely," Goldfarb answered. "Where are the snows of yesteryear?"

"Here in Edmonton, they're liable to still be stacked up in the odd places, waiting to get shoveled away," Walsh answered. "Still, though, I do take your point."

The door opened. In strolled Jack Devereaux. He was never late, but he never looked as if he hurried, either. "Hello, all," he said, and went to get himself a cup of tea. "What's on the agenda for today?"

"Cut and try," David Goldfarb said. "A lot of bad language when things don't go the way we want. Nothing too much out of the ordinary." He noticed Hal Walsh taking a deep breath and, with malice aforethought, forestalled him: "Oh, and Hal's getting married. Like I said, nothing important."

That won him the glare he'd hoped he would get from his boss. It also won him a raised eyebrow from Devereaux. "Really?" the other engineer asked Hal Walsh.

"Yes, really," Walsh said, still giving David a sour look. "I asked Jane, and she was rash enough to tell me she would." That sounded as if he was doing some forestalling of his own.

"Well, that's the best news I've heard this morning," the French-Canadian engineer said. "Of course, up till now I hadn't heard much in the way of news this morning, so I don't know exactly what that proves."

"Thank you so much," Walsh said. "I'll remember you in my nightmares."

Still helpfully slanderous, Goldfarb said, "He's been blaming me—and you, too, because I cut my finger on that sheet metal when I was giving you a hand. If I hadn't done that, he wouldn't have had to take me to the doctor, and she'd still be a happy woman today."

He supposed he would, one of these days, have to let Moishe Russie know Reuven's former lady friend would be tying the knot. He wondered how Reuven would take that. His second cousin once removed hadn't wanted to stay with Dr. Jane Archibald. As far as David was concerned, that meant very poor eyesight on his younger cousin's part, but he couldn't do anything about it. He wondered if Reuven had found anyone else after Dr. Archibald left Palestine. Maybe Moishe would tell him.

Meanwhile, he had plenty of work here. He and Devereaux were still refining the design of that speedy new *skelkwank*-light disk player. He had a side project of his own, too, one that was nothing but a few sketchy notes at the moment but that he hoped would prove important one of these days. Hal Walsh knew he was working on something there, but didn't yet know what it was. Walsh made a good boss. He didn't insist on finding out every last detail of what was in his employees' minds. Goldfarb hoped his notion would reward the younger man's confidence in him.

Between the disk player and his own idea—with time out for lunch, and for odd bits of banter through the day—his hours at the Saskatchewan River Widget Works went by so fast, he was startled when he realized he could go home. He was also startled to see how dark it had got by the time he went outside, and how chilly the breeze from the northwest was. Autumn was here. Winter wouldn't wait very long—and winter in Edmonton, he'd already seen, had more in common with Siberia than with anything the British Isles knew by that name.

Naomi greeted him with a kiss when he got home. "You've got a letter here from London," she said.

"Have I?" he said. "From whom?"

"I don't know," his wife answered. "Not a handwriting I recognize. Here—see for yourself." She handed him the envelope.

He didn't recognize the handwriting, either, though it had a tantalizing familiarity. "Let's find out," he said, and tore open the envelope. His voice had gone grim. So had Naomi's face. She had to be thinking the same thing he was: wondering what Basil Roundbush had to say to him.

"Oh!" they both exclaimed at the same time. Naomi amplified that: "You haven't heard from Jerome Jones for a while."

"So I haven't," Goldfarb agreed. "Better him than some other people I'd just as soon not name."

"Much better," his wife agreed. "We'd still be in Northern Ireland if it weren't for his help, and I always thought he was rather a nice chap from what I remember of him during the first round of fighting."

"Did you?" David asked in a peculiar, toneless way.

"Yes, I did." Naomi stuck out her tongue at him. "Not like that, though." She made as if to poke him in the ribs. "What does the letter say? I've been waiting since the postman brought it."

"Curiosity killed the cat," Goldfarb said, at which his wife *did* poke him in the ribs. He threw his hands in the air. "Give over! I surrender. Here, I'll read it. 'Dear David,' he says, 'I trust this finds you and your lovely wife and family well and flourishing.' "

"No wonder I liked him," Naomi remarked.

"Yes, he always did have a smooth line. A lot of girls fell for it," David said, which got him a dirty look. He held up the letter and went on, " 'I am doing as well as can be expected for one with such a dissolute past. You may perhaps be interested to learn that a certain unfriend of yours has had his own unsavoury past, or something of the sort, catch up with him—so it would appear, at any rate.' "

He looked up from the page. His wife made little pushing motions. "Don't stop," she said. "For God's sake, go on."

"I love it when you talk to me like that," David said, which made Naomi give him a good push—exactly what he'd had in mind. "Oh," he went on. "The letter. I thought you meant something else." He glanced down at it. "Where was I? Oh, yes . . . 'A certain—often a very certain, by all indications—Group Captain Roundbush is in hospital and not expected to pull through, the brakes to his Bentley having failed whilst he was negotiating a curve at a high turn of speed. Signs are that his brakes were encouraged to fail. "A highly professional job," someone from Scotland Yard writes on a report that just chanced to cross my desk.' "

"I wish I could say I was sorry," Naomi said at last.

"So do I," Goldfarb agreed. "But I can't, because I'm not. There's a bit more here: 'Not everyone is altogether displeased at this development, because his faction had close ties to the *Reich*, and the *Reich*, being more radioactive than not these days, is no longer seen as our stalwart bulwark against the Lizards. What our stalwart bulwark against the Lizards shall be now, I have no idea, but seeing Roundbush hoisted by his own hooked-cross petard doubtless pleases you more. As ever, Jerome.' " Goldfarb kissed his wife. "And do you know what, sweetheart? He's right." He kissed her again.

☆ 16 ☆

Kassquit stooped slightly to look at herself in the mirror. She made the affirmative gesture. Maybe the wild Tosevites weren't so daft to let their hair grow after all. She liked the way it framed her face. True, it did make her look less like a female of the Race, but she worried less about that than she had before she started meeting wild Big Uglies. She no longer saw any point to denying her biological heritage. It was part of her, no matter how much she still sometimes regretted that.

She looked down at herself. She was also growing hair under her arms and at the joining of her legs. That last patch still perplexed her. In long-ago days, had such little tufts of hair helped Tosevites' semi-intelligent ancestors find one another's reproductive organs? Animals both on Home and here on Tosev 3 often used such displays. Maybe this was another one. Kassquit couldn't think of any other purpose the hair might serve.

The telephone hissed, distracting her. "Junior Researcher Kassquit speaking," she said. "I greet you." She sometimes startled callers who knew she was an expert on Big Uglies but were unaware she was of Tosevite descent herself.

But this time the startlement went the other way. The image that appeared in her monitor was that of a Big Ugly—and not just any Big Ugly. "And I greet you, superior female," Jonathan Yeager said formally. Then he twisted his face into the Tosevite expression of amiability and went on, "Hello, Kassquit. How are you? It is good to see you again."

Her own face showed little. By the nature of things, it couldn't show much. Considering how she felt, that was probably just as well. Her voice, however, was another matter. She made it as cold as she could: "What do you want?"

"I wanted to say hello," he answered. "I wanted to say it face

459

to face. I fear I made you unhappy when I told you I was going to enter into a permanent mating arrangement—*to get married,* we say in English—with Karen Culpepper. I arranged this call from the Race's consulate here in Los Angeles to apologize to you."

Sudden hope leaped in her. "To apologize for entering into this arrangement with the Tosevite female?"

"No," Jonathan Yeager answered. "I am not sorry about that. But I am sorry if I did make you unhappy. I hope you will believe me when I say I did not intend to." He paused, then pointed at her from the screen. "You have let your hair grow since I was up in the starship with you."

"Yes." Kassquit made the affirmative gesture. She forgot—well, almost forgot—to be angry at him as she asked, "What do you think?" The opinions of members of the Race about her appearance meant little to her: they had no proper standards of comparison. Jonathan Yeager, on the other fork of the tongue, did.

"I like it," he said now, and used an emphatic cough. "Hair does usually seem to add to the attractiveness of a female—even though you were attractive before."

"But not so attractive as to keep you from seeking a permanent mating arrangement with this other female." Kassquit could not—and did not bother to—hide her bitterness.

The American Big Ugly who had been her mating partner sighed. "I have known Karen Culpepper for many years. We grew to maturity together. We come from the same culture."

Kassquit, of course, hadn't grown to maturity with anybody. She had no idea what doing so would mean. She suspected she was missing something because of that, but she couldn't do anything about it. For that matter, she sometimes suspected that the way she'd been raised left her missing all sorts of social and emotional development most Big Uglies took for granted, but she couldn't do anything about that, either.

She said, "Would you have found it impossible to stay up here and spend all your time with me?" She hadn't asked him that while he was aboard the starship. She hadn't known how much his leaving would hurt till he'd gone—and then it was too late.

"I am afraid I would," he answered. "Would you have found it impossible to come down to Tosev 3 and spend all your time here?"

"I do not know," she said. "How can I know? I have never experienced the surface of Tosev 3." She sighed. "But I do understand the comparison you are making. It could be that you are speaking a truth."

"I thank you for that," Jonathan Yeager said. "You were, I think, always honest with me. And I did try to be honest with you."

Maybe he had. Back then, though, she hadn't understood everything he'd meant, not down in her liver she hadn't. Did she now? How could she be sure? She couldn't, and knew it. But she understood more now than she had then. She *was* sure of that. With another sigh, she said, "You will do as you will do, and I shall do as I shall do. That is all I can tell you right now."

"It is a truth," the American Big Ugly said, nodding as his kind did to agree. "I wish you well, Kassquit. Please believe that."

"And I . . . wish you well," she replied. That was more true than otherwise—the most she would say about it. She took a deep breath. "Have we anything more to say to each other?"

"I do not think so," Jonathan Yeager said.

"Neither do I." Kassquit broke the connection. Jonathan Yeager's image vanished from her monitor. She sat staring at the screen, waiting for a storm of tears to come. They didn't. Not weeping seemed somehow worse than weeping would have. After a moment, she realized why: she had finally accepted that Jonathan Yeager wouldn't be coming back.

I have to go on, she thought. *Whatever I do, it will have to be in that context. If I seek another wild Big Ugly for sexual pleasure, I shall have to respond to him, not to my memories of Jonathan Yeager.* She wondered how she could do that. She wondered if she could do it. *Of course you can. You have to. You just figured that out for yourself. Have you already started to forget?*

She probably had. Emotional issues arising from sexual matters were far more complex, and far more intense, than any she'd known before Jonathan Yeager came into her life. That, she feared, was also part of her biological heritage. She'd done her best to pretend that heritage didn't exist. Now—she ran a hand across her hairy scalp—she was beginning to accept it. She wondered if that would result in any improvement. All she could do was see what happened next.

What happened next was that the telephone hissed again. "Junior Researcher Kassquit speaking," she said again, seating herself in front of the monitor. "I greet you."

"And I greet you, Kassquit," Ttomalss said. "How are you today?"

"Oh, hello, superior sir." Kassquit did a token job of assuming the position of respect—no more was needed while she was sitting down. Ttomalss might have asked the question as a polite commonplace, but she gave it serious consideration before answering, "All things considered, I am pretty well."

"I am glad to hear it," Ttomalss said. "I was listening to your conversation with Jonathan Yeager. I think you handled it with an emotional maturity to which many wild Big Uglies could only hope to aspire."

"I thank you," Kassquit said. Then, once the words were out of her mouth, she wasn't so sure she thanked him after all. This time, she spoke with considerable care: "Superior sir, I understand why you monitored my life so closely when I was a hatchling and an adolescent: I was, after all, an experimental subject. But have I not proved your experiment largely successful?"

"There are times when I think you have," her mentor answered. "Then again, there are other times when I think I may have failed despite my best efforts. When I see you imitating wild Tosevites, I do wonder whether environment plays any role at all in shaping an individual's personality."

"I *am* a Tosevite. It cannot be helped," Kassquit said with a shrug. "I am having to come to terms with that myself. But have we not established that I am also a citizen of the Empire, and able to provide important and useful services for the Race? In fact, can I not provide some of those services precisely because I am at the same time a citizen of the Empire and a Big Ugly?"

She waited anxiously to hear how he would respond to that, and felt like cheering when he made the affirmative gesture. "Truth hatches from every word you speak," he replied. "I cannot tell you how delighted I am to discover how seriously you take your obligations as a citizen of the Empire."

"Of course I take them seriously," Kassquit said. "Unlike a good many members of the Race—if I may speak from what I have seen—I take them seriously because I do not take them for granted."

"That is well said," Ttomalss told her. He used an emphatic cough. "Your words could be an example and an inspiration for many males and females of the Race."

"Again, superior sir, I thank you," Kassquit said. "And I am also pleased to have the privileges that come with citizenship in the Empire."

She waited once more. Ttomalss said, "And well you might be. Say what you will for the wild Big Uglies, but you are part of an older, larger, wiser, more sophisticated society than any of theirs."

"I agree, superior sir." Kassquit couldn't smile so that her face knew about it, as a wild Big Ugly could, but she was smiling inside. "And would you not agree, superior sir, that one of the privileges of citizenship is freedom from being arbitrarily spied upon?"

Ttomalss opened his mouth, closed it, and then tried again: "You are not an ordinary citizen of the Empire, you know."

"Am I less than ordinary?" Kassquit asked. "If I am, how am I a citizen at all?"

"No, you are not less than ordinary," Ttomalss said.

Before he could add anything to that, Kassquit pounced: "Then why do you have the right to continue to listen to my conversations?"

"Because you are different from an ordinary citizen of the Empire," Ttomalss answered. "You can hardly deny that difference."

"I do not deny it," she said. "But I do think the time is coming, if it has not already come, when it will not outweigh my need to be able to lead my life as I see fit, not as you reckon best for me."

"Here you are, trying to wound me again," Ttomalss said.

"By no means." Kassquit used the negative gesture. "You are the male who raised me. You have taught me most of what I know. But I have hatched from the egg of immaturity now. If I am a citizen, if I am an adult, I have the right to some life of my own."

"But think of the data the Race would lose!" Ttomalss exclaimed in dismay.

"Am I important to you as an individual, or because of the data you can gain from me?" Even as Kassquit asked the question, she wondered if she wanted to hear the answer.

"Both," Ttomalss replied, and she reflected that he could have said something considerably worse. But even that wasn't good enough, not any more.

"Superior sir," she said, "unless we can reach an understanding, I am going to take a citizen's privilege and seek to gain my privacy, or more of it, through legal means. And, should I learn I am in truth more nearly experimental animal than citizen, I shall have other choices to make. Is that not a truth?" She ended the conversation before Ttomalss could tell her whether he thought it was a truth or not.

"I think we're in business," Glen Johnson said. "By God, I really do think we're in business. We got away with it clean as a whistle."

"Congratulations," Mickey Flynn said. "You've just squeezed maximum mileage from a series of one case."

"Oh, ye of little faith," Johnson said.

"I have a great deal of faith—faith in the capacity of things to go wrong at the worst possible moment," Flynn replied. "Always remember, O'Reilly insisted that Murphy was an optimist."

"He usually is," Johnson agreed. "Usually, but not always."

Flynn shrugged. "If you think you're going to make me give way to unbridled optimism, you can think again. Either that, or you can put on a bridle and go horse around somewhere else."

With a snort more than a little horselike, Johnson said, "I wonder what will happen when the Lizards do find out."

"That depends," Mickey Flynn said gravely.

"Thank you so much." Johnson tacked on not an emphatic cough but another snort. "And on what, pray tell, does it depend, O sage of the age?"

"Vocative case," the other pilot said in something like wonder. "I haven't heard a vocative case, a real, living, breathing vocative case, since I escaped my last Latin class lo these many years ago." Johnson had never heard of the vocative case, but he was damned if he would admit it. Flynn went on, "Well, it could depend on a lot of different things."

"Really? I never would have guessed."

"Hush." Flynn brushed aside his sarcasm like an adult brushing off a five-year-old. He started ticking points off on his fingers: "First off, it depends on how soon the Race does figure out what's going on."

"Okay. That makes sense." Johnson nodded. "If they work that out day after tomorrow, they have a better chance of doing something about it than if they work it out year after next."

"Exactly." Flynn beamed. "You can see after all."

Now Johnson ignored him, persisting in his own train of

thought: "And things will be different depending on whether they find out on their own or if we have to rub their snouts in it."

"This is also true," Flynn agreed. "If the latter, they will probably be trying to rub our noses in things at the same time. That creates the need for a lot of face-washing, or else a mudbath—I mean, a bloodbath. See, for example, the late, not particularly lamented Greater German *Reich*."

Johnson shivered, though the temperature in the *Lewis and Clark* never changed. He felt as if a goose had walked over his grave. "What happened to the *Hermann Göring* could have happened to us this past summer, too. The Lizards made damn sure the Nazis weren't going to get themselves a toehold in the asteroid belt."

"It didn't happen to us because it happened to Indianapolis," Mickey Flynn said. "Thanksgiving is coming before long. Do we give thanks for that, or not?"

"Damned if I know," Johnson said. "But I'll tell you something I heard. Don't know whether it's true, but I'll pass it along anyhow."

"Speak," Flynn urged. "Give forth."

"I've heard," Glen Johnson said in low, conspiratorial tones, "I've heard that the *Christopher Columbus* has some turkeys in the deep freeze, to cook up for a proper Thanksgiving. Turkey." His gaze went reverently heavenward—which gave him nothing but a glimpse of the light fixtures and aluminum paneling on the ceiling of the *Lewis and Clark*'s control room. "Do you remember what it tastes like? I *think* I do."

"I think I do, too, but I wouldn't mind testing my hypothesis experimentally." Flynn raised an eyebrow at Johnson. "If you'd known you'd spend the rest of your days eating beans and beets and barley, you wouldn't have been so eager to stow away, would you?"

"I didn't intend to stow away, God damn it," Johnson said, for about the five hundredth time. "All I wanted to do was get my upper stage repaired and go home, and our beloved commandant hijacked me." He stuck to his story like glue.

"Anyone would think he'd had some reason to be concerned about security," Flynn said. "A preposterous notion, on the face of it."

"I wasn't going to tell anybody, for Christ's sake." That was also part of Johnson's story, and might even have been true.

"Brigadier General Healey, in his infinite wisdom, thought otherwise," Flynn replied. "Who am I, a mere mortal, to imagine that the commandant could ever be mistaken?"

"Who are you, one Irishman, to give another one a hard time?" Johnson shot back.

"Shows what you know," Flynn said. "Quarreling among ourselves is the Irish national sport. Of course, we have been known to put it by—every now and again, mind—when a Sassenach comes along." He fixed Johnson with a mild and speculative gaze, then sighed. "And we've also been known *not* to put it by when a Sassenach comes along. If it weren't for that, I suspect the history of Ireland would have been a good deal happier. A good deal more Irish, too, and less English."

Johnson didn't know much about the history of Ireland or, for that matter, the history of England. He knew the history of the United States from the patriotic lessons drilled into him in high school and from reading in military history since. He said, "The Irish aren't the only ones to quarrel among themselves. My great-grandfathers wore blue. You listen to some of the folks here from Texas or the Carolinas and you'll think the Civil War ended week before last."

"My great-grandfathers wore blue, too," Flynn said. "The Army was the only place that would give them anything close to a fair shake in those days. But over the past hundred years, America's been a dull place. Every time we've fought, it's been against somebody else."

Before Johnson could answer that, the intercom started blaring his name: "Lieutenant Colonel Johnson! Lieutenant Colonel Glen Johnson! Report to the commandant's office immediately!"

"There, you see?" he said, unstrapping himself. "Healey's been spying on us again." He thought he was joking, but he wasn't quite sure.

After swinging his way through the corridors of the *Lewis and Clark* and gliding past Brigadier General Healey's adjutant, he caught himself on the chair across from the commandant's desk, saluted, and said, "Reporting as ordered, sir."

"Yes." Healey's bulldog countenance seldom looked as if it approved of anything. So far as Johnson could remember, the commandant had never looked as if he approved of him. Healey went on, "Have you ever heard of an officer named Sam Yeager?"

"Yes, sir," Johnson answered. "He's the fellow who pretty much wrote the book on the Lizards, isn't he?"

"That's the man." Brigadier General Healey nodded. He leaned forward and glowered at Johnson. "Did you ever meet him?"

"No, sir," Johnson answered. "What's this about, if you don't mind my asking?"

His own bump of curiosity itched. He'd never met Yeager, no, but he'd spoken with him on the phone. Yeager was another loose cannon, a man with a yen to know. Johnson had sometimes wondered if the Lizard expert had tried finding out who'd attacked the ships of the colonization fleet. He said zero, zip, zilch about that to Healey.

"That man is a troublemaker," the commandant said. "You're a troublemaker, too. Birds of a feather, if you know what I mean."

"Sir, that's not birds of a feather," Johnson said. "That's a wild-goose chase."

"Is it?" Healey said. "I wonder. What would you have done, Lieutenant Colonel, if you'd found out that we were the ones who'd attacked the Lizards' colonization fleet?"

"I can't tell you, sir, because I really don't know," Johnson replied.

"That's the wrong answer," Brigadier General Healey growled, spearing him with the perpetually angry gaze. "The right answer is, 'Sir, I wouldn't have said a goddamn thing, not till hell froze over.'"

"What if I'd found out the Russians or the Germans did it, sir?" Johnson asked. "Wouldn't I sing out then?"

"That's different," the commandant said. Before Johnson could ask how it was different, Healey spelled it out: "That's them. This is us. Whoever spilled the beans to the Race has got Indianapolis' blood on his hands, and President Warren's blood, too. If I knew who it was . . ." He'd been out in weightlessness a long time. He could probably never go back to gravity again. If he could, he would without a doubt be permanently weakened. Somehow, none of that seemed to matter much. If he caught the bean-spiller, he *would* do horrible things to him.

"Sir . . ." Johnson said slowly, "are you telling me you think this Yeager was the one who told the Lizards we'd done it?" That fit in with his own speculations unpleasantly well. And Healey had access to a lot more secret information than he did.

"I don't know," the commandant answered, his voice a furious, frustrated rumble. "I just don't know, goddammit. Nobody knows—or if anybody does, he's not talking. But plenty of people want to find out—you can bet your bottom dollar on that. Yeager's a loose cannon. I know that for a fact. He was trying to find out about this place, for instance. I know that for a fact, too."

"Was he?" Johnson knew damn well Yeager was, or had been. He wondered if Lieutenant General Curtis LeMay had raked Yeager over the coals, too. He could hardly ask.

But he thought he got his answer anyhow, for Brigadier General Healey went on, "Whoever ran off at the mouth, he didn't just cost the president's neck, either. A lot of good officers are sitting on the sidelines now. They might have known this or that, and they kept quiet, the way they were supposed to. And what kind of thanks did they get for it? I'll tell you what," Healey said savagely. "They got the bum's rush, that's what. It isn't right."

"Yes, sir," Johnson said, and then, greatly daring, "Sir, did you know anything about what was going on?"

Brigadier General Healey's face was a closed door. "You are dismissed, Lieutenant Colonel," he said, and bent to the papers secured to his desk by rubber bands.

After saluting, Johnson pushed off from the chair and glided out of the commandant's office. He was thinking hard. Healey had done his best to put him together with Sam Yeager and to get him to say he thought Yeager was the one who'd let the Lizards know the USA had attacked their starships.

Johnson shook his head. "I'll be damned if I'll say that," he muttered. He wouldn't have said it even if he thought it true, not without certain proof he wouldn't. He knew one thing, though: he wouldn't have wanted to be in Sam Yeager's shoes, not for all the tea in China.

Sam Yeager brushed his wife's lips with his own and headed for the door. "See you tonight, hon," he said. "Don't know why they want me downtown today, but they do. Have fun with Mickey and Donald."

Barbara rolled her eyes. "I expect I will. They don't pay so much attention to me as they do to you."

"I'm bigger," Sam said. "That probably counts for something.

I've got a deeper voice, too. That would count for something with people. I'm not sure how much it matters to the Lizards. Maybe we ought to try to find out."

"Don't you think we ought to treat them as kids first and guinea pigs second?" Barbara asked.

"Part of me does," Yeager admitted. "The other part's the one that's seen Kassquit. It doesn't matter whether we say we're treating them as kids or as guinea pigs. They'll end up guinea pigs. They can't help it. We don't know enough to raise them the way the Race would."

"I'm not sure the Lizards really raise them at all when they're this young," his wife said. "They just try to keep them from eating one another."

"You may be right," Sam said. "Whether you are or not, though, I've still got to go downtown."

"I know," his wife answered. "Be careful."

"I will. I always am." Sam patted the .45 on his hip. "It's part of my uniform, and I wear it. There aren't all that many people who know about what went on and are dangerous—at least, I hope there aren't. But I'm not taking any chances any which way." Before Barbara could answer, he closed the door and went out to the car.

Driving into the middle of Los Angeles during the morning rush hour reminded him of why he didn't like to do it very often. Fighting his way to a parking space once he got off the freeway hammered the lesson home. And crowding into an elevator to go up to the offices where he worked when he couldn't stay at home added a final unwelcome exclamation point.

Just being here was enough to give him the willies. This was where Lieutenant General LeMay had chewed him out for getting too curious about the space station that became the *Lewis and Clark*. Had LeMay known what all else he was curious about, the lieutenant general would have chewed him out a lot harder.

Sam grimaced and walked a little straighter. He was still here, while Curtis LeMay didn't work for the U.S. Army any more. There was a small cadre of high-ranking officers—formerly high-ranking officers—who didn't work for the U.S. Army any more. None of them had ever said a word in the papers about why they didn't work for the Army any more. Yeager suspected something truly drastic would happen to them if they did try to go to the papers.

He wondered if Harold Stassen had succeeded in rooting out everybody involved in the attack on the colonization fleet. He supposed it was possible, but had his doubts nonetheless. Stassen had probably done just enough to keep the Lizards from screaming too loud, and not a lot more.

"Good morning, Yeager," said Colonel Edwin Webster, Sam's superior.

"Good morning, sir." Sam saluted. He cast a longing glance toward the coffee pot, but asked, "What's up?" Duty came first.

Webster saw the glance. "Pour yourself some joe if you want it, Yeager," he said. "World's not going to end because you take the time to drink a cup."

"Thanks." Yeager grabbed one of the plastic-foam cups that were steadily ousting waxed cardboard. He adulterated the coffee with cream and sugar, then came back to Colonel Webster. After blowing on the coffee and taking a sip, he said, "Ready when you are, sir."

"Come on into my office," Webster told him, and Yeager dutifully followed him back there. His superior went on, "We've had a devil of a lot more reports of animals and plants from Home in the Southwest and South the past couple of months. I know that's what you were working on when you went on detached duty there this summer, so it seemed logical to call you in to have a look at them."

"Detached duty," Yeager echoed in a hollow voice. "Yeah."

He eyed Colonel Webster. He'd been detached from his duty, all right, detached from it by a couple of fellows speaking in the name of the government of the United States and carrying pistols to back their play. He'd gone to Desert Center. After that, he might have fallen off the edge of the world. Detached duty was a cover story that could fit almost anything. Did Webster know more than he was letting on? If he did, Sam couldn't see it on his face.

You start looking for people who know more than they're letting on and you'll start hearing voices pretty soon, he thought. *They'll come after you with a net and put you in a rubber room. Of course, if you don't worry at all about what happens to you, you're liable to disappear again, and this time odds are you won't come back.*

"Something you wanted to say about your duty?" Webster asked.

"Uh, no, sir," Sam answered. "I was just thinking I was glad to get back to California."

"Okay," his superior said crisply. "Come on. I've got the reports waiting for you. This is a real problem. Maybe you'll be able to figure out what to do about it. If you can, that'll put you a long jump ahead of everybody else."

"I'm not sure there's anything we *can* do about it, sir," Yeager said, "at least if you mean in terms of stopping these beasts. We may have to see if we can make them useful to us instead. Sometimes God gives you lemons. If He does, you'd better learn to like lemonade."

"Could be." Webster didn't sound convinced. "So far, nobody has any idea how to do even that much."

"Well, azwaca and zisuili can be pretty tasty," Sam said. "The Lizards eat 'em. No reason we couldn't."

"They're ugly as sin," Colonel Webster observed.

"So are pigs, sir," Yeager answered. "I grew up on a farm. Nobody who ever took care of livestock thinks it's beautiful. And the people who don't take care of it don't usually give a damn what it looks like. All they'll see is the meat in the butcher case, not the animals it came from."

"Old McDonald had a farm, ee-i-ee-i-oh," Webster sang in a surprisingly melodious baritone, "and on that farm he had some azwaca, ee-i-ee-i-oh. With a *hiss-hiss* here and a *hiss-hiss* there . . ."

Sam stared at the bird colonel as if he'd never seen him before in his life. "You okay, sir?" he asked quizzically.

"How the devil should I know?" Webster answered. "Do the kind of work we do and there's something wrong with you if you *don't* start going a little squirrelly after a while. Or are you going to tell me I'm wrong?"

"I wouldn't think of it," Yeager said. "You want to point me at those reports now?"

"I sure will," Colonel Webster said. "For the time being, what I want you to do is flip through 'em fast. Cover as much ground as you can in the next couple of hours, then come back to my office and we'll talk some more."

"Okay, I can do that," Sam said. He didn't have an office here, though by his rank he would have been entitled to one. What he had was a sheet-metal desk in one corner of a room filled mostly by clerks and typists. It wasn't even exclusively his; he shared it with a couple of other itinerant officers, and his key opened only two drawers. For obvious reasons, he'd never put anything he worried about anyone else seeing inside that meager space.

"There you go." Colonel Webster pointed to the pile of papers in the plywood IN basket at the back right corner of the desk. "Skim those and head back to me at, oh, half past ten. Go ahead and set aside any you think you'll need to look at more later on, but I'm going to want a broad overview from you then."

"Right." Yeager saluted, then sat down in the swivel chair behind the desk. Webster headed back to his office. Sam got to work. He nodded to himself as he grabbed the report on top of the stack. At least his boss knew exactly what he wanted. Sam hated few things more than vague orders.

He hadn't had much to do with the spread of plants and animals from Home since getting kidnapped from Desert Center. Now, every report he read made his eyebrows rise higher. Zisuili were eating the desert bare in Arizona. Plants from Home had been spotted outside Amarillo, Texas. Barren places throughout the Southwest were getting more barren. *These creatures are worse than goats,* somebody had written. That made Sam purse his lips and blow out an almost silent whistle. He knew how bad goats were. Nobody who'd ever kept them could doubt that. Imagining beasts more destructive than they were wasn't easy. But the photos accompanying some of the reports at least raised the possibility that that writer knew what he was talking about.

And then there were the befflem. They'd got farther from the Mexican border and raised more kinds of hell than all the Race's meat animals put together. They killed cats. They killed some dogs, too. They raided henhouses. They stole from garbage cans. They bit people. They ran very fast for creatures with such stumpy legs, and their armored carcasses made them tough to harm.

"What will be interesting," Sam said when he returned to Colonel Webster's office, "will be seeing how all these animals—and the plants that are spreading, too—come through the winter. My guess is that cold weather will limit the northern range for most of them, but it's only a guess."

"There will be places where they can thrive year-round,

though," Webster said. "This is one of them." He tapped his desk as if expecting a herd of ssefenji to come trampling across it.

"Yes, sir, I think so," Sam agreed. "Unless I'm wrong, we'll have to learn to live with them as best we can."

"What do we do if their plants start crowding out our crops?" Webster asked.

"Sir, I haven't got any good answers for that," Yeager said. "I don't think anyone else does, either. Maybe the pesticide people will come up with something that kills plants from Home but leaves our stuff alone. Something like that's liable to be our best chance."

Colonel Webster eyed him with more than a little respect. "I happen to know that that's being worked on right now. I don't know when results will come, or even if they'll come, but it is being worked on."

"Stands to reason," Sam said. "But do you know what I think the real trouble spot could be?" He waited for Webster to shake his head, then went on, "Befflem. They're liable to be as much of a nuisance as rats and wild cats put together, and they don't seem to have any natural enemies here."

"Cold weather, like you said," Webster suggested.

Sam shrugged. "Maybe. But I've looked at a couple of reports there that talk about finding them in dens with nests, so maybe cold won't bother them as much as it would some other beasts from Home."

Webster scrawled a note. "I'm glad I called you in, Yeager. I don't think anybody else has mentioned that." He paused, scratching his head. "The Lizards keep befflem for pets, don't they? Maybe we could do the same."

"We keep cats for pets, too—or they keep us for pets, one," Yeager answered. "That doesn't mean they aren't a nuisance plenty of places." He managed a lopsided grin. "Of course, as far as the Lizards are concerned, we're nothing but nuisances ourselves, so I don't think we'll get much sympathy from them."

"Too goddamn bad," Webster said. Sam's grin got wider. He nodded.

"No." Johannes Drucker shook his head. "I don't think we can go back to Greifswald. There's a good-sized Lizard garrison there, and that male called Gorppet knows me much too well. We'd be under a microscope if we tried."

"Too bad." Both of his sons and his daughter spoke at the same time.

But his wife nodded. "I'd just as soon stay here in Neu Strelitz, or else go someplace where nobody has any idea at all who we are and start over there. Too many people back in Greifswald know why they took me away for a while."

Drucker watched his older son. That Heinrich had joined the band of holdouts in Stargard had probably saved Drucker's own neck; the major who commanded them had changed his mind about shooting him. But those holdouts were at least as fanatical about Party ideology as any SS men. If they ever found out Heinrich Drucker's mother was, or might have been, a quarter Jewish . . .

Very visibly, Heinrich figured that out for himself. He walked over and put a hand on his mother's shoulder. "All right," he said. "We'll go somewhere it's safe for you."

Letting out a small, silent sigh of relief didn't show, and sigh Drucker did. The Nazis made heroes of children who turned in their parents. He hadn't thought Heinrich would fall for such nonsense, but you couldn't be sure till things actually started happening.

Claudia turned to him and asked, "Father, if you can't fly into space any more, what will you do for a living?"

That was a good question. It was, in fact, *the* good question. Drucker wished he had a better answer for it. As things were, he said, "I don't know. Something will turn up. Something always does, if you're willing to work. I can be a mechanic, I suppose. I can make an engine sit up and do as it's told."

"A mechanic?" Claudia didn't sound very happy at that. The social difference between a *Wehrmacht* officer's daughter and a mechanic's could be measured only in light-years.

"Honest work is honest work," Drucker insisted, "and mechanics make pretty good money." Claudia looked anything but convinced.

Before he could say anything else, somebody knocked on the front door to Käthe's uncle Lothar's house. The Druckers crowded it to the bursting point, but Lothar, a widower, didn't seem to mind. He was Käthe's father's brother, and didn't let on that he knew anything about the possibility of Jewish blood on the other side of her family tree. Nobody talked about that where Uncle Lothar could overhear—*better safe than sorry* summed up everyone's attitude.

He came into the back bedroom now with a frown on his face: a big, rawboned man in his sixties, still physically strong but, like so many others, badly at sea in this new, diminished *Reich*. Nodding to Drucker, he said, "Hans, there's a soldier out front wants to speak to you."

"A soldier?" Suspicion roughened Drucker's voice. "What kind of soldier? *Wehrmacht* or *Waffen*-SS?" He wasn't at all sure he wanted to meet an SS man without an assault rifle in his hands.

But Käthe's uncle answered, "A *Wehrmacht* lieutenant, just barely old enough to shave."

"I'll see him," Drucker said with a sigh. "I wonder what he'll make of me." He wore one of Lothar's old shirts, which was too big on him, and denim trousers that had seen better days. He hadn't shaved this morning.

Sure as the devil, that wet-behind-the-ears lieutenant didn't look as if he believed his eyes. "*You* are Colonel Johannes Drucker?" He seemed to have to remind himself to come to attention and salute.

Drucker returned the salute, though he wasn't at all sure he remained in the *Wehrmacht* himself. "That's right, sonny," he answered, no doubt further scandalizing the lieutenant. "What can I do for you today?"

Visibly holding in his anger, the young officer spoke with exquisite politeness: "Sir, I am ordered to bring you to a secure telephone line and connect you to the *Führer* in Flensburg." Every line of his body screamed that he hadn't the faintest idea why Walter Dornberger would want to speak with such a derelict.

"A secure phone line?" Drucker said, and the lieutenant nodded. "Secure from the Lizards?" he persisted, and the kid nodded again. Drucker hadn't known such lines survived anywhere in the *Reich*, let alone in sleepy Neu Strelitz. Maybe he wouldn't have to be a mechanic after all. "I'll come."

He'd expected to be taken either to the telephone exchange or to the *Burgomeister*'s hall. Instead, the lieutenant led him to a fire station where men playing draughts looked up without much curiosity as he walked by.

The secure telephone looked like an ordinary instrument. But another *Wehrmacht* officer was in charge of it. He gave Drucker a fishy stare, too. When the lieutenant confirmed Drucker's identity, the other officer made the call. It took a couple of minutes to go through. When it did, the officer thrust the handset at Drucker and said, "Go ahead."

"Johannes Drucker speaking," Drucker said, feeling like an idiot.

"Hello, Hans. Good to hear from you." That was Walter Dornberger's voice, all right.

"Hello, sir." As soon as Drucker spoke, he knew he should have called Dornberger *mein Führer*. Now that the former commander at Peenemünde had the job, how seriously did he take it? Would he be offended if he didn't get the respect he thought he deserved? Drucker plowed ahead, trying to hide his gaffe: "What can I do for you? I thought I was retired."

"Nobody who's still breathing is retired," Dornberger answered. "If you're breathing, you can still serve the *Reich*. That's why I was so glad to hear you'd turned up in Neu Strelitz. I can use you, by God."

"How?" Drucker asked in real confusion. "The Lizards won't let us get back into space. Unless . . ." He paused, then shook his head. With radar watching every square centimeter of the *Reich*, clandestine launches were impossible. Weren't they? Hoping he was wrong, he waited for the new *Führer*'s reply.

"That's true—they won't," Dornberger said, which nipped his hope before it was truly born. The *Führer* went on, "But that doesn't mean I don't need you closer to home. I'm going to order you here to Flensburg, Hans. You've got no idea what a small cadre of men I can really trust."

"Sir . . ." Drucker's voice trailed away. Dornberger had him by the short hairs, and he knew it. Of course the *Reich*'s new leader could trust him. Dornberger knew why the *Gestapo* had seized Käthe. If Drucker gave him any trouble, the blackshirts could always grab her again.

"I'll have a car there for you—for all of you—in a couple of days," Dornberger said. He didn't mention the sword he'd hung over Drucker's head. Why would he? Smoother not to, smoother by far. The *Führer* continued, "You'll be doing important work here—don't kid yourself for a moment about that. And you'll have the rank to go with it, too. Major general sounds about right, at least for starters."

"Major general?" Now Drucker's voice was a disbelieving squeak. The young lieutenant who'd brought him to the fire station stared at him. He didn't look as if he believed it, either.

But Walter Dornberger repeated, "For starters. We'll see how you shape in the job when you get here. I hope to see you soon—and your whole family." He hung up. The line went dead.

"Sir . . ." The lieutenant spoke with considerably more respect than he'd given Drucker up till then. "Sir, shall I escort you back to your house?"

"No, never mind." Drucker walked back to his wife's uncle's in something of a daze. He didn't know what he'd thought Dornberger would have to say to him. Whatever it was, it didn't come close to matching the real conversation.

When he went into the house, the children, Käthe, and her uncle Lothar all pounced on him. The children exclaimed in pride and delight when he gave them the news. Lothar slapped him on the back. Käthe congratulated him, too, but he saw the worry in her eyes. She knew the grip Dornberger had on him through her. He shrugged. He couldn't do anything about it but hope things would work out all right. He wished he could think of something else, but what else was there?

The motorcar that came for them was an immense Mercedes limousine. People up and down the street stared as they piled into it. Drucker hoped it wouldn't tempt some ambitious band of holdouts into trying a hijacking. It purred away from Neu Strelitz in almost ghostly silence.

A few hours later, they were in Flensburg, in Schleswig-Holstein hard by the Danish border. "It's like another world," Käthe breathed as the motorcar pulled to a stop in front of the Flensborg-Hus, the hotel where the *Reich* was putting them up till they found permanent lodgings. And so it was: a world that hadn't seen war. In the *Reich*, that made it almost unique. It was the main reason Walter Dornberger had chosen the town at the west end of the Flensburger Förde, an arm of the Baltic projecting into the neck of land that led up to Denmark.

Some of the people at the hotel spoke more Danish than German. The monogram of Frederick IV of Denmark stood above the gate: he'd built the Flensborg-Hus as an orphanage in 1725.

A major general's uniform waited in the room to which the bellboy led Drucker. He put it on with a growing feeling of unreality. After he'd adjusted the high-peaked cap to the proper jaunty angle, Heinrich's arm shot out in salute. "You look very handsome," Käthe said loyally. If her heart wasn't in the words, how could he blame her?

The next morning, a lieutenant who might have been brother to the one back in Neu Strelitz took him to the *Führer*. Walter Dornberger was working out of another hotel not far from the downtown maritime museum. A servant brought Drucker pickled herring and lager beer. After he'd eaten and drunk, he asked, "What will you have me doing, sir?"

"We've got to rebuild," Dornberger said. "We have to conceal as much as we can from the Lizards. And we have to take full control of the country, put down the outlaw bands or at least bring them under government control. Until we've done all those things, we're hideously vulnerable. I'm going to put you to work at concealment. The more weapons we can keep from turning over to the Lizards, the better."

"What have we got left?" Drucker asked. "Explosive-metal bombs? Poison gas?" Dornberger just smiled and said nothing. Drucker found another question: "What do I do if the Lizards find some of it?"

"Give it up, of course," Walter Dornberger answered. "We can't afford to do anything else—not yet we can't. One of these days, though . . ."

"If the Lizards are patient, we have to be patient, too," Drucker said.

"Just so." Dornberger beamed at him. "You will do very well here, I think."

By God, maybe I will, Drucker thought.

"Well, well." Gorppet looked up from a listing of new appointments by the Deutsch government. "This may be interesting."

"What have you found?" Hozzanet asked.

"Remember that male named Johannes Drucker, with whom I had some dealings because he was associated with Anielewicz?" Gorppet waited for his superior to make the affirmative gesture, then went on, "He has turned up in Flensburg with a promotion of two grades."

"That *is* interesting," Hozzanet agreed. "What is he doing there, to earn such a sudden, sharp advance?"

"His title, translated, is 'commandant of recovery services,' " Gorppet replied after checking the monitor. "That is so vague, it could mean anything."

"I always mistrust vague titles," Hozzanet said. "They usually mean the Big Uglies are trying to hide something."

"We already know the Deutsche are trying to hide as much as they can from us," Gorppet said.

"Really? I never would have noticed," Hozzanet said. The Race didn't have an ironic cough to set beside the emphatic and the interrogative. Had it possessed such a cough, Hozzanet would have used one then.

"Here, however, we are in an unusual position, because this Drucker speaks our language fairly well and has interacted with us in ways that are not hostile," Gorppet persisted. "We have some hope of getting him to see reason and cooperate with us."

"Really?" Hozzanet repeated, still sounding anything but convinced. "Is this Drucker not the male who refused to tell you anything whatsoever about how the male who drove him to, ah, Neu Strelitz ended up dead something less than halfway there?"

"Well, yes," Gorppet said. "But that was an individual matter. This one pertains to the survival of his not-empire. If he sees he will endanger the *Reich* by refusing to cooperate, I think he will tell us at least some of what we need to know."

"My opinion is that you are far too optimistic, if not utterly addled," Hozzanet said. "But I can see you do not intend to listen to me. Go ahead, then: call this Drucker. I will warn you of one thing, though—accept none of his denials without proof. Distrust them even with thorough proof."

"You may believe otherwise if you like, superior sir, but I really must assure you that I did not hatch from my eggshell yesterday," Gorppet said stiffly. "I do know that Big Uglies will lie whenever it suits their interest to do so—and sometimes, I think, just for the sport of it. And . . ." His voice trailed off. He didn't go on with whatever he'd been on the point of saying. Whatever it was, in fact, he forgot all about it. He started to laugh instead.

"And what is so funny?" Hozzanet asked. "Give me something to make me laugh, too, if you would be so kind. I could use a good laugh, by the Emperor." He cast down his eye turrets.

So did Gorppet, who then answered, "It shall be done, superior sir. It just occurred to me: I believe I have the proper tool for persuading this particular Tosevite to listen to me and to do my bidding, or some of it."

"Tell me," Hozzanet urged. "Such a claim is usually all the better for proof. I do not think this likely to prove an exception to the rule."

"I agree, superior sir," Gorppet said. "Consider, though. When we first met Drucker, in whose company was he? In whose *friendly* company was he? Why, that of Mordechai Anielewicz." He pronounced the Tosevite name with care. "And who is Mordechai Anielewicz? A leader of the members of the Jewish superstition in the subregion called Poland. The ideology of Drucker's superiors requires permanent hatred for members of the Jewish superstition. If those superiors were to learn from us that he had violated their fundamental rule . . ."

He waited for Hozzanet's judgment. If he'd missed something obvious, the other male would take sardonic pleasure in letting him know about it. But Hozzanet bent into the posture of respect, a very sizable compliment when from superior to inferior. "That is good. That is quite good," he said, and added an emphatic cough. "By all means, make your telephone call. We may realize considerable profit from it. Blackmail is liable to prove more effective than friendship. This is Tosev 3, after all."

"I thank you, superior sir," Gorppet said. He had no trouble telephoning Flensburg. The Race often needed to do so, to tell Deutsch officials what to do. Even though he spoke none of the local Big Uglies' language, he was quickly connected to Johannes Drucker: plenty of Deutsche, especially those involved with communication, could use the language of the Race. The line was voice-only, but he didn't mind that; he was not good at interpreting Tosevite facial expressions.

"I greet you, superior sir," Drucker said once the connection went through. "How may I help you?"

He doubtless meant, *How may I hinder you?* Big Uglies were not immune to polite hypocrisy. Gorppet said, "I congratulate you on your promotion. And I believe I should also congratulate you on recovering your mate and hatchlings. Is that not a truth?"

"Yes, that is a truth," the Tosevite replied. "No harm in admitting it now."

"I hope they are all well?" Gorppet said.

"Yes," Drucker said again. "I thank you for asking."

"I suppose you want them to stay well?" Gorppet said. "You must, after searching so long and hard to find them."

This time, Drucker paused before answering. Gorppet had not thought him a fool. When he did speak again, what he said was, "I do not care for the way this conversation is going. What is your point?"

"My point is that I hope I will not have to tell anyone about your recent friendship with Mordechai Anielewicz," Gorppet replied. "I believe that would be unfortunate for all concerned. Do you not agree?"

Silence stretched a good deal longer now. At last, Drucker said, "In the language of the Race, I cannot call you all the vile names I am thinking in my own language. I wish I could. What do you want from me in exchange for your silence?"

He caught on quickly, all right. Gorppet said, "Is it not a truth that your government seeks to conceal weapons that should have been surrendered to the Race?"

"I have no idea what you are talking about," the Big Ugly said.

"No? That will probably mean I shall have to make some other telephone calls," Gorppet said.

Drucker spoke in his own language. Gorppet didn't understand a word, but it sounded impassioned. Then Drucker returned to the language of the Race: "You will want me to betray my own not-empire. That is very hard for me to do."

"The choice is yours," Gorppet said.

Another long silence. "You will hear from me from time to time," Drucker said, breaking it. "You will not hear from me very often, or I would give myself away."

"I understand," Gorppet said. "I think we may have a bargain. Do not forget your obligation, or the bargain will come undone. I warn you now. I do not intend to warn you again."

"I understand," Drucker said, and broke the connection with what struck Gorppet as altogether unnecessary violence.

But that was neither here nor there. Turning to Hozzanet, Gorppet said, "I believe he is recruited. The true test, of course, will be in what he reveals. If he fails us . . ." He shrugged. "If he fails us, he will pay the price."

"He will deserve it, too," Hozzanet said.

Before Gorppet could reply, his telephone hissed. It was another voice-only connection with a Tosevite on the other end. "I greet you," the Big Ugly said. "Mordechai Anielewicz speaking here."

"And I greet you," Gorppet said in some surprise. "I was just talking about you, as a matter of fact. How may I help you?"

"You need to know something has gone missing," the Jewish leader answered.

"Do I?" Gorppet thought for a moment. "In that case, I probably also need to know *what* has gone missing—is that not a truth?"

"Yes," Anielewicz said. "That is a truth." He used an emphatic cough.

When the Big Ugly didn't say anything more, Gorppet realized he would have to prompt him. He did: "Will you tell me what has gone missing, or did you put this telephone call through to tantalize me?"

Mordechai Anielewicz sighed, a sound much like that a male of the Race might have made. "I will tell you. You will have heard, I suppose, that the Jews of Poland possess an explosive-metal bomb captured from the Deutsche years ago, at the end of the first round of fighting."

"I have heard this, yes," Gorppet replied. "I do not know whether it is a truth or not, but I have heard it." His tailstump lashed in sudden alarm. "Wait. Are you telling me—?"

"I am telling you that we do indeed possess this bomb," Anielewicz said. "Or rather, I am telling you that we did possess it. At the moment, we do not. By *we* here, I mean the organized group of Jewish fighters who have held it for all these years."

Gorppet's head started to ache. "Do you mean to say that an explosive-metal bomb has been stolen?" That got Hozzanet's complete, and horrified, attention. "If you do not have it, who does?" That seemed a good question with which to start.

"There is no sign of violence in the place where it was kept," the Tosevite replied. "This leads me to believe some of my fellow Jews have taken it, and not Poles or Russians or Deutsche."

"I see," Gorppet said. "And what would Jewish hijackers be likely to do with an explosive-metal bomb?" He answered that for himself: "They would be likely to bring it here, into the *Reich*, and try to use it against the Deutsche, against whom they have strong motivation for seeking vengeance."

"That is also my belief," Mordechai Anielewicz said. "If the Deutsche still have any explosive-metal weapons of their own hidden away, they might be provoked into using them against you—and against us in Poland—if such a bomb destroyed one of their cities without warning."

"So they might," Gorppet said unhappily.

"I am sorry for the inconvenience," the Big Ugly said. "I do not know for a fact that the bomb can still burst. But I do not know for a fact that it cannot, either. We have tried to maintain it over the years. It is large and heavy. In my measure, it weighs about ten tonnes." He translated that into the Race's units.

Gorppet thought he must have made a mistake. "Are you sure?" he asked. "That seems an impossibly large weight."

But Anielewicz answered, "Yes, I am sure. Tosevite technology with these weapons was primitive in those days. We have improved since. That is our way, you will recall."

"Yes. I do recall," Gorppet said tonelessly. A hopeful thought occurred to him: "You Tosevites have many different languages. Would Jews in the *Reich* give themselves away by how they speak?"

"No," Anielewicz said. "I am sorry, but no. Yiddish, our tongue, is close to the Deutsch language as is, and many Jews are fluent in that language itself."

"Splendid." Gorppet turned an eye turret toward Hozzanet. "By the spirits of Emperors past, superior sir, what do we do now?"

"They let someone wander off with an explosive-metal bomb?" Atvar spoke in tones of extravagant disbelief. Extravagant disbelief was exactly what he felt. Even for Big Uglies, that struck him as excessive. "They do not know who? They do not know when? They do not know where? They do not know how?"

"It must have happened during the fighting in Poland, Exalted Fleetlord," Pshing replied. "Things were chaotic then, you must admit."

"Whose side are you on?" Atvar snarled. "I would not mind so much if another Deutsch city vanished from the map, but I fear the Deutsch Big Uglies could still retaliate against us. No matter what they claim, I find it unlikely that they have surrendered all of their explosive-metal weapons."

"Another round of fighting would leave the Deutsche extinct," his adjutant remarked.

"I wish they were extinct now," Atvar said. "But they have been damaged enough not to be dangerous at the moment, and the one set of reasonably reliable Tosevite allies we have had, the Jews of Poland, have turned on us."

"They did not mean to do so," Pshing said.

"I do not care what they meant to do." The fleetlord was in a perfect fury of temper. "They are letting their own private, trivial feuds influence the policy of the Race. That is intolerable—intolerable, do you hear me, Pshing?"

"Yes, Exalted Fleetlord," Pshing answered. "But what will you do? What can we do?"

That was a different sort of question. It painfully reminded the fleetlord that the intolerable was all too often commonplace on Tosev 3, and that the Race's policies here had to pay far more notice to the Big Uglies' whims and superstitions than anyone would have imagined possible before the conquest fleet set out from Home. "We have to try to get the bomb back," Atvar answered. "That much is obvious, but if we fail there, we also have to convince the Deutsche that we did not detonate it."

"That will be difficult," his adjutant said. "It also may not help much. The Deutsche dislike the Jews as much as the Jews dislike them."

"Both those points, unfortunately, are truths," Atvar said. "And the not-emperor of the Deutsche is sure to blame us for anything the Jews do." The Big Ugly named Dornberger would have reason to do so, too, but the fleetlord chose not to dwell on that.

"Will you warn the Deutsche this bomb may be on their territory?" Pshing asked. "I gather from the reports that the weapon is anything but inconspicuous."

"Until we have more definite information, I believe I will keep quiet," the fleetlord answered. "One more truth is that I would not be altogether dismayed to see the Deutsche punished further, so long as they fail to avenge themselves on us. It is not as if they fail to deserve it."

"The variable being whether we can escape their vengeance in the aftermath," Pshing said.

"Yes. The variable," Atvar agreed. That was a nice, bloodless way to ponder whether thousands or tens of thousands or hundreds of thousands of members of the Race might become radioactive dust on account of the reckless actions of a handful of headstrong Big Uglies. He sighed. No male since the unification of the Empire had had worries even remotely like his.

He skimmed the report again. The occupiers were doing what they could in secret to help the Jews find their missing bomb. How much was that? How secret was it? The report didn't say. The fleetlord took that as a bad sign.

And then the telephone hissed. "If that is Fleetlord Reffet, tell him I just jumped out the window," Atvar said to Pshing. "Tell him I have joined the Muslim superstition and am at prayer so I cannot be disturbed. Tell him anything. I do not wish to talk to him now."

"It shall be done, Exalted Fleetlord," Pshing said, and went off to do it. Atvar was one of the few members of the Race prominent enough to have another individual to block nuisances from him. Most males and females had to make do with electronics. He let out a self-satisfied hiss, enjoying the privilege.

But it turned out not to be the fleetlord of the colonization fleet. Pshing's image appeared on Atvar's monitor. "Exalted Fleetlord, it is Senior Science Officer Tsalas," Atvar's adjutant said. "He maintains that the matter about which he would speak to you is of some urgency. Shall I put him through?"

"Yes, by all means," Atvar replied. "Tsalas is not one to start laying eggs out of mating season." He winced after speaking. That slang expression for getting excited over nothing was perfectly good back on Home, but how much meaning would it have here on Tosev 3 in a few generations if he couldn't suppress the ginger trade?

Pshing vanished from the screen, to be replaced by an elderly, studious-looking male. "I greet you, Exalted Fleetlord," Tsalas said.

"And I greet you, Senior Science Officer," Atvar replied. "My adjutant tells me something urgent has come up. What is it?" He wondered if he really wanted to know. Urgent matters on Tosev 3 spelled trouble more often than not.

But Tsalas made the affirmative gesture. Atvar braced himself for the worst. It didn't come, at least not right away. The science officer said, "You will have been advised of the large meteoric impact on Tosev 4 not long ago?"

"Oh, yes." Atvar used the affirmative gesture, too. "This solar system, by everything I have been able to gather, is much more untidy than that of Home. It seems a fitting place to have hatched the Big Uglies."

Tsalas laughed. "That no doubt holds a good deal of truth,

Exalted Fleetlord. But there are data to suggest that this impact was not altogether the result of chance."

"I do not understand," Atvar said. "What else could it have been?"

"None of our probes out in the belt of minor planets between Tosev 4 and Tosev 5 noticed anything out of the ordinary among the American Big Uglies working there," the science officer said. "But a new probe traveling toward that belt had its forward camera operating, and caught . . . this."

His face vanished, to be replaced by a view of space and stars. Off to the right of the screen, a new star, not very bright, suddenly came to life. After Atvar watched it for a little while, he saw that it was moving against the stars in the background. "That is a rocket motor!" he exclaimed.

The display winked out. Tsalas reappeared. "Truth, Exalted Fleetlord," he said. "That *is* a rocket motor, and one of considerable power, or the probe would not have noticed it at such a long distance. I sped up the video for you to help you grasp its nature more quickly."

"But what motor is it?" the fleetlord asked. "It cannot belong to either of the two American spaceships now in the belt of minor planets, or the probes already there would have seen this burn. What *are* the Big Uglies doing?"

"I am not certain," Tsalas replied. "No one is certain—no one not an American Tosevite, at any rate. But it seems likely that the motor accelerated a good-sized chunk of rock from its normal orbit among the minor planets and toward the more inward regions of this solar system. It seems likely, in fact, that our outbound probe happened to catch the launch of this chunk of rock toward its eventual collision with Tosev 4."

"But Tosev 4 is an utterly worthless world," Atvar said. "Why would anyone, even Big Uglies, be so addled as to bombard it with meteors?"

"Perhaps," Tsalas said gently, "to give them practice in hitting other, more inherently valuable, targets."

That needed a moment to sink in. When it did, Atvar let out a hiss of unadulterated horror. "You are telling me that they could bombard us here on Tosev 3 from out in the belt of minor planets," he said.

"I believe so, yes, Exalted Fleetlord." Tsalas sounded no happier than Atvar felt. "I apologize for not bringing this to your notice sooner. Connecting several apparently unrelated pieces of data took longer than it should have. On the other fork of the tongue, perhaps we should count ourselves lucky that the connection was made at all. The American Tosevites plainly intended to keep it secret from us."

"Yes. Plainly," Atvar said. "And we shall have to see about that, too. Indeed we shall. I thank you, Senior Science Officer. I believe you may well have done the Race a great service." He listened with some small part of one hearing diaphragm to Tsalas' thanks, then broke the connection and shouted, "Pshing!"

His adjutant rushed into the office. "What is it, Exalted Fleetlord?"

"Summon the American ambassador to me this instant. This instant, do you hear?" Atvar said. "I do not care what that Big Ugly is doing. I do not care if he is eating. I do not care if he is mating. I do not care if he is standing in front of a mirror and watching his hair grow. I want him here at once. No delay, no excuse, is to be tolerated. Do you understand me?"

"Yes, Exalted Fleetlord. It shall be done, Exalted Fleetlord." Pshing fled.

Henry Cabot Lodge arrived quite promptly, even if not so soon as Atvar might have wished. "I greet you, Exalted Fleetlord," he said, his accent thick but understandable. "What can I do for you today? I gather from your adjutant that the business is urgent, whatever it may be."

"You might say so," Atvar answered. "Yes, you might say so. How does the United States dare to prepare to bombard Tosev 3 from the belt of minor planets between Tosev 4 and Tosev 5?"

He wondered if Lodge would have the nerve to deny the charge. But the Big Ugly said, "We are a free and independent not-empire. We are entitled to take whatever steps we choose to protect ourselves. So long as we are not at war with the Race, we do not have to make an accounting of our actions to you."

"Do you recall how close you came to being at war with the Race not long ago?" the fleetlord demanded.

"Yes. And I also recall the price we paid to avoid it," Henry Cabot Lodge replied. "It was just that we should pay it then, for we were in the wrong. But we are not in the wrong here, Exalted Fleetlord, and you have no right to protest our legitimate research in space."

Lodge was never a male to bluster and threaten. But he

sounded determined here. Even Atvar, no great expert on Tosevite intonation, could tell as much. He said, "Regardless of whatever installations you devise out there, Ambassador, the Race remains able to destroy your not-empire many times over."

"I understand that," the Big Ugly said steadily. "We are now able to treat with you on more fully equal terms, however."

And that, unfortunately, was a big, ugly, unpalatable truth. "We could wreck this entire planet, if necessary, to keep you Tosevites from escaping your solar system." Atvar had had that thought before. Now, suddenly, it seemed much more urgent—and also much harder to do. *Could* he give such an order, slaying all the colonists along with the Big Uglies? He wondered.

He or his successors would have to be the ones to do it, if anyone did. By the time he sent a query Home and waited for a reply at the laggard speed of light, that reply would come far, far too late to do any good. Not even the Emperors had borne such responsibility, not since before the days when Home was unified.

Henry Cabot Lodge said, "That is madness, and you know it perfectly well."

"Truth: it is madness," Atvar agreed. "But Tosev 3 is a world of madness, so who knows whether a mad answer might not be the best?" To that, the American Big Ugly had not a single word to say.

☆ **17** ☆

Bombs burst in Peking, shaking the ground. At the Central Committee meeting, Liu Han turned to Nieh Ho-T'ing and said, "We are making them work much harder this time."

"Truth," the People's Liberation Army general answered in the language of the little scaly devils. He went back to Chinese: "Thanks to the missiles we got from the Soviet Union, they cannot use their landcruisers or their helicopters or even their aircraft so freely as they would like."

Mao glanced across the table at them. "We have held Peking now since the uprising began. We hold a good many cities here in the north, and the countryside surrounding them."

Nieh nodded. "From there to the Soviet border, the scaly devils appear only at great peril to their lives."

"If Molotov wanted to, he could legitimately recognize us as the government of liberated China," Mao said. "But will he do it?" He scowled and shook his head. "He does not dare, the dusty little worm, for fear of angering the little devils. Stalin was ten times the man he is. Stalin knew no fear."

To Liu Han, Nieh murmured, "Anyone who isn't afraid of the little scaly devils has tiles loose on his roof."

"Well, of course," she whispered back. "You know how Mao is. Molotov hasn't given him everything he wanted, so of course he's going to rant about it. He isn't satisfied till things go exactly as he saw them in his mind."

"That makes him a great leader," Nieh said, to which she nodded. He added, "It can also make him *very* tiresome," and Liu Han nodded again.

Mao took no notice of the byplay; Mao took as little notice as he could of anything that didn't involve himself. He went right on talking. When Liu Han started paying attention to him again, he was saying, "—might be better off demanding recognition from the little scaly devils than from the Soviet Union."

Heads bobbed up and down along the table. Chou En-Lai said, "I think there is some hope they may give this to us. We have shown them we are determined and we are not to be trifled with. If we send them an embassy, I think they will listen. They had better listen, or they'll be sorry."

"That's right. That's just right," Mao said. Of course he thought anyone who agreed with him was right. He continued, "They're already sorry. We can send them an embassy under flag of truce. If they heed us, well and good. If they don't, we're no worse off." His forefinger shot out: "Comrade Liu Han! You have dickered with the scaly devils before, haven't you?"

"Uh—yes, Comrade," Liu Han said, taken aback.

"Good." Mao beamed at her, his face round as the full moon. "That's settled, then. We'll send you through our line. You know what you are to demand of them."

"Our independence, of course," she answered.

"That's right." He nodded. "Yes, indeed. No more imperialists in our country. We've seen too many—first the round-eyed devils, then the Japanese, then the little scaly devils. No more, not if we're strong enough to hold our own against them."

"What if they refuse us that?" Liu Han asked.

"Then the fight goes on, of course," Mao said.

But she shook her head. "I'm sorry, Comrade. What I meant was, what if they offer us something less than full independence but more than nothing? What if they offer us, say, some small area to rule on our own, or if they offer us some voice in affairs but not real freedom?"

"Refer such things back to me," Mao told her. "They will be checking with their superiors, too. I have no doubt of that."

"All right." Liu Han nodded. What Mao said made good sense, though she wondered whether the little scaly devils would have anything at all to say to a representative of the People's Liberation Army. She gave a mental shrug. The People's Liberation Army would contact the imperialist oppressors. If they wanted to talk after that, they would.

She spent the next couple of days discussing possibilities with Mao and with Chou En-Lai. Then word came back that the little devils would treat with her. She got into a motorcar with a white flag tied to the radio aerial. The driver took her out of battered

Peking and down to the scaly devils' shuttlecraft port. Voice cheerful, he said, "This road is supposed to be cleared of mines."

"If it isn't, I'm going to be very unhappy with you," Liu Han said, which made the fellow laugh.

A mechanized fighting vehicle like the one that had taken her out of the little scaly devils' prison camp blocked the road. An amplified voice blared from it, in the scaly devils' language and then in Chinese: "Let the negotiator come forward alone."

Liu Han got out of the motorcar and walked to the fighting vehicle. Clamshell doors at the rear of the vehicle opened. She got in. Three little scaly devils glared at her. They all carried rifles. "I greet you," she said in their language.

"We will take you to our negotiator," one of them answered— no politeness, only business.

That was the last they said till the fighting vehicle halted a couple of hours later. Liu Han had no idea just where she was. Her surroundings when she left the vehicle did nothing to enlighten her. She found herself in the middle of one of the little devils' encampments, full of drab tents.

A scaly devil was waiting for her. "You are the female Liu Han?" he asked, as if anyone else were likely to have emerged from the machine. When she admitted it, he said, "Come with me," and led her to one of the tents.

"I am Relhost," said the scaly devil waiting inside. "My rank is general. I greet you."

"And I greet you," Liu Han answered, returning courtesy for courtesy. She gave her own name, though he already knew it.

"You are not fond of us. We are not fond of you. These are obvious truths," Relhost said. Liu Han nodded. The little devil made his kind's gesture of agreement to show he knew what that meant. He continued, "Your side and mine have made agreements even so. Maybe we can do it again."

"I hope so. That is why we asked to talk," Liu Han said. "We have liberated a large stretch of China from your imperialistic grasp."

Relhost's shrug was amazingly like a man's. "For the time being," he said. He didn't reckon *imperialistic* an insult; to him, it was more likely to be a compliment. "I expect we shall retake all the territory you have stolen from us." He paused. One of his eye turrets swung toward a small portable stove in a corner of the tent, and to the aluminum pot bubbling on it. "Would you care for some tea?"

"No, thank you." Liu Han shook her head. "I did not come here to drink tea. I came here to discuss the fight with you. I think you are wrong. I think we can keep what we have taken. I think we can take more."

"It is usual, in a hard fight, for both sides to think they are winning," Relhost observed. "One of them proves to be wrong. Here, I think—the Race thinks—you will prove to be wrong."

"Plainly, we disagree about that," Liu Han said. "We can hold. We will hold. And we can bleed you white." That was how Liu Han thought of the phrase, anyhow; its literal meaning was, *We can crack all your eggs.*

"You have cost us a certain amount," Relhost admitted, and then tempered that by adding, "but not so much as you think. And I am certain that we have hurt you a great deal more."

That was true, gruesomely true. Liu Han had no intention whatsoever of admitting it. Instead, she said, "We can afford to lose far more than you can." She also knew that was true; it was an underpinning of Mao's strategy.

"What do you propose, then?" Relhost asked.

"An end to the fighting. You recognize our independence in the land we control now, and we promise not to try to gain any more," Liu Han said.

"No. Absolutely not." Relhost used the little scaly devils' hand gesture that was the equivalent of a human headshake. "You spoke of cracking eggs. Your promises are not worth cracked eggshells. We have seen that too many times by now. We will not be fooled again." He appended an emphatic cough.

Liu Han knew the People's Liberation Army's promise would be written on the wind, too. She wouldn't admit that, either. She said, "We have shown we can take and rule broad stretches of territory. We do not hold others where we can still disrupt you. You might do better to give up this land. You cannot hold it."

"We can. We shall." The scaly devil used another emphatic cough. "You think we are not ready for a long fight. I am here to tell you that we will fight for as long as it proves necessary. If we yield here to you now, we would have to yield elsewhere to other Tosevites later. It would mean the ruination of the Empire on this world. That shall not be."

You understand that you would lose face, Liu Han thought. *You understand this one stone would start an avalanche.* Very often, the little scaly devils were naive about the way people worked. Not here, worse luck. Here, they understood only too well. Liu Han wished they hadn't. She said, "Another bargain may be possible."

"I am listening," Relhost answered.

"You have seen that we are going to be a power in the land for a long time to come," Liu Han said. "Give us a share in ruling China. It is possible that you might control foreign affairs. But we can share in administering the land."

But Relhost said, "No," again. He said it with as little hesitation as he'd used before. He went on, "You want us to admit you have some legitimate right to be part of the government of China. We will never do that. This land is ours, and we intend to keep it."

"Then the fight will go on," Liu Han warned.

"Truth," Relhost said. "The fight will go on. It will go on, and we will win it. You would do better to accept that now, and to live within the Empire. You could become valued partners in it."

"Partners?" Liu Han asked sardonically. "Partners are equals. You have just said we cannot be equals."

"Valued subjects, then." Relhost sounded cross that she had pointed out the contradiction.

"We should not be subjects in our own land," Liu Han said. "We will not be subjects in our own land. That is why the fight goes on. That is why it will go on."

"We shall win it," the little scaly devil said.

Maybe he was right. Liu Han still had faith in the historical dialectic, but less than she'd had when she was younger. And the scaly devils had their own ideology of historical inevitability to sustain them. They believed in what they were doing every bit as much as the People's Liberation Army believed in its mission.

"I will send you back to your own side under safe-conduct," said the little scaly devil who was a general. "The war will continue. We will never agree to your independence. We will never agree to your autonomy."

"You will never defeat us." Liu Han wondered, not for the first time, whether she would live long enough to find out if she was right.

* * *

Queek, the Race's ambassador to the Soviet Union, was in a worse temper than usual. "Here, Comrade General Secretary," he said to Vyacheslav Molotov through his Polish interpreter, who as usual seemed to be enjoying himself. "I insist that you examine these photographs."

Molotov put on his reading glasses and looked at them. "I see a number of explosions," he said. "So what?"

"This caravan was intercepted from the air just on the Chinese side of the border with the USSR," Queek said. "These explosions you are generous enough to notice prove that it was carrying munitions—very large quantities of munitions."

"So what?" Molotov repeated. "The Chinese are in rebellion against you. Why is it surprising that they should use large quantities of munitions?"

"By everything we have seen, the Chinese are incapable of manufacturing many of these munitions for themselves," Queek said. "This leads us to the conclusion that the Soviet Union is supplying them."

"You have no proof of that whatever," Molotov said. "I deny it, as I have denied it whenever you have made that accusation."

"These photographs prove—" the Lizard began.

"Nothing," Molotov broke in. "If they were taken on the Chinese side—your side—of the border, they prove *nothing* about what my country is doing."

"Where else would the bandits and rebels in China have come up with such advanced weapons?" the Lizards' ambassador said. "They cannot make these weapons for themselves. The caravan carrying the weapons was intercepted near the USSR's border. Do you seriously expect the Race to believe even for a moment that the Soviet Union had nothing to do with them?"

"Were any of these weapons of Soviet manufacture?" Molotov asked—a little apprehensively, because there was always the chance that the Red Army, in its zeal to arm the People's Liberation Army, might have ignored his orders against such a blunder and added Soviet weapons to those obtained from the *Reich.*

But Queek said, "No. They were made by the Germans and Americans."

Molotov was confident his relief didn't show. Nothing showed unless he wanted it to, and he never wanted it to. And, as a matter of fact, the USSR hadn't supplied the Chinese with many

American weapons lately. *Nice to know we really are innocent of something,* he thought. *It makes my protestations all the more convincing.*

He said, "In that case, you would do better to talk with the Germans and Americans, don't you think, instead of making these outrageous false charges against the peace-loving workers and peasants of the Soviet Union."

"We do not necessarily view them as false," Queek said. "The Race understands that it is far from impossible to obtain weapons from the nation that manufactured them, and then to pass them on to bandits who support your ideology."

"On the basis of this presumption, you have made these provocative charges against the Soviet Union," Molotov said. "In view of the unsettled state of the world this past year, do you not think you would be wise to avoid provocation?"

"Do you not think you would be wiser to keep from provoking us?" the Lizard returned.

"As I have repeatedly told you, I deny that we have done any such thing, and it is plain that you have no proof whatever of any guilt on our part," Molotov said. Had the Race had any such proof, life would have grown more interesting than he really cared to deal with. He went on, "You might also inquire of the Japanese, who had their own imperialist ambitions in China before the Race came to Earth."

"We are doing so," Queek answered. "But they deny any part in supporting these bandits, who, as they accurately point out, are ideologically aligned with the USSR, not with Japan."

"They might well support them anyhow, merely for the sake of giving you trouble," Molotov answered. "Has this concept never occurred to you?"

"Before we came to Tosev 3, it probably would not have," Queek said. "You Tosevites have taught us several interesting lessons on the uses of duplicity. If we are less trusting now than we were just after we arrived, you have only yourselves to blame."

That, no doubt, held a lot of truth. But it had nothing to do with the business at hand. "You had proof against the Germans," Molotov said, "the best proof of all: they attacked you. You had proof against the Americans, because of the defector. With proof, war becomes justified. To threaten war without proof is foolhardy. I insist that you convey my strongest possible protest to the fleetlord. I demand a formal apology from the Race for making these unfounded and unwarranted accusations against the Soviet Union. We have done nothing to deserve them."

He sounded vehement, even passionate. Queek spoke in the Lizards' language. The interpreter sounded downcast as he translated: "I shall convey your insistence and your demand to the fleetlord. I cannot predict how he will respond."

An apology, of course, would cost Atvar nothing but pride. Sometimes that mattered very much to the Lizards. Sometimes it seemed not to matter at all. They were less predictable than people that way.

But then Queek went on, "It may be that we have no proof of the kind you describe, Comrade General Secretary. Regardless of your protests and your bluster, however, you must never forget that we do have a great deal of circumstantial evidence linking the USSR to these weapons. If the evidence ever becomes more than circumstantial, the Soviet Union will pay a heavy price—and it will be all the heavier to punish you for your deceit."

"As you must know, the peace-loving workers and peasants of the Soviet Union are prepared to defend themselves against imperialist aggression from any enemies," Molotov answered, once more suppressing a nasty stab of fear. "We taught both the Nazis and the Race as much a generation ago. Our means of defense now are more formidable than they were then. And, just as we were prepared to stand shoulder to shoulder with the United States, you may reasonably expect that the USA will also stand shoulder to shoulder with us."

He had no idea whether the Lizards could reasonably expect any such thing. Harold Stassen would act in what he reckoned his nation's self-interest, and Molotov had no good grip on that. He also had no notion whether Stassen would be reelected in 1968; political writers in the United States seemed dubious about his prospects. But Queek couldn't readily disprove his claim.

And it seemed to rock the Lizard. It rocked him, in fact, a good deal more than Molotov had thought it would. Queek said, "You have told us to mind our own business in our dealings with you. Now I tell you to mind your own business in respect to our dealings with the United States. You would be wise to heed and obey."

Well, well, Molotov thought. Yes, that was a more interesting response than he'd looked for. He wondered what had happened between the Lizards and the Americans to prompt it. No new crisis had come to the notice of the GRU or the NKVD. The NKVD, of course, was not what it had been. *Damn Beria anyhow,* Molotov thought, as he did whenever that unpalatable truth forced itself to his attention.

Aloud, he said, "I was not speaking of your dealings with the United States, but of my own country's. I have no control over how you and the Americans deal between yourselves, any more than you have control over how we and the Americans deal between ourselves." He yielded a little ground there, or seemed to, without committing himself to anything.

Queek said, "I have told you everything the fleetlord instructed me to convey. For your benefit, I shall repeat the gist: do not meddle in China, or you will regret it."

"Since we have not meddled in China, I do not see why you are telling us not to do so," Molotov replied. "You have never been able to prove otherwise."

"You remain under very strong suspicion." Queek got to his feet, and so did his interpreter. The Pole looked unhappy. He had come in hoping to see Molotov discomfited, but had not got what he wanted. Instead, his own principal was downcast while leaving. As Queek stalked toward the door, he added, "Sometimes strong enough suspicion is as good as truth."

The Soviet Union ran on exactly the same principle. Nevertheless, Molotov affected outrage, snapping, "It had better not be. If you attack us on the basis of suspicion, a great many innocent human beings and members of the Race will die as a direct result of your error."

He waited to see what Queek would say to that. The Lizard said nothing at all. He left the office, his interpreter trailing along like the running dog he was. When Molotov rose from his chair, sweat dripped from his armpits. He was good—perhaps better than any man alive—at simulating imperturbability. No one could gauge what he thought or whether he worried. But he knew. He knew all too well.

A crew of cleaners started vacuuming the office where he'd met with Queek and the hallway the Lizard and his interpreter had used coming to and going from that office. Molotov went back to the office he used for all business other than that involving the Race. Andrei Gromyko and Marshal Zhukov were sipping tea there.

"How did it go?" the foreign commissar asked.

"Well enough, Andrei Andreyevich," Molotov answered. He savored the sound of the words, then nodded. "Yes, well enough. Perhaps even better than well enough. Queek came in full of accusations—"

"Groundless ones, of course," Zhukov put in.

"Yes, of course, Georgi Konstantinovich," Molotov agreed: despite the best Soviet security precautions, the Race might still be listening here. "As I say, he came in breathing fire, but I made him realize he had no proof whatever for his false claims, and that he had no business making threats without proof."

"That's good, Vyacheslav Mikhailovich. That's very good," Zhukov said. "You do know your business, no two ways about it."

"I am glad you think so," Molotov said. If Zhukov didn't think so, he would be out of a job and probably dead. He raised a forefinger. "One thing I noted: the Lizards are unusually concerned with the United States at the moment. Do you have any idea why, Comrade Marshal?"

"No, Comrade General Secretary." Zhukov scribbled a note to himself. "I shall try to find out, though."

"Good. By all means do so," Molotov said, and Zhukov nodded in what was without a doubt obedience. Zhukov could unmake Molotov. The Red Army was, if he chose to wield it, the most powerful instrument in the USSR. But he seemed increasingly content to follow the lead of the Party and, especially, of its general secretary.

Molotov smiled, but only inside, where it didn't show. He'd been through a lot. He was convinced he'd been through more than any one man deserved to suffer. But he'd prevailed so far, and now, against all odds, he thought he could bring the Red Army and its commander to heel again. He tapped a pencil a couple of times on his desk. *I shall triumph yet,* he thought. *In spite of everything, I shall, and the Communist Party of the Soviet Union with me.*

"You want to make the acquaintance of a Tosevite historian?" Felless said. "Why would you seek to meet such an individual?"

"I do not necessarily have to meet the Big Ugly," Ttomalss replied. "But I would like to confer with a historian, yes. The

Race faces many more difficulties in assimilating this world to the Empire than we anticipated."

Felless let out a derisive hiss. "That has become painfully obvious." It was so obvious, in fact, that she wondered why Ttomalss chose to belabor the point.

He proceeded to answer her. "Because of large differences in biology and relatively small differences in cultural sophistication, I think the Big Uglies will cling to their ways far more tenaciously than either the Rabotevs or Hallessi did. If you like, I can go into detail."

"Please do," Felless said, intrigued now: this was her specialty, too. And, when Ttomalss had finished, she found herself impressed almost against her will. "You make an interesting case," she admitted. "But why do you seek a Tosevite historian?"

"I am interested in instances of acculturation and assimilation in the past on Tosev 3," Ttomalss replied. "The more I understand about such matters from the perspective of the Big Uglies, the better my chances—the better the Race's chances—of successfully planning for the full incorporation of this world into the Empire. And so . . . do you know, or know of, any Tosevite historians?"

"As a matter of fact, I do," Felless answered. "I even know one who is in my debt." She'd got Monique Dutourd a position, true. That she'd done so as a result of blackmail was something she kept to herself. She went on, "This Tosevite female's one drawback is that she does not speak the language of the Race, but only Français."

"Language is often a problem in working with Big Uglies," Ttomalss said. "I suspect you will be able to find me a translator. Please do get in touch with this historian, superior female, if you would be so kind."

"Very well," Felless said with poor grace; she wasn't so sure she wanted to deal with the Big Ugly again. But duty was more important than anything, except possibly ginger. "It may take some little while. She is no longer in Marseille."

Ttomalss made the affirmative gesture. "I understand. When you have the time, however, I would appreciate it." He was so grateful and reasonable, Felless found no way to refuse him. That annoyed her, too.

Arranging a call to Tours wasn't easy, especially since she needed an interpreter. She made sure she chose one who she knew tasted ginger. Dickering with the Tosevite was liable to involve topics that would horrify a prim and proper male or female: topics Ambassador Veffani, for instance, should never hear about. Even with a fellow taster, Felless knew she was taking a chance.

The call went through to Monique Dutourd's university office, at a time when she was likely to be in. And, sure enough, she said, *"Allô?"*—the standard Français telephone greeting.

"I greet you," Felless said in return, and the interpreter translated her words into Français. "Senior Researcher Felless here. Do you remember me?"

"Yes, very well." The Big Ugly came straight to the point: "And what is it that you want with me?"

"Your expertise as a historian," Felless answered.

"You are joking," Monique Dutourd said. "Surely you must be joking."

"Not at all," Felless said. "A colleague of mine wishes to discuss Tosevite history with you. He is turning an eye turret toward analogies between the present situation with respect to the Race and you Tosevites and possible past situations in your history. I do not know if there are truly comparable situations. Neither does he. Would you be willing to explore this matter with him?"

"It could be," the female Tosevite replied. "It could even be that it would be interesting. Is it that your colleague speaks Français?"

"Unfortunately, no," Felless said, thinking it wasn't unfortunate at all, but only natural.

"What a pity," Monique Dutourd said. "I do not speak your language, either. If we are to talk of the Romans, we shall need an interpreter, as you and I have here."

As an aside, Felless asked the male who spoke Français, "Who are these Romans?"

He shrugged. "Some Big Uglies or other, I suppose." He would not be the ideal translator for Ttomalss; Felless could see that.

So could Monique Dutourd. She said, "It might be better if the interpreter were a Tosevite, someone who was himself at least somewhat familiar with the folk and events about which he was translating."

"Yes, that does seem sensible," Felless agreed. Monique Dutourd seemed intelligent—*for a Big Ugly,* Felless added to herself. She asked, "Do you have anyone in particular in mind to translate for you, then?"

"As a matter of fact, I do," the Tosevite female answered. Felless' interpreter had to resort to circumlocution for a bit after that: "The Tosevite male she has in mind is the fellow hatchling of the male and female who engendered her. The Big Uglies can describe this relationship in one word, though we cannot. She assures me that he is fluent in our language—as fluent as a Tosevite can be."

"Big Uglies stress kinship as we stress friendship," Felless said, and the male with her made the affirmative gesture. She went on, "Ask her if she thinks this male Tosevite would be willing to do the work of translating, and what sort of pay both she and he would expect for working with Ttomalss."

"I am sure Pierre would be willing," Monique Dutourd replied. "There is a certain difficulty, however: the Race presently has him imprisoned for smuggling ginger. If you can do anything to get him released, I would be grateful."

"I would not mind seeing Pierre Dutourd released myself," Felless' translator remarked. "I have bought a good deal of the herb from him, and it is harder to find now—not impossible, but harder."

"Truth," Felless said. "But can we get him released for this project?"

"*I* cannot," the male said. "You may have better connections than I do."

"Tell Monique Dutourd I will try to arrange her kinsmale's release," Felless said with more than a little trepidation. "Tell her I can guarantee nothing, for I am not sure how far my influence will reach. Ask her if she would consider discussing these matters with Ttomalss even if I cannot arrange this other Big Ugly's release."

She had no great hope for that. She knew only too well that the Tosevites took an affront against their kinsfolk as an affront against themselves. But, to her surprise, Monique Dutourd replied, "Yes, I would be willing, though I am grateful for your making the effort to help him."

"I will do what I can," Felless said, hoping the Tosevite female could not hear her relief. "I hope you will also seek other possible interpreters."

"It shall be done," the Big Ugly said in the language of the

Race—that was one phrase a great many Tosevites knew, even if they knew no more.

After getting off the phone with Monique Dutourd, Felless thought hard about ignoring her promise. Having anything public to do with ginger was all too likely to get her in trouble with the Race's authorities. But she wouldn't have minded seeing Pierre Dutourd free, either.

And so, despite misgivings, she telephoned Ambassador Veffani. He was as suspicious as she'd known he would be. "You want to set that rogue free to cause trouble for the Race again?" he demanded. "How much ginger will he give you in exchange for this freedom?"

"I have not spoken with him at all, superior sir. How could I?" Felless tried to make herself the very image of righteousness. "His name was mentioned as a possible interpreter by a Tosevite historian whom I contacted at the request of Senior Researcher Ttomalss. You are welcome to confirm that with Ttomalss, if you like."

"Believe me, I shall," Veffani said. "How is it that a notorious ginger smuggler came up in a conversation with a Tosevite scholar? I find this hard to believe."

"Find it however you please, superior sir," Felless answered. "The scholar and the smuggler happen to share a mother and father. You know how Big Uglies are in matters relating to kinship."

Veffani let out an unhappy hiss. "I do indeed. It is that sort of difficulty, is it? And I suppose the Tosevite scholar will have nothing to do with us unless we release the Tosevite criminal?"

Monique Dutourd hadn't said anything of the sort. Felless didn't care to lie outright to Veffani, but she did want to accomplish her own goals as well as Ttomalss'. "You know how Big Uglies are," she repeated, and let the ambassador draw his own conclusions.

"So I do," Veffani said with a sigh. "Well, perhaps we can arrange to release him long enough to do the necessary work and then return him to prison." He caught himself before Felless could say anything. "No, the odds are it would not work. Let me speak with Ttomalss and find out just how important his work is. If he makes the request for this translator, I can release the Big Ugly with a better conscience."

"I thank you, superior sir," said Felless, who hadn't expected to gain even that much from the ambassador.

"I am not nearly sure you are welcome," Veffani answered. "As I say, I shall consult with Ttomalss. He has the respect and admiration of the fleetlord—and he has never been known to taste ginger." He broke the connection.

Felless glared at the monitor. No, Ttomalss didn't taste. That hadn't kept him from mating with her when she tasted. Not tasting hadn't kept Veffani from mating with her when she tasted, either. When females tasted, they *would* emit pheromones and males *would* mate with them. That, of course, was the problem with the herb.

She wondered how the two ginger-addicted members of the Race who'd sought an exclusive mating contract with each other were doing among the Tosevite barbarians of the United States. She didn't approve of what they had done. Big Uglies were supposed to take on the customs and usages of the Race, not the other way round. No, she didn't approve. But even so . . .

Ginger, she thought. Without the herb, the Race would have had a much easier time on Tosev 3. Easier, yes, but not nearly so enjoyable. The urge for a taste surged up within her. She tried to resist, but not very hard. And hadn't that been the way she'd dealt with ginger ever since her first taste? She hurried to the desk, took out the vial, poured some of the powdered herb into her palm, and let her tongue dart out.

Delight shot through her. So did a feeling of brilliance, of omnipotence. She'd learned the hard way it was only a feeling, not reality. The first thing she had to do with that supposed brilliance was figure out a reason for staying here inside her chamber till she wasn't emitting pheromones any more. If she failed there, she would have males mating with her—and she would have endless trouble from Ambassador Veffani.

She didn't care. No, she did care—but not enough to keep her from tasting. Never enough to keep her from tasting. What could she do while she was stuck in here? *Research Tosevite history,* she thought. *Why not? It has suddenly become relevant, and I can claim it is something I truly need to know. Who are, or were, these Romans, anyway?* She began seeing what, if anything, the Race's data stores could tell her.

* * *

When the telephone rang, Mordechai Anielewicz hoped it would be the landlord with whom he'd spoken a couple of days before. There was a sellers' market for flats in Przemysl these days, as there was throughout Poland. But he did have hopes of moving into a bigger place, which he knew his family sorely needed. He hurried to the phone and answered with an eager, "Hello?"

But it wasn't the landlord, who was a big, bluff fellow named Szymanski. Instead, he heard the hisses and pops of a Lizard's voice: "Do I speak to Mordechai Anielewicz, the leader of those who follow the Jewish superstition in Poland?"

"You do," Anielewicz replied in the language of the Race. "And may I ask to whom I speak now?" He had trouble telling one Lizard's voice from another's.

"You may indeed, Mordechai Anielewicz," the Lizard replied. "I am Gorppet, whom you met outside Greifswald, and with whom you have spoken since. I greet you."

"And I greet you," Mordechai said. "This will have something to do with the missing explosive-metal bomb, unless I miss my guess."

"Truth—it will," Gorppet agreed. "I would like you to do me a favor that, I believe, will make its recovery more likely."

"I will be glad to do so," Anielewicz answered, "as long as it is nothing that endangers any of my fellow Jews except for the ones who have taken the bomb."

"I do not believe that will be a problem," Gorppet said.

"Go ahead, then," Mordechai said. "I shall have to be the final judge of that, though. I warn you now, to avoid misunderstandings later."

"I understand," the Lizard said. "You may perhaps be interested to learn that we have recruited your acquaintance, the Deutsch officer named Johannes Drucker, to provide us with information and work with us from his new post in Flensburg."

"Have you?" Mordechai said. "How did you manage that?" He had trouble imagining Drucker working with the Race. But one possible way to get the rocket pilot's cooperation crossed his mind. "Did you threaten to tell his superiors that he and I worked together for a little while without trying to slaughter each other?"

"That is exactly what we did, as a matter of fact," Gorppet answered. "You must be well schooled in duplicity, to have figured it out so quickly."

"Maybe." Mordechai admired Gorppet for thinking of it. Not many Lizards would have. "However that may be, what do you want me to do?"

"We informed the Deutsche that this bomb might be on the territory of their not-empire. I have learned from Johannes Drucker that the Deutsch constabulary believe it to have been hidden not far from the city of Breslau. You are familiar with the city of Breslau?" Gorppet said.

"Yes, I am familiar with it," Anielewicz answered. "That is, I know of it. I have never been inside it. The Deutsche touched off an explosive-metal bomb near there during the first round of fighting."

"Indeed. And the Race detonated one on the city during the more recent combat," Gorppet said. "Breslau itself is not presently inhabited or inhabitable. But the surrounding towns and villages remain densely populated. If the bomb were to explode, it would do severe damage. It might cause new fighting, much of which would involve Poland."

That struck Anielewicz as probable, too, unpleasantly so. "I ask you again: what do you want me to do?"

"We of the Race have moved combat teams into the area," Gorppet replied. "The Deutsche have also moved combat teams into the area. But no one is eager to try to retake the bomb. Failure would be expensive."

"Truth." Mordechai used an emphatic cough to show how big a truth it was. He went on, "There are enough Tosevites with the bomb that you cannot wait for them all to sleep at the same time?"

"That appears to be the case, yes," Gorppet said. "And so we were hoping you might go to this town near Breslau and try to persuade the fellow members of your superstition to surrender, and to return the bomb. We are willing to promise them safe conduct and freedom from punishment, and we shall enforce this on the Deutsche."

"Why do you suppose these Jews will listen to me?" Mordechai asked. "If they were the sort who would listen to me, they would never have taken the bomb into the *Reich* in the first place."

"If they will not listen to you, to whom will they listen?" the

Lizard asked in return. "Suggest a name. We would be grateful for that."

Try as he would, Anielewicz couldn't come up with any names. "Maybe," he said hopefully, "they have not set off the bomb because they cannot, because it will not detonate any more."

"No one has seemed eager to experiment along those lines," Gorppet said. "Will you come to the environs of Breslau? If you choose to do so, both the Race and the Deutsche will obey your orders."

"I will come," Anielewicz said.

"Good," Gorppet answered. "Pack whatever you need. Pack quickly. Transportation will be laid on. Farewell." He hung up.

"What are you doing?" Bertha Anielewicz exclaimed when Mordechai started throwing clothes into the cheap cardboard suitcase that was the only one they owned. He explained as he went on packing. That made his wife exclaim again, louder than ever.

"I know," he said. "What choice have I got?"

He hoped she would come up with one for him. She didn't. All she said was, "You're doing this for the Germans?"

He shook his head. "I'm doing this to keep the war from hitting Poland again. If that helps the Germans . . ." He shrugged. "What can you do?"

Somebody knocked on the door. Bertha opened it. A man spoke in Polish: "I'm here for Mordechai Anielewicz."

"I'm coming," he said, and grabbed the suitcase. He kissed his wife on the way out, then followed the man downstairs to a beat-up motorcar. They got in. The car zoomed off to a park. A helicopter waited there, rotors spinning. He scrambled into it. He didn't fit well: it was made by and for Lizards. The helicopter roared off to an airstrip a few kilometers outside of Przemysl. A jet aircraft sat on the runway. Its motors were already running. As soon as Anielewicz boarded and sat down in one of the uncomfortable seats, the airplane took off. Half an hour later, he was on the outskirts of Breslau.

A male came up to him while he was still wondering if he'd remembered to bring a toothbrush. "I am Gorppet," the Lizard said. "I greet you."

"And I greet you," Mordechai answered. "What are you doing

here, if I may ask? Are you an expert on explosive-metal bombs?"

"Me?" Gorppet made the negative gesture. "Hardly. But my superiors have decided I *am* an expert on Johannes Drucker and Mordechai Anielewicz. That is the expertise that brought me here to meet you. Am I not a lucky male?"

"Very lucky," Anielewicz agreed. He didn't know how to say *cynic* in the language of the Race, but thought Gorppet's picture could have illustrated the dictionary definition. "Where near Breslau do you think the bomb is hidden?"

"Somewhere in the town called Kanth. Where, no one has bothered to tell me yet," Gorppet replied—a cynic, sure enough. "In this strange environment, it could be anywhere, and that is a truth. Altogether too much water on this world."

The vicinity of Breslau didn't seem so strange to Anielewicz. The city had sprawled on both sides of the Oder and over the numerous islands in the river. Dozens of bridges had spanned the Oder. These days, Breslau itself was wreckage and nothing else but, thanks to the explosive-metal bomb that had burst above the city. Considering what the Germans had visited on Poland—and anywhere else their bombs could reach—Mordechai had a certain amount of trouble feeling sympathetic.

He pointed ahead. "This little town here—Kanth?—hardly seems to have many hiding places for a bomb."

"Easy enough to hide a bomb," Gorppet answered. "Harder to hide that we are looking for it."

And there, as the Race would have said, was another truth. The Lizards had set up a command post outside of Kanth. The Germans had set up another one. If there were Jews holed up in there with ten tonnes' worth of explosive-metal bomb, they could hardly doubt they'd been noticed.

"What exactly do you want me to do?" Mordechai asked. "Go in there and ask them to come out without blowing up the town?"

"As I told you on the telephone, we and the Deutsche will obey your orders here," Gorppet replied. "These are your followers. The presumption is that you will best know how to deal with them."

Anielewicz wondered how good that presumption was. Any followers of his who really followed him wouldn't have absconded with the explosive-metal bomb in the first place. But he had no better notions, and so he said, "We had both better find out where your leaders believe the bomb to be."

"It shall be done, superior sir," Gorppet said, for all the world as if Mordechai were a Lizard of higher rank. "Come with me, then. We can both learn."

Inside one of the tents the Lizards had set up, a monitor displayed a map of Kanth. The map was in German, and must have been copied from a Nazi document. A red square blinked on and off on one street near the edge of town. Anielewicz pointed to it. "Is that the place?"

"Yes, that is the place," answered a Lizard whose body paint was similar to Gorppet's but somewhat more ornate. He went on, "I am Hozzanet. You are the male named Anielewicz?" At Mordechai's nod, Hozzanet went on, "What can we do to assist you in dealing with these individuals?"

"Get me a bicycle," Mordechai answered. "I do not want to walk all that way."

"It shall be done," Hozzanet said, and done it was. He had no idea where the Lizards came up with the bicycle—for all he knew, they borrowed it from the Nazis—but they got it. His legs ached when he started pedaling: the never-failing legacy of German nerve gas more than twenty years before. *Why am I doing this?* he wondered. *Why am I risking my neck to save a bunch of Germans who hate me?* That was the question his wife had asked. It seemed more urgent now. But the answer still came all too clearly. *Because this band of idiots is liable to make the Nazis visit more harm on people I don't hate, on people I love.*

People in Kanth stared at him as he rolled through the quiet, almost empty streets. They knew something was going on, but they had no idea what. If they started fleeing, what would the men with the bomb do? Probably try to set it off, so they could kill folk other than themselves. Anielewicz had played the role of a terrorist. He knew how such folk thought.

Here was the street. Here was the house, on the left-hand side. It had an attached garage that had probably been a stable before the turn of the century. It could easily have held the bomb. Nobody had trimmed the grass in front of the house for a long time, but that was far from unique on the street. With fall edging toward winter, most of the grass had gone grayish yellow.

Mordechai leaned the bicycle against a beech tree with a

couple of bullet holes in the trunk. As he walked up to the door, he felt eyes on him from inside. *What a fool I am for coming here,* he thought, and knocked on the tarnished brass knocker.

The door opened. The man who stood there aimed a submachine gun at Anielewicz's belly. "All right, you damned traitor," he growled in Yiddish. "Get your *tukhus* inside! Right now!" Mordechai went in. The door slammed shut behind him.

Ttomalss did not like using a sound-only telephone, but the Race didn't yet have a consulate in Tours from which he could have had a proper discussion with the Tosevite historian Felless had found for him. Making the best of things, he said, "I greet you, Professor Dutourd."

A male Big Ugly turned his words into Français. A female Big Ugly answered, presumably in the same tongue. The male Big Ugly spoke in the language of the Race: "And she greets you."

At least the historian and the interpreter were on the same circuit. As far as Tosevite telephone technology went, that was no small achievement. Ttomalss said, "Professor Dutourd, I gather the Romans whom you study are an important imperial folk among the Tosevites."

More back-and-forth between the Big Uglies. "Yes, that is a truth," Monique Dutourd answered through the interpreter. That interpreter, Ttomalss had been given to understand, was a notorious ginger dealer. But he was also a kinsmale to the historian. Knowing from painful personal experience how intimate Tosevite ties of kinship could be, Ttomalss had prevailed upon Ambassador Veffani to allow his release. He hoped he was doing the right thing. He did not want to have to deal with a hostile historian. That would make learning what he needed to know all the more difficult.

"I gather also that these Romans ruled many different kinds of Tosevites, some of them from cultures very different from their own," Ttomalss said. If he turned out to be wrong there, he would have to ask Felless to find him another historian.

But Monique Dutourd said, "Yes, that is also a truth."

"Good." Ttomalss knew he sounded relieved. He wondered if the Tosevite interpreter noticed. The very idea of different cultures had been alien to him before he came to Tosev 3. That of Home had been homogeneous since not long after the Race unified the planet. The Rabotevs and the Hallessi had quickly adopted their conquerors' ways. He could find more differences crossing a river on this world than he could in crossing light-years of space between worlds in the Empire.

"What is it you wish to know about the Romans and these other cultures?" Monique Dutourd asked.

"I want to learn how the Romans succeeded in incorporating them into their empire and into their culture," Ttomalss answered.

"Ah, I see," the Tosevite historian said. "This is relevant to your present situation, is that not a truth?" Either she or her interpreter let out a couple of yips of barking Tosevite laughter. Through him, she went on, "There are those among us who say history is not relevant to anything. I am glad to find the Race disagrees."

Plenty of males and females of the Race, Ttomalss knew, would not only have agreed but would have added emphatic coughs to their agreement. He did not mention that to the Big Uglies on the other end of the telephone line. Instead, he said, "Yes, I certainly think it is relevant. I am glad to find that you do, too. Whatever you can tell me will be of value to the Race."

"In that case, perhaps you will understand that I wonder whether I ought to tell you anything at all," Monique Dutourd said.

"If you do not, someone else will." Ttomalss did his best to sound indifferent. "Or we will eventually gain the information from your books. Whatever else we may be doing, we are not discussing secret matters here."

After a pause, the Tosevite female said, "Yes, that is so. Very well; you have reason. I will discuss these things with you."

"I thank you." Ttomalss did his best to treat her as he would have treated a savant of his own kind.

She said, "First of all, incorporation into the Roman Empire assumes Roman military victories. I do not think we need to talk about those."

Ttomalss found himself making the affirmative gesture, which did no good on a phone link without vision. "I would agree with you," he said. "Our military technology is very different from that of the Romans. And so is yours, nowadays." *And the Race will be arguing about why that is so for generations to come,* he thought. Never had his species been presented with such a rude surprise.

"All right, then," Monique Dutourd said. "Once a subregion was conquered, the Romans gave local autonomy to towns and areas that were not in rebellion against them. They did harshly stamp out rebellions where those arose."

"That is a sensible policy," Ttomalss said. "In large measure, we follow it here." The trouble with following it was that Big Uglies who were put in positions of authority often used that authority for themselves and against the Race. Ttomalss wondered if the Romans had had similar problems.

"With very few exceptions," Monique Dutourd went on, "the Romans allowed the males and females of the conquered subregions to practice whatever superstitions they chose to follow."

"That is also a sensible policy," Ttomalss said. "Why did they make exceptions?"

"On account of superstitions they thought dangerous to their empire," the Tosevite historian replied. "I can think of two examples. One was the superstition of the Druids, which had its center here in what is now France. The Romans feared that these Druids, who were the leaders of the superstition, would also lead the local inhabitants into rebellion against them."

"And the other?" Ttomalss asked when Monique Dutourd did not name it at once.

"The other, superior sir, was called Christianity," she replied. "You may perhaps have heard of it."

"Yes," he said automatically, before realizing she was being ironic. Then he asked, "But why did they try to suppress it? And why did they fail? This is the largest Tosevite superstition at the present time."

"They tried to suppress it because the Christians refused to acknowledge any other . . . spiritual forces," Monique Dutourd said, "and because the Christians refused to give reverence to the spirits of the Roman Emperors."

"Really?" Ttomalss said in surprise. "In that, they are much like the followers of the Muslim superstition today with respect to the spirits of Emperors past—Emperors of the Race, of course."

"Yes. Both Christianity and Islam are offshoots of the Jewish superstition, which disapproves of giving reverence to anything but the one supreme supernatural authority," Monique Dutourd said.

"Ah." Ttomalss scribbled a note to himself. He hoped and assumed the Race already knew that, but he hadn't known it himself. He asked, "Why are the Muslims so much more fanatically opposed to the Race at present than the Christians?"

"To get a proper answer to that, you would need to ask someone who knows more about Islam than I do," the Tosevite historian answered.

Her reply won Ttomalss' respect. He had seen a great many individuals—both members of the Race and Big Uglies—who, because they were experts in one area, were convinced they were also experts in other, usually unrelated, areas. When he said as much, Monique Dutourd started to laugh. "And what do you find funny?" he asked, his dignity affronted.

"I am sorry, superior sir," she said, "but I find it strange that you are making an argument like the one a famous Tosevite savant named Socrates used when he was on trial for his life almost twenty-four hundred years ago."

"Am I?" Ttomalss wondered who this Socrates was. "Did his argument succeed?"

"No," Monique Dutourd answered. "He was put to death."

"Oh. How . . . unfortunate." Ttomalss found a different question: "Did you use your years or mine there?"

"Mine," she said, so he mentally doubled the figure. She added, "At that time, the Romans were only a small and unimportant group. They later conquered the Greeks, one of whose subgroups, the Athenians, executed Socrates. The Greeks were culturally more advanced than the Romans, but could not unify politically. The Romans conquered them and learned much from them afterwards."

"I see," Ttomalss said. Ancientest history back on Home was full of stories like that, some true, others legendary, with scholars disagreeing over which was which. He asked, "What benefits did the Romans give to keep conquered subregions from rebelling?"

"Security from outside invasion," Monique Dutourd answered. "Security from feuds with their neighbors also within Roman territory. Local self-government, as I said before. A large area unified culturally, and also unified economically."

"I see," Ttomalss repeated. "These are, of course, advantages you Tosevites would receive on becoming subjects of the Empire."

"Ah, subjects," the Tosevite historian said. "One thing the Romans did that made them unusual among our empires was to grant full citizenship to more and more groups that had formerly been subjects."

"You could expect the same from us," Ttomalss said. "Why, already there is one Tosevite with full citizenship in the Empire."

"How interesting," Monique Dutourd replied. "Why only one? Who is he?"

"She," Ttomalss corrected. "That is a complicated story. It has to do with the unusual circumstances of her hatching." He said not a word about the continuing dispute with Kassquit over whether he kept the right to monitor her activities if she was a full citizen of the Empire. That was also complicated, and none of Monique Dutourd's business. Instead, Ttomalss asked, "If these Romans were such successful rulers of their empire, why did it fail?"

"Scholars have been arguing over that ever since it happened," the Tosevite female answered. "There is no one answer. There were diseases that reduced the population. The economy suffered as a result of this. Rulers grew more harsh, and their bureaucracy grew more stifling. And there were foreign invasions, most importantly from the Deutsche, who lived to the north of the Roman Empire."

"The Deutsche?" Ttomalss exclaimed in surprise. "The same Deutsche whom the Race knows only too well?"

"Their ancestors, rather," Monique Dutourd said.

"Yes, of course," Ttomalss said impatiently. "How interesting. That strikes me as an example of true historical continuity. I have not seen many on Tosev 3."

"They are here," Monique Dutourd said. "If you have not seen them, it is because you have not looked for them—or perhaps you have not known where to look."

"Yes, I suppose that could be," Ttomalss admitted. "Would you be willing to teach me more Tosevite history?"

"It could be," the female Big Ugly said. "There would be the question of payment, of course."

"Of course," Ttomalss said. "I am sure we can come to some sort of equitable arrangement about that."

"Payment might not necessarily involve money," Monique Dutourd said, "or not money alone. I would want my kinsmale fully pardoned, now that I am cooperating with the Race."

"Regardless of his unpleasant and unsavory dealings," Ttomalss said.

"Yes. Regardless of them." Ttomalss noted that the Tosevite female did not deny them. She wanted the ginger smuggler forgiven in spite of them. He sighed. *Kinship, not friendship,* he thought. That showed historical continuity among the Big Uglies, sure enough. He sighed. He could wish—he did wish—it didn't.

Monique Dutourd wished she hadn't come to Tours with fall heading toward winter. The city did not show itself to her at best advantage. She was a child of the warm Mediterranean; winter in Marseille was almost always mild, with snow a rarity. Not here. Sure enough, the Atlantic drove Tours' climate, and frost came to the city early and often. After Caesar's conquest of Gaul, Roman colonists in ancient Caesarodunum would have been as appalled at the weather as she was now.

The climate at the university was also a good deal less than warm. Monique knew she wouldn't have gained a position had Felless not pulled wires for her. By all the signs, every colleague in the history department knew as much, too. Her welcome ranged from unenthusiastic to downright hostile.

"Let me teach," she told her department chairman, a white-haired fellow named Michel Casson who'd been at the university since recovering from a wound he'd received defending Verdun in 1916. "Let me publish. I'll show you that I belong in this place."

"You will have the opportunity," Casson replied, peering at her through reading glasses that magnified his eyes tremendously. "We cannot prevent you from having the opportunity. It is to be hoped that you will not damage the reputation of the university too badly by what you do with it."

Ears burning, Monique left his office in a hurry. That she might prove an asset to the university had plainly never entered his mind. Her nails bit into her palms. *I'll show you, by God,* she thought. Having lost all her notes for the paper on the cult of Isis in Gallia Narbonensis that had occupied her before Marseille went up in nuclear fire, she was doing her best to reconstruct it despite a research library that wasn't nearly so good as the snooty professors and librarians believed.

Back in Marseille, having to deal with her brother and the unwelcome attentions of Dieter Kuhn had made her neglect the monograph. Here in Tours, Kuhn was gone from her life, for which she heartily thanked the Lord, the Virgin, and all the saints. Instead, though, she had to deal with the Lizard named

Ttomalss. He wanted nothing from her in bed. He even paid. But guiding him through Roman history stole time from the paper, no less than submitting to the German's less intellectual pursuits had done.

And she still had to deal with Pierre. Technically, she supposed he was a paroled prisoner. She tried not to have anything to do with him when he wasn't translating for Ttomalss. She sometimes wished she hadn't got him out of the Race's prison to interpret for her. Her life would have been simpler if she'd left him there to rot.

But he is my brother. Blood was thicker than water. She wondered if Pierre would go to a tenth the trouble for her that she'd gone through for him. She had her doubts. Pierre was for Pierre, first, last, and always.

One day, after they'd got off the telephone with Ttomalss, he said, "It's a pity that Lizard is such a straight arrow. If he weren't, I could have a fine new ginger network going already."

"Do you mean you don't have one?" Monique asked with what she hoped was withering sarcasm.

Predictably, her brother refused to wither. "Of course I do," he said. "I meant a new one, one that reached right up into his starship. That would be worth arranging, if only I could."

"Don't you ever think of anything but ginger and Lizards?" she demanded.

"Ginger is what I do for a living," Pierre said imperturbably. "The Lizards are my customers. Don't you ever think of anything else but those old Romans who've been dead forever?"

"Occasionally," Monique answered, acid in her voice. "Every now and then, for instance, I have to think about how to get you out of prison or whatever other trouble you wind up in on account of ginger."

Her brother didn't even have the grace to look shamefaced. "Took you long enough this time, too," he grumbled. "I thought I was going to rot in that damned cell forever. I got you out of the French jail faster than you sprang me."

Had he not added that last, reminding her he had helped her now and again, she thought she would have tried to hit him over the head with an ashtray. As things were, she said, "I never would have been carted off to jail if it weren't for Dieter Kuhn, and he wouldn't have cared about me at all if it weren't for you." One way or another, she was going to pin the blame on Pierre.

He said, "Would you rather have them take me back to jail?"

"What have I got to do with that?" Monique said. "You're selling ginger again. You don't bother hiding it from me. You hardly bother hiding it from anybody. Of course the Lizards will notice. They're not stupid. Do you think they're not watching you? Sooner or later, you'll annoy them enough that they'll scoop you up and throw you into another cell. I probably won't be able to get you out then, either."

"Somebody will." Pierre spoke with maddening confidence. "That's what connections are for. The more people you know, the more people you've got to do you a good turn when you really need one."

"And the more people you've got to betray you when they need something from the Lizards or the *flics*."

Pierre stared at her in some surprise. "Where'd you learn to think like that?"

Monique laughed at him. "And people say that studying history never does anybody any good!" she exclaimed, and swept out of the room before he could come up with an answer.

Somewhere south of the city of Tours, the Franks had hurled the previously invincible Arabs back in defeat more than twelve hundred years before. Monique knew that, but she had no interest in finding the battlefield. For one thing, nobody knew exactly where it was. For another, she had no motorcar to go gallivanting over the landscape. And, for a third, that battlefield didn't much interest her: it was several hundred years too modern. That amused her.

When she happened to mention it to Ttomalss, it amused him, too. "This is a difference in viewpoint between the Race and human beings," he said through her brother. "To us, a difference of a few hundred years would not matter much."

"That's strange," Monique said. "I would think that a chronological framework was important for your historians as well as for ours."

"Well, yes," Ttomalss said, "but everything that happened before the days of the Empire was a very long time ago for us. What real difference if something happened 103,472 years ago or 104,209? I pick the numbers at random, you understand."

In an aside, Pierre added, "When Lizards talk about years, cut everything they say in half. They count two for every one of ours, more or less."

"Thanks. I think I already knew that," Monique answered. It was still daunting. She tried to imagine keeping more than fifty thousand years of history straight. Maybe Ttomalss had a point after all. Even here on Earth, with only a tenth as much history to worry about, people specialized. She concentrated on Roman history. The faculty at the University of Tours also boasted a historian of pre-Roman (not ancient; that wasn't a word historians used since the Lizards came) Greece, one who studied medieval western Europe, one who specialized in the history of the Byzantine Empire (which struck even Monique as uselessly arcane), and so on.

Even so, she said, "Knowing the relative order in which things happened is important. Otherwise, you cannot speak of causation in any meaningful sense."

"Causation?" Her brother gave her a dirty look. "How the devil am I supposed to say that in the Lizards' language?"

"Figure it out," Monique told him. "If Ttomalss decides you're not doing a good job, *he'll* ask for a new interpreter, and I won't be able to do a thing about it."

Pierre's expression grew even more forbidding, but he must have managed to get the meaning across, for Ttomalss answered, "Yes, you are right about that: sequence and relative chronology must be preserved. Absolute chronology may be less important."

Monique wouldn't have said that, but she had less absolute chronology to keep in mind. And she found herself enjoying the give-and-take of the discussion with Ttomalss. The Lizard didn't think like a human being—*and why should he?* she thought— but he was a long way from stupid. He had trouble understanding how people worked as individuals, though he tried hard at that, too. When he dealt with groups, he did better.

"I thank you," he said one day. "I am learning a great deal from you. You are both intelligent and well organized. These traits are less common among Tosevites than I might wish."

After Pierre translated that, he added a two-word commentary of his own: "Teacher's pet."

Monique stuck out her tongue at her brother. She said, "Tell Ttomalss that I thank him and I think he's very kind." That was flattery, but flattery with a core of truth. It was also flattery with a core of worry. What exactly was he learning from her besides Roman history? Something that would help the Lizards rule their part of Earth more effectively? Did that make her a traitor to mankind?

Don't be silly, she said to herself. *Most people don't think Roman history matters to us these days, so how could it be important to the Lizards?* She relaxed for a while after that crossed her mind. But then she thought, *If the Lizards think it's important, maybe it is.*

When the telephone rang in her flat, she hurried to answer it. She'd dreaded the phone in Marseille: it was too likely to be Dieter Kuhn. Here, though, she hadn't had any trouble. *"Allô?"*

"Hello, Professor." Even if Rance Auerbach hadn't been speaking English, she would have known his wrecked, rasping voice at once. He went on, "How are things going for you up there?"

"Things are . . . very well, thank you. Thank you very much," Monique replied. She also used English, and was glad for the chance to practice it. Auerbach was a ginger dealer, too, but somehow that bothered her less in him than it did in her brother. She said, "Is it that I could ask you something?"

"Sure. Go ahead," he told her, and she poured out the substance of her conversations with Ttomalss and her worries about what the Race was learning. When she'd finished, Auerbach said, "The world would be a better place if everybody's troubles were so small."

"Thank you," Monique said again, this time in French: a breathy sigh of gratitude. She felt as if he were a priest who'd just given her absolution and a very light penance after a particularly sordid confession. "You have no idea how much you relieved me there. I want to be able to see myself in a mirror without flinching."

That produced a long silence. At last, Auerbach spoke in English again: "Yeah. Don't we all?" Monique suddenly wondered if she were the only one whose conscience bothered her.

☆ **18** ☆

"Yes, Colonel Webster," Jonathan Yeager's father was saying into the telephone. "I think we'll be all right if we keep cool. We have to stay firm out there, but we can't get pushy about it or we'll make them nervous. My professional opinion is, everybody'd be sorry if that happened." He listened for a moment, then said, "Okay, sir, I'll put it in writing for you, too," and hung up.

"More trouble about the motors on the rocks in the asteroid belt?" Jonathan asked.

His dad nodded. "You betcha. They can't blame me for that one, so they're asking my advice instead." Sam Yeager's chuckle sounded sour to Jonathan. "Hell, son, I didn't even know this was going on—though I've got to tell you, I've had suspicions ever since that big meteor slammed into Mars."

"Have you?" Jonathan raised an eyebrow. "You never said anything about it to me—or to Mom, either, that I know of."

"Nope." His father shook his head. "Not much point to talking about suspicions when you don't know for sure. Last time I was back in Little Rock, I did ask President Stassen about it."

"Did you?" That his father was in a position to ask questions of the president of the United States still sometimes bemused Jonathan. "What did he tell you?"

"Not much." His father looked grim. "I didn't really expect him to. He was probably afraid I'd go running to the Lizards with whatever I heard. That's nonsense, but it's nonsense I'm going to be stuck with for the rest of my life."

"That's not fair!" Jonathan exclaimed with the ready outrage of youth.

"Probably not, but I'm stuck with it, as I said." His dad shrugged. "I could go on and talk about what sort of lesson that should be for you, and that you should always keep an eye on

519

your reputation no matter what. But if I did that, you'd probably look around for something to hit me over the head with."

"Yeah, probably," Jonathan agreed. "You're not too bad as far as lectures go, but—"

"Thanks a lot," his father broke in. "Thanks a hell of a lot."

Jonathan grinned at him. "Any old time, Dad." But the grin had trouble staying on his face. "What are the Lizards going to do, out there in the asteroid belt? If they try doing anything, will we fight them?"

"It's like I told Ed Webster: if we don't do anything to get 'em twitchy, I think we can ride out the storm," his father answered. "But I also think they have to think we'd fight if they did try anything out there. A lot of the time, you end up not having to fight if you show you're ready to in a pinch."

"If we did fight the Race, we'd lose, wouldn't we?" Jonathan asked.

"Now? Sure we would, same as we would have last summer," his father replied. "But that's not the point, or it's only part of the point. The other part is how bad we'd hurt 'em if we went down swinging. They don't like what the Nazis did to them, and we'd do more and worse." He sighed. "If that outbound probe of theirs hadn't spotted our rocket lighting up, we could have built a much stronger position out in the asteroid belt before the Race caught on."

A strong position in the asteroid belt was something less than important to Jonathan. "Do you think there'll be a war, or not?" he asked. "The whole idea of fighting the Race seems like such a waste of everything worthwhile to me. . . ."

"I know it does," his father said slowly. "It seems that way to a lot of kids in your generation. I'll tell you something, though: when the Lizards first came to Earth, they shot up the train I was riding on, and I volunteered for the Army as soon as I made it into a town where they'd take me. So did Mutt Daniels, my manager, and he was about as old then as I am now. They took both of us, too. They didn't even blink. That's how things were back in those days."

Jonathan knew that was how things had been back in those days. He tried to imagine it, tried and felt himself failing. Stumbling a little, he said, "But the Race isn't so bad, really. You know that's true, Dad."

"I know it's true *now*," Sam Yeager said. "I didn't know it then. Nobody knew it then. All we knew was that the Lizards came out of nowhere and started beating the crap out of us. And if we—and the Reds, and the Nazis, and the British, and the Japs—hadn't fought like mad bastards, the Lizards would've conquered the whole world, and you and your pals wouldn't be looking at them from the outside and thinking how hot they are. You'd be looking at 'em up from under, and no way to get out from under 'em."

"Okay. Okay." Jonathan hadn't expected a speech. Maybe his dad hadn't expected to make one, either, because he looked a little surprised at himself. Jonathan went on, "I understand what you're saying, honest. Things do seem different to me, though. I can't pretend they don't."

"I know they do." His father's laugh was rueful. "You take the Race and spaceships and explosive-metal bombs and computing machines for granted. They're part of the landscape to you. You're not an old fogy who remembers the days before they got here."

"No, not me." Jonathan shook his head. *The old days, like Dad said,* he thought, and then, *The bad old days. People didn't know much back then.*

Now his father was the one who said, "Okay. You can't help being young, any more than I can help being . . . not so damn young." He ran a hand through his hair, which really was getting thin on top. But even if he wasn't so young, even if he was going bald, his eyes could still get a wicked twinkle in them. "Of course, if it weren't for the Lizards, you wouldn't be here at all, because I never would have met your mother if they hadn't come."

"I know. You've told me that before. I don't like thinking about it." Jonathan didn't like thinking about that at all. Imagining his own existence as depending on a quirk of fate was uncomfortable. Uncomfortable? Hell, it was downright terrifying. As far as he could tell, he'd always been here and always would be here. Anything that shook such foundations was not to be trusted.

"What do you like thinking about?" his father asked slyly. "Your wedding, maybe? Or your wedding night?"

"Dad!" Reproach rang in Jonathan's voice. His father *was* an old man. He had no business thinking about stuff like that.

"Just wait till you have kids," his father warned him. "You'll tell them about what it might have taken to make sure they weren't born, and they won't want to listen to you, either."

"I hope I don't go and do stuff like that," Jonathan said. "Maybe I'll remember how much I hated it when you did it to me."

His dad laughed at him, which only annoyed him more than ever. Sam Yeager said, "Maybe. But don't bet anything much on it, or you'll be sorry. I didn't like it when my father did it to me, but that's not stopping me. Once you get to a certain age and see your kid acting a certain way, well, you just naturally start acting a certain way yourself."

"*Do* you?" Jonathan said darkly. He wanted to think he'd be different when he turned into an old man, but would he? How could he tell now? A lot of years lay between him and his father's age, and he was in no hurry to pass through them.

"Yeah, you do," his father said, "however much you think you won't till you get there." He grinned at Jonathan again, this time less pleasantly. Jonathan scowled. His father could outguess him better than the other way round. That struck Jonathan as most unfair, too. Once upon a time, his dad had been young, and he still—sometimes, sort of—remembered what it was like. But Jonathan hadn't gotten old yet, so how was he supposed to think along with his father?

He gave ground now: "If you say so."

"I damn well do," his dad said. "How are you coming along with figuring out how to tie a bow tie?"

Jonathan threw his hands in the air in almost theatrical despair. "I don't think I'll ever get it so it looks right with a fancy tux."

That made his father laugh. "It wasn't anything I had to worry about when I married your mother. I was in uniform and she was wearing blue jeans. That great metropolis of—"

"Chugwater, Wyoming," Jonathan chorused along with his father. If he'd heard about the tobacco-chewing justice of the peace who'd married his folks once, he'd heard about him a hundred times. The fellow had been postmaster and sheriff, too. Not having to worry about a tux did give the story a slightly different slant, but only slightly.

His father's eyes went far away. "Things haven't worked so bad for Barbara and me, though," he said, more than half to himself. "No, not so bad at all." For a couple of seconds, he neither looked nor sounded like an old man, not even to Jonathan. He might have been looking forward to a wedding himself, not back on the one he'd had a long time ago.

"Chugwater, Wyoming." This time, Jonathan spoke the ridiculous name in a different tone of voice. "It must be pretty hot, to be able to remember getting married in a funny place like that. I mean, a church is probably prettier and all, but everybody gets married in a church."

"It was one of those crazy wartime things," his father answered. "Nobody knew whether the Lizards could take Chicago, so they pulled all the physicists and the typists—your mom was one—and the Lizard POWs and the interpreter—me—and sent everybody to Denver, where it was supposed to be safer. We almost got killed just when we were setting out. A Lizard killer-craft shot up our ship. That was the first time—" He broke off.

"The first time what?" Jonathan asked.

"Never mind. Nothing." His dad turned red. Jonathan scratched his head, wondering what that was all about. If he didn't know better, he would have sworn . . . He shook his head. Nobody was ever comfortable thinking about his father and mother doing *that*, especially before they got married. Sam Yeager went on, "Isn't there something useful you could be doing instead of standing around here jawing with me?" By his tone, he didn't want Jonathan thinking about that, either.

"Like what?" Jonathan didn't feel like doing anything useful, either. "Mickey and Donald are all taken care of." That was the chore he most often had to worry about. Not that he didn't enjoy dealing with the two little Lizards—though not so little now. He did. But he didn't want to get herded off to take care of them. That made him feel as if he were still little himself.

"I don't know," his father said. "Shall I think of something?"

"Never mind." Jonathan decamped from the kitchen, pausing only to grab a Coke from the refrigerator. He gambled that his dad wouldn't have time to come up with anything particularly nasty—yardwork qualified, in his opinion—before he did that, and he won his gamble.

Back in the safety of his own room, he took a big swig at the soda and started studying his assignment in the history of the Race: he had exams coming. *One more semester after this one, and then I can start making a living with the Lizards, just like Karen,* he thought. And, thanks to his dad, he had some of the best connections in the whole world. Friendship counted for an awful lot with the Race, and his father had more friends among the Lizards than any human being this side of Kassquit.

Poor Kassquit, he thought. Much as the Race fascinated him, he wouldn't have wanted to get to know it the way she had. Thinking about her made him sad and horny, both at once: he couldn't help remembering what they'd spent so much time doing up on the starship. Thinking about doing that with Kassquit made him think about doing it with Karen, and their wedding, and their wedding night. What with all that, he got very little real studying done, but he had a good time anyhow.

Rance Auerbach stared out the hotel window at the waters of the Mediterranean. Even now, with fall sliding toward winter, they remained improbably warm and improbably blue. Oh, the Gulf of Mexico pulled the same trick, but Marseille was at the same latitude as Boston, more or less. It seemed like cheating.

"We ought to get a blizzard," he said.

Penny Summers shook her head. "No, thanks. I saw too goddamn many blizzards when I was growing up. I don't want any more."

"Well, I don't, either," Rance admitted. "But weather this good this late in the year just doesn't feel right." He coughed, then wheezed out a curse under his breath. Coughing hurt. It always had, ever since he got shot up. It always would, up till the day they buried him. That, or something close to it, was on his mind these days. "Maybe I'm just antsy. Damned if I know."

"What's to be antsy about?" Penny asked. "We're doing great—a lot better now that they dropped on good old Pierre. Plenty of business, plenty of customers . . ."

"Yeah." Auerbach lit a cigarette. That would probably make him cough some more, but he didn't care. No, that wasn't right. He did care, but not enough to make him quit. "Maybe it's just that things are going too good. I keep waiting for the knock on the door at three in the morning."

Penny shook her head. "Not this time. If they didn't grab us when they got Pierre the Turd, they aren't gonna do it. You and me, sweetie, we're home free."

Now Rance eyed her with more than a little alarm. "Whenever you start thinking like that, you get careless. Remember what happened when we took that little trip down into Mexico? I don't want anything like that happening again. They owe us for a lot more now than they did back then."

"You worry too much," Penny said. "Everything's gonna be fine, you wait and see."

"You don't worry enough," Rance returned. "You go around acting like the Lizards and the Frenchmen can't see us, you're going to find out you're wrong. Then you'll be sorry, and so will I."

"I'm not the one who's been taking chances lately," Penny said. "You're the fellow who blackmailed that Lizard into finding good old Pierre's sister a job. Of course, that was just out of the goodness of your heart. Yeah, sure it was."

"Lay off me on account of that, will you please?" Auerbach said wearily. "I never messed around with her, and you can't say I did no matter how much you want to pin it on me."

"If I could, I'd be gone," Penny answered. "I don't stay where I'm not wanted, believe you me I don't." She glared at him. "But even if you didn't do anything, I could tell you wanted to."

"Oh, for Christ's sake." Rance rolled his eyes. He knew that was overacting, but he needed to overact a little, because Penny wasn't wrong. Picking his words with care and hoping that care didn't show, he said, "She's not ugly, but she's not anything special. I don't know what you're all up in arms about."

"Cut the crap, Rance," Penny said crisply. "I'm not blind, and I'm not stupid, either. I said you didn't do anything, but I know how a man looks at a woman, and I know how a man acts around a woman he's sweet on, too. You're not the sort of guy who charges out and does big favors for just anybody."

That held enough truth to hurt if Rance looked at it closely. He limped over to an ashtray and stubbed out the cigarette. Returning the glare Penny'd given him, he answered, "Yeah, that's why I threw you out on your can when you called me up out of a clear blue sky."

"You know how I paid you back, buster." She tugged at her skirt, as if about to pull it off. "Some other gal could do it the same way."

"After what Monique Dutourd went through with that damn Nazi, I don't think she pays in that coin," Auerbach said, though he would have been interested in finding out whether he was wrong. "And we've been round this barn before, babe. Like I said, I sicced the Germans on that goddamn Roundbush because I wanted a piece of David Goldfarb's ass."

When he'd used that line before, he'd made Penny laugh. Not this time. She said, "You sicced the Nazis on Roundbush because he pissed you off. That's the long and short of it."

That also held some truth, but only some. Stubbornly, he said, "I did it because I don't like to see anybody getting a raw deal. That goes for Goldfarb, and it goes for the French gal, too."

"Yeah, a knight in shining armor," Penny snarled.

"I already told you once, I didn't throw you out when you called me on the phone," Auerbach rasped. "I'll tell you something else, too—I'm getting goddamn sick of you ragging on me all the time. You don't like it, leave me half the cash and get your own room and run your own business and leave me the hell alone."

"I ought to," she said.

"Go ahead," Rance told her. "Go right ahead. We split up once before. Did you think we were going to last forever this time?" He was spoiling for a fight. He could feel it.

"That'll give you the excuse you need to hop on the next train for Tours and your little professor, won't it?" Penny blazed.

Rance laughed in her face. "I knew you were gonna say that. God damn it to hell, I knew you would. But there's something you don't get, sweetheart. If I'm by myself, I don't go to Tours. If I'm by myself, I go to the airport and hop on the first plane I can catch that's heading for the States."

Penny laughed, too, every bit as nastily as he had. "And you last about three days before the guys whose hired goons you plugged find out you're back and fill you full of holes for payback."

He shook his head. "I don't think so. Once I'm home, I can fade into the woodwork again. I did it for years before you barged in and livened things up. I figure I can do it again without much trouble."

"Go back to Fort Worth and finish drinking yourself to death? Quarter-limit poker with the boys at the American Legion hall?" Penny didn't hide her scorn. "You reckon you can stand the excitement?"

"It wasn't so bad," he answered.

Before Penny could say something else nasty, the telephone on the nightstand rang. She was standing a lot closer to it than Rance was, so she picked it up. *"Allô?"* That tried to be French, but ended up sounding a lot more like Kansas. She listened for a minute or so, then said, *"Un moment, s'il vous plaît,"* and held the phone out to Auerbach. "Talk to this guy, will you? I can't make out more than about every other word."

What that meant was, she had no idea what the Frenchman was saying. She spoke some French, but she'd always had a devil of a time understanding it when spoken. Rance limped over and took the phone from her. *"Allô?"* His own accent wasn't great, but he managed.

"Hello, Auerbach," said the frog on the other end of the line. "The shipment is early, for a wonder. You want to pick it up tonight instead of Friday?"

Now Rance said, *"Un moment."* He held his hand over the mouthpiece and spoke to Penny in English: "Want to get the stuff tonight?"

"Sure," she said at once. "Are we still in business?"

"You need me, or somebody who can really talk some, anyway," Auerbach answered. She made a face at him. He went back to French: *"C'est bon."*

"All right," the ginger dealer said. "Usual time. Usual place. But tonight." The line went dead.

Auerbach hung up the phone and folded his arms across his chest. "Like I said, you want to walk out on me, go right ahead. We'll see which one of us lasts longer as a solo act."

"Oh, screw you," she said, and then, half laughing and half still angry, she proceeded to do exactly that. She clawed him and bit his shoulder hard enough to draw blood. As he bucked above her, he was trying to hurt her at least as much as he was trying to please her. Afterwards, panting and sweaty, she asked him, "Where you gonna get a lay like that from your professor?"

"She's not my professor, dammit," he said. "If you listened as well as you screw, you'd know that."

"I don't want to listen," Penny said. "The more you listen, the more lies you hear. I've already heard too many." But after that she did stop putting him through the wringer about Monique Dutourd, for which he was more than duly grateful.

They got dressed and went downstairs to grab a taxi. "We want to go to 7 Rue des Flots-Bleu, in the Anse de la Fausse Monnaie," Rance said in French to the driver of the battered VW. In English, he remarked, "Just like Marseille to have a district named for counterfeit money." Then he had to squeeze into the cab's cramped back seat. "One more reason to hate the goddamn Nazis," he muttered as his leg complained.

The Anse de la Fausse Monnaie lay on the southern side of the headland whose northern side helped shape Marseille's Vieux Port. Being well to the west of the center of the city, it hadn't suffered badly from the explosive-metal bomb. The locals hardly thought of themselves as citizens of Marseille at all. They hadn't been till the Germans built roads connecting their little settlement to the main part of the city.

As soon as Auerbach paid off the cabby, the fellow drove away faster than a Volkswagen had any business going. Rance didn't care for that. "He doesn't much want to be around here, does he?" he said. "Next question is, what does he know that we don't?" The hotel couldn't have been more than a mile and a half away, but was effectively in a different world—and, with Rance's bad leg, a far distant one.

Penny, as usual, refused to worry. "We've been here before. We'll do fine this time, too," she said, and headed off toward the tavern that was their target. Sighing, wishing he were carrying a submachine gun, Auerbach followed.

Inside, fishermen and hookers looked up from their booze. The barkeep had seen the two new arrivals before, though. When he jerked a thumb at the staircase and said, "Room eight," everybody relaxed—even if the newcomers didn't look as if they belonged, they were known, expected, and therefore not immediately dangerous.

Rance's leg complained about the stairs, too, but he couldn't do anything about that. By the moans and low thumpings coming from behind the thin doors upstairs, most of those rooms weren't being used for ginger deals, but for a much older kind of transaction.

Rance knocked on the door with the tarnished brass 8. "Auerbach?" asked the Frenchman who'd telephoned.

"Who else?" he said in English. He didn't think the frog knew any, but that didn't matter. His ruined voice identified him as surely as a passport photo.

The door opened. A blinding light shone in his face. Another one speared Penny. The room was full of Lizards. They all pointed automatic rifles at the Americans. Rance's imagined submachine gun wouldn't have done him a damn bit of good.

"You are under arrest for trafficking in ginger!" one of the Lizards shouted in his own language. "We shall lock you up and eat the key!"

A human would have spoken of throwing away the key. As Auerbach raised his hands over his head, he wasn't inclined to quibble about differences in slang. He'd always known this day might come. He found himself less frightened, less furious, than he'd imagined he would or could be if it did. Turning his head toward Penny, he said, "I told you so."

"Oh, shut up," she answered, but he still thought he got the last word.

Nesseref always checked her telephone for messages when she got home after walking Orbit. As often as not, the messages she did get were advertisements, some delivered by real members of the Race reading from scripts, some altogether electronic. She deleted both sorts without the least hesitation. Nobody was ever going to convince her that she could set foot on the road to riches by responding to a phone call from someone far likelier to be out for his profit rather than her own.

Today, though, she had one of a different sort. A weary-looking male's visage appeared on her monitor. "I am Gorppet, of Security," he said. "I am calling from Kanth, near Breslau, in the Greater German *Reich*. We are both acquaintances of the Big Ugly named Mordechai Anielewicz. Please return my call at your convenience. I thank you." His recorded image disappeared.

What sort of trouble has Anielewicz found now? Nesseref wondered. Gorppet's phone code was part of the message. She let the computer reply, wondering if she would have to record a message for him in turn. But she got him. "Small-Unit Group Leader Gorppet speaking," he announced. "I greet you."

"And I greet you. Shuttlecraft Pilot Nesseref, returning your call."

"Ah. I thank you for being so prompt," Gorppet said.

"Mordechai Anielewicz is not just an acquaintance to me," Nesseref said. "As you will probably know, he is a friend. From your call, I presume that he is now a friend in trouble. How can I help him?"

"He is indeed a friend in trouble." Gorppet made the affirmative gesture. "He is being held hostage by several males of the

Jewish superstition here in Kanth. They may well kill him. It is even possible they have killed him already."

"Wait!" Nesseref exclaimed. "You must be mistaken. Anielewicz belongs to this superstition himself."

"I spoke truth," Gorppet said. "You do know that these Jews in Poland have an explosive-metal bomb."

"I know Anielewicz claimed to have one," Nesseref replied. "I never knew whether that was a truth, or only a fiction intended to impress me."

"It is, unfortunately, a truth," Gorppet told her. "And Jews, it seems, are no more immune to factional squabbles than any other Big Uglies. A faction that wanted to damage the Deutsche to the greatest possible degree seized control of the bomb during the late fighting and moved it to this vicinity."

"I . . . see." Nesseref saw only too well, and liked none of what she saw. "What will the Deutsche do if such a bomb bursts among them? What *can* they do?"

"No one precisely knows except for their own high-ranking officers," Gorppet said. "No one is eager to find out. We are operating on the assumption that they have more weapons than they surrendered to us. All evidence strongly points that way. That is why Anielewicz agreed to try to persuade these Jews to give themselves up."

"To help the Race? To help the Deutsche?" Nesseref said. "That is extraordinarily generous of him." She used an emphatic cough.

Gorppet's voice was dry: "I doubt those were his main motivations. I think he was more concerned lest Poland, his homeland, receive the brunt of whatever counterattack the Deutsche might make."

"Ah. Yes, that does make a certain amount of sense," Nesseref agreed. "But you have not answered the first question I asked you: how can I help him?"

"I have not thought of any direct way," Gorppet said. "Still, you know him well and you know Big Uglies well in general, especially for a female from the colonization fleet. Would you be willing to enter the *Reich* and become part of the team that is seeking to regain control over this bomb?"

"Provided my superiors approve, I would be happy to," Nesseref said.

"I have taken the liberty of making those arrangements before speaking to you," Gorppet said. "I will send transportation for you shortly."

"Have you? Will you?" Nesseref couldn't decide whether to be grateful or annoyed. "How very . . . efficient." She grudgingly gave the male the benefit of the doubt.

He proved as good as his word. Nesseref had just got Orbit's food and water ready for her own absence when an official motorcar pulled up in front of her apartment building. The driver telephoned from the motorcar, as if to leave her in no possible doubt: "I await you, Shuttlecraft Pilot."

"Coming." Nesseref hurried to the elevator, waited impatiently for it to arrive, and then rode down to the lobby. When she went out to the motorcar, she asked the driver, "Will you take me to this town by Breslau?"

"No, superior female," he said, and drove her out of the new town to where a helicopter waited on the yellowish, dying grass of a meadow. She did not care for helicopters, reckoning them unsafe. But she boarded this one with no more than a minimal qualm. It sprang into the air and flew off toward the west.

When it landed, it came down not far from the wrecked and radioactive Deutsch city, at an encampment almost as large as the nearby Tosevite town of Kanth. At first, Nesseref was surprised to discover that the encampment contained Deutsch Tosevites as well as members of the Race. Then she realized that made good logical sense. The Deutsche, after all, were the ones most intimately concerned with the explosive-metal bomb.

"Yes, it is a considerable embarrassment for us," Gorppet said when she was escorted to his tent. "The Jews, after all, are Big Uglies who are supposed to be under our control. For them to act so emphatically against our interest makes us look like fools to the Deutsche."

"And to other Big Uglies," Nesseref remarked.

"And to other Big Uglies," the male from Security agreed. "The problem the Jews pose the Deutsche is at present the most urgent, however."

"These Jews refuse to release Anielewicz?" Nesseref asked.

Gorppet made the affirmative gesture. "He went to them, they seized him, and he has not been seen since. We cannot prove he is still alive, but we presume he is, or the Big Uglies with the bomb would likely have tried to detonate it."

"I . . . see," Nesseref said, as she had when he telephoned her. "You have a lot of optimistic speculation resting on very little evidence, or so it seems to me."

"That may well be so," Gorppet said.

"Has anyone found a way to extract Anielewicz from his predicament?" Nesseref asked.

Now Gorppet used the negative gesture. "Not without unacceptable risk of having the bomb go off," he replied.

"That would be unfortunate," Nesseref said.

"Truth. And especially for Anielewicz." Yes, Gorppet's voice was dry. "Consideration is also being given to a bombardment so sharp and intense, it would kill everyone in the house before anyone could trigger the bomb."

"That would be wonderful, if it worked," Nesseref said. "How likely is it to work, do you think?"

"If either we or the Deutsche thought it likely, it would have been attempted by now," the male replied. "That no one has attempted it shows how risky it is. That it remains under consideration shows how seriously both we and the Deutsche view this situation."

"I understand," Nesseref said. "Have you come to any better notion of how I may help rescue Anielewicz and keep the bomb from going off?"

"Unfortunately, no," the male from Security told her. "But, since you know him well, I was hoping you might have insights and ideas that have not occurred to me." Another male came in. His body paint was slightly more elaborate than Gorppet's. To him, Gorppet said, "Superior sir, here is Shuttlecraft Pilot Nesseref. Shuttlecraft Pilot, I present to you Hozzanet, my superior."

"I greet you," Nesseref said.

"And I greet you," Hozzanet replied. "Welcome to the waiting room, Shuttlecraft Pilot. We hope we are far enough away to escape the worst effects of blast and radiation. We also hope we do not have to try to find out experimentally."

"I can see that you might." Nesseref swung an eye turret from Hozzanet to Gorppet and back again. "Are all Security males as cynical as the two of you?"

"Probably," Hozzanet answered. "It is a useful part of our professional baggage. Believing the males and females and Big Uglies we are in charge of investigating would only trap us in a net of lies."

"From your point of view, I suppose that makes sense," Nesseref said. "You must have endless trouble with such unreliable and ever-shifting circumstances. I am glad I deal with the physical universe, with constants rather than variables."

A couple of other males in the body paint of Security pushed their way into the tent. Nesseref paid them no special notice till one of them asked, "Small-Unit Group Leader Gorppet?" When Gorppet made the affirmative gesture, both males drew pistols and aimed them at him. The one who'd spoken before said, "You are under arrest, on suspicion of dealing in ginger and violent assault on the Race in the subregion known as South Africa. Your Tosevite accomplices have been captured in the not-empire of France, and have made full confessions."

Nesseref stared in astonishment. Gorppet said, "I deny everything." He sounded convincing. But he'd just shown he, like Hozzanet, believed in very little. He *would* sound convincing, regardless of whether he spoke truth.

Hozzanet spoke to the males with the pistols: "We are in an emergency situation here. For the good of the Race, I ask that you allow my subordinate to stay free till it is resolved. If it is resolved satisfactorily, he will probably have earned a pardon. If not"—he shrugged—"we are all liable to be dead."

The Security male who'd been quiet till then said, "We have no authority to bargain with you or with him."

"Then you had better get some." Hozzanet was as ready to bend the rules as a Big Ugly. "Go on. I give my pledge, in the Emperor's name, that he will not flee."

After whispering to each other, the Security males made the affirmative gesture. "On your snout be it," one of them said. He left. His partner stayed.

"I thank you, superior sir," Gorppet said quietly.

"I warned you when I recruited you for Security that we would not tolerate large-scale ginger operations," Hozzanet said. "But you have a chance to redeem yourself even there—if that bomb does not burst."

"If it does, spirits of Emperors past will judge us," Nesseref said, and cast down her eye turrets.

"That is a truth," Hozzanet agreed. "And they will judge harshly—they have never heard of ginger."

"What you need to do," Nesseref said, "is to get into communication with Anielewicz and help him persuade his fellow Jews not to detonate the explosive-metal bomb. If not . . ." She found herself puzzled and dismayed. She had never thought she would have any great use for a ginger dealer, but Gorppet plainly worked hard on his actual duties when he was not involved with the herb. And he didn't seem to use it as some males did, as a tool to get females to mate with him.

Now he made the affirmative gesture. "That is a truth, superior female. It is what I need to do—or you, if you think the Big Ugly more likely to heed a friend than an acquaintance. But do you have any idea how to accomplish it without inciting the other Jewish Tosevites to set off the bomb?"

Wishing she could do anything else but, Nesseref used the negative gesture.

Prevod was an excellent writer. Straha would never have asked her to collaborate with him had he not liked some of her work he'd seen. And, as he saw from the prose the two of them produced together, his memoirs would be an egg-smasher to set tongues wagging for years . . . if they were ever published. He'd always expected Atvar to prove an obstacle to publication. He hadn't expected the same problem from his coauthor.

"But, Shiplord, you cannot say that!" Prevod exclaimed, not for the first time, when Straha outlined another of the quarrels that had led to his barely unsuccessful effort to overthrow Atvar as fleetlord of the conquest fleet.

"And why not?" Straha demanded. He liked it that she was polite enough to call him *shiplord*, even though he was no longer entitled to wear the body paint showing him to be the third most powerful male in the conquest fleet. "It is a truth. I never stopped warning him that his half measures would lead to trouble. He continued them, and they did indeed lead to trouble."

"Have you got documentary evidence to support this?" Prevod asked.

"I am sure such evidence exists," Straha said. "I did not offer this advice in secret, but in meetings of the high-ranking officers of the fleet. Those records would have been preserved."

"Can we gain access to them?" Prevod asked. "Or are they concealed from general view under secrecy regulations?"

"The latter, I would suspect," Straha said. "Atvar would not be eager to have his ineptitude displayed for everyone to see." He hesitated. When he went on, his tone was grudging: "And, I admit, even now we might not want the Big Uglies to learn how divided and uncertain we were in those days. They might think that malady still afflicted us. And"—acid returned to his voice—"with Atvar still in command, they might be right."

Prevod sighed. "Without the documentation, Shiplord, how can I hope to include this incident in the book?"

Straha sighed, too. "I am not writing a history text here, you know. Footnotes are not mandatory." He studied Prevod. She was young and bright and highly skilled with words. When he engaged her, he'd thought that would be enough. He'd thought it would be more than enough, in fact. What he thought now was, *Maybe I was wrong.* Swinging an eye turret her way, he asked, "Have you ever felt inclined to challenge authority?"

"Why, no, Shiplord." She sounded astonished that he should put such a question to her. "Those senior to me are generally senior for good reason. They know more than I do, and have more experience. Should I not learn from them rather than trying to substitute my inferior judgment for theirs?"

That was the response a female of the Race should have given. It was the response the large majority of males and females would have given. Straha knew as much. But hearing it now frustrated him no end. "If those in authority make a mistake, should you not point it out? If you fail to point it out, will they not go on making it—and probably making other mistakes as well?"

"Their own superiors are the ones who should correct them," Prevod replied. "That is not an appropriate role for an inferior."

"Who was Atvar's superior?" Straha asked. "He made mistakes. He made them in huge lots. Who was to point them out to him? He had no superiors here. He still has none—and he is probably still making mistakes."

"In my opinion, rehashing a past that cannot be changed will not gain you many readers," Prevod said. "You would create a far more entertaining and exciting book by concentrating on the foibles of the Big Uglies and on your return to the Race with the information about which group of Tosevites attacked the colonization fleet. Do remember, most of those who read the book will have come here as members of the colonization fleet, not the conquest fleet."

"I understand that," Straha said. "You want this to be an entertaining and exciting memoir, then, not an important one?"

"If no one reads it, how can it be an important memoir?" Prevod said.

By the Emperor, how I want a taste of ginger, Straha thought. *By the Emperor, how I need a taste of ginger.* He refrained, though it wasn't easy. He knew he would have a harder time putting up with Prevod if he did taste. Picking his words with care, he said, "One of the so-called foibles you mention was an honesty so thoroughgoing, the male who possessed it gave me information that would harm his own not-empire and his own species because he judged that the right thing to do. How many males and females of the Race could hope to match him? But perhaps that would not amuse my readers enough to be entertaining."

He intended his words for sarcasm. But Prevod took them literally, saying, "Many would think well of the Big Ugly under those circumstances. Having a sympathetic Tosevite appear might make for an interesting novelty."

"We both use the language of the Race," Straha said, "but I wonder if we speak the same tongue. Maybe I should go on in English." He spoke the last sentence in the Tosevite language. He hadn't used it since fleeing the United States.

"What did you just say?" Now Prevod sounded interested. When he told her, she went on, "Did you have to learn that Tosevite tongue? Were the Big Uglies too ignorant to learn ours?"

"You really ought to know better," Straha said. "Some of them not only speak it but write it quite well." That was when he realized he'd lost his temper, for he added, "About as well as you do, in fact."

Prevod's tailstump quivered in anger. She said, "That is ridiculous."

"Is it?" Yes, Straha had lost his temper. He wrote an electronic message to Sam Yeager under the name of Maargyees that Yeager used to fool the Race's computer network: *I am trying to persuade a certain—a very certain—female that you are literate in our language.*

Luck was with him, for a reply came back almost at once: *I am sorry, Shiplord, but I cannot write it any more than I can speak it.*

I see, Straha wrote back. *And why not?*

Because I am only a Big Ugly, of course, Sam Yeager re-

turned. *How can anyone without a tailstump have any brains?*
That is where the Race keeps them, is it not?

I often wonder if we keep them anywhere, Straha wrote.

Well, in that case you are wasted as a male of the Race, his Tosevite friend answered. *You really ought to turn into a Big Ugly.*

Straha's mouth fell open in startled laughter. He swung an eye
turret away from the monitor and back toward Prevod. "Do you
see what I mean?"

The writer's tailstump was twitching more than ever. "If you
care for his writing so much, Shiplord"—now she used the title
as one of reproach, not respect; he could hear the difference in
her voice—"maybe you ought to get him to compose your memoirs with you."

"Do you know," Straha said slowly, "that is not the worst idea
I have ever heard. Of course, most of the worst ideas I have ever
heard have come straight from Atvar's mouth."

He meant the joke to soften what he'd said just before. It
didn't do the job. Prevod sprang to her feet. "Whomever you use
to help you write your memoirs, I shall not be that female," she
said. "As far as I can see, the Race was right to keep you far
away—you fit in better with the Tosevite barbarians than you do
with us." She punctuated that with an emphatic cough. And, before Straha could say anything, she stormed out of his chamber
in Shepheard's Hotel and slammed the door behind her.

"Oh, dear," Straha said aloud. Then he started to laugh. He
went back to the computer and wrote, *Are you still there, Sam*
Yeager?

No, I am not here, Yeager replied. *I expect to be back pretty*
soon, though.

That was, on the face of it, absurd. No male of the Race would
have thought to write any such self-contradictory sentences.
And yet, as an answer to a rhetorical question, why wasn't *no* as
good as *yes?* Straha returned to the keyboard and wrote, *How*
would you like to help me put my memoirs together?

What happened to the writer you were working with? the Tosevite asked.

You did, Straha answered.

This time, the only symbol Sam Yeager sent was the one the
Race used as a written equivalent of an interrogative cough.

It is, unfortunately, a truth, Straha told him. *I made an in-*
vidious comparison between her writing ability and yours, and,

for some reason or other, she took offense. I now find myself without a collaborator. Are you interested in becoming one? You know the story I aim to tell. You should: you have interrogated me about a good deal of it.

The Big Ugly didn't reply for some little while. When he did, he wrote, *Sorry for the delay. I had to find out what "invidious" meant. You must be joking, Shiplord.*

By no means, Straha wrote, and used the symbol for an emphatic cough.

Well, if you are not, you ought to be, Sam Yeager wrote back. *I do not write your language well enough for males and females of the Race to want to read my words. They would be able to tell I am a Big Ugly. Your computers figured out that I was, because I sound as if I am writing English.*

Computers do not read. Readers read, Straha insisted. *Your way of writing is interesting and unusual, whatever makes it so.*

I thank you, Shiplord, Sam Yeager replied. *I thank you very much. You have paid me a great compliment. But I cannot do this. And your chances of getting your memoir published go up if you have a member of the Race writing with you, and go down with me. You cannot say that is not a truth.*

If any Tosevite is a hero among the Race, you are that male, Straha wrote. *Your name would help the memoir, not hurt it.*

Maybe—but maybe not, too, his friend responded. *And having my name on your memoir would not help me here in the United States. I may be a hero to the Race, but many Americans still think I am a traitor.*

Straha hadn't considered that. He realized he should have. *Very well, then,* he wrote. *Farewell for now.*

Farewell, Sam Yeager wrote back. *Barbara has just called me to supper. Good luck finding another male or female to work with.*

"Good luck," Straha said mournfully. "I will need more than luck. I will need a miracle. Several miracles, very likely. And I do not believe in miracles. I have been in exile too long to believe in miracles."

He'd been an exile from the Race, and now he was an exile among the Race. He hadn't been at home in the United States, and he didn't feel at home now that he'd managed to return to the society the Race was building on Tosev 3. *I probably would not feel at home if I went into cold sleep and flew back to Home.* If he didn't fit in among the Race here, how would the smug and stifling society back on the homeworld seem to him?

He went over to the ginger jar Atvar had let him have. He took a big taste. As euphoria filled him, he patted the jar with an affectionate hand. With ginger, if nowhere else, he found himself at home.

David Goldfarb took a last long look at the notes he'd been fooling with for the past few months. The time for fooling was over. Now he had to get to work. He wasn't going to refine his concept any further on paper. He would have to see what he got when he turned scribbles and sketches into something real.

Part of him was nervous, heart-poundingly nervous. When he started working for real instead of on paper, he might turn out not to be able to make anything worth having. But the rest of him, the larger part, was eager. He'd learned electronics—or what people knew of electronics before the Lizards came—by tinkering. He still sometimes felt he thought better with his hands than with his head.

He got up from his table. "I'm going out for a bit," he told Hal Walsh. "I need to pick up a couple of things we haven't got here."

His boss nodded. "Okay. Bring the receipts back, too, and I'll reimburse you."

"Thanks," Goldfarb said. "I'm not sure you'll want to when you see what I've got, but . . ." He shrugged.

"I'm not sure I like the sound of that," Walsh said, but he was grinning.

Jack Devereaux looked up from the circuit he was soldering. "I'm almost sure I don't," he said, which made Walsh laugh. Goldfarb was grinning as he put on his overcoat. Hal was a pretty good chap to work for, no doubt about it.

His grin slipped when he went outside. Edmonton in late November was raw and blustery, with the wind feeling as if there were nothing at all between the North Pole and the street down which he was walking. People seemed to take it in stride. David didn't think he ever would. The British Isles lay this far north, too, but the Gulf Stream moderated their climate. Nothing Goldfarb had seen moderated the climate here.

Fortunately, the shop he wanted was only a couple of blocks

from the Saskatchewan River Widget Works. He bought what he needed and went back to the Widget Works with his purchases in a big paper sack. Before he headed back, though, he made sure he took the receipt out of the sack and stuck it in his pocket. If things went the way he hoped, Hal Walsh *would* pay him back. If they didn't, his boss would laugh at him.

He shook his head. Hal wouldn't laugh. Not everything worked out, and Walsh was smart enough to understand as much. But if this didn't work, it would fail rather more spectacularly than other failed projects at the Widget Works. And, Goldfarb suspected, Jack Devereaux would never let him forget about it, even if his boss did.

Devereaux and Walsh both looked up when David came in carrying the big sack. "Doughnuts?" Devereaux asked hopefully.

"That would be a lot of doughnuts," Hal Walsh observed. Devereaux nodded, as if to say that the prospect of a lot of doughnuts didn't bother him a bit.

"Sorry, blokes." Goldfarb upended the sack on his work table. Four large, fuzzy teddy bears spilled out. One spilled a little too far, and ended on the floor. He picked it up and put it with the others.

In interested tones, Devereaux asked, "Are those for your second childhood or for your children's first?"

"With a spot of luck, neither," Goldfarb replied. As if to prove as much, he seized an Exacto knife and slit one of the bears from neck to crotch. He started pulling out stuffing and tossing it in the wastebasket. Devereaux made horrified noises. Goldfarb looked up from his work with what he hoped was a suitably demented grin. "Didn't know you were working alongside the Ripper, Jack?"

Devereaux made more horrified noises, this time at the pun rather than at the carnage David was inflicting on the defenseless toy. Hal Walsh inquired, "What *are* you doing besides getting this place ankle-deep in fluff?"

"I hope I'm playing Dr. Frankenstein," Goldfarb answered, whereupon Jack Devereaux lurched stiff-legged around the office in one of the worst Boris Karloff impressions David had ever seen. Refusing to let the other engineer get his goat, or even his bear, he nodded. "That's right, Jack. Without the little motors and the little batteries the Lizards have shown us how to make—

to say nothing of their compact circuits—I never could have imagined this. As things are—"

"You've had the chance to go crazy in a whole different way," Devereaux said.

David shrugged. "Maybe. I'm going to try to find out."

"Dr. Frankenstein?" Walsh eyed him. The boss was nobody's fool. "By God, you're going to make an animated teddy bear, aren't you?"

"I'm going to try," Goldfarb answered. "They used to do this kind of thing with gears and clockwork, but I got to thinking that electronics are a lot more flexible."

Jack Devereaux's eyes lit up. "That's a damn good idea, David. I don't know if you can make it walk on two legs, but something that moves its arms, moves its eyes, and still stays cute as all get-out . . . We, or somebody, could sell a lot of those."

With another nod, Goldfarb said, "I'm thinking the same thing. And something that talks, too: those sound chips are cheap to make. And maybe . . ." He snapped his fingers in delight at coming up with an idea not in his notes; sure as hell, working with his hands was inspirational. "We could hide a little infrared sensor right on the thing's nose, so nobody would need to actually flip a switch to turn it on."

"The more I hear of this, the better I like it," Walsh said. "I really do. We get the design patent, then license it for manufacture, and we might rake in a very nice piece of change, a very nice piece of change indeed. We need a name for 'em, though. What'll we call 'em? Fluffies?" He batted at a wisp of teddy-bear stuffing floating in the air. "How's that sound? Fluffies." He cocked his head to one side, considering the flavor of the name.

"Not Fluffies," Goldfarb said. "Furries."

"David's right." Jack Devereaux nodded vigorously. "The fluff's on the inside, where it won't show. The fur's right out there in plain sight."

After a moment's thought, Walsh nodded, too. "Okay, Furries it is. We've got a name. We've got an idea. Now let's make it real." He beamed at Goldfarb. "How would you like to be driving a Cadillac by this time next year?"

"I don't like driving anything here," David answered. "It still feels like I'm on the wrong side of the bloody road. But if I have to drive anything, a Cadillac wouldn't be bad. This side of a tank, I couldn't very well get any more iron around me."

"This is putting the car before the horse—or before the Furry, I should say," Devereaux pointed out. "Like Hal said, we need a real one, so we can see if we've got anything worth having."

"If you hadn't interrupted me at my surgery, I'd be on the way there already." Goldfarb went over to the parts bin that ran along one wall of the office and started rummaging through them. Though he didn't know it, his face wore an enormous smile. Tinkering made him happy—yes, indeed.

Once he had the idea and the parts, the Furry presented no enormous technical challenges. The biggest was getting all the components into its belly and still retaining enough stuffing to keep it huggable. A teddy bear that wasn't soft, he reasoned, would lose half its appeal.

"*Now* what are you doing?" Devereaux asked a little later. "Brain surgery?"

Exacto in hand, David nodded. "You might say so. Occurred to me this fellow might have big blinking eyes instead of the glass buttons he came with. But if he's going to get them, I've got to open up his head."

He used the knife to slice up hollow plastic balls, and colored them with the pens in his shirt pocket. They required another little motor, this one inside the head. Jack Devereaux clicked his tongue between his teeth at the result. "If I saw anything with eyes like that, I'd run like hell."

"It's a prototype, dammit," Goldfarb snapped. "It lets me know what I can do and what I can't. The next one will be prettier."

He installed the infrared sensor in the Furry's nose, and some sound chips and a little speaker behind the mouth. When he aimed an infrared beam at the revamped teddy bear, it spoke in muddy tones: "Here, piss off."

"Hmm," Hal Walsh said. "We may have to work on that just a bit." Everybody laughed. Then Walsh asked, "Do you suppose you can make it move its lips while it talks, the same way it moves its eyes?"

"Hadn't thought of that," Goldfarb answered. "I can try. By the time we're done with the bloody thing, it'll do everything but make tea." He paused. "But maybe that's not so bad. The more it can do, the longer Junior will take to get bored with it."

Some more tinkering provided the Furry with plastic lips carved from another ball. They didn't move in a very lifelike way, but they moved. Walsh nodded. "That's better—or busier, anyhow."

"I think he's ugly as sin, myself," Jack Devereaux said.

David eyed him. "Some people might say the same about you, old chap. The Furry's a first try. He'll improve." He didn't spell out the implications. Devereaux made a horrible face at him just the same.

"Mutilate another teddy bear, would you, David?" Hal Walsh said. "See if you can do a neater job on this one. I'm going to get on the phone and talk with a couple of manufacturers I know— and with an advertising agent, too. With something like this, we want to make the biggest splash we possibly can."

"Right," Goldfarb said, and got to work. Somewhat belatedly, it occurred to him that he might have made more money had he developed this project on his own, not under the auspices of the Saskatchewan River Widget Works. He shrugged as he slit open the belly of a second plush bear. Walsh hadn't had to hire him, and had backed him up during his troubles with Basil Round-bush. His boss deserved recompense for that—and, if the Furries did even a quarter as well as the men of the Widget Works dreamt they would, there'd probably be plenty of money to go around.

Walsh said, "I just called Jane, too. She can come by and record some prettier phrases than the one you used there."

"Fair enough," David answered. Jane Archibald's voice wasn't so smashing as her looks, but it was an improvement over his lower middle class, East End London accent.

He was just affixing the second set of plastic lips when Hal Walsh's fiancée came in. The men from the Widget Works put both prototype Furries through their paces. Jane's eyes went wide. "Every little girl in the world will want one," she breathed, and then, "If you have them saying things in a man's voice—and maybe if they were different colors—you could sell a lot to boys, too, I think."

"I like that," Goldfarb said, and scribbled a note.

The toy jobber who came to the Widget Works the next day also liked it. He stared in astonished fascination at the second prototype Furry—by then, the first one was safely out of sight. "Oh, yes," he said once he'd seen it put through its paces. "Oh, yes, indeed. I think we'll be able to move a great many of these, provided the manufacturing costs aren't too high."

"Here." Hal Walsh handed him a sheet of paper. "This is my best estimate. Most of the parts are right off the shelf."

"Oh, my," the jobber said after glancing over it. "Well, I can see it's going to be a great deal, a very great deal, of pleasure doing business with you gents."

"David here gets the credit for this one," Walsh said; he was, sure enough, a good man to work for. He patted the Furry on the head. "David gets the credit—and, with a little bit of luck, we all rake in the cash."

Reuven Russie wondered when he'd last been so nervous knocking on a door. It had been a while—he knew that. When he'd come here to look at the widow Radofsky's toe, that had been business. Now he was coming to look at all of her, and that was anything but.

How long had he been standing here? Long enough to start worrying? He'd been worrying since before he left home, and the "helpful" advice from his twin sisters hadn't made things any better or easier. Had anybody inside here heard him? Should he knock again? He was just about to when the door opened. "Hello—Reuven," Mrs. Radofsky said.

"Hello—Deborah," he answered, at least as tentatively; he'd had to check the office records to find out her first name. "Hello, Miriam," he added to the widow Radofsky's daughter, who clung to her mother's skirt. Miriam didn't answer. She probably didn't like him much; he was the fellow who gave her medicines that tasted nasty and shots.

"This is my sister, Sarah," Deborah Radofsky said, nodding back toward a slightly younger woman who looked a lot like her. "She'll watch Miriam while we're out."

"Hello," Reuven said. "We've spoken on the phone, I think."

"Yes, that's right, Doctor," the widow Radofsky's sister said. "Have a good time, the two of you. Come here, Miriam." Reluctantly, Miriam came.

Deborah Radofsky stepped out onto the sidewalk. "Shall we go?"

"Yes, let's," Reuven answered. He cast about for what to say next, and did find something: "How is your toe doing?"

"It's getting better," she replied. "It's not quite right yet, but it is getting better." They walked on for a few paces. The night was clear and cool. It was also peaceful; the Muslims in Jerusalem, and in the Near East generally, had been calm of late, for which Reuven was very glad. Mrs. Radofsky also seemed to be looking for something more to say. At last, she asked, "Where are we going for supper?"

"I had Samuel's in mind," Reuven replied. "Have you been there? The food's always pretty good."

"Yes, I have." She nodded. "But not since . . ." Her voice trailed off. *Not since my husband was alive*—that had to be what she wasn't saying.

"Would you rather go somewhere else?" Reuven asked. "If eating there would make you unhappy . . ."

"No, it's all right." The widow Radofsky shook her head. "It wasn't a special place, or anything like that. It's just that I haven't been out to eat anywhere much since he . . . died. Things have been tight, especially with Miriam."

Reuven nodded. Samuel's was only about four blocks away; nothing in Jerusalem was very far from anything else. They had no trouble getting a table. Reuven ordered braised short ribs; Deborah Radofsky chose stuffed cabbage. He ordered a carafe of wine, too, after a glance at her to make sure she didn't mind.

The wine came before the food. Reuven raised his glass. *"L'chaim!"*

"L'chaim!" Deborah echoed. They both drank. She set her glass down on the white linen of the tablecloth. After a moment, she said, "Do you mind if I ask you something?"

"Go ahead," he answered.

Her smile flickered, as if uncertain whether to catch fire. She said, "You're the son of an important man—a famous man, even. You're a doctor yourself. Why haven't you been married for years?"

"Ah." Reuven had expected something like that, if perhaps not quite so blunt. But he liked her better for the bluntness, not worse. He said, "Up till I left the medical college, I was very busy—too busy to think a whole lot about such things. I was seeing somebody at the college for a while, but she emigrated to Canada as soon as she finished, and I didn't want to leave Palestine. I have a cousin in the same town she moved to. He says she's getting married soon."

"Oh." The widow Radofsky weighed his words. "How do you feel about that?"

"I hope she's happy," Reuven answered, much more sincerely than not. "She's always done what she wanted to do, and I don't think this will be any different." He looked up. "Here comes supper." Even if he didn't wish Jane any ill whatsoever, he didn't feel altogether comfortable talking about her with Deborah Radofsky.

She dug into her stuffed cabbage, too. For a while, they were both too busy eating to talk. Then she found another disconcerting question: "How do you like taking out one of your patients?"

"Fine, so far," he said, giving back a deadpan stare he'd learned from his father.

She didn't quite know what to make of that; he could see as much. After a sip of wine, she asked, "Do you do it often?"

"This makes once," Reuven said, deadpan still. He threw back a question of his own: "How do you like going out with your doctor?"

"This is the first time I've been out with anyone since Joseph . . . died," Mrs. Radofsky said. "I would be lying if I said it didn't feel a little strange. It doesn't feel any more strange because you're my doctor, if that's what you mean."

"All right." Now Reuven tried on a smile. It fit his face better than he'd thought it would. "I like your little girl."

That made Deborah Radofsky smile, too. "I'm glad. Someone at the furniture store asked me to go out with him a few weeks ago, but he changed his mind when he found out I have a child." She stabbed the next bite of stuffed cabbage as if it were her coworker.

"That's foolishness," Reuven said. "Life isn't neat and simple all the time. I used to think it was a lot simpler, back when I was still going to the medical college. The more real practice I see, though, the more complicated things look."

"Life is never simple." The widow Radofsky spoke with great conviction. "You find that out the minute you have a baby. And then Joseph went off to work one morning, and the riots started, and he didn't come home, and two days after that we had a funeral. No, life is never simple."

"What did he do?" Reuven asked quietly.

"He was a lathe operator," she answered. "He was a good one, too. He worked hard, and he was going places. His boss thought so, too. And then . . . he wasn't any more." She emptied her wineglass in a hurry. When Reuven held up the carafe, she nodded. He filled her glass again, then poured some more wine for himself, too.

As they finished supper, he asked, "Would you like to go see that new film—well, new here, anyhow—about ginger-smuggling in Marseille? I'm more interested than I would be otherwise, because my cousin—the one who's in Canada now—got forced into dealing ginger there when he was in the RAF."

"Vey iz mir!" Deborah Radofsky exclaimed. "How did that happen?"

"His superior was in the business in a big way, and David was a Jew, which meant he had a hard time saying no unless he wanted worse things to happen to him," Reuven answered. "Of course, the Nazis arrested him, and it's hard to get a whole lot worse off than that. My father got the Race to pull strings to get him out."

"Lucky for him your father could," she said, and then, after a moment, "Marseille's one of the places that got bombed, isn't it?"

Reuven nodded. "The film was made before the fighting, obviously. Otherwise, there'd be nothing but ruins. It's supposed to have some spectacular car chases, too."

"I'll come," Deborah Radofsky said. "Miriam won't give Sarah too hard a time. She'll go to sleep, and my sister can look at the television or find something to read."

"Oh, good." Whether it was too much trouble for her sister would have been Reuven's next question.

The theater wasn't far, either. It was the one Reuven and Jane Archibald had come to on the night they first made love. He glanced over at the widow Radofsky. He didn't think they'd be sharing a bed tonight. He shrugged. He'd known Jane a long time before they became lovers. He wasn't going to worry about hurrying things here.

"You've got about fifteen minutes to wait before this show lets out," the ticket-seller told him as he laid down his money.

"That's not bad," Deborah Radofsky said. Reuven nodded. They went into the lobby. Reuven got them both some garbanzo beans fried in olive oil and glasses of Coca-Cola. They were just wiping their hands when people started coming out of the film.

Reuven heard Arabic, Hebrew, Yiddish, and something that might have been either Russian or Polish. The film would be subtitled in the first two languages; the dialogue, he knew, was mostly in English. And then, to his surprise, a couple of Lizards came out. They were chattering away in their own tongue.

"What were they saying?" Mrs. Radofsky asked.

"They were wondering how much of the story was true and how much was made up," Reuven answered. "What I'm wondering is whether they were from Security, or if they were ginger smugglers themselves. One or the other, I'd bet. I wish I'd got a better look at their body paint."

"If they were in Security, wouldn't they be smart to wear body paint that said they weren't?" she remarked.

"Mm, you're probably right," Reuven said. "Come on—let's go in and grab the best seats we can."

The film wasn't one for the ages, but it wasn't bad, either, and the chase scenes were at least as spectacular as advertised. Reuven had no trouble following the English; it was the most widely used human language at the Moishe Russie Medical College. He saw the widow Radofsky's eyes drifting down to the bottom of the screen to read the Hebrew subtitles.

After the last explosion, after the policeman hero collared the villains, the lights came up. Reuven and Deborah Radofsky rose and headed for the exit. They'd just got out into the lobby again when he took her hand. He wondered what she'd do, what she'd say. She gave him a brief startled look, then squeezed his hand a little, as if to let him know it was all right.

"I hope you had a good time," he said as they neared her house.

"I did." If she sounded a little surprised at herself, he could pretend he didn't notice. And he might have been wrong.

Hoping he was, he asked, "Would you like to do it again before too long?"

"Yes, I'd like that a lot, I think," the widow Radofsky said. She smiled up at him as they got to her front door.

"Good," Reuven said. "So would I." He embraced her, not too tightly, and brushed his lips across hers. Then he stepped back, waiting to see what she'd do about that.

To his relief, she was still smiling. She took keys from her handbag and opened the door. "Good night, Reuven," she said.

"Good night, Deborah," he answered, and turned to go. He hoped she'd call him back to come inside with her. She didn't.

She closed the door; he heard the latch click. With a shrug, he headed home. He'd had a good time, too. Maybe it would be even better when they went out again.

☆ **19** ☆

In the encampment outside the little town of Kanth, Gorppet waited and worried. Every day that went by without the explosive-metal bomb's going off was something of a triumph, but no guarantee the accursed thing wouldn't detonate the next day—or, for that matter, the next instant. And one of the things he worried about was that the encampment might not be far enough outside Kanth. If the bomb went up, he was too likely to go up with it.

"Can we do nothing to rout out these Tosevites?" Nesseref asked him. "Can we do nothing to make them release my friend?"

Gorppet had asked her to come to Kanth precisely because she was Mordechai Anielewicz's friend. Now he wondered if that didn't make her more annoyance than asset. Trying to keep sarcasm out of his voice, he said, "I am open to suggestions, Shuttlecraft Pilot."

"Have we yet tried negotiating with these Jewish Big Uglies?" the female said. Before Gorppet could speak, she answered her own question: "We have not."

"That is a truth," Gorppet agreed. "The next sign of willingness they show for negotiations will be the first."

"Perhaps we should not wait for them to show signs. Perhaps we should seek negotiations ourselves." Nesseref waggled an eye turret at him. "Perhaps *you* should seek negotiations yourself. You can afford failure here even less than the Race can."

With deliberate rudeness, Gorppet turned both eye turrets away from her. Unfortunately, that he was rude didn't mean she was wrong. If the Race succeeded here—and especially if the Race succeeded because of his efforts—Hozzanet might have enough pull to set that in the balance against his ginger dealings down in South Africa. If not . . . If not, he was going to spend the rest of his days in some very unpleasant places.

Nesseref said, "Maybe you could use that Deutsch Big Ugly, that Drucker, as a go-between. I know he is acquainted with Anielewicz, and Tosevites know one another better than we can hope to know them."

"No." Gorppet not only used the negative gesture, he added an emphatic cough. "Remember, the Big Uglies with the bomb are Jews. They would be more inclined to listen to one of us than to a Deutsch male."

"Ah. Well, no doubt you are right. In that case, maybe one of us ought to go and talk with them," Nesseref said. "As things stand, I do not see how that could hurt."

"Do you not?" Gorppet said in hollow tones. He could see all too well how it might hurt: bullets, knives, blunt instruments, whatever other tools for torture Tosevite ingenuity—always too fertile in such areas—might devise.

But Nesseref also had a point. *Something* needed doing. The longer the Race and the Deutsche waited, the more things that could go wrong. Even more to the point, as far as Gorppet was concerned, the longer the Race waited, the more likely the disciplinarians were to seize him and take him away, concluding he was not helping in the present situation.

And so, without enthusiasm but also without anything he saw as choice, he approached Hozzanet the next morning and said, "Superior sir, if you need someone to approach the house where the Tosevite terrorists are staying, I volunteer for the duty."

"I am not sure we need anything of the sort," Hozzanet replied. "Anyone we offer to these Big Uglies would likely be seized as a hostage, as Mordechai Anielewicz was."

"I understand that, superior sir," Gorppet said. "I am willing to take the chance. You will understand why I am willing to take the chance. More than any other male of the Race here at the moment, I am expendable."

"No male is expendable," Hozzanet said. "Do you hope that you will be a hero if you succeed where few males would even have tried, and that that will be weighed against your present difficulties?"

"Yes, superior sir. That is exactly what I hope," Gorppet answered.

"Well, it could be that you are right," Hozzanet admitted. "Of course, it could also be that the Big Uglies will torment you or kill you, in which case you will gain nothing and lose that which is irreplaceable."

"Believe me, superior sir, I understand this is a gamble," Gorppet said. "It is, I repeat, one I am willing to make."

"I cannot give you permission for such a rash act myself," Hozzanet said. "I shall have to consult with my superiors."

Gorppet made the affirmative gesture. "Go ahead, superior sir. I hope they decide quickly. Would you not agree that we may not have much time?"

Hozzanet didn't say whether he agreed or disagreed. He just waved Gorppet away and began making telephone calls. Later that day, he summoned Gorppet back into his presence. Not sounding particularly happy, he spoke formally: "Very well, Small-Unit Group Leader. You are authorized to pursue negotiations with the Big Uglies at whatever level of intimacy proves necessary." He twisted an eye turret in a particular way. "Try not to get killed while you are doing all this."

"I thank you, superior sir," Gorppet said. "It shall be done."

"Wait," Hozzanet told him. "It shall not be done quite yet. We are going to make you a little more useful first."

And so, when Gorppet approached the house in Kanth from which Mordechai Anielewicz hadn't returned, he wore several small listening devices glued to his scales. They were covered with false skin, to make them as difficult as possible for the Big Uglies to detect.

Of course, he thought as he walked up to the house, *they could just shoot me now, in which case my superiors back at the encampment will hear nothing useful.* But no shots rang out. He looked for a speaker by the door with which he could announce himself. The house boasted no such amenity. Few Tosevite houses did. Lacking anything better to do, he knocked on the door.

The Big Uglies inside had to know he was there. They could surely see he carried no weapon (and they just as surely couldn't see the little patches of false skin). Why wouldn't they let him in? If nothing else, he gave them another hostage. They wouldn't know that a good many members of the Race—everybody who particularly hated ginger—wouldn't be sorry to see him dead.

But no one came to the door. Would he have to leave empty-handed? He didn't intend to do any such thing. He knocked again. "I come in peace!" he called in his own language. He could have said the same thing in Arabic, but no one in this part of Tosev 3 used that tongue. He knew none of the languages the Deutsche and the Jews spoke.

At last, the door did open, though not very wide. A Big Ugly gestured with an assault rifle—*come inside*. Gorppet obeyed. He'd come here to do nothing less. The door slammed shut behind him.

"I greet you," he said, as if he'd come on a friendly visit. "Do you understand my language?"

"No, not a word," the Big Ugly answered—in the language of the Race.

It could have been funny, had the Tosevite not been carrying that rifle and had he not been so plainly ready to use it. As things were, Gorppet said, "I thank you for letting me come in here."

With a shrug, the Tosevite said, "You came to this house. We can hold you here. You cannot give us any trouble."

"As you still hold Mordechai Anielewicz?" Gorppet pronounced the name, so alien to him, with great care: he did not want to be misunderstood.

And he was not. With a nod, the Jewish Big Ugly answered, "Yes, we hold him; that is a truth. But you will have nothing to do with him. Nothing, do you understand me? You two shall not plot together. I know you are our enemies."

"I have fought side by side with males of your superstition, and—" Gorppet began.

"It is not a superstition," the Tosevite snapped. "It is truth."

"We disagree," Gorppet said, wondering if that would get him shot the next instant. "But as I say, I have fought side by side with Jewish Tosevites against the Deutsche. Mordechai Anielewicz has led you. How can you say that we are your enemies?"

"Because it is a truth," the Big Ugly said. "Now you of the Race and the Deutsche work together against us. You do not want us to have the vengeance we deserve."

"We do not want another round of fighting under any circumstances," Gorppet said. "What good could it do?"

"Go down these stairs," the Jewish Tosevite said. Gorppet went. The Big Ugly stayed far enough behind him that he couldn't hope to whirl and seize the rifle. He didn't intend to try any such thing, but his captor couldn't know that, and took no chances. The Big Ugly resumed: "Destroying the Deutsche is worthwhile for its own sake."

"If you set off this bomb, you will not only be destroying the Deutsche," Gorppet said. "Do you not see that? You also put the Race at risk, and your fellow Jews in Poland."

"Destroying the Deutsche is all that matters to us," the Tosevite said implacably. He pointed to a door. "Go in there."

Gorppet opened the door. The chamber inside was small and dark. Before going in, he said, "You would also destroy yourselves, of course."

"Of course," his captor agreed with chilling calm. "Do you know the story of Masada?"

"No." Gorppet made the negative gesture. "Who is Masada?"

"Masada is not a person. Masada is—was—a place, a fortress," the Big Ugly answered. "Nineteen hundred years ago, we Jews rose up against the Romans, who oppressed us. They had more soldiers. They beat us. Masada was our last fortress. They put soldiers around it. They demanded that we surrender."

"And?" Gorppet asked, as he was obviously intended to do.

A melancholy pride in his voice that Gorppet could not mistake, the Jew said, "All the soldiers in Masada—almost a thousand of them—killed themselves instead of giving up to the Romans. We can do that again here. We are proud to do that again here."

Gorppet had seen plenty of Muslim Tosevites willing to die if in dying they could carry out their goal of harming the Race. Big Uglies who did not care whether they lived or died were the greatest problem the Race faced, because they were so hard to defend against. Gorppet said, "If you harm your own males and females more than you harm the Deutsche, what have you accomplished?"

"Harm to the Deutsche," the Tosevite said. "Revenge for all they have done to us. We need nothing more."

He was impervious to reason. That was the most frightening thing about him. Gorppet tried again nonetheless: "But harm will also come to those you care about."

"We shall punish the Deutsche." Yes, the Big Ugly was impenetrable. He gestured with his rifle. "Go inside."

"You will not listen to me," Gorppet protested.

"I did not ask you to come here. I did not say I would listen to you if you did. Why should I listen to you? You will only tell me lies." The Tosevite gestured with the rifle barrel again. "Go inside, I tell you, or you will never go anywhere again."

Despair in his liver, Gorppet went. The Big Ugly closed the door. The lock clicked. Gorppet found himself in almost total blackness; only the tiniest bit of light leaked under the bottom of the door. He had to explore by touch. He found nothing but a pad that might do for a sleeping mat and a metal pot he presumed he was to use for his excrement.

I should have let myself go to prison, he thought. *Anything would be better than this.*

Oddly, Johannes Drucker hadn't hated the Lizards while fighting two wars against them. He'd been a professional. They'd been professionals. Both sides had just been doing their jobs. Had the Lizards felt otherwise, they would have killed him after his attack on their starship.

Now, though, he hated them. He'd hated Gunther Grillparzer for trying to blackmail him, too. He'd been able to do something about Grillparzer, who he heartily hoped was dead. And he hated the Lizards for blackmailing him. The trouble was, he couldn't do anything about them.

He peered through Zeiss binoculars at the house in Kanth where the Jews had holed up with the explosive-metal bomb. An artillery shell or a conventional bomb from a dive-bomber might kill all of them before they could detonate the weapon they'd stolen. If it did, the crisis would be over.

Might. If. Those words didn't carry a lot of punch, not till you measured them against the risk. If the shells, if the bombs, didn't do the trick . . .

In that case, Kanth and a good deal of the surrounding countryside would go up in radioactive fire. The Jews would have a measure of revenge on the *Reich*, and who could guess what would happen next?

He even understood why the Jews holed up in Kanth wanted their revenge. Before the *Gestapo* hauled Käthe away, he didn't think he would have. He hadn't seen Jews as people till then, only as enemies of the *Reich*. But, considering what he felt toward the goddamn blackshirts, why shouldn't they feel the same way, only more so? Sure as hell, Germany had given them reason enough.

And Mordechai Anielewicz hadn't been anything but a husband and father trying to find his family, the same as Drucker himself had been doing. Christ, each of them had even named a son after the same man. Yes, Jews were people, no matter what the SS said.

But Drucker hated Anielewicz anyhow, not for himself but because, through the Jew, the Lizards had been able to ensnare him. If they told his superiors what they knew, he wouldn't be able to protect Käthe any more.

He also hated Gorppet, and hoped the Jews had cut the miserable Lizard's throat. For all he knew, they might have. Gorppet had gone into that house, but he hadn't come out, any more than Anielewicz had.

Despite his loathing of the Race, Drucker found himself having to work through and with the Lizards. He couldn't very well approach that house in Kanth himself, not in his fancy new major general's uniform. That would be all the Jewish terrorists needed. They'd set off their bomb just for the fun of blowing up a high-ranking Nazi. Hell, in their shoes he would have done the same thing.

Since he couldn't approach the Jews, he went into the tent where Gorppet's superior, a male named Hozzanet, was still working. Another Lizard was talking with Hozzanet, one whose style of body paint he recognized. "I greet you, Shuttlecraft Pilot," he said—talking with that one was bound to be more interesting than talking with the male from Security.

The Lizard to whom he'd spoken swung a startled eye turret in his direction and asked, "How is it that you know what my body paint means?"

"I have also flown in space, as pilot of the upper stage of an A-45," Drucker answered. "I tried to destroy one of your starships, but I did not quite succeed." Since he did not think he had met the pilot before, he also gave his name.

To his surprise, the Lizard said, "Oh, I remember you. I was the shuttlecraft pilot who flew you back to Nuremberg after you were released from captivity. I am Nesseref."

"Are you?" Drucker said, and knew that sounded foolish as soon as it came out of his mouth. "We have a saying in my language: small world, is it not?"

"So it would seem," Nesseref said. "It is small enough. I am given to understand that we share Mordechai Anielewicz as a friend."

"As an acquaintance, at any rate," Drucker said, though he

wondered why he bothered splitting hairs. His acquaintanceship with the Jew was close enough to let the Lizards squeeze him because of it. If that didn't make it friendship, it came close enough. He asked, "And how did you become acquainted with Anielewicz?"

"My home is in Poland," the Lizard answered. He—no, she, Drucker recalled—went on, "We met quite by chance, but found we liked each other. That is how any friendship between two individuals begins. Is it not a truth?"

"I suppose so," Drucker said. "The question now is, what can we do to help him stop the terrorists from setting off that bomb?"

"Truth," Nesseref said, and Hozzanet echoed her.

The male from Security went on, "I know that your government now perceives we were not responsible for allowing the terrorists to enter the *Reich* with this bomb. We did not give it to them. In fact, as you will recall, it is of Deutsch manufacture."

But Drucker shook his head. Walter Dornberger had given him specific instructions on this point. "The Jews are your puppets. You let them keep the bomb for all those years. If they use it against us, we shall hold you responsible for that act of war against the *Reich*."

"You would fight us again?" Hozzanet demanded. "You truly would, in view of what happened the last time?"

"I can only tell you what my *Führer* tells me," Drucker answered. "We are an independent not-empire even now, and you may not treat us as if we were of no account."

"If you fight us again, you shall be of no account," Hozzanet said. "Can you not see that? Whatever you try to do to us, we shall do to you tenfold."

Back during the Second World War, before the Lizards came, the Germans had always said they would punish their foes ten times harder than they were hurt. Hearing that phrase aimed at the *Reich* made Drucker wince, especially since he knew the Lizards could so readily carry out their threat. Nevertheless, he spoke as he'd been ordered to speak: "But we will also hurt you again. You know we can. How soon will you be weaker than the Americans and the Russians?"

He knew a good deal about Lizards. He didn't watch Hozzanet's face. He watched the tip of the Lizard's stumpy little tail. Sure enough, it quivered. That meant Hozzanet was upset. The male made a good game effort not to show it, though, saying, "First, the *Reich* does not have the power to do that to us. Second, regardless of any other concerns, none of you Deutsche would be here to learn the answer to that question."

Dornberger had foretold that he would say something like that. The former engineer and commandant at Peenemünde was shaping as an effective *Führer*—as effective as he could be in a crippled *Reich*. Just as in a well-planned chess opening, Drucker had the next move waiting: "Do you think we are unprepared to sacrifice ourselves now so that Tosevites triumph in the end?"

Hozzanet's tailstump quivered again. But the Lizard said, "To be perfectly frank, yes. That is exactly what I think. You Big Uglies are very seldom able to think or plan for the long term. Why should this occasion be any different?"

He had a point. Drucker did his best not to acknowledge it, saying, "Precisely because we have so little to lose."

"Any individual's life is a lot to lose," Nesseref put in. "No one can lose anything more important."

That was sensible. Drucker somehow wasn't surprised. Anyone who flew into space had to have good sense. Otherwise, you ended up dead before you got the chance to gain much experience.

Hozzanet said, "Let me see if I understand something. The *Reich* is interested in attacking this house in Kanth, to attempt to put the Jewish Tosevites out of action before they can detonate the bomb."

"That is a truth," Drucker agreed.

"But if you try this attack and fail, so that the bomb detonates, you will blame the Race," the Lizard persisted.

"That is also a truth," Drucker said.

"How can both these things be true at once?" Hozzanet demanded. "How can you blame us if your assault fails?"

"Because we should not even have to consider the possibility of making an assault," Drucker answered. "Because these Tosevites had no business having a bomb in the first place, let alone smuggling it into the *Reich*. That they had it and that they could smuggle it are both the fault of the Race."

"Whose fault is it that these Tosevites hate the *Reich* so much?" Hozzanet said. "Whose fault is it that Poland was attacked, which created the chaos that let them move the bomb? Both these things are the fault of the *Reich*."

He was probably right about that. No: he was certainly right about that. But Drucker said, "I have stated the *Führer's* views on the matter."

"So you have," Hozzanet said sourly. "The Race's view is that they are foolish and irresponsible. The Race's view is also that, if you will blame us for the failure, you shall not be allowed to make the attempt."

"I protest, in the name of my government," Drucker said.

"Protest all you please," Hozzanet replied. "I tell you, this thing shall *not* be done." He added an emphatic cough. "I tell you also that, if your government launches combat aircraft, we shall do everything in our power to shoot them down before they can attack Kanth."

"What you are saying, then, is that the *Reich* is depending on a male of the Race and a Jew to save it from this explosive-metal bomb," Drucker said. Before either Lizard could speak, he held up a hand to show he hadn't finished. "I have seen that not everything my government has said about the Jews is true. But Anielewicz has reason to hate us, not to wish us well."

"When Gorppet called him, Anielewicz could have let these other Jewish Tosevites detonate their bomb and punish the *Reich*," Hozzanet said. "He did not. He came here to try to stop them. You should remember that."

By the nature of things, Hozzanet couldn't know about the parable that spoke of the Pharisee who passed on the other side of the road and the good Samaritan who stopped to help a man in need. Even without knowing it, though, he got the message across.

And, just in case he hadn't, Nesseref drove it home: "These other Jews, the ones with the bomb, hate the *Reich* more than Mordechai Anielewicz does. If that were not true, he would not have come here at all."

Drucker suspected Anielewicz worried more about further damage to Poland than about damage to the *Reich*. In Anielewicz's place, he suspected he would have felt the same way. But that didn't make the Lizards wrong. With a stiff nod, Drucker said, "I shall report your words to the *Führer*."

He went back to the German encampment alongside that of the Race and telephoned Walter Dornberger. After he'd given his old commander the meat of the conversation with the two

Lizards, Dornberger let out a long sigh. "What you're telling me, Hans," the *Führer* said, "is that we have to rely on this Jew? There's more irony in that than I really want to stomach."

"I understand, sir. I feel the same way, pretty much," Drucker replied. "But I don't think Anielewicz will leave Kanth alive without getting those terrorists to give up their bomb. The Lizards seem sure he'll do everything he can." He didn't want to let Dornberger know he knew the Jew well enough to have his own opinion.

"But will it be enough?" Dornberger demanded.

"Right now, sir, we can only hope," Drucker said. He also suspected he hoped even more urgently than the *Führer* did. Walter Dornberger, after all, was back in Flensburg. He wouldn't turn to radioactive dust if something went wrong here in Kanth. *But I will,* Drucker thought. *Dammit, I will.*

There were, Mordechai Anielewicz thought, nine Jews holed up with the explosive-metal bomb. That was enough to let them have plenty of guards for him, for any other captives they might have, and for the bomb itself. In the end, though, the probably nine boiled down to only one: the Jews' leader, a fellow named Benjamin Rubin. Mordechai knew that, if he could reach Rubin, everything else would follow.

But could he reach him? For a long time, Rubin hadn't even wanted to talk to him. Nobody'd wanted to talk to him. He counted himself lucky that the Jews hadn't just shot him and tossed his body out on the porch as a warning to anyone else rash enough to think about talking to them.

At first, he'd thought they were going to do exactly that. Nobody called him anything but "traitor" till he'd been there for several days. Finally, that made him lose his temper. "I fought the Nazis before most of you *mamzrim* were born," he snapped at one of the trigger-happy young Jews who reluctantly came in pairs to bring him food. "I killed Otto Skorzeny and kept him from blowing up Lodz with the bomb you're sitting on now. And you call me a traitor? *Geh kak afen yam.*"

That could have got him shot, too. Instead, it got him what he'd hoped it might: a chance to talk with Benjamin Rubin. He didn't know Rubin well; the fellow hadn't been any kind of bigwig till he hijacked the bomb. But he was now. One of the toughs who followed him led Mordechai into his presence as if into that of a rabbi renowned for his holiness.

Rubin didn't look like a rabbi. He looked like a doctor. He was thin and pale and precise, about as far removed as possible from the ruffians he led. "So you want to convince me I'm wrong, do you?" he said, and folded his arms across his chest. "Go ahead. I'm waiting."

"I don't think I need to convince you," Anielewicz said. "I think you see it, too. The way it looks to me, you just don't want to admit it to yourself."

Benjamin Rubin scowled. "You'd better come to the point in a hurry, or I'll decide you haven't got one."

"Fair enough." Mordechai hoped he sounded more cheerful than he felt. He was doing his best. "Suppose you blow up Kanth. What have you got? A few thousand Germans at the outside. I wouldn't bet on even that many, though—they're sneaking away every chance they get. Hardly seems worthwhile, for an explosive-metal bomb."

"We were heading for Dresden," Rubin said petulantly. "The truck kept breaking down. That's how we ended up here."

"Too bad." Now Anielewicz did his best to simulate sympathy. "But you could do things in—and to—Dresden you can't even think about here."

"Maybe. But we've still got the bomb, and we can still do plenty with it, even if it's not so much as we hoped." Rubin nodded, as if reassuring himself. "I can die happy, knowing what I've done to the damned Nazis."

"And what will the damned Nazis do once you're dead?" Mordechai asked. "They'll hit back with whatever they've got left, that's what. How many Jews in Poland are going to die on account of your stupidity?"

"None," replied the Jewish leader who'd stolen the bomb. "Not a single one. The Germans know what will happen to them if they try anything like that again."

Anielewicz laughed in his face. Rubin looked astounded. None of his henchmen would have done anything so rude. Maybe, having henchmen, he'd forgotten there were people who didn't think so well of him. Mordechai said, "You're here. You're willing to die to take revenge on the Nazis. You think there won't be plenty of Nazis willing to die to take revenge on a pack of kikes?"

He used the slur deliberately, to rock Rubin back on his heels. The other Jew said, "They'd never have the nerve."

That only made Mordechai laugh some more. "You can call the Nazis all sorts of things, Rubin. I do, every day. But you're an even bigger idiot than I think you are if you think they don't know how to die well. Dying well is half of what fascism is all about, for God's sake."

"And how do you know so much about it? You've been in bed with them, that's how," Rubin said.

"Yes, and that's a load of shit, too," Mordechai said. "Anybody who's not blind can see as much."

One of the bully boys who'd brought him in to Benjamin Rubin tapped him on the shoulder. When he turned, the fellow hit him in the belly and then in the face. He folded up and sank to the floor. He tasted blood in his mouth, but none of his teeth seemed broken when he ran his tongue over them. Somehow, that mattered very much to him. If by some accident he came through this alive, he didn't care to spend any time sitting in a dentist's chair.

Slowly, painfully, he got to his feet. What he wanted to do was kill the bastard who'd slugged him. But he couldn't, not when said bastard's pal was pointing a rifle at his chest. That being so, he didn't even waste time glaring at the bully boys. Instead, he turned back toward Rubin. "If you don't want to listen to me, you don't have to. If you want your bully boys here to pound on me, they can do that. That's what I bought when I came through the door. But it doesn't mean I'm not telling you the truth, even so."

"Maybe you call it that," Rubin said. "I don't. I call it a pack of lies and foolishness. I'd sooner go out like Samson in the temple."

"I've noticed," Mordechai answered. He'd also noticed that, unlike Samson, Rubin and his pals hadn't killed themselves as soon as they got in trouble. He didn't say anything about that, not wanting to goad them into anything. Instead, he went on, "You're like Samson one way: you don't worry about what'll happen to the rest of the Jews once you're gone."

"They'll get by," Benjamin Rubin said. "They always have. And we'll punish the Nazis for all they've done to us."

Anielewicz sighed. "You keep saying that. I keep telling you to look out the windows here. You just won't do them all that much harm."

Rubin glowered at him. "I don't have to listen to this. I don't have to, and I don't intend to." He nodded to his henchmen. "Take him away."

"Come on, pal," said the fellow who'd slugged Anielewicz. "You heard the boss. Get moving."

With a rifle pointed at him, Mordechai had no choice. *The boss,* he thought as they led him away. *Why don't they just call him the* Führer*? It's only one step up.* He didn't say that; he judged it too likely to get him killed.

When the bully boys got him back to the basement room where they kept him on ice, they slammed the door behind him with needless violence. Maybe they hoped the bang would make him jump. It did, a little, but they didn't have the satisfaction of seeing as much.

Nobody could have seen much in that room. It had no lamps and no windows. He got colossally bored when they parked him there. He didn't know how long at a time they left him in cold storage. He did know, or thought he knew, that he spent inordinate stretches of time asleep. He had nothing better to do. No matter how much he slept, though, he always felt logy, not well-rested.

He tried the door every so often when he was awake. It never yielded. Had he been the hero of an adventure novel or film, he would have been able to pick the lock—either that, or to break down the door without making a sound. Being only an ordinary fellow, he remained stuck where the terrorists had stowed him.

A couple of times, he heard them speaking the language of the Race, and a Lizard answering them. They didn't mention to him who the Lizard was. He hoped it wasn't Nesseref. Enough that he was in trouble without dragging his friend in with him. He also hoped it wasn't Gorppet. If the male from Security hadn't taken in Heinrich's beffel, he never would have found his family again. He owed the Lizard too much to want him endangered.

But he didn't know. He never got the chance to find out. The terrorists efficiently kept him and the Lizard, whoever it was, from having anything to do with each other. In their place, he would have done the same. That didn't keep him from wishing they'd proved less professional.

And then—it couldn't have been more than a couple of hours after he'd reluctantly admired their professionalism—they all started screaming at one another. It was like listening to a horrible family row. But everybody in this family packed an assault rifle, and the explosive-metal bomb sat only a few meters away. A family row here could have extravagantly lethal consequences.

At last, silence fell. Nobody'd shot anybody, not so far as Mordechai could tell. But he hadn't the faintest idea what *had* happened—he hadn't been able to make out the words—or why they'd started screaming at one another in the first place, either. All he could do was sit there in the darkness and wonder and wait.

Instead of waiting, he fell asleep. He didn't think he'd been asleep very long when the door flew open. One of the bully boys shined a flashlight in his face. Another one growled, "Come on. You're going to see the boss."

"Am I?" Anielewicz yawned and rose and did as he was told.

He was still yawning when the two toughs escorted him into Benjamin Rubin's presence. Rubin didn't beat around the bush: "Is it true that, if we surrender, we can surrender to the Lizards and not the damned Nazis? And there's supposed to be a safe-conduct out of here and a pardon afterwards. Is that true, or isn't it?"

"Yes, it's true," Mordechai answered, more than a little dazed. "Does it matter?"

"It matters," Rubin said bleakly. "On those terms, we give up." He took a pistol off his belt and handed it to Anielewicz. "Here. This is yours now."

Two more of his followers brought in the Lizard Mordechai had heard. It wasn't Nesseref; he would have recognized her body paint. "I greet you," he said. "Are you Gorppet?" When the Lizard made the affirmative gesture, Anielewicz went on, "They are surrendering to the Race, in exchange for safe-conduct and pardon. Will you go make the arrangements for picking them up and getting them out of the *Reich*?"

"It shall be done," Gorppet answered. "And you have no idea how glad I am that it shall be done."

"Oh, I might," Anielewicz said.

One of the Jews who followed Rubin led the Lizard toward the front door. It opened, then closed again. Rubin said, "I'm counting on the Race to keep its promises."

"It's a good bet," Mordechai said. "They're better about things like that than we are." He raised an eyebrow. "What made you change your mind at last?"

"What do you think?" Benjamin Rubin said bitterly. "We tried to touch off the damned bomb, and it wouldn't work." He looked as if he hated Anielewicz. "These past twenty years, I thought you were taking care of it."

"So did I," Mordechai said. "But do you know what? I've never been so happy in all my life to find out I was wrong."

"Well, there is one crisis solved." Atvar spoke in considerable relief. "Solved without casualties, too, I might add. That is such a pleasant novelty, I would not mind seeing it occur more often."

"I understand, Exalted Fleetlord," Pshing said. "I hope such proves to be the case."

"So do I." Atvar used an emphatic cough. So much time on Tosev 3, however, had turned him from an optimist to a realist, if not to an outright cynic. "I would not bet anything I could not afford to lose. Given the present sorry situation on too much of Tosev 3—and, indeed, throughout too much of this solar system—my larger bet would too likely prove doomed to disappointment."

His adjutant made the affirmative gesture. "I understand," he repeated. "Shall we now proceed to the rest of the daily report?"

"I suppose so," Atvar replied. "I am sure I will not like it nearly so well as the news from the *Reich*."

Next on the agenda was the latest news on the fighting in China. Atvar promptly proved himself right: he didn't like it nearly so well as he'd liked the news from the *Reich*. From somewhere or other, the Chinese rebels had come up with revoltingly large quantities of Deutsch antilandcruiser rockets and antiaircraft missiles. The fleetlord had a strong suspicion where *somewhere or other* was: the SSSR, with a long land border with China, seemed a far more likely candidate than the distant, shattered *Reich*. But he couldn't prove anything there, the Race's best efforts to do so notwithstanding. And the SSSR, unfortunately, was able to do too much damage to make welcome a confrontation without secure proof of wrongdoing. Molotov, the SSSR's not-emperor, had made his willingness to fight very clear.

"One thing," Atvar said after reading the latest digest of action reports from China. "Fleetlord Reffet can no longer object to recruiting members of the colonization fleet to help defend the Race. A few more campaigns like the one now under way there and we will not have enough males from the conquest fleet left to give us an armed force of the size and strength we require on this world."

"As a matter of fact, Exalted Fleetlord, Fleetlord Reffet is still objecting," Pshing said. "If you will see item five of the agenda—"

"I shall do no such thing, not now," Atvar said. "Reffet is welcome to hiss and cough and snarl as much as he likes. He has no authority to do anything more. If he tries to do anything more than object—if, for example, he tries to obstruct—he will learn at first hand just how significant military power can be."

He relished the thought of sending a couple of squads of battle-hardened infantrymales to seize Reffet and force him to see reason when it was aimed at him from the barrel of a rifle. If the fleetlord of the colonization fleet provoked him enough, he just might do it. So he told himself, at any rate. Would he ever really have the nerve? Maybe not. But thinking about it was sweet.

He needed a few sweet thoughts, for the next agenda item was no more satisfactory than the one pertaining to China: the American Big Uglies were going right ahead with their plan to turn small asteroids into missiles aimed at Tosev 3. Probes had found several new distant rocks to which they'd fitted motors, and analysts were warning in loud and strident tones that they were sure they hadn't found them all.

"Spirits of Emperors past turn their backs on the Americans," Atvar muttered. He swung an eye turret toward Pshing. "Our analysts believe the Americans will resist with force if we try to destroy these installations, even if no Big Uglies are presently aboard them. What is your view?"

"Exalted Fleetlord, it might have been better had we not threatened them with war if they attacked our automated probes out in the asteroid belt," his adjutant replied. "Now they can reverse that precedent and hit us in the snout with it."

"No doubt you are right about that," Atvar said unhappily. "But I am more concerned with practical aspects than with legalistic ones here. If we ignore the precedent and resort to force, will they respond in kind?"

"By every indication from Henry Cabot Lodge, they will," Pshing said. "Do we wish to ignore the express statements of their ambassador? Can we afford to ignore those statements? If we ignore them and find we were mistaken, how expensive and how embarrassing will that prove?"

"Those are all good questions," Atvar admitted. "They are, in fact, the very questions I have been asking myself. I wish I liked the answers I find for them better than I do."

"And I also understand that," Pshing said. "The more technically capable the Big Uglies become, the more difficult in other ways they also become."

"And the more unpredictably difficult, too." Atvar swung both eye turrets toward the monitor. "Why are so many American and Canadian manufacturing companies suddenly ordering large quantities of a particular small servomotor from us? To what nefarious purpose will they put the device?"

"I saw that item, Exalted Fleetlord, and checked with our Security personnel," Pshing said. "The stated reason is, this motor will be the central unit in a toy for Tosevite hatchlings."

"Yes, that is the *stated* reason." Atvar bore down heavily on the word. "But what true reason lurks behind it?"

"Here, I believe, none." Pshing spoke to the monitor, which yielded Atvar a view of a goggle-eyed, fuzzy object that looked like a cross between a Big Ugly and some of the large wild beasts of Tosev 3. "This thing is called, I believe, a Hairy. By the excitement with which the Tosevites speak of it, it is already remarkably popular, and seems on the way to becoming more so."

"Madness," Atvar said with great conviction. "Utter madness, and an utter waste of good servomotors, too."

"Better they should go to fripperies than to devices that truly would trouble us," Pshing said.

"Well, that is a truth, and I can hardly deny it." Atvar looked at the next item on the agenda. It involved talking with Reffet about recruiting males and females from the colonization fleet. "Reffet is a nuisance, and I can hardly deny that, either. Go call him, Pshing. Perhaps the shock will make him fall over dead. I can hope as much, at any rate."

"It shall be done, Exalted Fleetlord," Atvar's adjutant said, and went off to do it.

Reffet remained among those breathing. Atvar had known his untimely demise was too much to hope for. "I greet you," Atvar said when his opposite number's image appeared in the monitor. He'd given up trying to be friendly to Reffet. Perhaps he could still manage businesslike. "Have you seen the latest casualty figures from my males trying to put down the Chinese revolt?"

"They are unfortunate, yes," Reffet answered. "This planet should never have cost so much to pacify."

"If you know how to make the Big Uglies ignorant, perhaps you will tell me," Atvar said. "Since we must deal with them as they are, though, perhaps you will draw the obvious conclusion and stop obstructing what needs to be done."

More earnestly than Atvar had expected, Reffet said, "Do you not yet grasp how alien this world is to me—indeed, to all the colonization fleet? Do you think we imagined independent Tosevite not-empires, spacefaring Big Uglies armed with explosive-metal bombs, when we set out from Home? Do you think we imagined how disrupted our carefully planned economy would become when we discovered that the Tosevites were already doing so much of the manufacturing we had expected to have to do ourselves? Do you think we dreamt of the staggering effect ginger would have on our whole society? Can you truthfully say you looked for any of these things before going into cold sleep?"

"I looked for not a one of them. I have never claimed otherwise," Atvar replied. "But what I and what the conquest fleet as a whole have tried to do is adapt to these things, not pretend they do not exist. That pretense is what we see too often from the colonization fleet, and what infuriates and addles us."

"How long did you take before you began to adapt?" Reffet asked. "If you tell me you did it all at once, I shall not believe you."

"No, we did not do it all at once," Atvar said, relieved to find Reffet so reasonable. "But, because we were so outnumbered, we could not pretend that the Big Uglies are in fact what we wish they were, an attitude we have seen too often among you colonists. Sooner or later, we shall grow old and die off. Sooner or later, you will have to defend yourselves. Such is life on Tosev 3, like it or not. Until such time as this planet is fully assimilated into the Empire—if that day ever comes—we shall have to maintain our strength, because the wild Big Uglies assuredly will maintain theirs."

Reffet sighed. "It could be that you are right. I do not say that it is, but it could be. But if it is, this world will be a long-lasting anomaly within the Empire, with a permanent Soldiers' Time and with the disruptions springing from ginger. If you think I like or approve of this, you are mistaken. If you think I am incapable of dealing with it, however, you are also mistaken."

"Do you know what?" Atvar said. Without waiting for a reply, he went on, "I have no difficulty whatsoever in accepting that,

Reffet. On that basis, I think we can get along well enough. I certainly hope we can, at any rate."

Atvar knew he sounded surprised as well as pleased. So did Reffet: "I also hope so, Atvar. Let us make the effort, shall we?"

"Agreed," Atvar said at once. After he broke the connection, he stared at the monitor in astonished delight. *Maybe we really can work together,* he thought. *I never would have believed it, but maybe we really can. And maybe, just maybe*—a stranger thought yet—*Reffet is not an idiot after all. Who would have imagined that?*

A moment later, Pshing's face appeared on the monitor. His adjutant said, "Exalted Fleetlord, you have a call from Senior Researcher Ttomalss. Will you speak to him?"

"Yes, put him through," Atvar said, and then, as he and Ttomalss saw each other, "I greet you, Senior Researcher."

"And I greet you, Exalted Fleetlord," Ttomalss said. "As you will know, I have been examining the ways in which the Big Uglies administered their own relatively successful empires, in the hope that we might learn from their history. In this effort, the empire administered by the Big Uglies called Romans has proved perhaps the most instructive."

"All right, then," Atvar said. "How did these Romans administer their empire, and how might we imitate their example?"

"Their most important virtue, I think, was flexibility," Ttomalss replied. "They treated areas differently, depending on their previous level of civilization and on how well pacified they were. They had several grades of citizenship, with gradually increasing amounts of privilege, until finally the inhabitants of a conquered region became legal equal to longtime citizens of their empire. And they did their best to acculturate and assimilate new regions into the broader fabric of their empire."

"These sound as if they may be ideas we can use," Atvar said. "The concept of multiple grades of citizenship strikes me as particularly intriguing, and as being worth further exploration. Please prepare a more detailed report and send it to me for consideration and possible action."

"It shall be done, Exalted Fleetlord," Ttomalss said. "I thank you."

"On the contrary, Senior Researcher: I may be the one who should thank you," Atvar said. After Ttomalss was off the line, Atvar made the affirmative gesture. Maybe, just maybe, the

Race would find ways to incorporate Tosev 3 into the Empire after all.

Liu Han sat behind a table on a dais. A disorderly crowd of city folk and soldiers of the People's Liberation Army filled the hall. Here and there, braziers had been lit, but they did little to fight the chilly wind that howled in through shattered windows. Liu Han brought her hand down sharply on the tabletop. The noise cut through the babbling of the crowd. People looked her way. That was what she wanted.

"We are ready to bring in the next defendant," she told the soldiers nearest the table. "His name is"—she glanced down at a list—"Ma Hai-Teh."

"Yes, Comrade," their leader said. Then he bawled out Ma Hai-Teh's name at the top of his lungs. More soldiers dragged a man through the crowd till he stood in front of the dais. He wore a frightened expression and the filthy, torn remains of a Western-style business suit. His hands were bound behind him.

"You are Ma Hai-Teh?" Liu Han asked him.

"Yes, Comrade," he answered meekly. "I want to say that I am innocent of the charges brought against me, and I can prove it." He spoke like an educated man—and only an educated man was likely to have, or to want, Western-style clothes.

"You don't even know what those charges are," Liu Han pointed out.

"Whatever they are, I am innocent," Ma replied. "I have done nothing wrong, so I cannot possibly be guilty."

"Did you serve as a clerk for the little scaly devils while they ruled Peking?" Liu Han asked. "Did you help them rule Peking, in other words?"

"I moved papers from one folder to another, from one filing cabinet to another," Ma Hai-Teh said. "That is all I did. The papers were school records, nothing more. Nothing in them could possibly have harmed anyone."

Liu Han nodded. Ma looked relieved. That was a mistake, and would doubtless prove his last. Now she wouldn't even have to bother calling witnesses to confirm that he had been a clerk for the scaly devils. She said, "You have confessed to counter-revolutionary activity, and to being a running dog of the little scaly imperialists. There is only one penalty for this: death. Soldiers of the People's Liberation Army, take him away and carry out the sentence."

Ma Hai-Teh stared at her as if he couldn't believe his ears. He hadn't understood what sort of trial this was, and he would never get a chance to improve his understanding. "But I am innocent!" he wailed as the bored-looking soldiers dragged him off.

A minute later, a volley of gunfire outside cut off his protests. Liu Han looked at the list again. "Next case," she said. "One Ku Cheng-Lun."

Unlike the luckless, naive Ma, Ku Cheng-Lun labored under no illusions about the sort of proceeding in which he found himself. As soon as he had given his name, he said, "Comrade, I used my clerical position to make as many errors as I could and to sabotage the little scaly devils every way I could."

"I suppose you have some proof of this?" Liu Han's voice was dry. She supposed no such thing. She'd listened to a lot of running dogs and lackeys trying to justify their treason to mankind. She'd heard a lot of lies.

But, to her astonishment, Ku, whose hands were also bound, turned to his guards and said, "Please take the paper from my shirt pocket here and give it to the judge." When a soldier did so, the clerk went on, "Comrade, this is a reprimand from my supervisor, warning me not to make so many mistakes and saying I put his whole department in danger because I did. But I kept right on, because I hate the little devils."

"I will look at this paper." Liu Han unfolded it and rapidly read through it. It was what the prisoner said it was, and was even written on the stationery of the Ministry of Public Works. Had he written it, to protect himself after the scaly devils were expelled from Peking? Had his boss written it because he was nothing but a lazy good-for-nothing? Or was he really a patriot and a saboteur, as he claimed?

He spoke now with unhesitating pride: "I am *not* a traitor. I have never done anything but fight for freedom, even if I did not have a rifle in my hands."

"I suppose that is possible," Liu Han said: as great an admission as she'd made in any of these summary trials. She scratched the side of her jaw, considering. After half a minute or so, she said, "I sentence you to hard labor, building roads or entrenchments or whatever else may be required of you."

"Thank you, Comrade!" Ku Cheng-Lun exclaimed. Hard

labor was *hard* labor; his overseers might well end up working him to death. He probably knew that, too—he seemed very well informed. But to come through one of these trials without getting executed was something close to a miracle. Ku had to be aware of that.

Sure enough, Liu Han sent the next man brought before her to the firing squad, and the one after him, and the one after him as well. Revolutionary justice ruled in Peking now. The little scaly devils had held sway for a generation. Traitors and collaborators and running dogs by the thousands, by the tens of thousands, needed to be hunted down and purged.

The fourth man after Ku Cheng-Lun claimed to be in the service of the Kuomintang. That presented Liu Han with another dilemma. The Kuomintang had risen along with the People's Liberation Army, but, having less in the way of armaments, was very much a junior partner in the struggle against the little scaly devils. Still, Liu Han didn't want to damage the popular front, so she sentenced the fellow to hard labor. If his fellow reactionaries chose to rescue him later, she wouldn't worry about it.

Nieh Ho-T'ing had also been trying traitors. They met for supper after nightfall ended the trials till morning. Over buckwheat noodles and bits of shredded pork, Nieh said, "Even if the little devils do end up putting down this revolt, they will have a hard time finding anyone to help them administer China."

"That is good . . . I suppose," Liu Han said. "Better would be driving them back so we go on ruling here."

"Yes, that would be better," Nieh agreed. "I do not know if it can happen, though. Wherever they concentrate their strength, they can beat us. That remains true, even with our new weapons—and we've used up a lot of those."

"The Russians will have to send us more, then," Liu Han said.

"That won't be so easy, not any more," Nieh Ho-T'ing replied. "The scaly devils have already shot up a couple of caravans—and Molotov, damn him, doesn't dare get caught in the act of helping us. If he does get caught, the little devils land on him instead, and he won't take that chance. So we're liable to be stuck with what we've got."

"Not good," Liu Han said, and used one of the scaly devils' emphatic coughs.

"No, not good at all," Nieh said. "And we had an unpleasant report today from down in the south."

"You'd better tell me," Liu Han said, though she was anything but sure she wanted to hear.

"Here and there, the scaly devils are starting to use human troops against us," Nieh Ho-T'ing said.

"They've tried that before," Liu Han said. "It doesn't work well. Before long, the soldiers go over to us, or enough of them do, anyhow. Humans naturally have solidarity with one another."

But Nieh shook his head. "This is different. Before, they would try to use Chinese soldiers here in China, and you're right—that didn't work. But these men, whoever they are, aren't Chinese. They're mercenaries in the pay of the little devils. They don't speak our language, so we can't reach them. They just do what the scaly devils tell them to do—they're the perfect oppressors."

"Now that is not good. That is not good at all." Liu Han scratched her jaw, as she had while judging Ku Cheng-Lun. What she decided here was a good deal more important than her verdict in the clerk's case—though Ku would not have agreed with that. After some time, she said, "We will have to speak in the little scaly devils' language. The mercenaries are bound to understand that, or some of them are. Otherwise, the scaly devils couldn't give them their orders."

Nieh Ho-T'ing nodded. "Yes, that is a good idea. Better than anything we've tried yet—it's bound to be. Some people say these soldiers are from South America, others say they're from India. Either way, they might as well come from Home for all the sense we can make of what they say."

"We have to make them understand," Liu Han said. "Once we do, the rot will start."

"Here's hoping, anyhow," Nieh said.

Before Liu Han could answer, jet engines started howling low over Peking. Antiaircraft guns barked. Antiaircraft missiles took off with roaring whooshes. Bombs burst. The ground started to shake. Little waves shimmered in Liu Han's bowl of broth and noodles. She picked it up. "I wish we had airplanes of our own," she said. "The way things are, the little devils can hit us, but we can't hit back."

"I know." Nieh Ho-T'ing shrugged. "Nothing we can do about that, though. Molotov isn't about to pack fighter planes on camelback, any more than he's likely to send us landcruisers. But now, at least, we make the scaly devils pay a price when they use those things."

"Not enough," Liu Han said. More bombs burst, some not very far away. She glanced at the oil lamps that lit the inside of the noodle shop. So easy for a hit to knock them into the rubble and start a fire . . . Broad stretches of Peking had already burned from fires of that sort.

"If we fail this time, we try again," Nieh said, "and again, and again, and as often as need be. Sooner or later, we win."

Or we give up, Liu Han thought. But she would not say that; saying it seemed to make it more likely to come true. Part of her realized that was nothing but peasant superstition, but she kept quiet all the same. She'd grown up a peasant, never expecting to be anything else, and couldn't always escape her origins.

Bombs fell again, some nearer, some farther away. Nieh Ho-T'ing said, "If they keep doing this, there won't be anything left of Peking but ruins."

"Maybe not," Liu Han said, "but they'll be *our* ruins."

Nieh eyed her with more than a little admiration. "You would say that about all of China, wouldn't you?"

"If it meant being rid of the little scaly devils for good, I would," she replied.

He nodded. "You always have taken the hard line against them."

"I have my reasons, even if some of them are personal and not ideological," Liu Han said. "But I am not really a hardliner. My daughter, now, she would say, 'Let all of China be ruined even if it doesn't necessarily mean getting rid of the little devils for good, just so they can't have it.' "

Nieh Ho-T'ing nodded again. "I see the difference. Mao would probably agree with Liu Mei, you know."

"Well, he'll have his chance with this uprising," Liu Han said. *Unless the people refuse to fight any more—unless they would sooner have peace regardless of who rules them.* She kept that to herself, too.

"Mao has been a revolutionary his whole life," Nieh said. "A lot of us have. We will go on fighting, however long it takes. We are patient. The dialectic is on our side. We will bring the country with us."

"Of course we will," Liu Han declared. But then the doubts that never quite went away came out: "The only thing that worries me is, the little scaly devils are patient, too." Nieh Ho-T'ing looked at her as if he wished she hadn't said any such thing. She too wished she hadn't said it. But she feared that didn't make it any less true. More bombs rained down on Peking.

Just seeing Tosevite railroads had convinced Nesseref that she didn't like them. Instead of being clean and quiet, they roared and puffed and chugged and belched filthy, stinking black smoke into the air. One of these days, she was told, the Race would replace the horrible engines in Poland with more modern machinery. But it didn't look as if that would happen any time soon. There were so many more urgent things to do. No matter how filthy the locomotives the Big Uglies built, they did work after a fashion, and so they stayed in service.

And now she found herself in a passenger car behind one of those noxious locomotives. The rolling, swaying, jouncing ride was even worse than she'd expected, and left her as nervous as a wild Big Ugly would have been to fly in a shuttlecraft for the first time.

Fortunately, few Tosevites saw her discomfiture: one car on each train was reserved for males and females of the Race. In fact, Nesseref had the entire compartment to herself. A Tosevite conductor came through and spoke in her language (a relief, because she'd learned only a handful of words in either Polish or Yiddish): "Przemysl is the next stop. All out for Przemysl."

Out she went, in some anxiety. If no one was waiting for her here at the station, she would have to brave a taxi. That would be doubly difficult: first finding a driver who understood her and then surviving a trip through terrifying Tosevite traffic. Having experienced both, she vastly preferred space travel, which had fewer things that could go wrong.

But a Big Ugly on the platform waved to her, waved and called, "Shuttlecraft Pilot! Nesseref! Superior female! Over here!"

With more than a little relief, Nesseref waved back. "I greet you, Mordechai Anielewicz. I am glad to see you."

"And I am glad to see you," her Tosevite friend replied. "I was even gladder to see you when I came out of that house in Kanth. Seeing any friends there was very good indeed."

"I can understand how it would have been." Nesseref's eye turrets swiveled this way and that. To her, this crowded platform in Przemysl, full of shouting, exclaiming Big Uglies, was a frightening place; she would not have wanted to be here without a friend, and especially a Tosevite friend. But this was different from what Anielewicz had gone through inside the *Reich*. She was, fortunately, sensible enough to understand as much. No one wanted to kill her here—she certainly hoped not, at any rate. But Anielewicz could have died at any moment in Kanth, and he'd volunteered to go there understanding that was so.

Now he said, "Come with me. My apartment is not very far away. My mate and hatchlings look forward to meeting you. Well, Heinrich looks forward to meeting you again. And he looks forward to showing you his beffel."

Nesseref's mouth fell open in amusement. "Ah, yes—the famous Pancer." She pronounced the Tosevite name as well as she could. "He may be interested in meeting me, too—I probably smell like a tsiongi, and that is an odor that will always get a beffel's attention."

Anielewicz spoke three words in his own language: *"Dogs and cats."* Then he explained: "These are Tosevite domestic animals that often do not get along with each other."

"I see," Nesseref said. She skittered after Anielewicz so she wouldn't lose him in the cavernous train station. Tosevites stared and pointed at her and exclaimed in their unintelligible languages. Many of them inhaled the burning herb that always struck her as noxious; its acrid smoke filled her scent receptors.

Outside, the cold smote her. Mordechai Anielewicz repeated, "It will not be far."

"Good," she said, shivering. "Otherwise, I do believe I would freeze before I got there. This winter weather of yours makes me see why you Tosevites deck yourselves in so many wrappings."

"I have seen members of the Race do it, too," Anielewicz said. "Staying warm is nothing to be ashamed of."

"I suppose not." Nesseref hurried down the street after him. "But wrappings are rarely necessary back on Home. We do not like to think they should be necessary anywhere we live."

"What you like to think is not always what is true," Anielewicz remarked, a comment with which she could hardly disagree.

She sighed with relief on entering the lobby to his block of flats, which was heated. "You must understand, you have more tolerance for cold than we do," she said. "Here, frozen water falling from the sky is something you take for granted. Back on Home, it is a rare phenomenon at the North and South Poles and at the peaks of the highest mountains. Otherwise, for us, it is unknown."

That made the Big Ugly let out several of the barking yips his kind used for laughter. "It is not unknown here, superior female," he said, and tacked on another emphatic cough. "If the Race is going to live in large parts of Tosev 3, you will have to get used to cold weather."

"So we have discovered," Nesseref said, with an emphatic cough of her own. "The males of the conquest fleet have had more of a chance to grow accustomed to your weather than we newcomers have. I must tell you, my first winter here was a dreadful surprise. I did not want to believe what the males had told me, but it was true. And seasons here on Tosev 3 last twice as long as they do on Home, so that winter seemed doubly dreadful."

"Without winter, we could not enjoy spring and summer so much," Mordechai Anielewicz said.

Nesseref answered that with a shrug. Suffering to make pleasure seem sweeter struck her as more trouble than it was worth. She didn't say so; she didn't want to offend her friend and host. Instead, she followed him upstairs.

That the apartment building had stairs instead of an elevator said something about the level of technology the local Big Uglies took for granted. Nesseref remembered the fire that had destroyed not just Anielewicz's apartment but his whole apartment building. Such a disaster would have been impossible in her building, with its sensors and sprinklers and generally more fireproof materials.

On the other fork of the tongue, this building was more spacious than the one in which she lived. Part of that was because Tosevites were larger than members of the Race, but only part. The rest . . . The Big Uglies didn't seem to build as if every particle of space were at a premium. The Race did. The Race had to. Home, and especially Home's cities, had been crowded since before the Empire unified the world. The Tosevites' architecture said they still felt they had room to expand.

Their technology has come very far very fast, Nesseref thought. *Their ideologies lag behind.* In a way, that was a comforting thought; it let her view the Big Uglies as primitives. In another way, though, it was frightening. The Tosevites had the means to do things they could scarcely have imagined a few generations before.

She wished she hadn't thought about how expansive they were.

"Here we are." Anielewicz led her down the hall and opened the door to what was, she presumed, his apartment. It did not seem so very spacious, not with so many Big Uglies inside it. They greeted her in turn: by their wrappings, she identified two females and two more males besides Mordechai Anielewicz.

And there was a beffel: a very fat, very sassy beffel who swaggered out as if he owned the apartment and the Tosevites in it were his servants. He stuck out his tongue at Nesseref, taking her scent. For a moment, it was as if he had to condescend to remember what a member of the Race smelled like. But then he caught Orbit's odor clinging to her, and swelled up in anger and let out a sneezing, challenging hiss.

"Pancer!" Heinrich Anielewicz said sharply. He spoke to the beffel in his own language. Nesseref had no idea what he said, but it did the trick. The beffel deflated and became a well-behaved pet once more.

"You have him well trained," Nesseref told the youngest Tosevite. "I have known many males and females of the Race who let their befflem become the masters in their homes. That is not so here."

"Oh, no," the hatchling said. "My father would not allow it."

Mordechai Anielewicz laughed again. "Convincing Heinrich of that was easy enough. Convincing Pancer of it has been harder."

Nesseref laughed, too. "Even among us, befflem are a law unto themselves."

Anielewicz's mate did not speak the language of the Race nearly so well as he did, but she spoke with great intensity: "Superior female, I thank for to help Mordechai for to find us. I thank you for to help to go to Kanth, too."

"You are welcome, Bertha Anielewicz." Nesseref was pleased she'd recalled the name, even if she didn't pronounce it very well. "I am glad to be a friend to your mate. Friends help friends—is that not a truth?"

"Truth," Anielewicz's mate agreed, along with what was surely intended to be an emphatic cough.

Nesseref had wondered what sort of food the Tosevites would serve her; Anielewicz had made it plain that following the Jewish superstition limited what he and his kinsfolk could eat. But the shuttlecraft pilot found nothing wrong with the roasted fowl that went on the table. Big Uglies ate more vegetables and less meat than the Race was in the habit of doing, but if Nesseref enjoyed more pieces of the bird and less of the tubers and stalks that went with it than did her hosts, no one seemed to find that out of the ordinary.

"Here." Mordechai Anielewicz set a glass half full of clear liquid in front of her. "This is distilled, unflavored alcohol. I have seen members of the Race drink it and enjoy it."

"I thank you," Nesseref said. "Yes, I have drunk it myself."

"We have a custom of proposing a reason for drinking before we take the first sip," he told her. Raising his glass, he spoke in his own tongue: *"L'chaim!"* Then, for her benefit, he translated: "To life!"

"To life!" Nesseref echoed. Imitating the Tosevites around her, she raised her glass before sipping from it. The alcohol was potent enough to make her hiss; after it slid down her throat, she had to concentrate to make her eye turrets turn in the directions she wanted. She asked, "May I also propose a reason for drinking?"

Anielewicz made the affirmative gesture. "Please do."

Raising her glass, the shuttlecraft pilot said, "To peace!"

"To peace!" The Tosevites echoed her this time, Anielewicz again translating. They all drank. So did she. The alcohol was strong, but it was also smooth. Before Nesseref quite noticed what she was doing, she'd emptied the glass. Anielewicz poured more into it.

Seeing everyone in the apartment having a good time and no one paying any attention to him, Pancer let out a plaintive squeak. Heinrich Anielewicz patted his own lap. The beffel jumped up into it and rubbed himself against the young Big Ugly as he might have against a member of the Race.

Maybe the alcohol had something to do with the solemnity with which Nesseref spoke: "Watching something like that makes me hope our two species really will be able to live in peace for many years to come."

"Alevai," Mordechai Anielewicz said in his language. As he had before, he translated for her once more: "May it be so."

"May it be so," Nesseref agreed, and then tried the Tosevite word: *"Alevai."* Maybe it was the alcohol, but she had no trouble saying it at all.

☆ **20** ☆

Car keys clinked as Sam Yeager fished them out of his pocket. "I'll be back in a bit," he called to Barbara and Jonathan. "I'm going to see how the alterations for my tux look."

"You'll be dashing," his wife said. Sam snorted. That wasn't a word he'd ever thought to apply to himself. Jonathan just snickered. His tuxedo already fit fine, so he didn't have to worry about return trips to the tailor.

Out on the street, cars slid past, their lights on. It was just a little past five-thirty, but night came early in December, even in Los Angeles. Yeager unlocked the door to his own Buick in the driveway, got inside, and fastened his seat belt. As he started the engine, he shook his head in bemusement. Back before the Lizards came, nobody'd bothered putting seat belts in cars. Nowadays, everyone took them for granted: the Race's attitude toward minimizing risk had rubbed off on people.

He backed out of the driveway and drove south down Budlong toward Redondo Beach Boulevard, on which the formalwear place stood. Maybe he really would look dashing by the time the Japanese-American tailors were done with him. Jonathan did, sure enough. But Jonathan, of course, was a young man, and it would be *his* wedding day. Sam knew he needed more help to look sharp than his son did.

He'd gone only a couple of blocks—he hadn't even got to Rosecrans yet—when he spied motion in the rearview mirror. He needed a heartbeat to realize it wasn't motion behind the car. It was motion *inside* the car: somebody who'd been hiding, lying down on the back seat or maybe between the front and back seats, coming up and showing himself.

That heartbeat's hesitation was at least half a heartbeat too long. By the time Sam took one hand off the wheel and started to go for his .45, he felt something hard and cold and metallic pressed to the back of his head. "Don't even think about it, Yeager," his uninvited guest told him. "Don't even *start* to think about it. I know you're heeled. Keep both hands where I can see 'em and pull on over to the side of the road if you want to keep breathing even a little longer."

Numbly, Sam obeyed. He'd known this day might come. He'd known it ever since he gave Straha the information he'd uncovered. He'd known it before then, as a matter of fact. But he'd been extra careful since that day. This once, he hadn't been careful enough. *One mistake, that's all you get.*

"Attaboy," his passenger said when he parked the car by the curb. "Now—tell me where it's at, so I can pull your teeth. Don't get cute with me, either. I'd sooner ice you someplace where it's quieter than this, but I'll do it right here if I've got to."

"Right hip," Yeager said dully. Smooth and deft, the man in the back seat half stood, reached forward, slid his hand under the safety belt, and plucked out the pistol. *I was stupid twice,* Sam thought. *I couldn't have got it very fast there myself.* Right now, though, that didn't look as if it would matter.

"Okay," said the man with the pistol—with two pistols now. "Get moving. Go down to Redondo Beach and turn right."

I was going to do that anyhow, Yeager thought as he pulled back into traffic. In an idiot sort of way, it was funny. Or maybe his brain was just spinning round and round without going anywhere, like a hamster's exercise wheel.

The light at the corner of Budlong and Rosecrans turned red. Sam hit the brake. As he did, one small light went on in his head. "You're Straha's driver!" he blurted. Gordon, that was the fellow's name.

"Not any more, I'm not," Gordon answered. "That's your fault, and you're going to pay for it. President Warren's dead. That's your fault." The light turned green. Yeager drove south, not knowing what else to do. Straha's driver—no, his ex-driver now—continued, "Indianapolis went up in smoke. *That's* your fault. And a hell of a lot of good men lost their posts. That's your fault, too. If I could kill you four or five times, I would, but once'll have to do."

"What about all those Lizards?" Sam asked. The light at Compton Boulevard was green. He wished it were red. That would have given him a few extra seconds. "They never had a chance."

"Fuck 'em." Gordon's voice was flat and cold. "And fuck you, buddy."

"Thanks a lot," Yeager said as he stopped for the red light at Redondo Beach Boulevard. "Fuck you, too, and the horse you rode in on."

Straha's driver laughed. "Yeah, you can cuss me. You'll be just as dead either which way. Now go on down to Western. Turn left there and keep on driving till I tell you to stop."

Sam waited till the way was clear, then turned onto Redondo Beach. He had a pretty good idea where Gordon would have him go. Western ran all the way down to the Palos Verdes peninsula, where there were plenty of wide open spaces without any houses close by. Kids drove down to P.V. to find privacy to park; he wouldn't have been surprised if Jonathan and Karen had done that a time or two, or maybe more than a time or two. Palos Verdes offered privacy for murder, too.

Coming up was Normandie. The next big street after it was Western. Yeager swung into the left lane as he drove west on Redondo Beach. He was nearing the light at Redondo Beach and Normandie when it went from green to yellow to red. Cars on Normandie started going through the intersection.

Sam slowed as if he were going to stop at the light, then stamped on the gas for all he was worth. Gordon only had time for the beginning of a startled squawk before the Buick broadsided a Chevy station wagon.

It had been a good many years since Sam's last traffic accident. He'd never caused—he'd never imagined causing—one on purpose. As they always did in pileups, things happened very fast and seemed to happen very slowly. Collision. Noise—incredible racket of smashing glass and crumpling metal. Yeager jerked forward. His seat belt caught him before he could spear himself on the steering wheel or go headfirst through the windshield.

Gordon wasn't wearing a seat belt. Sam had counted on that. Straha's driver hadn't been sitting directly behind him. He'd been more in the middle of the back seat. At the impact, he too was hurled forward, half over the top of the front seat. The pistol flew out of his hand. Sam had counted on that, too—he'd hoped for it, anyway. With the reflexes that had let him play a pretty fair left field once upon a time, he snatched it up from the floorboard and hit Gordon in the head with it, as hard as he could. Then he got back his own .45 from Gordon's belt.

All that happened as quickly as he could do it. He hadn't had time to think about it. He couldn't remember thinking anything since deciding to run the light at Normandie, any more than he'd done any thinking while chasing down a long fly ball in the alley in left-center. Thinking was for afterwards.

Afterwards, however much against the odds, seemed to have arrived. Time returned to its normal flow. Sam suddenly noticed blaring horns and squealing brakes as other drivers somehow missed adding to the accident.

The first thing that ran through his mind was, *It wasn't an accident. I meant to do it.* The next thought made a lot more sense: *I'd better get the hell out of here before the car catches on fire.*

When he tried to open the door, it wouldn't. He twisted in his seat and kicked at it. At the same time, somebody outside yanked at it for all he was worth. It did open then, with a scream of tortured metal.

"You son of a bitch!" roared the man outside, a stocky, swarthy fellow whose ancestors had come from Mexico if he hadn't. "You stupid motherfucking son of a bitch! You trying to get me killed? You trying to get yourself killed?"

He must have been driving the other car. Sam was proud he'd managed such a brilliant deduction. "No, I was trying to keep from getting killed," he answered—literal truth. He realized he sounded mushy. There on top of the dashboard, quite undamaged, sat his upper plate. He reached out with his left hand and stuffed it into his mouth.

"Man, I oughta beat the living shit outta you, and—" The man standing in the intersection suddenly noticed the pistol in Yeager's right hand. His eyes went enormously wide. He stopped roaring and started backing away.

That let Sam get out of the car. One look at the stove-in front end told him he'd never drive the Buick again. He shrugged. He'd have the chance to drive some other car one day. Almost as an afterthought, he dragged Gordon out of the wreckage. Gordon's head thumped on the asphalt, but Sam wasn't about to lose any sleep over that.

A couple of other cars had stopped. Their drivers jumped out to lend a hand. But nobody seemed eager to come very close to Yeager, not with one pistol in his hand and another on his belt. "Don't do nothin' crazy, mister," a tall, skinny blond guy said.

"I don't intend to," Yeager said—he'd already been crazy

enough to last a lifetime, and to prolong one. "I'm just waiting for the cops to get here."

He didn't have to wait long. Siren howling, red lights flashing, a squad car raced up Normandie and stopped in the intersection, which was already a lot more crowded than it needed to be. Two of Gardena's finest got out and looked things over. "Okay," said one of them, a burly fellow with black hair and very blue eyes. "What the hell happened here?"

As far as Sam could see, that was pretty obvious. He sighed with relief for a different reason, though—he'd met the policeman before. "Hello, Clyde," he said. "How are you tonight?"

The Mexican man who'd been driving the station wagon let out a wail of anguish. His car was wrecked—and it was totaled, bent into an L—and the guy who'd rammed him knew the cop by his first name?

Clyde needed a couple of seconds to pull Sam out of his mental card file, but he did. "Lieutenant Colonel Yeager!" he exclaimed. "What the hell happened here?" This time, he asked it in an altogether different tone of voice.

Briefly, as if making an oral report, Yeager told him what had happened. "Yeah, and that's all a bunch of bullshit, too," Gordon said from the street. Sam jumped. He hadn't noticed Straha's driver coming to. Gordon went on, "This guy kidnapped me, dragged me off the street. He was babbling about ransom money."

Sam handed Clyde both pistols. "You'll probably find both our prints on both of them. You want to know where I was going when I left home, call my wife and son. You can check with the formalwear place, too—it's right down the street here."

"Whaddaya think?" the other cop asked Clyde.

"Yeager here, he's had some nasty stuff happen to him that nobody ever got a handle on—nobody this side of the FBI, anyhow," Clyde said slowly. "You ask me, this looks like more of the same." He bent down and put handcuffs on Gordon. "You're under arrest. Suspicion of kidnapping." Then he pointed at Sam. "But you're coming down to the station, too, till we find out whose story checks out better."

"What about me?" cried the man who'd been driving the station wagon.

Nobody paid any attention to him. "Sure, I'll come," Sam said. "But please do call my wife, will you, and let her know I'm okay."

"We'll take care of it," the second cop said. He went back to the police car and spoke into the radio. Then he walked back toward the accident. "Tow truck's on the way. Another car, too, so we can get both these guys to the station."

"Okay, good," Clyde answered. "Like I said, we'll sort it out there." He hauled Gordon to his feet.

"I want my lawyer," Gordon said sullenly.

Whoever his lawyer was, he'd be good. Sam was sure of that. But, as he walked toward the squad car, he didn't worry about it. He didn't worry about anything. By the odds, he should have been dead, and he was still breathing. Measured against that, nothing else mattered.

Jonathan Yeager fiddled with his tie in front of the mirror in the church's waiting room. He'd practiced tying a bow tie under a wing collar ever since he'd got the tux, but he still wasn't real good at it. One side of the bow definitely looked bigger than the other. "I don't think I'll ever get it right, Dad," he said in something close to despair.

His father clapped him on the shoulder and advised, "Don't worry about it. Nobody's going to care much, as long as you're there and Karen's there and the minister's there. And you probably won't have to worry about it again till you're marrying off your own kid—and nobody'll pay much attention to *you* then, believe me."

"Okay." Jonathan was willing—more than willing, eager—to let himself be convinced. He glanced at his father. Sam Yeager's tie was straight. The bulge under the left shoulder of his tuxedo jacket hardly showed at all. Jonathan shook his head. "I wonder when the last wedding was where the father of the groom carried a pistol."

"Don't know," his father said. "Usually it's the father of the bride, and he's carrying a shotgun."

"Dad!" Jonathan said reproachfully. His father grinned, altogether unrepentant. Jonathan shook his head. He and Karen had been careful every single time—no need for Mr. Culpepper to go out and buy shotgun shells. Even so, he changed the subject: "Will you and Mom be okay watching Mickey and Donald while Karen and I are off on our honeymoon?"

"We'll manage," his dad replied. "If we really start going crazy, we can call one of the Army's other Lizard-psych boys, like the fellow who's baby-sitting them today. But I don't expect we'll need to. They're getting big enough to be easier than they were even a few months ago."

Somebody knocked on the door. "You fellows decent in there?" Jonathan's mother asked.

"No," his father answered. "Come on in anyway."

The door opened. Jonathan's mother came in. "Karen looks lovely," she said. "She's wearing the dress her mother got married in, you know. I think that's so romantic."

Jonathan hadn't seen Karen yet. He wouldn't, not till she came down the aisle. Not everybody followed that old custom these days, but her folks approved of it. Since they were footing the bill, he could hardly argue with them. His father asked, "Everything okay out front, hon?"

"Everything looks fine," his mother said. "And nobody's come in who hasn't been vouched for by somebody. No strangers at the feast."

"There'd better not be." Just for a moment, his father's right hand started to slide toward the shoulder holster. Then he checked the motion. He went on, "The judge refused to let Gordon out on bail yesterday. He was the biggest worry."

"I hope he stays there till he rots," Jonathan's mother said.

"Yeah." That was Jonathan. He added an emphatic cough. His father had told him some of what went on the night the Buick met its end. He had the feeling his dad hadn't told him everything, not by a long shot.

"Well, now that you mention it, so do I," Sam Yeager said.

Another knock on the door. The minister said, "About time to get ready, there."

"We are, Reverend Fleischer," Jonathan said. His heart thumped. He was ready for the ceremony, sure enough. Was he ready to be married? He wasn't so sure about that. He wondered if anybody was ready to be married before the fact. His mother and father had made it work, and so had Karen's parents. If they could manage it, he supposed Karen and he could, too. He turned to his mother and father. "Shall we do it?"

His father started to say something. His mother gave his dad a look, and his dad very visibly swallowed whatever it had been. Instead, he said, "We'd better round up your best man, too. He ducked out for a cigarette, didn't he?"

"Yeah." Jonathan nodded. "Greg goes through a pack a day, easy."

"With everything they're finding out these days about what cigarettes do to you, I think young people are foolish to start." His mother's grin was wry. "That doesn't mean I don't use them myself, of course."

"I was going to point that out," Jonathan's father said. "I've got a pack with me, too."

The minister opened the door. Jonathan's best man stood behind him. Greg Ruzicka and he had known each other since the fourth grade. Greg's head was also shaved; like so many of his generation, he found the Race at least as interesting as humanity. He gave Jonathan a thumbs-up. Jonathan grinned.

"If you'll just come along with me now, and take your places," Reverend Fleischer said. "Then I'll give the organist a nod, and we shall commence."

When Jonathan got to the door that led to the aisle down which he'd walk, he looked at the backs of the guests' heads. His friends, his parents' friends—Ullhass and Ristin were there; Shiplord Straha, for obvious reasons, wasn't—and a few relatives, and those of Karen and her folks. He gulped. It was real. It was about to happen.

Karen and her mother came out of the other waiting room. She waved to him and smiled through her veil. He took a deep breath and smiled back. Reverend Fleischer bustled up to the altar and gave the organist the signal. The first couple of notes of the Wedding March rang out before Jonathan realized they had something to do with him. His best man hissed. He jumped, then started walking.

Afterwards, he remembered only bits and pieces of the ceremony. He remembered his own parents coming up the aisle after him, and Karen on her father's arm, and her maid of honor—she'd known Vicki Yamagata even longer than he'd known Greg. After that, it was all a blur till he heard Reverend Fleischer saying, "Do you, Jonathan, take this woman to have and to hold, to love and to cherish, till death do you part?"

"I do," he said, loud enough for the minister and Karen to hear him, but probably not for anybody else.

It seemed to satisfy Reverend Fleischer. He turned to the bride. "Do you, Karen, take this man to have and to hold, to love and to cherish, till death do you part?"

"I do," she answered, a little louder than Jonathan had.

Beaming, the minister said, "Then by the authority vested in me by the church and by the state of California, I now pronounce you man and wife." He nodded to Jonathan. "You may kiss the bride."

That, Jonathan knew how to do. He swept the veil aside, took Karen in his arms, and delivered a kiss about a quarter as enthusiastic as he really wanted to give her. That still made it pretty lively for a kiss in church. When he let her go, he saw almost all the men and what was to him a surprising number of women looking as if they knew exactly what he had in mind.

"We're really married," he said: not exactly brilliant repartee from a new bridegroom.

"How about that?" Karen answered. That was commonplace enough to make him feel a bit better.

They went up the aisle this time, and over to the hall next to the church for the reception after the wedding. Jonathan drank champagne, fed wedding cake to Karen and got fed by her, and shook hands with everybody he didn't know and most of the people he did.

"Congratulations," Ristin told him in hissing English.

"I thank you, superior sir," Jonathan answered in the language of the Race.

As his red-white-and-blue body paint showed, Ristin was an ex-POW who'd made himself thoroughly at home in the USA. He kept right on speaking English: "This is an enjoyable celebration. I almost begin to understand why those two of my kind who fled to this country would desire it."

"Weddings are supposed to be fun," Jonathan agreed, now sticking to English himself. "From everything I've heard, though, it's the settling-down part later on that makes a marriage work."

Ristin shrugged. "I would not know. Most of us have no interest in such unions. But I know your kind does, and I wish you every success."

"Thanks," Jonathan said again.

People pelted Karen and him with rice when they went out to his elderly Ford. He hoped it would start. It did. He was glad to be out of the tux and in ordinary clothes again. Karen ran a comb through her hair, getting the rice out of it. "How about that?" she said again.

"Yeah. How about that, Mrs. Yeager?" Jonathan said. "You're going to have to get used to signing your name a new way."

Karen looked startled. "You're right. I will. And I'll have to get used to being at the end of the alphabet, too, instead of near the front. Culpepper was good for that."

The hotel they'd picked for their wedding night was close to the airport. When they got up to their room, he picked her up and carried her over the threshold. Inside, they discovered a bottle of champagne waiting in a bucket of ice. Karen read the little card tied to the bottle. "It's from your folks," she said, and sighed. "My mom and dad wouldn't have thought of anything like that."

"Your parents are nice people," Jonathan said loyally.

But he didn't want to think about his new in-laws—or his own parents, for that matter. That wasn't what a wedding night was for. He wasn't very interested in more champagne at the moment, either. It might make him sleepy. He didn't want to be sleepy, not tonight.

Karen might have been reading his mind. "We don't have to hurry," she said, glancing toward the bed that dominated the hotel room. "We don't have to worry about getting caught, either. I like that." Her eye went to the ring with the very little diamond Jonathan had set on her finger. "I like this, too."

"Good." Jonathan had a slim gold band on his own finger. He wasn't used to wearing rings; it felt funny. "That's the idea." He walked over to her. Their arms went around each other. Who kissed whom was a matter of opinion. This time, in privacy, they didn't have to hold back any enthusiasm.

Not very much later, they lay side by side on the bed. Jonathan's hands wandered. So did Karen's. She said, "This is a lot better than parking in a drive-in, you know?"

"Yeah!" Jonathan couldn't take his eyes off his bride. They'd never had the chance to be fully naked together before. "You're beautiful. I already knew that—but even more so."

She pulled him to her. "You say the sweetest things." After they'd kissed for quite a while, Karen pulled back perhaps half an inch and said, "I'll bet you tell that to all the girls." She poked him in the ribs.

He squeaked—she'd found a ticklish spot. And, just for half a second, the corny old joke put him off his stride. He *had* told Kassquit something pretty much like that, or as close to it as he could come in the language of the Race, which wasn't really made for such sentiments. He wondered how Kassquit was doing, and hoped she was doing well.

But then his mouth found its way to the tip of Karen's breast again. She sighed and pressed his head against her. He stopped thinking about Kassquit. He stopped thinking about everything. A moment later, the marriage became official in a way that had nothing to do with either the church or the state of California, but that was as old as mankind nonetheless.

"Oh, Jonathan," Karen said softly.

"I love you," he answered.

They made love a couple of times, fell asleep in each other's arms, and woke up to make love again. Over the course of the night, the champagne did disappear. It wasn't enough to make them drunk; it was enough to make them happy, not that they weren't pretty happy already.

The wakeup call at eight the next morning interrupted something that wasn't sleep. Afterwards, Jonathan said, "I don't know why we're flying up to San Francisco for our honeymoon."

"It'll be fun," Karen said. "We'll see all sorts of things we haven't seen before."

"If we ever get out of the hotel room, we will," he said. "I don't know about that."

"Braggart." She wrinkled her nose at him. They both laughed. Jonathan squeezed her. They went downstairs for breakfast, and then back up to the room to find something to do in the couple of hours before the plane took off. To Jonathan's considerable pride, they did. On the basis of a bit more than half a day, he liked being married just fine.

Kassquit stooped slightly to look in the mirror in her cubicle. That she had to stoop reminded her she wasn't biologically part of the Race: the mirror was at the perfect height for a male or female from Home. She'd had to start stooping even before she reached her full growth. Either she'd tried not to think about it or she'd let it mortify her, as did every difference between herself as she was and the female of the Race she wished she were.

Now she knew those differences were even larger than she'd thought before she met wild Big Uglies. That knowledge could mortify her, too. "I am a citizen of the Empire," she said. "I am a Tosevite, but I am also a citizen of the Empire."

It was a truth. Sometimes—perhaps, even, more often than not—it helped calm her. But the converse held, too. She was a citizen of the Empire, but she was also a Tosevite. And, at the moment, she was engaged in a task which proved exactly that.

Her hair—the hair on her scalp, that is, not the hair that sprouted elsewhere on her body—had got long enough to need combing. The black plastic comb she held had come up from the surface of Tosev 3 at her request. The Race didn't make anything like it: what point, with scales instead of hair? She'd needed to send an electronic message to Sam Yeager to find out how the Big Uglies kept hair in any kind of order. "Comb," she said as she used it. The word was English. The Race did not have the thing, and so did not have a term for it.

After she finished using the comb, she studied the result. Her hair was neater, no doubt about it. She suspected any Big Ugly who saw her would have approved. She also suspected neither males nor females of the Race would care one way or the other. Members of the Race disapproved of her hair on general principles. Not long ago, that disapproval would have crushed her. Now, every once in a while, she enjoyed annoying males and females. If that wasn't her Tosevite blood coming out, she had no idea what it was.

The intercom panel by the door hissed for her attention. "Who is it?" she asked.

"I: Ttomalss," came the reply.

Kassquit stuck on an artificial fingerclaw for a moment, so she could prod the switch to let him in. "I greet you, superior sir," she said, bending into the posture of respect.

"And I greet you," Ttomalss replied. "I hope you are well?"

She made the affirmative gesture. "Yes. I thank you. And yourself?" After Ttomalss used the same gesture, Kassquit asked him, "And what can I do for you today, superior sir?"

"You mentioned to me the ambiguities involved in recording every action of an individual who is a citizen of the Empire with the same privileges as those enjoyed by other citizens of the Empire," Ttomalss said.

"I certainly did mention that to you, yes," Kassquit said. "And I do not believe the issue is in the least ambiguous."

"You will, I hope, understand that I did not and do not altogether agree with you," Ttomalss said. "But a review committee of higher-ranking individuals has come to a different conclusion. I am now able to tell you that the routine recording of your actions has ceased and will not resume."

"That is . . . very good news, superior sir." Kassquit added an emphatic cough. She knew she sounded astonished. She *was* astonished. That the Race would put her wishes ahead of its own research was something to be astonished about. Then she checked her swelling delight. "Wait."

"What is it?" Ttomalss asked.

"You say you are able to tell me the routine recording of my actions has stopped," Kassquit answered. "You do not say that this is a truth. *Is* it a truth, superior sir?"

She watched him narrowly. She was not a female of the Race, to have instinctual cues about what his body language meant, but she'd been watching him all her life. When he flinched now, the motion was tiny, but she saw it. And when he said, "What do you mean?" she caught the startled alarm in his voice.

"I mean that you were lying to me," she said sadly. "I mean that you thought I would not pay close enough attention to your words. When I was a hatchling, I would not have. But I am an adult now. When you lie to me, I have some chance of realizing it."

"You do not understand." But Ttomalss didn't deny what she'd said.

She wished he would have denied it. "I understand you have lied to me. I understand I cannot trust you any more. Do you understand—do you have any idea—how much pain that causes me? I am sorry, superior sir, but I do not think I want to see you again for some time to come. Please go."

"Kassquit, I—" Ttomalss began.

"Get out!" Kassquit shrieked at the top of her lung—no, lungs; being a Tosevite, she had two. They seemed to make her voice doubly loud, doubly shrill, inside the little cubicle. Ttomalss cowered in alarm as her cry echoed and reechoed from the metal walls. Without a word, he fled.

As the door hissed shut behind him, Kassquit fought the urge to run after him and do him an injury. Assuming she actually could, what would it do except land her in trouble? *It would make me feel better,* she thought. But, in the end, that proved not quite reason enough, and she let her mentor escape.

She made the negative gesture. "No. I let him escape physically," she said, much more quietly than she'd ordered him to go.

"But he will not get away with it, by the spirits of Emperors past."

After casting down her eyes as any other citizen of the Empire would have, she made a telephone call. A female of the Race said, "Office of Fleetlord Reffet, fleetlord of the colonization fleet. How may . . . I help . . . you?" Her voice faltered as she saw herself facing a Tosevite rather than the member of the Race she'd expected.

"I am Junior Researcher Kassquit," Kassquit said. "I should like to speak to the Exalted Fleetlord, if that is possible."

"I doubt very much that it will be," the female replied.

Such a lack of acceptance didn't even anger Kassquit any more; she'd encountered it too often. She said, "Please mention my name to the fleetlord. You may possibly be surprised."

To another member of the Race, the females surely would have said, *It shall be done.* Here, she plainly debated refusing Kassquit altogether. At last, with a shrug, she replied, "Oh, very well." Her image disappeared as she set herself to finding out whether Fleetlord Reffet would indeed condescend to speak to this Big Ugly who bore the title and name of a female of the Race.

If Reffet decided he didn't care to speak with Kassquit, she probably wouldn't see the female in his office again; the connection would just be broken. But Kassquit knew she'd done the Race—and Reffet—a considerable service in identifying the male who called himself Regeya on the electronic network as Sam Yeager, wild Big Ugly. She hoped the fleetlord would remember, too.

And, for a moment, she wished she could forget. Had she not unmasked Sam Yeager, she would never have become intimate with Jonathan Yeager. She would have come closer—much closer—to remaining a good counterfeit female of the Race. But that hadn't been how things worked out. Now Jonathan Yeager was permanently mated to another wild Big Ugly. And now Kassquit knew she was doomed always to stay betwixt and between. She could never make herself into a proper member of the Race, but she could never fully be a Tosevite, either.

The female reappeared. "The fleetlord *will* speak to you," she said in startled tones. She vanished again. Reffet's image replaced hers.

Kassquit folded into the posture of respect. "I greet you, Exalted Fleetlord," she said. "Is it not a truth that I have been adjudged a full citizen of the Race?"

"Let me examine the facts before I answer, Junior Researcher," Reffet said. One of his eye turrets swung away from her, presumably to look at another monitor. No matter how she tried to make them behave so, her eyes refused. After a little while, Reffet swung both eye turrets back toward her. "Yes, that does appear to be a truth."

"Do I have all the privileges of any other citizen of the Empire, then?" she persisted.

"I would say that would follow from the other." Reffet added the affirmative gesture.

"In that case, Exalted Fleetlord . . ." Kassquit took a deep breath. "In that case, I request that you formally reprimand my mentor, Senior Researcher Ttomalss, for falsely assuring me that he had stopped recording my every activity when in fact he has not. He admitted as much when I caught him in the lie. And I daresay you can see and hear him admit as much on the recording he has denied making. I also request that you order him to cease such recordings in the future."

"Junior Researcher, are you sure you wish to pursue this formally?" Reffet asked.

"Exalted Fleetlord, I am," Kassquit replied. "I see no other way to gain at least some of the privacy a citizen of the Race is entitled to. Being who I am, being what I am, I know I can never hope to lead a normal life. But a citizen of the Empire should not have to lead a life in which she is on constant display."

"Truth," the fleetlord of the colonization fleet said. He let out a soft hiss as he pondered. At last, he made the affirmative gesture to show he had decided. "I shall order Ttomalss to cease this recording. But I shall not reprimand him. As you note, your situation is not and cannot be normal."

"I thank you," Kassquit said. "But perhaps you misunderstood. I do not want him reprimanded for the recording. I want him reprimanded for the lie."

"Think carefully on this, Junior Researcher," Reffet said. "I understand your reasons, I believe. But do you truly wish to alienate your mentor? For one in your . . . unusual position, having a prominent friend could prove valuable, and not having one could prove the reverse." He used an emphatic cough.

Kassquit started to answer with something sharp, but checked herself while she thought. Reluctantly, she decided the fleet-lord's advice was good. "I thank you," she said. "Let it be as you suggested. But could you please informally let Ttomalss know you are displeased with him because of the lie?"

Reffet's mouth fell open in a laugh. "Perhaps you do not need a prominent friend after all. You are a strong advocate for your-self. I shall do that. Farewell."

Well enough pleased with herself, Kassquit began checking the areas of the electronic network in which she was interested. Before long, Ttomalss telephoned her. Without preamble, he said, "I suppose you are responsible for the tongue-whipping I just got from Fleetlord Reffet."

"Yes, superior sir, I am," Kassquit answered.

"I am certain you think I deserve it, too," Ttomalss said. "Things are now arranged as you desired. You are no longer being routinely recorded, and that *is* a truth." He used an em-phatic cough.

"Good," Kassquit said, and used one of her own. She and Ttomalss both broke the connection at the same time. She hoped she wouldn't have to go on without his help. If she did, though, she expected she would manage. She was fundamentally alone. Being who and what she was, how could she be anything else? "I just have to live with it," she murmured, and set about to do ex-actly that.

Vyacheslav Molotov was walking past his secretary's desk on the way to his own office when his legendary impassivity cracked. Stopping in his tracks, he pointed at the object that had startled him and said, "*Bozhemoi,* Pyotr Maksimovich, what on earth is *that*?"

"Comrade General Secretary, it is called a Furry," his secre-tary replied. "My cousin is the protocol officer in our embassy to the United States, and he sent it to me. They are, apparently, all the rage there—by what he said, he had to fight a mob of house--wives at a department store to get his hands on any of them."

"I had forgotten you were related to Mikhail Sergeyevich," Molotov said. He peered over the tops of his spectacles at the so-called Furry. "I fail to see the appeal. There must be many more attractive stuffed animals."

"But this is not an ordinary stuffed animal, Comrade General

Secretary," his secretary said. "Here, let me show you." He aimed a handheld control at the toy's nose. The Furry opened its eyes and swung them over the room, for all the world as if it really were waking up and looked around. It waved a hand and spoke in English.

"Bozhemoi!" Molotov said again. "I see what you mean. It is almost as if the devil's grandmother lives inside the little thing." When he spoke, the Furry's eyes turned toward him. It said something else in English. For all he knew, it was answering him. "Does it hear me?" he asked.

"Literally, no," his secretary said. "In effect, yes. It has all manners of sensors and circuits stolen from the Lizards' technology, which make it much more versatile than toys commonly are."

"Versatile," Molotov echoed, watching the Furry. It had been looking at the secretary, but its alarmingly lifelike eyes returned to him when he spoke. "Amazing," he murmured. "The Americans are foolish to use so much of this valuable technology in something to amuse children. They are, in some ways, very much like children themselves."

"My cousin writes that a Canadian actually invented the Furries, though they're being made in the United States," his secretary said.

"Canadians. Americans." Molotov shrugged. "Six of one, half a dozen of the other. There are no big differences between them, the way there are between us Russians and the Ukrainians, for instance." He warily eyed the Furry. Sure enough, it was eyeing him, too. "Turn it off, Pyotr Maksimovich."

"Certainly, Comrade General Secretary." His secretary wasn't about to tell him no. When he used the control again, the Furry yawned, waved good-bye, said one last thing in English ("That means, 'Good night,' " Molotov's secretary said), and closed its eyes. It truly might have been falling asleep.

"I hope your children enjoy it," Molotov said. He had to repress the urge to sidle around his secretary's desk as he finally went on into his office. *It is only a toy, a machine,* he told himself, *nothing but plush and plastic and circuits programmed to perform one way or another.* He was a thoroughgoing rationalist and materialist, so that should have been self-evident truth. And so it was—when he forced himself to look at it rationally. When he didn't . . . When he didn't, the devil's grandmother might have animated the Furry.

Sitting down at his desk, going through paperwork—all that seemed a great relief. He'd done it every day for years, for decades. Getting up for some tea and a couple of little sweet cakes dusted with powdered sugar was routine, too. The more he stuck to routine, the less he had to think about the Furry and what it implied. So much technology, casually lavished on a toy! The USSR had stolen the same technology from the Race, and could have matched the Furry—but any economic planner who dared suggest such a thing would have gone to the gulag the next minute.

Molotov wondered how many Furries would be imported into the Soviet Union, and what sort of demand for such fripperies they would create among the majority who would not prove able to get their hands on them. He shrugged. He cared very little whether or not people clamored for consumer goods. What sensible planner would? The Red Army got what it needed. The Party got what it needed. If anything happened to be left over after that, the people got it. *Unlike the capitalist Americans, we have our priorities straight,* Molotov thought smugly.

After a while, he glanced at the clock. It was after ten. Zhukov and Gromyko should have been here on the hour. Molotov tapped one finger on the desk. Most Russians were hopelessly unpunctual, but those two had learned to come and go by the clock, not by their own inclination. Where were they, then?

Almost as soon as the question formed in his mind, he got the answer. Squeaky English came from the anteroom. Molotov's secretary's Furry had captured the head of the Red Army and the foreign commissar no less than it had ensnared Molotov himself. He went out to the anteroom and said, "Good morning, Comrades. Have you begun your second childhoods, to play with toys instead of conducting the business of the Soviet Union?"

Gromyko said, "It *is* a clever gadget, Vyacheslav Mikhailovich. It is also a funny gadget, if you speak English."

Zhukov nodded. Delight glowed on his broad peasant features. Plainly, he would sooner have gone on fooling around with the Furry than dealing with state business. He said, "I'm going to get some of these . . . for my grandchildren, of course."

"Of course," Molotov said dryly.

With obvious regret, the diplomat and the soldier allowed themselves to be led away from the American toy. Even as Zhukov sat down in front of Molotov's desk, he said, "That's a damn fine toy, no two ways about it."

"There are always two ways about everything, Georgi Konstantinovich," Gromyko said. "The second way here is that the Americans waste so much energy and technological expertise on this piece of frivolity when they could be using them to some advantage on their own defense."

"All right, something to that," Zhukov allowed. "But a little fun's not against the law every now and then." He still sometimes thought like a peasant, all right.

Molotov said, "Can we forget the toys for the time being and discuss our plan of action for China? That was, if you will recall, the reason we were to assemble here today. Had I known of the Furry in advance, I assure you I would have put it at the head of the agenda."

His sarcasm seemed to get through where nothing else had. Instead of blathering on about the stuffed animal, Zhukov said, "Mao's done better than we thought he could, hasn't he?"

"Indeed," Molotov said.

"Now the question is, has he done too well for his own good?" Gromyko said.

"Exactly so, Andrei Andreyevich—exactly so," Molotov agreed. "If he keeps giving the Lizards as much trouble as he has lately, how soon will they start using explosive-metal bombs to suppress him?"

"Too many of those bombs used already, all over the world," Gromyko said.

"If the Lizards do start using explosive-metal bombs, they may not get rid of the whole People's Liberation Army, but they're liable to wipe out the leadership cadres," Zhukov said.

"You are right, Georgi Konstantinovich, and that is not desirable," Molotov said. "We want the People's Liberation Army to remain a thorn in the side of the Race for years—indeed, for generations—to come." He turned to Gromyko. "Andrei Andreyevich, I want you to work closely with Japan and the United States. If all three powers express their displeasure at the use of explosive-metal weapons in China, that may well give the Lizards pause."

"I shall do my best to arrange a joint declaration, Comrade

General Secretary," Gromyko replied. "Too many sovereignties have already used too many explosive-metal bombs, as I said a moment ago."

"It bears repeating. We should also emphasize it with the Race," Molotov said. "And I believe we should make it less urgently necessary for the Race to have to think about using explosive-metal bombs in China." His gaze swung back to Zhukov. "Do you understand what I mean, Comrade Marshal? Do you agree?" He wished he could simply give Zhukov orders, but the head of the Red Army would have had an easier time giving him orders than the other way round.

Zhukov grunted now. "You want us to stop sending the People's Liberation Army the German rockets that let them take out tanks and helicopters and airplanes."

Molotov, for once, did not grudge a smile. "Exactly!"

"Mao will pitch a fit," Zhukov predicted. "This isn't the first time we've sold him down the river."

"And it may not be the last, either," Molotov replied with a shrug. "Is weakening the People's Liberation Army not what seems best for the Soviet Union and for the world as a whole?"

He waited. If Zhukov said no, he would have to backtrack, and he hated the idea. But, after another grunt, Zhukov said, "Yes, I suppose so. The Chinese will still keep the Lizards in play. They just won't be able to do such a good job of it. If the Lizards didn't have explosive-metal bombs, I'd answer differently. Of course, if the Lizards didn't have explosive-metal bombs and the technology that goes with them, they'd still be stuck on Home."

"The world would be a different place," Gromyko said musingly. "Better? Worse? Who can guess?"

"Who indeed?" Molotov said. He thought the Soviet Union would have survived the attack the Nazis were unleashing in 1942 when the Race arrived, he hoped the Soviet Union would have survived, but he was anything but certain. Would anyone have tried flying into space by these early days of 1966 if the Lizards hadn't shown it could be done? He doubted that.

"No point to such airy-fairy questions," Zhukov said. "We can only deal with what is, not with what might have been."

Gromyko's heavy eyebrows came down and together in a frown; he didn't care to be casually dismissed like that. But his voice showed none of his annoyance as he asked, "If we make it harder for the Chinese to annoy the Lizards, shall we find some other way to make their lives interesting?"

"What have you got in mind?" Molotov asked.

"When we launched those missile warheads loaded with ginger at the Race's Australian settlements, the results were highly disruptive—and highly entertaining," the foreign commissar observed.

But this time Zhukov spoke before Molotov could: "*Nyet.* We got away with it once, but that is no guarantee we could do it twice. And the hot water we would land in if we got caught . . . *Nyet.*"

Reluctantly, Molotov nodded. "I agree with Georgi Konstantinovich. Smuggling ginger is one thing. Bombarding them with it is something else if we get caught: an act of war." Gromyko sulked. He didn't show it much—he never showed anything much—but he sulked. Molotov would much sooner have backed him than Zhukov. That would have enhanced his own power and diminished the marshal's. But he would have no power at all if the USSR went the way of the Greater German *Reich. Survival first,* Molotov thought. *Everything else afterwards, but survival first.* He'd lived by that rule for three quarters of a century. He wondered how much further he could go.

Monique Dutourd turned to—turned on—her brother with even more annoyance than usual. "Isn't there anything you can do?" she demanded.

"Me?" Pierre didn't just shake his head. He laughed in her face. "If I tried to get Auerbach out of the Lizards' prison, do you know what would happen? I'd end up back inside it myself, that's what. No thanks, little sister."

He was likely right, worse luck. Even so, Monique said, "It's not fair. The American got me up to Tours, and now he's locked away."

"I notice you don't say anything about his girlfriend," Pierre remarked.

He was right about that, too. Monique hadn't said a word about Penny Summers, although she'd also been arrested. Truth was, Monique had little use for Penny, and suspected the feeling was mutual. Trying not to sound defensive, she said, "He did more for me than she did."

"And what would you like him to do for you?" Pierre asked

insolently. Monique looked around for something to throw at him. Before her eye—and her hand—settled on anything, her brother went on, "Remember, I'm not the one who's got clout with the Lizards any more. *You* are. Like I've said before, you're the teacher's pet. And that Ttomalss is sure as hell a Lizard with pull. He'd have a lot better chance of getting the Race to spring Auerbach than I would."

"Do you really think I could?" Monique heard the astonishment in her own voice. She needed a moment to figure out why she was so astonished. But then she did: she'd never had much power to do things or change things. She'd been done to and changed instead. The idea that she could be an active verb rather than a passive one startled her.

Pierre shrugged. "Suppose he says no. That's the worst that can happen, and how are you worse off if it does? At the very least, you'll know you tried."

"You're right." Monique knew she sounded surprised again.

"When's Ttomalss going to call again?" her brother asked.

"Tomorrow, isn't it?" Monique answered.

"Yeah, I think that's right." Pierre paused and lit a cigarette. "All right, tomorrow you tell him no Auerbach means no ancient Romans. Sound like you mean it and you've got a chance."

"Peut-être." Monique started to laugh. "You're going to be the one who sounds like I mean it. I don't know the language."

"We'll see how it goes," Pierre said. "If he tells you no flat out, then he does, that's all." He blew a smoke ring. Whether the American got out of prison didn't matter a centime's worth to him one way or the other.

Ttomalss did telephone the next day. "I greet you," he said through Pierre. "We were discussing, as I recall, the ways in which the Romans used gradations in status between full subject and full citizen to integrate foreign groups into their empire. Do I understand correctly that a group's degree of citizenship would depend on the degree to which it had assimilated itself to Roman customs and practices? That strikes me as a very rational approach to administration."

He did indeed understand correctly. He wasn't stupid, or anything close to it; he reminded Monique of that with every conversation they held. But he was alien, very alien. He reminded her of that with every conversation they held, too.

"Well," Pierre said, not translating any more. "Do you try, or don't you?"

"I do," Monique replied. "Tell him there is a personal matter we need to discuss before we go on with the Roman history."

"It shall be done," her brother said, one of the scraps of the Lizards' language she understood. He went on with a long sentence of hisses and pops and coughs that were Greek to her—or would have been, save that she knew Greek.

After Pierre finished, Ttomalss let out an amazingly human-like sigh. "I might have known this would happen," he said. "In fact, this has already happened, when you arranged to have your brother released from prison to translate for you. What do you want from me this time?"

"I want you to release an American named Rance Auerbach, who, I believe, has been unjustly imprisoned as a ginger dealer," Monique answered. She said not a word about Penny Summers. If Pierre wanted to tease her more about that, he could. Her conscience didn't trouble her too much. Auerbach was the one who'd helped her. Penny wasn't, and hadn't.

"It always comes down to ginger dealers," Ttomalss observed. "This herb causes us more trouble than any drug does for people." (As an aside, Pierre added, "He really said, 'Big Uglies.'") The Lizard went on, "Let me consult our records about this Auerbach. Then I will tell you what I think."

Silence fell on the other end of the line. Into it, Pierre asked, "What was the name of the Lizard who got you this place in Tours?"

"Felless," Monique said. "Senior Researcher Felless. Auerbach knew she tasted ginger, and he blackmailed her into helping me."

"Senior Researcher? Same title as Ttomalss," her brother observed. "I wonder if they know each other. I wonder if he likes her, which is even more to the point. Felless . . ." He scratched his cheek. "I think she was one of Business Administrator Keffesh's pals. Keffesh is in jail, too, you know."

"They do know each other. Felless recommended me to Ttomalss. Do you think we can use all that to push him?" Monique asked.

Her brother shrugged a very Gallic shrug. "Don't know yet. Like I said, a lot of it's going to depend on what he thinks of her."

Drumming her fingers on the desktop in front of the telephone, Monique waited to see what Ttomalss would say. After a couple of minutes, the Lizard began to speak again: "I am sorry, but that does not appear possible. His crimes include some in the subregion known as South Africa in which members of the Race fired on one another in pursuit of ginger."

That didn't sound good. But Monique had expected him to refuse at first. After all, doing nothing was easier and more convenient than doing something he didn't much care to do. She said, "If males of the Race were shooting at one another, there's no evidence Auerbach was shooting at anybody, is there?" She hoped there wasn't.

To her relief, Ttomalss said, "No. But he has admitted being there, admitted being part of the plot. He has implicated males of the Race."

"If he's given evidence that helped the Race, doesn't he deserve leniency?" Monique asked.

"He has leniency, as far as imprisonment goes." Ttomalss paused, then fired back a question of his own: "Why are you so interested in this Tosevite male, Monique Dutourd? Do you want to mate with him?"

Pierre translated that rather more bluntly. Monique gave him a dirty look. He laughed at her. But Ttomalss definitely was not a fool, for the thought had been in the back of her mind. While she wondered what to say, Pierre offered his advice: "If you mean yes, say yes. If you mean no, say yes anyway. They think we're all sex-crazy all the time, anyway. It'll help push him."

"All right. Thanks. Translate this . . ." Monique thought, then said, "Yes. We've never had the chance yet, and I can hardly wait. We've just been friends up till now."

After putting that into the Lizards' language, her brother nodded vigorously. "Good. Real good. Friendship counts for a lot with them."

"I've seen that from the questions he asks about the Romans," Monique said.

Ttomalss sighed again. "In spite of your desire, however urgent it may be, I doubt I have the influence to do as you wish . . . Why are you two Tosevites laughing?"

Monique and Pierre looked at each other and started laughing again. "How do we explain he sounds like the worst bad film ever made?" Monique asked.

"We don't," Pierre said, which was also probably good advice.

"Back to the main argument, then," Monique said. "Tell him Auerbach did me a large favor, and I want to pay him back."

"What sort of favor was this?" Ttomalss asked. "I suspect it was no favor at all. I suspect you are inventing it to fool me."

"I am not," Monique said indignantly, though Pierre probably wouldn't be able to translate the indignation. "If it weren't for Rance Auerbach, I wouldn't have my position here at the University of Tours."

"Now I know you are lying," Ttomalss said. "I happen to know for a fact that Senior Researcher Felless of the Race obtained that position for you. She was the one who suggested I talk to you about the history of the Romans."

Monique nodded to herself. Now the question was, were Felless and Ttomalss friends or just professional colleagues? She said, "Senior Researcher Felless got me the position because Auerbach urged her to."

"Urged her to, you say?" Ttomalss echoed. "Do you mean he threatened to publicize her ginger habit again?" (" 'Again'?" Pierre said. "So she's got caught before, has she? Isn't that interesting?")

"Auerbach hasn't said anything about it to the Race's authorities since, not that I know of," Monique told Ttomalss. "Not yet, anyhow."

"Not yet?" Once more, Ttomalss repeated her words. Once more, he sighed. "You will next tell me that, if he stays imprisoned, he will accuse Felless of using ginger. The question you should ask yourself is, do I care?"

"No, superior sir," Monique said. "That's the question you should ask yourself, don't you think?"

Sure enough, there was the nub of it. If Ttomalss didn't care at all what happened to Felless, he'd be less likely to help get Rance Auerbach out of prison. Instead of directly replying right away, he said, "You want to help the Tosevite gain his freedom because he did you this favor. Do you remember that Senior Researcher Felless also did you the favor of obtaining this position for you? Is it just that you should threaten her after she gave you that assistance?"

"She wouldn't have, if it hadn't been for Auerbach," Monique said.

"Do remember something else as well," Ttomalss added. "If

you got your position thanks to the Race, you can also lose it thanks to the Race."

"I know. Believe me, I know," she said. "But I was working as a shopgirl before Rance Auerbach did me that favor. I can find work as a shopgirl again."

"I daresay I could find another Roman historian, too," Ttomalss warned.

"What do you think?" Monique asked Pierre.

"If he meant to tell you no, he'd have done it already," her brother replied.

"I think you're right. I hope you're right," Monique said. "Tell him this: I'm sure he's right. If he wants to do that, he can. But if he wants to keep working with *this* Roman historian, he needs to give me some help here. He's not paying me much money to work with him, and remind him of that, too."

After Pierre translated, Ttomalss let out another sigh. "I can make no promises, but I will see what influence I can bring to bear," he said at last. ("You won't get any more than that out of him," Pierre said.) "Can we now continue with our discussion of grades of Roman citizenship?"

"Yes, superior sir," Monique answered, as meekly as if she were only a scholar of classical civilization, and not a black-mailer at all.

Glen Johnson had company as he rode his scooter through the scattered drifting rubble of the asteroid belt, though he was alone in the cabin. He couldn't see his company with the naked eye, either. But his radar assured him he wasn't alone in this stretch of space. One of the Lizards' probes followed him on his rounds.

This wasn't the first time a probe had shadowed him as he went hither and yon, either. He wondered if the machine had received instructions from back on Earth to keep an electronic eye on him, or if the computer controlling it had decided to follow him on its own. Mankind remained behind the Race when it came to computer-guided machinery. Just how far ahead the Lizards were wasn't quite clear.

"Okay, pal," Johnson said to the probe, not that it could hear him. "You want the grand tour, I'll give you the grand tour."

He remained convinced that, no matter how smart the probe was, he was smarter. It was faster and stronger and more accurate. But he was more deceitful. If the probe wanted to learn more about what all the Americans were up to out here in the vicinity of Ceres, he would cheerfully lead it down the primrose path.

His radar guided him toward one of the rocks on which a work crew had mounted a motor: a weapon, in other words, aimed at the Lizards back on Earth. He used his little maneuvering jets to go all around the asteroid, examining it in microscopic detail. The Lizards' probe also went around the rock, though it stayed several miles farther out than he did.

After finishing his inspection, he radioed the *Lewis and Clark*: "Asteroid code Charlie-Blue-317. All installations appear to be operating according to design."

That done, he took the scooter away from the asteroid and on toward another one of similar size about twenty miles ahead. He gave the second floating chunk of rock the same meticulous inspection he'd given the first one. As before, the Race's probe followed him. As before, it also went all around the asteroid. There was only one difference: this asteroid didn't boast a motor.

Even so, Johnson sent a radio message to the *Lewis and Clark*: "Asteroid code Charlie-Green-426. All installations appear to be operating according to design."

Having said that, he went on to the next rock on his list. This time, the Lizards' probe didn't follow him quite so quickly. Instead, it kept prowling round and round the asteroid he'd code-named Charlie-Green-426. He knew exactly what it was doing. It was trying to figure out why he'd gone there and what installations he was talking about. He wondered how long the Lizards would take to figure out that he was yanking their tailstumps. The longer, the better.

By the time he was done inspecting the next asteroid—which also remained untouched by human hands—the probe had caught up with him. He sent off the usual kind of message: "Asteroid code Charlie-Green-557. All installations appear to be operating according to design."

Then he had a new thought. Instead of heading off toward another drifting hunk of rock, he pointed the scooter at the Lizards' probe and used the radar to steer toward it: it was so efficiently blackened, he couldn't see it till he got very close. The scooter mounted machine guns. He didn't know what sort of weaponry the probe mounted, and didn't want to find out here.

Instead, he flew around the probe at about the same range as he'd flown around the past several asteroids. The probe maneuvered, too, making it more like a dance than anything else. When Johnson had finally finished, he fired up the radio again and said, "Asteroid code Edgar-Black-069. All installations appear to be operating according to design."

What will the Lizards make of that? he wondered. If he were a Lizard monitoring the Big Uglies out in space, he wouldn't care for the implication that his probe was one of their installations. He hoped his hypothetical Lizard wouldn't like it, either.

After that bit of confusion, he went on to visit several more asteroids, some with motors mounted on them, others without, on a long, looping trajectory that took him back to the American spaceship from which he'd departed. He guided the scooter into the airlock, which closed behind him. When the inner door opened and he emerged from the scooter, the airlock operator said, "The commandant wants to see you right away."

Fighting back a strong impulse to groan, Johnson said, "Oh, God, what now?"

"Beats me," the operator said. "But that's what he told me, and when he says something, he usually means it."

"Isn't that the sad and sorry truth?" Johnson answered. "Okay, Rudy, thanks." He swung off to beard Brigadier General Healey in his den.

When he got to the commandant's office, deep in the heart of the *Lewis and Clark*, Healey fixed him with a fishy stare and said, "Asteroid code Edgar-Black-069? We have no asteroid with that code designation."

"Oh." Johnson fought against another groan. The commandant was at least as literal-minded as any Lizard ever hatched. He explained his *pas de deux* with the Race's probe. "I made up the code name. Let the Race go nuts trying to figure out my signals. The probe is black. That's what made me think of it."

Healey drummed his fingers on the desktop. "I see. Very well. Dismissed."

"Sir?" Johnson said in surprise.

"Dismissed, I said." Healey's expression turned suspicious, which wasn't a very sharp turn. "Why? Did you think I would keep grilling you once I found out what I needed to know?"

Johnson shrugged. "Never can tell, sir. It's happened before, Lord knows." He didn't have to worry about keeping the commandant sweet. Brigadier General Healey was going to despise him till one of them died.

He hoped Healey would erupt now. For a couple of seconds, he thought the commandant would. But no such luck. After a long exhalation, Healey growled, "I haven't got time to play games with you today, Lieutenant Colonel. Get the hell out of my office."

"Yes, sir," Johnson said, and glided away. He wondered if the commandant would throw something at him to speed him on his way, but Healey didn't.

Out in the corridor, Johnson looked at his watch. He'd made better time out among the asteroids than he'd expected; he wasn't due back in the control room for another hour and a half. That left him to ponder whether he felt more like sleep or company. He yawned experimentally, then shook his head. He could do without sleep a while longer. Which left . . . "The refectory," he murmured, as if giving orders to his chauffeur.

But he was his own chauffeur. He brachiated down the corridor till he came to the entrance to the large chamber. It was the middle of the afternoon, ship's time: not a meal period. The place was crowded anyway; because it was the biggest chamber in the *Lewis and Clark*, and because people did assemble there for meals, they'd got into the habit of gathering there to chat and socialize whether it was mealtime or not.

Lucy Vegetti spotted him floating in the entranceway and waved. He waved back and swung his way toward her. As he drew near, he spotted Mickey Flynn hanging on to a nearby handhold. "You two plotting together?" he asked.

"Of course," Flynn said solemnly. "What else would we be doing? This is, after all, a ship full of conspiracies about to hatch."

"And if you don't believe him," Lucy added, "just ask the Lizards."

"Oh, I believe him," Johnson said. "After all, could a man with a face like that possibly tell a lie?"

"Why, the mere idea is ridiculous," Flynn said.

"Besides," Johnson went on, "I just spent a few hours in the scooter adding to the Lizards' paranoid fantasies." *And to Brigadier General Healey's,* he thought, but he didn't say that out loud.

Lucy Vegetti wagged a finger at him in mock indignation.

"You've been visiting rocks with no motors on them again." She paused. "Did you notice anything interesting on any of them?"

"Spoken like a geologist," Glen said, at which she stuck out her tongue at him. He continued, "I didn't see anything that struck me as strange, no. Sorry. But I did do a little buck-and-wing with the Lizard probe that was trundling along after me." He described how he'd treated it as if it were an American installation, not a spacecraft belonging to the Race.

"I like that." Lucy nodded, then turned to Flynn. "What do you think, Mickey?"

"How could I presume to disagree?" the backup pilot asked. "If I did, you would presume me presumptuous."

"Anybody who knows you is more likely to presume you preposterous," Johnson said.

"I am affronted," Flynn declared, letting go of the handhold so he could fold his arms across his chest and show how affronted he was. As far as Johnson was concerned, that only made him look more preposterous. And, since air currents started to move him away from the handhold, he had to reach out and grab it again.

"To the Lizards, we're all preposterous," Lucy said.

"That's part of the game," Johnson said. "The less seriously they take us—*us* as people generally and *us* as the people out here—the better off we are."

"If they didn't take us seriously, would that probe have followed you everywhere you went, like Mary's little lamb?" Mickey Flynn enjoyed playing devil's advocate.

"Maybe not," Johnson admitted. "But if I run around doing crazy things, after a while the Lizards will just be sure I'm nuts, and then they won't take me seriously any more. That'll be good, like I said."

"It would have been better if they thought we were just out here mining," Lucy said. "Now that they know we're turning little asteroids into weapons, they're going to keep a closer eye on us."

"They'll keep a closer eye on us *while we're doing that*," Flynn said.

Johnson nodded. "Mickey's right. The asteroids are useful as weapons, but they're also useful as camouflage. The Race is paying an awful lot of attention to those rocks, and to the motors on them. The Race is paying attention to us when we go to them.

It's paying attention to us when we set up motors on new rocks, and when we look rocks over to see if they'd be good with motors on them."

"I know." Lucy nodded, too. "And the Lizards aren't paying so much attention while we go on about our real business—our A-number-one real business, I mean—out here." She looked from Johnson to Flynn and back again. "Do you really think we'll be able to launch a starship by the turn of the century?"

"I'll be an old man by then," Glen Johnson said. "Too old to be in space, by rights. But I hope I'll still be around to see it."

"Me, too," Lucy said. "The Lizards got here. We ought to be able to go see Home."

"Who knows where the Russians will be by then, either?" Mickey Flynn said. "Maybe they'll be right behind us—or right beside us. I wouldn't mind."

"Home. Ten light-years away—a little more. Something to look forward to," Johnson said. "We should always have that." His friends nodded once more.

The Great War is over but the conflict continues…

American Empire: Blood & Iron
by Harry Turtledove

The Great War has ended, and an uneasy peace reigns around most of the world. But nowhere is the peace more fragile than on the continent of North America, where bitter enemies share a single landmass and two long, bloody borders.

In the North, proud Canadian nationalists try to resist the colonial power of the United States. In the South, the once-mighty Confederate States have been pounded into poverty and merciless inflation. U.S. President Teddy Roosevelt refuses to return to pre-war borders. The scars of the past will not soon be healed. The time is right for madmen, demagogues, and terrorists.

At this crucial moment in history, with Socialists rising to power in the U.S. under the leadership of presidential candidate Upton Sinclair, a dangerous fanatic is on the rise in the Confederacy, preaching a message of hate. And in Canada, another man—a simple farmer—has a nefarious plan: to assassinate the greatest U.S. war hero, General George Armstrong Custer.

With tension on the seas high, and an army of Marxist Negroes lurking in the swamplands of the Deep South, more than enough people are eager to return the world to war. Harry Turtledove sends his sprawling cast of men and women—wielding their own faiths, persuasions, and private demons—into the troubled times between the wars.

Published by Del Rey Books.
Available at bookstores everywhere.

Coming in July 2002...

American Empire:
The Center Cannot Hold
by Harry Turtledove

It is 1924—the roaring twenties. In the United States, the
Socialist Party, led by Hosea Blackford, battles Calvin Coolidge
to hold on to the Powell House in Philadelphia. And it seems as
if the Socialists can do no wrong, for the stock market soars and
America enjoys prosperity unknown in a half century. But as old
names like Custer and Roosevelt fade into history, a new generation faces new uncertainties.

While the Confederate States suffer poverty and natural calamity,
the Freedom Party promises new strength and pride. But if its
chief seizes the reins of power, he may prove a dangerous enemy
for the hated U.S.A. Yet the United States take little note.
Sharing world domination with Germany, they consider events
in the Confederacy of little consequence.

As the 1920s end, calamity casts a pall across the continent.
With civil war raging in Mexico, terrorist uprisings threatening
U.S. control in Canada, and an explosion of violence in Utah, the
United States are rocked by uncertainty.

In a world of occupiers and the occupied, of simmering hatreds,
shattered lives, and pent-up violence, the center can no longer
hold. And for a powerful nation, the ultimate shock will come
when a fleet of foreign aircraft rain death and destruction upon
one of the great cities of the United States...

Published by Del Rey Books.
Available at bookstores everywhere.

Counting Up, Counting Down
A visionary collection of
science fiction, fantasy, and alternate history tales

by
Harry Turtledove

From Harry Turtledove, bestselling author and
critically acclaimed master of alternate history, comes
a classic collection of science fiction tales and what-if
scenarios. In narratives ranging from fantastic to
oddly familiar to eerily prescient, this compelling
volume illustrates Turtledove's literary skill and
unbridled imagination.

In *Counting Up, Counting Down* Harry Turtledove
offers the entire spectrum of his own short stories
in one collection of seventeen thrilling,
unforgettable tales.

Published by Del Rey Books.
Available at bookstores everywhere.

Look for Harry Turtledove's thrilling Worldwar series…

Worldwar: In the Balance

The allied forces of the Axis powers grapple for victory as the Second World War rages across the globe. And then, from outer space, comes a new enemy that will unite Earth's warring nations in a battle to save their planet.

Worldwar: Tilting the Balance

The marauding extraterrestrial invaders that struck at the height of WWII lay waste to the German, Russian, Japanese, and American forces with their superior weapons and firepower. But Earth is determined to resist enslavement…and slaughter.

Worldwar: Upsetting the Balance

Once sworn enemies, Hitler, Roosevelt, Churchill, Stalin, and Mao are now bound together as comrades in the devastating war against a brutal intergalactic scourge. And now once-forbidden weapons and unthinkable tactics are being used to combat the inhuman invaders bent on conquest.

Worldwar: Striking the Balance

Time has nearly run out in the battle between Earth and the monstrous alien invaders from the stars. And as city after city across the globe is consumed in radioactive firestorms, the combined Allied and Axis forces struggle to stave off world domination…even as they risk humanity's annihilation.

Published by Del Rey Books.
Available at bookstores everywhere.

Colonization

The exciting continuation of the Worldwar epic by Harry Turtledove

It's been twenty years since World War II became a war between worlds, and humans and their would-be alien conquerors must now co-exist peacefully on Earth. But when a new wave of invaders sparks a new war for domination of the planet, thus begins the stunning sequel series to the Worldwar saga...

Second Contact

Down to Earth

Aftershocks

In these towering tales of struggle and tyranny, Harry Turtledove combines a lavish cast of twentieth-century leaders, their countries, and a terrifying threat of earth-shattering proportions. Packed with action, adventure, and sacrifice, *Colonization* is a masterpiece of the imagination.

Published by Del Rey Books.
Available at bookstores everywhere.